Exile's Children

This bound copy consists of uncorrected page proofs.
Material for quotation should be checked
against the regular edition.

Trade Paperback Publication Date: January 1996
On sale: December 1995
Spectra Fantasy   592 pages   6¹/8″ × 9¹/4″
ISBN 0-553-37486-9 $12.95/$17.95 in Canada

BANTAM BOOKS

Also by Angus Wells

Book of the Kingdoms #1:
    Wrath of Ashar
Book of the Kingdoms #2:
    The Usurper
Book of the Kingdoms #3:
    The Way Beneath
The Godwars #1: Forbidden Magic
The Godwars #2: Dark Magic
The Godwars #3: Wild Magic
Lords of the Sky

Exile's Children

Angus Wells

BANTAM BOOKS
New York Toronto
London Sydney Auckland

EXILE'S CHILDREN
A Bantam Spectra Book/ January 1996

Spectra and the portrayal of a boxed "s" are trademarks of Bantam
Books, a division of Bantam Doubleday Dell Publishing Group, Inc.

Book design by Donna Sinisgalli

Library of Congress Cataloging-in-Publication Data

Published simultaneously in the United States and Canada

Bantam Books are published by Bantam Books, a division of Bantam
Doubleday Dell Publishing Group, Inc. Its trademark, consisting of the
words "Bantam Books" and the portrayal of a rooster, is Registered in
U.S. Patent and Trademark Office and in other countries. Marca
Registrada. Bantam Books, 1540 Broadway, New York, New York 10036.

PRINTED IN THE UNITED STATES OF AMERICA

BVG   10 9 8 7 6 5 4 3 2 1

For Anne Lesley Groell
and Jamie Warren Youll.
With special thanks to Stephen Youll.

Exile's Children

1 The Meeting Ground

When Morrhyn came out of the Dream Lodge the first thing he saw was a heron chased across the sky by three harrying crows. The ungainly fisherbird swooped and dove, its wide wings beating heavily, but the crows were relentless in their pursuit, and as the heron reached the stand of hemlock flanking the Meeting Ground, it squawked a protest and gave up its catch to the robbers. Morrhyn wondered if this was an omen, and if any of the other wakanishas attending the Matakwa had observed the drama. He would mention it later, he decided, and perhaps they would discuss its meaning; meanwhile, he had much else to occupy his mind.

After the heat of the lodge, the early morning air struck chill on his sweated skin and he shrugged his bearskin closer about his shoulders. The year was young yet, the New Grass Moon barely full, but the sky promised benevolence, and when he turned to make obeisance to the Maker's Mountain, he saw the great peak shining brilliant in the rising sun. Perhaps that, too, was an omen; perhaps the Maker sent a sign to balance the other. Morrhyn was unsure: lately, his dreams had left him turbulent with uncertainty. He felt some dreadful threat approached the People, but what its nature or when it should arrive remained mysterious. This past night, as before, he had dreamed of strange creatures all clad in shining metal, and mounted on such beasts as defied imagining, and knew their purpose was evil. At their head rode a figure whose armor shone sun-bright, and whose mount was huge and bloodred with wickedly curling horns and eyes that blazed fiery. No such folk, or such weirdling beasts, existed in all Ket-Ta-Witko, and he feared the meaning of the dream, and prayed earnestly that it not be realized. When it came his turn to speak in the Dream Council, he would tell all this to his fellow wakanishas and seek their advice. Perhaps others had shared the dream: he could not decide if he hoped for that confirmation of his oneiric power or dreaded its corroboration.

Sighing, he made his way through the sleeping lodges to the stream that crossed the Meeting Ground and stooped to lave his face and chest. Farther down the brook he saw Rannach watering his prized stallion, laughing with several of the other unmarried warriors. The young man stood bare-chested in the cold, and for a moment Morrhyn envied him his youth and the overweening confidence it brought. He had never enjoyed such confidence, but then, he had come early to his calling, recognized as a Dreamer and claimed by old Gahyth before he had opportunity to ride out after the wild plains horses or go alone against the bear or the lion to earn the right of the warrior's braids. He was wakanisha: his hair hung loose; Rannach's was tied in braids these seven winters now.

And now the young man prepared to choose a bride. There were maidens enough amongst the lodges of the Commacht who looked favorably on him, and their parents would welcome his bride-visit. Morrhyn wished he would choose one of them; it should be so much simpler. But Rannach had eyes only for Arrhyna, as if his first sight of the Tachyn girl had hooked his heart and bound it firm. Had Morrhyn not known better, he might have wondered if the maiden had entranced Rannach, delivered him some love potion that enslaved him with ropes of blind desire; but from Matakwas past he knew her for a modest girl, seemingly unconscious of her beauty. He did not believe she had worked some magic on Rannach but only been herself, and Rannach fallen honestly—and totally—in love with her. Which, of course, was the strongest magic of all, and in the circumstances perhaps the worst.

Morrhyn grunted as he straightened, absently cursing the years that tolled their count in the stiffening of his limbs, and nodded greeting as Rannach smiled and waved, hoping his silence should indicate to the warrior his aversion to conversation. He had no desire at that moment to speak with the young man: he knew where the conversation must go, what he would say and what Rannach would reply, and that it must leave him further troubled. He needed to think, to ponder his dream and the days to come, to determine what part Rannach and Arrhyna might play in the future of the Commacht; indeed, in the future of all the People.

It would all, he thought as he burrowed deeper into his robe and turned from the stream, be so much easier if Vachyr did not court the girl: if Vachyr were not Chakthi's son, or Chakthi so intransigent. But these things were immutable as the Maker's Mountain. Intermarriage amongst the clans was not unusual, and if Rannach paid court to any other Tachyn maiden, likely Chakthi could find no cause for objection. The Maker knew the Tachyn akaman held little enough love for the Commacht, but he would likely not argue Rannach's pursuit of some maiden other than Arrhyna, only urge the parents set an exorbitant bride-price. That his only child pursued the same maiden changed everything: Chakthi would bring all his influence as akaman to bear, seeking to deliver Vachyr whatever—or, in this case, whoever—the warrior desired. Chakthi's love of his son was blind and, since his widowing, untempered by feminine influence.

Nor did Morrhyn believe Hadduth likely to do other than second his akaman, even though it was the wakanisha's duty to consider the greater good, the welfare of all the People. Hadduth, he could not help thinking, was a cringing dog to Chakthi's wolf: when Chakthi howled, Hadduth barked his support. It needed no dreaming to prophesy this looming future. Rannach was headstrong in his pride, and should Vachyr contest with him, should it come to a challenge . . .

That, Morrhyn thought, he had rather not consider. Save he must, for he was wakanisha of the Commacht and his burden was the contemplation of fate's weaving. It was a burden he accepted, delivered when Gahyth saw him for a Dreamer, but it brought him little pleasure. Its weight sat heavy; nor was it shared, for amongst the young men of the Commacht he could discern none with the talent. He was not yet so old he need worry about that absence, but the time must surely come when he need teach another the art. He thought that then he must perhaps turn to another clan, to persuade some likely candidate to take the oaths and vow fealty to the Commacht. And did it come to that, he would not look for his successor amongst the Tachyn.

A voice intruded then on his musings, and he saw that he had come absentminded amongst the lodges. Lhyn called to him from the mouth of Racharran's tent and he smiled at sight of her, old memories, old longings, stirring ruefully. Gray strands wove through her hair now, but they seemed only to make the gold glow brighter, as if silver joined the molten flow; and were there lines upon her face, they served only to emphasize her beauty. Once, perhaps . . . But Morrhyn shoved the thought away. Lhyn had made her choice and he would not argue it; had not then, when he saw her eyes grow moist as she denied him and told him she went to Racharran, and could not now, when he saw her happy. He raised a hand and went toward her, still not quite able to stem the swift thudding of his heart. Perhaps, he thought, I am not so old after all.

"I've pan bread readying," she told him, "and Racharran brought home a deer. Shall you eat with us?" She held the lodge flap open as she spoke, knowing he would not demur.

Morrhyn beamed as the smells wafted tempting to his nose and said as he entered the lodge, "Our akaman is, indeed, a great hunter of deer."

"As our wakanisha is of dreams," Racharran answered, chuckling from across the lodge fire. "Sit, my friend, and fill your belly."

Morrhyn thought of the meager breakfast set by in his own lodge: this should surely be better, and give him chance to speak with the akaman of his dream and doubts. He sat, shucking off his bearskin, savoring the odors as Lhyn took the pan bread from the flames.

They ate, as was custom, in silence, speaking only when all were done and Lhyn filled cups of Grannach manufacture with sweet herb tea.

"I saw Rannach," Morrhyn began. "He's of the same mind?"

Racharran nodded, his handsome face darkening somewhat. "My son is obstinate," he murmured. "This day he intends to go to Arrhyna; tomorrow Bakaan will make formal approach."

"The Maker grant Vachyr not be there," Morrhyn said.

"Surely not even Vachyr would sully the Meeting Ground." Lhyn made a sign of warding as she spoke.

Her husband grunted, shrugging, "Vachyr's a temper fierce as our son's pride," he declared. "I wonder if there's much to choose between them."

Lhyn gave him a disapproving frown. "I'd not liken our son to Chakthi's," she said. "Rannach is—"

"Obstinate," Racharran interrupted.

"His father's son," said Lhyn.

"Perhaps." Racharran spread his hands wide. "But he'll not listen to me in this, and his choice could not be worse."

"He loves her," Lhyn said, "and she him. Would you argue that?"

"Not that they share a passion," Racharran said. "Only that it's a passion such as can deliver us to war." He turned to Morrhyn. "How say you, wakanisha?"

Morrhyn wiped deer fat from his chin and pondered awhile. Then: "I see both sides, I think. I'd wish the Maker had guided Rannach's eyes elsewhere, but they fell on Arrhyna and they'll not be shifted. We cannot forbid the marriage; neither can Chakthi. What comes of it . . ."

The akaman said, "Trouble. Were it in my power, I'd forbid it."

"And make an enemy of our son," said Lhyn. "He'd take Arrhyna and go away."

"Yes." Racharran ducked his head in unhappy acceptance. "And so, instead, we make Chakthi our enemy. Come summer, our folk must ride careful on the grass—the gift of Rannach's desire."

"But you'll support him," Lhyn said, "does Chakthi take it before the Council?"

"Of course." Racharran's smile was sour with resignation. "He's my son. I've spoken with him, and my words ran like water off stone. He knows my feelings—and Morrhyn's—and he'll not be diverted. But I shall support him in Council."

Lhyn smiled and filled their cups. Morrhyn said, "I dreamed again."

Racharran said, "The same?" And when the wakanisha nodded his confirmation: "Aught of Rannach?"

Morrhyn said, "No; and that troubles me. It's as if this dream is so great, it drives all others out. It burns through my nights like a prairie fire." He shuddered despite the lodge's warmth. "It frightens me."

Racharran studied his old friend, reading concern like spoor on the weathered face. That disturbed him, and when he spoke, his voice was soft. "Can you put a meaning on it?"

"No." Morrhyn shrugged a negative. "Save danger threatens, and a danger far greater than Chakthi alone. Ach!" He sighed and shook his head. "I am not a very good Dreamer, that I cannot interpret this."

Racharran said, "You are the best," echoed by Lhyn.

Morrhyn favored them with a smile. "Thank you for your faith," he murmured, "but it troubles me that I sense this yet cannot discern its import." Conscious that he slumped, he straightened his back, forcing a more confident tone. "I shall speak of it in the Dream Council. Perhaps others have known this dream."

Racharran nodded: these were matters for the Dreamers, not yet of immediate concern to the akamans. Was Morrhyn's dream shared, could the wakanishas of all the clans gathered for the Matakwa put a meaning to it, then it would become a thing for the Chiefs' Council. Until then he had worry enough contemplating Rannach's suit.

He anticipated a summer of war, and could not help the kindled anger that it was Rannach lit the flame. In the name of the Maker, why could the youth not see reason? Arrhyna was a prize, but there were others aplenty, and did Rannach only set the good of the clan before his own desire, then he would forsake the girl and find some other whose taking was less likely to bring the Tachyn raiding. Rannach was not, Racharran thought sadly, the stuff of which akamans were made.

"You think of Rannach?"

Lhyn's soft voice intruded on his dark contemplation, and he answered her with a silent nod. She sighed and looked to Morrhyn.

The wakanisha said, "The stallion roped, you'd best not let go."

Racharran grunted irritably. "This stallion is likely to trample us."

"But still," Morrhyn returned, "the rope is on and we must make the best of it."

"Did you offer Chakthi compensation?" Lhyn suggested.

Her husband snorted. "For a bride whose price is already paid? I've some pride yet." His aquiline features softened and he touched his wife's hand. "Besides, I suspect Chakthi would see that only as added insult."

"There's no easy answer," Morrhyn offered. "Save pray the Maker gentles Chakthi's temper."

"And Vachyr's," Racharran said.

When Morrhyn quit their lodge, the great encampment was awake. His conversation had delivered no enlightenment, and he felt still no desire to converse with any others, so he drew up his robe to cowl his head and walked away from the lodges to where the toes of the Maker's Mountain rested on the earth. The stone shone silvery in the risen sun, aged as time and furrowed with cracks like the skin of an ancient. Higher, the slopes rose steep, lofting above the Meeting Ground as they climbed to shape the flanks of the great peak. That stood smooth, carved by wind and untold years, a pinnacle that stabbed the clouds, the pillar holding up the heavens: the Gate through which the People had come to Ket-Ta-Witko. Perhaps up there, closer to the Maker's weaving, he might find answers.

He set to climbing, the ascent soon warming him enough that he shed the bearskin, leaving it where a clump of thorn bushes jutted spiny from the rock. He clambered up until he reached a shelf that overlooked the Meeting Ground and squatted there, surveying the lodges of the gathered clans.

Once each year, always in the New Grass Moon, they came to this place in Matakwa. Here they offered to the Maker, giving thanks for bounty past and prayer for bounty to come. Here disputes were settled, and marriages made. What could not be resolved by the akamans and wakanishas of the individual clans was settled by the Chiefs' Council, and the will of the Council was final. Here the wakanishas met in Dream Council, speaking of their visions, seeking the advice of their fellow Dreamers, initiating novices. Here the People met with the Grannach, the Stone Folk, who lived inside the hills and came out to trade their

metalwork for skins and beadwork and bone carvings. The Matakwa
was a celebration both secular and holy, bound by one overriding com-
mandment: that no blood be spilled. Morrhyn prayed earnestly that it
continue so. He could not say how, but he felt that was connected in
some fashion to his dream—that no blood sully the Meeting Ground,
lest it bring on the burning horses of his vision with their dreadful
riders.

He chanted his prayer and heard the words carried away on the
wind that blew up. He hoped the wind carried them to the Maker's ears.

Then, seeking calm, he studied the camp.

The lesser limbs of the Maker's Mountain curved horn-shaped
about the great verdant bowl, fending the wind. There was grass for all
the horses and sufficient timber to augment the dung fires with ample
wood. The stream that wandered across the bowl turned and twisted
serpentine, so that none need pitch their lodges far from water. It was as
fine a place as any in Ket-Ta-Witko, and surely the only place where all
the clans might gather.

The lodges spread colorful below him, painted with the emblems of
the five clans and those personal to the occupants. The horse head of the
Commacht stood proud across the brook from the Tachyn buffalo; he
saw the wolf of the Aparhaso and the turtle of the Naiche, the eagle of
the Lakanti. Past the lodges the herds cropped the grass, watched by the
older children, the younger scurrying agile and loud between the tents,
their games joined by barking dogs. Streamers of smoke rose blue from
the cookfires, swirled and lost where they met the wind. Folk wandered
the avenues between the tents, pausing to hail friends, renew old acquaintances. Toward the center, warriors displayed horses for barter,
women the blankets woven through the long moons of Breaking Trees
and Frozen Grass. It was a sight that always stirred Morrhyn's heart, of
which he never tired. He hoped that when the Maker took him back, it
might be here, where his bones could forever lie close to this wondrous
symbol of unity.

He knew he smiled as he watched it all; and then his smile froze at
the sight of Rannach splashing through the brook.

The warrior was dressed in his finest, no longer bare-chested but
wearing a shirt of pale buckskin, bead-woven and painted with the horse
head. His breeches were of the same hide, dyed blue and fringed in red
and white, and his dark hair gleamed from recent washing. Over his left
shoulder he carried a blanket. He went directly toward the lodge of
Nemeth and Zeil, Arrhyna's parents. At least, Morrhyn thought, he
bears no weapons; and then: he gave Racharran his word.

Even so, the wakanisha could not entirely quell his presentiment and looked past the young warrior to Vachyr's tent, pitched beside his father's. He let out his relief in a long sigh as neither Tachyn appeared. Still, his heart beat fast as he returned his gaze to Rannach, for he knew the absence of Arrhyna's other suitor was no more than temporary respite, the quiet preceding impending storm. What shape that storm should take he knew not, only that it surely came on.

"You who made us all," he said, unaware he spoke aloud, "grant this goes smooth."

Then he held his breath, as if he stood close by Rannach's shoulder and not far off and high, as the young man halted before the lodge. The flap stood open and Nemeth came out, speaking awhile with Rannach before turning to call inside. Arrhyna appeared, and on the instant Morrhyn saw she had awaited this visit: her hair shone a fiery red, falling loose over her shoulders, and she wore a gown of deerskin worked so soft it was almost white. Morrhyn imagined she had spent the winter moons shaping that garment, in anticipation of this moment.

Rannach spoke and the maiden smiled, demurely lowering her head as she stepped toward him. He shrugged the blanket from his shoulder, raising his arm so that it fell in a swoop of red, blue, and white. Arrhyna stepped into its folds and Rannach settled his arm around her, lifting the blanket to hood them both. Then, moving as one, they walked away, first amongst the lodges of the Tachyn, then over the stream to wander the lines of the Commacht.

Morrhyn drew his eyes away: the declaration was made, now only formalities remained. Formalities and Vachyr's response, and Chakthi's. The wakanisha craned his head around, staring up at the Maker's Mountain. He sensed his dream thundering closer, but the pinnacle offered him no sign of what approached, and after a while he rose and began the descent.

It was time to face the future.

2 Ceremonies of the Horsemen

"Three hands of horses were offered." Chakthi flung out his fingers in emphasis. "Prime stock, every one."

"No doubt, for the blood of the Tachyn herds is the envy of us all." Juh of the Aparhaso spoke mildly, his tone a gentle contrast to Chakthi's venom. Racharran smiled faintly: the old man was ever a keeper of the peace. "But still the decision rests with the girl."

Chakthi's hand sliced air, dismissive.

"Who chooses Rannach," said Yazte of the Lakanti. "Whose bride-offer was accepted by Nemeth."

Beyond this inner circle of akamans and wakanishas, Racharran heard a nervous shifting and guessed that was likely Nemeth. The man had courage, he thought, to defy the Tachyn leader. He wondered if Nemeth and Zeil might not soon come seeking the shelter of the Commacht lodges: it was theirs for the asking.

"Rannach offered only ten." Chakthi pressed his point, his lupine features painted sharper in the firelight. His pale eyes flashed a challenge. "Ten against Vachyr's fifteen. How can that be right?"

"Our women are not beasts, my friend." Juh frowned, his wrinkles spreading like sun-cracks over the ancient clay of his face, but still his tone was mild. "They are not bought and sold like horses. Arrhyna has a say in this."

"And tells Rannach *yes*." Yazte spoke with studied calm, only the barest hint of contempt in his voice.

Does this all come to war, we've an ally there, Racharran thought. Yazte's no more liking for Chakthi than I. He turned his attention to the others, wondering where their allegiances would lie. Juh, he thought, would seek to hold his Aparhaso aloof from any conflict. He looked to Tahdase of the Naiche but the young man's face was veiled, as if he'd not yet cast his stone. Racharran could not blame him: Tahdase was not long akaman of his clan—this was his first Matakwa as leader—and, sensibly, he sought no enmities. Even so, Racharran thought, Chakthi forces this to a vote, and then Tahdase must make his choice.

He returned his eyes to the Tachyn akaman as Chakthi spoke again. "I do not say our women are beasts." Chakthi attempted a placatory smile: it seemed to Racharran like the grin of a wolverine. "Only that any sensible father, any sensible maiden, must surely choose the better price. Indeed, the better man."

Racharran had promised himself he would play the diplomat in this Council, not invoke Chakthi's anger, but this was too calculated an insult to ignore with honor. He raised a hand and said, "You say that Vachyr is the better man?"

Morrhyn's elbow dug hard against his ribs, but he ignored the wakanisha as he faced Chakthi. The Tachyn smiled stonily and ducked his head. "Vachyr is Tachyn: yes, he is the better man."

Racharran stiffened even as Morrhyn's hand clasped his wrist. None bore arms in Council, but had Racharran worn a blade then . . . "Careful." Morrhyn's voice was a breeze against his ear. "He rants; he seeks to provoke you. Do not rise to his bait."

It was not easy. Yazte stared at Chakthi as he might at some night crawler found in his bedding. Old Juh frowned in open disapproval. Even careful Tahdase looked shocked. At their sides, the wakanishas of their clans scowled. Racharran reined in his anger, forcing back the challenge that sprang to his lips. Carefully, measuring his words, he said, "Your opinion is your own to hold, brother. As is mine."

A shadow crossed the Tachyn's face, anger and disappointment flashing an instant in his eyes. In the name of the Maker, Racharran wondered, does he truly look to begin a fight here, now?

"We are the Council of the People." Juh's voice was no longer so gentle; now it was edged with the steel that made him akaman. "It is unseemly that we trade insults here, in Matakwa."

Yazte grunted agreement; Tahdase nodded as solemnly as his youth allowed.

Chakthi stared fiercely around for a while, then Hadduth spoke softly in his ear and he lowered his head. "My brother Racharran speaks the truth. Our opinions are our own to hold. I intended no insult to the Matakwa."

It did not sound like an apology, but under the pressure of Morrhyn's fingers, Racharran nodded his acceptance.

"So, then, do we return to this matter of Arrhyna?" Juh sounded relieved.

"What's to discuss?" Yazte smiled with deliberate calm. "An offer has been made, an offer rejected; the maiden has chosen. What else is there?"

Chakthi's teeth ground behind his thin-pressed lips and the eyes he turned on the Lakanti were cold as winter ice. "As akaman of the Tachyn, I object to her choice." His voice was no warmer than his gaze. "As akaman of the Tachyn, I ask that the Council decide this matter for her."

This was without precedent, but it was no more than Racharran had expected. Times were, a maiden could not decide between two suitors or her parents might object to her choice, then the matter could be decided in Chiefs' Council, all concerned presenting their views and the Council's decision final. In this case there was nothing for the Council to decide: Arrhyna had chosen, her parents did not object. Chakthi pushed too far—as Racharran had feared—solely on behalf of his son. He looked past the Tachyn akaman to where Vachyr sat amongst the warriors. The young man was glaring across the Council fire—at Rannach, Racharran guessed.

"Does my brother Racharran object to this?" asked Juh.

Racharran shook his head even as Yazte murmured, "You need not do this, brother. This is a farce."

He flashed the Lakanti a smile and made a small, quieting gesture. It *was* a farce: he had no doubt of the immediate outcome, for all he might wish Arrhyna would stand up and renege her promise to Rannach, declare her mind changed, and go to Vachyr. The future should be easier that way. But still—he could not help the small flame of malice—it should be good to see Chakthi humbled.

Ceremoniously, he rose to his feet, blanket cradled, and said, "I have no objection. Let those concerned be heard."

Old Juh nodded. Yazte scowled dark as Chakthi. Tahdase looked nervous. The ancient Aparhaso chief raised a hand. "Then I summon them," he intoned. "Let the maiden and her parents step forward and be heard. Let the warriors step forward and hear our judgment."

The protagonists moved through the crowd encircling the Council. Vachyr and Rannach trod proudly, glowering at each other like young buffalo bulls in rut. Arrhyna came with downcast eyes, nervous as a deer, Nemeth and Zeil close behind and no more confident. The crowd fell silent.

Juh said, "Let the maiden Arrhyna speak," and smiled encouragingly. "Child, you are much honored—two brave warriors ask your hand and offer many horses. Which would you have?"

For a moment, Arrhyna's hair curtained her face, red as the fire's glow. She spoke from behind its veil, too soft she might be heard. Yazte said, "Child, do you speak up? You've naught to fear; none shall harm you here, nor say you nay."

Arrhyna raised her head at that, green eyes wide as they fixed on Rannach. "My choice is Rannach," she said.

Vachyr's scowl darkened, the corners of his angry mouth downturned. Rannach beamed. Juh said, "Now we hear the parents."

Nemeth glanced at Chakthi, clearly loath to earn the akaman's further disfavor. Juh motioned that he speak, and the man touched his wife's hand. With his eyes fixed on the ground he said, "Vachyr's brideoffer is generous, but my daughter has made known her choice and I cannot deny her."

"You name Rannach your choice?" Juh asked.

Nemeth swallowed and said quietly, "I do."

"And there is agreement with your wife in this?"

Nemeth nodded. Zeil said, "There is. I would abide by my daughter's choice. I name Rannach."

Racharran heard Chakthi's furious grunt, saw the tightening of Vachyr's jaw. No good at all, he thought. This shall be a troubled summer. But even so . . . He could not deny that the Tachyns' discomposure afforded him a degree of pleasure.

"Then it is agreed by all who have a choice in this," Juh said. "How speak my brothers?"

Yazte said, "It is agreed," beaming at Vachyr.

Slower and softer Tahdase said, "It is agreed."

Chakthi snarled and shook his head. "I say *no!*"

Juh turned to Racharran. For an instant the Commacht thought he might shock them all by siding with Chakthi, but that should only make an enemy of his son, and likely drive him away. Then those headstrong warriors who followed Rannach would go with him and the clan be weakened. Nor, was he honest with himself, could Racharran perform so dramatic a turnabout: it would be a diminishment of his honor. Loud, he said, "It is agreed."

Juh climbed stiffly to his feet, his arms raised as he turned slowly around the circle. "Then let all present know it is decided." His voice was pitched to carry to the outermost ring. "The maiden Arrhyna shall wed the warrior Rannach with the blessing of this Council. Let none argue this, nor speak against it."

Chakthi did not speak against the decision—could not—but instead sprang upright with a furious snort and stalked from the circle, Hadduth trailing his heels. Vachyr hesitated a moment, glaring first at Arrhyna then at Rannach before following his father.

Into Racharran's ear Morrhyn said, "Chakthi cannot argue this."

"No?" answered Racharran.

Morrhyn said, still soft, "To argue this is to go against the Council. He would be cast out; no less Vachyr."

Racharran grunted, then looked to his son, who came past the fire with his bride-to-be. Rannach's smile was wide and proud; Arrhyna stood modestly beside him.

Racharran climbed to his feet and took the girl's hands. "I welcome you to the Commacht, daughter." He glanced at Rannach. "Perhaps you'll tame this stallion."

Arrhyna smiled shyly. "Thank you, my akaman. I am honored to live amongst your lodges."

Rannach said, "Thank you, father. For a while there I feared you might take Vachyr's side."

"For a while," Racharran said quietly, "I thought I might. For the good of the clan."

The shock he saw on Rannach's face was gratifying, but then he shrugged and smiled more warmly. "But how could I, after Chakthi's insult? Vachyr the better man? Ach, no! Only—" he placed a hand on both their shoulders—"tread wary about those two, as you would about a wounded buffalo."

Rannach nodded gravely. "I'd see Arrhyna in our lodges this night," he said. "And ask you offer her parents our hospitality."

Perhaps, Racharran thought, there's yet hope for him. Perhaps marriage *will* gentle him. Aloud, he said, "That's wise. Yes: I'll speak with them now."

"Thank you," Arrhyna said. "The akaman of the Tachyn bears them little love for this, I think."

"Chakthi," Rannach declared, grinning, "bears little love for anyone. Save Vachyr."

"Go." Racharran dismissed them with a wave. "Take your cohorts with you. And remember your promise!"

"As my akaman commands."

Rannach spread his blanket to encompass Arrhyna and jerked his head. On the instant, Bakaan and the others came hurrying up to form an honor guard. Racharran went to where Nemeth and Zeil stood. They looked to him like buffalo separated from their herd, and frightened.

"Your daughter sleeps under my protection this night," he said, "and soon shall wed my son. Would you name yourselves Commacht, then you are welcome in my clan."

Nemeth looked at Zeil, who nodded and smiled nervously. "My thanks," he said. "We've angered Chakthi with this, and . . ." He shrugged helplessly.

"Chakthi is not a man to forgive a perceived slight," Racharran finished. "Do you bring your tent across the water now, and tomorrow we'll cut your horses from the Tachyn herd."

"And does Chakthi object, my Lakanti shall be there." Yazte came up to join them, clapping Racharran cheerfully on the shoulder. "In the name of the Maker, my friend, that was a thing worth the seeing. Chakthi had the look of an old bear driven from his wintering cave. His discomfort was a thing to relish."

"Old bears are grumpy," Racharran said. "And often dangerous."

"True." Yazte's smile faded. "But should this particular bear show his claws, you've but to ask my help."

Racharran nodded. "I'll see them wed soon as possible," he murmured. "Perhaps the ceremony will cool Vachyr's ardor and he look elsewhere for a bride."

"Perhaps." Yazte snorted. "But Chakthi's pride? That shall not be cooled, I think."

"Ach, pride!" Racharran chopped a dismissive hand. "Such pride is a curse."

"But what should we be without our pride?" Yazte asked. "You'd not take the Tachyn's insult. Was that not pride?"

"It was." Racharran smiled, somewhat ashamed. "I rose to that."

"As would any warrior," Yazte said. "Chakthi stepped beyond the pale with that. I've not your calm. Had he said that to me . . ."

Racharran nodded, wearying of the conversation. He felt a need to forget the bellicose Tachyn for a while. "I've tiswin in my lodge," he said, "do you care to celebrate this decision."

"I do," Yazte declared eagerly. "Lead on, my friend."

"A moment." Racharran motioned that Yazte wait, and went to where Juh sat, deep in conversation with the Aparhaso wakanisha, Hazhe. He waited politely until they looked up, then extended his invitation.

"Thank you," murmured Juh, "but these old bones of mine crave rest, and the days when I could sit with you youngsters drinking the night away are long gone. The wedding, though, I shall attend."

Racharran ducked his head, accepting the subtle dismissal. He turned toward young Tahdase, but the Naiche akaman was already quitting the circle, surrounded by a protective band of warriors.

He returned to where Yazte waited. "We drink alone," he said.

Yazte chuckled. "Then the more for us."

Racharran smiled and looked about for Morrhyn. The wakanisha was deep in conversation with Kahteney of the Lakanti and Isten of the Naiche, and when Racharran caught his eye and motioned the lifting of a cup, he shook his head. Racharran shrugged—so it would be him and Yazte, and therefore, no doubt, further discussion of Chakthi and his famous temper. He went from the circle with the Lakanti, hoping Yazte did not drink him dry.

"I've known the same dream," Kahteney said. "I fear it bodes ill for the Commacht. I believe it means war with the Tachyn."

"That may well come," Morrhyn allowed, "but I cannot believe the dream refers to that. I fear it is something larger."

He looked to Isten, hoping—or fearing—for confirmation, but the Naiche Dreamer only shook his head and said, "This is a thing for the Dream Council, not"—he glanced around as if fearful of eavesdroppers—"so public a place."

Morrhyn frowned. Isten and his akaman shared the same cautious nature; or the one fed the other: it was hard to decide. They both prompted him to think of nervous deer, waiting, testing the wind, before venturing forth. Surely neither would come readily or swiftly to any decision; and he felt in his bones that swift decisions would be needed ere long. But, by custom, he must allow Isten was right: was the dream forewarning of events momentous as he feared, then it was a thing for the Dream Council, for all the wakanishas. And after, when interpretation was agreed, for the full Council. He wondered if, after that night's events, concord could any longer be reached. He lowered his head in silent acceptance.

"Best then we sit in council soon," Kahteney declared tersely, favoring the Naiche wakanisha with an irritated glance.

"Yes." Morrhyn nodded, wishing it might be now. It seemed that since arriving at the Meeting Ground his trepidation grew apace, as if this gathering of the clans somehow accelerated his concern.

"But best Rannach and Arrhyna are wed first," said cautious Isten. "Let that particular thorn be blunted before we seek Hadduth's aid."

Morrhyn doubted the marriage ceremony would do much to blunt any of the Tachyns' feelings, but it would, he supposed, finally resolve the minor problem. "My brother Isten speaks wisely," he declared diplomatically. "But once that is done?"

"We hold Dream Council," said Kahteney, and smacked his lips, grinning. "Now, Morrhyn, did Racharran not invite my akaman to drink tiswin? And do you not think we wakanishas should attend them?"

Morrhyn hesitated. He would sooner speak of the dream or be alone to contemplate its meaning. Save, he thought, Isten will not lend us his advice; and Kahteney believes it means war; so . . . He ducked his head and said, "I suppose so. Isten, do you join us?"

"I think not." The Naiche smiled apology. "Likely Tahdase would have my counsel."

He nodded his farewell and left them. Kahteney watched his retreating back and said, "A careful one, that. Like his akaman."

"Caution," said Morrhyn, "is no bad thing."

"Save it become vacillation," said Kahteney. "And those two are like skittish colts. They prance and run directionless when the stallions stamp their hooves."

Morrhyn refused to be drawn into criticism. Instead, he pointed in the direction of the Commacht lodges. "Do we join our akamans before they finish all the tiswin?"

Kahteney needed no further urging: together the wakanishas strode from the circle.

Their path took them through the Tachyn camp, and there folk watched them pass in silence. It was impossible to know their feelings. Morrhyn saw light in Chakthi's lodge and the outlines of three men cast shadowy against the hide. Chakthi and Vachyr spoke with Hadduth, he surmised; he wondered of what. Kahteney appeared oblivious, or careless, but the Commacht was relieved when they forded the stream and came amongst the lodges of his own clan.

From where the tents of the unmarried men were pitched there came a great clamor, laughter and shouts and dancing. They celebrated Rannach's triumph with tiswin: Morrhyn hoped they would not drink so much as to carry their merrymaking across the stream. He wished he could share their carefree joy.

Racharran and Yazte sat outside the Commacht akaman's lodge, a pitcher passing from hand to hand. They laughed and jested, but more soberly than the young men, as befitted mature warriors. Space was made for the two wakanishas, and Morrhyn accepted a cup that Racharran filled. Lhyn, he saw, was not present, and assumed she saw to the settling of Arrhyna and her parents, whose lodge the girl would continue to share until the ceremony was concluded—the usual safeguard against a groom rendered overly amorous by tiswin.

"Nemeth and Zeil are settled?" he asked.

Racharran nodded, his face a moment dark.

Yazte chuckled and said, "Chakthi watched their going like some bile-ridden buffalo, then announced them banished from the Tachyn. Ach, it was a sight to savor, his black face."

Morrhyn essayed a smile, not wishing to offend.

"We spoke of the Grannach," Racharran said.

Yazte said, "Of their absence."

Morrhyn felt a fresh prickling of doubt. The Stone Folk attended the Matakwa each year, coming down from their high caves and secret tunnels to trade their metalwork with the People—had since first the clans came to Ket-Ta-Witko—but the Meeting Ground had been filled for three days now and usually the Grannach would have appeared on the first. That they had not seemed to the wakanisha a further confirmation that all was not well. Lacking any explanation of their absence, he only shrugged.

"When shall you hold Dream Council?" Racharran asked.

"Once Rannach and Arrhyna are wed," Morrhyn replied. "When shall that be?"

"I'd see her parents' horses safe," Racharran said, "and then announce the wedding. The horses tomorrow, the wedding the next day?"

"Yes." Morrhyn stifled a sigh and took the pitcher, filling his cup. Perhaps tiswin would still his fear a little. "You'll feast them?"

"Modestly," Racharran said. "I'd not see my son's pride too swollen, nor seem to flaunt the thing in Chakthi's face."

"That's wise," the wakanisha said. "And perhaps the Grannach shall be here by then."

"I'd throw a great feast," Yazte declared, laughing, "and make a point of inviting Chakthi and Vachyr." He paused, still laughing. "Or perhaps a point of *not* inviting them."

Morrhyn thought the akaman had taken his fair share and more of the tiswin. Racharran said, "I shall invite Chakthi and Hadduth—it should be insult otherwise."

Yazte snorted, but Kahteney nodded approvingly. Morrhyn said, "Might you not ask Juh to arrange it? Will Chakthi listen to anyone, it must be him. And does Chakthi accept, then it must surely be a step toward settling these differences."

"That should be a wise move, I think—if it works," Racharran said soberly.

"I am outvoted, then," said Yazte, reaching for the pitcher. "But I tell you, that sour face will spoil my appetite."

Racharran reached out to grasp the Lakanti's wrist. "Does he accept, my friend, then I ask that you bear that spoiling. I charge you to curb your tongue and not give him cause for further offence."

"Me?" Yazte's eyes rounded and he slapped a hand to his chest in mockery of innocence. "Offend Chakthi, me?"

"Yes," Racharran said. "Have I your word?"

Yazte's lips pursed as if he contemplated the matter, then he shrugged. "It shall be hard, but yes. I'd not see your son's wedding feast spoiled. Though . . ." His smile grew broader. "I think Chakthi's presence shall not improve it much."

Racharran said, "Perhaps not; but peace between us shall."

The morning of the wedding dawned fine. The sun lit the pinnacle of the Maker's Mountain as if in blessing, and when Morrhyn emerged from his lodge he perceived no ill omens—save, perhaps, that he had again dreamed of the fire-footed horse and its blank-eyed rider. Nor was he comforted by the continued absence of the Grannach, and as he bathed he cast his eyes toward the mountains, hoping all the time to see the Stone Folk coming.

He was disappointed, and struggled to shake off pessimism as he returned to his tent to dress in his finest buckskins, readying for the ceremony.

Such affairs were conducted simply by the People, though the Commacht lodges and, to a lesser extent, those of all their neighbors, were abustle as the time approached. Usually, Rannach's chosen man would have gone amongst the Tachyn to summon forth the bride and present her suitor, then lead them back to the groom's clan, but now that Nemeth and Zeil were taken into the Commacht, Bakaan went to their tent and called that they come out.

Rannach stood behind him. His hair was woven in the warrior's braids and his wedding clothes shone with beadwork bright as his eyes. Three times Bakaan called, and at the third cry Nemeth and Zeil threw back the flap and led their daughter out. Arrhyna wore pale deerskin, bracelets of Grannach work glinting on her wrists, little combs of the Stone Folk's precious silver glittering in her fiery hair. Bakaan took her hand and brought her to where Rannach stood, then motioned that they follow him to the cleared center of the Commacht encampment.

Morrhyn waited there, with Racharran and Lhyn, and as the procession drew near he was reminded of their wedding. Gahyth had presided then, and he had stood behind the aging Dreamer, fighting to curb his envy that his closest friend won the woman he loved. He had thought such memories long buried, but as Rannach and Arrhyna approached, he felt them rise anew, and must fight down the same sense of loss. He hid behind a wakanisha's gravity as he motioned the pair kneel and raised the sacred rattle over their heads.

The crowd fell silent as he intoned the ritual and the couple gave back their responses. He touched them both with the rattle, asking that the Maker regard them with favor, and it was done. Racharran led out a piebald mare, her coat brushed to gleaming smoothness, and saw Arrhyna mounted; Lhyn brought her son's favorite horse. Then Morrhyn gestured that they follow him, the parents falling into step behind the bridal pair as the wakanisha led them amongst the Commacht lodges and then on in a wide circuit of the Meeting Ground, through all the encampments.

As they passed, he proclaimed the traditional words: "Let the People see these two are wed. Let the People ask the Maker bless them." But as they went by the Tachyn lodges he was unpleasantly aware of the muted response—even more of Hadduth's unsmiling visage, the wakanisha's lips moving silently in what might have been either agreement or curse. Few there came out to follow the procession, and of Chakthi or Vachyr there was no sign. It was a relief, like sunlight breaking through storm clouds, to go amongst the Lakanti, and after them the Aparhaso and the Naiche, where folk shouted joyously and came trotting behind calling greetings and good wishes, laughing as they showered the bridal pair with dried petals and sweet-scented herbs.

Bakaan and those other warriors closest to Rannach had erected a lodge for the pair, set apart from the others on the edge of the Commacht camp, close by the Maker's Mountain, that their first nights together be spent close under the watch of the Maker and they have privacy. There they would remain until the Matakwa was ended and they pitched their lodge with the other married folk. Looking at their smiling faces, Morrhyn thought they had sooner go there immediately, but first they must partake of the feast.

That was ready on their return, the guests trailing them in a great laughing crowd: a marriage made at Matakwa was considered most lucky. And perhaps it is, Morrhyn thought as he watched the informal celebration commence. But like a blade, luck has two sides, and he wondered should that luck be good or bad.

He found a place at Racharran's side, where the most favored guests sat. Lhyn was on her husband's left, next to Nemeth and Zeil, with Rannach and their daughter; Juh and Yazte and Tahdase were there, each sided by their wakanishas and their wives. Kahteney favored Mor-

rhyn with a smile the Commacht Dreamer returned even as he wondered, Where is Chakthi? Where is Hadduth? Do they intend to insult
the Commacht with their absence?

He grunted his relief as the two Tachyn appeared, for all they
seemed in no wise happy to be there. Chakthi offered only the curtest of
formal greeting to his hosts, and even terser to the bridal couple; Nemeth and Zeil he ignored.

Racharran climbed to his feet—smiling, Morrhyn thought, less in
genuine welcome than relief similar to his own. "I bid you welcome,
brother." Racharran gestured that Chakthi and Hadduth take their
places. "And you, wakanisha. You favor us with your presence."

Chakthi ducked his head as if receiving no more than his rightful
due; Hadduth's thin lips stretched in parody of a smile. They sat in
silence, accepting the tiswin Racharran himself poured.

"This is an auspicious day," he said, raising his cup in toast. "My
son weds a Tachyn maiden, and at Matakwa. Do we put by those things
that have stood between us and celebrate this wedding in friendship?
Do we drink to future amity?"

It was an unfeigned offering of peace. Juh beamed and nodded his
silvered head in commendation; Tahdase murmured encouragingly.
Even Yazte hid his dislike and showed the Tachyn his teeth in approxi-
mation of friendship.

Chakthi stared awhile at Racharran, then slowly raised his own cup.
"To the future," he said.

"A toast." Juh's voice filled a moment of awkward silence. "I drink
to Rannach and Arrhyna. May their joining join their clans."

Again Chakthi's cup was raised an instant slower than the others,
but still he drank. And still, Morrhyn thought, it is like inviting a vicious
dog to share the feast, all the time wondering if he'll eat or turn on the
guests.

Tahdase intoned a toast: "To Rannach and Arrhyna. May their union
bless this Matakwa."

Chakthi drank again, but again a moment late, as if he used the
tiswin to wash away the words.

Now Yazte spoke. "I drink to Rannach and Arrhyna. And to peace
at this Matakwa."

Morrhyn sighed gratefully as he raised his cup. Likely Kahteney had
reinforced Racharran's admonishment that the Lakanti not offend
Chakthi. But then Yazte spoke again: "And your toast, brother?"

His round face beamed amiably at the Tachyn akaman, and surely
there was no overt hostility in his question save, Morrhyn thought, it is a
kind of challenge.

Chakthi smiled then and raised his cup. "I drink," he said, "to Rannach and Arrhyna. May they receive all they deserve."

It was no clear indication, but neither was it possible to find offense in the words. They were ambiguous, perhaps, but not insulting. Those present drank, and for the first time Chakthi's smile seemed genuine.

3  Ill Omens

The feast lasted long into the night, thankfully without incident for all Chakthi and Hadduth seemed less to celebrate than brood. They spoke little, and then only when addressed directly, and their smiles seemed to Morrhyn furtive and empty of humor, save they shared some private jest. As soon was meet, Rannach and his bride made their excuses and departed for their lodge and, once they were gone, Chakthi and Hadduth offered unsmiling farewells and quit the Commacht camp. None were sorry to see them go, and the feast grew more lively for their absence: tiswin flowed in renewed abundance and, as if the cloud were blown away to reveal the sun, the camp rang loud with laughter and bawdy songs.

Morrhyn drank his fill, but not so much that his senses were fuddled, and he saw that all those of the inner circle—save Yazte, who sat cheerfully swaying, his attention alternating between a cup of tiswin and a rib of buffalo—shared his caution. He listened alertly as Juh beckoned Racharran closer.

"This was well done," the old akaman declared. "That Chakthi attended is a good sign, I think."

Racharran hesitated before replying, and from his expression, Morrhyn saw that he did not share Juh's optimism. "I hope it be so," he murmured. "I had hoped to dissuade Rannach from this courtship, but . . ." He shrugged eloquently. "You know my son."

"Indeed." Juh smiled. "A warrior proud as his father. And as determined."

"Headstrong," Racharran said. "He sets his own desires before the good of the clan."

"Perhaps," Juh allowed mildly. "But marriage between the clans is not forbidden, nor necessarily a bad thing—are your hopes realized, then this wedding may bind the Commacht and the Tachyn closer. And even I am not yet so old I forget what it is to love." He reached out to touch his wife's hand, at which Guyan, whose hair was silver as her husband's, beamed and nodded.

"Yes." Racharran sipped tiswin, his expression thoughtful. "But still Chakthi loves Vachyr fierce as a bear sow her only cub; and I think Vachyr is sorely disappointed."

"Young men often are," said Juh. "But they get over it. Vachyr will turn his attention elsewhere—he's no choice now."

"I hope it is so," Racharran said; but Morrhyn guessed that he, too, thought on Chakthi's dark face and equivocal toasts.

"Ach, is this a wedding feast or a mourning?" Yazte interjected. "The girl made her choice and Rannach has his bride. Let Vachyr and his miserable father whine all they want, they can do nothing."

"Not in Matakwa." Racharran nodded, unsmiling. "But after? Our grazing shares a border, and that's ever easy cause for disagreement."

Yazte snorted laughter. "Does Chakthi come raiding, send for me. I'll bring my Lakanti against him and between us we'll crush him."

"Best not speak of war here." Tahdase made a gesture of warding, his youthful face worried. "That's to bring ill luck down on all."

"True." Juh nodded gravely. "The Matakwa is for peace, not talk of war. Nor is this a war council, but a wedding feast. So . . ." He lifted his cup. "I drink to friendship."

They drank, but as he raised his own cup, Morrhyn glanced to where the moon struck silvery against the flanks of the Maker's Mountain and saw an owl drift silent across the face of the disc. Symbol of wisdom and death, both: he wondered which this bird presaged, and felt a sudden chill. There was too much strange at this Matakwa—the dream, the ill feeling, the absence of the Grannach. All felt to him the disparate pieces of some momentous puzzle that he could not yet comprehend.

Abruptly, he said, "I'd sit in Dream Council tomorrow or the next day."

Across the fire Kahteney ducked his head and said, "I too. As soon we may."

"The next day, if you will." Hazhe, whose years were not much fewer than his akaman's, smiled and gestured with his cup. "I shall need a while to recover."

"And Hadduth must be informed," said cautious Isten.

Morrhyn said, "The next day, then, but no later, eh? There are matters we need discuss."

It was agreed and set aside: this feast was not the place for such debate as Morrhyn sought. But still he could not help finding Kahteney's ear to ask if the Lakanti had seen the owl.

"I did," he answered, "I believe it was a sign that Racharran was wise to seek peace with Chakthi."

Or, Morrhyn thought even as he shrugged and ducked his head, that death shall soon visit us.

That night—what little was left when the guests finally departed—he elected to pass in his sweat lodge. Less, were he honest, in search of enlightenment than from the desire to sweat out the tiswin, that his head be entirely clear for the talks to come.

Even so, he dreamed: of a heron that fought uselessly with harrying crows that fell like black thunderbolts from a stormy sky where fires seemed to burn behind the louring clouds. An owl spun circles above the combatants, its white wings painted red as blood, and when the heron was driven down, the owl swooped after, driving off the crows; but still the heron fell and lay broken-winged upon the ground. The owl flew off, toward the snow-white pinnacle of the Maker's Mountain, where the sky became all red, as if the heavens bled. There was thunder then, like an uncountable herd of horses running wild across the grass, and a shouting.

Morrhyn woke. Wind beat a tattoo on the hide of the lodge and the fire was burned down to glowing coals, the stones dulled and vaporless. His head throbbed somewhat, but nonetheless felt cleared of the tiswin's effects. He found the water bucket and drank deep, then realized the shouting continued: swiftly, he drew on his buckskins and unlaced the lodge flap.

Racharran stood outside, his braids whipped by the wind, his blanket drawn tight across his chest. His chin was lowered against the draft, and when he raised his head Morrhyn saw trouble in his eyes.

"The Grannach are come." The akaman spoke without preamble, the absence of greetings a further mark of his concern.

Morrhyn reached back to fetch out his bearskin. "Where are they?"

"Lhyn feeds Colun; the rest are settled about the camp."

This was not untoward: usually the Stone Folk would come first to the Commacht lodges. Their leader, Colun, was long a friend of Racharran, and it was to the akaman's tent he customarily paid his first visit. Now, however, Morrhyn sensed all was not well. "What's amiss?" he asked.

"I've but a little piece of it." Racharran shook his head as if that little piece were more than he could properly comprehend, and not at all to his liking. "I'd have you hear the entirety with me, then we must take it to the rest."

Morrhyn nodded, pausing a moment to glance in the direction of the Maker's Mountain. The sun was not yet fully over the horizon and the sky pierced by the peak was tinged with pink. It brought back the images of the dream and the wakanisha shivered inside his fur. The wind was chill—not unusual in the Moon of New Grass—but he knew the cold he felt came from another source. He fell into step beside Racharran, matching the akaman's long stride, neither man speaking.

The lodge was warm, Lhyn piling wood on the central fire so that tongues of flame rose crackling toward the smoke hole. There was the savory smell of pan bread and hot tea, the spitting of roasting meat. Morrhyn shed his bearskin as Racharran closed the tent flap and laced it tight. Then he frowned as he saw Colun.

The Grannach chief was small, like all his people: standing, his head would reach no higher than Morrhyn's chest. His hair was gray but no indication of his age, for the Stone Folk all resembled the rock they tunneled, as if they were carved from the same material. But Morrhyn had never seen a rock look so miserable.

"Greetings, Morrhyn." Colun spoke from where he sat, like a stumpy child ensconced in furs. His teeth flashed briefly from the density of his beard. "You are hale?"

"I am." Morrhyn stared at the little man with a mixture of sympathy and frank curiosity. It was a reflex to add: "And greetings to you. What has happened?" There was no need to inquire after Colun's health: it was written in his wounds.

Lhyn had already wound a bandage about his craggy head, and now knelt to bathe the long cut scoring his cheek. His right hand wore a filthy wrapping, and Morrhyn saw a red-stained gash in the thigh of his leather breeches. His belt lay close to hand, as if he'd not be parted from the weapons sheathed there: a wide-bladed sword and a curve-headed ax. He winced as Lhyn sluiced off dried blood and set a potion of curative herbs down the length of the cut.

"A long story," Colun said, "and one that troubles me to tell it. A cup of tiswin would lubricate the tale."

Racharran brought out a pitcher. Morrhyn was vaguely surprised that any of the spirit was left. He shook his head in refusal of the cup Racharran offered and waited impatiently as Colun drank.

"That's good." The Grannach smacked his lips and raised his brows in anticipation of more.

The Stone Folk, Morrhyn thought as the cup was refilled, downed tiswin even faster than Yazte, but it seemed to them no more than water. His own head still ached somewhat, and he wished Colun would tell his tale without protraction. A useless wish, he knew: the Grannach spoke as they lived, at their own pace and to their own rhythms.

Racharran settled himself on the furs, placing the pitcher in Colun's short reach. Lhyn glanced at it and frowned, but made no comment as she dressed the Grannach's wounds.

"There was a battle." Colun extended his bandaged hand in evidence. Lhyn took it and began to unwind the dirty cloth. She made a disapproving sound at the sight of the damage, and Colun said, as if apologizing to her, "I deemed it best we come immediately to the Meeting Ground with the news. These are only scratches."

"Who fought?" Morrhyn knew that sometimes the Grannach contested amongst themselves for ownership of the tunnels, the lodes of metal they worked, but such internecine struggles were not of such import that Colun would hurry wounded to the Meeting Ground.

"All the tribes." Colun grimaced as hot water was splashed across his hand. "In the western passes."

"Against the Whaztaye?" Morrhyn frowned in disbelief: he had it from Colun himself that the People Beyond the Hills were peaceful, friends to the Grannach as were his own Matawaye.

"No." Colun shook his head, his face become as mournful as anything so stonelike could look. "I think there are no Whaztaye any longer. I think they are all slain—or worse."

Morrhyn heard Racharran's sharp intake of breath; even calm Lhyn paused in her ministrations. He stared in perturbed wonder at the rugged little manling.

The People knew of the Whaztaye, for all they had no contact with any who dwelt beyond the mountainous boundaries of Ket-Ta-Witko. The Maker had set down all humankind in their appointed places when the world was made, and to venture beyond those limits was to go against the Will, the Ahsa-tye-Patiko that holds all things in their rightful place. Nor was there reason: Ket-Ta-Witko was spacious and bountiful, and fed all the People's needs. Thus it had been since first the sun rose over the world; the Maker had given the Matawaye their place, and the Whaztaye theirs, and ringed both lands with such peaks as defeated trespass. Only the Grannach moved through those rocky barriers, and only through those—never out of sight of their home-hills. What news passed between the peoples of the world, they carried along their secret ways, and denied passage to all others. Sometimes they were named the Stone Guardians, for they were fierce in defense of the Maker's boundaries.

Morrhyn heard himself ask, "How? Do the Whaztaye defy the Will?"

Colun refilled his cup before he spoke again. "Not the Whaztaye. Some other folk."

He drank, impervious to his listeners' impatience as the rock he resembled. Morrhyn stifled a sigh, knowing he must wait on Colun. That the Grannach had come hasty with this news did not mean he would tell it swift.

"We saw them—the Whaztaye—first in what you name the Moon of Cherries Ripening." Colun glanced at the clean bandage Lhyn wound about his hand and murmured, "Thank you. So, yes—it was in the Moon of Cherries Ripening that they came in numbers to the east of their land, hard against our mountains. They were refugees and they were more than the land there could feed, but still the clans gave them shelter. They were a sorry lot—the Whaztaye are not like you Matawaye, but farmers and hunters, without much skill in battle—and their sole baggage was sad stories. They sent some of their chieftains and holy men into the hills, to bring the tale to us, and I tell you, in the name of the Maker, the tale was doleful." He broke off abruptly as Lhyn touched his thigh.

"I must clean this," she said. "Take off your breeches."

Colun swallowed. "A pinprick, nothing worse." Morrhyn thought he blushed, though it was hard to tell on a face so flinty.

Lhyn said, "Made by a very large pin. Now, shall you remove these leathers, or must I ask my husband and Morrhyn hold you down and I do it?"

Colun studied her defiantly awhile and found no retreat in her gaze. Had Morrhyn time for laughter, he would have chuckled at the Grannach's expression.

"Well?" Lhyn asked.

"In the Maker's name!" Colun fumbled, awkward with his bandaged hand, at his belt buckle, grumbling all the while. "I had not thought the women of the Matawaye so forward. Were you my wife . . ."

"You'd likely obey swifter," Lhyn said, and knelt to remove the Grannach's boots. "Ach, think you you're the first man I've seen without his breeches? Or the first I've tended? Now . . ."

She frowned as the wound was exposed. It seemed a lance had pierced Colun's thigh. The cut was deep and lipped with swollen purple flesh, crusted with old blood. Lhyn muttered something too low for the men to hear and filled a bowl with steaming water into which she sprinkled herbs. "This," she murmured, "will likely hurt somewhat."

"In which case . . ." Colun downed a cup of tiswin and readied another. Then, as if to hide his embarrassment: "Where was I?"

"The Whaztaye sent a delegation," Racharran prompted.

Morrhyn saw the akaman shared his own impatience—and the same resignation.

"Yes. Ach!" Colun stiffened as Lhyn began to wash the ugly wound. "So, they sent a delegation of their chiefs and holy men to the hills. Like you, they've a gate-place where the Maker brought them to their land, and where, like you, they meet with us. This, however, was not the time, and they said they waited there full half a passing of the moon before my people noticed them. They were very hungry when we came, but even more intent on telling their tale than eating. Which reminds me of my own hunger."

His bushy brows rose in question, like two caterpillars arching their hairy backs on a stone.

Lhyn said, "Soon. Let me first finish this, and then I'll see your belly filled."

Colun mumbled something that sounded like "Women!" then promptly smiled an apology as Lhyn glanced up, saying, "Forgive me, but your culinary skills are legend, and the scent of that meat whets my appetite so keen."

Lhyn snorted and set to plastering the wound with salve. The Grannach looked disappointed, and then, almost reluctantly, resumed his tale.

"Yes, they told their story, which was most disturbing. . . . They spoke of their people—those who lived—fleeing in great numbers out of the west, driven in panic and disarray before a dreadful army. All their land, they said, was riven by this horde, which none of their seers or holy men had foretold. They spoke of awful slaughter and asked our help. They asked that we should take their defenseless ones into our tunnels and send our warriors to join in battle against the horde." He paused, frowning as if even now he marveled at the request. "In all our history, none have asked this of us; it was a thing that seemed defiance of the Will. It was a thing we debated amongst ourselves."

He shook his head, his frown deepening. Morrhyn wondered how long that debate had lasted, how many of the Whaztaye had died meanwhile.

"Finally, it was decided that we could not accede to all they asked." Colun sighed noisily. "The Maker set us down where we belong and charged we Grannach with the securing of the hills. Besides, we had not enough food to satisfy them all, nor are you folk who live under the sky happy in our caves and tunnels, and we could not know how long this war might last."

Morrhyn wondered if the shadow that flitted across the craggy features then was doubt at the charity of that decision. Even so, he thought, Colun does no more than speak the Will correctly. "It was not a decision we reached easily." Colun drank tiswin, as if to cleanse the memory. "But it *was* reached, and by all my people. We told them *nay,* and that we would instead send our strongest warriors out into the foothills and fight this stranger horde did it come there."

"Lift your leg," commanded Lhyn, "so I can bandage it."

Morrhyn marveled that she could remain so practical as Colun unwound his tale. His own attention was focused entirely on the Grannach's words. He should likely have let Colun bleed to death telling this story.

Colun raised his leg and then, with obvious relief, tugged up his breeches. "Ach, I do grow somewhat faint. Perhaps I might eat now, that I not lose my strength?"

Lhyn turned to the cookfire, filling a platter with bread and meat that she passed to the beaming Grannach. When she raised the kettle, he shook his head and patted the pitcher of tiswin. Morrhyn and Racharran each took a platter, absently transferring food to their mouths as they waited on Colun.

He emptied his dish and asked for more before resuming. "Where was I? Yes, we made our decision known—which saddened the Whaztaye—and sent our strongest down with them to the foothills. Ach, but they were truly a sorry lot we found there. It seemed as if all the folk were gathered like animals driven from their grazing by a fire, come up into the hills in hope the flames not reach so far.

"But they did . . . The Maker knows, they did! We spoke with them there, to learn what manner of foe we faced, and what we heard was strange."

His second platter cleaned, he set it aside and drank tiswin. Then: "They spoke of such creatures as I'd not ever heard of; of terrible warriors whose only love seemed slaughter, who rode aback strangeling beasts of no better humor than their masters. They came, the Whaztaye told us, out of the western hills, out of the Maker's gate.''

"That cannot be!" Racharran's patience dissolved at this announcement. "The gates are closed by the Maker's own hand. What you describe surely could not be."

He looked to Morrhyn for support, and in his eyes the wakanisha saw both stark rejection of Colun's statement and a measure of dread. Morrhyn was abruptly reminded of his dream—of all his recent dreams—and felt a terrible fear. Was this their inspiration? Did they portend this horde? He heard a clatter, and turned from Racharran's agitated gaze to see Lhyn retrieve a fallen dish. Her eyes were wide, darting from him to her husband to Colun. He said carefully, "Do we hear all of this tale before we declare 'yea' or 'nay,' and looked to the Grannach.

Colun shrugged. "I did not believe it at first either, but I saw the Whaztaye gathered there like frightened beasts, by the Maker! They had what sheep they'd not eaten with them, though they did not last long, and I knew some terror was abroad. Whether it came through the gate or was some thing of the Whaztaye's own making I did not at first know, but then I saw them . . .''

His skin, as much as was visible under his beard, was the color of old stone, but Morrhyn thought it paled. And when he drank this time it was as though he needed the tiswin to fortify his tongue against the telling.

"They came like a storm, like a grass fire. Swift as that, and as heedless." He paused and drained his cup, shaking his head. "By night, it was. I think they prefer the night: they fight fiercest then, as if they are creatures of darkness and abhor the sun. It was in what you name the Moon of Melting Snow: the time before your New Grass Moon rises, when snow still covers the high hills and the rivers run strong with melt. We saw them from our heights, like a black wave lit by the moon, rolling across the grass to where the Whaztaye had set their lodges. They came so swift! Nor was there halt or hesitation—they only attacked, like rabid wolves, and just as senseless. They seemed uncaring of hurt, almost—Almost, it seemed they welcomed death, as eager as they slew.

"It was a terrible slaughter. The Whaztaye are not fighters, and they fell before these . . . creatures . . . like . . . like their sheep to wolves! The children and the women, the old folk—the defenseless ones were slaughtered as thoughtless as you'd crush a bug. I confess that I wished then we had granted them leave to enter our tunnels! I'd sooner we had done that and asked the Maker forgive us after, for I wept at what I saw done there.''

He broke off, reaching for the pitcher. Morrhyn wondered, as his head lowered, if he hid a tear.

"The men died too. Some fled and were cut down; others stood their ground and died. We Grannach are of sterner stuff, however, and rallied to defy the horde. It was like . . ." He frowned, staring awhile into the flames of the cookfire as if he saw the battle refought there. "It was like defying an avalanche, like damming a flood with no more than your bare hands. Remember, we fought on our own ground, those hills as familiar to us as your plains to you—we'd that advantage. But even so we were driven back, steady as snow under the springtime sun. We retreated, so ferocious were our enemies, and had we not our caves and tunnels, I think we should have died there, like the Whaztaye.

"Ach!" He chopped air as if he held his battle-ax still. "It shames me to say it, but retreat we did. Though"—he smiled wickedly—"we left not a few of them slain. I believe we taught them not all the world's folk are such easy prey as the poor Whaztaye."

"What are they?" Racharran's voice was soft, his expression troubled. "What cause do they follow?"

"I did not," Colun said somewhat tartly, "engage them in conversation. What they are, where they came from, why they engage in such slaughter—these are things I do not understand. I know only that they are savage beyond belief, and now command all the land of the Whaztaye. For all I know, they hold the lands beyond too."

He shrugged and drained his cup, his face abruptly a mask of disappointment when he found the pitcher empty. Unspeaking, Lhyn brought another, and he drank with relish.

"But you held them?" Racharran asked.

"In a way." Colun nodded doubtfully. "We slowed their advance somewhat in the ravines and the defiles. But only slowed it—they are careless of losses. In the Maker's name! I saw them press on across the bodies of their dead and wounded with no more thought than they gave the Whaztaye fallen. On and on they came, even when we sent rocks crashing down, avalanches that buried them by the score; and every time we thought them halted, they came again. Like ants, they were: remorseless. We had no choice but to fall back until we reached our secret places. Had we not those refuges . . ." He sighed and shook his head. "We went into the tunnels and sealed the entrances behind us. Then we licked our wounds awhile and debated what to do."

Morrhyn asked, "The seals held? These . . . invaders . . . could not breach them?"

"Not then," Colun answered. "When I left, the seals held intact. But . . ." He spread his hands wide. "Did the Whaztaye speak aright and they *did* come through the farther mountains, then they've such powers as I've not seen before; nor ever believed could be. Still, when I departed the tunnels were secure. And do these creatures gain entrance, the passage shall cost them dear. But if they suceed . . . I deemed it wise to warn you."

"And our heartfelt thanks for that," Racharran said.

Morrhyn said, "What did they look like?"

Colun shrugged again and told him, "I never saw their faces—I saw only their armor, which is not like any I have seen before. Like insects they were, all bright, shiny colors that hid their faces and their forms."

"They were not men?" asked Morrhyn.

"They have two arms, two legs," Colun said, "and they've each a head. But are they men, I cannot say. I thought them demons."

Wakanisha and akaman exchanged a look. Racharran said, "This news must be brought before the full Council."

Morrhyn nodded and said, "Yes, and must be discussed in Dream Council." He turned to the Grannach. "You'll tell all this again?"

Colun said, "Do you ask it," and favored them both with a somber stare. "I fear this threatens us all. Perhaps all the world."

"I'll send word now." Racharran stood, crossing to the lodge's entrance.

When he stepped outside, Morrhyn saw that the sun was up, the wind abated. Streamers of white cloud ran out across a sky of pure blue and all the Matakwa camp was awake, loud with cheerful laughter. He turned as Colun's gruff voice intruded on his thoughts.

"You dreamed of this?" the Grannach asked.

"Perhaps; I'm not sure." He felt that doubt dissolving even as he spoke. "I've had such dreams as deny clear interpretation."

He told the detail of his recurring dream, and when he was done Colun said, "And the other Dreamers?"

"One at least," Morrhyn advised. "Save he believes it a scrying of different trouble."

Colun gestured that he explain and Morrhyn told him of Kahteney's interpretation. "Perhaps," the Grannach murmured, "you are both right."

"How so?" asked Morrhyn. "Trouble with the Tachyn is scarce so fearful as what you've described."

"Save," Colun said grimly, "that does this horde find a way into Ket-Ta-Witko, it were better the clans fight unified, not betwixt yourselves."

Morrhyn felt a hollow place open inside him at that, and for a while could only stare aghast at the craggy little man. Then all he could find to say was "Yes."

Racharran came back on the heel of the affirmative, halting as he saw Morrhyn's face. "What is it?" he demanded. "Some new alarm?"

Morrhyn reached out to clutch his wrist. "There must be no trouble with Chakthi!" His voice was urgent. "There must be peace between the clans."

Racharran studied his friend and ducked his head in confirmation. "All well, there shall be. In light of Colun's news, I doubt even Chakthi can harbor such petty grudges."

"Even so." Morrhyn did not release his hold. "Do you impress that on Rannach? And in Council seek to bind Chakthi with solemn vows?"

"I shall," Racharran promised. "Even now messengers go out with word. I've asked that we sit in Council this night."

Morrhyn had sooner it be earlier, but it was not a thing to be decided by a single akaman' and he could only wait until the messengers returned with their answers. He loosed his hold and reached unthinking for a cup. He had raised it to his lips and drunk before he knew Colun had filled it. He did not taste the tiswin, only the heat spilling through the void inside him. Across the fire he saw Lhyn watching him, her eyes clouded.

"Rannach," he said. "I'd ask him to hold to our camp this day—to his lodge, if he will—that he not flaunt Arrhyna before Vachyr or Chakthi."

"I'll go." Lhyn spoke before her husband, motioning that Racharran remain seated. "Likely he'll take it easier from me."

Morrhyn said, "It matters little how he takes it, only that he obey."

Lhyn nodded, pale-faced, and was gone, and then the three men could only wait.

4 The Stolen Bride

Arrhyna hid giggling and naked beneath a fur as Rannach cursed and tugged on his breeches. It was not unusual that a new-wed couple find themselves the target of friends' tricks, and already her husband's had played their share. She supposed this calling of his name was another, but for all she wanted nothing more than to be alone with Rannach, she could not find it in herself to object overmuch. These Commacht were a cheerful folk, unlike her own Tachyn, whose mood reflected their akaman's. Since Chakthi's wife had died, he had become a surly, sullen man, his temper short, his judgments swift and brutal, and that dour temperament seemed to infect all the clan. There was not so much laughter amongst the Tachyn lodges. She frowned as she thought on how he had treated her parents, then smiled at the thought that they were now taken in by the Commacht. Racharran seemed a kind man, if somewhat stern, and most assuredly of far graver disposition than his son. She watched as Rannach—her husband now!—laced his breeches, admiring the way muscle corded and flexed across his broad shoulders. Did he curse, it was good-natured, and the Maker knew, he was so handsome, she so fortunate.

Her smile faded as he flung back the lodge flap, an oath dying on his lips, replaced with a mumbled apology.

"Mother, forgive me. I thought . . ."

He stepped back, inviting Lhyn to enter. Arrhyna drew the fur up to her chin, wishing there had been more warning of this visit. What would Lhyn think of her, lying abed with breakfast not even thought about yet? She bit her lip at sight of Lhyn's face, but then the older woman smiled.

"What apologies are needed are mine to offer." Lhyn ducked her head in Arrhyna's direction as Rannach settled a blanket about his shoulders. "You're settled, daughter?"

Daughter. Arrhyna liked that: it seemed a further seal laid on the happiness of her future. She nodded from behind the fur and said, "I am . . . Mother."

"My son"—this with a mock stern glance at Rannach—"treats you well?"

Arrhyna blushed and giggled and said, "He is a fine husband."

"Whose attentions I'd not deprive you of." Lhyn smiled still, but behind her friendly expression Arrhyna could detect . . . She was not sure: fear was her strongest impression. Despite the fur, she felt a sudden chill.

Rannach, too, she thought, for he said, "What brings you, Mother? Not, of course, that we are anything but happy to see you."

"Ach!" Lhyn waved a hand, dismissing his solicitous words. "A new-wed couple happy to welcome visitors? Rannach, even were you not my son I'd know better than that. Nor would I disturb you, save . . ."

Her smile disappeared entirely and Rannach frowned. "What is it?" he asked. "Some trouble with Vachyr? Chakthi?"

"Not yet." Lhyn shook her head. "Nor, the Maker willing, shall there be. Your father calls Council this night, and I've a thing to ask you."

Swiftly, she described Colun's news. Rannach's frown grew deeper; Arrhyna was abruptly aware of her nudity. She wished she were dressed: it seemed somehow more fitting that she receive such news clad.

"I shall attend the Council," Rannach declared.

"As should you," Lhyn said. "But more . . ." She spoke of Morrhyn's fears.

"My father would have me skulk in my lodge?" Rannach shook his head in angry denial. "Am I an embarrassment, then? Have I not given my word I'll not raise hand against the Tachyn whilst this Matakwa lasts? Is that not good enough for my father, for my akaman?"

"It is Morrhyn, also, who asks this," Lhyn said patiently. "And I. Nor does your father believe you would break your given word. But Chakthi, Vachyr . . . Their tempers are short, and doubtless they still chew on defeat. I ask only that you not give them cause for resentment, but hold to this lodge until the Council sits."

Rannach chewed on this awhile, then turned suspicious eyes on Lhyn. "I am not *commanded?* My father does not *bid* me remain hidden?"

"No." His mother sighed, the shaking of her head a weary movement, as if this were ancient ground they trod. "He—and Morrhyn, and I—only *ask* it of you. This news that Colun brings, it frightens me; it . . . worries . . . your father. And Morrhyn—it was he pressed hardest that you not give Vachyr or Chakthi the least cause—"

"This is my wife!" Rannach cut short her words, stabbing a finger in Arrhyna's direction. "I courted her as custom demands; she made her choice. The council denied Chakthi's objections and now we are wed, with the blessing of all this Matakwa. What *cause* might my presence give him?"

Lhyn sighed again and looked to Arrhyna, who said softly, "Chakthi needs no cause for resentment, husband. It festers in him like a poisoned wound."

"His problem," snapped Rannach, "not mine."

"Save are these creatures all Colun describes," Lhyn said slowly, "then the People surely face such problems as transcend these petty squabbles."

Rannach scowled and said, "I've no squabble with any present at this Matakwa." He smiled fondly at his wife. "I've all I want."

Arrhyna returned the smile, but fainter, her eyes drawn irresistibly back to Lhyn's face. Racharran's wife was beautiful in an older, dignified way: she hoped she might look like that when she owned as many years as Lhyn. But now she looked drawn, as if trepidation etched the passing of time deeper into her features. It was hard to take such news hid under furs, naked; harder to see the worry in Lhyn's eyes and know that differences existed between the man she loved and his father. She caught Lhyn's eye and saw a plea there: she knew she must make some contribution or accept the role of docile wife.

"Mother speaks sense," she said, ignoring the flash of anger that lit Rannach's eyes, tightened his jaw. "The Maker knows, I've spent my life amongst the Tachyn lodges, and so can tell you that neither Chakthi nor Vachyr need reason for resentment, or honest cause for squabble—they find such where they will. Do you only comply with this request . . ." The gratitude in Lhyn's gaze was pleasing.

"And hide myself away like some skulking dog"—Rannach shook his head—"for fear I offend Chakthi and his sorry son?"

"For the good of all the People," Lhyn said. And smiled, "Besides, had you other plans? The Maker knows, when I wed your father we did not emerge from our lodge for days."

Arrhyna blushed and giggled. Rannach's scowl eased somewhat. "Mother," he said, "you are shameless."

Lhyn shrugged. "It was hunger drove us out in the end . . . different hunger. Had your father only thought to lay in sufficient supplies . . ." Her smile grew warmer, encompassing her son and his bride. "But we were not wed in so propitious a place—our lodge was, from choice, isolated—and so there was no one to leave food outside."

"We've food enough."

Rannach refused to be mollified yet, but Arrhyna saw him weakening and, encouraged by Lhyn's frankness, said, "And so no reason to quit this warm lodge."

She felt her cheeks grow hot at her boldness, and was glad of Lhyn's approving smile.

Lhyn said, "It should be a mother's pleasure to feed you both."

"And therefore"—Arrhyna allowed her covering fur to slip a fraction—"we've no reason to go out. Save you grow bored, husband."

Rannach swallowed, his scowl quite lost under the flush that suffused his cheeks. Arrhyna saw Lhyn fighting laughter and let the fur slip farther.

"Ach!" Rannach cleared his throat noisily, looking from one woman to the other as if torn between amusement and embarrassment—and perhaps, also, irritation. He threw up his hands. "I am defeated. Do you ask it, Mother, then so be it. Tell my father I shall quit this tent only to do what I must, naught else. But I shall attend the Council."

"All shall attend that," Lhyn said gravely, "for it shall affect all. But my thanks; I'll advise your father of your decision."

Rannach nodded. Arrhyna said, "I've not yet prepared our breakfast," and blushed anew. "But do you give me a moment . . ."

"Stay there, daughter." Lhyn waved her back as she moved to rise. "Let me honor my promise—I'll bring you food betimes." She smiled and favored Arrhyna with a private look. "And leave it outside, eh?"

"Thank you," Arrhyna said.

Lhyn rose and was gone. Rannach laced the lodge flap tight behind her and loosed his breeches. Arrhyna threw back the sleeping furs, but when he came to her she set a hand against his chest and said, "Tell me of your father."

"My father?" Rannach's face was a mockery of outrage. Arrhyna thought it not entirely assumed. "You'd discuss my father now?"

"I'd know what stands between you," she said, fending off his hands. "He is the akaman of the Commacht, but you defy him. No Tachyn would argue Chakthi's wishes like that."

"We are not like the Tachyn," Rannach said.

"No." It was difficult to ignore his exploring hands, the touch of his lips against her skin. "But it is more than that. There is something stands between you and your father that sets you to bristling like a dog with hackles raised."

"So I am a dog now?" Rannach's voice was muffled against her breasts. "Your husband is a dog?"

"Dogs are not so strong," she said, fastening her hands in his unbound hair that she might draw his face up. "Dogs are not such great warriors, nor such mighty hunters—nor so handsome. But dogs acknowledge a leader."

"I am a man," he said.

Doggedly, she thought, and almost laughed, but stifled the sound for fear she offend him. "Tell me, husband. Please? I am come a stranger into your clan, and I'd know these things."

Rannach sighed and gave up his amorous expedition. He rolled onto his back, settling an arm beneath her shoulders. Arrhyna turned into his embrace, running fingers through his hair. Which, she thought with pride, she would braid later, and he be the most handsome warrior in all the Meeting Ground.

He said, "My father is a wise man. He is a great warrior who leads our clan as could no other. I am not like him, but he'd have me so. I lack his patience, his wisdom. I cannot be he, and so I am a disappointment to him."

Arrhyna said, "No!"

"Yes! He'd school me that I become akaman when he grows too old, but I'd not shoulder that responsibility."

"It should be a great honor," Arrhyna said. "Already Chakthi names Vachyr his successor; and I think the Tachyn shall not argue him."

"I am not Vachyr!" Rannach's voice was suddenly harsh; she tensed against him, abruptly aware of things she had not sensed before. "Nor is my father Chakthi."

His voice softened and she heard admiration in it, and love. She said, "No, I'd not compare either of you to those two. But why should you not become akaman?"

He groaned. "And carry all that burden? My father took it up when he was not much older than I, and I saw the years it set on him. I'd be no more than a warrior—free to ride and hunt where I will, not always thinking on the clan. I'd"—he chuckled into her hair—"go out to steal Tachyn horses without concerning myself with Chakthi's feelings. I'd be free, Arrhyna! I've no interest in the politics of akamans and wakanishas."

"But," she began, and was silenced by his finger against her lips.

She bit it gently as he said, "Listen. This is such decision as my father makes—when I told him I'd approach you and ask you to be my wife, he looked to dissuade me. He told me Vachyr courted you, and I should offend the Tachyn; that were I Vachyr's rival, I'd offend Chakthi, and likely he find reason to come against us. He pointed out all the Commacht maidens I might have. Their beauty, their parents' wealth . . ."

Arrhyna loosed her teeth from his finger as he chuckled and said, "Many of them were very lovely. Indeed . . . Ach!"

Her teeth fastened again, harder.

"But none compared to you," he said, his hand no longer against her lips, but tracing the contours of her body. "I told him I'd have no other. That could I not have you, then I'd live solitary and never wed. He told me I was crazed; that I risked the welfare of all the Commacht in pursuit of blind love. He did his best to dissuade me . . ."

"But," she said, "did not succeed. For which I thank the Maker."

"As do I," he said earnestly. "But my father would have it otherwise. Had he his way, then you should now be wed to Vachyr."

She shuddered: the notion was horrible. But still . . . "He has shown me only kindness," she said. "Him and your mother both."

Rannach said, "He *is* kind. That makes it harder. Think on it." His voice grew fierce and she cringed, but against him. "To know what someone wants—what they desire fierce as life itself—and tell them 'No, do otherwise.' To tell them 'So you love this woman, but forget her, quit her. Choose another, for the good of the clan.' I could not do that, but my father did."

"Surely," she said even as she thought how glad she was Rannach had ignored him, "he had to. For the good of the clan. And he supported you in the end."

"Yes." Rannach loosed a gusty breath. "But only when he saw I'd not be shifted from my course."

"He's akaman," she said.

Rannach said, "Yes," again and sighed again. "And for such reasons I'd not be. And that disappoints him."

"What," she asked, "would you have done?"

"Were I akaman?" He laughed. "I'd have given my blessing and told Chakthi to set his head under his horse's tail; and did it come to war, then so be it."

Arrhyna felt pride warm her: that he could love her so well. But even so, he seemed foolhardy. She remembered friends and said, "It shall not, eh? Not now, not after what your mother told us?"

Rannach said, "Not by my hand. Ach, my father thinks I am foolish

—he fears I'll vaunt you before Vachyr and Chakthi! He thinks me a fool, even though I gave him my word. He thinks me entirely irresponsible."

Against his shoulder she said, "Perhaps he is only careful of all the People. And knows the course Chakthi's temper takes."

"And so," Rannach said, "he sent my mother to speak with me? Not come himself?"

"Had he?" she asked, thinking she already knew the answer, that she discovered momentarily layers of this relationship she had not suspected. "What then?"

Rannach snorted humorless laughter. "Likely," he admitted, "we'd have argued. And I taken you out on that fine piebald mare, all around the Meeting Ground, both of us dressed in our finest, that all here could see my prize."

"And rub Vachyr's nose in it?" she asked. "And Chakthi's?"

"Yes!" he said, and laughed honestly. "But you see how wise my father is? He sent my mother instead, knowing she might persuade me."

Arrhyna feared his pride might get the better of his sense and moved closer against him. "I am glad," she said, "that your mother succeeded."

For a moment she thought this little battle lost, but then he relaxed and turned toward her. "As am I," he said.

Neither of them heard Lhyn's discreet cough as she left the promised food outside their lodge, and by the time they found it, it was cold and the dogs had eaten most of it.

The night was cool, the sky above the Meeting Ground a star-pocked expanse dominated by the gibbous moon that shone silvery on the pinnacle of the Maker's Mountain as Rannach quit the lodge. Arrhyna had braided his hair, fixing the plaits that marked him as a warrior with little silver brooches of Grannach manufacture that glittered bravely in the moonlight. She thought he looked magnificent as he settled his blanket about his shoulders and bade her farewell.

"You'll not attend?" he asked again.

She shook her head, smiling. "I'd not spoil so good a day with sight of Vachyr. His sullen face would surely sour it." The Maker knew, but she became diplomatic; Lhyn would be proud of her. "You can tell me what's decided when you return. Or in the morning."

Languidly, she stroked their sleeping furs. Rannach laughed. "You grow forward, wife."

She grinned. "Also, I'd tidy this lodge. I'll not have your mother think me a slattern."

"My mother," he said, "likes you."

"And I her," Arrhyna replied. "And so I'd show her how good a wife I shall be to her son."

"You are," he said.

"So, now go." She rose to touch his cheek. "The drums are calling, and I've work to do."

Rannach smiled, studying her awhile as if he would fix her forever in his memory, then nodded and ducked through the lodge flap.

Folk were already moving toward the center of the camp, where a wide-spaced ring of fires marked the inner circle where the akamans and wakanishas gathered. The more senior warriors sat between the flames, an informal barrier between the gathered mass and those who would debate Colun's news. Thus the clan leaders might talk with some degree of privacy, without undue interruption. Later they would speak with their clans, make their suggestions and hear the views of their own folk before returning to the Council, that consensus be reached. Such was the way of the People.

As Rannach approached the Commacht lodges, Bakaan stepped from the shadows. Zhy and Hadustan were with him, falling into step like a bodyguard.

"We waited for you." Bakaan sounded excited. "By the Maker, I thought you'd never quit your lodge."

Rannach grinned with all the lofty pride of a new husband. "I had good reason not to," he said, "but I'd hear what Colun's to say, and what the akamans decide."

"Arrhyna does not come?" asked Zhy.

Rannach shook his head, trusting they'd see the splendid brooches. "She was"—he glanced from one to the other—"too tired."

His friends howled laughter. Hadustan said, "And you? Do you need a shoulder to lean on?"

"I," Rannach declared solemnly, "am strong. I can still stand without your help. Just."

More laughter at that, then a sobering as they crossed the stream and skirted the edge of the Tachyn lodges. Bakaan said, "It is likely wiser she not attend. I hear that Vachyr and Chakthi spent the better part of this day skulking in Chakthi's lodge." He turned to study Rannach's face. "You've made an enemy there, my brother."

"Those two," Rannach said loftily, "are beneath my contempt."

"Even so." Bakaan's homely face grew serious. "A vicious dog is best watched, lest it creep up and bite you."

"Or slain," Zhy muttered.

"Is this why you escort me?" Rannach looked from one to the other, frowning. "Did my father ask this of you?"

They looked a moment shamefaced. Zhy shook his head; Hadustan laughed nervously. Bakaan said, "No, not Racharran."

There was something hesitant about his answer and Rannach demanded: "Who, then?"

Bakaan licked his lips and said, "It was your mother."

Rannach snorted. Hadustan said, "She'd not see her son harmed. And we know how fragile you are; so when she asked us, how could we refuse?"

"Your mother," said Zhy, "is very persuasive."

"And most careful of her son's health," said Bakaan. "Now, my own would never show such care for me. Why, did I walk in your boots, I think she'd send me into the Tachyn camp with her blessing."

Rannach swung up a hand in mock attack. Bakaan aped terror as Zhy laughed and Hadustan said, "We told her a warrior so mighty as you knows no fear, that Vachyr will likely hide behind his lodge flap at your passing. But you know what mothers are."

"And fathers," Rannach said, then shook his head resignedly and laughed. "So you *are* my bodyguard."

"Your devoted followers," said Hadustan.

"A guard of honor," said Zhy.

"That you come to the Council as a new groom should," said Bakaan, and flipped a finger against a brooch hard enough that Rannach winced. "Looking splendid."

Rannach said, "Gifts from Arrhyna's parents," and let his irritation fade away.

They came to the camp's center and eased through the outer throng to the fire circle. The talking was begun, Colun standing as he told his story, his people in a group amongst the senior warriors. Rannach saw his father seated beside Morrhyn, Yazte and Kahteney on one side of them, Tahdase and Isten on the other; then Juh and Hazhe, Chakthi and Hadduth. There was silence as the Grannach spoke, and for a while after he was done, still silence. It was as though his words imposed a weight on the night the Council found hard to bear.

Then Juh spoke. "This is alarming news," he said. Rannach wondered if the ancient face wrinkled in concern or doubt.

"It is a matter hard of believing," said Tahdase. "That a horde breaches the Maker's wards?" He turned swiftly as Colun grunted. "It is not that I name our Grannach friend a liar, but this is unprecedented."

Chakthi said, "I find it hard to believe."

Rannach looked past the Tachyn akaman, thinking to see Vachyr standing close to his father. There was no sign of Chakthi's son, and he wondered if Vachyr hid himself in shame. Then all his attention was focused on the Council as his own father spoke.

"It is surely," Racharran said, "hard to believe. But that does not mean it is not true. I have no doubt but that Colun speaks the truth."

"Nor I," said Yazte. "And so it seems to me that our decision must be what we do about it."

"How so?" Chakthi's tone was a challenge. "Is it true, then some horde has come into the land of the People Beyond the Mountains. What concern is that of ours? We've no dealings with the Whaztaye. They are not our brothers—what is their fate to us?"

"Did they enter the Whaztaye country through the gate," Racharran said, "then they might well come down through our own mountains. And then it must surely be of great concern to us."

"We should prepare for war," said Yazte.

Rannach felt a thrill: was Colun's description of these strangeling invaders told true, then they should surely be far finer enemies than even the Tachyn. He felt his blood run swifter along his veins: there would be glory to be won in such fighting.

"I think," he heard Juh say, "that it is early to speak of war. The Maker set us Matawaye down here in Ket-Ta-Witko because this is our land: the place we belong. The Maker ringed the land with the holy mountains that we not be threatened, neither threaten those other folk who live in the places beyond. I wonder if we do not question the Maker's wisdom when we assume the gates may be breached."

He turned to Hazhe for confirmation; the Aparhaso wakanisha nodded his agreement.

Tahdase said, "Juh speaks wisely. Surely the Maker will protect us, and not allow this horde passage through the hills."

"They slew the Whaztaye!" Colun said, rising to his feet. "In the Maker's name, I tell you I saw them!" He raised his bandaged hand; slapped it against his thigh. "I got these wounds off them! They are not like any folk I have seen—they fight like demons, and they came over the lands of the Whaztaye like fire across the plains."

"But, like fire, were halted," said Tahdase. "Against the mountains."

"For now." Colun ducked his head, returning to the ground. "For now."

Yazte asked, "You think they'll come through?"

"That should be a hard-fought passage," Colun declared. "Do they attempt our ways, we Grannach shall fight them down all the tunnels; down all the caverns. But we are not so many, and they are like a locust swarm. Do they attain the high passes . . ."

"Surely none can," said Juh. An arm still corded for all it was thinned by age thrust up to indicate the encircling hills. "Men cannot breathe up there. Thus the Maker decreed."

"Men cannot," said Colun, "but I am not sure these creatures are men like you and me."

"You slew them, no?" Chakthi asked; and when Colun nodded: "Then surely they are men."

Colun made a helpless gesture and said, "Perhaps some. But you would as easily stem a prairie fire with flapping hands." He looked around the circle, staring fiercely from under overhanging brows. "I tell you, they are a *horde;* a terrible flood. And you had best prepare."

"Do you?" asked Chakthi.

"Yes!" Colun nodded vigorously. "My Grannach are ready to seal the secret ways with rock and magic. Our manufactories are turned to blades and shields and arrows; to spear points and armor. Oh, yes, we prepare."

"Then," Chakthi said, "we've both the Maker's wards and your strength to defend us; and so Ket-Ta-Witko is likely safe."

"These are our friends!" Racharran cried. "Shall we leave the Grannach to fight alone? To fight our battles for us?"

Rannach was proud of his father at that moment, disgusted with Chakthi's response.

"It is not our battle yet," the Tachyn said. "Does this horde move against the Grannach, then I'll give them my support. Does this horde look to enter Ket-Ta-Witko, then I'll bring my warriors to battle. But that time is not yet come! I say we trust in the Maker—these invaders shall not pass through the sacred hills. I say that Juh and Tahdase speak wisely when they tell us to trust in the Maker. I say we take no decision now, but wait."

Rannach saw Yazte's hand rise angry, halted by Racharran's gesture. His father said, "Wait? Wait for what? This horde to come? Or Colun's people to come tell us we are invaded? Shall we wonder if the fire burns and not go look? Only *wait* until we see the flames rise?"

"What do you suggest?" asked Juh.

"That we set watchers, at the least," Racharran answered. "Warriors to guard the hills and speak with the Grannach. That we may know what threatens us."

"I think my brother doubts the Maker," Chakthi said. "Surely the Will promises us safety here."

Tahdase leaned toward Isten, whispering a moment, then said, "This *is* the promise of the Ahsa-tye-Patiko: that we be secure here."

Chakthi nodded gravely. Rannach saw Colun stiffen, and Racharran murmur with Morrhyn even as he reached out to touch the Grannach's hand, silencing his angry retort.

Carefully, Racharran said, "I do not question the Will. But I ask the Council to consider a question: Are we tested? Perhaps the Maker chooses to test us."

"And finds some wanting," said Chakthi.

Juh motioned for silence. "It may be so." He looked to Racharran, to Colun, at each akaman and wakanisha in turn. "If all we have heard is true, then it may well be a great test comes to us. If this horde our Grannach friend speaks of owns such strength as he describes, then we face a dreadful test; and we must think carefully about what we are to do. I say this is not a thing we can decide in a single Council, but a matter to sleep on, to ponder and approach with caution."

Caution? Rannach thought. Colun brings warning of a horde come out of the Maker-knows-where with blood and fire, and we must ponder it? What we should do, old man, is what my father says—ready for the fight.

"This is wise." Tahdase's voice interrupted his angry thoughts. "We need time to think on this."

"What's to think on?" Yazte stabbed a finger in the direction of the Maker's Mountain. "Do you doubt Colun? Are we to sit talking—*think-ing!*—until this horde comes to us?"

"Shall it come tomorrow?" Tahdase addressed himself to Colun, who—irritably—shook his head. "Surely we've a little time?"

The Grannach shrugged and nodded reluctantly. Juh said, "And the wakanishas sit in Dream Council tomorrow, no? Can we not give it that long, at the least?"

"I support my elder brother," Chakthi said.

"And I," said Tahdase.

Juh smiled. "Then shall it be so? Shall this Council form again after our wakanishas have spoken? And we decide then?"

Tahdase and Chakthi ducked their heads in ready accord; Racharran and Yazte were slower, but—with scant choice left them—agreed.

"Then so," Juh said, "let the wakanishas speak of this and all other matters on the morrow, and all well, this Council shall reconvene and we reach a decision."

They seemed to Rannach blind as horses grazing downwind of a lion: oblivious of impending danger. All save his father and Yazte. He thought that Chakthi likely argued for procrastination only because

Racharran argued for preparation. Juh, he thought, was an old man dreaming of a peaceful old age, disinclined to consider such turmoil as Colun warned of; and Tahdase was aged beyond his years, cautious as a rabbit with fox-scent on the air. He snorted his disgust loud enough one of the older warriors turned to fix him with a disapproving stare. Rannach knew what he would do were he akaman of the Commacht.

He turned his head to see the faces of his friends, and knew that they should be with him: their eyes burned with dreams of glorious battle.

"I'd speak with Colun of these warriors," Bakaan whispered.

"When my father addresses the clan," Rannach answered, "you shall have your say. And Colun will be about our camp tomorrow."

Hadustan said, "Think you Racharran shall speak for war?"

Zhy said, "It must be the decision of all the People. How say you, Rannach?"

"That my father," he said slowly, "would do as he says—prepare."

"And you?" Zhy pressed.

Rannach laughed. "I'd send warriors out now, to watch the hills. By the Maker! I'd lead them into the Grannach tunnels myself, to meet these invaders and defeat them before they set foot on our grass."

"And we," Bakaan said, "would follow you into battle."

"Yes," said Zhy.

"Save," said Hadustan with a lubricious grin, "that we are unwed warriors, whilst Rannach is now a married man."

"I am myself," Rannach declared, frowning. "Wed or not, what difference?"

Hadustan's grin spread wider and even more lascivious. "I wonder," he said, draping an arm about Rannach's shoulders, "if there are not matters that need explaining to you, my friend. Had I the choice of riding out to face such creatures as Colun describes, or lingering snug beneath my furs with a woman like Arrhyna . . . Well, that should be no decision at all."

Rannach caught his wrist and turned, twisting Hadustan's arm even as he laughed. "Which?" he demanded.

"Why," said Hadustan, "I'd send you out to fight, and I"—he fell to his knees, mimicking pain, pitching his voice high—"Oh, Rannach, you're so strong. Stay warm under the furs, Rannach. Please, don't leave me."

Rannach chuckled and let him go as faces turned toward them. "Envy!" he said. "Perhaps someday you shall find a woman like Arrhyna. It is not likely because of your resemblance to an ugly horse, but perhaps the Maker will take pity on you."

Hadustan rose, grinning, "And meanwhile she lingers lonely in your lodge . . . Oh, Rannach, I'm so alone."

"Yes." Rannach nodded solemnly. "For a fool, you speak wisdom." He glanced toward the circle of the Council. The akamans spoke now of clan affairs, of disputed grazing and such other matters: none of interest. "I've duties you'd not understand. I shall go."

"Oh, Rannach!" Hadustan cupped hands between his legs. "I believe I understand."

Rannach smiled and shook his head, turning away. The others fell into step around him as he pushed back through the crowd. They passed through the surrounding lodges and forded the stream, traversing the Commacht camp, where he waved them back.

"I think I am safe now," he said. "I thank you for your brave duty as my bodyguard, but now . . . The rest, I believe I can manage alone."

"Are you sure?" Hadustan asked. "You'll not require our aid?"

Rannach stooped to scoop up a round of horse dung and fling it at his friends. As they ducked and laughed, he strode toward his lodge, ignoring the catcalls that followed him.

Light showed through the hide and around the edges of the entrance. He thought on Arrhyna, wondering what she might have cooked, or if Lhyn would have delivered a meal. Mostly, he thought on Arrhyna, and his step quickened.

When he thrust the flap aside and found her gone, the lodge in disarray, his anguished scream split the night.

It was like the shriek of a pained lion, full of anger and anguish. Bakaan and the others halted in their tracks, spinning around to run, swift, to Rannach's lodge. They found him readying his war gear, his eyes wild with rage and loss.

"What is it?" Bakaan glanced about the disordered tent, seeing there the signs of a struggle. "Where's Arrhyna?"

"Stolen!" Rannach's voice was a snarl. "Vachyr did not attend the Council; now I know why."

Bakaan said, "I'll saddle your horse. And mine."

"This is my fight." Rannach snatched up his bow and quiver, his expression softening a moment as he turned to his friend. "When I find Vachyr, it shall go ill for him, and that shall not please my father. I'd not have you suffer his wrath."

Bakaan shrugged. "I'm your brother; Arrhyna is my sister. Your loss is mine."

Hadustan said, "And Vachyr might not be alone. I'm coming with you."

An instant later Zhy said, "I too. We ride together."

Rannach looked at them and said, "My father will be angry."

Bakaan shrugged again, said, "Wait for us," and beckoned the others to follow him.

Rannach shouted after them, "Hurry!"

The lodge was disordered and he had little time, but amongst the litter he found his paints and a mirror of Grannach silver: when his companions returned they saw the bands of black and yellow striped across his cheeks and nose. Silently, Bakaan took up the pots and decorated his own face in the colors of vengence, then Hadustan and Zhy.

"Where will he run?" Zhy wondered.

Hadustan suggested to the Tachyn grass, but Rannach shook his head and said, "Too obvious. He'll look to hide his trail, confuse pursuit; and Arrhyna will slow him."

Zhy swallowed nervously and said, "If she can. Likely she's tied or unconscious." His voice faltered.

Rannach fixed him with a gaze both hot with fury and cold as ice. "Has he harmed her, his life is mine."

Zhy nodded and glanced at Bakaan, who said, "Remember your promise."

"He's stolen my bride: he reneges all promises!" Rannach's mouth stretched in a wolfish smile that contained no humor, only threat. "Now do we find his trail?"

They moved out, leading their animals, their eyes downcast, searching the ground for sign. Around the lodge the grass was trampled, but they were hunters, and as they cast wider afield they found spoor, the tracks of two horses angling to the southwest. They mounted then and rode under the moon, slowly at first, casting back and forth where the trail was confused with earlier hoofprints, but then swifter as the tracks cleared the Matakwa grazing and became a double line pointing into the doubtful future. They were each armed with blades of Grannach steel and hatchets, and each one carried a bow and full quiver, a lance and a hide shield.

And all were painted for war.

5 A Thief Is Taken

Rain drummed out a rhythm on the roof tiles of Davyd's crib, counterpointed by the steady dripping where slates had torn loose in the last gale. It was too much to ask that Julius repair his property, even at the exorbitant rate he charged for the tiny under-the-eaves chamber. At five guineas a week—in advance, or else—to find a decent place with no questions asked and dinner thrown in was as much as the young thief could expect. So he forwent any notions of complaint and consoled himself with the thought that at least he had a roof over his head and need not daily face the problem of accommodation. Best of all, Julius cared only that his rent be paid—not how it was acquired.

And, Davyd told himself, it was not a very large hole. The pot placed beneath caught the inflow and—a bonus—gave him fresh water without the need to traverse the winding corridors and circuitous stairways of the rookery to the well. There were some there who would not scruple to waylay and rob a fellow lodger; some who'd not hesitate to denounce a dreamer to the God's Militia, did they suspect; and in Evander, under the rule of the Autarchy, suspicion alone was enough to speed a body to the scaffold. Julius, at least, could be trusted to keep his mouth closed—so long as the coins found their weekly way into his purse.

The greater danger lay outside, in the streets, in the risk of capture and subsequent revelation. That thought Davyd pushed assiduously aside: he was uncertain just how far the powers of the Inquisitors stretched and he was absolutely certain he did not want, at first hand, to find out.

And there lay the crux of his problem.

His last theft had netted him sufficient to rest awhile, not worry about the rent, and eat fairly well. Now that haul was all but gone and he must replenish his funds—which his dreams suggested was not a good idea. It was a quandary: to risk detection or risk losing his room. Neither was much palatable.

He rose from the age-mottled chair and went to the corner where wall and rafters met, finding the nook in which he hid his purse. Counting the pennies again did nothing to increase them. He must, somehow, find the coin Julius would demand before the week was out. That or find some other lodgings: Julius's only rule. He hid the few coppers and moodily resumed his place in the ancient chair, staring at the rippled surface of the catchpot.

Begging held neither much appeal nor much hope. He could, at a pinch, beg with the best of Alehouse Bob's crew—he was young enough, and thin enough of face and frame that folk felt sorry for him and pitched him small change when he stooped to such activity—but he considered it beneath his dignity. He was a thief, not a beggar. Besides, in such miserable weather—which looked to set to continue for some time—there would not be many folk abroad, at least not on foot, and the gentry in their carriages never thought to toss out a share of their easy-found wealth. More likely that some Militia patrol would come upon him and, at best, deliver him a sound drubbing, at worst arrest him. Davyd fancied neither.

Endeavoring to take a more optimistic view, he told himself that the rain would keep the Militia as surely under cover as it would honest folk. That it would also render rooftops slippery was of no great consequence —he was surefooted as a cat when it came to rooftop work.

The problem was the dream.

He had survived as a thief to the ripe age of thirteen thanks to the dreams. He did not understand them, or much care to. It was enough to know them reliable, and had come to trust them surer than he did any living soul. They told him when he might successfully mount a larcenous venture, and when not. This was not, they had told him, an auspicious time. Indeed, the last had featured red-coated Militiamen and faceless, black-clad Inquisitors, and had brought him gasping up from sleep to stare wild-eyed around his crib, his chest heaving as he anticipated the pounding on his door, the shouts of warning.

But ninepence would not pay Julius's rent, and if he did not go to work soon he must go hungry and homeless: he had procrastinated long enough.

He felt his heart begin to flutter and reached to the table where the last of his brandy stood. He poured a small measure—enough to calm his nerves or fortify his courage—and brought the battered silver cup to his lips. That was worth a crown or two, but not five guineas; and besides, it held a sentimental value. Aunt Dory had told him his mother owned it—before the Militia took her, before they took Aunt Dory and left him entirely alone—and he would not part with it. So he drank and set the cup down, finding no alternative but to venture out.

The dream had told him *no,* but what else could he do?

He sat awhile longer, pondering it, images running apace through his mind. There was a merchant's office on the edge of the port quarter where he was confident of finding coin—a watchful eye and attentive ear had told him that much—and he doubted the hexes would be stronger than his skill with the picklocks. He could see himself opening the strongbox, filling his pockets with crowns and even golden guineas. Enough to pay off Julius and leave himself secure for a few weeks.

On the other hand, he could see—or, at least, imagine—the Inquisitors' dungeons and the instruments there. Vividly, he could see the last witch burning. It had taken place in Bantar's chief plaza, the great square formed by the cathedral, the palace of the Autarchy, the Temple of the Inquisitors, and the Militia barracks. The condemned had been a woman, not very old, found guilty of soothsaying. He could not understand how, were she truly able to foresee the future, she had not predicted her fate and fled. But she had not, and the Militia had taken her. The Inquisitors had put her to question, and on a dull gray day the flames of her burning had lit the plaza bright.

Davyd could hear her screams still; he felt no wish to echo them, as surely he would, were his own ability discovered. The Autarchy frowned upon any but its own agents wielding the power of magic, and what the Autarchy frowned on was ruthlessly eradicated. Which was why Aunt Dory had impressed upon the orphaned child the need to keep his dreams secret, once the old woman recognized their nature. To that end she had taken him to the plaza and forced him—no more than five or six years old then—to watch as a condemned warlock was given to the flames. He had taken the lesson to heart, firm as the officers of the God embraced their faith. Had he one fear greater than all others, it was of that awful consumption by fire. Only his dread of water came near that terror. It had served him well; it had kept him alive. But now he had only ninepence and the rent soon due.

He groaned, his mouth gone dry, and filled his cup again, swallowing the last of the brandy. The rain still tapped against the roof like impatient fingers, as if awaiting his decision. He made it in a rush—no time to doubt; not now, when Julius would any day demand his tithe. He took his coat from the bed and shrugged it on. It was a good coat, quite waterproof, and of a blue-black shade that blended into shadows or the color of slates. Concealed within the lining were pockets for his picklocks and the rewards they gained him. He settled a cap over his telltale red hair, and before he might change his mind—come to his senses, said a loud voice inside his head—he thrust open the crib's one window and clambered out.

Across the sloping roof to its gable he crept, then down and across, to the overhang of the rookery's neighbor. Along the ledge there to an attic window, loose-hung and opening on a dusty, web-draped storeroom. His nimble fingers sprung the door easy enough and locked it behind him—caution, always caution; Aunt Dory had impressed that on him too—and down the narrow stairs to the lowest level. Another easily picked door lock saw him in the alley behind, and he marched briskly toward his destination.

The rain-slick streets were mostly empty—this was not a quarter frequented by upright citizens even in dry daylight—and soon he was hurrying down the narrow alleys of the docklands.

The merchant's building was as easy of access as he'd anticipated— for a rooftopper. There was a yard at the rear, overlooked only by the blank windows of warehouses, and he climbed astride the bricks, then along to where a drainpipe afforded purchase for the upward climb. He found the roof and paused a moment. The rain still fell, but here it was scented with the tang of the ocean, and dark in the twilit distance he could see the skeletal outlines of masts and crossbeams where ships lay at anchor in the harbor. He suppressed a shudder at the thought of venturing out onto the open water in one of those vessels, and then another as his imagination replaced the twigs of rigging with images of flame. He spat and crossed his fingers, and went spiderlike over the tiles to the small window set flush with the slates. It was dusty and water-swollen and it creaked horrendously as he worked it open, but there were no ears save his to catch the sound. Even so, he waited awhile before dropping into the room below, and then again at the door, listening.

The building was quiet. From what he'd heard, this merchant was too mean toinvest in dogs or watchmen. He hoped the same parsimony applied to hexes. He fought off the images of his dream that sought to penetrate his mind as he descended to the ground floor, where the owner located his personal office.

That door yielded easy as any other, and Davyd slipped into a bare-boarded room with one window that looked onto the yard behind. He found a lantern and struck a lucifer. The strongbox sat square and bulky in a corner. Too heavy to lift, it was secured with a padlock that would have defied a less skilled thief: Davyd took out his picks and set to work.

It was not long before he sprung the lock and raised the box's lid, grinning triumphantly as he surveyed the contents. The sundry papers interested him not at all, but on them lay three pouches that weighed heavy as he snatched them up. He loosed the drawstrings and his grin spread wider as lamplight shone on gold and silver—there was enough there to last him some months. He spilled the coins into his secret pockets and trimmed the lantern's wick. His coat was heavy now, and he chuckled, quite forgetting the dream.

Then remembered every vivid detail as he heard the sound of a door opening, a commanding voice, and the thud of approaching feet.

For an instant he froze, panic curdling in his belly. Boots beat a threatening tattoo on the floor outside the office, and through the open door he saw the glitter of lamplight on metal and polished leather, heard the same voice bark the order to watch the outer door.

It seemed his mind ran out of gear: thoughts came with a dreadfl clarity, but he could not set his feet in motion. Hexes, he thought. There *were* hexes! And then: They'll burn me!

As if touched by the flames, he sprang into action.

Crouching, he moved to the office door. There were two lanterns, held aloft by Militiamen—five of them and a lieutenant, the silver insignia on his cap like a vigilant eye, watchful for thieves. They were in the outer hall, moving purposefully between the desks there. All save the lieutenant held muskets. The stairway was to Davyd's left: he might reach it, were he quick enough.

Still bent over, he eased out from the office and began to shuffle toward the stairs. A gap showed, three yards or so of open floor. He drew a breath and crossed his fingers, then flung himself desperately for the stairway.

Shouts echoed, then were drowned by the roar of musket fire. Davyd felt splinters strike his face and screamed in unalloyed terror, his nostrils filled with the reek of burning power.

"Halt, or you're dead!"

The command sounded loud as the musket's shot. He chanced a backward glance and saw the lieutenant at the stairway's foot, a pistol in his hand. He wished he'd heeded the dream. He raised his hands and took a half-step downward, then reversed his movement and scrambled pell-mell up again. The pistol discharged, and it seemed that all the long, tall chamber was filled up with the muzzle flash. He felt the ball pluck at his coat; he heard the clatter of coins falling as a pocket tore.

The lieutenant cursed and bellowed an order. The stairs stretched out before Davyd, long and straight, offering no obstacle to the muskets that were now aimed at him. It seemed the bare wood clutched at his feet and he felt his limbs grow heavy.

"Come down. Now, else we fire!"

Five muskets: not all could miss. Davyd swallowed and clenched his eyes against the tears that threatened to spill. He nodded and raised his hands. This time he did not attempt to fool them.

"God, he's but a boy."

There was a hint of sympathy in the Militiaman's voice, but his aim did not waver.

"Devil's spawn." The lieutenant's voice was hard, contemptuous. "A sneaking, misbegotten thief, no matter his age. Take him."

"Please, sir." It was worth a try. "I'd not have done it but that I'm starving."

The officer cuffed him, setting his ears to ringing, and whilst his head still spun, his hands were dragged back and bound with cord. He did not attempt to halt the tears now, but they won him no more sympathy.

"Thought you'd defeat hexes, eh?" The lieutenant's voice was calmer now; gloating, it sounded to Davyd. "Well, boy, you did not, and you've earned yourself a place in the dungeons. Starving, you said? Well, they might feed you there. What think you of that?"

What Davyd thought was: only let them not learn I dream.

As they searched his pockets and he stared numbly at the lantern flames, a dreadful fear gripped him, pinching his tongue and his innards so that all he saw, all he knew, was that fiery glow. It seemed, almost, he could feel it on his skin.

It was not the first time Davyd had been imprisoned, though it was the most serious charge. Once he had spent a month in jail for begging, and once been sentenced to six on charges of picking pockets. He had been somewhat younger then, and supposed that counted in his favor—certainly he had gotten off lightly—nor had there been Inquisitors in either court. This time, however . . . This time he was older, and the charge more serious. He thought he likely faced some years in the prison barges or the quarries, perhaps even the mines. He did not relish the notion, and the relative comfort of his cell was small consolation in face of such a future.

It had been a surprise to find Julius come with bribe-money for the jailer—enough that the food was decent and the cell lit by a good lantern, clean bedding provided, and even a somewhat rickety chair and table. He had not thought Julius so kind, but the big, bluff fellow had come armed with coin and his knowledge of Bantar's ways, and shrugged off Davyd's startled gratitude as if embarrassed to be found out. His largess, however, did not extend to the hiring of a lawyer, and Davyd must play his own advocate when he came to trial.

At least Julius had managed to find out when that should be, thus rescuing Davyd from the torment of speculation. Tomorrow, it was; and thanks to Julius, he was able to assuage his worry with a bottle of good wine. That had been Julius's farewell gift: he did not anticipate seeing Davyd again, would not—for sake of anonymity—attend the trial. At least he had wished his former lodger well.

Now Davyd drank his wine and prepared to sleep. He did not think the morrow should provide any great surprises, not beyond the judge's choice between the barges, the quarries, or the mines. He supposed he preferred it be the quarries: at least there he should see the sky.

If he had only, he thought as he dimmed his lantern and readied himself for slumber, heeded his dreams, he would not be in this predicament. But he had not, and there was no point to dwelling on that foolishness now. Life had taught him to be pragmatic, and save for learning what lessons experience taught him, he saw no point in conjecture. He would, however, he vowed as he closed his eyes, always heed the dreams in future.

The one that came that night, though, was mightily difficult to interpret.

He floated on a vast expanse of water and could not tell whether he stood alone, somehow suspended above the waves, or on the deck of a ship. It mattered little either way: Davyd was afraid of water, and in this oneiric state it represented a terror as great as that of burning. He looked about and saw no shoreline, no hint of land at all, but only the gray and rolling ocean all around, the waves white-topped under a blue sky absent of any feature other than the unwinking eye of the sun. There were things beneath the waves—he *knew,* for all they remained invisible —that slowly rose to drag him down into the deeps or swallow him like some morsel of flotsam.

He woke sweaty, his heart beating arrhythmic, dread tearing a cry from his gasping mouth. Panting, he flung himself from his bed to find the lantern and extend the wick until the honest yellow flame drove off the afterimage of waves and eternity and lost hope. He reached for the wine bottle and cursed long when he found it empty. He contented himself with water instead, splashing some against his face that he fully regain his senses. After that he dressed and waited full-clad for dawn. He did not want to return to that dream; he did not understand it, only that it filled him with an awful fear.

It was a lengthy wait, but in time the prison made those sounds that prisons make in announcement of another day. Light came pale past the bars on the window and the nocturnal rustlings, the moans of other inmates, the night cries, gave way to muted conversation, the jangle of keys, the clatter of the breakfast trolley.

Davyd felt no appetite for the porridge, white bread, and aromatic coffee that should be Julius's final purchase on his behalf. His belly felt filled with liquid that rolled and shifted like sea swell, and he only tidied himself and waited to be summoned.

His case was not heard until noon, and when the Militiamen came to fetter him and bring him before the judge, his belly rumbled protestingly. He thought that might perhaps serve him well—that he appear not well fed but as a starveling orphan forced by unkind fate to a life of crime. He hoped the judge would not inquire too deeply of his circumstances and confrères, for he knew he would not live long—no matter where he be sent—did he give up Julius and the others. Most strongly, he hoped the magicks warding the court would not reveal him for a dreamer; he prayed there be no Inquisitors present.

He need not have worried: such inquiries seemed not to have occurred to the judge, whose aim appeared to be the swiftest possible dispensation of the Autarchy's justice. Nor did any Inquisitors attend, only the watchful Militiamen and a tipstaff.

Davyd was asked his name, to which he answered, "Davyd Furth, sir," doing his best to sound utterly miserable and equally penitent. It was not difficult to manage the misery. His age was established as thirteen and his abode as the street, after which the judge pronounced his sentence.

When he declared that Davyd be indentured and held prisoner until the next transportation ship sailed for Salvation, Davyd broke down. He shrieked his objections, pounding manacled fists against the ledge of the accused's box, quite oblivious of the hexes that burned his skin. He begged that he be sent to the quarries, to the mines—even the barges. Only not condemn him to crossing the ocean. He wailed as the Militiamen dragged him away.

He was sobbing as the door of his cell closed. He *knew* that he must surely suffer a horrid fate upon the Sea of Sorrows and, had he not been left chained and his belt and foulard taken from him, he would likely have become a suicide.

6 Virtue Assaulted

Work as a tavern wench in the Flying Horse was not the employment Flysse Cobal had hoped to find in Bantar, but she bore her disappointment as cheerfully as she could. She had hoped to find a position as a lady's maid, or perhaps a seamstress, but the bustling city had proven unkind to her dreams and she had been forced to settle for serving ale and avoiding the groping hands of amorous patrons. And it was easier here, she told herself, than in Sieur Shaxbrof's mansion in Cudham. There, it had been quite impossible to escape the master's attentions or, though it was no fault of hers that he pursued her, the animosity of his wife. She had thought it a fine thing to be accepted as a parlormaid, a great honor for a farmgirl whose family could barely support three daughters when the harvest had failed for two years running, and she had gone eagerly to her new post. She had not anticipated that so elevated and aging a man as Sieur Shaxbrof would prove so lecherous, nor that his wife should blame her rather than him and order her dismissal. That had been a terrible blow for Flysse, and she had elected to seek work in the city before burdening her family again.

At least, she told herself, she had been able to save a few silver crowns, and Bantar was surely a wondrous place, even though working in a tavern was not the life she had envisaged. One day, she promised herself, she would find more congenial employment. But for now, the

Flying Horse was the best she could find, and she would make the best of it.

If only the inn's patrons did not assume she was as available as most serving wenches, forever praising her beauty . . . Flysse supposed she *was* pretty, but almost wished she were not. It would make life easier.

She studied her face in the mirror she shared, like the room, with the other seven girls. It seemed to her an ordinary enough face—round and framed with blond curls, the eyes and nose a little too large to her mind, the mouth too wide. But men told her it was a sight to behold, especially Lieutenant Armnory Schweiz of the God's Militia, who seemed quite deaf to her reiterated protestations that she did not—most definitely and unrelentingly not—wish to become his mistress.

Most men, their advances once rejected, accepted they'd not have her and contented themselves with flirtatious comments, laughing at her blushes. But not Armnory Schweiz, who appeared determined to break down her resistance and ignored her honest avowals that she wished only to be left alone. He would be there tonight—he was there every night—and Flysse sighed unhappily at the thought. It seemed to her that the lieutenant's watery blue eyes pierced through her clothing to study the naked flesh beneath with gloating anticipation; and no matter how she tried to avoid his hands, they always found a way to her waist or thigh or backside. She had believed the officers of the Autarchy above such behavior—before she came to Bantar. Now she knew better: since Armnory found her, she knew the men of the God's Militia were not much different from Sieur Shaxbrof, or any other men—save in the powers they held. Were he not a lieutenant in the Militia, she thought, I'd spill a tankard over his grinning head, or dent it on his skull. But he was, and she'd been warned of the consequences.

With a last long sigh she finished the tidying of her hair and readied herself to go down to the taproom. She was already late, and Master Banlyn's patience was not inexhaustible.

When she entered the long, already smoke-filled room, the first thing she saw was Armnory Schweiz. He looked to be in his cups, but even so his eyes were focused on the door and a lecherous smile stretched his narrow lips as he spotted her. Instantly, he raised his tankard, and Flysse had no choice but to nod and go to his table.

His smile grew broader as she approached, exposing uneven teeth stained brown by tobacco, and he brushed at his moustache like some gallant on the stage of the playhouse. As Flysse came near and reached to take his empty mug, he seized her hand, gazing earnestly at her face. She forced herself to stand, and if she did not smile, at least she did not recoil in disgust.

"Flysse, dearest Flysse." He raised her trapped hand to his lips. "Have you thought on my proposal, my dear?"

"'Sieur, you've had my answer," she told him not for the first time, repeating the lie that seemed her best defense: "I've a sweetheart awaiting me in Cudham."

"Pah!" Schweiz dismissed with a careless wave the notion of a patient sweetheart. "Some yokel stinking of dung and sweat? Flysse, I tell you, you've captured my heart and I'll not rest till I have you."

Flysse glanced round, hoping Master Banlyn—anyone—would come to her rescue, but there was a space about Schweiz's table, as if his scarlet uniform created an aura that defied approach surely as any hex. There was no hope of rescue save by her own wits.

"'Sieur," she extemporized, "it's as I've said—we are engaged, and I cannot forswear that vow. Surely you, an officer in the God's Militia, understand the import of such a promise?"

Schweiz snorted. He seemed to Flysse more drunk than usual, more pressing. He said: "An officer in the God's Militia, yes! And consequently of far greater position than any yokel. You must forget your promise, Flysse. Shall it make your mind easier, I'll have our padre bless you and absolve you. Only—"

"'Sieur!" She feigned amazement, shock. "You suggest I renege a vow made in God's name?"

Schweiz said, "I do; you must. Listen to me, Flysse—I think of you hourly, and I swear I cannot live lest you agree to my proposal."

Now her shock was genuine. "That I allow you to set me up as . . . as your *doxy* . . . your *kept woman?*"

"As my *mistress,*" Schwiz said. "There's a difference, you know."

"I think not, 'sieur. I think you suggest the unthinkable." She captured his tankard, hoping he'd free her to gain more ale. "I'm not some street woman, to be bought and housed for your pleasure."

"For my love," he argued. "Only for my love."

But there was not, now or ever, Flysse thought, any mention of honest marriage. She felt fear stir—Schweiz seemed mightily determined this night, and did he continue in this vein and not leave her go, she thought it should be very hard to rein her temper, her disgust. It should prove very hard not to strike him, and damn the consequences.

"I think," she said, hoping her voice did not tremble, "that I'd best refill your mug, no?"

"No," said Schweiz, "for I've made up my mind this day. I *shall* have you, Flysse."

He jerked his arm free then, tugging her forward and down, reaching out with his free hand to grasp her shoulder so that she was toppled and turned to land across his knees. He set an arm around her and a hand beneath her chin, holding her head still as he planted a beery kiss on her lips.

Flysse closed her mouth tight and struggled furiously, pounding at his shoulders and back. But he was strong and ignored her blows, endeavoring to force his tongue between her lips even as the hand that clutched her chin descended busily down her body to find its way beneath her skirts.

Flysse felt nauseated, and the queasy feeling galvanized her to a more ferocious defense of her honor. She raked nails down her attacker's cheeks, gratified even through her panic to hear Schweiz's pained cry. His hand left off its clumsy fumblings and rose to touch the wounds. When he saw the blood upon his fingers, he gaped in disbelief. Then snarled in anger.

"God's blood, girl, you've marked me! You'll pay for that in kind."

He took a handful of her hair and slapped her hard. Flysse felt her eyes water, then shrieked in outrage as he cupped a hand about a breast and squeezed viciously. Dimly, she was aware of an abrupt silence throughout the taproom, so that Schweiz's panting sounded unnaturally loud. She wondered why no one came to her aid. Surely Master Banlyn would not stand idly by; surely there must be someone would take this creature off her. But none came: there was only Armnory Schweiz's hand tearing at her bodice and his face descending again. She supposed it was not so unusual, a patron disporting with a tavern wench; likely the other girls would laugh it off and return the kisses, nor object to the hand unlacing her bodice to delve at the flesh beneath. Some, she knew, would invite him to bed.

But she was not like them. In Cudham she had fought off Sieur Shaxbrof—and others since coming to the Flying Horse—and she would not willingly submit to attentions so distasteful. She felt his tongue probe into her mouth. It tasted of ale, tobacco, and stale food. She felt her breast freed from the confines of the bodice, and his fingers toy there, then slide down her waist, her hip, to lift her skirts, exposing her legs. She clamped them tight, but ragged nails scratched between her thighs, forcing crudely upward to her undergarments. He laughed as the cotton ripped under his exploring fingers. She thought that he would surely rape her.

She did not think of what she did then, nor of the consequences. She was hardly aware of her hand—which still, somehow, held the emptied tankard—rising to strike his temple, slamming the pewter mug against his skull.

Lieutenant Armnory Schweiz gasped and fell back on the bench.

Flysse leapt up and, as he stared at her and reached out a hand, struck him again, full in the face. The blow jarred her knuckles; the tankard was dented. Schweiz's nose spread wide across his cheeks, spurting blood that splattered over his tunic, darkening the scarlet. He grunted, and clutched at her again, and she drove the mug straight into his face. He yelped as teeth shattered, spitting fragments from between his pulped and bloody lips, his eyes glazing. Flysse felt dizzy, dropping the mug as she instinctively adjusted her disordered clothing, her eyes wide as Schweiz moaned, cursed, and dribbled blood.

Across the taproom, Master Banlyn said softly, nervously, "In God's name, girl, do you know what you've done?"

Defended my honor, Flysse thought. Only that.

Armnory Schweiz touched cautiously at his ruined face. When he raised his head, his eyes were furious. When he spoke, his voice came thick.

"To attack an officer of the God's Militia is a crime, you bitch. You'll pay for this!"

He fumbled his pistol from the holster. Master Banlyn cried, "No! For God's sake, Lieutenant, don't shoot her!"

"Shoot her?" Schweiz shook his head, sending a spray of blood and mucus arcing over the floor. "I'll not shoot the bitch. Oh, no—I'll not end it so easy."

Flysse took a step back: there was a madness in his eyes that filled her with dread. She flinched as he cocked the pistol, but he only set the muzzle on her chest and grimaced a horrid smile.

"In the name of the Autarchy, I arrest you, bitch." He flourished the pistol at the door. "Now come with me."

Flysse had cleaned her share of stables and pigpens, and even they were preferable to her cell. For one thing, they were sunlit, not sunk in the perpetual gloom of the prison with its few sputtering tallow candles and small, barred windows; and the straw on their floors was considerably fresher than the noisome, insect-infested stuff littering the flagstones of this tiny cubicle. Nor were the inhabitants so threatening as her neighbors here—the catcalls and lewd comments that greeted her arrival had made Flysse blush. She had not known women did such things together as were suggested, and she was grateful—a small mercy—that none other shared the cell.

She wondered how long she should be confined, and what the outcome of her trial might be. The jailer—a gaunt woman who seemed to Flysse no kinder than her charges—told her that such injury as she had inflicted on an officer of the God's Militia must guarantee a strict punishment. It seemed the lieutenant's nose was soundly broken and several of his teeth knocked loose, and that amused the jailer as much as it amused her to frighten Flysse with speculation of her impending fate. Almost, she wished she had not struck the man, but what else might she have done? Certainly not submit to his desires; and surely a judge would understand that, no matter what the jailer said.

She had determined from the first to tell the truth and, did the court allow it, call upon Master Banlyn and the other girls from the Flying Horse to stand as witnesses. Surely they must confirm her story, that Armnory Schweiz had persecuted her with his attentions, suggesting such liaisons as no God-fearing woman should be asked to accept. The trouble was she had no more experience of courts than of jails, and no real idea whether or not she might summon witnesses to her character and conduct. She had asked the jailer, but for such information the woman demanded payment, in coin or kind, and Flysse lacked the one and had no taste for the other. She wondered if her meager savings were safe. She could not, currently penniless, send word to those she named her friends, nor had any visited her in the few days of her incarceration. She believed her only hope was truth, and the understanding of the judge; but the jailer's ominous declarations filled her with dread. Even so, she hoped her hearing might be soon: at least it would remove her from this stinking cell—for ever or awhile. Beyond that she could not—dared not—think. She must cling to the hope of freedom, anticipate her return to the Flying Horse and a resumption of her life. The alternative —whatever it be—was altogether too terrifying to consider. She slumped despondent on the splintery bench that was both seat and bed, watching the roaches scuttle busily amongst the straw, then rose as a lantern illumined the corridor outside and the rattle of the jailer's keys heralded the woman's approach.

She came with two Militiamen, their expressions scornful as they ignored the obscene suggestions echoing their footsteps. They halted outside Flysse's cell, waiting as the wardress applied her key and flung open the cage. Flysse saw that one held manacles, and in her sudden nervousness came close to giggling that it be thought needful she go chained. Perhaps they feared she should attack them. But manacled she was, wrists and ankles fettered, a chain between her legs that caught up her skirts immodestly and made her totter as they brought her from the cell and up the old stone steps to the hall beyond.

She asked them, "Where are we going?" and had back a curt, "To court," after which she had no time for questions. Nor did she see any point in pleas, so stern were their faces.

She had not known the courtroom stood above the cells until she was brought in and ushered to a walled stand raised some three steps from the floor. Sudden fear rendered her giddy, and she set her hands upon the ledge before her, only to gasp and snatch them back as the magic in the hexes there burned her palms. Through watered eyes she saw a small, thin man dressed all in red-edged black seated behind a high desk. He wore a powdered wig and she assumed him to be the judge. There was another official she did not know was a tipstaff, and the only other person present was Armnory Schweiz, his face masked with bandages. He did not look at her.

"You are Flysse Cobal, formerly employed in the tavern named the Flying Horse?"

The judge's voice rasped like a file drawn across protesting metal. It sounded to Flysse as hard. She said, "I am. I—"

"Silence." The judge raised a hand. "It is true that some nine days ago you attacked Lieutenant Armnory Schweiz of the God's Militia?"

"No!" she cried. "That's not true!"

"You deny you struck the lieutenant violently in the face with a tankard?"

There was no hint of sympathy, only a dry indifference tinged with boredom and irritation.

Flysse said, "No . . . yes, I struck him, but . . ."

The judge looked up from the papers spread before him and fixed Flysse with an angry glare. "Young woman, do you answer me aye or nay, and no more save I tell you so. Confine yourself to only that, else it shall go harder with you."

"But," said Flysse, and fell silent in face of his pursed lips and narrowed eyes.

"You confess that you did strike the lieutenant?"

"Aye," said Flysse.

"Thereby inflicting considerable injuries to both his person and the dignity of the uniform he wears."

Flysse was not sure whether a question was asked or a statement made, so she remained silent. She was trying hard not to cry now; she wished there were some friendly face in the room.

The judge glanced at his papers, then at Schweiz. "Lieutenant, do you describe your injuries."

Schweiz rose to his feet. "My lord, my nose was broken and four of my teeth shattered." His voice was thick and lisping. "Also, she scratched me and struck me about the head."

"And you were at the time in the uniform of the God's Militia?"

"I was."

"And was there any justification for this attack?"

"My Lord, there was not."

"Liar!" Flysse could not help it: she must protest. "He's lying! He molested me. He said—"

The judge motioned at the two Militiamen standing behind Flysse. Abruptly she felt her arms seized, and before she could turn her head or say another word, a ball of leather was forced between her jaws and secured in place about her neck. She gagged, afraid of choking now. Tears ran helplessly down her cheeks and she thought she should likely faint.

"So," the judge declared, "without provocation an attack was launched on an officer of the Autarchy. A grave offence, indeed, and one demanding of a grave penalty." He looked at Flysse with eyes cold as winter ice. "Do you heed me, Flysse Cobal."

To her surprise, she did. Her ears were ringing and she fought the impulse to vomit against the gag. Her eyes were blurred with tears, but somehow she still saw the spiteful face clear and clearly heard the sentence pronounced.

"I decree that you shall be sent into exile. To Salvation, where you shall be indentured for the remainder of your life."

The last thing Flysse saw before she fainted was Armnory Schweiz smiling as best he could with his ruined mouth.

7 Honor Betrayed

"La!"

As he said it, Arcole Blayke lunged forward, driving his sword almost casually past the defending blade, the point entering his opponent's chest. The viscount Ferristan gasped, an expression of absolute disbelief clouding his face. As he withdrew the rapier, Arcole wondered why they always looked surprised. God knew, they engaged in the duel with the intention of killing the other man—that was his own purpose; what point else?—but seemed never to think they might themselves be harmed. Always, that look of disbelief.

He stepped a pace back, blade lowered as the viscount tottered, frowning, and opened his mouth. Had he intended to speak, he was not successful; instead, he emitted only a coughing sound and fell on his face. Arcole shook a kerchief loose from his sleeve and wiped his blade, handing both cloth and sword to his second.

Dom said, "A fair fight, fairly won," in a voice intended to carry to Ferristan's men as they rolled their master onto his back and shouted for the surgeon to come forward.

Softer, to Arcole, he said, "But even so, best you lie low awhile, or even quit Levan. The House Ferristan has friends in high places."

"He called me out," Arcole returned, extending his arms to take the jacket a servant offered. "He impugned my honor, and it was *he* issued the challenge."

"Even so," said Dom.

"Is the aristocracy entirely without honor now?" Arcole demanded. "The fight was fair—and witnessed. What reasonable charge might be brought?"

"Does the Autarchy need a reason?" Dom gave him back, cautiously modulating his voice that none save Arcole hear him. "Those black-garbed bastards make their own rules since the Restitution."

"And forget the ancient laws of Levan?" Arcole shrugged, idly studying the surgeon's fruitless attempt to restore life to the dead. "Surely not, my friend."

"God!" Dom shook his head, thinking his own efforts to instill some measure of caution in Arcole were useless as the surgeon's. "The House Ferristan walks hand in hand with the Autarchy. His father"—this with a nod toward the corpse—"entertains the governor to dinner. Think you he's not their ear? Or that he'll forgive this?"

Arcole shrugged again and beckoned a servant, who passed him a cup. He drank the brandy and sighed contentedly. The surgeon rose from his labors to pronounce, officially, that Luis, viscount of House Ferristan, was dead. Dom, addressing the Ferristan seconds, said, "The fight *was* fair, no? You stand witness to that."

The Ferristan seconds gave no reply, only looked dour and nervous as they lifted up their dead master and bore him away to his carriage.

"You saw it, no?" Dom turned to the surgeon, wiping blood from his hands. "There can be no question, eh?"

"No." The surgeon shook his balding head vigorously. "No, none. The duel was fought fair."

"And is he questioned by Ferristan men or the Autarchy's lackeys," Dom said, eyeing the surgeon's retreating back, "he'll swear the opposite with equal enthusiasm."

Arcole smiled. "You grow cynical, old friend."

"I grow realistic," said Dom. "And I'd wish the God gifted you with as much sense."

"But he did not," Arcole declared. "He gave me a certain skill with a blade and as much with the cards. I thank him for that, and that I've yet some notion of honor."

"Notions of honor," said Dom, "are oftimes the cerements of the foolish."

"Do you name me a fool?"

Dom shook his head: friend though he was, Arcole Blayke was no less unpredictable. And, to say the least, incautious. A gambler and a duelist—both of repute—he did not go unnoticed by Levan's new masters. He made, Dom thought, no attempt at caution; rather, he flaunted his habits. And in these years since the Evanderans had conquered Levan, such habits were disapproved of. The Autarchy had scant affection for such independent spirits—and a way of rendering them docile. He wished Arcole might make himself less noticeable, but then he'd not be Arcole. Dom sighed, knowing he'd as well beat his head against a rock.

"Still, a . . . holiday . . . might be advisable," he said. "There are salons in Bantar, no?"

"Rubbish." Arcole set a companionable arm about Dom's shoulders, steering the smaller man toward their carriage. "I've too many friends here; and what should I do in the very seat of those glum God's men? Why, I'd languish in Bantar."

Dom sighed and shrugged, abandoning the attempt, and allowed his friend to hand him into the coach.

Inside, Arcole leant back against the velvet plush of the seats. The carriage rocked, the matched pair moving eagerly to the coachman's bidding, drawing the phaeton over the rutted track to the paved road beyond. They passed through the city gates and came to the hotel in which Arcole had taken rooms. It was amongst the finest, all painted panels and crystal chandeliers—memories of a time before the Restitution, before Evander had conquered the surrounding countries and the Autarchy established its governors and their Militia, puppet masters holding the strings of a tamed and toylike class that now ruled solely in name. Save, Dom thought as the carriage was dismissed and they entered the luxurious foyer, that some had the ear of the true rulers and might well be heard, did they whine loud enough.

Arcole called him from his gloomy musings with a hand on his shoulder. "Breakfast? I confess myself quite famished." He seemed to have forgotten the duel. Was it so easy to dismiss the taking of a man's life, Dom wondered. But he kept the thought to himself and only nodded.

As they made their way to their customary table, conversation ceased a moment, then started up again, louder. Heads turned toward them—or, more correctly, Dom thought, toward Arcole. He saw admiration on some faces, disapproval on many others. That Arcole Blayke fought a duel that morning was common knowledge amongst the patrons of the Hotel Dumoyas. Before the morning was out, it would be known across the city that the viscount Ferristan was dead. Dom saw money change hands, and marveled that there were yet folk foolish enough to wager on Arcole's defeat.

At his side, Arcole was bowing and murmuring greetings, his smile sunny; Dom saw more than one lady return that smile with an unspoken invitation. He, too, ducked his head and voiced pleasantries, but that was only formality: attention was focused on his companion. He was not at all surprised, nor any longer put out—he was not unhandsome, but Arcole was possessed of a charisma that surpassed mere looks, though he had those in abundance as well. The God had favored him with more than just skill with a sword and cards, and if he lacked a measure of common sense, then that vacancy was balanced with charm and wit and education and . . . (Dom had sometimes amused himself by compiling a list of Arcole Blayke's winning characteristics. It had proved a long list.)

They reached their table and allowed a waiter to seat them. Arcole ordered a bottle of Levan's famous sparkling wine; Dom asked for coffee. They agreed on deviled kidneys and kedgeree, fresh fruit and toast. As they ate—Arcole with the appetite he'd claimed—Dom was aware of the eyes that shifted constantly in their direction.

"They wonder at your future," he remarked, "what measures House Ferristan will take."

"What measures can be taken?" Arcole returned. "Luis was their only decent swordsman. Think you they'll hire some mercenary?"

His smile suggested he found the notion amusing, the likelihood a hired sword could defeat him ridiculous. Dom only sighed and shook his head.

Arcole washed down a mouthful of kidneys with a measure of wine, dabbed a napkin to his mouth, and said, "I've promised young Alleyn Silvestre a hand of cards this noonday. Shall you join us?"

"You've an appointment with your tailor," Dom reminded him.

"Of course." Arcole pushed away his emptied plate. "But there's time enough before I relieve Alleyn of more coin."

"And we're to attend the duchess this evening."

"Dear Madelyne, yes." Arcole nodded solemnly. "I'd not forgotten, but I doubt it will take me long to empty Alleyn's purse."

"The Duchess Fendralle would be a valuable ally," Dom remarked. "Did the count of Ferristan bring some charge, her affections might prove most useful."

"Her affections? Do you suggest I bed her, Dom?" Arcole's brows rose in feigned surprise. "Why, she's almost old enough to be my mother, nor gifted with much in the way of looks! And what of the duke?"

"A husband," Dom murmured in answer, "has never stopped you before."

"True enough," Arcole acknowledged cheerfully, "but I think not Madelyne."

"At least sweet-talk her?" Dom asked. "And young Silvestre, might you not let him win a hand or two?"

"Dom," said Arcole, "you worry too much. I tell you, nothing will come of Ferristan's demise. Levan's known duels too long; the Autarchy will take no notice of this morning's squabble. So, do we attend the tailor?"

They returned to the hotel to find Alleyn Silvestre awaiting them with three companions, but before the cards were dealt a commotion in the foyer caught Dom's attention. It went unnoticed by the players until he saw the scarlet uniforms of Militiamen appear in the doorway of the gaming room and coughed a warning.

Arcole glanced around. Dom gestured toward the captain advancing at the head of ten men, all bearing muskets save the officer. He wore only a saber, a pistol, and an expression of grim resolution.

Arcole set down his cards as the captain said, "Arcole Blayke? I've a warrant for your arrest."

"On what charge?" Arcole demanded.

His tone suggested a mistake was made, and the officer scowled as he fumbled in his sabertache for a document bearing the heavy seal of the Autarchy. Unfolding the sheet, he intoned: "That you did, in the early hours of this morning, take the life of Luis, viscount Ferristan. And for that offense—"

"Offense? It was a duel! And fought honestly."

Arcole was genuinely outraged. The captain ignored his protest. "You confess, before witnesses, that you slew the viscount?"

Dom said, "There were witnesses to the duel. I'm one; there were others."

"Indeed," the captain said. "Who shall all, in due course, give testimony. You are?"

"Dom Freydmon," said Dom.

The captain nodded. "Doubtless you'll attend the hearing, Master Freydmon. Meanwhile"—he turned his attention back to Arcole—"you, sir, will come with me."

Alleyn Silvestre said, "This is ridiculous! All Levan knows Arcole fought Ferristan; all Levan knows it was a fair fight. Arcole would not have it otherwise."

"My thanks," Arcole said, smiling.

"You saw it?" the captain asked, and when Silvestre shook his head: "Then I'd suggest you hold your tongue, else you'll accompany this duelist to the cells."

"The cells?" Arcole sprang to his feet, right hand touching the hilt of his rapier. "You'd jail me like some common criminal?"

Dom cried a warning as the ten muskets were cocked and raised to fix their sights on Arcole's chest.

"Or shoot you down," said the captain, "do you not come peaceably."

"I've committed no crime," Arcole protested. "In the God's name, is this Evanderan justice?"

"You question Evander's justice?" The captain's eyes fixed hard on Arcole's face. "You'd add that to the catalogue of your crimes?"

"I'd claim my innocence."

Arcole's hand closed on his sword's hilt. Dom said, "Arcole, no! Go with them—I'll find an advocate."

"Your friend"—the captain managed to make it an insult—"gives sound advice. Now, do you give me your blade, or do I take it from you?"

Arcole said, "Alone you could not, 'sieur. Dismiss your men and try to take it."

"Threatening the life of an officer of the God's Militia is another offense," the captain replied, "punishable by execution!"

"He did not threaten you," Dom said. "That was an invitation."

"The court shall decide," the captain promised. "Now, 'sieur, I grow impatient. Do you obey me, or shall you die here?"

Dom said, "You've no chance, Arcole! Go with them. An advocate shall surely have you loose ere dusk."

"And we've the duchess's soirée to attend, eh?" Arcole smiled with far more confidence than Dom felt. "Indeed, I'd not miss that. So, shall we settle this ridiculous matter?"

He took his hand from the rapier and, with his left, loosed the belt. The captain took the proffered sword and nodded at the door. A crowd was gathered there, Dom saw, thankful the Militiaman did not attempt to cuff or bind Arcole.

"Gentlemen." Arcole bowed to young Silvestre and his companions. "It seems you shall keep your money today."

"It shall be spent on an advocate," Silvestre declared.

Arcole smiled and turned to the impatient captain. "So, do you lead the way?"

The captain glowered, motioning for his men to hold their muskets ready as he marched from the gaming room. Dom watched them go before he asked urgently, "Alleyn, you've the name of a reliable advocate?"

■   ■   ■

At least, Arcole reflected, Dom had managed to bribe his jailers so that he need not appear before the court disheveled and shabby as some common criminal. Indeed, as he stood in the box reserved for the accused, Arcole decided he was the best-dressed man in the room—save for the manacles about his wrists and ankles. They quite spoiled the hang of his cuffs, and likely scored his polished boots beyond repair. No matter; as soon as these tiresome formalities were dispensed, he would rid himself of these clothes. He would, he thought as he watched the officers of the court take their places and the tipstaff call the chamber to order, arrange a celebration at which all memories of this interlude would be ritually burned. That should certainly be amusing, and as the charge against him was read, he began to compile a list of guests.

". . . And knowing yourself the superior swordsman did thus conspire to murder him. How plead you?"

Arcole realized the question was addressed to him. He stared at the prosecutor, thinking the man had poor taste in tailors. Or perhaps Levan's rulers paid their officers too poorly to afford to dress decently. He frowned and said, "Not guilty, of course."

The prosecutor smiled back. He was a Levanite, by his looks—one of the turncoats who curried favor with the Evanderans, like old Ferristan there. Arcole glanced at the count and got back a glare of such unalloyed hatred, he wondered if the old man lost his mind. Surely he understood his son had died in a duel: a matter of honor that he, born of Levan's oldest stock, should comprehend. In better days—those lost to Evander's conquest—this affair would never have been allowed come thus far.

But, to Arcole's bemusement, it had; and now Raymone of House Ferristan glowered at him from behind that oiled white beard as if he were some rabid dog to be slain on sight before he might spread his infection. Was it not enough Militiamen had taken him captive as if he were a criminal? And more—oh, yes, far more indignity—had he not been locked with chains on his feet in a filthy cell that stank of urine and vomit, been forced to eat slop he'd not feed the lowest servant, allowed to shave and bathe and change his clothes only when faithful Dom handed over an exorbitant amount of coin?

And now they accused him of murder?

It was ridiculous. His frown deepened into an expression of genuine outrage and he looked away from Raymone, letting his gaze wander over the courtroom.

Two Militiamen guarded the door and two more stood at his back, even though the box he occupied was painted with hex signs he recognized as powerful. The judge was an Evanderan, as were the two advocates attending him. Tipstaff and prosecutor were Levanites; there was no jury—the Autarchy had dispensed with juries—but the accused was allowed his own counsel. Arcole's advocate was a bewigged young man whose sallow face was drawn, his movements nervous as if he were the one on trial. Which, in a way, Arcole supposed, he was—the Levan's new rulers had little affection for any who argued their authority. Perhaps this advocate—Arcole could not quite recall his name—was braver than he looked. Surely he wasn't the only lawyer Dom could find willing to take the case.

"You find these proceedings amusing?"

The judge's voice was querulous, his florid face darkening in irritation; Arcole shook his head and said, "I find them pointless."

Dom winced; the defending advocate climbed heavily to his feet. "My lord, if I may?"

The judge waved a hand and the advocate bowed and continued: "My client was born in the Levan, my lord; he was raised here, in the customs of his country. One of those customs is that matters of honor be settled by the duel."

"He murdered my son," Ferristan cried.

The judge failed to order him silent. Instead, he said, "The Levan now resides under protection of the Autarchy; and in Evander, matters of honor are *not* so crudely settled."

"Of course, my lord." The advocate bowed again; Arcole thought he cringed. "The Autarchy leads us on a more civilized path, but still . . . old customs die hard."

"Had he a quarrel," said the judge, "he should have brought it before the courts. *That* is the civilized way—not these bloody brawls you Levanites resort to."

"It was not," Arcole declared, "a brawl."

Eyes beady and cold as a raven's studied him a moment; then, disdainfully, to the Militiamen at his back the judge said: "Does the accused interrupt again, gag him."

Arcole opened his mouth to protest, to ask if this was *civilized* Evanderan justice, but his advocate spoke first, urgently, motioning him silent.

"Please forgive my client, my lord. He is not accustomed to legal proceedings—he intends no offense."

"But gives it nonetheless," the judge said. "Continue."

"The sadly departed viscount Ferristan was engaged in a game of petanoye with Sieur Blayke," the advocate said, "and lost a considerable amount of money."

Arcole was tempted to remark that the dead man was an excruciatingly bad player, but Dom was shaking his head and grimacing at him, so he bit back the words and only stood silent, listening.

"He had been drinking heavily throughout the game," the advocate was explaining, "and grew offensive. I've depositions to that effect, my lord, do you care to study them."

The judge beckoned and the tipstaff took the affidavits and brought them to the bench. The judge glanced at them and pushed them away.

The prosecutor asked, "Where are the witnesses? Depositions are useless without witnesses."

"Quite," said the judge.

Arcole's lawyer looked to where Raymone Ferristan sat and said, "I fear the witnesses are unavailable, my lord. Three are gone to country estates and two are incapacitated; one has simply disappeared."

"Then I'll not allow their testimony," the judge announced. "These depositions are worthless."

The young advocate sighed, but the count of House Ferristan was smiling now. By God, Arcole thought, the old bastard's bribed or beaten them! No wonder I've no friends here save Dom. He felt a little of his certainty wither.

"Sieur Freydmon is present," the advocate said.

Dom rose, but the prosecutor cried, "My lord, Dom Freydmon is a known associate of the accused. They are old accomplices—"

Arcole's lawyer said, "I object! Sieur Freydmon is a respected man. To suggest he is an *accomplice* . . ."

The judge motioned him silent. To Dom he said, "Is this true?"

"That I am Arcole's friend?" asked Dom. "Yes. I've known him seven years now."

"Then I find this man unsuitable as a witness," the judge declared. "Clearly any testimony he may give will be colored by his acknowledged association with the accused. Sieur Freydmon, seat yourself."

Dom stood a moment with open mouth, disbelief in his eyes. The judge fixed him with a beady stare and he sat. Arcole felt a little more of his confidence dissipate.

"The viscount grew offensive," the advocate went on, weary as a man pushing a heavy weight uphill, "and insulted Sieur Blayke. Aspersions were cast as to Sieur Blayke's antecedents, and accusations made of his honesty—"

The prosecutor interrupted. "All hearsay! These are no more than allegations. Without corroborative testimony the court is asked to accept the word of the accused alone. And Luis, viscount Ferristan, is not here to defend himself."

"No," said the judge ponderously, "he is not."

Helplessly, Arcole's man said, "My lord, do you refuse to allow the depositions and Sieur Freydmon's testimony . . ."

"I apply the law," said the judge. "No more than that. Do you accuse me of error?"

The count of Ferristan's smile grew wider, fiercer. Arcole felt the last of his confidence dissolve, to be replaced with growing outrage. This is a farce, he thought, Raymone and this damn Evanderan judge work hand in glove.

He heard his advocate say quickly, "No, my lord. Nothing of the sort."

"Then present your case."

"I am left with little to present," said the advocate helplessly. "Sieur Blayke is well known in Levan as a man of honor. He has never faced such charges before. It is common knowledge that the viscount insulted him and challenged him, and that Sieur Blayke acted as must any man of honor—he accepted the challenge. To do less should have been an insult to House Ferristan. I assure you, my lord, that the duel was fairly fought. There were witnesses . . ."

"My lord." The prosecutor darted in like a terrier on a rat. "I've no doubt that Sieur Freydmon will be one of these alleged witnesses. Where are the others?"

Bought off, Arcole thought, or else terrified into silence.

"Were I allowed time," pleaded the advocate, "I might find them."

"Too late," the judge declared briskly. "Are they not now present, I'll not grant more time. Have you aught else to say?"

The advocate shook his head. The judge waved the prosecutor forward.

"I'll not take up much of your time, my lord," he promised. "I've but a few plain questions for the accused, and I believe this matter may be soon settled." He turned to Arcole. "You are known as a gambler and duelist, no?"

Arcole looked down on the thin-faced prosecutor and said, "I've some skill with cards, and with a blade."

"Do you make a living from your gambling?"

Arcole shrugged and answered, "Aye."

"And you have fought numerous duels?"

Arcole nodded.

"How many?"

"I've not kept count."

"Two? A dozen? A score? A hundred?"

"Less than a hundred. Perhaps fifty."

"And won them all?"

Arcole smiled coldly. Hope seemed lost; his pride remained. "I am here, no?" he said.

"So you have slain perhaps as many as fifty men. That suggests you are greatly skilled. Were you a soldier?"

"I fought for the Levan," Arcole said.

The prosecutor smiled. "In the Restitution? Did you kill men then?"

Again Arcole only nodded: there seemed no point to words.

"My lord." The prosecutor turned to the bench. "Luis, viscount of House Ferristan, had fought only three duels in his young life; he was never a soldier. I put it to you that the accused boasts such skill as surely rendered this fight unfair. He might have refused the challenge, but knowing he held the upper hand, he engaged with the unfortunate viscount confident of victory. It was no less than murder, my lord, and I ask you pronounce Arcole Blayke guilty of that crime."

The judge nodded. "Do you have aught to say?" he asked of Arcole.

It seemed a bitter taste filled Arcole's mouth and he was tempted to spit. Raymone was beaming triumphantly; the prosecutor oozed confidence. Arcole's lawyer stood with downcast eyes; Dom stared aghast. The judge waited with obvious impatience.

"Save this be a travesty and House Ferristan entirely devoid of honor," Arcole said, "no."

"Then it is my duty as an officer of the Autarchy," said the judge, "to pronounce sentence. I find you, Arcole Blayke, guilty of murder. I sentence you to die."

8 Branded

"You did *what?*"

The chains fettering Arcole's ankles rattled as he rose. Dom started back, so angry was his friend's voice, so outraged his expression. For a moment he thought Arcole about to strike him, but instead the fists struck only empty air and Arcole shook his head, his eyes wide now in disbelief.

Dom said, "I thought it best. I thought you'd be pleased. At least . . ."

"Oh, Dom." Now Arcole's voice came weary and Dom saw his shoulders sag. "What have you done? Why did you not ask me first? That, at the least." He slumped on the wooden bench, his back against the dirty wall, careless of his shirt.

"I had little enough time," Dom said, "and none too much money. By God, Arcole, it costs fifteen golden guineas to buy my way in here. And most of our coin is taken by the court . . ."

"Stolen by the court!" snarled Arcole. "I tell you, Dom, there's as little justice left in the Levan as there's honor."

"Be that as it may," Dom went on, more aware than Arcole of the ticking minutes: fifteen golden guineas did not buy many. "The bulk of our savings was taken in fines and compensation to House Ferristan"— he ignored Arcole's snort—"and what I managed to rescue, I thought to employ on your behalf."

"And now it's gone?"

When Dom nodded, Arcole tipped back his head and groaned, then sank his face in his hands and from behind that barrier muttered, "Dom, what have you done to me?"

"Saved your life," his friend said. "I thought you'd be pleased."

The face that rose to meet his was at first difficult to recognize as Arcole's. The eyes were leeched of their usual sparkle and marked beneath by dark crescents. Stubble decorated cheeks and chin, and the hair—usually so carefully barbered—was lank and uncombed. Then Arcole smiled, and Dom saw a flash of the old sardonic humor.

"Is there any left?"

Dom said, "A few guineas."

"So what shall you live on? Have you enough?"

"I'll get by," he said, and waved a dismissing hand. "It's you we need concern ourselves with."

"I?" Arcole chuckled: a cynical sound. "My fate's decided, no?"

"I thought you'd be pleased," Dom repeated. "They were planning to hang you."

"I had prepared myself for that, old friend. But this . . . ?" He shook his head. "There's no chance you might get the money back?"

Before Dom could reply, while he still stared in disbelief at his friend, Arcole answered himself: "No, of course not. That God-cursed Evanderan judge would never return it, not once in his thieving pocket."

"He's already signed the papers," Dom said.

Arcole nodded, less like a man reprieved than one hearing himself condemned. He had taken it better in court, Dom thought. He seemed far better disposed to death than to this news. Warily, he said, "They'd have hung you, Arcole, and left your body on the gallows for the crows to pick. That was the verdict—Raymone of House Ferristan made sure of that."

"Then you risk his anger," Arcole said. "When this gets out, he'll likely seek to take your life."

"I know." Dom nodded. "I leave for Tarramor at dawn. He'll not find me there—I've friends—"

"How shall you live?"

It seemed odd that Arcole should concern himself with that, and typical. Dom shrugged and said, "I can teach . . . whatever. I'll find something. Perhaps"—he vented a small, sad laugh—"perhaps I'll write a book about your exploits."

"Lie low awhile," Arcole advised him. "House Ferristan has a long arm, and Raymone a long memory. The old bastard," he added.

"At least you'll thwart him," Dom said.

"Aye." Arcole's smile showed briefly, then: "Do you know what they do, Dom?"

Dom nodded, not wanting to say it. It seemed to him that anything was better than hanging: he was not, he knew, of Arcole's mettle.

"Exiles are branded," Arcole said. "On the cheek, are they male; women on the shoulder."

"But you'll be alive," said Dom quietly. "Is that not something, at least? Surely that's preferable to the gallows."

"Is it?" Arcole asked in a voice Dom found horribly reasonable. "They'll put their mark on me as if I were a . . . a common criminal! A footpad, or some highwayman. They'll put me in the hold of some stinking ship and send me over the Sea of Sorrows to Salvation—the wilderness! *And I shall never return!* Is that truly better, Dom?"

Dom swallowed, close to wishing he'd not invested such coin, such time—and both at some considerable risk to himself once word reached House Ferristan—to save his friend's life. Then Arcole took his hand and smiled and said, "Dom, I know you've acted for what you believe the best. Do I seem ungrateful, forgive me. It's that I was ready to die, not live in exile. I cannot envisage myself indentured in the wilderness."

"It may not be so bad," Dom said, trying hard himself to smile. "There's at least one town there. Grostheim, they name it."

"Indeed." Arcole affected a tone of languid interest. "And think you it's gaming salons? And I shall be allowed to play a hand or two of petanoye? Perhaps there shall be dances?"

Sorrowfully, Dom said, "I'm sorry."

Arcole laughed with sudden humor and slapped a hand to his friend's shoulder. "Oh, Dom; Dom, it's I should apologize, not you. You risk your own safety to save my life and I reward you with curses and mockery—forgive me." He rose, bowing. "Likely, in time I'll come to make some life there, and thank you for it. Only now put off that mournful face and accept my thanks, and my earnest apologies."

"I do." Dom forced his lips apart in semblance of a smile. "Not that you need to apologize."

"So." Arcole returned to the bench. "When do I depart on this great adventure?"

"Tomorrow, so I understand," Dom said. "You go first to Bantar, overland; a ship from there."

"Then this is our farewell," Arcole said.

"Aye," said Dom. "By the day after tomorrow Raymone will know you're not hung. But you'll be on your way by then, and he'll not have chance to stop you."

"And you'll be bound for Tarramor. Fare well there, old friend."

Dom nodded. There seemed little else to say, and he could hear the turnkey approaching: fifteen golden guineas bought so little time. He took Arcole's hand and then was drawn into his friend's embrace. Almost, he wept against Arcole's shoulder, but that should not do, and so he only held his friend a moment and then drew back.

"May the God protect you, Arcole."

"Better, I hope, than he's done so far," Arcole declared, and grinned.

Dom heard the turnkey cough noisily outside the cell. He wanted to say more, but could think of nothing; and knew he *should* weep did he linger. So he bowed, as if they stood in some grand salon, and went out through the door the turnkey held for him. He heard it slam behind him and the key turn in the lock, and then tears did come, for he knew he would never see Arcole again.

In the cell, Arcole rubbed absently at his cheek, wondering what it should feel like when the red iron was pressed there. Soon enough, he thought, he would know—and that brand would mark him all his life. There'd be no hiding it from the ever-watchful eyes of the cursed Autarchy. He damned Evander then, and all its priests and Inquisitors and Militiamen, and vowed that had he ever the chance to bring them down, he would seize it and laugh as they fell.

The branding came soon enough—at dawn the next day—which suited Arcole better than waiting.

The turnkey came with four Militiamen, who took hold of Arcole even though he did not struggle, and drew his hands behind his back, locking them there with heavy cuffs that were connected to the manacles around his ankles by a length of chain. He must perforce go tottering, with a Militiaman to either side, their hands upon his arms, and two vigilant behind, to the low, dark hall where a brazier glowed red and a man clad all in scorched and greasy brown leather tended his irons.

There was a chair of wood and metal, high-backed and bolted to the floor, its purpose obvious. Before the Militiamen might prod him onward, Arcole shuffled of his own accord toward the seat.

"Master Torturer, good day." He nodded a greeting to the leather-clad man, and had the satisfaction of seeing the fellow gape in startlement at his casual tone. "Shall I sit here?"

The man nodded dumbly and looked to the Militiamen as if for reassurance that the prisoner was secured safely. Three favored Arcole with reluctantly admiring smiles; the fourth's was scornful. "You'll use a different voice when you feel the iron," he said.

"Think you so?" Arcole determined he would not scream.

The Militiaman said, "Take his arms," and two of them grasped Arcole firmly as the speaker produced the handcuff key and removed the shackles.

He was pushed down onto the chair, where bands of dark iron locked about his wrists, more around his ankles. A leather strap was bound tight around his chest, and another across his forehead, holding his head rigid against the chair's high back.

"He's secure."

The Militiamen stepped back; the one now wore a grin of horrid anticipation, the rest watched stoically. The torturer drew on a heavy gauntlet and took an iron from the brazier. The head glowed bright in the dim light. Arcole gritted his teeth: he would not cry out.

The torturer stood before him, and he closed his eyes against the iron's heat as it was thrust close.

Such was the pain, he could not prevent the shout that burst forth. He heard it echo off the indifferent stone; his nostrils filled with the stench of burning flesh. He was grateful for the darkness that encompassed him.

He woke suddenly, unwilling to leave the soothing blankness. Cold and wet denied him that solace, however, and he spluttered indignantly as he realized a bucket of water had been thrown over him. A hand took his chin, steadying his head as another smeared some salve over the raw pain that covered one side of his face. The pain subsided to a dull throbbing, and he opened his eyes to find the same four Militiamen studying him with calm indifference.

"Not so brave now, eh?"

He recognized the speaker and forced a smile that seemed to crack his face apart. "Have you a mirror?" His voice was thick, and every word sent shafts of pain through his skull. "Perhaps I shall start a new fashion."

The Militiaman scowled; his companions smiled. Then they hauled Arcole upright and locked the cuffs about his wrists again, this time at the front, and marched him from the hall.

He thought they might return him to his cell and that should be a small blessing, for he felt very weak and would stretch out on his bench and sleep awhile, but instead, he was led down a long corridor to a flight of steps that rose to an arched doorway opening onto a courtyard. Blue sky showed above high walls, and somewhere a bird sang. The air smelled clean and fresh after the malodorous cellars of the prison, and rain glistened on the flags as Arcole was brought to a wagon.

It was such a vehicle as he had seen often enough in the streets of Levan: painted black, with high, solid walls and roof, a single window in the rearward door covered with a metal grille. It was such a vehicle as transported prisoners; he had never thought to ride in one himself.

A ladder granted access to the interior, and the Militiamen stood back as Arcole climbed awkwardly inside. He grimaced at the smell that succeeded in combining all the body's fluids in one overpowering fetor, then he was pushed down onto a narrow bench and the chain unlocked from his shackles and fixed to a ring set in the wall above his head. The Militiamen departed and he looked about.

Five other prisoners sat watching him with the numb indifference of lost men. All were branded, their cheeks displaying the letter *E* that was the damning mark of the exile. Arcole winced at the sight.

"None too pretty, eh?"

The speaker was a hulking fellow, his dirty black beard serving to throw the scar into vivid relief against the prison pallor of his cheek. Arcole prayed he did not look so dreadful. He said, "No. I think we'd none of us win prizes for our looks at present."

The bearded man coughed laughter and asked, "What they got you for?"

"I killed a man," Arcole said.

The bearded man was unimpressed. "So'd I," he said. "In a tavern. Bastard pulled a knife on me, so I broke his neck. They'd've hanged me, save they want slaves out there in Salvation."

"Salvation," Arcole grunted. "Hardly our salvation."

"Better'n hangin', no?" the giant said.

"Think you so?" Arcole replied.

The bearded man gaped at him as if he were deranged. "Livin's better'n dyin', no?"

"It depends," said Arcole, "on the manner of one's existence."

"You one o' them philosophers?" the giant demanded. He pronounced it *fill-oss-off-er*.

Arcole shook his head and sucked breath as the movement set his cheek to burning. "No," he replied, "I'm"—he corrected himself—"*was* a gentleman of leisure."

The giant guffawed. He seemed not to feel any pain. "Not no more," he hooted. "A gentleman o' leisure, eh? Won't be much leisure in Salvation, friend. Hard labor's what you'll get out there—same as the rest o' us. Just hard labor til you're spent, an' then you die. Gentleman o' leisure, hah!"

He leant back against the wall, grinning through his beard. Arcole closed his eyes and fervently wished he were somewhere else; he thought the gallows should have been preferable to weeks in such company.

Then the door was flung closed and the interior was abruptly dark. A key grated in the lock; the wagon rocked as the driver climbed to his seat, then lurched as he cracked his whip over the team and the horses flung themselves into the traces. Faint came the clatter of hooves as the escort of Militiamen formed about the vehicle. It began to move, across the prison yard and out through the gates Arcole could not see. The wheels rumbled over cobblestones. Someone whimpered; someone else began to hum unmelodiously. Arcole closed his eyes. He thought this should be a most unpleasant journey.

Davyd stared around the barnlike hall at his fellow exiles. They looked to him like any crowd found on the lesser thoroughfares of Bantar, save that all wore manacles, and all were branded. His own scar no longer pained him, but the cuffs about his wrists chafed. He thought that had he his picklocks, it should not be too difficult to get free; but those were long lost and, even could he use them, the brand decorating his cheek marked him for all to see. Not even Julius would offer refuge to one bearing the mark of exile.

No: he was condemned now, without hope of rescue. He sniffed noisily and tried to tell himself that he was lucky, that it could be worse —had the Autarchy discovered he was a Dreamer, he should likely have been burned by then. It failed to help: he faced a fear almost as great. Soon he would be herded out of this solid, safe, *earthbound* hall and onto a ship that floated on water. And that ship would slip its moorings and turn from the harbor toward the open sea. Its sails would fill and it would progress westward, to the Sea of Sorrows and beyond, out where there was nothing but ocean. An ocean that was filled with monsters, like the creatures in his dream.

He shivered, trying without success to drive those oneiric images from his mind, and his shivering became a trembling that set his teeth to rattling and, against his will, the tears to flowing helplessly down his cheeks. He drew up his knees, hugging himself as best he could with shackled wrists, his eyes screwed tight as he rocked back and forth, chased by the monsters he *knew* awaited him.

It was a while before he felt the hands that stroked his shaking shoulders and heard the voice that murmured soothing words such as he'd not heard since Aunt Dory died. Unthinking, he turned toward the sound, burrowing into the consolation of the arms and the warm body that offered him temporary refuge.

"There, there. It's not so bad, eh? Don't cry; please don't cry. It's not so bad."

"It is," he mumbled, and almost added, I know it is, because I dreamed it. But the habit of that concealment was grained too deep, and so he only repeated: "It is."

"I'll look after you," the voice promised, and Davyd opened his eyes and blinked back the tears that he might see his comforter.

She was not that much older than he, and he thought she looked like an angel, one of the carved and gilded angels that decorated the churches he so seldom visited. Her face was an oval framed by golden curls, that managed even in disarray to tumble artfully as if arranged by a coiffeuse. Her eyes were big and blue as cornflowers, and her mouth was wide, the lips full and red. She was, he decided, absolutely beautiful. Suddenly he was embarrassed and drew back a little.

She smiled and said, "My name's Flysse. What's yours?"

"Davyd Furth," he answered, sniffing. He saw that his tears had marked her blouse, which had once been white. "And it *is* bad."

For an instant her smile faltered, became forlorn, but then she rearranged it in the shape of confidence. "The ships cross the ocean all the time," she said. "They come and go, and they're really quite safe."

"They sink," he said.

"How do you know?" she asked gently.

"My mam was drowned," he said gruffly. It was difficult to talk about it even then, so many years later, but it was the only acceptable reason he could offer. He couldn't mention his dreams, the fluid visions that had haunted him since childhood, his mother's death by water only enhancing their terrifying import. It was his dreams that had always told him that. Turning back to his companion, he added, "She went out on a fishing boat, and there was a storm, and she was drowned. So I know!"

"Oh," she said, "I'm sorry."

He shrugged, swallowing noisily. "It was long time ago. I don't hardly remember her, but it made me scared."

"But we'll be on a big ship," she said, trying to comfort him. "Much bigger than a fishing boat. I'm sure it will be safe."

"On the ocean?" He shook his head miserably. "There are storms and sea monsters. And they get becalmed and everyone starves, or goes mad because they've no water."

"How do you know?" she asked again.

"Because," he said, "I do. How do you know they don't?"

"I used to work in a tavern," she said, "and sometimes sailors came there."

"Sailors lie a lot," he said.

"And sea captains," she said, "who are respectable and don't lie; they told me about it. And if they could, then they must've crossed the ocean, no?"

He thought about that a moment, then frowned and shrugged again. She still held him, though not so close, and he did not want to quit her embrace. Nor did he wish to seem a sniveling coward in her eyes, but that was hard—he was still very afraid.

"I suppose so," he allowed. "But I don't want to go."

She laughed at that, not mockingly but softly, as he remembered Aunt Dory laughing when he brought her some childhood fear. It was a comforting sound, and he felt a flash of anger. He was no child, to be fed soft words and meaningless noises.

"I'm not a coward," He said.

"No, I didn't think you were."

He felt a little better for that. He suspected she said it only to soothe him, but he liked her the more for it.

"I'm afraid too," she said, "do I tell the truth."

Davyd forgot his tears then, and that he was by several years the younger. He straightened his back and said, "I'll protect you."

"Thank you," she said, sounding absolutely sincere. "Perhaps we might protect each other?"

"Yes." He nodded vigorously. "What did you say your name was?"

"Flysse," she said. "Flysse Cobal."

He held out a hand and they shook as best the manacles allowed, sealing their bargain. They were both encouraged: it was good to find a friend in hardship.

"When do you think we'll"—Davyd hesitated: he still did not like to think of the imminent future—". . . sail?"

"I heard a guard say soon," Flysse answered him. "They're waiting for some other prisoners. When they arrive, we depart."

"I hope they take a long time. The longer the better."

Flysse laughed at that. The sound was odd in this miserable place, like a hurdy-gurdy in a graveyard. Davyd found his smile become genuine. He saw faces turn their way, most frowning as if the owners wondered at their sanity, and he began to laugh himself, defiantly.

He thought perhaps he *was* a little crazed, for the memory of the dreams remained and he knew past any doubting that his dreams told the truth. Danger waited for them on the open sea. He wondered if he should tell this newfound friend, but habit bade him not. In his life he had learned more of mistrust than of faith, and it occurred to him that Flysse might buy her freedom with revelation of a dreamer. Likely the thought was unworthy, but even so—wiser for now that he hold his tongue. Did he come to trust her fully, perhaps then—but not now, when careless words might save him from the sea only to give him to the flames. It was an unpleasant choice, but the fire was certain; the sea . . . Well, while the dream had threatened horrors, it had not *specifically* foretold his death, so perhaps there was hope. He clung to that straw like a drowning man.

Two more days they waited in discomfort and ignorance. They were fed, albeit poorly, and were free to move about the hall, but most remained huddled in their places as if staking some claim to that sad patch of ground. When the guards came in with their food, the briefly opened doors admitted a wafting of air that smelled of the sea and tar and wet rope, reminding them they were held in the harbor quarter. Davyd thought the hall must once have been a warehouse—faint through the overlaid scent of unwashed bodies there were more exotic odors of spices and tobacco—and the few windows were set high and very dirty. It was still, he supposed, a kind of warehouse, save now its contents were human—living goods awaiting shipment across the ocean. He thought he might have lost his mind were it not for Flysse.

She remained determinedly cheerful, so that he must match her and pretend he was no longer afraid. He hoped they might be indentured together, when they reached Salvation—if they survived the Sea of Sorrows.

For her part, Flysse was grateful for the company of this odd boy, and—though she hid it—as much shocked as intrigued by his tales of robberies and rookeries, of pockets picked and locks undone. He was, unashamedly, a thief; indeed he was rather proud of his larcenous skills, which sat ill with her honest upbringing. Yet as he told her of his sad childhood, of a mother barely remembered and of the woman—Aunt Dory—who had raised him, she could not help but feel sympathy. He seemed to her less a genuine criminal than a luckless victim of unkind fate. In Cudham a home should have been found for him, a place to sleep, and honest work. He might well have had no more than a corner of some hayloft, but the folk of her village would have seen him fed and clothed, not left him to his own devices.

Such a reminder of home saddened her, for she knew she would never see Cudham again, and likely her parents never know her fate. She wondered if they would assume her dead, or—far worse—believe she had forgotten them, seduced by the city. She did not believe word would ever reach them of her exile, and with that thought tears threatened. Then it was Davyd who comforted her, with tales of daring thievery and colorful accounts of folk who seemed to her quite bizarre, so that before long she smiled again and listened eagerly to his yarns.

So the days passed until, around noon on the third day, the last of the exiles arrived.

Davyd and Flysse were deep in conversation. Flysse was speaking of the summer fair in Cudham, which seemed to Davyd a marvelous thing. She broke off as the doors opened and six men were ushered in. They were unshaved and dirty and none too steady on their feet, as if walking were a thing they had forgotten. The doors banged shut behind them and they stared around, blinking and squinting in the poor light.

Five were dressed in the clothes of ordinary workingmen, but the sixth was in gentlemanly attire; and though his coat was soiled and his boots scuffed, and his chin as stubbled as the rest—save for one giant fellow who sported a voluminous beard—he managed an air of elegance that set him apart. He looked about with narrowed eyes, his lips pursed in an expression of distaste, as if he found himself in unfamiliar surroundings not at all to his liking. Flysse thought she had never seen a man so handsome.

"I wonder what he did to end up with us."

Flysse blushed as Davyd spoke, thinking her observation overly brazen; but then she saw that she was not alone in remarking the newcomer. He was, after all, the only man present to wear such finery, or such an air of disdain.

"Looks like a toff," Davyd murmured, and chuckled. "And if he keeps his nose in the air like that, someone's likely to dent it for him."

Flysse thought that should be sad—it seemed to her a very attractive nose.

"Nice clothes," Davyd remarked, watching as the stranger picked a way between his fellow prisoners in search of a space. "I wonder if he managed to bring any coin?"

"How could he?" Flysse asked, turning toward Davyd whilst still managing to watch the man from the corner of her eye. She found herself hoping he might find a place beside them, then berated herself for such silly notions. He was clearly a gentleman fallen on hard times, and unlikely to consider her worthy of notice.

"It can be done," Davyd assured her from the depths of his worldly wisdom. "It all depends on who you know, who your friends are."

"What good would money do?"

Davyd winked and told her, "Guards can be bribed—to give you extra food, light work, that kind of thing."

Flysse nodded, thinking not for the first time that she was an innocent in such matters.

"But I reckon not," Davyd continued. "A toff like that—why, if he had any coin, he'd surely have bought himself a barbering, likely had his boots polished . . ."

There was a hint of regret in his voice, and Flysse gave him all her attention. "And if he had?" she asked. "What good to you?"

"To *us*," Davyd corrected her, and waved expressive fingers.

"You'd pick his pockets?" Flysse was shocked.

Davyd grinned and shrugged, quite unabashed. "Likely not," he said ruefully, "while I've got these cuffs on. But are they removed . . ."

"You'd steal his money?" Now Flysse frowned, prompting Davyd to a perplexed expression.

"I'd make our journey as easy as possible," he declared. "What's wrong with that?"

"It would be stealing," Flysse said.

"That's what I do," Davyd replied. "I'm a thief."

"And see where it's got you." Flysse was stern now.

"Aye." Davyd glanced around. "Here—where I've not much to lose. Except"—he turned his gaze back to the stranger—"perhaps my life."

"No!" Flysse was suddenly afraid: she'd not lose this new-won friend. "You mustn't. Promise me!"

Davyd was still watching the man. He shook his head absently and said, "I doubt I'll have the chance, even if he does have coin. Look at him. See how he moves?"

Flysse obeyed: he seemed to her most graceful. In her ear she heard Davyd whisper: "I'd wager he's a duelist. He's that look about him."

Flysse had no idea what a duelist looked like.

Davyd said, "Am I right, he'd make a good friend. And we could use a friend."

Flysse thought it unlikely so gentlemanly a fellow would have much inclination to befriend an urchin thief and a tavern girl, but before she had time to voice such pessimism, Davyd was calling to the man.

"Hey, 'sieur! We've room aplenty here."

The man looked toward them. As his eyes met hers, Flysse blushed anew and lowered her head.

"A smile would help," Davyd whispered.

She refused to look up or answer, and the next thing she knew the boots halted before her and a deep voice said, "Madam, may I join you?" as if she sat not in this dingy hall all filled with branded prisoners but in a salon, free.

She heard Davyd say, "Of course, 'sieur, and welcome. I'm called Davyd, Davyd Furth. This is Flysse Cobal."

There was a movement. Flysse looked up from under lowered lashes and saw the man bow. Along the hall someone laughed.

"I am Arcole Blayke. With your permission?"

She nodded and managed to mumble an affirmative. Arcole Blayke said, "Thank you," and settled himself beside her.

"So," asked Davyd, "what brings you here, Sieur Blayke?"

"I killed a man in a duel," Arcole replied, and chuckled bitterly. "Unfortunately, he had a powerful father."

"I thought as much." Davyd sounded triumphant. "You're a duelist."

Arcole nodded gravely. "And you?"

"A thief," Davyd said.

Arcole frowned as if this news did not please him and looked to Flysse. "And what was your crime, Mistress Cobal?"

"She struck a lieutenant in the God's Militia," Davyd answered for her. "He tried to seduce her and she broke his nose, and most of his teeth."

Flysse saw Arcole duck his head approvingly, then turn a bright smile on her. "Then you've my congratulations, mistress. Such an act deserves applause."

Flysse could not help but smile back, even as she felt her cheeks grow warm.

"You're not from Evander," Davyd said.

"No, I come from the Levan," Arcole replied.

"And," Davyd began, then halted as the doors opened again and Militiamen appeared, framed in afternoon sunlight, a captain at their head.

"On your feet!" the captain shouted. "You're Salvation-bound."

9 The Die Is Cast

Throughout the Council, Morrhyn felt a niggling doubt tug at his mind. He wondered at Chakthi's expression: it seemed to him sly, and he did not understand why the Tachyn akaman drew out the debate. Surely the vital question was the People's response to Colun's alarming news, not the trivial matters Chakthi brought up. What could grazing rights and disputed boundaries count against the possibility of impending invasion? It was as if the Tachyn would have the Council sit longer than any there cared for. And why was Vachyr not in his usual position, behind his father? He sensed the rest growing wearied with the seemingly endless procession of petty matters, but—conscious of the delicate balance of allegiances—said nothing.

It was plump Yazte, in the end, who said what was in all their minds. He raised a hand as Chakthi waxed loquacious on the subject of a stream that boundaried the Tachyn grass and asked bluntly, "Can this not wait? The Maker knows, but we've larger decisions to take, and much to ponder."

Chakthi said, "I'd have these smaller matters settled that they not trouble us when we come to these greater things."

To which Yazte replied, "And I'd find my bed. My ears ache with all this talking, and I'd speak privately with Kahteney. Remember, the wakanishas would sit in Dream Council on the morrow."

"Yes, I remember." Chakthi nodded, his smile unctuous. "So surely better no little troubles disturb their concentration."

Yazte snorted, shaking his round head, and looked to Racharran for support.

The Commacht akaman shrugged, diplomatic, not wishing to offend Chakthi.

Yazte frowned and turned to Juh. "How say you, brother? Do you not grow weary?"

Juh smiled his ancient smile and lowered his head. "It is not for me to bid my brother silent," he said, "but I think we might set aside these lesser things."

"Do we vote on it?" asked Tahdase.

Yazte said, "I vote for sleep. I say we leave all lesser matters for another day."

Juh nodded and raised a hand in agreement, soon followed by Tahdase. Racharran raised his hand. Hadduth whispered in Chakthi's ear and the Tachyn akaman smiled and said, "So be it." Morrhyn hid a frown: he sensed something went on here that he could not interpret.

He quit the Council at Racharran's side. Lhyn emerged from the crowd to join her husband, and Colun walked with them.

The Grannach was grumpy. "My belly aches for want of sustenance," he complained. "And a pitcher of tiswin would not go amiss."

Lhyn laughed and promised him both. Racharran said, "Chakthi does not usually speak so much. I wonder what oiled his tongue this night."

"There was something about him." Morrhyn shook his head, perplexed. "As if he and Hadduth shared some secret. Nor was Vachyr present."

"No." Racharran's eyes narrowed in sudden suspicion and he looked to his wife. "Rannach quit the fires soon after Colun spoke. Have you seen him?"

She said, "I suspect our son was eager to return to his bride. Like any new-wed young man."

"Perhaps." Racharran nodded. They came amongst the Commacht tents and he looked to where Rannach's lodge was pitched. The moon was bright, the tent a shadow on the grass, faint firelight visible at the entrance. A grunt escaped his lips and he said, "His horse is gone, and Arrhyna's."

Morrhyn suddenly felt all his doubts knot tight in his belly.

Lhyn said, "Likely they ride under the moon," and jabbed an elbow against her husband's ribs. "Once you had such romantic notions."

Racharran frowned, ignoring the sally.

Mournfully, Colun asked, "Does this mean I go hungry?"

"No." Lhyn favored her husband with a disapproving glance. "Do you and I go on, and I'll see that belly of yours filled. My suspicious husband will meanwhile go skulk about our son's lodge—and we'll laugh at his blushes when he returns."

"And tiswin?" Colun demanded.

"And tiswin," Lhyn confirmed. She pushed Racharran forward. "Shall you embarrass yourself, husband? Or shall you leave them be?"

Racharran, not looking at her, said, "Feed Colun; all well, I'll join you soon. Morrhyn?"

Akaman and wakanisha crossed the open ground to the lodge. As he saw the unlaced entry flap, Morrhyn groaned. Racharran cursed, shouldering the flap aside to enter. The interior elicited a louder, fiercer oath.

This, Morrhyn thought with dreadful realization, is why Chakthi delayed us so long. To give his Maker-cursed son time. Damn them both! He snatched at Racharran's arm as the akaman moved away.

"No, you cannot! Think on it—even is Vachyr gone, what proof have we he'd anything to do with this? Shall you accuse Chakthi without clear proof?"

"Think you this is not his work?" Racharran demanded.

"I think it is." Morrhyn set himself before his akaman like a man facing an angry bull buffalo, he thought. He set his hands against Racharran's shoulders. "But even so, we've no proof."

"What proof do we need?" Racharran pushed against the wakanisha. "Shall we wait for Rannach to bring him back across his saddle?"

"Is he alive, then yes," Morrhyn cried. "Pray for that. Do you go storming through the Tachyn lodges now, you only give Chakthi cause for greater insult, and legitimate!"

For a while Racharran stood rigid, straining against Morrhyn. Then he slumped, the tension leaving his frame. He nodded wearily. "We're caught, no?" He raised his face to the moonlit sky as if in supplication. "Oh, by the Maker! Had Rannach only listened, found some other bride . . ."

"But he did not," Morrhyn said. "He found Arrhyna and wed her, with the blessing of the Council. Has Vachyr stolen her, then he stands condemned before all the Matakwa."

"Does he live to be condemned." Planed by the moonlight, Racharran's face was haggard. "But does Rannach slay him within the boundaries of the Meeting Ground, then it shall be my son who stands condemned."

Morrhyn said, "He gave his word."

A barking laugh escaped Racharran's tight-drawn mouth. "Did

some wife-stealer take Lhyn, think you *I'd* remember such a promise when I faced him? Would you?"

Almost, Morrhyn said no, but he held that back and instead said, "Then the Maker grant Rannach remembers."

They were blooded warriors, accustomed to the hunt and—sometimes—clan warfare. They could read a trail and, with the Maker's blessing, outguess their quarry. But those skills were also Vachyr's, and he could ride hard and fast, thinking only of escape and the obscuration of his spoor, while they must seek out his tracks by night, and ensure which were his and which those of other riders. With all the People come to Matakwa, the country around the Meeting Ground was busy with trails: they must ride slower, and carefully, lest they lose the sign.

"Ach!" Bakaan rose from his examination of the trampled grass and swept out an arm, indicating the profusion of tracks. "I'd guess a party of Tachyn came to meet him, then scattered two by two."

Hadustan leaned from his saddle, scanning the ground. "All two by two," he murmured. "And look." He pointed to the dung piles littering the area. "They waited for him."

"Chakthi's hand!" Rannach said it like a curse. "His father must have aided him, sent warriors out to hide his trail."

"Then," said Zhy, "it was all planned in advance. And it might be," he surveyed the tracks, "they join later, and we face . . . what? Two hands of warriors?"

Bakaan asked, "Do you say we turn back?"

"No." Zhy shook his head. "Only that we ride cautious."

"Ten warriors are too many." Rannach held the stallion in check as the animal pranced, sensing his urgency. "The absence of ten warriors from the Council would be noticed."

"How so," Zhy asked, "amongst so many?"

Rannach thought a moment, then: "Chakthi would not give such a task to any save his most trusted men. And I saw none of those absent from the Council fires."

Bakaan asked, "What do you tell us?"

Under the moon's light it was hard to decide whether Rannach snarled or frowned. Perhaps it was both; he said, "That earlier this day Chakthi sent men out to hide his son's tracks. They gathered here, as if meeting Vachyr, then rode out in pairs in different directions. Vachyr came here and rode on, thinking to confuse any pursuit."

He dropped from the saddle, tossing the stallion's rein to Bakaan as he walked an impatient circle around the hoof-marked ground.

"See? These are older; harder." He stooped, fingers delicate as they probed the prints. He checked them all, then: "These, they're more recent. And one animal has smaller hooves—like Arrhyna's mare." He pointed northward. "Vachyr goes that way."

Bakaan asked, "You're sure?"

Rannach said, "I pray the Maker I am."

He leapt astride the stallion and heeled the big horse into the night.

Lhyn was unhappy with Racharran's decision, and her displeasure encompassed Morrhyn. He cringed under her frown.

"Alone?" She expressed her anger with the spoon, ladling stew into their bowls hard enough they must clutch the platters two-handed, lest gravy splatter them. "You send no senior warriors after him? To . . . protect him? Or prevent him from slaying Vachyr?"

Colun, already emptying his second bowl and his second pitcher of tiswin, beamed and said, "He's a warrior, no? He's my old friend's son —he'll come to no harm."

"Be quiet!" Lhyn withered the Grannach leader with a single furious glance. "Eat, and drink your tiswin, and hold your tongue. This is my son we speak of."

Colun belched and shrugged. "Forgive me," he said, and filled his cup.

"I've explained it, no?" Racharran looked to the wakanisha for support. "It's as Morrhyn says—do I send riders out, then Chakthi can claim I took a hand in whatever happens."

"And is Rannach slain?" Lhyn asked. "Or he slays Vachyr? What then?"

"Does he slay Vachyr," Racharran said, "then likely we shall have war with the Tachyn when we need peace, alliance against these invaders. I think that Chakthi planned this well."

Lhyn settled by the fire, and when she spoke her voice was no cooler than the flames. "And is our son killed?"

Morrhyn ventured an opinion. "He is not alone," he said. "Those comrades of his ride with him—Bakaan and the other two, Hadustan and Zhy."

"And has Chakthi sent warriors to halt them?"

Was this, Morrhyn wondered, what marriage was like? Was it this furious exchange of views? Did the presence of children bring forth such differences? He thought how difficult it must be for Racharran: father and akaman of the clan, both.

He said, "I doubt Chakthi risks that."

Lhyn stared at him and he thought of lions.

He said, "I think that Chakthi agreed this with Vachyr, but would not risk sending others. I think that Vachyr rides alone, whilst Rannach has his companions."

"And shall likely slay Vachyr," Lhyn said, granting him no release. "And stand condemned for breaking the Matakwa truce."

Morrhyn lowered his face: it was hard to meet the burning of her eyes.

Racharran said, "Does it come to that, then surely the Council will understand. By the Maker, Vachyr stole our son's bride! He must be condemned."

"And we Commacht," Lhyn said coldly, "then find ourselves at war with the Tachyn. Which you, my husband, and you"—her icy gaze took in Morrhyn—"say that is what we must avoid at all costs."

"There is no other way." Racharran's voice sounded empty, bereft. "It's as we say—Chakthi's tied our hands."

"Oh, Chakthi's clever." Her answer was a snort of contempt that gathered in her husband and Morrhyn and Chakthi in one maternal basket. "He's tied your hands, eh? And does Vachyr slay our son?"

Morrhyn sympathized with Racharran even as he felt grateful that question was directed at the akaman. He knew what he wished his answer should be, and what it must be. He fixed his eyes on the fire as Racharran spoke. He thought he could not bear to look at either face, the father's or the mother's.

"Then I must go before the Council and demand Vachyr be condemned as a bride-thief and a murderer." Racharran's voice reminded Morrhyn that they were none of them any longer young: it was the voice of years, weighted with responsibility. "But I must also remember that I am akaman of the Commacht; and that our clan—and all the People—face an unknown threat."

"And our son?" Lhyn asked.

"Is one man," Racharran said. "The Maker help me, but does it come to it, I must sacrifice him."

"Our son?" she demanded.

Her husband ducked his head. As if, Morrhyn thought, a terrible dread hand pressed it down in rueful acceptance.

As Racharran said "Yes," Colun belched noisily and pitched sideways over the furs, spilling the dregs of his tiswin.

The tracks went north into the stones of the foothills. The moon bleached the pinnacle of the Maker's Mountain the color of old bone.

The timber spanning the long legs of rock disgorged owls that hooted soft protest at their passage. The needles the trees dropped were soft and resilient, not given to the holding of tracks—the bride-thief was not stupid.

Nor were the hunters.

There were always signs to be read: a twisted branch, a scarred root, a place where water oozed and held the spoor. They followed: up into the wide spurs where the rock shone white under the moon and only the gravel drift below afforded mark of hoof-passage. Along ravines where turned stones guided them, lit blue and black by the silent moon. Up and around, along a wide circle that as dawn came on fell into a line moving south and east, skirting the Meeting Ground; likely to traverse the boundary of the Commacht and the Tachyn grass before moving onto the safer ground of Vachyr's own clan.

Rannach pushed them hard, allowing but a single halt to rest and water the horses, riding through the night as if demons bayed at his heels.

In time, the eastern horizon shone pink as the heart of a river-washed mussel shell, and the moon faded reluctantly behind the mountains. The landscape ahead glowed gold and red as the sun came up, chasing herds of white clouds across the paling sky. Birds rose in chorus of the dawn and insects joined their song.

The tracks turned eastward, and showed the tired signs of weary horses.

Bakaan said, "Soon; he's slowing."

Rannach hefted his lance, the Grannach blade sparking sunlight in glittering shards against the morning. "Yes, soon."

It was the voice of a questing wolf, scenting prey.

Bakaan said, "Remember your promise."

"To Arrhyna?" Rannach spoke harshly. "Or to my father?"

Bakaan shrugged. "Better alive, eh? That he face the humiliation . . ."

Rannach looked into his friend's eyes and offered no answer.

Hadustan said, "He's not running for the Tachyn grass. Look." He angled his lance in the direction of the tracks glistening dewy in the rising sun. They went toward a dense stand of pine and maple that shone dark green in the burgeoning light. "I think he looks to lose us there, but if we ride hard around . . ."

"We might lose his trail," Rannach said.

"Or get ahead of him," Hadustan answered.

Rannach said, "He might double back, and then we lose him."

Bakaan said, "This is your hunt, brother; it's your decision, but I believe Hadustan is right."

Rannach's hands flexed indecisive on lance and rein. His head dropped as he thought, chin resting awhile against his chest before he looked up and said, "We ride for the wood. It might be Vachyr watches us. So . . ." He thought a moment longer; then said, "It's not so large a wood, eh? So—Bakaan, do you patrol this side in case he does double back; Zhy and Hadustan, you ride the edges. I'll go around."

"And if we find him?" Zhy asked. "Remember, we're still within the Meeting Ground."

"Take Arrhyna from him!" Rannach's voice was the snarl of an outraged lion. "How, I don't care. Only take her back."

Zhy said, "I doubt he'll give her up easy."

"Do we find him," Hadustan said, "then we'll ask him gently to release her. And if he refuses, well . . ." He raised his lance, turning the pole so that the blade caught sunlight.

"Does it come to that," Rannach declared, "the crime is mine. I take responsibility."

Bakaan said, "We'd not let you do that, brother."

"Does Vachyr fall to me, I want to boast his slaying," Hadustan said.

Rannach shook his head, slower now, and smiled. "I could not ask for finer friends, or better brothers. But is there payment to be made, then I claim it. You agree?"

"Time passes." Zhy glanced skyward. "Do we ride, or sit here talking?"

Rannach said, "We ride!" And heeled the stallion onward.

Morning came warm, shifting transitory with the moods of this New Grass Moon: one day chill, the next like summer. Morrhyn stepped from his lodge with the sun on his face and stared up into a sky all decked with drifting billows of white cloud, like snow-colored buffalo charging across the blue. The only birds he saw were the crows that gathered annually about the Meeting Ground: none ill-omened, nor had he dreamed. He had sunk weary into his furs, to wake hoping Vachyr and Rannach both lived, and there be no cause for war between the Commacht and the Tachyn.

Oh, Maker, he asked as he looked toward the Mountain, Might it not be so? Could you not intercede and stay their hands, their anger?

He did not anticipate an answer. The Maker moved mysterious; and did the deity hear, then the reply would come in kind, not plain words.

The wakanisha sighed and spat into the grass, and settled to the preparation of his breakfast. He thought he could not expect Lhyn's hospitality this morning.

Rannach held the stallion to a gallop around the edgewoods. His companions rode slower behind him, and as he left them behind he told himself they must be right. Hadustan's guess must be correct. The Tachyn grass lay that way and the Maker-cursed wife-thief would run for that safety. He'd not dare risk the Meeting Ground, not with a stolen bride.

Rannach felt the pulsing of the stallion's brave heart between his legs. It matched the pulsing of his own. The blood ran hot and heavy in his head, dispelling hunger and lack of sleep. He knew only desperate hope and the heat of anger. The promises made to his father were forgotten: his wife was stolen—a crime demanding blood-payment.

He rounded the wood as the sun touched its midmorning point, and eased the tired stallion to a halt. Not far off, the grass ran smooth and green to the banks of a river that sparkled blue and silver. Willows bowed over the water and herons waded there, and from the timber, crows rose in raucous chorus. Rannach scanned the wood and turned his horse toward the stream. He walked the animal until the beast was cooled and no longer panting, all the while praying he not be wrong, that Vachyr *should* appear. Then he watered the horse, even knelt and slaked his own thirst; splashed water on his face and told himself that if he could, he would try to leave Vachyr alive.

It should not be easy, not after what Vachyr had done. But if it were possible . . . Yes, perhaps even better than killing him, to bring him back captive, slung shamed over the saddle of his own horse, to face the condemnation of the Matakwa—of all the People. To see Vachyr and his father both condemned. That, and keep his promise to Racharran.

Save only Vachyr had not harmed Arrhyna: that he could not tolerate.

He swung into the saddle and walked the stallion back toward the wood.

The crows were not rising now in morning's flight. They came in waves, first from their central roosting, then closer, as if riders disturbed them. Rannach hefted his lance, fixed his shield firmer about his left arm, and faced the timber.

Vachyr came out. He rode a chestnut gelding that moved tired. He held a lead rein in his left hand, attached to Arrhyna's piebald mare.

Rannach's wife lay across the saddle, her hands and feet lashed firm, her auburn hair spilled loose about her face, so that Rannach could not see it.

He raised his lance and shouted, "Ho! Wife-stealer!"

Vachyr halted. He looked weary, and angry. Long scratches ran down both his cheeks. He let go the lead rein and allowed Arrhyna's piebald to walk toward the water.

"So, you found me."

Rannach said, "Yes. And now I am going to take you back—so all the People see what you are."

Vachyr smiled an ugly smile and said, "And also tell them what I've done to your wife. Shall you be proud of that?"

Rannach looked at the mare as she passed him. Arrhyna groaned and raised her head, the curtaining hair parting so that he saw the bruises decorating her face. She said, "Kill him," through swollen lips.

"I've had her," Vachyr shouted. "Last night I took her!"

Rannach watched the piebald mare go by. Then he vaulted from the saddle and ran to halt the horse. He cut Arrhyna's bonds and eased her to the ground. The horse walked free as he cradled his bride in his arms. He stroked her face, easing her hair away. It was painful to look at the bruises.

Arrhyna said, "I fought him. In the Maker's name, I swear I fought him!"

Rannach said, "I know. He dies for this." All thoughts of returning Vachyr alive were forgotten, burned away in the heat of his rage. He vaulted astride the bay and couched his lance.

Vachyr laughed and said, "Remember, we're not off the Meeting Ground yet."

Rannach shouted back: "Fight or die!"

Vachyr answered: "Do you harm me, you shall be condemned for shedding blood at Matakwa. Can you bring me back alive, then your wife faces disgrace. Listen! Let me go and I'll say nothing of the pleasure I took of her. How say you?"

Rannach glanced at Arrhyna. Her lips moved, and though he could not hear what she said through the pounding of the blood in his head, he recognized the words she shaped: "Kill him!"

He shouted, "Yes!" and heeled the stallion to the charge.

Vachyr brought his shield across his chest, leveled his lance. The bay gelding sprang forward as he drove his heels against its ribs. Both horses were battle-trained: they attained their full pace in instants. Both men were warriors: they steered their mounts with knees and heels, shields protective, lances poised to strike.

They came together and Rannach caught Vac
shield, turning it up and away as his own drove at
Vachyr twisted sideways in his saddle, using his sh
thrust. Rannach's lance scored a bloody line across l
pitched sideways across his horse.

Momentum carried them apart; both hauled thei
charge again.

Rannach's lance took Vachyr in the groin. He
pierce his shield and ride up fiery across his should
sensation: he was entirely concentrated on Vachyr's fa
wide and awful grin. He saw Vachyr lifted from the sa
ward off the gelding even as he seemed to slide alon
lance; it protruded from his back. Rannach went by ar
depositing Vachyr on the grass.

He swung the stallion around.

Vachyr rested on hands and knees. His breeche
between his legs was dark. His head hung down, ar
wounded buffalo. Long streamers of bloody spittl
mouth.

Rannach shouted, "Look at me!" And when Vac
rose, "For Arrhyna!"

He charged and drove his lance through Vachyr's
Tachyn pinned like a bug to the grass.

He came out of the saddle before the stallion halt
to clutch Arrhyna in his arms and stroke her hair, her c
held her gently, afraid of giving further hurt.

She said, "I am spoiled, husband."

He shook his head and said, "No! Not in my eye

She put her arms around him, nestling into his emb
his chest, said, "He forced me."

Rannach said, "His sin, not yours."

"And what shall you tell the Council? When th
about this?"

"That Vachyr stole you," he said, "and rode awa)
that I slew him for that."

"On the grass of the Meeting Ground?"

She raised her head to look into his eyes. When he
again, it was hard to hold back the tears, but he nodded
And am I condemned for that, it shall be worth it—to 1

"I must tell them," she said, "that all the People kno
him."

Rannach hesitated an instant—there was pride, disap

sidered, gossip—then he smiled and said, "All that matters to me is
t I have you back. Must you speak of what transpired, then so be it.
I do not ask you to do that. You need say only that Vachyr stole you,
I won you back. That is all that matters to me."

Arrhyna looked a long time into his eyes. Then she said, "I am
tunate in my husband."

Rannach shrugged and smiled and said, "No less than I in my wife."

10 Of Things to Come

Morrhyn chewed on the pahé root, his gums and tongue numbing as the drug took effect. He saw Hazhe reach out to toss a scoop of water over the coals, and it was as if the Aparhaso Dreamer moved in slow motion, the rising steam billowing no faster than a lazy cloud in the summer sky. Hazhe caught his eye and smiled solemnly, his gray head nodding in decorous rhythm. Morrhyn smiled back and rested against the hide-covered frame, letting his gaze rove—slowly—about the Dream Lodge.

The sides of the wa'tenhya glowed in the morning sun and fragrant steam hung misty about the interior. Kahteney lounged to Morrhyn's right, his eyes already fogged, mouth gone slack. On Morrhyn's left, Isten beamed; past him, Hazhe went on nodding. Across the seething coals Hadduth sat with closed eyes. Morrhyn wondered how much the Tachyn wakanisha knew of Arrhyna's kidnap, how much was his design. He thought it likely Chakthi's idea, but probably embellished by Hadduth. He thought that sooner or later—inevitably—there must be a confrontation; as he had warned Racharran, it had been planned cleverly, leaving no opportunity for accusation without insult.

Then he felt the numbness in his mouth spread out through his skull, encompassing his mind so that he fell back, his eyes wide and blank, incapable of closing as they stared at the unfolding images of the dream he now shared with all the wakanishas of the Matawaye.

.   .   .

Racharran sat with Colun outside the akaman's lodge. The Grannach was entirely recovered from his drunkenness— a recuperative ability Racharran envied—and sat cross-legged before the six of the folk he had brought with him, all eager to speak of their experiences with the strangeling invaders. Lhyn, not yet ready to forgive her husband, bustled within the tent, emerging to shake blankets or comb furs with sidelong glances of disapprobation at the men.

Racharran maintained a dignified, if somewhat nervous, expression. It was not easy: he worried no less than Lhyn about their son. Often, as his clan came to speak with him of Colun's news and the deliberations of the Council, he thought that it were better he go to Chakthi and plead with the Tachyn akaman for peace, for unity. But he doubted Chakthi would listen, nor could he quite bring himself to go supplicant to a man he despised.

So he sat and listened to the folk of his clan, told them what he knew and what he believed, and watched them hear out Colun and his Grannach, then walk away, knowing they should come back to express their opinions, that he take back the decision of all the Commacht to the Council.

He looked to where the Dream Lodge was pitched on a shelf of stone above the Meeting Ground. It was set apart that the wakanishas not be disturbed, close to the flank of the Maker's Mountain, where wide-limbed cedars shaded the grass and the pinnacle of the holy Mountain rose above.

He wondered what they dreamed with the pahé in them and what answers they would bring out from the wa'tenhya. He felt afraid.

There was fire, and dread riders on beasts that stamped flame from the grass, fanged jaws clacking in anticipation of prey. They were unknown and horrid, but their masters were worse. They rode in rainbow colors that should have been beautiful but were not: were, rather, malign as a cyclone-spoiled sky, like once-bright flesh decayed and spoiled. They carried poles on which skulls rattled, those empty sockets no less empty than the bearers' eyes. Mouths opened in soundless laughter and shrieks of triumph, all proclaiming the same awful challenge: "We come!"

Before them stood a mountain wall Morrhyn did not recognize but nonetheless knew to be the farther side of those peaks that ringed Ket-Ta-Witko, seen as once the Whaztaye must have seen them. There were no Whaztaye in the dream, only the strangelings who came on inexorable, like a brilliant, dreadful tide, closer and closer to the hills.

Morrhyn shuddered in his trance. He wished to wake—this vision

awed and terrified him—but knew he must not, that he must suffer the
images and glean from them what knowledge he might for the sake of all
the People. He knew that sweat beaded his face: it was chill as the wind
in the Hard Frost Moon and hot as the sun in the Moon of Ripe Berries.
He felt afraid.

Rannach wound Vachyr's body in the Tachyn's blanket as Arrhyna
bathed. He wondered what should happen when he brought the corpse
back to the Meeting Ground, and found it hard to care. He had got
back his bride, and he had slain Vachyr in honest battle. How could he
be blamed? Was he accused of truce-breaking, surely the Matakwa must
understand: Vachyr had stolen his wife. Surely that was the greater sin.

He waited until Arrhyna was done with her bathing and then loaded
the body across Vachyr's horse. He helped Arrhyna into her saddle and
climbed astride his stallion.

Arrhyna said, as he took up the rein of Vachyr's animal, "Do you
want to do this? Do you want to go back? You had best be sure, husband."

Rannach said, "As I told you, yes. But you need not say anything."

"Still, he did what he did."

"Do you love me?" Rannach said.

Arrhyna said, "Yes. More than life."

"Then it does not matter what he did. Only that you love me, and I
you."

Arrhyna smiled. Rannach heeled his stallion, Vachyr's bay gelding
snorted protest at the weight of the body, and they rode toward the
wood.

"I cannot doubt the word of the Grannach." Racharran gestured at the
squat folk seated around him. "Does Colun say the Whaztaye are slain,
then I'd not gainsay him. It is my belief that such folk as might broach
the gate are come; it is my belief we should prepare. But you must make
up your own mind. Speak with the Grannach, if you wish; and tell me
later what you'd have me do."

Zeil nodded and said, "Yes, that's wise. Chakthi would not speak so
openly."

Racharran said, harsher than he intended, "I am not Chakthi."

Zeil said, "No, and I thank you again for accepting me into your
clan. You've news of our daughter?"

"No." Racharran shook his head. "Only what you know—that she was taken and Rannach went after her. You shall know as soon as I when news comes."

"Thank you." Zeil ducked his head.

Racharran sighed and looked to where Lhyn busied herself with the fire. The day aged now, the descending sun hurling red light against the slopes of the Maker's Mountain. Eastward, the moon rose into a swath of gentian blue, like a teardrop on a blanket. Crows roostered loud and heavy-winged herons flapped homeward. The Meeting Ground was hung over with the smoke of cookfires, the air redolent of roasting meat, loud with the sound of the People. All of it as it should be, and always had been, save that . . .

Save that he sat with Grannach, who brought alarming news.

Save that the wakanishas still sat up there in their Dream Lodge.

Save that his son was gone, likely to slay Vachyr and deliver the Commacht to war.

Save that his wife ignored him . . .

He rose and went to where Lhyn sat by the fire, motioning that Colun remain. Let the Grannach answer awkward questions for a while.

"I ask your forgiveness," he said, and—warily—set a hand on her shoulder. "I'd not . . ." He shrugged, unsure what he should say, what she might answer. "I'd not see our son hurt, but . . ."

Lhyn said, "I know," and turned toward him. "I was angry. That Rannach suffer . . ."

"He might still," Racharran said.

"Yes." She turned farther, so that she moved into the compass of his arm, leaning her head against his chest. "But you are akaman of the Commacht, and must think of all the clan. I thought only of our son."

Racharran said softly, "Yes. I wish it were not so."

"But it is," Lhyn said, and smiled for the first time that day. "Now go do your duty, eh?"

Racharran brushed his lips against her cheek and thanked the Maker for so understanding a wife, then went back to speak with his people.

It was impossible to reach agreement. Each wakanisha had shared the dream, and none doubted it was a true dream, but as to its interpretation, what it portended for the People, there was only discord.

Hadduth insisted the invaders must remain beyond the mountains, that the fate of the Whaztaye was none of the People's affair, that likely the western folk had somehow offended the Maker and suffered consequent punishment. To believe these creatures might broach the gate was, he suggested with a veiled glance at Morrhyn, an insult to the Maker, whose wards must surely hold the People free from harm. Better, he claimed, to set their trust in the Maker and do nothing.

Isten supported him. It was a subtle argument, and the Naiche Dreamer was naturally cautious.

Morrhyn disavowed the suggestion of blasphemy and struggled to conceal his contempt of Hadduth. The Grannach had brought this news, he pointed out, and had fought the invaders, and surely none would question the integrity of the Stone Folk. Did these strangelings come against Ket-Ta-Witko, he said, then would their presence not be an affront to the Maker? Would it not be the duty of all the People to deny them?

Kahteney voiced his agreement, adding his suggestion that any prevarication might well be considered dereliction of the Matawaye's duty to the Maker, and surely a betrayal of their Grannach friends.

Morrhyn looked to Hazhe, who had not yet spoken, but only listened. The Aparhaso Dreamer nodded gravely and declared that the dream had provided much food for thought, but no obvious answers. They needed, he said, more time to ponder the import of the vision.

It was the only agreement the Dreamers could reach.

Full dark had fallen by the time they emerged from the wa'tenhya and walked down the mountainside to their respective clans, and Morrhyn felt a weariness upon him that was sour with his certainty the future must find the People unprepared.

11 Homecoming and Accusal

It was dusk before Rannach found all his comrades again.

Hadustan was the first, his face a mirror of Zhy's and Bakaan's when they saw Arrhyna and the body slung across the bay gelding, their words neither so different: "Sister, it is good to see you safe," and "You slew him, then, brother," and "I wish I'd see that fight." Carefully, not one of them commented on Arrhyna's bruises other than to ask was she well, or wondered aloud on the time she had spent with Vachyr. It was as if they all recognized a step had been taken that must likely affect all their futures, and left it to Rannach to say where the trail might lead them.

They made camp close to the edgewood, Vachyr's body left wrapped a little distance off. None spoke of the morrow, but only ate and slept, and wondered at the Council's reaction.

The horses were wearied from the chase and Rannach set an easy pace on the return. None, anyway, were overly eager to face the Chiefs' Council. The strictures of Ahsa-tye-Patiko had been broken and, no matter the cause, some punishment would surely be assigned them. His comrades unaware, Rannach had made himself a promise that he would take full responsibility: he, after all, was the one who had slain Vachyr. He thought none could blame Arrhyna, but Bakaan and the others would surely earn Chakthi's anger, and the Tachyn akaman seek to encompass them in his demands for retribution. When they came before the Council, Rannach had decided, he would endeavor to deflect that vengeful temper, draw it to himself alone. He glanced back to where the chestnut gelding bore its carrion bundle and thanked the Maker the season was not so warm the flies came out. Vachyr had been obnoxious enough alive; even dead he caused trouble.

The New Grass Moon was full when they came in sight of the Meeting Ground, and Close to its apex. It shown serene from a sky, bathing the flanks of the Maker's Mountain in light of the color of bone, washing over the lodges that spread like sleeping buffalo across the grass. The camp was oddly silent, the central fires sending up a glow that spoke of long debate, attended by all the Matawaye. Talk of Colun's news, Rannach thought, and what conclusions the Dream Council had reached, the People's response. He wondered how his arrival would affect the debate.

They halted on the edge of the Commacht camp and Rannach saw that they waited on his word.

"I'd have this done," he said. "Do we see to our horses and then . . ." He looked to where the fireglow lit the sky. "Do you meet me at my lodge?"

Bakaan nodded, unspeaking, and walked his mount away, followed by Hadustan and Zhy. Rannach and Arrhyna went to their tent. The entry flap was laced shut, and when they looked inside they saw the interior restored to order, even the fire low-banked in anticipation of their return.

Softly, Arrhyna said, "Lhyn's work."

Rannach nodded and said, "You need not witness this. You could stay here."

Arrhyna shook her head. "I am part of it, no? And I am your wife. What is done to you is done to me."

Rannach said, "There will be hard words spoken. It shall likely be ugly."

Arrhyna shrugged.

He asked, "Do you wish to change? To tidy yourself?"

"No." She looked him in the eye. "Let the People see what Vachyr did."

He said, "As you wish," and picketed their horses.

He shed his weapons, and they waited awhile until the others came. All looked grave now, the laughter and the boasting of their return forgotten in face of the imminent future.

"So." Rannach took up the halter of Vachyr's horse. "Do we go?"

Arrhyna fell into step at his side, and they made their way through the Commacht tents, watched silently by the old ones who remained to tend sleeping children. They crossed the stream and paced the gauntlet of the Tachyn lodges, to where the Council sat.

Folk parted at their approach and a buzzing murmur went through the crowd so that before they reached the inner circle all knew they came, and none could doubt the burden the chestnut gelding carried.

Rannach heard a shout and guessed the news reached Chakthi. He saw his mother standing with Nemeth and Zeil, all wide-eyed. Lhyn raised a hand as if she'd touch him but did not quite dare. He smiled at her and ducked his head in greeting. Arrhyna said, "Thank you for tending our lodge." And to her parents: "I am well; be calm." Lhyn essayed a faint smile and made a helpless gesture; Zeil put an arm about his wife's shoulders.

The senior warriors parted, ushering them through, and as they entered the circle a tremendous silence fell.

Rannach offered the assembled akamans and wakanishas formal greeting and into the silence said, "I ask forgiveness for this interruption, but I deemed it best I came immediately. I have slain Vachyr."

Yazte of the Lakanti sat closest to where he stood, and he thought he heard the akaman murmur, "No bad news," but he could not be sure because a second shriek from Chakthi split the night.

The Tachyn was on his feet, staring at the gelding and what it carried. Hadduth stood close behind, his expression unreadable.

Morrhyn said, "Oh, Maker, help us now."

Rannach looked to his father and said, "I had no choice; he left me none."

He saw Racharran's stern features cloud and stiffen, eyes a moment closed, then staring at his son as if he looked on a stranger, or past him to some dread future that he had sooner not envision.

Chakthi cried, "My son is killed! Blood is shed in Matakwa—I demand vengeance."

Rannach led the horse across the circle. It shied at the fires and Chakthi's shouts, but he held its halter tight and thrust the rein at the Tachyn akaman.

"This is your son's horse. It bears his body. He was fairly slain."

Chakthi stared at the proffered rein; at the blanket-wrapped bundle across the saddle. His lips peeled back so far and wide, his gums showed pink, and from between his gritted teeth erupted a snarl akin to a wolverine's. He sprang at Rannach with upraised hands.

Rannach stood his ground as Chakthi's fingers fastened on his throat, and made no attempt to defend himself. Arrhyna screamed. Then Yazte was there, and Tahdase, dragging the enraged Tachyn back, shouting for his warriors to hold him. Rannach coughed and massaged his neck. He wondered why Racharran sat so still.

Old Juh, his wrinkled face sear with shock, rose to his feet and spread his arms wide. "Hold, I tell you. Hold!" His voice was harsh from speaking and creaky with age, but still it carried. "Let there be no more violence. Not here! Already there is enough."

Yazte and Tahdase handed Chakthi to his liegemen, who held him nervously as Hadduth spoke urgently in his ear. The Lakanti and the Naiche stood waiting, until Chakthi was calmed somewhat. He loosed the fastenings on the blanket and stared at his son's dead face, touched it, then handed the rein to a warrior who led the horse away. Yazte and Tahdase resumed their places; Chakthi was slower to sit. His eyes burned like coals in the night of his face, locked firm on Rannach.

Juh said, "I think we must set aside all other matters for now, and speak of . . ." He hesitated, distaste etched into his frown. "Of this other matter. It is a very grave thing, this."

Chakthi said, "It is a breaking of the law, of the Will!" His voice was harsh. "My son is murdered in Matakwa. His blood is shed—and blood calls for blood!"

Racharran spoke for the first time: "Not murdered." He stared stone-faced at the Tachyn akaman, then glanced at Rannach. "Slain fairly, my son says."

"Your son!" Chakthi made the words an insult. "Vachyr is murdered; your son lives."

Racharran's mouth tightened. Morrhyn touched his elbow and spoke too softly for Rannach to hear. The Commacht akaman turned to Juh, to Tahdase and Yazte. "Do we hear from all those concerned, that all this picture be drawn clear?"

Yazte said swiftly and loudly, "Yes! We need hear all of it."

Tahdase ducked his head, his eyes darting about like those of a man frightened by his responsibilities and seeking guidance.

Juh said, "I agree. Chakthi, my brother, I mourn your loss; but we must hear the full tale before any judgment is delivered."

He waited for the Tachyn's sullen nod, then turned to the four, standing nervously now, the eyes of all the People on them. "Who speaks first?"

Rannach said, "Vachyr stole my bride. She is innocent of any crime; neither did my brothers have any part in Vachyr's death. I alone slew him."

Bakaan said, "No! We are as one in this."

Juh raised a hand to silence them. "Then speak one by one." He looked at Rannach. "Your bride was stolen?"

Rannach said, "Yes."

"Then," Juh said, "let her speak first."

Arrhyna found Rannach's hand—comfort in his firm grip—and said, "He invited Vachyr to surrender, but Vachyr . . ." She shook her head, hiding her face behind the curtain of her hair. "Vachyr boasted of . . ."

Rannach drew her close, silencing her. "Vachyr would not surrender," he said. "He . . . lied to me. He offered such insults as I could not take. I lost my temper and charged him."

"Only after . . ." Once again Arrhyna found herself tugged close to her husband. This time she fought free, refusing to be silenced. "No, Rannach, let it be said clear, that all the People understand." She held her head high, meeting the eyes of each akaman. "I swear in the name of the Maker that what I say is true—Vachyr took me by force from our lodge and, though I fought him, I could not prevent him. He beat me; then and again, and when I woke the second time he . . ."

She shuddered, and Rannach said, "You need not speak of this."

Arrhyna sniffed and said, "I must. The . . . the second time he was on me, I fought him as best I could, but he is—was—strong, and I was dizzy from his blows . . ."

When she was done, she could hear her mother weeping.

Juh leveled a finger at Rannach, who told of finding Arrhyna gone and his determination to rescue her. Bakaan, Hadustan, and Zhy, he said, had come only to aid him in tracking the kidnapper—their intention to bring him back alive. He spoke of finding the trail obscured, and locating it again, of the final meeting.

When he was finished, Juh looked to Chakthi. "This thing of the tracks, of aid in the kidnap," he asked, "was this known to you?"

Chakthi shook his head. "Neither that or aught of any kidnap." He spat the words. "I say this Commacht slew my son in spite alone."

Juh frowned. "In spite alone? Forgive me, brother, but that makes no sense. Why should Rannach slay your son in spite? Certainly, they vied for the woman's hand, but that was given to Rannach. Why should he be spiteful?"

Chakthi shrugged and sneered at Arrhyna. "Perhaps this wanton looked to share her blanket with more than one. Perhaps she seduced my son and her husband found them together."

Arrhyna clung to Rannach's hand as he lunged forward. Racharran shouted, "No!"

From out of the crowd Zeil bellowed, "He lies! I know my daughter."

Almost, Arrhyna was dragged off her feet. She locked a second hand on Rannach's hair, snatching at a braid so that his head was hauled back and turned toward her.

"No!" she cried. "Do you not see what he attempts?"

Strong hands fell hard on Rannach's arms, and into his ear he heard his father say, "Your wife speaks sense; heed her."

He struggled awhile, enraged, the more for Chakthi's smile, which seemed to him triumphant. Racharran set an arm around his neck, another on his wrist. Hoarse, he said, "Do you insult my wife again, I'll slay you as I slew your misbegotten son."

Chakthi said loud, "Now he threatens me. He's a madman. What would he not do?"

Yazte joined Racharran and Morrhyn, and together they fought Rannach down.

"Boy," Racharran said as he struggled, "you do your cause no good with this. Now calm yourself!"

Into his father's face Rannach snarled, "Would you allow my mother insulted so?"

Racharran's face was an instant stone, then he shook his head. Rannach was too furious to see the misting of his eyes.

"Then why," Rannach grunted, "do you grant Chakthi such privilege?"

Racharran sighed. "There's more afoot than you understand. Trust me."

"Trust you?" Rannach glared into his father's eyes, and for a moment Racharran thought his son would spit in his face. "You hear out that whoreson's insults and ask me to trust your silence?"

Pain aged the akaman at that, and he looked to Morrhyn, who said, "Rannach! This goes past insults. All the People stand in jeopardy, and Chakthi has some part in that pattern. Do you love the People—do you love the Commacht and Arrhyna—then rein in your anger and trust your father!"

Rannach still fought their hold. "Not save he side me!" His voice was harsh as steel on stone. "Not save he stand up and name that whoreson a liar!"

Morrhyn set a hand against his mouth: Rannach bit him.

Then a deep voice said, "Would you continue this discussion of yours, give him to me. We'll hold him."

The Grannach were scarce half the height of a Commacht, but when one took his arms, and Colun sat upon his legs, Rannach knew truly how strong they were. A third squatted at his back, a hand upon his shoulder, ready to gag him. He fought them awhile, but it was as useless as if stone encased him. He was grateful that Arrhyna came solicitous to sit beside him; he hated his father then, and Morrhyn for taking his father's side. He wished he had not come back but gone wild and renegade into the hills, anywhere there was honesty without the seduction of whatever politics went on here. He would give his life for the People, for his clan; but here, now, there was only indignity and embarrassment.

Still he must listen, and did he raise his voice in protest or argument, a grainy hand clamped hard over his mouth and he could only gasp for breath and lie still under the imponderable weight of the Grannach. Thus he lay and heard Bakaan speak of the pursuit, and and then Hadustan, and after him Zhy. Then he heard Chakthi deny all involvemena and suggest again that Vachyr was unfairly slain, likely murdered by all four Commacht, that likely Arrhyna shared her favors with all four. It was a sour tirade, and as he heard it, Rannach vowed that someday he would slay Chakti.

When the Tachyn was done the akamans sat awhile in silence, each beckoning their Dreamers close. Then the younger men waited on Juh, whose seniority gave him precedence in such matters. He studied Arrhyna, who sat resolute beside her husband, and slowly shook his head. "I think grief trips my brother's tongue." He spoke carefully. "That is understandable, but not"—he shrugged, his old eyes troubled—"hardly fair to this woman. Were she so wanton, would Vachyr have sought to wed her? Are there any here will attest to such promiscuity?"

From amongst the Commacht, Zeil shouted, "Only to her virtue!"

Juh motioned that Arrhyna rise and come forward. When she stood at the center of the circle, he said, "Forgive me, I would not question your chastity, but this must be settled clear, that there be no misunderstanding."

Arrhyna nodded and Juh waved Hazhe forward.

The Aparahaso Dreamer rose stiffly to his feet and paced to where Arrhyna stood. He pointed to the holy mountain and said, "We stand in the gaze of the Maker. This is a holy place, where any who lie must surely bring down his wrath. Do you then swear that you are chaste?"

Arrhyna said without hesitation, "In the Maker's name, I do. I am . . . Before my husband, I knew no man. Since I was wed I have known only him. Save . . ." Tears rolled slowly down her cheeks; Rannach struggled with the Grannach to go to her. "Vachyr took me by force, and beat me until. . . ." She looked from the wakanisha to Chakthi. "Do you go look at his face and see the marks I put there, fighting him!"

Hazhe declared, "I find her true."

Chakthi shouted, "I am not satisfied. She lies! This is some Commacht device, that my son's murder go unpunished!"

There was a loudening murmur ran through the crowd then, as if bait were tossed over water and the fish rose. Then Juh spoke again.

"This is no easy thing," he said. "There can be no doubt a crime has been committed; indeed, two. Shall my brothers hear my thoughts on this and then we decide what measures be taken?"

He waited until all voiced agreement, then rose and walked to the circle's center. Firelight and moonglow cast his face like worked stone. "First," he said, "it is my belief that Vachyr was maddened by loss of the woman he'd have for his wife. I believe he stole Arrhyna, the which was ill done and a heinous crime."

Chakthi's cry of "No!" went ignored, as was Yazte's enthusiastic "Yes!"

"But wrong cannot justify wrong." For an instant, the ancient eyes fell on Rannach. "And it cannot be argued that the shedding of blood in Matakwa is also a crime. This is the second: that Rannach slew Vachyr even as the Matakwa truce bound him to peace. He scorned the Ahsa-tye-Patiko in that."

"And must die for it," Chakthi shouted.

Juh ignored this as he had ignored the other. "Two crimes," he said. "The one punished; the second . . . We must speak of this."

He returned to his blanket, seating himself as Racharran called to be heard.

The Commacht akaman took the speaker's place, his head a moment lowered. Then he looked up, eyes moving slowly about the circle. "Rannach is my son," he said, "and I do not argue that he is headstrong, but this I swear in the name of the Maker—that before we came to this Matakwa, where I knew he would seek Arrhyna's hand, I had from him a promise that he would accept whatever judgment the Council delivered in that matter, nor raise his hand against Vachyr."

"So much for Commacht promises," Chakthi snarled.

"I trust his word," Racharran continued, "and I tell you that what he has done he did because he had no other choice. Would any here"—he turned around slowly, his eyes encompassing the assembled akamans and all the crowd—"would any here, finding their wife stolen, not go after her kidnapper? Would any here, finding her beaten, not look to slay her taker?"

"The Ahsa-tye-Patiko!" Chakthi bellowed. "Shall we overlook the Will? Does the law no longer matter?"

"Your son stole Arrhyna. His was the crime. Rannach did only what any other warrior would do, in honor." Racharran let his eyes move out over the crowd again. "Is that not true?"

Yazte was the first to answer. "Yes!" he cried, and his shout was taken up by others until all the Meeting Ground rang loud and roosting birds shifted nervous in the trees.

When there was silence again, Racharran said, "Then I ask that the Council look lenient on my son. Had Vachyr not stolen Arrhyna, there would be no crime. Let the blame be Vachyr's!"

Chakthi rose to speak, but Hadduth clutched his arm and whispered in his ear and the Tachyn akaman fell back silent as Yazte asked to speak.

"I am with my brother Racharran in this," the plump Lakanti said. "That Chakthi has lost a son is a sad thing. But the crime *was* Vachyr's— Rannach did no more than would I, or any other man. I say we should not punish him."

Chakthi said, "My son is dead."

"Then let there be a blood-price agreed," said Yazte. "Let that be settled and put aside. We've other matters to discuss."

Chakthi said, "My son's death is of no account?"

Doggedly, Yazte said, "Let the Council decide a blood-price."

"No!"

Yazte shrugged, spread his hands in exasperation, and looked to Juh, who turned to Tahdase and asked, "Do you speak, brother?"

The young Naiche akaman whispered with Isten and then rose nervously to his feet. "I agree that Vachyr was wrong." He glanced swiftly around, his eyes flickering from face to face. "It *was* a crime to steal Rannach's bride, but I think it is as my brother Juh says—wrong cannot justify wrong. And as my brother Chakthi says—blood has been shed in Matakwa and reparation must be made."

Chakthi said, "I call for Rannach's execution."

Racharran said, "Let the Council decide a blood-price and it shall be paid. But how can any call for my son's death?"

Tahdase looked helplessly to Juh.

The old akaman said, "This is not a thing we may decide easily, or swiftly. Do my brothers agree, I suggest that we speak on this. Save . . ." He ducked his head at Racharran, at Chakthi. "Save that two fathers are involved, and their loyalties are consequently divided. I say that neither Chakthi nor Racharran have say in this, but only we who have no part."

Tahdase nodded his agreement abruptly; Yazte glanced at Racharran before he ducked his head.

Racharran said carefully, "So be it."

Chakthi whispered again with Hadduth, then allowed it be so.

Juh said, "Then we three shall speak on this and deliver our decision."

Chakthi asked, "When?"

Juh sighed and said, "This Council is already long, and we've much yet to discuss. Do we sleep tonight, and Yazte and Tahdase come to my lodge on the morrow? The People shall know our thoughts this next night."

Chakthi grunted his agreement, then demanded: "And the while? Shall the murderer be guarded, or shall his father set him free?"

Racharran tensed at that slur, but held his temper checked and said nothing.

Juh's face expressed disapproval; he looked to Racharran. "Your word is good, brother. Shall you ward your son, that he attend our judgment tomorrow?"

Racharran said, "I shall."

Juh said, "That's good enough for me."

Chakthi looked to argue, but again Hadduth restrained him, and he lowered his head in curt agreement.

"Then," Juh said, "when the sun sets tomorrow, let us all attend and this thing be settled."

The Grannach released Rannach on his father's nod. He rose and set an arm about Arrhyna's shoulders; he felt very confused and a little afraid. He felt he tottered on the brink of a precipice, flailing for balance, and he was unsure whether the chasm was his death or the love and hate—both inextricably mingled—he felt for his father.

Racharran said, "Shall you remain?"

"Is my word still good, yes."

"Your word was always good. But you are like an unbroken horse: it's hard to know who you'll kick next."

Warriors moved about them, shielding them, and they began to walk toward the Commacht lodges.

Rannach said, "I thought you betrayed me. But then you spoke and I . . ."

Racharran sighed and looked to the westering moon, then back to where the pinnacle of the Maker's Mountain stood bone-white and bleak against the sky, and said, "Do you not think I love you?"

Rannach was taken aback: he shrugged.

Racharran said, "You are my blood, my son. And you are a warrior of the Commacht, and the clan is my blood. I need consider both: the burden of any akaman."

Rannach frowned and said, "I slew him fair."

"I know; I never doubted that. Nor, likely, would I have done different."

Rannach said, "Then why . . . ?"

Wearily, Racharran said, "Because I am akaman of the Commacht and I must think of the clan and all the People, and things come toward us that frighten me."

Rannach had never heard his father speak before of fear, and it frightened him. He looked at his father's face and began to ask a question, but Racharran raised a hand to silence him. "Not now. Do you come home and we shall eat and drink tiswin, and then I'll tell you."

Rannach nodded and drew Arrhyna closer, letting his father lead the way. At least he remembered, as he saw Morrhyn sucking on his bitten hand, to ask the wakanisha's pardon for that injury.

"No matter." Morrhyn shrugged, and Rannach thought his face looked haunted. "It will heal. Though, by the Maker, you've powerful teeth."

Rannach smiled at that, but could not quite summon a laugh.

Racharran's lodge was crowded. Lhyn met her son with a smile, embracing him and Arrhyna, then the two women busied themselves at the fire as Colun reached for the tiswin and began to pour. Racharran turned to Morrhyn and asked that the wakanisha speak of the Dream Council.

"You need to know this," he said to Rannach, "that you understand why we must have peace."

His tone boded no good, and Rannach nodded and sat silent as Morrhyn spoke. When the Dreamer was done, Racharran told of the akamans' debate, interrupted by Rannach's return, and of his fear—and Morrhyn's—that save the clans swear binding oaths of peace, the People would likely fall in disarray before the invaders.

"But is this so," Rannach said when the ominous tale was told, "then Hadduth agreed the truce, and Chakthi. How could they do that, knowing of Vachyr's crime—likely privy to his escape?"

"Now you show sense," Racharran said, and ruefully, "if somewhat late in the day."

Rannach bristled. "What else should I have done? What else could I have done? My wife was stolen!"

"Brought the matter to the Council," Racharran answered, "that Vachyr's crime be known from the start. Had the Council sent out riders, perhaps Vachyr might have been taken alive, and Chakthi have no chance to accuse you."

Rannach met his father's eyes awhile and then lowered his head. "I did not think," he said slowly. "I knew only that Arrhyna was taken and I must go after her."

"And now," Racharran said, "there's a price must be paid."

Morrhyn said, "I suspect it was a well-thought trap. I wonder if Chakthi did not gamble on Vachyr escaping—which should likely have led to war. And if Vachyr was taken? Why, Chakthi could deny all knowledge. And was Vachyr slain? Then, again, an end to peace—without blame attaching to Chakthi."

Rannach studied the wakanisha in amazement. "You say that Chakthi gambled his own son's life?"

"I believe he did." Morrhyn sighed, his brow creased in a frown. "I suspect all this was hatched by Chakthi and Hadduth, in spite and hatred of the Commacht."

"But . . ." Rannach spread his hands, indicating bafflement. "Are your worst fears aright, Chakthi plays into the hands of these invaders."

Morrhyn nodded.

Rannach said, "How could he? Is he crazed?"

"Perhaps." Morrhyn shrugged. "That he bears us Commacht no love is common knowledge. Then at this Matakwa he saw his son's desires thwarted, and Zeil and Nemeth taken into our clan. Perhaps that was more than he could bear."

"But to gamble his own son's life?" Rannach shook his head. "And when all the People are likely threatened?"

Mildly, Morrhyn asked, "Did you think of all the People when you aimed your lance at Vachyr?"

Shamefaced, Rannach shook his head.

Morrhyn said, "I think there's a poison in Chakthi, and in Hadduth. It addles them. Perhaps—" He hesitated, eyes a moment closed, his face a moment haggard. "Perhaps it's to do with these strangeling invaders."

Lhyn gasped at that and clutched her husband's shoulder. Arrhyna drew closer to Rannach, as if the chill, dread breath of nightmare invaded the lodge, a black and ominous mist.

"Be that as it may," Racharran said heavily, "there are more immediate problems. A judgment shall be delivered tomorrow, and I must accept it."

"No!" Lhyn's fingers drove hard into the muscle of his shoulder. "Rannach acted honorably!"

"But still broke the law," Racharran said. "Still shed blood in Matakwa."

"Had he not," Arrhyna said, "I should be with Vachyr now, likely brought to the Tachyn grazing. What then?"

"War with the Tachyn." Racharran spoke hollow-voiced. "Chakthi's wish still granted."

"Shall Juh and the others not see that?" Lhyn asked. "Not see Chakthi for what he is?"

"Perhaps." Her husband ducked his head as if it sat heavy on his neck. "But without proof they can know only that Vachyr was slain and Rannach admits the deed. That the Ahsa-tye-Patiko *was* ignored."

Rannach squared his shoulders and asked, calmly as he was able, "What shall their judgment be? My death?"

He ignored Arrhyna's horrified cry; Racharran ignored Lhyn's. The akaman said, "Perhaps they will consider the circumstances. Perhaps Yazte can convince Juh and Tahdase. Perhaps they will consider my plea and their judgment be clement."

"And is it not?" Rannach asked.

Racharran faced his son. "I am akaman of the Commacht. I must abide by their judgment, no matter what it cost me."

12 Judgment

The moon stood aloof over the Meeting Ground, this night veiled in fast-blown streamers of dark cloud so that patterns of shadow and light pursued a dance across the encampment. From the center, where the Council fires burned, sparks rose to join the dance. From all the People gathered there to hear the judgment of the akamans there rose not a sound; it was as if the Matawaye held their breath, waiting, knowing these events momentous.

They had talked enough that day, all the men and women, debating amongst themselves what their decision might be were they seated with Juh and Tahdase and Yazte in the Aparhaso chieftain's lodge.

It was a day unlike any other in the memory of the People. The Matakwa's usually festive air was dulled and glum. Racharran asked of his warriors that they hold close to the Commacht lodges and not venture where their paths might cross those of the Tachyn. Chakthi stalked amongst his folk with the white clay of mourning a rigid mask over his lupine face. He vowed his son would lie within his lodge until judgment be delivered, and only then, avenged, be given burial.

None were sure where: no man had before died by violence during Matakwa, and none could say for sure whether or not the Ahsa-tye-Patiko allowed that the trees of the Meeting Ground might take such a body. The Tachyn thought perhaps Chakthi would take Vachyr back, to lay him in the ancestral burial wood, but Chakthi would not sat—only cry for vengence and spill ashes on his loosened hair. Hadduth, his own face streaked white, trailed on Chakthi's heels like a skulking dog.

Rannach, in deference to his father and his own promise, remained mostly in his lodge. When he bathed or went to tend his horse and Arrhyna's, an escort of senior warriors went with him. He kept a brave face. Arrhyna endeavored to conceal her fear, to stem the tears that threatened when her parents came or Lhyn sat with her outside the lodge.

As if his eyes were opened in a moment, Rannach understood what it was to be an akaman. He saw the barely hidden dread in his mother's eyes and the unmasked pain in his father's, and knew that Lhyn's fear was entirely for him, her son, whilst Racharran must fear for him, for the Commacht, and for all the People. It seemed to him a terrible burden.

As the time approached when his future should be decided, he said to his father, "I am sorry."

Racharran smiled: a thin stretching of his lips. "As am I."

"Whatever judgment comes," Rannach said carefully, "I shall accept."

Racharran nodded and turned his face toward the Maker's Mountain. The pinnacle was bathed in the light of the westering sun, its flanks and peak reddened as if wounded. "I know you are brave," he said. "I would also have you understand."

Rannach said, "I think I do."

"Were this another time, another place," Racharran said, "it should be different. Had Colun not brought his news, had Morrhyn not dreamed his dreams . . ."

"I know. I'm sorry," Rannach said again.

Racharran smiled again, warmer now: the heat of pride there. "You've courage," he said, and took Rannach's right hand between his own. "You were always brave and I have always been proud of you, but I must think past you. Do you understand that?"

"Now," Rannach said.

His father said, "I cannot argue the judgment."

It sounded like a farewell. From behind him, where Arrhyna sat sewing, Rannach heard a gasp. He said, "I know. I'd not ask that you do."

"What I can do," Racharran said, "I shall. But the People cannot be in disarray are Morrhyn's worst fears aright."

"No." Rannach held his father's hands tighter. "I understand."

■   ■   ■

The clay masked Chakthi, his face unreadable. Only the dark eyes showed his hatred as he studied Rannach, his unbound hair falling matted and ash-smeared about his shoulders, as if he were some vengeful ghost unleashed by the Maker to take his toll on the quick.

And if he were a spirit, Rannach thought, then Hadduth was his familiar, crouched whispering at his master's side, his own features all distorted by clay and ash, as if Vachyr had been his own son and Chakthi's loss his. But Rannach stifled his contempt: he had made his father a promise and would not break it, for Racharran's sake and his own honor.

His father sat across the circle from the Tachyn, Morrhyn close by, and Lhyn with Zeil and Nemeth, the two mothers with their arms about Arrhyna. Colun squatted surrounded by his Grannach, a cluster of living rocks, their bearded faces grave as stone. Behind them, allowed such precedence for their part in this drama, stood Bakaan and Zhy and Hadustan. Juh sat with Tahdase and Yazte, their Dreamers in a group beside. And all around there was silence as the People waited.

Juh rose and walked to the circle's center, where Rannach stood. He must raise his head to look the younger man in the face, and when he did, Rannach could not interpret his expression. He adjusted his blanket about his shoulders and turned slowly around, speaking loud that all hear.

"As was agreed, I have spoken long with Tahdase of the Naiche and Yazte of the Lakanti, and we have reached a decision. Shall our judgment be accepted by all?"

Rannach was the first to answer yes, Racharran the second. Chakthi said, slower and enigmatic, "Be it fair."

Juh turned hooded eyes on the Tachyn and said, "It was agreed by you, brother. Will you argue now?"

Chakthi's lips worked, the clay splitting in myriad lines that distorted his features even further. Hadduth touched his elbow and spoke in his ear, and Chakthi lowered his head so that his ashy hair curtained his face. From behind that camouflage he said, "I will hear your judgment."

Juh took this for assent and turned to Rannach.

"This is our judgment; it was not easily reached. There are many arguments, both for you and against you. That you broke the law cannot be denied . . ."

From Chakthi's mask, like a ghostly moan, came: "The law is clear —his death."

Juh ignored him. ". . . But neither can it be denied that Vachyr transgressed when he stole your wife, and we believe her testimony. Therefore, the first crime was undoubtedly Vachyr's."

Rannach stood stock-still. Like the sparks lofting from the fires, he felt an ember of hope rise.

"So," Juh continued, "there is a balance here. It is our belief that had Vachyr not gone against the Will, you would not have broken it. But"—he raised a hand from under his blanket as if to quench the disagreement none had voiced—"still it is as I have said: that wrong cannot be justified by wrong."

Rannach felt the ember die.

Juh said, "Our brother Chakthi has called for your life. Your father has offered blood-payment. Chakthi has refused that and would see you slain. What say you?"

Rannach was startled. He had anticipated judgment—readied himself for death—assuming the verdict already decided: the one way or the other. He had not thought to be asked his opinion.

He looked at Juh and saw no dissemblance in the ancient eyes, only patience and sorrow. He fought the impulse to turn toward his father. He said carefully, "I slew Vachyr in fair fight. I told him I would take him back to face judgment of his crime, but he taunted me and my temper rose—I took up my lance and slew him."

"And these taunts? What were they?"

Rannach said, "Insults," and glanced swiftly at Arrhyna. "I'd not speak of them."

Arrhyna broke from her mother's arm, and Lhyn's, and rose to shout, "Vachyr boasted of raping me!"

Softly, that only Rannach hear him, Juh said, "There's honor in you." Then louder: "Our judgment is this: that Rannach of the Commacht had just cause to slay Vachyr of the Tachyn, and so we would not take his life. But that he shed blood at the time of Matakwa was wrong, and therefore we have decided that Rannach be banished from the lodges of the People. Let him go away and live lonely. Let none succor him, neither his own clan nor any other. And should he come again onto the grass of the People, then his life is forfeit. This is our judgment: let it be done."

Rannach bowed his head, accepting.

Chakthi sprang to his feet, shrieking, "No! I'll see him dead. I do not accept this!"

Hadduth clutched at his shirt, but the Tachyn akaman would not be silenced. He slapped the wakanisha's hand away and strode to where Rannach stood, and Juh, looking furious from one to the other. Juh set himself before Rannach even as Racharran and Yazte rose, moving forward. Even shy Tahdase was on his feet.

"He must be executed!" Where the clay split around his mouth, Chakthi's lips spat foam. His eyes burned fierce as flames. "He slew my son and I'll have his death!"

Undaunted, Juh said, "Judgment is delivered, brother."

Chakthi raised a hand. Warriors of the Tachyn and the Commacht surged forward. The men of the Lakanti came to Yazte, those of the Naiche to Tahdase, the Aparhaso to Juh. Like the fires' sparks, voices rose bellowing against the night. Men roared and women screamed; dogs set to barking, and from the corrals the horses shrilled.

It was a Council like no other.

Only Rannach was still in the midst of the turmoil. He wondered if death was not preferable to banishment. He saw Chakthi's enraged face, the clay all split and broken now like a shed concealment, glowering at him, and old Juh shielding him. Then his father and Yazte and Tahdase were there, confronting the Tachyn akaman, their warriors facing Chakthi's men. He saw Chakthi's fisted hand come down against Juh's face, and the old man stagger. He caught him and held him turned from the attack, feeling blows land hard against his head and shoulders before the maddened Chakthi was fought back.

Juh said, "My thanks. Now let me go."

Rannach nodded and released him to his men. The warriors of the clans stood faced against one another. Juh touched his bruised cheek and pulled his blanket about his shoulders as if he felt a chill wind blowing, then moved to stand between the angry factions.

"Is it come to this?" His voice rang out vigorous for all his years. "Is all the Will forgotten? Are we become squabbling dogs?"

Slowly, driven by his outrage, the warriors drew back. Hadduth took hold of Chakthi's shirt and tugged hard, wary as if he clutched a rabid hound. Racharran took his son's arm and pulled Rannach back. Yazte and his Lakanti formed a defensive line between the Commacht and the Tachyn.

"Judgment is delivered," Juh shouted. "It is as was agreed, and it is binding. Rannach shall quit this place by the setting of tomorrow's sun, and not again come to the grass of the People, else his life be forfeit."

Small amongst the bodies of his Aparhaso warriors he looked to where Chakthi stood. "And any who deny this or defy it breach the Ahsa-tye-Patiko. Let Rannach be gone by tomorrow's sunset. Let none hunt him or seek to delay him. Until this Matakwa is ended, it is so."

Chakthi looked him back, and in no less a voice said, "This Matakwa is ended now. There is no peace now. There is only war."

Juh gasped and raised a hand as if to touch Chakthi. "What do you say, brother? Your grief speaks wild and I ask you to think again. We've much to discuss yet, for the good of all the People."

Chakthi glared hot-eyed at the older, smaller man. His lips curled in an expression that was sneer and snarl together, the clay fragmenting further. "I say there is no justice here." A hand swept a dismissive arc. "I say that I am not your brother—save you give me Rannach."

Doggedly, Juh said, "Judgment is delivered on that, brother, and in the name of the Maker I ask you accept it."

"No!" Chakthi howled his answer.

To Racharran, Yazte said urgently, "Do you go? Take your son away and swift, before this comes to blows!"

Racharran hesitated, then nodded and motioned for his people to quit the fire circle. Behind them the night echoed with angry cries.

It was a Matakwa like no other.

Arrhyna wept, clinging to Rannach as they were hurried away. Tears rolled down Lhyn's cheeks; Racharran's face was held in rigid composure. Morrhyn stared back at the tumult they left, his belly knotted and cold with dread. Nemeth and Zeil went pale-faced and troubled, Colun and his Grannach trotting to hold pace with the longer-legged Commacht.

As they reached the akaman's lodge, the Tachyn were already quitting the Council fires, led by Chakthi and Hadduth, storming shouting through their camp. Children began to wail; dogs barked furiously. Racharran paused, issuing brisk orders that warriors align themselves along the stream for fear Chakthi's rage engender an attack. Yazte and some thirty or forty warriors of the Lakanti, the Aparhaso, and the Naiche came running, skirting the edge of the Tachyn lodges to join the Commacht men.

"Ho, brother!" The Lakanti akaman was flushed, waving a large hand to halt Racharran. "Old Juh suggests we play guardian."

Racharran frowned and said, "We need no guardians, brother. We can defend ourselves."

"Juh is a cautious man." Yazte was panting, more accustomed to riding than running. "But in this I agree with him, Chakthi is crazed, and should his clan share his madness, it were better they face us than your warriors, that there be no further claim of insult or injury. He thinks—and I think him right—that Chakthi will not dare attack all the clans."

Racharran's eyes narrowed and Morrhyn said, "This is wise. The Maker knows, we've trouble enough without there be more bloodshed."

Racharran looked toward the Tachyn lodges and grunted his assent. "So be it. Now I'd speak with my son, and . . ." Like the clouds scudding across the moon, a shadow darkened his face. "See him on his way."

"Soon and safely, eh?" Yazte nodded toward the shouting Tachyn. "Likely Chakthi will have riders seeking him ere long."

Morrhyn said, "The judgment was that none pursue him or raise hand against him until this Matakwa ends."

Yazte grinned sourly and said, "This Matakwa *is* ended. Chakthi takes his clan away."

"He cannot!" Morrhyn stared aghast at the Lakanti. "What of the invaders? What of the truce?"

Yazte shrugged, grimacing. "Kahteney shall explain—I'd best attend here. Ho, Kahteney! Where are you?"

The Lakanti wakanisha came hurrying out of the crowd. He took Morrhyn's arm, leading him aside as Racharran and the others went on.

"Chakthi quits the Matakwa," he said. "The Tachyn strike camp this night, and none can dissuade him. He swears vengeance on Rannach and all the Commacht."

"Oh, Maker!" Morrhyn turned toward the great white peak of the holy mountain. Its pinnacle was dark with windblown cloud, as if it hid its face. The play of moonlight and shadow across its flanks suggested falling tears. "What madness is this?"

Kahteney said, "Tachyn madness; Chakthi's madness. Listen—after you quit the fires he called again for Rannach's death, and had men not stood between him and Juh, I think he'd have struck the old one again. Juh and Tahdase and Yazte tried to reason with him, but there's no placating a wounded lion, eh? He'll quit the Meeting Ground tonight, and he declares the Matakwa therefore ended and Rannach fair game. Also, he promises war with the Commacht soon as he's buried Vachyr."

Morrhyn began to speak, but the Lakanti Dreamer hushed him. "You'll need tell this to Rannach, and advise Racharran also. Tell them the Lakanti stand with them, but no other. Tell them to ride wary, for Chakthi is crazed and I think he'll stop at nothing."

"But the truce?" Morrhyn cried. "The invaders?"

"The one forgotten," Kahteney replied, "and the other? Chakthi and Hadduth deny the danger; Juh and Tahdase prevaricate." He barked a sour laugh. "Are our fears fleshed, my friend, the People are in terrible danger."

Morrhyn looked again toward the mountain, but its apex was still hidden. Worse comes to worst, he thought, like nightmare taking form. He took Kahteney's hand. "As you say, I must inform Racharran. My thanks, friend."

Kahteney nodded, mouth stretching in an unhappy smile. "We Lakanti stand with you. Now go."

"Yes." Morrhyn turned and ran after his akaman.

Behind him, from across the stream, warriors of the Tachyn bellowed insults and challenges. He prayed none cross that fragile barrier; there was already enough broken this night.

"Would he dare?"

Morrhyn looked at Lhyn's teared face and wished he might offer her better comfort. But that was not his place, nor now within his capability, and so he ducked his head and said, "Kahteney believes he would; I believe he would."

Racharran looked to Rannach and said, "Then you must go tonight. Now!"

Rannach said, "I am not afraid of Chakthi. I'd not run like a frightened dog from that whoreson."

Racharran inhaled a deep breath and let it out slow, holding back the anger and the disappointment that threatened to edge his response. His son, he thought, was like some youngling buffalo bull newcome to his prime: all bristling and audacious and aware only of his strength and desire and pride. "Were it Chakthi alone," he said, "I'd back you in the fight. But it would not be Chakthi alone. He'll hunt in a pack like the dog he is, and not even you can defeat all the Tachyn."

Rannach said, "Then send warriors with me. Or,"—he looked about the fire, at the kindred and friends who sat there—"let me come back to the Commacht grass."

Racharran shook his head, avoiding his wife's eye. "I cannot. You heard the judgment."

"Chakthi defies it," Rannach said. "Is it then still binding?"

Racharran said, "I thought you understood. You said you understood."

"That was then. This is now."

Racharran sighed and said, "You did not understand. Those are the arguments of youth, without forethought. Honor is honor; my honor is mine, Chakthi's his."

"Chakthi," Rannach said, "has no honor."

"No." Racharran shook his head in agreement. "But I do, and you do. And so we are bound by promises that men like Chakthi ignore. Judgment was delivered, and it binds us, else we forfeit our honor."

Rannach frowned, pondering this. At his side, Arrhyna stifled tears, a hand across her mouth.

Morrhyn said, "There's more to think on. The Tachyn strike camp: the Matakwa is ended. Chakthi promises war: shall he find us on the trail? Better were the clan on our own grass before the Tachyn come against us. As your father says, Rannach, you must go quickly, and alone. The Ahsa-tye-Patiko is already broken, and does your father defy the judgment of the Council, then surely we further offend the Maker. I think we shall need his goodwill in the times to come."

As he spoke, he kept his eyes firm on the young man's face that he not see Lhyn's expression; but he could not block his ears to her moan, and it cut him deep.

Colun spoke then, his voice startling them, as if a boulder ground against its moorings overhead. "We Grannach are not bound by this judgment," he rumbled. "Juh spoke only of the People, that none of the Matawaye succor him. Is that not so, Dreamer?"

Morrhyn said, surprised, "I suppose . . . Yes. What do you say?"

Colun shrugged, succeeding in spilling tiswin down his shirt. "That he come with us. The Matakwa is ended; those fools blind themselves to what threatens Ket-Ta-Witko and there's no reason for us to linger here, so we go. Let Rannach come with us. We'll ward him, should Chakthi attempt anything." His beard opened to expose teeth parted in a wolfish grin. "Let him try attacking Grannach warriors."

Racharran asked, "You'd take him into your tunnels?"

"Perhaps not that, but into the hills, into the wild places where you do not go. Nor could Chakthi come against him."

"It should need be this night," Racharran said. And looked to Rannach. "Would you agree to this?"

"Have I another choice?"

His father answered, "Death is your other choice."

For a while their eyes locked, then Rannach lowered his head. Lhyn loosed a cry that was part anguish, part relief. Arrhyna said, "I come with you."

Rannach said, "It will not be easy. You would fare better with the clan."

She said, "I am your wife; you are my husband."

He said, "Yes," and took her hand and smiled. "So be it."

Racharran said, "There's another thing, do you agree."

"What?" Rannach frowned. "Have I not agreed enough?"

Racharran shrugged and glanced at Morrhyn. "You might be our sentry. Do these invaders breach the mountains, you might bring word."

"And defy the judgment?" Rannach mocked his father with his pantomimed outrage. "Come forbidden back to the grass?"

Racharran refused the bait. Gravely, he ducked his head and said, "Do these invaders come, then the judgment will surely be forgotten. To have word early would surely absolve the crime."

He looked to Morrhyn for confirmation. The wakanisha pursed his lips. "These are strange times," he said. "The Ahsa-tye-Patiko offers no guidance in this. But . . . Yes, I think it must be so. It should be for all the People, no?"

"Even," Rannach said, "for Chakthi and his Tachyn?"

Morrhyn asked, "Would you give even them up to what I fear comes?"

Rannach thought a moment, then grinned and said, "I'd sooner slay Chakthi myself."

"Then your answer is yes?"

Rannach nodded. His father smiled sadly and said, "Then do we strike your lodge and see you equipped?"

"As," Rannach replied, "my akaman commands."

Arrhyna said, "Might I bid my parents farewell?"

Rannach told her, "Of course. But swift, eh?"

She nodded and rose to embrace Lhyn, then hurried from the tent. Rannach held his mother close and whispered, "I shall see you again. I thought to die this night, but now I think the Maker smiles on me and I shall live."

Lhyn took his face in both her hands and said, 'I pray it be so, my son. I pray we meet again in better times."

She touched her lips to his cheek and let him go. Morrhyn could see the tears she held in check. Almost, he wept himself: it seemed all order was disrupted and he could not know what blame to apportion to Rannach, what to Chakthi, nor what to himself or even—he made the sign of warding—to the Maker. He rose and took Rannach's hands.

"For what worth it has, you go with my blessing. The Maker guard you and see you safely home again."

"Thank you." Rannach turned to Colun. "So, do we go?"

The Grannach grunted and emptied his cup. "Strike your lodge and fetch your animals," he said. "We'll be ready."

Rannach nodded and took his father's hand. They did not speak, but there was again some kind of understanding between them, and Rannach quit the tent.

Bakaan and Hadustan and Zhy waited for him, and when he told them he departed, they announced they'd accompany him.

"No." Rannach shook his head. "You heard the judgment—no succor. I'll not see you condemned for my crime."

They argued, but he remained unbending and they contented themselves with helping him prepare for departure.

It was soon enough done. The lodge was struck, its hides and all its contents stowed on two horses, the bay stallion and Arrhyna's piebald saddled, then Rannach took up his weapons. Lhyn came with food, and Nemeth and Zeil came sad with their daughter. To them Rannach said, "I ask your forgiveness that I take your child away so soon."

"Not you," Zeil returned, scowling as he looked toward the Tachyn camp. "This is Chakthi's doing. Go with my blessing."

"And come back safe," Nemeth added.

Rannach bowed his head. "No harm shall come to Arrhyna while I live," he promised. "This is I swear."

Then Colun and his Grannach, all bearing weapons, came shuffling up.

Racharran set hands upon his son's shoulders. "Go now, and the Maker with you. We'll confuse your trail somewhat, and delay Chakthi as long as we can."

Rannach could not resist it: "But without bloodshed, eh?"

Before Racharran had chance to reply, he embraced his father, then his mother, and swung astride the stallion. Arrhyna mounted the piebald and took the lead reins Bakaan offered.

"So." Colun raised a hand. "My thanks for your hospitality. What further news we get, I'll send you somehow. Farewell."

He lifted his ax, and his Grannach shaped a phalanx before the horses, Colun at the head. He broke into a trot that surprised Rannach with its speed. The young Commacht looked once at his wife, once at his parents and people, then urged the bay forward after the speeding Stone Folk.

They went swift away, toward the hills where the Maker's Mountain stood still hidden behind the veil of cloud.

13 Wild Places

It was an arduous trail the Grannach took, and by the day's ending they were in a place only the wakan-ishas had visited. Colun left men behind to watch their backtrail and set guards on their camp, which was in a corrie where the rocky walls hid their fire and a single man might watch down the mountain for sign of pursuit. Rannach noticed that Colun had another watch the high slopes also, as if the Grannach feared not only Chakthi's pursuit but also what might come from above: more than words, that impressed on him the gravity of Colun's warning.

They rose with the dawn and continued upward, on narrow trails that rose steep enough it was often necessary to dismount and lead the horses, which—accustomed to the plains of Ket-Ta-Witko—liked this climbing not at all. Without them the Grannach should have gone much faster, for they moved like mountain goats, surefooted and fleet where the horses stumbled and balked.

When they halted at noon, Colun said, "You'd do better to leave those beasts behind. Let them find their way back to your clan herds and you go on afoot."

Rannach looked at the bay stallion, cropping grass beside Arrhyna's mare, and shook his head. "I hunted that horse a full moon before I got my rope on him; and it was another moon before he'd accept the saddle. I'll not give him up so easy."

"They slow us," Colun said.

"And should Chakthi find them coming down the mountain?" Rannach gestured downslope. "Then he'll know where we go."

"Chakthi!" Colun turned his head to spit. "He's not coming after us."

"How can you know?" asked Rannach.

"These are our mountains." Colun gestured at the encircling peaks, steeper and craggy now, dominated by the massive bulk of the Maker's Mountain. "We Grannach know who comes and goes here. Besides . . ." His knobby face creased in a mischievous grin. "My watchers came back last night whilst you flatlanders slept, with news."

"News?" Rannach could not conceal his urgency: the circumlocution of the Grannach was sometimes frustrating.

Colun nodded and chewed deliberately on a piece of meat. Rannach must contain himself and accept that Colun would speak in his own good time, and only then; and that all depended on the goodwill of the Stone Folk, for without them survival should be perilous. Still, it was no easy lesson to learn.

Eventually, Colun swallowed and said, "Ach, but I miss the tiswin your people make. However . . . Yes, my watchers came back and told me your father and Yazte thought to mark the ending of the Matakwa with horse races, which took place about the foothills. The Naiche and the Aparhaso joined in, and"—he reached for the meat, selecting a cut —"and so, when Tachyn warriors came riding up, they found their path quite blocked. Now Chakthi takes his people away."

"He might still send scouts," Rannach said.

"On a cold, old trail?" Colun shook his head, chuckling. "And one, the Maker knows, that does not favor horses."

Rannach nodded and thought a moment. "Still, I'd keep the horses," he said. "Should these invaders come, I'll need a mount to carry word. But can they live up there?" In his turn, he gestured at the high slopes.

Colun shrugged. "The getting there will be hard, but can they climb, they'll live. We've animals of our own, you know."

"I didn't." Rannach smiled an apology. "I thought you Grannach lived entirely in your tunnels."

Colun laughed hugely. "Like moles, eh? Or rats?" He opened his eyes wide in semblance of some subterranean creature, his hands groping blindly at the empty air. "Wandering about in the dark, down in the deep stone?"

Somewhat embarrassed, Rannach nodded.

"We've more than our tunnels," Colun said. "You'll see."

Then, before Rannach could question him further, he sprang up-right and shouted that they go on.

The way grew steeper still, until it was quite impossible to ride and they must go on foot, with ropes on the animals and the Grannach shouldering the beasts from behind. Rannach thought it would be no easy descent, but he no longer feared pursuit. He felt instead another fear, and wished he had spoken at greater length with Morrhyn. He and Arrhyna were now in a place none of the People had visited. The after-noon sun shone bright on the pinnacle of the Maker's Mountain, and he thought on the stories of the People and the Ahsa-tye-Patiko, and that he now trod sacred ground. It was not forbidden, but the People ac-ceded this land to the Grannach, deeming them the guardians of the passes and the gate, and none of the Matawaye came here. He had shed blood in Matakwa, broken the Will, and albeit he believed he could not have changed that slaying, still he wondered how the Maker might re-gard his presence here.

He raised his eyes to the Mountain and shaped a sign of warding. Am I bloody and sinful, he thought, then punish me, but not my wife. Arrhyna is innocent, and surely cannot be condemned.

But the Mountain gave back no obvious answer, though he saw an eagle ride the sky and a flight of ravens winging black across the azure and wondered if he observed some sign that only a wakanisha could interpret. He felt breathless and oddly dazed. The light seemed brighter here and the landscape startlingly clear, as if the slopes and trees and boulders bruised his eyes. The lore of the People had it that the First Folk had come to Ket-Ta-Witko from that mountain, brought to the land through the gate. Most had gone down onto the grass of the plains to become the clans of the Matawaye, those who elected to remain amongst the peaks becoming the Grannach. He had not thought much on that—it was a thing of the Dreamers, not for warriors—and in the hinder part of his mind he had always entertained a doubt, thinking it strange a people who loved the grass so well should come from moun-tains. But now, as he came ever closer to the Mountain—closer than any of his kind in living memory had come—he wondered. It was so vast a hill: a gigantic column that seemed to support the sky, majestic in its sheer enormity, and he less than an ant on even these lesser slopes he climbed.

He had not realized he halted until a Grannach shouted for him to go on, save he wished to pick up his cumbersome horse and carry the beast himself. The hoarse voice rang in his ears and he shook his head, but the terrain still shimmered around him, impaling him on the vision of the pinnacle, and he thought he must remain immobile, like a votary statue staring forever at the Mountain. Then Colun's hand came down to clasp his face and shake him, and he heard the Grannach say, "Flatlanders! Ho, Rannach, do you move, or shall you stand all goggle-eyed until you starve?"

He said, "I . . ." And aimed a trembling finger at the peak.

Colun said, "Yes, I know. Now move!"

It seemed impossible. He looked back and saw Arrhyna brought up between two Grannach, her horse in care of others, still more with the laden packhorses. Her eyes were wide as his, and on her face an expression of rapture.

Pain then: he realized that Colun had slapped him, and the Grannach was very strong. His eyes watered and his head spun a moment, but then he grunted and took up the rein and continued on.

That night was cold, their camp made in a cleft where a thin column of white water spilled out from black rock to pool amidst dressed stones before trickling away downslope. Moss grew on the rock, and little stunted bushes like clutching hands. Arrhyna slept soon as she had eaten, but Rannach must force himself to the effort of grooming the animals and seeing them blanketed against the chill. He was grateful for the warmth of his wife's body as the thinning moon looked down impassive.

In the morning, mist draped the cleft and the fire sputtered and spat, affording little heat. Rannach was miserable, and Arrhyna seemed dulled by the cold; moisture sparkled on the horses' manes, and they fretted. The Grannach were themselves: cheerful as ever, speaking eagerly of homecoming. Rannach looked up and saw only a narrow band of gray that did no more than hint at the possibility of sunlight, and thought that they must face days of such traveling before they could hope to reach the high slopes where the tunnels began. He wondered if they had not done better to remain on the grass and take their chances with the Tachyn.

And then he saw his first example of the Grannach's wondrous work.

They left the cleft behind and toiled up a sweeping traverse overhung with looming cliffs and stubby, wind-twisted pines. The trail looked to turn back on itself to the east, near vertical, and Rannach could not see how the horses should manage the ascent. Ahead, Colun halted, awaiting his little column. He was beaming as Rannach and Arrhyna labored up to join him, as if anticipating some great joke.

"See?" He stabbed a finger at the blank rockface.

Rannach stared wearily at the stone and shrugged.

"What do you see?" Colun asked.

Rannach glanced at Arrhyna and said, "Stone. I see stone."

Colun nodded and said, "You've not the eyes of a Grannach. Watch and you'll see what none of your people have ever seen."

He set both hands flat against the rock and muttered, too low and guttural for either Matawaye to make out the words. They only stared in amazement as the stone trembled, like water rippled by a flung pebble, and became an opening. Rannach gasped and clutched at the stallion's rein as the horse skittered, backing from the impossible ingress. He dragged the plunging head down and blinked, scarce able to believe his eyes. Where smooth gray stone had been, there was now a semicircular opening large enough to accept a horse. The arch was carved with intricate symbols, and within was light, bright as the sun, shining from nowhere to reveal a smooth floor running back into the mountain.

"Moles, eh?" Colun's grin spread wider. "Rats, eh? Enter and see for yourselves." He stepped through the arch, bowing elaborately like some genial host delighted with his guests' surprise.

It was the promise of hope and hospitality, but still Rannach felt a strange reluctance to enter. He was accustomed to open places, to the sky's wide space and the spread of the plains. He looked at Arrhyna and saw her similarly disinclined. But they had nowhere else to go, so he took in a deep breath, took her hand, and walked into the tunnel.

The horses balked at first, but then allowed themselves to be led in, urged on by the Grannach. Colun stood by the arch and, when all had entered, spoke again and again touched the stone. The blue sky wavered and darkened as if a mist blew up, and was replaced with solid rock.

Rannach stared about. The air was warmer than was right, and smelled dry. He could not tell where the light came from: it surely could not come from the stone itself, alone. He felt threatened by the imponderable weight of the mountain, and was grateful for the soft touch of Arrhyna's hand.

"Come." Colun beckoned them and, without waiting to see if they obeyed, struck out along the tunnel.

The air was still and silent, flinty in their nostrils. It was very quiet, so that the clatter of the horses' hooves dinned loud, like raucous voices raised lewdly in some holy place. Rannach hurried after the Grannach, who now speeded ahead, and all the while looked around in abashed wonder at the legendary way he walked.

In time they came to a wider place and Colun announced it night, and that they should halt. Numbed, Rannach and Arrhyna obeyed and looked to the animals. They were in a vaulted cavern they could not tell was carved by the Grannach or nature, or perhaps both working in union. Ribs of blue stone curved upward out of walls that were more gold than white, conjoining in a sunburst circle overhead. At the center of the smooth floor was a walled pool of dark water, and about its circumference stood benches of dressed blue stone, darker than the arcing ribs above.

"We've no more food than we carry," Colun said as if this were the most ordinary place, needless of explanation. "But come tomorrow . . ."

He beamed and would not be further drawn out: they fed the horses from the packs and themselves ate cold food, the jerky and fruits Lhyn and the others had given them.

"Did you make all this?" Rannach asked.

"Over the ages." Colun lounged on a bench. "I myself did not, but this is all Grannach work. Ours and the Maker's." He shaped a sign Rannach did not understand. "You can sleep peaceful here."

That was said easier than it was done. It was strange to lie down aware that a mountain's weight lay overhead, where the light dimmed on a spoken word and only a pale glow from the sunburst ceiling shone, no moon or stars, nor the lodgefire's glow. Neither could they lie together, but each on their stone pedestal, like ambitious godlings or corpses laid to rest. Rannach was thankful for the waxing of the light and the bustle of the Grannach as they readied a cold breakfast; nor any less Arrhyna, who tasked herself with the horses and the dressing of her hair as if she'd soon as not be gone swift on their way.

On: through a longer length of tunnel, the Grannach padding fleet, the two Matawaye uneasy followers after their rescuer hosts, the horses trotting clattery loud behind, fretful at their strange surroundings. All day they moved, halting only once to eat and rest, and throughout all the tunnel showed no change, as if they traversed an eternal day governed by Grannach magic—a day that might, Rannach thought, go on forever, deeper and deeper into the mountains until there be no emerging but only everlasting travel. He began to wonder if he was being punished for slaying Vachyr.

Then the tunnel ended in another blank wall, and again Colun set his hands against the rock and spoke his oddly syllabled words, and the stone evaporated. Rannach was a moment blinded, his mind no less bedazzled than his eyes. He heard Arrhyna gasp and knew her dumbfounded as himself; he heard Colun chuckling. When his sight cleared he could not speak, only grunt out his amazement.

Beyond the carved arch of the tunnel's egress was a balustraded shelf that overlooked a valley embosomed within the mountains. The peaks rose guardian above, marching away into misty distances from which, like an impossibly vast sentry, rose the Maker's Mountain. About the valley the slopes fell gentler, as if smoothed by the Maker's hand or centuries of Grannach labor, and across them ran planted terraces, and down them little streams and stands of luxuriant timber. All down the valley's bowl there was grass that ran green and thick as any on the plains, and the streams that sparkled down the slopes fed into a wider brook that meandered away into the distance, disappearing into haze. Copses and larger hursts rose dark from the floor, and Rannach saw bighorn sheep grazing, and deer. It seemed to him as if a piece of his familiar grasslands was lifted up and brought to the mountains.

"Not all tunnels, eh?" Colun's hand fell heavy on his back, laughter bubbling in the Grannach's throat. "Not all grim stone and groping, eh?"

Rannach could only shake his head and mumble, "No." He stared, marveling, at the incredible vista. It was a fine, wide place, and the farthest limits stood beyond his sight.

Beside him, Arrhyna said, "Do your folk live here, Colun?"

"Not live," the Grannach answered. He walked to the balustrade, which reached to his waist, and swept out an arm. "We've such valleys all through the hills. We grow our crops here, and raise what meat animals we need. We hunt here, and come simply to see the sky and the grass, the woods, when the need's on us. Our dwellings are inside the stone."

He turned, beckoning them closer, and they joined him, wary of the low balustrade. It was a long drop to the valley floor.

"You, though, shall make your home here. You've water and grass, the crops on the terraces, and game for the taking. You'll be comfortable here, I think."

There was the hint of a farewell in his words, and Rannach asked, "Where shall you be?"

"I must go to my people." The dense-bearded face darkened, his smile fading. "I must tell them what happened below, at the Matakwa. I must tell them what your Council decided concerning the invaders. Or, rather, what your people could not decide."

"The Commacht are with you," Rannach said. "And the Lakanti."

Colun snorted dismissive laughter. "They *would* be—save likely your clan shall be fighting Chakthi's Tachyn. Perhaps with the aid of the Lakanti, but nonetheless engaged in petty war, whilst . . . Ach!" His fist pounded the balustrade's rim. "Do they look to come out of the

Whaztaye country through our hills, we'll fight them. Perhaps they'll not attempt that passage; perhaps Chakthi shall be slain and your folk make peace. It's in the Maker's hands now."

Rannach nodded, reminded of his role in that confusion. "Do they come," he said awkwardly, "I'll take word to my father. You'll have allies then—surely the Commacht, likely the Lakanti."

Colun grunted, his eyes fixed on the valley below. "Perhaps; save they're too busy fighting amongst themselves. But timely? Do those creatures breach our defenses, I think we shall none of us have too much time. Ach, I wonder if I shouldn't have challenged Chakthi myself, put my ax in his skull and let in a little sense."

"That should be my battle," Rannach said. And softer, "I was the one fired his rage."

"No." Colun turned from his observation of the valley to look up at the young Commacht. "Chakthi's rage is all of his own making. Had Vachyr not"—he glanced at Arrhyna and shrugged—"he left you no honorable choice save what you did. And Chakthi was a part of that—he knew of his son's plans and approved them. His, the sin. I only wish your folk saw it clearer, that your Council had condemned *Chakthi* to banishment, not you."

Rannach smiled thanks for that support and said, "You'd sooner have Chakthi for a neighbor?"

Colun's laughter belled across the sky. "As soon I'd bring a wolf pack to this place! I've no love for Chakthi. Do you not know the story?"

"Only that my father names you true friend." Rannach shook his head. "And that you come always to our lodges."

"You Commacht," Colun said, "make the best tiswin. But there's more to it; perhaps I'll tell you later. Now, however, do we go down?"

He moved from the balustrade, waving his followers to him, and they began the descent to the valley floor.

It was a wide way and smoothly carved, but vertiginous for all its width and easy surface. Rannach brought the horses down wary, aided by Arrhyna, and it was a relief to tread the floor, to be once more on grass.

The sun that had lit the strath so bright touched the peaks now, and shadow fell down the walls even as the sky remained bright. Stars showed, and the shaved round of the New Grass Moon. Rannach thought on how the Matakwa should be continuing until that disc was at least half waned, and felt a melancholy that he could not know how his clan fared, or be with his people when Chakthi attacked. He thought it would be good to face the Tachyn akaman down the length of a lance, and better still to see the head go in to Chakthi's belly.

He shaped a furtive sign of warding, reminding himself it had been anger delivered him to this place, his clan to war, and vowed that when he and his bride were settled here, he would perform rites of absolvement, express to the Maker his contrition. But first he would see Arrhyna safe and settled: he owed her that for her courage and all she'd suffered. She was his first concern. He looked to where she led her piebald mare alongside and smiled. She smiled back, and he thought how brave she was and how lucky—no matter what—that she had chosen him.

They went on awhile until they reached the stream and Colun called a halt.

"We'll camp here this night," the Grannach said, "and in the morning leave you."

Rannach asked, "Shall you come back?"

"In time." Colun nodded toward the valley's farther end. "As I say, I must speak with my folk. How long that shall take, I cannot tell, but I'll bring back word or come avisiting. Now, what's to eat?"

A fire was soon built and the packs ransacked for the makings of a farewell feast. Rannach insisted his supplies be used, assuring his Grannach hosts that he could easily hunt food in so hospitable a place. None argued, save that Colun mourned the absence of tiswin.

When their bellies were filled and they lounged on the grass about the fire, Rannach asked Colun what was the story he had earlier mentioned.

"Well . . ." Colun chuckled, the sound like the rumbling of a bear's belly. "Perhaps it's not my place."

For all he like this squat man, Rannach thought then of taking him and shaking him, save that the Grannach was too strong, and would likely embarrass him with that blunt power. So he smiled and said, "I'd hear it, save you are forbidden to tell it. . . ."

"Not forbidden." Colun smiled a reminiscent smile, staring at the fire. "It was agreed we'd not spread the tale wide, for fear of . . . upsetting . . . those concerned. Your father's a tactful man, Rannach, and thinks beyond his own pride."

Rannach ducked his head. "I know. But still I'd hear this tale."

"Perhaps." Colun glanced around at his fellows. "How say you?"

Like befurred rocks, the Grannach faces grinned. "Tell it, why not? It's a fine story."

Arrhyna said, "Please, Colun. I'd know this tale."

"And your smile," Colun said gallantly, "is hard to refuse. So, listen. . . . It was my first Matakwa. I was but newly named a creddan—which is somewhat like the title of akaman amongst your folk—and you, Rannach, were but a mewling babe, carried by your mother. Racharran was not long akaman of the Commacht, and I knew him not at all then, save from a distance.

"So, I came down to the Meeting Ground all prideful in my new-found status and drank your fine tiswin and, I am ashamed to say, took more than I could then manage." He paused as his comrades laughed, waiting for their merriment to die before he continued. "The next day I found my head akin to that rattle you shook in those days, and my belly not very easy. I thought to go off alone awhile and gather my senses. And what did I find?"

He broke off again, grinning. "What I found was a sizable bear, not long woke from his winter's sleep. The bear and a certain Tachyn warrior, whose name I did not then know. We came together in a wood some distance from the Meeting Ground, in a clearing there—me, the bear, and this Tachyn. He was ahorse, but his beast took fright and threw him, and he fell down on the ground. When he rose, he saw what I saw—that the bear was not in the best of humors and intent on eating one of us. Save he could not decide whether to chase the horse, the Tachyn, or me.

"Well, the horse made up its own mind and fled—wise animal!—which left the bear with but the two choices. I thought of following after the wise horse, but then that the bear would likely overtake me. Nor did I think it manly to leave the Tachyn warrior to face the beast alone. I had no weapons; the Tachyn had been hunting and carried a bow. I thought he'd use it, but he looked at the bear and took to his heels instead. The bear took after him and I picked up a fallen branch and threw it.

"I should not have done that: I should have let the bear take the coward. But I am Grannach and we know no fear, so I threw my stick and the bear turned about and came after me.

"At this point—as I wondered how fast I might climb a tree, and whether or not the bear should climb it swifter—your father came riding up. He was concerned for my health, he told me later, and had come looking for me. Praise the Maker that he did! However, he also carried a bow, and he put arrows into the bear faster than any man I've seen. He feathered the beast! It turned from me and went after him, and he led it away across the clearing and through the trees.

"Well, I ran after him and saw him slay the bear. Later we skinned it and ate its meat, and he gave me the hide which your mother had prepared." Colun beamed, stroking the skin that draped his shoulders. "This is that same animal, and that is why I am your father's friend and yours."

The fire crackled, sending sparks into the night. Rannach said, "And the Tachyn?"

"Why, he was Chakthi, of course." Colun grinned wickedly. "The bear slain, your father took me up on his horse—which I like not at all! —and we returned to the clearing. We found Chakthi there. His bow lay on the ground and he was high in a tree. By the Maker, but he clung to his branch like a possum, and took a long time coming down, even though your father assured him the bear was dead. I watched him descend, and I do believe his breeches were wet!"

Laughter echoed into the night. The Grannach rolled about, holding their sides. Rannach said, "What then?"

Colun said, "Diplomat that your father is, he assured Chakthi no word would be spoken of what transpired. Then he bound me to silence, telling me that it were better I not say anything, lest I make an enemy of the Tachyn akaman. Then he caught Chakthi's horse and brought it back, and we rode away to drink tiswin."

Rannach said, "Then Chakthi should be grateful to my father."

Colun's smile went away. *"Should be,"* he said. "But is not. Chakthi is such a man as regards gratitude as a hateful debt."

"So," Rannach asked, "is that why Chakthi bears us Commacht such enmity?"

"In part, I think." Colun nodded, grave now, and stared serious at Rannach and Arrhyna. "Neither has he much liking for me, or any Grannach, for like your father I was witness to his cowardice."

Arrhyna frowned and said, "But Racharran told him no tales would be told, and surely he must know that word stands good. . . ."

Colun shrugged. "I think that matters less to Chakthi than that we *know,* that we saw him up that tree all pale with fright, his bow forgotten on the ground. I think that such a man as Chakthi is broods on such matters, and they become like a festered wound that he cannot forget." He nodded as if in confirmation of his own assessment and fixed them both again with solemn eyes. "You two are the only others who know of this. Morrhyn does not, neither your mother. You see? Your father holds to his promised word."

Rannach said, "Had a man saved my life, I'd announce the debt. I'd feast him and name him blood-friend."

"You are not Chakthi," Colun replied. "His head follows a different trail, some other poison enters him."

"The invaders?" Rannach followed the direction of the Grannach's gaze. The mountains looked to him impassable, all cold and crenellate, looming moonwashed as snarling fangs. "How could that be?"

"How could I know?" Colun poked at the fire, encouraging brighter flames. "I am a Creddan, not a golan or a wakanisha. I cannot interpret signs or dreams. But . . ." His bulky shoulders rose and fell as he sighed. "There's surely a madness come to the borders of this land, and it seems to me a madness enters your people. Ach! The world knows a Grannach's word is good—but who listened to my warning?"

"My father," Rannach said, "and Morrhyn. Also Yazte and Kahteney."

"Whilst Chakthi and that hangdog Dreamer of his ignored it." Colun tossed a stick at the fire, sending sparks flurrying. "And old Juh and his wakanisha prevaricate; and Tahdase and his dither look to Juh for guidance like puppies to the leader of their pack. And all the while . . ." He looked again at the hills. "Is that not madness? When a true friend warns of danger the wise man listens and readies, no? But your Council only dithered and blocked its ears, like children who close their eyes tight to deny what's before them."

At Rannach's side, Arrhyna shivered and drew closer to her husband. Colun saw her shifting and essayed a smile. "You'll be safe here. Do they come, you'll have warning enough to get yourselves back down the mountains." He fetched the kettle from the flames and filled their cups, sipped the tea, and sighed mournfully. "Ach, but I wish this were tiswin."

One of his fellows chuckled and said, "There'll be beer when we reach home."

"It's not the same." Colun shook his head, grinning at the two Matawaye. "Of all the things you flatlanders make, it's my conviction tiswin is your greatest achievement."

"Perhaps I can brew it here," Arrhyna said.

Colun's face lit up. "You think that possible? Might you teach my wife?"

"I don't know." Arrhyna smiled. "I must explore this place, see if the right ingredients grow here. But can I, yes: I'll teach your wife."

Rannach said, "I didn't know you were wed."

"Since your father took his first step," Colun replied, and beamed a huge grin. "I married late, but wisely—Marjia is the most beautiful woman in all these hills. Or any others."

Rannach wondered how old the Grannach was. He knew the Stone Folk lived slow, long lives, but Colun's innate vitality seemed that of a young man: he had thought the Grannach no more than his own father's age, perhaps less, but Colun's words suggested a far greater length of years. It was not the custom of the People to speak much of age, and so he assayed a different question. It seemed to him he should learn all he might of his hosts.

"What's a . . . golan, you said?"

"One gifted by the Maker."

"The wakanishas are gifted by the Maker," Rannach said. "Do your golans dream, then?"

"No." Colun drank his tea and shook the cup clean. "Their gift is that magic that allows us to shape the stone. They read its pathways, its flow and ebb, and use their gift to follow those ways. To open them to our tools. You flatlanders think stone is dead, but it's not—it lives. Slow, I agree; and hard of comprehension save to the golans."

This seemed to Rannach quite incomprehensible, and he said, "They use their magic to cut the tunnels? Like that one we used?"

"To open the ways," Colun answered. "To persuade the stone to let us through. Then we ordinary folk come with our tools and refine the work. The entrances, they're all golan work. I can explain it no better."

"I'd like to meet one of these golans," Rannach said.

Colun said, "Perhaps you shall. They've little to do with any others, but who knows? These are strange times. Two flatlanders come to live in our hills, and a darkness stirs across the world. So who knows what meetings might come about?"

Rannach said, "Yes," and would have spoken further of the Grannach ways and all the world beyond these mountains, but Colun yawned massively and announced it time to sleep and Rannach knew he was done with talking.

He left the horses hobbled, cropping on the rich grass, and spread his blanket beside Arrhyna. It seemed wrong to pitch their lodge while their hosts slept open on the ground. He touched his bride's cheek and composed himself for sleep. The last thing he saw was the pinnacle of the Maker's Mountain shining like bleached bone under the moon.

He woke to shadow, realizing that dawn came late to this valley, and lay awhile listening to the morning. Birds rose chorusing, and from afar he heard the belling of a stag. He thought the hunting should be good here, and felt a sudden and tremendous excitement that he trod grass none of the People had before trod—as if he and Arrhyna were reborn as First Man and First Woman, raised by the Maker from the clay to walk this new land. He rose, draping his blanket about his shoulders, and fed the fire. Across the sky ran a great wide beam of golden light that fell upon the flanks of the Maker's Mountain and lit the peak so that it shone all silvery white, no longer like bleached bone but bright and radiant as newfound hope. He bowed his head and made a gesture of obeisance, promising the Maker that he would from now serve him as best he could, following the Ahsa-tye-Patiko and warding his wife and people even to the giving of his life.

Then he started, embarrassed, as the others woke and gathered about the fire. Arrhyna went to the stream, and after her ablutions were performed, came back and set to preparing breakfast.

When they'd eaten, Colun declared it time to part. Rannach asked where they went, and when the Grannach indicated the valley's invisible farther end, offered to ride with them.

"Stay here for now," Colun said. "Pitch your tent and see your wife comfortable. Hunt; explore. Learn the valley and find a place to live. When I can, I'll come back. Perhaps with Marjia"—he looked to Arrhyna—"that you fulfil your promise."

Arrhyna said, "I shall, is it possible."

"Ach, tiswin!" Colun chuckled. "I shall offer prayers that it is."

Arrhyna smiled; Rannach said, "Shall I not ride with you at least a little way?"

Colun beckoned him off then, out of earshot, and said, "Make your camp here a few days before you wander farther. And when you do, go no higher than that." He thrust a finger at the pines standing above the topmost terrace. "Let that be the limit of your exploration, eh?"

Rannach ducked his head and said, "As you will. But why?"

Colun sniffed noisily. "I am but one Creddan, as your father is but one akaman. My clan claims this valley, and it was my decision to bring you here. It might be that . . ." He grinned somewhat shamefaced. "That not all agree with my decision, especially when I tell my people of your Council's indecision. It would be wiser that you stay safe here, not risk offense. None shall harm you here, but some might take affront did you go wandering about our hills."

Rannach nodded and again said, "As you will." He no longer felt quite so secure.

Seeing this, Colun said, "No harm shall come to you here. I'd have said this earlier, save I'd not frighten Arrhyna. She's had frights enough of late, no?"

Rannach said, "Yes," and took the Grannach's horny hand between his own. "My thanks for all you've done, Colun. I deem it an honor to name you friend."

"And I," Colun said. "You're your father's son."

"Save I lack his wisdom."

"That shall likely come." Colun held Rannach's hands hard: it was as if stone ground his bones. "Time makes some men wise, if they live long enough. I think you'll learn it."

Rannach said, "I hope I may."

"The Maker stand with you," Colun said, and turned away.

In a while the Grannach were gone, trotting up the valley to where the stream turned around a stand of juniper and was lost.

Arrhyna said, "I think I might make tiswin from those berries." And then: "What did Colun say to you?"

Rannach shrugged and said, "Farewell," and for a moment thought to hide from her what else. But they were together now and alone, and he'd not hold any secrets from her. So he told her.

When he was done she said, "But we are safe here, no?"

"Colun said that."

She took his hand and smiled. "Then all is well. Do we pitch our lodge and begin this new life?"

Rannach said, "In a while," and took her in his arms.

14 Departure

Militiamen with bayonets fixed threateningly to their muskets lined the wharf from warehouse to waterside, a red-coated corridor from the land the prisoners were leaving forever to the ship that would take them into the unknown future. She was a schooner—the *Pride of the Lord*—and the sailors hanging from her rigging greeted the exiles with jeers and whistles as the column shuffled miserably toward her. Their catcalls joined the mewing of the swooping gulls in a chorus of derision, but Flysse paid them no heed—she was too concerned for Davyd, whose fear of water threatened to overcome his fear of the Militiamen's anger. The soldiers brooked no delay, nor hesitated to use musket butt or bayonet to urge on the tardy, as if the exiles were no more than cattle driven to slaughter. Ahead of Flysse, a weeping man turned back, and was forced on at bayonet point, his sobs becoming a shriek of pain as steel pricked his buttocks, decorating his breeches with bloody patches. The perpetrators laughed as if it were a great joke; Flysse felt Davyd's hand seek hers and grip hard. She looked at his face and saw his lips drawn tight over clenched teeth as he stared fixedly ahead. She thought he looked very young, and very afraid. Glancing around, she saw Arcole Blayke behind her, his expression disdainful as he eyed the chuckling soldiers. He seemed unaware of Davyd's terror.

The line moved slowly on, across the cobbles to the gangplank. At the head of that gently undulating ramp stood a captain. He held a heavy key with which he unlocked the prisoners' handcuffs, tossing them to a pile on the deck. More Militiamen stood there, alert as the exiles were freed and herded to the hold. Flysse felt Davyd shudder as he stepped on board. He looked around, wild-eyed, as his manacles were removed, eyes roving over deck and swaying masts to the gunwales to the sea beyond. He made no move, but for a moment she feared he would attempt to flee, though she could not imagine where.

The officer favored the boy with a contemptuous look and was about to speak, when Arcole forestalled him.

"Go on, lad. Don't give these bullies the pleasure."

Flysse turned, smiling gratefully as Davyd moaned and allowed her to lead him toward the hold, but Arcole was staring at the captain and she realized his words were intended less for Davyd than in challenge of the Militiaman.

The captain only sneered and loosed Arcole's manacles, motioning for him to follow the others. Arcole made a show of adjusting his shirt cuffs, bowed to the officer in a manner that succeeded in being insulting, and strolled leisurely to the ladder descending into the bowels of the ship. Flysse thought him very brave, and very foolish.

For her own part, she was terrified. Perhaps not so much as Davyd —whose fear seemed to rob him of volition, rendering his legs rubbery, his movements disjointed as a poleaxed steer—but still more afraid than she had ever been. She was grateful for the boy's presence, for his helplessness that enabled her to ignore her own terror to some extent. She concentrated on helping him down the ladder—she thought that he must fall without her hands to guide him.

But when she reached the bottom and saw her charge safely down, she found herself abruptly confused. She had never set foot on board a ship before, and she was immediately disorientated. The hold was a long, dim area divided by stacked ranks of narrow bunks that left barely enough space for passage between. Many of the bunks were already occupied, and Flysse peered around, wondering where she should lead Davyd. He had guided her in the warehouse, but now he only stood blank-eyed and shuddering like a mindless babe. She started as a hand touched her elbow.

"What's wrong with him?" Arcole asked, indicating the trembling boy.

"He's afraid of water," she replied.

"As are too many here." Arcole looked around, his nostrils flaring, and Flysse realized that the hold did, indeed, bear an odor of unwashed bodies. "Still, do you follow me?"

As he moved past her, she blushed and took a firm grip on Davyd's hand, leading him unprotesting after the tall man.

Arcole made his way between the bunks to a section overlooked by a hatch. The metal grille let in sufficient light, it was easier to see, and the air here was a little fresher. He halted, indicating the tiers.

"Save you object to the observation of the sailors, Mistress Cobal, I suggest you take the topmost. It shall be the airier." He extended a hand to help her up. "I'll see the boy settled."

"Thank you." Flysse allowed him to aid her climb. She noticed that his hand was very smooth.

She settled herself on the bunk and watched as Davyd took the middle level, and Arcole the lowest place. Each bunk had a straw pallet and a thin gray blanket. They were barely wide enough to accommodate the occupants, and surrounded by raised planks that formed low walls. Looking up through the hatch, Flysse could see a mast and the spars outlined against a blue sky. It occurred to her that it was the sky above Evander and that this should be the last time she would ever see it. She closed her eyes and told herself she would not cry.

"I must confess," she heard Arcole declare in his Levan drawl, "that I've known better quarters."

She wondered if he sought to cheer her, and then how Davyd fared. At that, she dismissed her own trepidation and hung her head over the bunk's edge to study the boy. He lay curled on his pallet, a blanket spread over him—had Arcole draped him thus?—so that only his head and the tight-clasped hands he pressed against his mouth were visible. She said his name but he gave no reply, nor offered any sign he heard her. She sighed and directed her gaze along the hold.

From her vantage point atop the tier, she could see the bunks were filling up. She thought there must be a hundred or more. Some exiles carried small bundles that they clutched close, afraid of losing whatever pitiful valuables they had managed to bring with them. Flysse wished she had been able to bring something—a comb would not go amiss, nor a change of clothing. She had no sure idea how long the voyage would last, and the notion of spending weeks at sea in garments not laundered since her arrest was unpleasant. No less that of spending the entire voyage in this dim, malodorous hold.

"Sieur Blayke?" she ventured. And when Arcole's face appeared below her: "Shall we spend all our time here, or shall they let us out? Shall we be allowed to wash? What shall we do when . . ."

She fell silent, embarrassed by the flood of questions. She was suddenly afraid he would find them insulting; how should a gentleman be familiar with the procedures of an exile ship?

His smile, albeit faint, put her better at her ease. "I've really no idea," he said. "This is as new an experience for me as it is for you."

Flysse blushed—she seemed to spend much of her time in his presence blushing—and said, "Of course. I'm sorry; forgive me. I just . . . I thought . . . Forgive me, please."

She was babbling again. She set a hand against her mouth to dam the spate, and bit on a knuckle as she fought the renewed threat of tears.

"Mistress Cobal," she heard him say, "there's nothing to forgive, I assure you. I think we are none of us much at our ease here. Our circumstances are unusual to us all. But . . ." She heard his voice come closer and opened her eyes to find his face looking over the rim of her bunk. "I believe they place some value on our lives—as indentured folk, at least—and so shall likely provide us with the basic amenities. Even the Evanderans tend their animals, no?"

Flysse nodded, taking no offense at his slighting reference to Evanderans. She did not feel she belonged to any particular nation, save that exile was, in itself, a kind of community. She essayed a smile, realizing he sought to comfort her.

"I imagine they'll see us fed and watered," he continued. "And I trust they'll allow us to wash. God knows, we shall have an ocean at our disposal, eh?"

He smiled then, and Flysse could not, despite all her fear, help thinking how handsome he was. She wiped at her eyes, thinking she must look a sight. A comb—a hairbrush—would be most welcome. Unconsciously, she touched her hair, smoothing the errant curls. "What should we do?" she asked. "For now, I mean."

Arcole shrugged. "Wait, I suppose. There seems little we *can* do, no? I imagine they'll issue instructions betimes. Meanwhile, I think it wise we remain here, to stake our claim." He gestured at the filling hold, smiling sardonically. "Should we quit these desirable quarters, we'd likely find them taken on our return."

Flysse nodded sadly. She thought things came to a sorry pass where folk prepared to squabble over such miserable beds, but still could see the sense of Arcole's advice. These bunks would be infinitely preferable to those situated away from the ventilation of the hatches, around the edges of the hull, where the light was dimmest and the air thick. She saw him smile and nod, and then his face was gone as he took his own place.

She settled back, watching the hold fill up as the enormity of her situation sank in. There were other women present, but the majority of the human cargo was male and she saw more than one pair of eyes turned her way, some merely curious, others openly speculative. She knew such looks from the taproom of the Flying Horse, but at least there she had been able to deflect the attentions of admirers. Here, she was not sure any rules *could* govern, save those the strongest saw fit to impose. She saw the massive black-bearded fellow who had entered the warehouse with Arcole watching her and turned away, not wishing to give him any encouragement. She remembered Arcole's reference to animals and wondered why men and women were not separated. The answer came with the memory of an overheard conversation between Master Banlyn and a sea captain, and with it a horrid quickening of fear.

The mariner had captained such a ship as this, and Master Banlyn had asked him, winking lewdly, what provision was made for the quartering of women and men. The captain had chuckled and reminded him that such folk as the exile ships carried were all indentured, and did they breed during the voyage, why, their children were born indentured and thus to lifelong service in Salvation.

Flysse felt her mouth go dry. She knew she lacked the strength to repel such attentions as might be forced on her. She could fight—would fight—but did some man look to rape her, she knew in her heart she should be helpless. Davyd might try to defend her, but he was only a boy. And Arcole? Would he protect her honor? She was nothing to him save a chance companion in hardship. Had he laid eyes on her in the Flying Horse, he'd likely not have noticed her at all, save perhaps as another tavern wench, beneath his dignity. She felt a lump grow in her throat and her eyes water. She squeezed them tight shut, telling herself she must be strong: she must not cry, show weakness. She could not help a stifled sob.

"What ails you now?"

There was a faint hint of irritation in Arcole's voice that added to Flysse's desolation. She swallowed and rubbed at her eyes. "I'm afraid," she said, and when Arcole sighed: "I'm sorry."

His tone sounded mollified somewhat. "What is it you fear? The Sea of Sorrows, monsters of the deep?"

Flysse stared at him in horror. Those dangers had been farthest from her mind, and she had rather he not remind her of them. She shook her head, annoyed now that she could not entirely stem the tears. "No," she said, and waved a hand at the hold in general. "It's this. All of it. These people."

Arcole turned, surveying the hold as if he looked over some unsavory gaming room. "Not, I'll admit, the company I'd choose." He gave her an ironic grin. "But still . . . comrades in adversity, no?"

"No," said Flysse. "You don't understand."

"Then tell me," he said.

Flysse thought he spoke out of politeness and nothing more. He seemed indifferent to her upset, even slightly bored, as if he saw her as inferior, or tiresome. She shook her head, afraid he tone was querulous as she said, "No; it's nothing."

When he sighed and she saw his brows rise a fraction, she scowled and turned her back, revising her opinion of him. Handsome he might be, but also arrogant, and she would not show him weakness. All around, she heard the sounds of her fellow exiles: their low-voiced conversations, some weeping, some chanting prayers, the shifting of bodies, the creaking of the bunks. There were unfamiliar noises, too, that came from the timbers of the ship and the sea beyond its hull, the sailors overhead. She heard the tramp of boots and the faint shout of orders, and then a growing silence that prompted her to open her eyes and sit up.

Descending the ladder granting access to the hold, she saw a man. An officer in the God's Militia by his uniform, but that not one she recognized. He did not wear the familiar scarlet, but a jacket of dark blue, crossed by white straps that supported a sword and a holstered pistol. He held a tricorn hat with a cockade of scarlet and white beneath one arm, one hand rested on the butt of the pistol. It was difficult to make out his face clearly, but she saw that his hair was fair and his features regular. He halted a few steps from the bottom and surveyed the hold as the silence spread.

When all was quiet he said, "I am Tomas Var, Captain of Marines in the God's Militia. I command fifty men, whose duty is to defend this vessel against all harm—be it from without or within."

He paused, allowing the significance of his words to sink in. Flysse heard Arcole murmur, "Our guards, by God."

Var let his gaze wander across the watching faces, then went on: "Do you give offense, do any of you think to foment mutiny or any kind of trouble, know that my men will shoot you down. You will obey such orders as I or any of my men give you, or those issued by Captain Bennan, who is master of this ship. Do you refuse, you will be flogged. Do you raise a hand against any soldier or sailor, you will be executed. Do you raise hand against one another, you will be flogged. Neither will I tolerate rape. Any who offend will be flogged within an inch of their life.

"Do you follow these rules, this voyage shall not be overly unpleasant. But remember always—you are the outcasts of decent society. You are exiles and you have no rights, only such charity as we elect to grant you.

"You will be fed twice a day, and, does the weather allow, come in groups on deck to exercise and bathe . . ."

He proceeded to outline those routines by which they must live. Flysse listened intently, seeking to persuade herself that the regime, and the presence of the marines, would impose order and a degree of safety. She thought this captain, this Tomas Var, seemed a decent man, whose care of his charges extended to delivering them whole and undamaged to Salvation. Or so she hoped . . .

Arcole listened to the clipped Evanderan voice with a cynical half-smile. Fifty marines should certainly be sufficient to maintain order and discipline amongst the exiles, nor did he doubt that Var would make good his promises of executions and floggings. He knew something of the Autarchy's marines. They had been the spearhead of the Evanderan armies, and a sharp, swift spear at that. They were undoubtedly fine soldiers, and likely no less efficient as warders. He did not share Flysse's optimism: to him Var's men represented the same authority that defiled his land and sent him into unjust exile.

He waited until Var was finished speaking and had gone back up the ladder, then stretched—as best his height allowed—on the bunk, staring morosely at the slats a few scant inches above. He anticipated a long and boring voyage. He wondered how many of the prisoners would survive unscathed. He could not believe all there would adhere to Var's rules. Indeed, were his companions on the journey to Bantar typical of his fellow exiles, he shared this miserable hold with a crew of ruffians. Save perhaps the young woman, Flysse, though even she represented something of an unwelcome problem.

He had acted instinctively when he helped her with the young thief, and she appeared to have taken that as some kind of commitment. He hoped she would not seek to attach herself to him: it would be an embarrassment. She was, he must admit, pretty enough, but a tavern wench—even one who had struck an officer of the God's Militia— was beneath his dignity. His friends would scorn him were he to dally there.

He chuckled then. Dom was his only real friend, and all those others who called themselves his friends should soon be left far behind. He would never see them again, so why should their opinion matter? It did not, he decided, save insofar as it reflected and echoed his own, and that did not permit attachments to tavern wenches, no matter how appealing. He was Arcole Blayke, gentleman, and must hold on to that concept of himself, else he descend to the level of the common folk around him. Besides, the girl was obviously vulnerable, and did he allow her to perceive him as her champion, it could only lead to her ultimate disappointment. He did not seek emotional attachments, but to survive this tedious voyage and make the best of his unwelcome fate.

He did not think that should prove too difficult once landed in Salvation. The place must surely be a wilderness—the God knew, it lay on the far side of the world—and there must surely be opportunities there for a gentleman, even one branded and indentured. He could read and write, which he doubted were attributes owned by many of his companions. He was a master swordsman, though he wondered if the Evanderans would trust him in reach of a blade. He could read music and play the harpsichord, and his singing voice was considered melodious. He was an able pugilist. His work with sketchpad and watercolors was more than efficient. And, of course, he was most handy with the cards. Was there a town of some kind, and inland farms, he supposed there must be some kind of society. There was, he believed, a governor, and he supposed that authority would entertain some kind of court. Therefore—surely—there would be a place for a gentleman of Arcole's talents. Perhaps as a tutor, something of that ilk. Surely even the uncouth Evanderans could not ignore his skills, but put them to use at something other than rough manual labor.

He nodded to himself, confirming his own logic. He need only survive the tiresome voyage, then make the best life he could in Salvation. It must be under the Evanderan thumb, without hope of return to his beloved Levan, but so be it. And perhaps . . .

He turned his head from side to side, studying the folk spread around the hold. God knew, there were enough of them: more sent before and no doubt more to come. Perhaps someday there might be even more exiles than Evanderans—more indentured servants than masters. So perhaps one day . . . The thought excited him. It was beguiling, almost terrifying in its promise . . . Perhaps one day the exiles might rise up and overthrow the masters, take Salvation for their own.

He pushed the notion away, afraid of the hope it offered. The Evanderans commanded magic and stamped out that faculty in all others. Doubtless they'd have practitioners in Salvation, perhaps even Inquisitors, whilst the exiles would have none. Certainly there would be a strong garrison. Better that such ideas be set aside until he gained a clearer picture of the life awaiting him on the farther side of the world. Learn all he could, and then decide. It was not dissimilar to a duel: one might have some knowledge of one's opponent, of his reputation, but until the first tentative moves were made, the engagé, the parry and riposte, one could not be sure. So one approached cautiously, learning, probing, until the counters, the skill of the enemy, were perceived. Only then did one strike.

That must be his course, and until he had gleaned all the information he might of his opponent, he would play the part of prisoner, submissive. It would not be easy—in all of this, one thing remained firm: his hatred of the Evanderans and their Autarchy—but he would do his best. And to do that he did not need a dewy-eyed girl clinging to his coattails, even less a stripling thief. Did they continue to attach themselves to him, he would rebuff them.

His mind made up, Arcole did his best to relax.

It was not easy. The bunk was too short, and scarcely more comfortable than his prison cell. The hold was filling up with the smell of unwashed humanity and the noises it made: he was not accustomed to mingling with such people. He wished he had a book to read, a pomander to protect his nostrils. He wished he might take a leisurely bath, or stroll about the deck. He touched his branded cheek, reminding himself that such basic amenities were denied him: he was an exile.

He heard unfamiliar sounds—shouts from the deck above and the creak of timbers—and felt the schooner shift. He was not much familiar with the ways of oceangoing craft, but he guessed the ship was towed from its moorings, out from Bantar's docks to the open sea beyond. He did his best to block out the cries of alarm that rose up to accompany the movement, and the scorn he felt at such caterwauling. There was no point to complaint—exile was inevitable. All that remained was to make the best of it. He hoped he would not be seasick.

He listened carefully awhile, then rose to stand beside the bunks, looking up. Through the grille of the hatch he could see a mast, and sailors clambering like squirrels about the rigging. Then, with a sound like massive sheets shaken by a giant, the sails unfurled and the deck lurched beneath his feet. He clutched unthinking at the rim of the topmost bunk, and felt a hand cover his as Flysse gasped. He turned and found her eyes huge and blue, staring at him as if in search of answers or reassurances.

"We must be under way," he said, and retrieved his hand. "We depart the harbor."

Flysse swallowed and nodded, feeling her cheeks grow warm at the cool indifference of his tone. She had hoped . . . But no. Whatever kindness he had shown her was no more than gentlemanly politeness. She had no right to expect more, nor would she. She directed her eyes upward, marveling at the vast billows of white canvas that filled the sky above, then looked downward as Davyd moaned and stirred, writhing on his bunk as if in nightmare's grip.

Forgetting her own discomfort and ignoring Arcole, she clambered down to perch beside the restive boy. His hand clutched hers, and his eyes opened.

"We're out to sea," he groaned. "Oh, God protect us."

Over her shoulder, Arcole said, "We quit the harbor, no more than that."

"For the sea!" Davyd cried. "We'll all drown! There are monsters there, waiting for us."

"Sailors' stories," Arcole said.

"They're true," said Davyd mournfully. "I know!"

Flysse squeezed his hand. "We're safe, Davyd," she said. "Why, we must be still in sight of Evander, and everyone knows there are no monsters in these waters. Besides, there are marines on board, all with muskets and swords. They'll surely protect us from any monsters. Did you not hear the captain?"

Davyd shook his head, but Flysse could not tell whether he denied her or told her he had not heard. She feared that he must sicken did he continue stricken by such terror. Barely knowing what she did, she turned to Arcole, her eyes imploring.

Arcole had rather not meet her gaze. It asked that he involve himself; it asked for his help—though for the boy alone, and that prompted his grudging admiration. He thought that this Flysse Cobal was perhaps made of better stuff than the common folk, of sterner mettle. He did not want to admire her; he wanted to ignore her. But he was, after all, a gentleman, and no gentleman could ignore a lady in distress, no matter what her station. He sighed and bent toward Davyd.

"As Mistress Cobal says, there are marines on board, and I saw cannon. Likely those alone would fend off any monsters." He could not help a slight smile: sea monsters, indeed! "But did you not see the hexes painted about the ship?"

Davyd shook his head or shuddered, Arcole could not tell which.

"Well, they are there, and no doubt are designed to protect all on board. I'd say that should be enough, no?"

Davyd grunted something that might have been a negative. Flysse put an arm about his narrow shoulders, cradling him as she might have done a baby. "Do you hear, Davyd?" she asked gently. "Sieur Blayke tells you we're safe, and he should know, eh?"

Arcole wondered how that should be. The Levan was landlocked, and the only waters he had ever crossed were rivers or lakes, and those by bridge or ferryboat. Horses he knew about, and cities, but the open sea was totally unfamiliar. He wished Flysse would not look at him so gratefully, but the boy had stopped shaking now and stared at him as if he were the fount of all knowledge. He sighed again and went on.

"We're valuable cargo, no? Exiled and indentured—property of some worth to the Autarchy, which guards its possessions jealously. I doubt me they'd risk losing us, or this ship. No, boy, you'll be safe."

Now two pairs of eyes studied him as if his words were the corner-stones of their lives. It occurred to him that Flysse was near as frightened as the boy but hid her fear for Davyd's sake. She rose higher in his estimation—which irritated him somewhat. He forced a smile and said, confidently as he was able, "Trust me, eh? You're safe."

Very soft, less to Arcole or Flysse than to himself, Davyd murmured, "But I dreamed . . ."

"Dreamed what?" asked Flysse.

Davyd caught himself and shook his head. "Nothing. It was just a dream. Only that."

His face—already pale—grew ashen, as if some fear greater even than his terror of water leeched the blood from his cheeks. Arcole saw the muscles of his jaw lock tight around clenched teeth and his head drop, eyes averted. Arcole was a gambler and a duelist, skilled in the reading of faces—of those small, unbidden signs that give a man away: he sensed something was hidden. He wondered what greater terror possessed the boy than his fear of the sea.

Flysse said, "Fear makes us dream sometimes, Davyd," and the boy nodded without looking up and said, "I'm thirsty."

Arcole thought he deflected further talk of his dreams. Almost, he pursued the matter, but Flysse looked to him and asked, "Would you be kind enough, Sieur Blayke?"

He frowned, at first not sure what she asked of him—he was not accustomed to fetching and carrying. But then he nodded brusquely and rose, walking to the hatchway ladder, where he recalled a water butt was located.

The deck shifted more steeply under his feet now, and he must adjust his step, balancing the tin cup carefully as he returned. He noticed that several of the human cargo were already sick, and wondered how long it would be before the hold stank of vomit. But he brought the cup back and handed it to Flysse. She smiled thanks and lifted the mug to Davyd's mouth.

When the boy had done drinking, he licked his lips and said huskily, "My thanks, Sieur Blayke."

Arcole waved a dismissive hand and took the empty cup, returning it. When he reached their bunks again, Davyd seemed a little calmer. Or in greater control of his fear. He no longer trembled, but he still clutched Flysse's hand as if it were a rock, anchoring him in a stormy sea.

Flysse said, "You are very kind, Sieur Blayke."

Arcole grunted. It seemed an attachment grew, whether he liked it or not. And he could not shake the feeling that Davyd hid something, something about his dreaming. He thought it must be a long voyage. He looked at the young woman and at the boy awhile, and then he said, "We are to be companions on this journey, no? So, do we dispense with formalities? My name is Arcole."

And against his will, he could not help but feel pleased by Flysse's smile.

15 For a Lady's Honor

Routines became established as the *Pride of the Lord* sailed steadily westward.

The exiles were each issued with a bowl, a spoon, and a cup, and soon after dawn each day they were fed. Sailors escorted by armed marines lowered tubs of porridge into the hold and the prisoners formed into lines to partake of the frugal meal. It was thick, unpalatable stuff, but after a few complainers had suffered beatings, there were no more objections. Throughout the day, in groups of twenty, they were allowed on deck to bathe and exercise as best they might in the small space allowed. Tomas Var ordered an arrangement of canvas sheets that afforded a degree of privacy for their ablutions, though sailors leered from the rigging as the women took their turn; and when Arcole pursued those exercises learned in the gymnasiums of the Levan, he attracted the catcalls of mariners and prisoners alike. He ignored them: such common folk could hardly be expected to understand the activities of a gentleman. Around sunset, thick soup and hard bread were issued. If the exiles were lucky, the soup contained pieces of meat. Inevitably, the larger part of each day was spent below decks.

And there hierarchies began to form.

The strongest, or the most vicious, of the prisoners attracted coteries of sycophants, and those groups carved out tiny kingdoms within the hold's small world. Had they not already claimed the most propitious areas for themselves, they set about the conquest. Those too weak to oppose them were banished to the less favorable sections: around the perimeter of the hull, where the air circulated slower and thicker and the journey to water butt or soup tub was longer. Some were required to pay a toll for the journey, in food or physical favors.

Arcole had not looked to establish himself as a leader—he had far rather been left alone—but early in the voyage a ruffian with broad shoulders and a wide chest, one of Karyl Oster's group, suggested he vacate his position beneath the airy hatch, taking the boy with him. The woman he could leave.

Arcole told him, "No. Why should I?"

The man—Arcole never bothered to learn his name—said, "Because I want it."

Arcole digested this and smiled. It was, on a level beneath his dignity, akin to the challenge of a duelist. He thought that he must adjust his attitudes in this new environment. Still smiling, he drove his fist into the man's stomach, and then, as the fellow doubled over, struck him twice—very precisely, just as he had been taught by Smiling Jacques, the prizefighter—about the head. The man fell down and did not get up. Arcole suggested to his minions that they carry him away, which they did instantly and nervously. After that, none others attempted to take over that section of the bunks, and Arcole found himself something of a hero.

Certainly Flysse saw him as such, and Davyd; and consequently he found himself further entangled with them, the which he found irritating and flattering in equal measure. The boy had calmed somewhat, but was still clearly troubled. He ate and drank automatically, as if from habit rather than desire, but when he slept he tossed and turned and cried out about sea monsters and destruction and then, on waking, denied memory of the dreams with averted eyes and new-paled face. He looked to Flysse for comfort and Arcole for protection, and when he walked on deck it was always with anxious looks toward the sea.

Arcole's curiosity about this went some way to fixing their relationship. He felt that Davyd possessed some knowledge he kept hid, and as much to escape the inevitable boredom of the journey as for any other reason, he determined to unlock the boy's secrets.

Flysse was another matter entirely.

He could not deny her beauty, but neither the differences between them. He respected her courage—especially that bravery that had prompted her to strike an officer in the God's Militia—and he admired the way she concealed her own fears in support of Davyd, but he could not forget that she had been a tavern wench. For all she spoke well, and possessed manners unusual for a serving woman—imitating the gentlefolk in whose mansion she'd once worked, he supposed—he could not help but think of her as beneath his station. Nor did he seek such entanglements as must surely hamper his advancement in Salvation. He looked on them both as curiosities: common folk come somehow under his protection, not properly understood, like inherited servants. And yet, when he saw the scar decorating Davyd's cheek exactly like his own, and the brand on Flysse's arm, he must remember that they were all of them exiles and in the eyes of the Autarchy no different.

For all he had told himself he must accept the situation and make the best of it, it was not easy to consider himself one with the other inmates of the hold, one with the human cargo of the *Pride of the Lord*. In too many ways he felt a greater kinship with the marines who watched him as he exercised and understood better than his fellow exiles what he did and why. He had sooner dined with Tomas Var—for all the man was an officer of the Autarchy, and an Evanderan—than take his bowl and eat on his bunk with folk who spoke in common accents and smelled of sweat and vomit. And yet he was consigned with them to exile: he wore the brand, and faced only a life of slavery, indentured. And those secret hopes he held—well, perhaps it did not hurt to make friends amongst his fellows.

And—a constant, growing curiosity—there were Davyd's dreams.

He knew of Dreamers. The Autarchy destroyed them mercilessly: they possessed some measure of that magic power that won Evander its wars. It was a strength greater than muskets or blades, and jealously guarded. He had not lied when he told Davyd of the hexes that warded the *Pride of the Lord*—they were strong, likely set there by Evanderan Inquisitors who were the strongest of all the magically gifted. Those sigils could hold a man back from jumping ship, or an exile from electing to drown rather than become a servant in Salvation. They would— did sea serpents exist—hold off those monsters. They were the truest strength of the Autarchy.

But there were other strengths, other magicks, and the dreaming was one. It prophesied, which was why the Autarchy sought out and burned all those outside its ranks who owned the gift.

Arcole was uncertain whether or not Davyd owned that gift. He knew only that the boy had spoken of dreams and exhibited unreasonable fear at mention of them. Was he a Dreamer, then his aversion to discussion was understandable; were he revealed, he would be executed. But if it was so—if Davyd *was* a Dreamer—then he was a potential ally, surely a useful tool.

He did not think Flysse entertained any suspicion of Davyd's potential ability, but the boy looked to Flysse for support, so Arcole could not overlook or dismiss the woman. He recognized, with a gambler's instinct, that the one card must depend upon the other, and if he were to succeed in his duel with the Autarchy, he might need them both.

So he allowed them to look to him for protection, and it was, he had to admit, not altogether unpleasant.

Flysse could not make up her mind about Arcole. As he had suggested, she called him by his first name now, and he addressed her by hers, and that would usually have confirmed their friendship. But she was not sure she could genuinely call him her friend—he remained somehow aloof. Oh, he was unfailingly polite and she was grateful for his guardianship, but there remained something about him that denied real intimacy. It was as though he erected an invisible barrier around himself, and often when they spoke—which was more usually on her or Davyd's instigation than Arcole's—she felt he talked down to her. That irritated her, for while she regarded him as a gentleman, she considered herself respectable and felt he might well treat her on a more equal footing. But her irritation was balanced by gratitude and the knowledge that without his protection, her situation on board the *Pride of the Lord* would surely be far worse.

Not that it was what she would call pleasant. The lack of privacy offended her, and the food was none too good. When she bathed, the leering faces that observed her from the rigging frightened her; and when she washed her clothes, she blushed at the catcalls and lewd whistles that prompted her to dress again, quickly, and suffer the dampness and the scratching of the saltwater. Almost, she wished she were as unashamed as some of the other women, who flaunted their nudity at the sailors. But perhaps worst were the nights, when the hold echoed to the sounds of copulation, and sometimes then she could not resist wondering what she would do were Arcole to approach her.

These thoughts she kept secret, though, and her unhappiness, for she must consider Davyd.

Although the terror that had possessed him on boarding was gone, she knew he was still very frightened. He did his best to hide it, but by day he was never far from her side or Arcole's, as if their presence firmed and calmed him, and by night he could not conceal his dreams. At first she tried to persuade him to speak of them and saw that Arcole did the same, but Davyd remained resolute, denying that he could remember what had set him to screaming in the night save it be his innate fear of the sea.

That seemed to Flysse a reasonable explanation, and it was soon obvious that Davyd was uncomfortable enough speaking of his oneiric experiences that she accepted his reasons and said no more. But she noticed that Arcole still pressed the boy with questions until Davyd would moan and hold his head, and look to Flysse to rescue him from interrogation, and she wished he would desist for Davyd's sake.

One day, on deck, she spoke to him of her concern.

He had completed his exercises and washed. She held his shirt, unable to resist studying his muscular torso as he performed his routine. Davyd was a little distance away, staring dully at the sea, as if awaiting the arrival of a monster so inevitable that fear became pointless. She passed him his shirt and said, "Arcole, I'd speak with you of Davyd." She kept her voice low, that the boy not hear. "Why do you question him so about his dreams? It serves only to upset him."

She wondered if she saw interest flicker in his eyes. Surely there was a momentary tightening of his jaw. But then he shrugged and said, "Do you not think it better a man face his fears?"

"Davyd's hardly a man," she answered. "He's but a frightened boy, and you frighten him the more with your interrogations."

Arcole looked a moment thoughtful, then asked her, "Do you not think he might exorcise his fears through confession?"

Flysse's brow wrinkled. Arcole noticed that she grew tanned, her hair become pale gold. For a moment he wondered how she would look in a decent gown, how she would sound without that harsh Evanderan accent. Then she shook her head and told him, "No. I think his fears are locked too deep, and shall remain until he sets foot on land again."

"Perhaps," Arcole said. "So you believe his dreams shall end when we reach Salvation?"

"Surely they will. It's the sea that frightens him, no?"

Again Arcole said, "Perhaps."

"How mean you, perhaps?" Flysse asked. "Is it the sea that frightens him, then surely dry land must comfort him."

For a third time Arcole said, "Perhaps."

Flysse found him enigmatic, and somewhat irritating. "Why are you so interested?" she demanded.

Arcole frowned, then hid that look behind a smile. "I've never spent time with anyone like Davyd," he said honestly. "The boy intrigues me; I'd learn what makes him dream so."

That sounded to Flysse as if Arcole relegated Davyd to the position of a specimen, some curious creature worthy of study for its oddity. She glared at him and said, "Is Davyd only some *thing* you observe?"

Arcole was taken aback by her vehemence. He felt a moment embarrassed, for there was a measure of truth in her accusation. Also he found himself disturbed that she grew so vexed, that he found himself concerned by her anger. He told himself he must assuage her for fear he lose a potential ally, that it was not personal. He bowed and said, "I ask your forgiveness, Flysse. I see that I've been clumsy in my attempt to aid the boy. Do you truly believe my questions worsen his condition, I'll put them up. My word on it."

He offered her a tentative smile. By God, what did it matter that he anger her? Save that he'd not; and he must admit, against his will, that he wished that less in fear of losing an ally than for the simple reason he'd sooner see her smile than glower at him. The admission troubled him, and he pushed it aside, to some hinder part of his mind.

Flysse hesitated an instant, then let herself smile back. "I think it should be for the best," she said. "For Davyd's sake."

"Then as I say." Arcole set a hand over his heart. "I shall desist."

"Thank you," Flysse said.

Then they started as Davyd cried out and sprang away from the rail. So vigorous was his jump that he flung himself some distance back, sprawling full length on the deck. Flysse and Arcole hurried to him, clutching him as he crabbed backward over the boards.

"Monsters!" His voice was hoarse and his eyes rolled, the whites exposed. "Sea monsters!"

Arcole left him in Flysse's care and went to the rail where now a small crowd was gathered, pointing and shouting, sharing Davyd's panic. He stared at the sea. The swell was a deep blue-gray, and from it emerged darting shapes of a similar color that raced alongside the schooner, sometimes flinging themselves high into the air like living missiles. For a moment Arcole felt his heart lurch, his skin crawl cold. Beside him a woman screamed.

Then, on his left, a marine lowered his musket and laughed. "Dolphins," he said. "Only dolphins, and no harm in them at all."

Arcole went back to Davyd and told him what the marine had said. "Harmless dolphins," he assured the trembling boy. "They're a kind of fish, I think. Certainly they're not sea monsters."

Davyd's hand gripped Arcole's wrist with a strength that belied his scrawny frame. "They'll come," he muttered. "I know they'll come. I dreamed it."

There was such awful certitude in his voice, Arcole wished he had not made Flysse that promise. He watched as she smoothed the frightened boy's hair, murmuring gently, and thought that he must find some subtle way to question Davyd further.

There was no immediate opportunity, however, for when Davyd's prostration caught the attention of the marines on watch, several came to stare at the boy. He saw them, and Arcole saw his terror arise again, now prompted by the soldiers. Some laughed, and Davyd forced himself to join them, hiding his fear behind a rueful smile and a shaking of his head. He allowed Arcole and Flysse to help him to his feet and took a drink of water, pretending calm. Arcole saw that his shirt was heavy with fear sweat, but said no more, only played the part of concerned friend. It would not be easy, but he determined to unlock the secret of the boy's dreams.

They approached the Sea of Sorrows now, and the days grew steadily warmer, no less the nights. Folk shed clothes like molting beasts, all modesty forgotten as the mounting heat pervaded the hold. The more brazen of the women went about in only their shifts, and emotions matched the rising temperatures. Arcole was gratified to see that Flysse did not demonstrate such abandon, though he could not properly define why.

Then, one stifling night, all became changed.

Arcole slept fitfully, bare-chested and awash with sweat. He could hear Davyd moaning in the bunk above, the grunts and cries of copulation loud amidst the snoring of those exiles fortunate enough to find sound sleep. He drifted in a limbo closer to wakefulness than slumber, and consequently was aware of stealthy footfalls moving toward him. He opened his eyes and began to raise his head, when a hand closed over his mouth, others clamping over his wrists, and abruptly he was hauled from the bunk.

In the light descending through the hatch, he saw that he was held by the man he had beaten and another of his coterie. A third held the wriggling Davyd. Flysse slept on, oblivious. Then Karyl Oster's bearded face drew close. His breath was redolent of decayed teeth.

"We've decided, Sieur Blayke"—he made the title an insult—"that we'll wait no longer. We've had enough of your highfalutin ways, an' since you don't take the woman, we will. Me first, an' then my mates. An' you can watch. How'd you like that, eh?"

The one holding Davyd said, "An' the boy for me."

Arcole struggled as Oster turned away, but the two holding him were strong. He saw faces watching from the surrounding bunks, but none came to his aid or raised any outcry. He supposed they were more afraid of the immediate retribution of Oster's bullies than the threat of Tomas Var.

Oster clapped a hand over Flysse's mouth and snatched her from her bunk in a single movement. Sleeping, she wore only a shift. It rose to expose shapely legs as Oster deposited her on the deck, still gagging her with his hairy hand. She fought him, her eyes wide with terror and outrage. He leered and told her, "Play easy, girl, an' this'll pleasure you. Fight me, an' . . ." He raised a fisted hand in threat.

Flysse went on struggling, and Oster struck her.

Something snapped in Arcole then. It was a strange sensation. He had killed men in duels of honor, but always with a cold precision; this was different—a hot, red rage seemed to loan him an unnatural strength. Barely aware of what he did, he stamped the heel of one bare foot down hard on the toes of one captor, feeling bones break. The man yelped, and his hold loosened enough that Arcole was able to tear an arm free and fling himself backward, driving the other would-be rapist against the bunk behind. He drove an elbow into the fellow's rib cage, and the hand across his mouth came loose. Still held by one arm, he kicked out, his foot sinking deep between the first man's legs. There was a shriek of pain and the man collapsed onto Oster. His grip on Flysse was broken and she took the opportunity to rake nails down Oster's cheek. He snarled and shoved his acolyte away, striking Flysse again.

The rage that consumed Arcole was fueled fiercer at that. He turned, wrenching clutching hands from his arm, not now in emulation of Smiling Jacques's lessons but in blind fury, seeking only to damage, to inflict pain. The man gasped as Arcole's fists landed against his ribs and face, and he raised his arms helplessly. Arcole batted them aside, clutched the bloodied face, and slammed the man's skull against the edge of the bunk. As he fell, Arcole spun round, seeking Oster, the architect of this outrage.

The giant was clambering to his feet, beating at the hands Flysse set about one wrist. Beyond them, Arcole saw Davyd fight loose of his captor and drop to the deck. The man who had held him gaped, then turned and scuttled into the shadows. Davyd flung himself at Oster and was hurled away.

Arcole said, "Flysse, let him go. Leave him to me."

Oster grinned and wiped a hand across the scratches running down his cheek. "Aye, girl, you do that. An' when I've done for the popinjay, I'll be back for you. I'll . . ."

The sentence ended as Arcole's fist smashed teeth. Oster spat blood and lumbered forward. He stood a good head taller than Arcole and his build was massive, apelike. In a gymnasium, with room to maneuver and employ well-learnt techniques, Arcole would have held the advantage, but here he had none. The spaces between the tiered bunks were narrow, denying movement, and Oster was clearly the stronger man. But

Arcole remained possessed by rage, and what he gave away in weight and reach was more than balanced by sheer fury.

As the leering giant advanced, Arcole set his hands upon the topmost bunks to either side and swung himself up, thrusting both legs forward. His feet slammed against Oster's chest, and the giant's advance was halted on a gust of fetid breath. Before he could recover, Arcole dropped to the deck and sprang forward, driving clenched fists rhythmically into Oster's abdomen. The blows were low—deliberately; Smiling Jacques would have called a foul—and Oster squealed, exhaling blood and spittle. His arms flailed, landing blows that Arcole scarcely noticed as he kicked Oster between the legs. The giant's eyes sprang wide, his head dropping as he curled instinctively around the pain. Arcole stepped forward to snatch handfuls of black hair and bring the man's head lower, down to meet his rising knee.

He felt no pain as broken teeth cut his flesh, only a savage satisfaction as he raised the head again, and again brought it down to smash against his knee. Cartilage broke in Oster's nose, and he snorted crimson froth. Still holding him by the hair, Arcole dragged him forward, tumbling him off balance so that the larger man pitched onto his knees. He swung the head then, a fleshly metronome that ended each arc against the solid wood of a bunk. Oster no longer resisted, but Arcole went on pounding the yielding skull.

He was dimly aware of Flysse's voice, entreating him to stop, but he ignored it until she grasped his arm, her weight slowing him.

"Arcole! For God's sake, Arcole, you've killed him!"

He blinked and let loose Oster's head. It fell to the deck and he saw the ruined temple, the blood—slick and black in the moonlight—that matted the hair and oozed from the ear. Flysse pressed against him, holding him back from further violence, and without thinking he put his arms around her, wondering vaguely why she wept.

"Arcole! Oh, God, Arcole, what have you done? What will they do to you? You know the rules."

He thought that for slaying such vermin as Oster he perhaps deserved applause, but then the import of Flysse's words sank in. He recalled Var's promise, exactly: *Do you raise hand against one another, you will be flogged.*

Surely not, when he had acted only in her defense. And Davyd's, he remembered, looking past Flysse's tearful face to where the boy stood wide-eyed with admiration. But then he thought that these were the strictures of the Autarchy, of Evander, and therefore it was likely to be so. He was not sure he could accept the indignity of a whipping—that was such punishment as was meted out to common criminals. And then he could only chuckle at his own foolishness, for in the eyes of the Autarchy he *was* a common criminal, an exile, branded and indentured. And now likely to be flogged, his objections of no more consequence to the Evanderan marines than his dignity.

Well, was it to be, he would act the man. He held Flysse at arm's length, making his smile careless. "Mistress," he declared, "am I to be punished, why, that it be for sake of your rescue shall make it worthwhile."

For a long moment she stared at him as if she thought him deranged, then she came close and, somewhat to his surprise, kissed him on the lips. No less surprising was the comfort he took from her gesture. He stared at her, and she blushed and drew back, tugging her shift closer about her as if only then aware of her immodest dress.

"I'll tell them what happened," she promised.

"And I," said Davyd. "They'll not flog you when they know."

"Perhaps not." Arcole felt a wetness against his bare sole and moved aside as he realized he stood in Oster's blood. "Perhaps there's some honor left in these Evanderans yet."

At his back someone said, "You'll find out soon enough," and he turned to see the companionway hatch flung back, lanterns flaring there as marines with cocked muskets descended the ladder.

A voice he recognized as belonging to Tomas Var said, "What goes on here?"

It was not, for Tomas Var, an easy decision. He supposed that were he made of sterner stuff, of such temper as so many of his fellow officers, then it should have presented no problems. The regulations covering the transport of exiles were very clear. One prisoner had slain another; he had also broken a man's head and another's foot. Two indentured servants would arrive in Salvation crippled, a third not arrive at all. Var could, therefore, order Arcole Blayke's execution; he was, undoubtedly, required to administer at least a flogging. Captain Bennan recommended the full fifty lashes. Var had doubts: he could not help but think he would have acted in similar fashion, had he been in Blayke's place.

He had listened to the pleas offered by Blayke's companions—the potential victims—and accepted that the dead man and his bullies had been intent on rape. Indeed, when the two hurt men named their missing accomplice and he had been dragged from his hiding place, all three had confessed, pleading for mercy and claiming they had acted solely in fear of Oster. Var had entertained no hesitation in ordering they each receive thirty lashes—in the case of the worst hurt, to be delivered when the ship's surgeon pronounced them fit enough to survive.

But Arcole Blayke was a problem. Var knew he must order punishment of some kind lest his authority over all the prisoners be weakened, but he was loath to accept Bennan's recommendation. He could not help but grant Blayke a grudging respect, and indeed, were he honest with himself, he felt that in other times, in other circumstances, they might even have been friends. He had checked the records of all involved, and found the thwarted rapists to be no more than he suspected —common criminals, footpads, and murderers. Davyd Furth was a thief: Var dismissed him. But the woman, Flysse Cobal, he thought honest, and—a notion he swiftly dismissed as traitorous—cruelly condemned to exile. And Arcole Blayke; well, he was a curiosity.

He was a gentleman. Of that, Var held no doubt at all: it was obvious from his speech and bearing, even had the records not revealed it. Nor had he acted from malice, but in defense of the woman. Had he not worn the brand upon his cheek, such action must have been considered honorable.

But he *did* wear the brand: he *was* an exile. And therefore Var must punish him.

He studied the man standing before him on the quarterdeck. Blayke was dressed now, in clothes of fashionable cut, but crumpled and somewhat soiled by the voyage. He wore a growing beard—the exiles were forbidden blades of any kind—but still he managed an air of elegance. He was flanked by two burly marines, ten more at attention to either side. He showed no remorse, nor any fear. Var thought of him exercising and knew that he was likely one of the few fit enough to take fifty lashes and survive. He did not want to give Blayke fifty lashes, but neither could he renege his duty or allow his authority to be questioned.

"You confess to the slaying of Karyl Oster," Var said.

Arcole nodded. "I killed him, yes."

"And grievously wounded Petyr Rayne."

"Which one was that?"

"You cracked his skull."

"Ah, him. Yes."

"And also wounded Matrym Greene. You broke his foot and . . . ah, unmanned him."

"I did. Had I my blade, I'd have slain them all. Swifter and cleaner."

Var wished the man were less defiant, and admired him for it. "You exhibit no remorse, Blayke," he said. "These men are—in Oster's case, *was*—the property of the Autarchy. As are you. Rayne and Greene shall likely be cripples now, and thus of lessened value. Oster is now quite worthless."

"Oster was worthless before I slew him," Arcole said. And hung Var from the crux of his dilemma: "Would you have done less?"

Var was not sure whether he wanted to smile or curse the man for his arrogance. He knew the answer to Blayke's question—and he could not admit it. He said, "Such theorizing is irrelevant. Have you aught to say in your defense?"

"Is it worth my speaking?" Arcole touched the brand on his cheek. "I've witnessed Evanderan justice."

Var's face darkened. Damn the man! He pushed too hard. And yet . . . Var must sympathize with him. He paused, reining his temper. "I have heard the woman, Flysse Cobal, and Davyd Furth plead on your behalf. They say those men were bent on rape and you acted only in defense of them both. Was that so?"

"I could hardly stand by," said Arcole, "and call myself a man. Much less a gentleman."

"Then you did act to protect the woman and the youth?"

Arcole wondered why the captain did not simply pronounce his Evanderan version of justice and be done with it. Could it be that he sought some loophole? Could an Evanderan officer be so honorable?

"Well?" Var prompted.

"Well, then, yes," Arcole said. "Oster and his bullies intended to rape Flysse and Davyd, both. No gentleman could fail to defend them and retain his honor."

Mostly to himself, Var murmured, "No."

At his side, Bennan snorted scornfully. Var ignored him, studying Blayke's face. Finally he said, "My orders are clear. You have damaged property of the Autarchy—raised hand against other exiles, for which the punishment is a flogging."

He heard Bennan vent an anticipatory chuckle and decided he did not much like the captain. "But," he continued, "I find such extenuating circumstances exist as persuade me to relax that punishment somewhat. So I hereby order that all the exiles be paraded on deck to witness administration of your punishment. Which shall be twelve lashes; to be delivered immediately."

16 Across the Sea of Sorrows

The full complement of marines lined the bulwarks as the exiles were summoned up from the hold. It was a little past noonday, and the sun glinted on the bayonets and polished buckles of the soldiers who stood at rigid attention. The exiles milled nervously, not sure what they should anticipate. And all they knew for certain was that Karyl Oster was dead, his corpse already delivered to the sea, and that four of their number were taken by the marines. Flysse and Davyd had no better idea of Arcole's fate than any others—they had been questioned by Tomas Var and immediately returned to their quarters. Flysse smiled as she caught sight of Arcole, standing erect between two blue-coated marines, and scowled at the other prisoner, recognizing him as the man who had threatened Davyd.

For his part, Davyd was nervous. He had far less faith in—and far more experience of—the Autarchy's justice than Flysse, and when she whispered "Arcole is well, no? Surely they'll not punish him?" he could only shrug and hope she spoke aright.

When sailors were ordered forward to raise a hatch and lash the grille upright, his doubts grew.

Then Tomas Var stepped out before the assembly. He wore full-dress uniform, tricorn set straight on his fair hair, left hand on the hilt of his sword. He climbed partway up he quarterdeck ladder and halted, surveying the crowd awhile before he spoke, his voice pitched to carry to them all.

"You see before you two men sentenced for crimes against the Autarchy. Let their punishments be an example to you all! Do any of you think to perpetrate such crimes as these are guilty of, let their fate dissuade you."

He paused as a nervous murmur ran through the crowd. Davyd felt Flysse take his hand.

"First," Var continued when silence fell again, "know that none escape. For their part in the attempted rape, Petyer Rayne and Matrym Greene are sentenced to thirty lashes apiece, which shall be delivered immediately the ship's surgeon declares them sufficiently recovered. Meanwhile, for his part in that heinous crime, Anton Gryme shall now receive thirty lashes."

He nodded toward Gryme, and the marines flanking the man motioned him forward toward the raised hatch. A sergeant, his tunic removed and his shirtsleeves rolled back, let fall the coils of a heavy whip. Gryme licked his lips. Davyd saw the sweat that trickled down his face, and experienced a savage satisfaction at the impending flogging.

Gryme took an unsteady step in the direction of the hatch, then shook his head as if denying the reality of his situation. A marine pushed him on, and suddenly Gryme let out a wailing cry and spun around. He ducked beneath the soldiers' outflung arms and ran screaming down the deck. For a moment Davyd wondered why the musketeers lining the rail failed to shoot, then saw the reason as Gryme flung himself wildly up the ladder to the foredeck and vaulted the rail there.

It was as though he struck a solid wall, save it was invisible: a wall of magic, set there by the hexes inlaid along the bulwarks. Gryme's leap halted in midair, his body bouncing back to crash onto the boards of the deck. He yelled anew and sprang to his feet, crossing to the farther side. This time he did not jump, but set his hands upon the rail and swung a leg upward, over the metal. He brought up his other leg—and was once more flung back. Moaning in frustration, he clambered to his feet, eyes darting madly, like an animal trapped by circumstances beyond its comprehension. Twice more he attempted to find the sea, and twice more was denied escape as the two men of his escort marched briskly toward him.

As they brought him back, Var said, "Another lesson. You shall none of you find that release—the hexes warding such escape are too strong. Now, sergeant, do you administer punishment."

For all Davyd bore Gryme no love, he winced as the lash cut stripes over the man's pale flesh. Screams dinned against his ears and he glanced at Arcole, who stood grim-faced; Davyd thought of his friend cut by that savage whip, and smiled his sympathy.

Before it was done, Gryme had passed out. He hung limp from the hatch as a seaman doused his bloodied back, and was still unconscious as two marines dragged him away.

"Now, the case of Arcole Blayke," Var declared. His voice rang loud in the hushed silence. "In that this man acted on behalf of others, I will not inflict such punishment as might be his. However, in that he damaged property of the Autarchy, I sentence him to twelve lashes."

Davyd heard Flysse cry, "No! That's not fair!"

He felt her grip tighten on his hand and said, "Arcole's strong, and twelve lashes are not so bad."

Flysse shook her head and moaned "No!" again. Tears ran down her cheeks, but she did not take her eyes from Arcole's face.

Arcole did not flinch when his escort motioned him forward, but stepped out as if taking a promenade about the deck. When he stood before the hatch, he removed his frock coat and held the jacket out to a marine as if the man were his second. The soldier stared at the garment, perplexed, not quite sure what to do.

Var called out, "Someone take it, eh?"

Before any other had chance to move, Davyd tugged his hand loose from Flysse's grip and darted to Arcole. A marine moved to halt him, but Var said, "No, leave the boy be," and Davyd took the coat.

"My thanks." Arcole ducked his head, smiling at Davyd. "And be so kind as to take my shirt too? I'd not see it needlessly soiled."

Davyd nodded, quite unable to speak in the face of such magnificent courage. He waited as the shirt was removed, then carefully folded the linen and retreated backward to where Flysse stood, his eyes intent on Arcole all the way.

Arcole stretched leisurely and favored the sergeant with a quizzical smile. "I trust your efforts do not fatigue your arm, sergeant?"

The marine grunted and shook his head. Someone in the crowd laughed nervously, another heartily. In the rigging overhead, a sailor called, "Bravely said!" From his station on the quarterdeck ladder, Tomas Var could not help smiling—though he swiftly hid the expression.

"So, gentlemen." Arcole stepped to the hatch and rested his weight against the metal frame, his arms upraised. "Shall we commence?"

The two men of his escort secured his wrists. One set a wad of leather between his teeth, murmuring, "Bite hard on this. It'll ease the pain somewhat."

They stepped clear and the sergeant uncoiled his whip. Davyd felt Flysse's hand clutch his shoulder as the plaited leather swung back. As it fell on Arcole's shoulders, her fingers dug deep, and she gasped as if she shared the pain. Davyd remained silent, only grimacing in sympathy each time the lash descended. It left long, angry stripes of red across the skin, and at each blow Arcole's body jerked. He did not cry out as Gryme had, but Davyd could hear the stifled grunts the pain elicited.

Tomas Var watched with an impassive face. He was pleased to see his sergeant follow the instructions given—that he place his blows with care, not overlay them but deliver each stripe separately. That would make it easier on the victim, and Blayke recover swifter. It was as much as he could do for the man and still do his duty by the Autarchy.

Down the length of the schooner he saw Captain Bennan watching from the poop deck and noted the look of disapproval on the man's face. He wondered if the shipmaster would find occasion to set his disagreement in the log or make report on his return to Evander. Var thought it likely: Bennan was something of a martinet.

Well, no matter, he decided. The punishment of the exiles was his territory, as was their care; and should his superiors in the God's Militia find cause to question his judgment, then he would justify his lenience with the explanation that he'd not see valuable property needlessly damaged. That he felt a sympathy for Blayke need not be known. That he felt—almost—a kinship with the man, he dared not admit even to himself. He was an officer in the God's Militia, a captain of marines with hope of advancement to come and a sincere belief in the Autarchy. Arcole Blayke was an exile, a criminal—it was not for Tomas Var to question that sentence. Neither to wonder if they might, ever, have been friends.

And so the captain of marines and his men watched in stolid silence, and the exiles nervously, and none there knew they shared a common emotion: admiration for Arcole.

But Arcole knew only pain, and anger that an honorable act be punished with the indignity of a flogging. He bit on the gag, determined to show no sign of weakness to the Evanderans, and it was easier than the branding, for he was sustained by his anger. When the final blow was given and the flogging ended, he still braced himself against the hatch, not knowing it was over.

That awareness came with the saltwater that splashed against his back, a sudden, sharper pain on the fiery throbbing of his ravaged skin. He had not known tears clouded his vision until then, when he gasped and blinked, and grew aware that his wrists were freed. He spat out the gag and forced himself to stand upright, unaided as he moved back from the hatch.

The sergeant was coiling the whip, his face fixed and rigid as a statue's, but as he carefully wound his loops of leather, he murmured,

"The saltwater helps. It hurts, but have someone bathe the wounds each day."

Arcole looked toward him, but it was as though the man had not spoken, even when—barely moving his lips—he added softly, "You were lucky. The captain ordered I flog you easy."

Arcole would have asked him why—would know why an Evanderan officer should show mercy to a Levanite exile—but his mouth was too dry to shape words, and the sergeant's blocky figure was suddenly vague, the masts and watching faces beyond him suddenly revolving in a slow and stately whirligig. So he only nodded his head and took a weak-kneed step forward toward where he thought Flysse and Davyd stood. And then he must concentrate on the next movement of his foot, and the one after, for he would not show weakness.

He reached the two and halted. Davyd still held his coat and shirt, but when the boy extended the garments he shook his head and mumbled, "Not yet. I'd not spoil a good shirt. When I'm healed . . . Now, water, if you would."

Davyd ran instantly to the nearest water butt. Arcole looked at Flysse's horrified face and forced his lips to stretch in semblance of a smile. "Might I borrow your shoulder a moment, Flysse? Else I think I shall fall down."

She came close, taking one arm and setting it gently about her shoulders. He leant on her, surprised by her strength, and waited until Davyd brought him the water. It was tepid: he thought he had never enjoyed a drink so much.

When the taste of leather was washed from his mouth, he said, "I think I should like to retire now, do none object."

Davyd came to his other side and, leaning on them both, Arcole made his unsteady way toward the hold. The crowd parted before the trio, none speaking, only watching in silence. Arcole's legs felt simultaneously lead-weighted and insubstantial. Each step was an effort, as if he wore impossibly heavy boots; and yet his knees were rubbery: had Flysse and Davyd not supported him, he should have fallen. He knew he lacked the strength to crawl, and that increased his anger. He forced his head upright and saw Tomas Var watching him. The captain's expression was unreadable. Arcole essayed a brief smile and ducked his head as if bidding the man farewell. He was surprised when Var returned the gesture.

Then he must concentrate on the ladder, which was now becoming a serious obstacle. Flysse went down before him, Davyd behind, and together they got him to the foot where he must rest a moment before finding his bunk. He was glad it was the bottommost—he did not think he could find the strength to climb.

Gritting his teeth against the pain each movement brought, he eased onto the pallet, stretching out facedown. That was a little better: the fire lit on his flesh became a single throbbing ache. He wondered how Gryme felt, and supposed—a small consolation—that the man experienced far worse.

"Is there anything we can do?"

He turned his head to find Flysse crouched beside him. Her eyes were large with concern, reddened by weeping, and moist with tears.

"I think not." He found it difficult to construct his thoughts in coherent fashion: he had much rather close his eyes and drift away. "The sergeant said the wounds should be bathed each day in saltwater. But otherwise . . ."

He realized he had closed his eyes only when he heard her voice again.

"Arcole? Arcole, the ship's surgeon attends you."

He focused on the breeches standing before his bunk. They stretched tight over an ample belly. It was too much effort to raise his head, so he did not see the man's face, but he thought the fellow's boots would benefit from polish. He grunted.

The surgeon grunted back and Arcole saw a bulky valise set down on the planks, opened by chubby pink hands that extracted a small pot.

"I've seen worse." The voice was genial, coming from a point above and behind Arcole. "The other fellow, f'r instance. Now . . ."

Arcole felt his back massaged. He supposed the surgeon applied a salve; certainly the throbbing pain abated.

"That'll help the healing. Tomorrow, wash him with seawater; do that every day until he's mended. Best he doesn't move until then."

The chubby hands returned the pot to the valise, snapped the bag shut, and lifted it out of sight. Flysse's face came back into view, Davyd close behind her. Arcole tried to speak, but his mouth was dry and his eyes very heavy. Shaping words was too much effort, so he only smiled and retreated into sleep.

When he woke, the hold was dark and filled with night sounds. He could hear Davyd grunting overhead. He was thirsty beyond endurance. He lay still, trying hard to ignore the thirst, but he could not. His mouth was arid and he attempted to rise. Pain lashed his back anew and he groaned. He did not think the sound loud enough to carry through the multitude of other noises, but on the instant he saw a shapely leg descend and moonlight fall silvery over Flysse's hair. She drew a shawl about her shoulders as she knelt beside him. Lit by the moon, he thought she resembled an angel.

"What is it?" she asked softly. "Do you hurt?"

Through gummy lips he said, "Water."

Flysse nodded and was gone. He thought to call her back—he feared for her, wandering the nighttime hold alone and he helpless to protect her—but it was too late and he could only lie there, cursing his weakness. He hoped the lesson of the floggings was taken by the bullies.

Then she was back, bringing a brimming pannikin to his lips.

It was not easy, drinking prone, endeavoring to lift only his head, for any other movement inflamed him. He must sip when he would have gulped, but Flysse was patient—more than he—and knelt holding the cup until it was emptied.

"Enough?" she asked. "Or shall I fetch you more?"

"No," he murmured. "Thank you."

She smiled and stroked his hair. He remembered she had stroked Davyd's hair, and wondered if the touch had comforted the boy as much. When she clambered back up to her own bunk, he felt a pang of guilt as he watched her ankles. They were very trim, and he recalled the touch of her body when he had held her.

In the days that followed, the order that had become established was reversed. Flysse and Davyd nursed the helpless Arcole. They brought him food and water, and once daily carried a bucket from the deck, bathing his wounds. One or the other was always with him, talking when he wished, silent as he slept, but always there when he woke. He came to take it for granted and would have missed their presence had they been less attentive.

He was, if anything, more in Davyd's company than in Flysse's, for the boy seemed loath to risk the deck without Arcole, as if the man had become a kind of talisman. It afforded him the chance to speak somewhat of Davyd's dreams—cautiously, for he remembered his promise to Flysse, and felt newly guilty that he broke it. He told himself it was for all their good—that if Davyd was a Dreamer, then that talent might benefit them all. But he was careful to make his inquiries casual, so that it should seem, almost, that Davyd spoke of his own free will, not through inducement.

"How do you sleep now?" he asked as if he did not lie listening to the boy's nocturnal cries. And when Davyd shook his head and lowered his eyes, "The nightmares still?"

Davyd nodded and Arcole laughed and said, "You saw Gryme try to jump the rail? You saw the magic that halted him? Strong magic, no?"

It was a slow process, but Arcole had little else to occupy his time as the *Pride of the Lord* entered the Sea of Sorrows and the easterly winds died away. Indeed, as the schooner ventured deeper into those latitudes, it was often necessary to put the ship's longboats over the side and have them tow the larger vessel. On those occasions the boats were crewed by exiles, marines stationed at tiller and bow. Arcole and Davyd were excused this exercise—the one because he was still weak, the other because he was too scrawny, too young. Then the hold was emptied, and Arcole might easier draw Davyd out.

"We've come to no harm yet," he said. "Surely you cannot still think we're in danger."

Davyd shrugged, and softly, looking not at Arcole but at the deck beneath his feet, said, "It will come. I know."

"Then best I mend," Arcole declared, "so that I can protect you."

Davyd smiled at that: a forlorn expression that denied solace, as if he knew better than to question the warnings of his dreams. "What comes comes," he said.

"How," asked Arcole, "can you be so sure?"

"Because I've dreamed it," Davyd whispered.

"And your dreams are true?" Arcole said. "Always?"

Davyd ducked his head as if he would sooner it were not so, and said, "Always."

He gasped then, aware that he had made such admission as could bring him to the flames. He swallowed and licked his lips, staring with tormented eyes at Arcole.

The man said, "I wondered. But . . . are they always true, how were you caught? Did they not warn you then?"

Wordlessly, Davyd lowered his head. The movement seemed to Arcole as much surrender to implacable fate as gesture of agreement. He felt momentarily ashamed that he forced the boy to this. He said, "I'll speak of this to no one. No one, Davyd! On that you've my solemn word."

Not looking up, Davyd said, "I dreamed of danger—I knew I shouldn't try to crack that crib. But I was short of coin, so I took the chance—and was caught."

Arcole said, "And now you dream of perils from the ocean."

Davyd nodded. Slowly, as if he lifted a great weight, he raised his head, facing Arcole at last. His eyes were haunted. He said, "Aunt Dory warned me not to tell anyone. They burn people like me."

"Only if they find out," Arcole declared, and reached out to take the boy's hand. "Do you trust me, Davyd?"

"Of course." There was such simple faith in the statement, Arcole felt embarrassment. "You saved me, no? And Flysse, too. Without you those bastards would have . . ."

He shuddered, lip curling in distaste. Arcole said, "Then trust me now when I tell you your secret's safe with me. I swear on my honor as a gentleman."

Davyd said, "I do trust you, Arcole."

"Then no one shall have this from me. Not even Flysse."

"I don't suppose it really matters now," Davyd said. "I dream of sea serpents, so sea serpents will come. And then . . ."

He sighed. Or perhaps he sobbed: Arcole was not sure, only that this hardened thief seemed at the moment no more than a frightened boy whose odd gift condemned him to secrecy and terror. He squeezed Davyd's hand, smiling with a confidence he no longer felt.

"And then they must face the hexes that guard this ship. And the cannon, and the marines. I think we can withstand even sea serpents, Davyd."

"Truly?"

There was a plea in the question: Arcole ducked his head solemnly. "Truly."

"And you'll not tell anyone else?" Davyd hesitated a moment. "Not even Flysse?"

"Not even Flysse," Arcole promised. And affected an expression of hurt dignity. "Do you doubt my word?"

Davyd shook his head, his face set in such earnest lines, Arcole had to chuckle. "It shall be our secret," he promised. "Ours alone."

"Thank you." Davyd smiled then, as if somehow this sharing of his secret lessened its weight.

Flysse found them like that, the boy settled beside the man with such a look on his face as she'd not seen before. She thought she'd not seen him so calm, so cheerful, since first they'd met. And Arcole . . . She could not properly interpret his expression: it seemed somehow both content and embarrassed, as if he had recently performed some act of kindness he had sooner be kept hid. They looked, she thought, almost like father and son, and she felt, almost, that she intruded.

The *Price of the Lord* progressed slowly over the Sea of Sorrows. There were no more disturbances. Apart from the obvious threat of flogging, the exiles were so wearied by their labors that none had the energy to foment trouble. They ate and slept only when they were not rowing; and, slow it seemed as the schooner's progress, Arcole healed.

He had suffered wounds before—at swordpoint and, twice, by pistol ball—but then he had been attended by surgeons of renown and had convalesced in luxurious surroundings. Faithful Dom had been there to fetch and carry, and acquaintances had visited. Yet even then, in such comfort, he was always impatient to recover; now, in the schooner's heat-baked hold, he grew frustrated beyond endurance. As soon as he was able to rise and walk unaided, he went on deck. Flysse urged him to wait, but he ignored her as he ignored the tugging of his healing wounds and made his way topside with her and Davyd fussing about him as if he were an invalid quite incapable of looking after himself. Which, of course, he was, though he refused to admit it, transforming grimaces of pain into careless smiles. He doubted either Flysse or Davyd believed him when he assured them he felt no pain, but they pretended and for that he was grateful. It was the truth when he told them he felt better for the sun on his back, and that he must surely go mad did he remain in the hold.

And he would study the ocean: awaiting confirmation of Davyd's ability.

They had spoken no more of that talent, and Flysse had no idea they had spoken at all. It was their secret, shared and exclusive, and did Flysse observe a change in their relationship, she assumed only that Arcole mellowed, accepting the young thief.

Arcole did, indeed, mellow. He acknowledged a debt of gratitude to them both, and found that he no longer looked down on them but regarded them as equals in adversity. He realized that he had not known such loyal friends since parting with Dom; he realized that this voyage changed him. He came—to his surprise—to hope they should not be parted when they reached Salvation.

And daily he watched the sea.

It was a featureless expanse, here. There was no swell, no waves, only a bland blue that spread remorseless to all the points of the compass. The sails hung usually limp, and when a breeze arose, it was weak and warm, doing nothing to aid their progress. The longboats scarcely disturbed the surface, and the *Pride of the Lord* seemed scarcely to move but rather hang suspended in timeless limbo. Food and water were rationed, and for the first time it occurred to Arcole that they might starve or die of thirst. He began to think that the proving of Davyd's dream might be a welcome interruption of such monotony.

Meanwhile, he slowly gathered back his strength. His back healed, and though it would be always scarred, the wounds no longer pained him. He recommenced his exercising, at first carefully but then with steadily increasing vigor. Davyd joined him, initially in those practices that put muscle on his narrow frame but then pleading that Arcole teach him the meaning of the apparently pointless movements that followed. As the days passed, Davyd learnt to box and the rudiments of the fencer's art—though that was difficult without swords.

Once, Tomas Var came by as they worked and stood awhile watching them. When they halted, he said, "Your back is healed, eh?"

Arcole nodded and returned him, "Yes," not sure of the officer's interest.

Var said, "Good," and then: "You teach the boy to fight."

Again Arcole said only, "Yes," wondering if he should feel grateful to this Evanderan.

"Who taught you?" Var asked, and when Arcole replied that he had trained with Smiling Jacques, he nodded as if he appreciated what that meant, saying, "He taught you well, I think."

Arcole gave him another, "Yes," and Var smiled faintly and strolled on.

When he was gone, Davyd said, "Who's Smiling Jacques?"

"A prizefighter," Arcole replied. "A famous pugilist."

"I thought you were a duelist," Davyd said, "and a gambler."

With mock solemnity Arcole said, "I was a gentleman. I gambled and fought some duels, yes; but a gentleman commands various accomplishments, don't you know?"

"I don't know much about gentlefolk," Davyd said, grinning. "Except they usually carry fat purses."

Some weeks earlier Arcole would not have found that statement so amusing—now he laughed. And Flysse, who watched them from beneath the shade of a limply drooping sail, smiled and thought that they seemed, almost, a family. It seemed to her the best of times. Oh, she had sooner have more to eat and be able to drink when she wished, to wash in private and have a change of clothes, but she was uplifted by the friendship arisen. Arcole had changed—he no longer irritated her—and she sometimes, secretly, thought that did he approach her bed, she would find it impossible to refuse him.

As man and boy returned to their exercising, she moved to the rail, looking out across the empty sea. Save it was no longer empty: in the heat-hazy distance lay a darkness that had not been there before. For an instant she thought to cry out, but then she thought of Davyd's nocturnal terrors, and feared to frighten the boy anew. Of late—since Arcole had accepted him—he had seemed calmer, as if come to terms with his horror of the sea. She'd not afright him and so she remained silent: the darkness did not seem to offer any threat.

Then a sailor shouted from the masthead and she caught his words: "Weed! Weed!"

The activity the shout produced alarmed Flysse. She turned to Arcole—beside her now, an arm around Davyd's shoulders—as sailors ran to their stations and marines primed the cannon.

"What is it?" she asked.

Arcole shook his head helplessly: it seemed to him only that—seaweed, albeit in vast quantity. He felt Davyd shudder and gave the boy a grin, holding him tighter.

The schooner drew gradually closer to the weed, and by nightfall it was clear that it was far more than some solitary floating mass. It stretched across the horizon, exuding a sulphurous odor that permeated the ship, foul as a midden. When darkness fell it lit the night with an eerie green phosphorescence. It was dense—the oarsmen in the longboats must labor hard to carve a way through, and when they were relieved they came back on board stinking of the stuff. Nor did the night bring any relief, for Captain Bennan feared entrapment and demanded the longboats stay out to maintain their slow passage westward.

The next day the ship lay deep within a sea of green that seemed so thick, a man might walk across it. Crabs scuttled over the weed—great misshapen things with ugly pincers, pursuing a kind of worm that writhed and oozed when taken. On board, folk wound cloths about their mouths and nostrils to fend off the stench and none bathed, for none cared to sample the water here. Men with boathooks were stationed in the longboats, to cut a passage clear.

Worst—for they boded ill for all on board—were the hulks that now became apparent.

They seemed exhibits preserved in a macabre oceanic museum: ships from yesteryear, and others of more recent design, lay becalmed amidst the weed. Their rigging hung empty from masts unpleasantly reminiscent of bones, and weed clung to their hulls, grew up over the bulwarks so that some appeared less wooden constructions of man's making than organic things, creations of this strange sea. On some, human remains rested amidst the weed, skulls and rib cages wound all round like horrid ornaments. Others were of fresher vintage and stood still proud of the engulfing weed, as if halted only recently—but empty, their crews gone, presumably in a final desperate attempt to escape by boat.

The *Pride of the Lord* moved with an agonizing languor, inch by slow inch. The longboat crews were soon exhausted and must be replaced sooner. Even the marines took their tur, and Arcole was deemed sufficiently recovered that he found himself ordered to the oars.

This alarmed Davyd, for he was convinced his dreams should soon come true, and he feared for Arcole's safety—the open boats were very vulnerable. Flysse must encourage him as best she could for all the time Arcole labored in the boats, and when he returned—sweat-drenched and reeking of the weed—Davyd would smile as if he came back alive from a dreadful war. She was herself by no means at ease—none were, for this horrid weed-strewn sea momentarily threatened to hold them in its embrace forever.

Tension gripped the schooner, not least because the cannon remained always manned and the sailors were issued cutlasses, as if some danger greater even than the weed were expected.

Had Arcole not come back on board exhausted, wishing only to eat and sleep until he must go out again, he might have questioned Davyd, asked after the boy's dreams. But he did not; and Davyd did not tell him that the dreams returned manifold. Neither did Tomas Var see fit to speak to the prisoners, save to issue the orders that sent them out to the boats. They were, after all, only exiles.

17 From the Depths

The week continued thick for several days, closing astern of the *Pride of the Lord* as if to obliterate all sign of her passage, while ahead it stretched dense, seemingly to the ends of the world. The entrapped hulks dwindled as the schooner labored on, until finally there were none; only the green, crab-infested wrack. Then, when it seemed it must be their fate to forever sail this horrid sea, the strange vegetation began to thin. That should have been a relief, but Arcole noticed that Var's marines and Bennan's sailors grew more tense. Cannoneers stood ready by their weapons and the seamen watched the ocean with increased vigilance. Bennan stationed extra lookouts on the mastheads, and the officers wore both swords and pistols, as if they readied against ambuscade.

Arcole observed all this with a strange fascination. He said nothing to either Flysse or Davyd, but he saw that the schooner prepared for danger and could not help wondering if Davyd's gloomy predictions should soon be proven true. It seemed to him that such monsters as the boy dreamed of would more likely infest the depths of the weed-sea than this perimeter, where the open ocean should likely soon appear, but still he wondered. Almost, he hoped for the materialization of Davyd's nightmares, for that would irrevocably prove the boy's ability, and he still believed that talent might somehow benefit him in the days to come.

Then one day, as the weed continued to thin out and the ship began to move swifter, Davyd beckoned him aside. He pulled down the cloth covering his nose and mouth that he might be heard. On his face Arcole saw a warning.

"I think," Davyd whispered, glancing around to be sure none might overhear him, "that it shall come soon."

"Your sea serpent?" Arcole frowned. "You're sure?"

"Not when exactly." Davyd shrugged helplessly. "The dreams don't tell me that. Only that . . . something . . . approaches."

All the while he spoke, his eyes roamed over the sea. Arcole felt his nervousness as a cold prickling down his own back, as if the scars of his whipping tingled in anticipation. Like Davyd, he studied the weed shimmering green under the relentless sun. It shifted now, undulating slightly. That meant, he thought, a current, a swell beginning, and that must surely mean the weed would soon end.

"Can you not say it clearer?" He did not mean to speak so sharp: it was a product of Davyd's nervousness, the tension of the crew and the marines. He smiled to soften the words. "What shall this beast do?"

"I don't know," Davyd answered. "I know only that we're in danger."

Arcole set a hand on the boy's shoulder. "Then best stand ready," he said. "But I tell you again, we've much protection on this vessel."

"I hope it's enough," Davyd said.

Then Flysse approached and Arcole forced a smile, saying, "Put on a cheerful face, eh? We'd not want Flysse alarmed."

Davyd tried a smile: it looked to Arcole more like a grimace of pain. Flysse said, "What ails you, Davyd?"

He drew the protective cloth closer about his face and from behind that camouflage said, "This stink. It sickens me."

He was, Arcole thought, a good liar.

"It afflicts us all," Flysse said. "But surely it shall soon be gone? Folk say the weed must end soon."

"I think it shall. See?" Arcole pointed to where the vegetation shifted. "The sea moves it now, it grows less thick. We'll soon enough leave it behind, I think."

They all three studied the wrack-laden ocean. And so were amongst the first to see the creature that rose from the depths.

At first it was only a greater undulation of the weed, as if a wave moved toward the ship. Then—even as a sailor bellowed warning from the masthead—it gathered speed, and a head appeared.

Flysse screamed. Davyd groaned as if all his worst nightmares were come true. Arcole gasped and took hold of Flysse and Davyd both, backing away from the rail. He was not sure any part of the schooner could be safe from such a monster, but instinct urged him back, to set as much distance as the deck allowed between them and it.

The head was not unlike a horse's, but vastly enlarged, with dead yellow eyes set under ridges of bone, a long jaw all lined with serrated fangs that sprouted from a scarlet mouth wide enough to swallow a man whole. From its lips, clusters of oily-looking tendrils dangled, like an obscene beard, and running from its skull to its broad back there was a scaly crest of a livid green that contrasted with the duller blue-gray of the serpentine neck. Abruptly, the monstrous beast hurled itself toward the ship.

A cannon roared, the smoke of its discharge momentarily obscuring the creature, then Arcole saw the shot splash weed high behind the rushing monster. A second boomed, and missed.

Arcole shouted, "Get below!" And pushed Flysse and Davyd in the direction of the hold. They resisted, as if his presence could protect them, and he shoved them forcibly toward the ladder. "Flysse, for God's sake, get below! It must be safer there!"

He saw them reach the ladder, two amongst a screaming, panic-stricken crowd. He hoped they would find safety there: he thought there could be none on deck, and did not know why he remained. He looked again toward the sea as muskets volleyed, and briefly glimpsed the creature as it dove under the schooner.

The *Pride of the Lord* shuddered as the beast swum beneath her keel. For an instant a tail edged with jagged fins lashed the surface on the port side, and Arcole gasped in naked wonder as he saw the creature's head appear above the starboard rail. The snakelike body appeared long enough to wind itself around the schooner. He saw the head loom high, jaws gaping as a cannon boomed. A ball struck the monster a glancing blow that gouged a line of red along its rising flank, but it appeared unhurt, only enraged by the wound. Swift as a striking snake, the massive head darted forward and a cannoneer was lifted screaming between the jaws, another sent tumbling as the beast shook its prey as a terrier shakes a taken rat. The man's screams ended abruptly as the sea serpent writhed back and gulped the body down. Then it struck again, even as marines emptied their muskets at a range so short, no ball missed its target. But none even dented the scaly hide, only bounced uselessly off, like as pebbles thrown at a charging bull. Three more marines were struck down and the morning was filled with the roar of the cannon, the rattle of musket fire, and the shouts of prisoners, sailors, and marines.

Arcole crouched by the midmast. It occurred to him that the hexes supposed to protect the ship had no effect on this weirdling beast. It seemed immune to magic; certainly it attacked at will, undeterred by hexes, muskets, or cannon.

Then it was gone, and for a while an eerie silence fell.

Then the men in the longboats began to scream. They were turning back toward the schooner when the great head came sweeping up and the monster's jaws closed around one boat. The fragile craft was lifted high in the air, men flinging themselves desperately clear as timbers cracked and broke easily as the bones the serpent snapped. Up and up it rose, the longboat splintering and dividing, falling away in two riven pieces as the beast came down across the second. That was sunk on the instant, carried down beneath the thinning weed by the creature's weight. A handful from the first boat attempted to swim to the *Pride of the Lord,* but they were hampered by the clinging weed, and the monster rose amongst them like some awful diner selecting tidbits at a ghastly feast.

A few succeeded in reaching the lines still hanging from the schooner's prow, and Arcole darted to the bows to aid them. He hauled one to uncertain safety, but then the serpent rose up before him, so close he smelled the salty, fetid odor of its breath, and for an instant he stared into an unwinking yellow eye. Then the jaws snapped shut and he fell back, clutching a hand, a length of arm severed at the elbow. He flung the grisly relic away and crabbed backward over the planks, thinking that surely the beast must strike again.

Instead it disappeared, only to strike again at the schooner's port side. The ship rocked with the impact as the great head drove forward like a battering ram, tearing at the bulwarks and threatening to stove in the deck.

Arcole risked the bow, but there were no more survivors, only ravaged bodies that floated amidst the disturbed weed and the pieces of a longboat. He retreated down the deck as the cannon fired again at point-blank range. It seemed this time that the creature was hurt, for it emitted a shrill, squealing sound and writhed, lifting monstrous coils in furious convulsions that sent reeking seaweed spraying over the ship. It submerged, and the schooner rocked wildly as the sea serpent swam under the keel and rose anew.

It reared higher now, snapping at spars that broke and splintered between its jaws easily as a man might snap a toothpick. At the head of the mainmast, a lookout cowered behind the useless shelter of the crow's nest and was snatched up. The monster let him fall and then itself came crashing down across the deck. Men were crushed under its bulk and others suffered hurt as the taloned flukes scrabbled over the planks, the

serpent crawling now like some gigantic worm until all its body draped
the schooner and its tail came lashing after. The *Pride of the Lord* threatened to capsize as the beast completed its journey, tumbling back under
the seaweed, leaving behind a trail of slime and carnage.

Arcole saw a musket at his feet, dropped by a marine who moaned
as he clutched a broken arm. He snatched the weapon up, then relieved
the wounded soldier of powder horn and pouch of shot. The musket
seemed entirely inadequate against such a monster, but it afforded him
some small comfort, and he held it firm as he stared around, wondering
from which direction the serpent would next attack.

Along the deck, Tomas Var was bellowing orders, gathering his marines about him, and Arcole ran to join them.

Var saw the musket in his hand and nodded approvingly. That he
was an officer of the God's Militia and Arcole an exile—forbidden by
law to carry such a weapon—seemed not to matter now, when they
faced death together.

"Fire in volleys," he commanded. "This God-cursed thing looks
armored, but perhaps . . ."

"Musket fire doesn't hurt it!" Arcole spoke, unthinking. "Use the
cannon."

"How?" Var ignored the presumption. "Save my gunners have clear
aim, the damn thing moves too fast."

"What if it boards again?" Arcole ventured. "Were the cannon directed inward?"

Var shook his head. "Does it board again, it shall likely sink us.
Besides . . ." He might have been about to add "We've no time," but
there was none, for the sea serpent chose that moment to resurface and
attack again.

Var led his force to the bulwarks. The rail was broken where the
beast had crashed through, the deck scoured and splintery, a cannon
torn from its trunnion and the gunners dead. The marines grouped tight,
aiming at the beast that now rushed furiously toward the ship, seemingly
intent on ramming the schooner again. Arcole found himself next to Var
and raised the borrowed musket to his shoulder, hoping it aimed true
even though it would do no good.

Var shouted, "Aim for the head. Ready . . . Fire!"

The muskets rattled. The sea serpent slid swift beneath the weed
and, was it hurt, it gave no sign. Arcole thought it likely possessed some
primal intelligence, or had attacked ships before: it dove as the guns
discharged, as if it knew them dangerous. Var ordered his men to the
farther rail, anticipating the beast should press its attack from that quarter. Arcole moved to obey, then hesitated as he saw a rope spilled loose

from its neat coil, close to the damaged cannon, and an idea took shape. It was likely impossible and undoubtedly perilous; yet did it fail, the ship must be sunk and all on board drown or be swallowed by the monster. He thought of Flysse and Davyd, and that they deserved a better fate.

He dropped his musket and took up the rope. It was a line such as raised and lowered the sails, and he hoped it was strong enough. He secured the line firmly about the wrecked cannon and ran out the other end, fashioning a noose. Musket fire and cannon's booming brought his head around in time to see the serpent rearing up beyond the starboard rail and the jaws close over the head and shoulders of a marine. Var sprang forward, sword raised, and was sent tumbling back as the creature swung its head. Arcole hefted the rope, glancing round. The line was heavy—too weighty that he might accomplish his stratagem alone. As the beast fell back into the sea, he crossed to Var.

The captain was disheveled, his tricorn lost and his shirt soiled. An ugly bruise decorated one side of his face, but he seemed more angry than afraid. Arcole touched his shoulder and explained his plan.

Var looked a moment amazed, but then he said, "Why not? We've naught to lose."

"I can't do it alone," Arcole said. "I need at least one other man."

Var said, "You've got him," and beckoned his sergeant.

Arcole assumed the captain would order the noncommissioned officer to assist him, but Var surprised him by bidding the sergeant take command of the musketeers. He turned to Arcole, motioning him on. The schooner rocked again as the sea serpent grated against her keel.

A dinghy lay between the main- and foremasts, and Var shouted for sailors to help launch the little boat. The seamen gaped as if he had lost his mind, and he must bully them into action. Arcole drew one aside, needing his help to spill loose the rope and drop a length into the dinghy. Then, with Var at his shoulder, he climbed on board.

The dinghy shipped weed and water as it hit the ocean, rocking wildly. Arcole took up the noose and Var the oars, and they moved a little distance from the schooner.

"God be with us," Var gasped as he rowed.

Arcole was not a religious man, but he echoed the prayer, thinking they needed all the luck any power might bestow. Even then he scarcely dared hope they should succeed.

"There!" he yelled as the serpent's wide-mouthed head appeared. "Stand ready!"

Var let the oars drop and snatched at the noose. Each clutching the rope, they moved apart to bow and stern.

The monster's blank-eyed face was not expressive, but Arcole thought it smiled rapaciously as the head went under. The finned back showed as great lengths of the body slid down. Arcole hoped it would attack as it had before.

It seemed slow minutes passed in silence. Var's face was pale, his eyes darting hither and yon over the weed. Arcole saw his knuckles white on the rope; his own hands felt sweat-slickened.

The dinghy trembled as the water under its keel was disturbed. Then it was hurtling upward, propelled high even as the clinkered sides stove in between the serpent's jaws. The massive head rose—through the noose.

Arcole let go the rope as fangs longer than a saber's blade clashed viciously before his face. The creature's breath overwhelmed even the reek of the seaweed, and he gagged as he tumbled helplessly through the air. Then he was choking as weed and water engulfed him, and for a while his world was a place of darkness and confusion, filled with the dreadful anticipation of those jaws closing about him.

Then blue sky shone bright above and he spat, tugging layers of wrack from his face. The monster still rose, the noose drawing tight about its throat. Arcole saw the *Pride of the Lord* off to his right, and Var's weed-littered head appeared. Pieces of the dinghy fell in a wooden rain. The sea serpent seemed to climb the sky, and when it dropped, Arcole was pushed toward the schooner by the wave it made. The ship seemed horribly far away, and he feared he would not reach it before the monster took him. He began to swim, awkwardly for the obstruction of the weed.

He saw Var was ahead of him, pausing at the foot of the rope ladder flung down by his marines to assist Arcole. They climbed together, propelled by desperation.

Overhead, the line ran taut. A soldier shouted warning and they both flattened against the schooner's side as marines and sailors threw their weight against the cannon, sending it after the tightening rope. It hit with a great splash and sank.

Arcole and Var reached the deck and turned panting to observe the serpent. The beast thrashed furiously, caught like some gigantic fish on the line, its movements hampered by the weight of the sinking cannon. It was not enough to drag the creature down but sufficient for Arcole's purpose—or so he hoped.

Var coughed, unable to speak as yet, and motioned that the sergeant order the cannoneers to fire.

Two pieces remained intact on the port side, and now the gunners had an easier target. They sighted carefully as the monster coiled and splashed and struggled against the rope. One gun roared, its charge hitting true, carving a bloody wound in the serpent's flank. The second boomed and a fresh gash spread blood over the turbulent wrack. The serpent shrilled in pain; on the ship a cheer went up. Again and again the cannon blasted, and though they sometimes missed as the monster writhed, still they scored enough hits that the creature's thrashing slowed, its blue-gray hide becoming speckled with red wounds. In time its struggles ceased and it floated atop the weed, fixing the schooner with a sullen stare. The cannon fired three more shots, and then the serpent opened its vast mouth a final time and sank.

Arcole stared long at the bloodied weed, waiting for the beast to surface. It seemed impossible that it should be at last slain. But nothing appeared save the lesser worms that wriggled up to feed on the blood and chunks of riven flesh.

He felt a hand on his shoulder and turned to find Tomas Var grinning at him. "By God, I thought us dead then. That was a wild venture."

"But it worked," Arcole replied.

"Indeed it did." Var clapped him vigorously on the back. "By God, Sieur Blayke, you saved us all."

For the moment there were no differences between them, only the comradeship of shared peril: they were only two men who had faced death together and survived. Arcole answered Var's grin with his own, and when the officer extended a hand, he took it. Then there was a crowd about them, soldiers and sailors all shouting their approval. Even Captain Bennan came to add his voice to the congratulations. Arcole felt a blanket draped about his shoulders and turned to find Var's sergeant at his back, that impassive face split by a huge smile.

"This calls for celebration," Var declared. "Sergeant, issue a tot to all present."

The sergeant saluted; his eyes shifted to Arcole, a brow raised in silent question. Var nodded and said, *"Everyone,* sergeant."

The exiles began to emerge from the hold, and when they saw the serpent was gone they, too, began to cheer. Flysse and Davyd came forward, hesitating as they saw the company about Arcole. He caught sight of them and beckoned them on, and the marines cleared a way until they stood beside him. He put his arms about them both.

"It's gone?" Davyd asked.

Arcole nodded, grinning at the boy. Flysse, her eyes bright with tears of joy that he survived, clung close. Then she sniffed and made a moue of distaste. Arcole realized that he stood soaked, draped with seaweed, and stinking. He laughed, and Tomas Var laughed with him.

Then the sergeant approached, carrying a keg. Rum was issued, but as Var raised his cup in toast, Bennan said, "Captain, this is hardly fitting." He frowned at Arcole.

"Even so"—Var held out his cup in Arcole's direction—"I drink his health. Exile or no, he saved us all."

Bennan's frown became a scowl, and he shook his head. "I cannot join in such a toast."

He turned away, passing his cup to a soldier, and strode back to his position at the helm, from where he watched the proceedings in open disapproval. Var ignored him, holding his cup high. "To Sieur Blayke," he cried, the toast echoed by his marines and not a few of the sailors.

Arcole drank deep. The rum was strong, but it seemed only to warm him, and no sooner was his cup emptied than the sergeant refilled it. He raised it, saying, "To Captain Tomas Var."

At that moment it seemed not at all odd that prisoner and guard should toast one another.

But when that was done the mood shifted subtly. There came an awkwardness, for the moment of danger was passed and now they must look to the future. The marine cleared his throat. "I must change," he said, "and I imagine you would welcome dry clothes."

Arcole shrugged. "Unfortunately, I was not able to bring my wardrobe on board."

"Of course." Var smiled, somewhat shamefaced. "Forgive me, I was not thinking." Then he frowned, as if wrestling with a difficult decision. "But I cannot see you remain in those stinking garments, Sieur Blayke. Do you come with me to my cabin, and I'll see outfitted."

Such generosity surprised Arcole, and he bowed, murmuring thanks. Var gestured awkwardly and motioned that Arcole accompany him.

His cabin was small and spartan, but from a sea chest he produced shirt and breeches, clean undergarments. Two soldiers brought in a tub of seawater, boiled clean and now cool. It was a luxury Arcole had not anticipated, and he eagerly washed the stink of the weed from his body.

"This is difficult," Var said. "I'd sooner we had met under different circumstances."

"The cards fall as they will," Arcole replied. "It's up to us how we play them."

Var nodded, his expression unhappy. "I've little choice in the matter." As if to emphasize the point, he buttoned on a clean tunic.

Arcole said, "No, I suppose not."

"Your actions, though . . ." Var's face grew thoughtful. "They shall not be forgotten. When we reach Salvation, I shall inform the governor of your bravery."

"My thanks." Arcole ducked his head in formal salute, then grinned: "And I suspect Captain Bennan will speak of your actions."

Var snorted. "Bennan's a stiff-necked fellow, for sure."

"And how," asked Arcole, "shall your masters take it, that you entertain an exile in your cabin? That you toast him and clothe him?"

Var looked a moment doubtful, then shrugged. "They must take it as they will," he declared. "And surely take into account that you saved them a ship."

Arcole felt less confident of the Autarchy's sense of justice, but he held his tongue. Var appeared disposed to talk and there was information to be gleaned that might be useful. Casually, Arcole said, "The hexes did nothing to deter that beast."

"No." Var drew a cloth over his sword. "Such magicks as are set on these transport vessels are designed to hold their prisoners, not to deter the monsters of the deep."

"We're not so valuable, then." Arcole made his voice careless. "I'd thought us prized cargo."

"Oh, Salvation needs its servants." Arcole wondered if it was bitterness he heard in Var's tone. "But exiles are plentiful, and the hexing that would protect a craft of this size is hard to work. What matter if some find a watery grave?"

"And the crews and your marines?" Arcole asked.

Var snorted a sour laugh. "We take our chances with you, no? And the serpents are not so often found."

"That seems"—Arcole hesitated, not sure how far he could draw Var out—"somewhat careless of your welfare."

"We do our duty." Var drove his sword home into the scabbard and faced Arcole. "And I fear I perhaps say too much. Forgive me, but I've matters to attend, and you—"

He broke off, embarrassed again. Arcole finished the sentence for him: "Am an exile."

"Yes." Var fidgeted with his sabretache, clearly torn between the refuge of formality and the odd relationship that began to form. "You understand? I cannot . . ." He shrugged. "I'd have it different, but I must return you to the hold. But you've my word I shall not forget what you've done."

Arcole bowed. He had expected no less, had perhaps gotten more than he had hoped. He went to the door and strode across the deck to where Flysse and Davyd stood.

Repairs were already begun. Exiles were set to work on the broken railings and damaged planks; the dead were drawn into neat lines, hidden beneath tarpaulins. Var came up and with Bennan at his side, commenced a brief funeral service, after which the corpses were pitched overboard. All the while they watched, Flysse and Davyd stood close by Arcole, as if they would reassure themselves he lived. Had he thought about it himself, he might have felt the same surprised relief. But he was thinking on what Var had let slip, that the *Pride of the Lord* and, therefore, he presumed, all the transports, were not hexed against external attack. And that Tomas Var, for all he did his duty, seemed not entirely happy with the task. There was food for future thought in that.

And further, Arcole now knew Davyd dreamed true. He was not yet sure how he might fit together such tidbits of knowledge, but like the gambler he was, he felt instinctively that such cards should be held close, against their future use.

As soon as he was able to speak privately to the boy, he asked that Davyd tell him of any future dreams. Davyd promised; now more than ever, Arcole was a hero in his eyes.

Nor less in Flysse's. She had seen little of the battle, and only after it was done learnt of Arcole's reckless venture, but she had known he remained on deck while she was below. She had believed they all might die and realized with a shock that her fear was less for herself, less for Davyd even, than for Arcole. She had not known she cared so much until she came out on deck and saw him safe. Then she had felt her heart pound wildly, and must hold herself back lest she fling herself into his arms and hold him tight. When he hugged her, she had struggled not to blurt out her feelings, afraid she presumed too much and that such declaration embarrass him and drive him from her. To tell him she loved him was too blatant, but to herself she admitted it was true: she loved Arcole.

Davyd's nightmares enede with the destruction of the sea serpent. The ocean still disturbed him: it seemed unnatural to float atop those unknowable depths, but he was able to come to terms with that. The absence of warning dreams assured him no further perils threatened, and had he a fear left, it was that Arcole might let slip some careless word that should condemn him to the Inquisitors' fires. But that was a very small fear—he trusted Arcole as he had trusted no one save Aunt Dory.

Indeed, had he thought about it, he would have realized that the place Aunt Dory had occupied in his life, the place that had been empty since her demise, was now filled by Arcole and Flysse. They were like newfound parents, or elder brother and sister. He had been alone so long, living on his wits and the deftness of his fingers without true friends that it was a joy to know them. He refused to think about their impending landfall, when fate might well separate them.

When such glum prospect did intrude on his happiness, he dismissed it, telling himself that Grostheim could not be so large a place they be parted. Sometimes he allowed himself to imagine them together there, that Arcole would take Flysse to wife and they would adopt him. Even did that not happen, he would surely see them often enough. Arcole would surely arrange it so.

Davyd had absolute faith in Arcole: he thought there could be nothing Arcole could not do. By God, he had slain the sea serpent! He had saved Flysse from rape, and even the marines—stern agents of the Lord's Militia—had hailed him hero. Now even Captain Var treated him with respect and had promised to speak out on his behalf when they reached their destination. He hoped Arcole would arrange it that they three remain together. It did not occur to him, dazzled by his admiration, that Arcole might entertain other plans.

And the *Pride of the Lord* continued on across the Sea of Sorrows, laboring slowly through the final limits of the weed sea, then swifter as the clinging wrack gave up its hold and freshened breezes filled the sails. No more serpents attacked, though three were sighted and the remaining cannon primed and aimed. Had Davyd dared speak out, he would have told Tomas Var there was no danger, but Arcole was the only one to share his knowledge and so he only watched, pretending a trepidation he no longer felt.

Then one day, when the sky spread bright above and the sea blue all around, three gulls came swooping overhead, their mewing answered by the sailors who shouted that landfall was nigh. The next day a line of darkness lay across the western horizon, and on the day after that the schooner came in sight of Salvation's coast.

18 The Long Night Falls

The New Grass Moon was flattened like a shield
dented in battle as the Commacht returned home.
The clan had ridden a distance with the mass the People and then, when
the Aparhaso and the Naiche went their ways, somewhat farther with
Yazte's Lakanti. But that trail parted in a few days and the doubled
strength of the two clans was split. Consequently, the Commacht
akaman rode wary, knowing Chakthi's promise and the man's temper.
He set his warriors about the defenseless ones as the column wove
homeward, with scouts and outriders and a rearguard about the main
body of the clan. It was, for all Yazte's promises of support, a sadder
journey than was usual, and Racharran looked constantly for sign of
ambush and all the time hoped Chakthi might see sense.

Forlorn hope, he knew, but still could not resist.

They came down a grassy avenue banded by tall oaks, sloping toward a
river with the sun lowering, shedding red light over the treetops, all the
clan spread out in long defile with the scouts ahead and the outriders
pressed in close by the timber, the rearguard watchful behind. Racharran thought to camp that night beside the water.

Then horsemen came out from the trees. Their shields carried the
buffalo-head emblems of the Tachyn and their faces were war-painted:
all bands of black and red, with daubs of white on the cheeks. They

came screaming their battle cries and firing bows that took three of the outriders from their saddles on the first pass, arrows driven deep into their ribs and chests, and then were gone still howling back into the wood. The Commacht warriors slew two of them, but then a second wave came from ahead, cutting in behind the scouts to send shafts like savage rain onto the column before turning back to the safety of the timber.

Racharran rallied his clan, calling in his warriors tight about the column, and urged them to a gallop for the river. He shouted down the younger men who would go after the ambushers and bade them hold the flanks. By the time they reached the water, the Tachyn were gone.

Four Commacht were dead, and more wounded. A dog snapped, howling, at the black and red Tachyn shaft driven through its ribs until a warrior ended its misery with an ax. All looked to Racharran for guidance.

He could do no more than bid them camp in tight formation beside the river, which should protect their backs, and set his warriors guardian about the camp, more ringing the horse herd. The young men and not a few of the older warriors were for riding out in search of the enemy. They pointed out—and rightly—that to attack a clan homebound from Matakwa was open breach of the Will, and had Chakthi himself not, by his action, set himself beyond the Will? Racharran could tell them only yes, and no—that did Chakthi elect to ignore the Will, that was his choice, but that the Commacht would not thus soil their hands. And when they asked him must they then ride all the way home in fear of Tachyn raids, he could only say yes, and bid them fight only defensive, adding, "On our own grass, the Will no longer ties our hands, and are we attacked, it shall be war."

This pleased them, for the treacherous raid heated tempers that might be cooled only in blood, and many set to speaking of the numbers they would slay and the punishments they would inflict on the Tachyn.

Racharran left them to it. His spirit was sunk low, for he saw the hoped-for peace was all lost, wisdom burned away in the flames of Chakthi's rage, and he foresaw chaos descending when the People stood in great need of common sense and common purpose. He walked a distance off alone, to where the waning moon painted the green grass all silvery and the river ran quick between its banks, babbling as it conversed with itself and the night. He looked to where the sentries patrolled, and past them to the trees, and then beyond toward the mountains, distant now and dark, the Maker's Mountain a pale pillar upholding the sky. He wondered how Rannach fared, and Arrhyna, and what newborn terrors Colun might find on his return home.

He spun, his Grannach blade in hand, as soft footsteps came up.

"Ho, it's me." Morrhyn raised hands in gesture of calming. "Think you a Tachyn might come so close?"

Racharran shook his head, returning the blade to its sheath. "This talk of war troubles me," he said. And beckoned the wakanisha to his side. "Shall we walk aways?"

Morrhyn fell into step beside his friend. "I should have dreamed of this," he murmured.

Racharran's laugh was a souring of the night. "We'd no need of your gift to foretell it." He glanced sidelong at the Dreamer. "That Chakthi's crazed enough to break the Will? I *knew* that; but still men died."

"That was not your fault," Morrhyn said. "You did all you could."

Racharran said, "I hoped too strong. I set too much faith in men. I hoped Chakthi yet retained some honor."

Morrhyn said, "Because you are a good man; an honorable man. Men like you see the best in others; you seek to see it, and overlook their weaknesses."

"And so my people die." Racharran stooped to lift a pebble from the river's shore, flung it out over the water. It splashed and was gone. "Do such 'good men' make good akamans?"

Firmly, Morrhyn answered, "Yes. You hold to the Will and seek only the good of all the clan, of all the People. That must be our hope, for I think that every breaking of the Ahsa-tye-Patiko now must be an offense against the Maker, and we shall need his goodwill in the times to come."

Racharran grunted, folding his blanket tight around his shoulders as if a chill wind blew, though the night was warm as the New Grass Moon faded toward its rebirth as the Moon of Dancing Foals. "And what shall come?" he asked. "More attacks? More die along the way? Until the young men fret and perhaps rebel? And then? War with the Tachyn? When we should all of us think on what Colun told us, and prepare for the worst."

Answers were hard to find: Morrhyn sighed and said slowly, "Perhaps; likely. There's a blind madness come to Ket-Ta-Witko, I think. It's as if"—he hesitated, looking toward the distant bulk of the Maker's Mountain—"as if some dark wind blows through the mountains to soil our minds and make us mad. You see the danger, and Yazte. But the others are like children hiding under their blankets, waiting for the night to go away."

"Shall it be a long night?" Racharran asked. "And shall it go away?"

Morrhyn closed his eyes a moment. He thought it might be no bad thing to find his own blankets and draw them firm over his head and play the child. But he could not: he was wakanisha of the Commacht, as Racharran was akaman, and they could neither of them forsake their duties. He said, "I think it shall likely be a very long night, and I cannot say if it will go away."

Racharran halted. The river folded here, a steep bank sliding down to a sandy beach. He lowered himself to the ground, legs dangling, and motioned Morrhyn to sit beside him. "What does your dreaming say of this long night?"

"Nothing." Morrhyn spread helpless hands wide. "Since I sat in the wa'tenhya, I've not dreamed at all."

Racharran turned to study his face. The akaman's was lit stark and hard-planed by the moon. Morrhyn found it hard to meet his eyes: they held no accusation, but still he felt accused. He said, "Since then I've slept like a child—either sound or waking frightened through the night. But what wakes me, I cannot say. There's nothing here." He tapped his head as if to dislodge some clogging hindrance. "No dreams, no warnings—only fear."

Racharran nodded, unspeaking. He stared at the river, running oblivious of their presence or their concerns, like passing time that flows and changes and is the same and always different.

Morrhyn said, "I'm afraid. I feel unarmed—as if I were a warrior hunting a man-eating lion in a thick, dark wood without weapons. I know the beast is there . . . somewhere . . . but I cannot see it or smell it or hear it. Only know that it watches me. And waits to pounce."

He felt Racharran's hand upon his shoulder then, squeezing. The akaman said, "Perhaps when we come home?"

"Perhaps." Morrhyn smiled sadly. "But meanwhile, what use am I? A Dreamer bereft of dreams? Useful as a blind horse."

Racharran's hand squeezed harder. "A blind horse can still carry a load, my friend."

"Save," Morrhyn said, "it's not much use in battle, eh?"

"You wakanishas do not fight," Racharran said. "Yours is the harder part."

"I am afraid." Morrhyn paused so that Racharran could not decide whether he stated a simple fact or voiced a wider fear. "I am afraid that in the days to come we shall all of us be called to fight. Against men or . . . something else. And my weapons are my dreams. Are they lost, then I am . . . what? Truly useless."

"No!" Racharran shook his friend as he might a despondent child. "You are what you are—wakanisha of the Commacht! Not only our Dreamer, but also arbiter of the Will. You interpret the Ahsa-tye-Patiko, and in that I think I shall need your help in the days to come."

"The Ahsa-tye-Patiko?" Morrhyn found a turf loose between his knees and worried it up and tossed it into the edgewater. It fell soggy and bobbed awhile, then took the current and was borne away. He could not look at Racharran's face as he said, "I wonder if the People do not all forget the Ahsa-tye-Patiko. Surely Chakthi disregards it; Vachyr did. Rannach was driven to that . . ." He bit his tongue. "Forgive me, old friend."

"No." Racharran shook his head. "For what you say is true. Rannach *did* . . . what you say."

"With cause," Morrhyn said.

"Yes." Racharran nodded. "But still, to no good effect. And did Chakthi plan it all, or only Vachyr, then the end's the same, no? The Matakwa ended in chaos and we all go our separate ways when we need harmony. But still we need the Will. Let the Tachyn forget it; we Commacht shall not."

"You see things straight," Morrhyn said. "True as an arrow."

"Because I see them simpler," Racharran gave him back. "To draw the bow and sight the shaft? That's easy—any warrior can do that. But you? Your task is the hard one, brother. You're the one communes with the Maker and must translate his Will for us."

"Save part of that is the dreaming," Morrhyn said. He tried to find the turf along the river's length and could not. He wondered if it floated on or sank.

Racharran said, "A part, yes. But another is the Ahsa-tye-Patiko, and that part you can still carry."

"Like," Morrhyn asked, "the blind horse with its load?"

"If you will," Racharran answered. "It's a load needs bearing. I think that I shall need your strength when the warriors grow restless."

Morrhyn said, "You shall have it—for what it's worth."

Racharran said, "It's worth much. Now, do we go check the picket lines and then find ourselves food? I think Lhyn's a flask of tiswin yet unopened. Save Colun found it."

Morrhyn smiled and nodded his assent, and they rose from their melancholy contemplation and returned to where the clan built the fires and wondered what the morrow held.

They crossed the river with a vanguard established on the farther bank and warriors watchful on the near. There was no attack, and by midmorning all were safely over, even the slain whom they carried with them that they might be set to rest in the trees of their own country. They went swiftly as a clan might, which was not very fast with old folk and children to tend, horses to herd, laden pack animals and travois to haul. Racharran took to halting early did some readily defensible place appear, and each night the camp was guarded. But still they moved inexorably toward their own country, and that was their beacon and their hope.

They came to a place where the land ahead was open, spreading wide between far ridges topped with birch and tamarack. The sky was oyster blue and laced with drifts of high cloud that strung out like the tails of racing horses on the sweet-scented wind. Off to the south a small herd of buffalo grazed, the bulls ringing the cows and calves as they scented the passing clan. Racharran led the column, his shield firm on his left arm, Grannach-bladed lance tall in his right. Bow and shafts lay quivered across his back. That morning, as Lhyn readied food, he had honed his knife. It was not the way he would usually have come home, and it seemed a weight upon his shoulders and his soul. He wished it might be different, yet knew it was not and could not be, and that he must accept it as he had urged Morrhyn to accept the weight of the wakanisha's burden.

He saw the Tachyn as his people reached the end parts of the ridges and the full width of the plain beyond spread out, sloping down to a deep and fast-running stream that marked the boundary of the Commacht grass. There were twenty men by his count, riding their animals slow along the ridgetop to his right, and when he looked to the left he saw twenty more, pacing their horses to match the column. They made no move to attack, only rode in insulting escort, as if daring the Commacht to charge them. Forty warriors were scarce enough to halt or defeat the clan, but they could inflict a damage Racharran had sooner avoid. He wondered what they planned, and if more men waited in hiding ahead, behind the last slopes of the ridges. He thought of the Ahsa-tye-Patiko, which forbade him to make the first move, and that the water ahead should be a barrier, his people penned by river and ridges.

His own warriors danced their horses around him, urging him to attack, telling him they could easily sweep these upstarts from the slopes.

He said, "No! We are yet bound by the Will. Find Morrhyn and bring him."

A man raced back along the nervous column to where Morrhyn rode with Lhyn and brought the wakanisha to Racharran.

The akaman pointed his lance at the Tachyn and then at the river. "Twenty and twenty to either side," he said, "and likely as many hidden ahead. I'd not fight them if I can avoid it, but they may not grant us that choice. What are your thoughts?"

Morrhyn nodded, recognizing the true purpose of Racharran's question, of the summons: to emphasize the wakanisha's position, establish his authority. These last nights, there had been mutterings amongst the impatient warriors—that their Dreamer lost his power, could no longer warn of hazards to come. Even now he saw faces turned dark and doubting toward him, waiting on him.

"The Ahsa-tye-Patiko is clear on this," he said. "Each clan is granted safe passage home, and to deny that is to deny the Will, to risk the Maker's anger."

From amongst the warriors came a voice he recognized as Bakaan's: "Chakthi denies the Will at his pleasure! Are we to die at his whim?"

Racharran's voice cracked through the morning. "We are Commacht! Would you forget the Will, then go join the Tachyn."

Morrhyn saw Bakaan frown and lower his face. He said, "They do not attack yet."

"Not yet." Racharran looked again toward the river. "But when we reach the ford?"

Maker guide me, Morrhyn thought. Have I offended you, punish me, not all the clan. "That would surely be the place," he said. "But why reveal themselves? I wonder if Chakthi has some other design in mind."

"What else could it be?" Racharran asked.

Morrhyn turned in his saddle to study the watching Tachyn, the river ahead. "Perhaps . . ." He gathered his thoughts, not knowing if the Maker granted him insight or if it was his own intuition. "Perhaps Chakthi seeks to share his sin. None saw him when they attacked before." He looked around: men shook their heads. "Perhaps this is like the kidnap—that Chakthi would draw us into a trap and claim his hands clean, that these warriors act unknown to him. Perhaps he'd lure us into a breaking of the Will."

A man barked laughter and shouted, "What matter? Are we attacked now or at the ford, the defenseless ones shall suffer. Why do we not charge them?"

Morrhyn thought that Racharran would answer, but the akaman sat silent, leaving the response to him. He said, "It is as Racharran says—we are Commacht: we hold to the Will. Let Chakthi bloody his hands, not ours."

The same man demanded: "And so we go like dew-eyed deer to the slaughter?"

Racharran was about to speak, but Morrhyn reached out to touch his wrist and silence him—the akaman had passed him this burden: now he would carry it as best he could. "I think they may not attack," he said. "I think perhaps they look to draw us into a charge, and after claim it was *we* made the first move."

"I would," the man declared. "Make the first move."

His cry was answered with shouts of agreement and approval, and all the while the column moved slowly on toward the ford and Morrhyn knew he must do something to hold his people to the Will, that the angry warriors not defile the Ahsa-tye-Patiko. He looked again at the Tachyn: they waved their lances in challenge, and the breeze carried their jeers.

He said, "No! The first move is mine."

His voice was loud and firm: it stilled the warriors. Racharran stared at him, eyes framing a question. He said, "I shall go to them and ask them what they do."

He felt afraid. He thought the Tachyn should likely slay him, and then was ashamed of his fear, thinking that did he fail to act, the Commacht should likely charge and the Will be further broken. He heeled his horse forward.

Racharran moved to halt him, said: "Not alone."

"Yes, alone." Morrhyn forced a smile and lied. "I think not even Chakthi's warriors would slay a wakanisha."

And do they, he thought, then what shall it matter? If I can no longer dream, what use am I? No matter what Racharran says. And if I succeed, then perhaps I shall strengthen the Will, perhaps persuade the hotheads to observance. He fixed Racharran with his eyes and turned his horse past the akaman's and drove his heels against the flanks, lifting the animal to a canter, shouting back in as firm a voice as he could manage: "Wait here!"

The day was warm: he felt chilled as he rode away from his people and his belly felt hollow. He let his eyes wander sidelong, seeing the Tachyn riders match his pace. As he passed the ridges' ends and came toward the river and the narrow ford, they descended and swung toward him. He could see none others hidden and reined in a little way from the water. The Tachyn closed on him, and he gentled his mount as the animal scented his fear and began to prance. His throat was dry and still he felt a great desire to spit, which he resisted, endeavoring to sit calm as he anticipated an arrow driving into his back, his ribs, his chest, or the sudden charge that would plant the lance's point in his belly and lift him from the saddle.

Instead, the Tachyn warriors wheeled their horses in a circle about him, round and round, as he sat holding his own in check. They called out, jeering, telling him the Commacht were cowards and afraid of the mighty Tachyn that they send a Dreamer in place of warriors. Some came in close to strike him and he swayed in the saddle, wincing at the blows, waiting for them to tire of the ritual.

When they did and slowed their circling to ring him, waiting, he said, "Why do you do this?"

They seemed a moment taken aback, then a warrior he did not recognize answered, "Because you are a Commacht and a coward."

He said, "I am Morrhyn, wakanisha of the Commacht. Who are you?"

The man hesitated, then said, "I am Dohnse."

Morrhyn nodded and asked, "Are you Chakthi's man, Dohnse?"

The Tachyn frowned, confused, and said, "Of course."

Morrhyn assumed him the leader and stared at him. It was very hard to ignore the men milling about, the weapons they brandished. He asked, "And where is Chakthi?"

Dohnse said, "He takes our people home. He takes Vachyr's body home."

Morrhyn said, "And Hadduth? Where is the wakanisha of the Tachyn?"

Dohnse's frown grew deeper, the bands of color decorating his face twisting. He said, "Hadduth rides with the clan."

"He should be with you," Morrhyn said. "That he might interpret the Ahsa-tye-Patiko for you."

Dohnse drew his rein tight, prompting his mount to dance. He looked uncomfortable, hid it behind a scowl. "What of the Will, Commacht?"

"We are homebound from Matakwa." Morrhyn angled his head back, indicating his own waiting clan, not taking his eyes from Dohnse's face. "And the Will is clear on that—to attack is to defy the Maker."

Under the paint, the scowl, it was hard to read the Tachyn's face, but he thought Dohnse looked an instant ashamed. He watched as the man shook his lance and then his head.

"Rannach broke the Ahsa-tye-Patiko when he slew Vachyr."

Morrhyn said, "Yes; but Vachyr broke it first when he stole Arrhyna. And the Council decided Rannach's punishment. Even now he lives in the wild places, alone." He stabbed a hand toward the west, toward the distant shadow-shapes of the mountains and the faint, shining bulk of the Maker's Mountain. "It is for the Maker to decide whether he lives or dies now. As it is for the Maker to decide the right and wrong of defying the Will. Shall you accept that, Dohnse? Shall you accept the Maker's wrath?"

Dohnse looked in turn toward the mountains and shaped a sign of warding. "Chakthi has declared war," he said, less confident now. "Why should I not kill you?"

Morrhyn said, "Because you would then break the Ahsa-tye-Patiko, Dohnse, and would surely earn the Maker's displeasure. I am a wakan-isha, and I tell you it would be so. Must be so! The Will is clear on this, and do you break it *you* must suffer his anger. You and all others who defy him. Shall you accept that anger alone? Or shall you go back and ask Hadduth, Chakthi, to take a share?"

Dohnse chewed awhile on his lower lip, his horse curveting, then grunted and said, "Why should I listen to you, Morrhyn of the Com-macht?"

Morrhyn said, "Perhaps because I came to you alone, that I might speak with you of the Will and find a way whereby you can avoid the Maker's anger. Perhaps because I'd not see further bloodshed in defiance of the Will."

Dohnse said, "Our clans are at war, Dreamer. How can there not be further bloodshed?"

Morrhyn would have sighed, save that must be interpreted as a sign of weakness, and he thought that if he showed any sign of weakness now he would die, and then the Commacht ride down on these misguided men and the Will be all shattered. So he steeled himself and said, "Perhaps there cannot. Save do you take lives now, you condemn yourselves in the eyes of the Maker and I'd not see you suffer that fate. Neither you or my clan."

"You weave clever words." Dohnse shook his lance in frustration and fury, but Morrhyn thought he saw a measure of doubt in the man's eyes. "I am Chakthi's man. I obey my akaman."

"Who is not here." Morrhyn said. "And thus able to claim his hands were clean, does this all come to killing. Neither him nor Hadduth, eh? Only you and your men—who shall suffer alone the Maker's judgment."

He saw the doubt grow larger. "Listen," he said, "there is a way past this. A way that leaves you with honor, nor condemned before the Maker."

Reluctantly, Dohnse asked, "How? What way is this?"

Morrhyn pointed at the river. "The boundary of our grass, that. Leave us cross—let the defenseless ones go over unharmed—and then the strictures of the Will are obeyed. Once over, we are on Commacht grass and this war Chakthi brings us shall no longer defy the Ahsa-tye-Patiko. Grant us that crossing and you shall not be condemned. I tell you this as a wakanisha."

Dohnse pondered awhile, then said, "I must speak of this with my people."

Morrhyn nodded. He sat his fretful horse as the Tachyn spoke amongst themselves. Before him the river burbled unconcerned, and above the sky stretched blue and hard in the spring sun, the mare's tails all strung out on the wind. He saw a hawk riding the aerial currents, hovering still as the cold chilled the center of his being as he waited for the Tachyns' decision. It seemed to him a frozen moment in which he could hear the nervous pounding of his own heart, and he thought that if the Tachyn decided in favor of his suggestion, then perhaps there was still some little hope, some honor left. He saw the hawk stoop as Dohnse spoke again.

"It shall be as you say." The Tachyn thrust his lance in the direction of the ford. He seemed torn, between, Morrhyn thought, fear of the Maker and fear of Chakthi. "Let your defenseless ones cross, and all your coward warriors. We shall not attack."

"My thanks." Morrhyn ducked his head. "It is good to find honor yet exists amongst Chakthi's people."

Dohnse frowned and spat onto the trampled grass. "Do not try my patience, Dreamer." He flourished his lance. "Go tell your people they cross with my permission."

Morrhyn waited no longer, but turned his horse and heeled the animal back. The Tachyn parted for him, watching him with sullen, angry eyes, and all the way he felt an unpleasant prickling between his shoulders, resisting the urge to gallop or to look back.

"They say we can cross unharmed," he told Racharran.

A warrior—Bakaan again, he thought—snorted and said, "They say? We could ride them down."

Racharran asked, "Are there more? Could it be a trap?"

"I think not." Morrhyn shook his head. "I saw no others. I spoke to them of honor and the Will."

Racharran nodded and said, loud, "That was a brave thing you did. So . . ." He raised his lance, waving the clan onward. "We cross in peace. Let no man break the Will."

He urged his horse forward and the Commacht came down between the ridges in an eager human tide. It was ever good to reach home again, but now the sweeter for what lay behind them; and if war lay ahead, then at least it should be fought on their grass, where the bones and blood of the ancestors nurtured them and made them strong. They came cautious to the river, the warriors yet alert along the flanks and to the rear, then forming defensive as the women and children and old folk made the crossing. The Tachyn disappeared back into the copses and Dohnse kept his word, so that all came over unscathed.

As Morrhyn waited, watching the horse herd and the dogs go

splashing over, Lhyn came up beside. She rode a paint pony, leading a roan that dragged a travois on which was loaded hers and Racharran's lodge, and all they had brought with them to Matakwa. The sun shone bright on her hair, so that the strands of silver glittered, enhancing the gold, and for all her face still reflected the loss of her son, she was smiling.

She said, "That was bravely done. I was afraid for you."

Morrhyn said, "I told Racharran they'd not dare harm a wakanisha," even as he felt a flush of pleasure that she had been concerned for him.

"They might have," she said. "They are Chakthi's people."

He shrugged, wishing he might reach out to touch her. It was as if those moments of danger heightened his senses and in their passing left him restless and needful of contact. He wished he might hold her; that it was his lodge loaded on the travois, and his blankets she'd come to that night. He thought that at that moment he had never desired her more.

"I was afraid," he said, and smiled sheepishly. "I feared they'd kill me. But . . ." He shrugged again.

"But what?" Lhyn asked, and reached out to touch his hand.

He shivered at her touch; it seemed he could feel the pulsing of her blood. He felt sure she must know this, and what his eyes surely said to her. He stretched his smile wider in camouflage and said, "Some of them yet honor the Will."

"Then we've hope," she said. "Are there such warriors amongst the Tachyn still. And such men as you with us."

He said, "Perhaps," and wished they not have this conversation and she go on to leave him lonely with his thoughts: it was hard to love another's wife.

Then Racharran came splashing back across the river and the moment was—thankfully for Morrhyn—ended as the akaman saw to Lhyn's crossing, and afer that the last of the clan went over, and then the rearguard and all the commacht came again onto their grass.

The Tachyn struck thrice more as they moved toward the summer grazing. The New Grass Moon waned and the nights were lit only by stars as the Moon of Dancing Foals gathered strength and the attacks were fought off with no Commacht slain and only minor casualties, but still they were savage reminder of Chakthi's vengeance-bent rage.

And still Morrhyn did not dream. He could not, it seemed: as if a darkening veil fell over him when he found his blankets. He slept—as he had told Racharran—like a babe: either dreamlessly sound or always waking unaware of what roused him, other than unknown terror. Once on the relative safety of the summer grass he raised himself a sweat lodge and passed long nights there seeking communion with the Maker and that oneiric world that foretold—or should have—the events of the mundane, but nothing came save sweat and blank, dark night. He ate the pahé root and still did not dream: he came to fear the Maker had taken away the gift and he become useless to his clan and all the People. He wondered if he had failed his duty, or if Colun's invaders stole his ability, and could not decide. He knew only tha the no longer dreamed, and could no longer forewarn or guide his clan. He felt then that the fear he had known when he faced Dohnse was just a small thing, and not at all to be compared with this.

And as his inner darkness grew, so did the war, as if the one thing were somehow linked to the other, or both controlled by some greater darkness that spread like malign twilight across Ket-Ta-Witko.

Racharran took his clan deep into the Commacht territory, far from the boundaries where usually they would be safe. Then, when no attacks came for a while and the Commacht were somewhat lulled into a sense of security, the clan divided, as was customary, into lesser family groups that drifted to their preferred grazing. It was not the way of the People to fight great battles, but rather skirmishes, fast raids, and ambuscades, small bands of warriors striking into a clan's territory to hit and run. Usually when they fought, it was over horses or disputed grazing, hunting rights. That Chakthi sent his people into battle envenomed purely with his own malice was a strange thing that the Commacht found hard to understand. But send them he did, and himself at the head, his face painted with the colors of war and vengeance, his shield daubed all black in mourning for Vachyr. He wore his hair still loose and foul with ashes and dirt, so that those who saw him and lived said that he wore the look of a ghost or a demon. Neither did his belligerence follow any pattern familiar to the clan. He brought his warriors in large bands, deep into the Commacht grazing, and after striking did not return to his own territory but pressed on, like a prairie fire blazing unchecked across the grass. Nor did he spare those considered by custom and the Ahsa-tye-Patiko inviolate: women and children, old men—the defenseless ones—died. He poisoned springs with corpses and damned streams with the rotting bodies of slain horses; where food was grown he trampled and befouled; and when no Commacht were available, he slew game, leaving the meat to rot. It was a war such as the Commacht had never known: it filled them with both fear and hatred. And still Morrhyn could not dream, but only give what advice he could.

He suggested to Racharran that the akaman bring in the scattered groups, that the clan band all together in such size as might daunt the Tachyn. It was an unknown thing, but they fought an unknown war, so Racharran sent out riders and all the Commacht drew together in one great defensive mass.

This in itself created problems, for with so large a band the grazing was soon worn out and they must often move nomadic, and the presence of so many people in one place frightened off the game so that hunters must travel farther afield after the buffalo and the deer, which left them vulnerable to the raging Tachyn. It was as if Chakthi's madness infected his clan, and Morrhyn wondered what insanity must grip Hadduth, that the Tachyn wakanisha raised no objection. But that, in light of his own problems, was a small consideration.

Despite Racharran's oft-voiced support, his standing amongst the Commacht diminished like water dribbling through gravel. He could not dream: he could not warn of attacks or fouled waterholes, buffalo herds or deer slaughtered or driven away. The clan began to mutter; the hotheaded young men first, but before too long also the older warriors.

"The Maker takes away his gift," he heard them say; and, "What use a Dreamer who cannot dream?" and "He's named no one to succeed him." When they knew he heard them they looked shamefaced and turned away, but the soft-spoken words rang condemnatory in his ears and he was ashamed: he thought he failed his people.

When the young men, and more than a few of the older warriors, spoke of raiding into the Tachyn lands to strike the enemy's camps as Chakthi did theirs, he argued with them, speaking urgently of the Ahsatye-Patiko and the importance of its continued observance. He said to them what Racharran had said—that they were Commacht and should not stoop to the Tachyn's low ways for fear of earning the Maker's displeasure. And they gave him back that it seemed to them they already suffered, and that surely what Chakthi did must justify any measures they took; and he could only answer that wrong could not justify wrong, which satisfied them not at all. Some even dared question him outright, asking if he could still, dreamless, properly interpret the Will. It was Racharran who intervened then, exercising his authority to forbid such counterattacks, and though he supported Morrhyn, still that intervention eroded the wakanisha's own standing. He felt he became shadowy, ever more insubstantial, as the clan's belief in him slipped away. He felt his belief in himself shrink, as if he drifted powerless on a tide he could neither control nor properly comprehend. He grew morose.

He spent long days alone in the sweat lodge, praying to the Maker for guidance, for enlightenment, and knew only the unanswering darkness. He ate the pahé root until Racharran and Lhyn came to him, together and separately, and begged him to cease for fear the narcotic leach out all his senses and leave him mindless. To which he answered: "And what matter? Undreaming, I *am* senseless: I am useless." And laughed bitterly and said, "That blind horse we spoke of? I am less use than that. I am become nothing."

"You are our wakanisha," Racharran said as Lhyn wiped sweat from his fevered face, his chest.

That touch would, not long ago, have excited him, but now he felt only a terrible weariness, an aching and unnamable void that left him despondent and weak so that he only lay beside the fire and knew vaguely she wiped him dry and brought broth to his mouth. He would not have eaten had she not forced him. He said, "I am a Dreamer without dreams. They talk about me when they think I shall not hear."

Racharran said, "I'll speak to them of that."

"No." Morrhyn shook his head. "They speak only the truth. Why should they not? I betray them."

Lhyn said fiercely, "No! You do what you can."

He laughed at that, feebly, and raised himself up. "What I can do is not much, eh?"

It seemed to him the darkness invaded his soul, and even when he sought the light he could not find it, as if it were dimmed or taken far away from him. He took the bowl from her hands and drained it and gave it back; she filled it from the pot she had brought and passed it to him. He looked at it and felt no appetite and shook his head.

She said, "That would be betrayal, Morrhyn—to let yourself grow weak when we need your strength. Eat!"

He looked at her and wondered how she could care so much for him when he was useless and she had lost her son. He looked at Racharran, who sat cross-legged and unhappy, his eyes narrowed in concern. He took the bowl.

Racharran said, "I've sent riders to the Lakanti, to ask for Yazte's help."

Morrhyn felt his belly grow warmer as the broth filled him. He felt weak and sick. He was not sure how long he had lain in the sweat lodge, nor how long since last he ate. He said, "Surely we need it. But what shall it mean? That this war is fought the fiercer? That more die?"

Racharran said, "I hope it shall mean we defeat Chakthi."

"Or slip deeper into this chaos?" Morrhyn let Lhyn drape a blanket about his shoulders. "I feel a long night coming."

"What do you say?" Racharran asked.

Morrhyn sipped the broth. It strengthened him; or perhaps it was the concern of these true friends. It did not matter: he felt his spirit climb a little way up from the darkness. It was as if he lay in a deep pit, but now a glimmer illuminated handholds, showed how he might ascend into the light again. He said carefully, "That this war blinds us to the other. That we fight the Tachyn, and does Yazte lend us men, then three clans fight. Shall Chakthi seek alliance with the Naiche or Juh's Aparhaso?"

Racharran said, "I think he'd not find it, nor we. I think both Juh and Tahdase would sooner stay clear of this."

Morrhyn shook his head and felt it spin. He closed his eyes awhile, gathering his confused and random thoughts. "I think it makes no difference," he said at last. "Colun brought us warning of that war the Whaztaye lost. He told us the impossible had become real, and of the Grannach's fears—that the invaders breach the mountains and come to Ket-Ta-Witko. *And we ignored him!* We had our own concerns, no? That Vachyr stole Arrhyna and Rannach slew him for that sin."

"And was punished for it," Racharran said, his face gone tight.

"And was punished for it," Morrhyn agreed. "And did we not then wonder what part Chakthi had in that, and Hadduth? What darkness had entered them that they played so dangerous a game? That Chakthi had likely chanced his own son's life to strike at us?"

Racharran said, "I do not understand."

Lhyn sat silent, her gaze fixed firm on Morrhyn's face, as if she sought the answers he was not sure he owned behind his eyes.

He said, "I wondered then if some greater darkness entered Chakthi. Think on how that Matakwa ended—in chaos and rage. Now we fight a war such as we've never known—the Ahsa-tye-Patiko is forgotten by the Tachyn, and our own young men speak of ignoring the Will. I think there's chaos abroad—and what better time to invade a land?"

He licked his lips as Lhyn flinched. He saw Racharran's hands tighten into fists. He wondered if the Maker guided his tongue, or only his own worst fears. He said, "I eat the pahé root and still cannot dream. My head is all clouded and dark. The Tachyn ignore the Will and every custom: chaos. We are divided. And should Colun's warning prove true?"

He saw Racharran's hands close tight again, this time the right folding about the Grannach knife he wore. Lhyn reached out to touch his wrist, her other hand nervous at her throat. Like her husband before her, she asked, "What do you say?"

He answered: "That a madness is on us. And I fear worse to come."

Her hand clenched tight. He dropped the bowl he held, the broth spilling unnoticed between his legs.

Racharran said, "Wakanisha, if this is your true belief, what must we do?"

Almost, he shrugged and answered, "I am a wakanisha who cannot any longer dream—why do you ask me?" But he could not shrug off that duty: he *was* wakanisha of the Commacht, and if he was to fulfil that duty, then he must accept it wholely or else be nothing: fail his clan and all the People. He wished the burden were not his—that he might turn from it and pass it to another; but there was—as the whispers about the camp had said—none other to whom he could hand it. And so, he thought, I must shoulder it like that blind horse, and trust to those instincts left me to carry it safely on. But to where, and to what end?

The entry flap of the sweat lodge faced west, looking toward the invisible mountains. It was closed now, but it was for a moment as if his sight grew vital enough that he saw through the hide and across the grass beyond the woods and the hills and the valleys and the rivers to where the Maker's Mountain loomed. It was as if he saw that peak standing bright into the sky, as if it came to him and stood above him and called him. He felt afraid and at the same time excited. For an instant he remembered the time Gahyth had named him a Dreamer and revealed to him those mysteries that belonged to the wakanishas alone.

He heard Lhyn say, "Morrhyn?"

And Racharran, "What ails you?"

He smiled then, a thin and narrow spreading of his lips, and answered them both: "I must go away."

It seemed not his lungs that pumped the air that vitalized the words, nor his throat that drummed the cords, nor his lips that shaped their forming, but some other's. Perhaps the Maker's. He thought that likely presumption, but still the words came clear, and he knew as he spoke them that there was no retraction possible, nor any turning back. He was compelled by a force he did not understand, nor wanted to: it was too strong. It was if he climbed those handholds he had envisioned, clambering from the pit toward the hope of light, driven by hope and fear together to ignore the pain and grip where no grip was possible, only the frail strength of himself and his own hope, which was no less fear. There was now only forward to . . .

He could not name it. Only know that it must be, else he be less than nothing.

He said, "I must go to the Maker's Mountain."

Racharran said, "No! Not now. We need you."

He laughed again and rose. The blanket fell from his shoulders as he went to the entry flap and flung it aside. It was dusk. The Moon of Dancing Foals waned; the sky was full of stars. The cookfires and the watchfires lit the encampment, and he heard the voices of his clan raised like sparks into the night. There was laughter and the sound of children, of dogs and the horses, and he felt a great love encompass him, and a terrible dread that he might never see this again. He stepped outside and felt a hand upon his bare shoulder and turned to look into Racharran's eyes. Lhyn stood beside her husband, her face all filled with such emotions as he'd not seen since her son was banished. He smiled at them.

"I must go the Maker's Mountain," he said again. "I am no use here. But there . . ."

He looked again toward where the mountain stood. It was no longer as in that brief vision, but its memory stood proud and he knew he had no other choice.

"I think I might find answers there."

19 Sanctuary

The Moon of Hairy Horses hung low above the valley, filling the strath with yellow light. The timber cascading down the terraces whispered a gentle song as the summer breeze caressed the leaves, and the stream murmured in counterpoint. The breeze was warm; nightingales trilled and were answered by the soft hooting of owls. It was a fine and perfect night: Rannach felt at ease.

He raised his head from where he lounged on the moon-washed grass to look to where Arrhyna sat. The fire emphasized the perfect lines of her face, and the moon dusted her hair with dancing silver. She caught his eyes and smiled.

"What are you thinking?" she asked.

"That I am very lucky," he replied. "That the Maker is kind to me."

She said, "To us," gravely, and looked toward the great stark peak that dominated all the hills, and then lowered her eyes and looked at the fire.

He saw thoughts hidden and asked her in turn, "What are *you* thinking?"

She raised her face from contemplation of the flames and said, "That we are lucky, but—" She paused, her teeth a moment on her lip as if she were not certain she should speak. He motioned that she continue. '. . . That perhaps our people are not so blessed. I wonder how they fare."

He sat up, crossing his legs and resting his elbows on his knees. He shrugged. "You are my clan now," he said. "My father agreed to my banishment, so I am no longer truly of the Commacht."

She frowned. "He is still your father. And what of your mother? What of my parents?"

His features darkened a moment. Sometimes, Arrhyna thought, his moods shifted so swift, he frightened her. He was like an untamed horse, a stallion not yet broken to the saddle and as like to stamp and bite as allow itself ridden. Was there a constant, it was his love for her, which she could not deny. She knew he loved his mother; nor any less his father, although that love was all caught up in troubled emotions as if— she thought again of stallions—Racharran were the old horse and Rannach the young: new blooded, prideful and . . . She was not sure. Envious? Ambitious? Or only young? She could not define it: he was too quixotic.

He said, "Likely they're safe. The clan will be on the summer grass now, and that's a long ride for the Tachyn. Likely Chakthi rants and does nothing. And if there's worse, what can I do? I am banished, fair game should I go back."

"No!" She shook her head, hair spilling so that moonlight danced there, suddenly afraid he might decide to go. "I do not say that you should go back. I only wonder how they fare."

He shrugged again and laughed. "I'll not go back. Why should I?" He swept out a hand in indication of the valley, of her. "I've all I want here. I've you and good hunting—this is a fine place."

She nodded and asked, "But what of Colun's news?"

The Grannach had not visited them often since delivering them to the valley. He had gone away with his people, and they had spent weeks exploring the confines of the place before deciding on a permanent campsite. It was a valley large enough that an entire clan might have lived there and not gone hungry: it was as if they two were delivered alone into a newborn world, separate and distinct from the wider country that was Ket-Ta-Witko. They had erected their lodge where the stream bent round in an oxbow, lush grass bordering the water, osiers behind. Rannach had hunted and she had planted: they were happy. The moons had faded, one dying to birth its successor, and it had been a good time, free of those concerns that had driven them from the People. Rannach accepted his banishment with a stoic indifference that she knew concealed his hurt, but that had waned as he settled and grew content, and she had wanted only to be with him, thinking there could be no true life for her without him. It had seemed to them both perfection, and were it not for the world beyond their idyllic confines, it might have been, had they been able to forget the larger world beyond the hills.

But then Colun had come back when the Fat Moon waned, telling them of the invaders beyond the mountains who, he said, massed about the foothills, now seemingly masters of all the Whaztaye country.

"And of what beyond that?" he asked rhetorically. "Where did they come from? What are they?"

Rannach shrugged then and said, "I've never seen them and cannot say. Can your golans not tell?"

"The golans speak with the stone, not dreams," Colun replied. And no, they cannot tell. But I have seen what I have seen."

His tone, his face, was grim, and Arrhyna asked, "Shall they breach your defenses?"

The Grannach shrugged then, and said, "Not yet. And a hard fight if they attempt it. But they are so many. They camp in the foothills as if they'd settle there, or wait for something. They herd their beasts on the plains below and, the Maker knows, but such creatures as they ride are past my imagining."

Rannach asked, "Do they not ride horses?"

Colun shook his head and answered, "What they ride are more lion than horse. I told you they had slain the Whaztaye, no? I was wrong—their animals feed on the Whaztaye!"

He shuddered then, and Arrhyna felt a cold dread invade her, her world. Rannach frowned as if he found this impossible to consider and asked, "They ride lions?"

"Not lions," Colun replied, "but things like lions, as if lions and horses and lizards had combined. They roam the plains to hunt the Whaztaye sheep—and anything else that lives and has blood in its veins. And their riders hold those of the Whaztaye who still live in pens and feed them to these animals—still quick. They are like some sickness come into the world. By the Maker, they make Chakthi look benign!"

Arrhyna asked, "What are they?"

But Colun could only shake his head and shrug and tell her he did not know, nor any of his people, and Rannach asked, "How do you know all this?"

"We watch," Colun said. "From the hills where our golans have cut new tunnels so that we may observe them." And he shook his head and added, "It is not a pleasant observation."

"Is that not dangerous?" Rannach asked. "Might they not find such tunnels?"

"Perhaps." Colun shrugged then, and looked uneasy. "But better we know what they do, eh? And if they find those openings, we can bring the stone down on them."

"Shall they?" Arrhyna said. "Find the tunnels?"

"Not save they've Grannach eyes," Colun told her. "Nor the high passes, which are well guarded now. All well"—he looked toward the holy mountain and shaped an obeisance—"the Maker shall see us safe."

"All well," Rannach said, "then, yes. But if not?"

"Then we fight a bloody war," Colun replied. "But not for a while. And you'll have warning enough. Now . . ." He dismissed concern, staring intently at Arrhyna. "What news of tiswin?"

It had been hard to shake off the fear his news induced, but she had essayed a smile and told him, "I believe I can make you tiswin when the junipers grow ripe."

"When shall that be?" he asked eagerly.

"In the Moon of Ripe Berries," she answered, and for all her fear could not resist smiling at his expression as she added, "And then the winter to ferment."

"Ach!" He grimaced at that. "So long?"

"I thought," she said, laughing at his exaggerated unhappiness, "that you Grannach were patient."

"We are," he said. "But patience is patience, and tiswin is tiswin. And I had hoped that bringing you flatlanders here meant I should have my own supply."

"So you shall," she promised, and thought, *If the Maker grants us the time.*

It had been a souring of their idyll they had worked to forget—which was not difficult because they were in love and alone in a new world, and could do nothing to change events beyond the valley. So they had settled to their new life and built for themselves a happiness that, by consent, precluded overmuch discussion of that dark, black wind that seemed to blow against the mountains from the west and perhaps found a way through the hills to pervade the plains of Ket-Ta-Witko. But still it was there, like the breath of the Wolf Moon skirling about the entry of their lodge, seeking to intrude, and though they did not speak of it, still it chilled them in those hinder parts of their minds that yet looked past the valley. It was as if a shadow hung behind them, just out of eye's range, so that when they turned to seek it, it was gone, darting round to another quarter, where it lurked hidden but yet present, like a skulking wolverine invisible in the night but *there*—unseen and unscented, unheard, only *present*.

But there was also lightness, an easy forgetting of the dark and what it held, or might. Marjia was such a beacon. Colun brought her to them when the Moon of Dancing Foals was old in the sky. Rannach thought she looked not unlike the moon in its fulness: all round and beaming, like a gold-haired boulder dressed in lavishly embroidered shirt and swaying skirt, her hair coiled and pinned with bright silver fixings about a plump face from which cheerful blue eyes sparkled and a rosebud mouth seemed fixed in an everlasting smile.

She bustled, bee-busy and happy as those honey-gatherers, into their camp, kissing first and Arrhyna and then him—they both must stoop to accept her embrace—firmly on both cheeks, then cheerfully ordering Colun to unload their gifts. There were needles for Arrhyna, a metal comb, a mirror of polished metal ornate in its design, and a thin knife edged fine to trim hide. For Rannach there was a knife and a small ax, both sharper and stronger than any he owned, a supply of arrowheads, and a new tip for his lance.

"There was not much trading this year," she said, "and so we've much to give."

Rannach was embarrassed. "We've nothing to compare," he said. "You shame me."

"Ach!" Marjia waved a cheerfully dismissive hand and with her other poked Colun in the ribs. "You promised my husband tiswin, no? And me the knowledge of its making. That's gift enough. The Maker knows, but have I that art, I'll make my husband happy—and have something to trade that drunkards like him will beg for."

"I am not," Colun said as dignified as he could as he laughed, "a drunkard."

"But fond of tiswin, no?" his wife returned, and before he had chance to reply said to Arrhyna: "Shall we look to our dinner and leave these men to manly talk?"

Arrhyna would sooner have heard whatever fresh news Colun brought, but it was clearly Marjia's purpose to lighten the day, and she knew Rannach would advise her of what was said, so she allowed the tiny woman to take her off and regale her with casual conversation as they prepared the food.

Marjia had never met with a flatlander before—only the Grannach men attended the Matakwas—and she found it hard to accept that Arrhyna could be happy with no company save Rannach's. Her own people lived close, in subterranean enclaves that sounded to Arrhyna quite horrible. The villages were lit, Marjia assured her, but the very idea of dwelling beneath that unimaginable weight of stone, families all crowded together with room piled on room, house atop house, prompted Arrhyna to shudder. But then, it was no less odd to Marjia that the People dwelt as they did, in lodges under the open sky.

"The sky," she said gravely as her blunt fingers worked with deft efficiency on the vegetables Arrhyna had gathered, "is all very well. Indeed, once in a while, it's good to venture out. But . . ." She glanced up at the wide panoply of stars and moon and shuddered herself. "I'd not want to be out here all the time. It's so . . . open."

Arrhyna could only nod and agree that their two peoples were different in their attitudes.

"But what does that matter?" Marjia beamed. "We are all the Maker's children, no? And did he see fit to make you to wander the open places and we to dwell within our hills, then that's as it should be."

Arrhyna smiled and voiced heartfelt agreement: she liked this woman on the instant. She could not help, looking at her, thinking of those stones the old folk heated in the lodgefire to warm their sleeping furs of a winter's night: Marjia was as round and solid, and as comforting.

And when, the next day, the Grannach woman departed, Arrhyna found she missed her. It had been a comfortable time, that first visit, and there was a small vacuum came with her going. For a while Arrhyna thought nostalgically on the companionship of the clans, of neighbors and shared duties, of all the things the women of the Matawaye did together. But she had Rannach, and before long the little sadness went away.

She asked her husband what news Colun had brought, and Rannach had shrugged and told her little that was new—the invaders still massed about the foothills, the Grannach still watching them; no more. They both of them wondered what purpose drove the stranglings and if they would attempt the crossing of the mountains, but that was only speculation and idle in light of their isolation. They prayed that the Maker deny the invaders passage, which was all they could do, and returned to their solitary life.

Nor did the subsequent visits of Colun and Marjia shed further light. They came again when the Red Berry Moon sat high and plump over the peaks, and in the Moon of Ripe Berries, but with nothing new to tell. It was as if all the world hung in stasis, or the Maker's wards defeated the invaders: hope in that, but still the ugly suspicion of *something* impending, still that sense of the wolverine lurking rapacious outside the fire's glow.

But it was ever easier to set that nagging doubt aside: the invaders made no move and there was nothing they could do, so they worked to set aside the doubts and turned their conversation to more cheerful matters.

Chief amongst these was the manufacture of the promised tiswin. Colun had brought kettles and pots at Arrhyna's request, and he and Marjia joined in the harvesting of the juniper berries and those other herbs required. She had versed Marjia in the quantities and the method of preparation. It seemed at first strange to instruct a woman likely old enough to be her grandmother or more in a thing she had learned at her mother's side, but Marjia was so enthusiastic a pupil—and urged on by her anticipatory husband—that Arrhyna soon forgot that difference and only enjoyed the Grannach woman's company. Together they set the brew to ferment, laughing at Colun's downcast face when Arrhyna told him the tiswin should not be ready until at least the Hard Frost Moon, or even later.

"Ach, so long!" He sighed dramatically, his craggy face a pantomime of disappointment. Then brightened, asking, "There's no chance I might have a taste now?"

"Not save you want a sour belly," Arrhyna told him. "It would taste foul now, and make you sick."

He slumped like a disconsolate stone and murmured, "Then I suppose I must make do with our beer."

"Which is no bad thing," Rannach said.

There were kegs of the Grannach ale stored in a lean-to, barrels of worked wood banded with staves of metal, strange to the two Matawaye who used no such storage: Arrhyna thought such constructions would be a fine way to keep meat. Colun had brought them on a handcart he and Marjia hauled like two sturdy ponies, the cart itself of as much interest to the Matawaye as the beer. The idea of carving wood into discs and fixing those discs to axles fixed in turn to a walled platform was unknown to the People. Their portage was done all on horseback, or on travois, and the notion of utilizing wheels was as novel to them as was the idea of riding to the Grannach.

"This," Rannach declared, touching the cart's round wheels as if they were holy objects, "would make traveling easier. A horse could be set in front to pull, and it all move faster than a travois."

"Likely," Colun agreed, without much interest. "But now, do we open a keg?"

Rannach had acquired a taste for the beer, and insisted that their hosts accept deerskins and meat in return. It was a time of learning for them all, marred only by that lingering, unspoken presentiment and one other thing.

Arrhyna had been the first to broach it. "We are your guests, and you are always welcome in our lodge," she said. Nervously, for she feared she might offend. Indeed, had Marjia not beamed at her, she might have fallen silent then; but the Grannach woman sat all agog and her smile was invitation to continue. "But only you come. Why do no others?"

There was a moment of hesitation, Colun glancing at his wife and Marjia at him as if they shared some silent, somewhat embarrassed communication. Then Colun said bluntly, "Not all welcome you here. There are some claim I was wrong to bring you, that you should be sent back to the lowlands. Some say I defy the Order—that which you name the Ahsa-tye-Patiko—in giving you this valley. They say your presence offends the Maker and weakens our defenses."

He shrugged apologetically while Marjia laughed and said, "They are fools! Should friends not aid friends in time of trouble? How can that offend the Maker?"

"Still," Colun said, "some claim that."

"Should we go?" Rannach asked. "I'd not see you suffer on our behalf."

"Ach, no!" Colun flung a dismissive hand at the sky. "This valley belongs to the Javitz, and I am creddan of the Javitz. It is other families —envious families—who make these claims."

"But no other . . . Javitz? . . . come," Arrhyna said.

Colun smiled sheepishly and told her, "I'd not give offense, save I must. The right and wrong of my decision is still debated and no conclusion reached, but meanwhile . . ."

He shrugged and found his mug. Marjia continued: "My brave husband would see you safe—and does. But he must also consider the welfare of our family, and so would hold all claims of wrongdoing to himself alone. Should the debate decide against him, then he'd not see any other Javitz blamed, but only him."

"And you?" Arrhyna suggested.

Marjia chuckled then, her round form shaking as if a boulder trembled. "I've no doubt that what he did was right," she said. "And am I condemned for that, then so be it."

"What shall happen," Rannach asked, "if the decision goes against you?"

"Who knows?" Colun replied, and grinned. "No flatlander has ever come here before—it's no easy decision."

"And so," Marjia added cheerfully, "will take a long time to decide. The elders will argue back and forth, and you two likely grow old before any minds are made up."

"Still," Rannach said, "I'd not bring you to harm. Were it better we go, then we shall."

Marjia then said, "Hush. We'll not hear such talk. Eh, husband?"

"No. You are our friends: you are guests of the Javitz. I should . . ." He drew himself up: a stone bristling like an offended dog. "I should take that as insult. Indeed . . ." He assumed as haughty a mien as might a stone. ". . . I forbid it; and any further talk of departure."

Save, Arrhyna thought even as she smiled her thanks—letting her eyes wander briefly to where the Maker's Mountain loomed high under the afternoon sun—that we and you are all forced to depart, fleeing like the Whaztaye before whatever menace lurks beyond these ringing hills.

But she hid that unpleasant thought behind her smile, which was entirely genuine, for she thought she'd never known such staunch friends.

So it went, idyll and menace, the days blending one into another as the moons waxed and waned and waxed again, time turning seemingly unconcerned with the events of men. Sometimes Arrhyna thought of the valley as a refuge, an island in a wide river, buffeted by hard floods but yet impregnable, safe. At others she thought of it as a beautiful prison in which she lay happily trapped, able to ignore the world outside.

And Rannach, she wondered as she studied her husband's face in the light of the Moon of Hairy Horses, what does he feel? What does he not tell me?

She asked again, "What of Colun's news?"

He shrugged and said, "The Maker's wards hold yet, no? So the invaders probe, but the Grannach defenses still hold them back."

"Colun told us," she said, "that they move deeper into the hills, that Grannach have died fighting them in the passes and the tunnels."

"And I," he returned, "have said I'd fight with the Grannach. And Colun tells me no, that his folk can hold the tunnels and the passes and have no need of me."

"But," she said, "what if . . . ?"

Rannach reached out to take her hand, raising it toward the shape of the holy mountain, now luminous under the moon. "It is in the hands of the Maker," he said. "His wards shall hold or not. Do they, then such talk as this is pointless. Do they not, then I shall fight."

"And what," she asked, "of the People? What of the Grannach?"

"I shall fight," he said. "I shall do what I can do. But for now I can do nothing save wait. It is in the Maker's hands."

20 Quest

Morrhyn lay across his horse's neck, a hand clamped over the muzzle, and listened to the hoofbeats drumming through the sun-heated earth. The slope rose gently before him and he prayed to the Maker that the hollow hide him from the Tachyn he had seen, and they had not spotted him.

A band of fifteen or twenty by his swift count, riding hard from the north, their faces all painted for war. He had sighted them as he climbed the slope—too far from the woods behind to risk retreat and nowhere to run save this shallow depression that might, were the Maker kind, conceal him. If not, if they found him, then all was lost, for they would surely slay him, wakanisha or not.

Or fool, he thought not for the first time. Perhaps only a fool on a fool's errand. Perhaps only a dreamless Dreamer riding to his death, one way or the other. Why am I doing this? Why have I left my people behind to go seeking . . . what?

It was not a thing he could properly explain to himself, and therefore quite impossible to define to others. No dream had summoned him to this quest, he had perceived no sign: there was only that inward certainty. He *knew* he must go; but when that was the only reason he found to give and got back sound arguments for his remaining, he could not help but feel doubt. The Maker sent him no guiding dreams—he could not claim that imperative—and he sometimes wondered, even as he prepared to leave, if some other agency lured him away, or even if he lost his mind. And, the Maker knew, there were sound enough reasons to stay.

"Chakthi runs loose," Racharran told him, "and I've not the warriors to spare to bring you safe to the hills."

Morrhyn had shaken his head at that and smiled sadly. "I'd not ask for an escort, old friend."

"I doubt," Racharran had said, "that the Tachyn will respect even a wakanisha now. If they find you, they'll likely kill you."

And Morrhyn had shrugged asked, "Shall that matter?"

"Yes!" Racharran had replied, staring fiercely at his friend. "To me and all the clan. We need you."

"Blind horses travel slow," Morrhyn had returned, "and need much care. As I am now, I am of no use. Do I go the mountain . . ."

"If you get to the mountain," Racharran had said.

"If," Morrhyn had agreed.

"Then what?" Racharran had turned to gesture westward, a hand sweeping wide in indication of the distance to be traveled. "If you get safely past the Tachyn and climb the mountain. Then what?"

"I don't know." Morrhyn had looked then to where the hills stood, too far off they might be seen. The Fat Moon was yet young, a slender crescent decorating a sky so serene, it belied the turmoil below. It shone over the massed lodges of the Commacht and the woodland to the south of the camp. There were more bodies scaffolded in the trees now, and amongst the tents women keened in mourning: the fighting had been fierce. He said, "I know only that I must go."

"And leave us," Racharran had said.

"I am not a warrior." It had been hard to look Racharran in the eye. "I am a wakanisha robbed of his dreams. Perhaps . . . do I go to the mountain . . ."

"Perhaps!" Racharran had said, irritation a moment exposed, like a knife part-drawn, then again sheathed. "Perhaps and perhaps and perhaps. Can you offer no better reason?"

Morrhyn had said, "No," and decided then he had best leave quickly.

"How will you find us again?" Racharran had asked, resigned now. "When you come back?" The way he said it made the "when" a lingering doubt.

"All well," Morrhyn had replied, "I'll find my dreams again and they'll guide me."

It was a measure of Racharran's trust that he nodded then and only asked, "When shall you leave?"

"With the sun," Morrhyn had said.

He had left the next day, mounted on his favorite paint horse with what few supplies he carried lashed behind his saddle. He took no weapons save a knife and a bow, a quiver of arrows tipped for hunting, not war—he felt no desire to fight, and hoped no Tachyn impede his progress: he wanted only to reach the Maker's Mountain and find what answers lay there, if any did. He could not help that nagging whisper of doubt that murmured its traitorous pessimism in his ear.

He felt alone, even as he rode with Racharran and two hands of warriors to the farther perimiter of the clan's temporary grazing. Dreamless, it was as if a part of his being had been taken away, a function so vital he no longer felt whole. He thought of men who had lost limbs or sight or hearing, and it seemed to him like that: that some vital and integral part of him had been cut off, leaving him less than he wished to be. He felt like a hunter whose left hand was gone, denying grip on a bow: useless. And so he must cling to that single hope, that the certainty he had felt *was* a promise of enlightenment and optimism. That in the mountains he should find his dreams again, find again that communing with the Maker that made him wakanisha.

But it was hard. The doubts dinned always in his ear and he wondered if he clutched at phantasms, or if somehow the strangeling invaders sent malign influences into Ket-Ta-Witko to lure and twist and weaken. He could only hold hard to that vision of the holy mountain, trust in the Maker, and commit to his chosen path.

He heard the hoofbeats fade and wondered how long he had held his breath. He was not much used to fear, not this kind, and he licked his lips and wiped a hand across his brow as the paint horse rose grumbling to its feet. He walked the beast up the slope, halting awhile below the ridgetop until he was certain the Tachyn riders had gone. Then he mounted and continued westward.

There was dust to the south where the riders had gone, and he wondered if the Tachyn rode against his own clan or the Lakanti: Yazte had answered Racharran's call with war bands that struck into the Tachyn grazing. But not enough: the Lakanti had their own affairs to tend, the summer hunting, the planting, and must also ward their borders against Chakthi's madness. Morrhyn wished he might have spoken with Kahteney, but that had not been possible, as if, somehow, fate turned and twisted to deny sensible dealing and turn the world all to chaos.

And the others, he thought as he heeled the paint down the ridge's farther side toward a stream flanked with sun-washed alders, choose not to see or know, but rather ignore the madness. Juh holds his Aparhaso aloof, and Hazhe offers no help; neither Tahdase nor Isten, who follow Juh's lead and wander to the farthest reaches of their grazing, as if this war has no concern for them. If they came to us, to stand against Chakthi's insanity, then perhaps it might be ended and the People stand together.

Against what? doubt whispered in his ear.

Against those dreams I had, he answered himself.

But those were only vague and you've none now. You're dreamless.

Colun's warning, he told the speechless sky. The invaders who have conquered and slain the Whaztaye.

Who are beyond the mountains, held back by the Maker's promise. Do you now question that? Do you question the Ahsa-tye-Patiko? Do you set yourself above the Maker?

No, he moaned into his horse's mane. But I question men, and Chakthi, and what comes to this land.

He saw the country ahead blur, and realized that tears filled his eyes. He wiped them away, telling himself he must be strong and go on, because there was no other way. He thought then of that vision of the Maker's Mountain and for a moment felt its strength again, and that spurred him so that he went onward, knowing he had no other choice.

He crossed the stream and rode up through the alders to a wide plain where buffalo grazed. The herds migrated southward now, and in better times the clans would have drifted with them, the People and the beasts joined in natural union: the Maker's providing. Now there were only the buffalo, the Commacht living slim, the warriors without time to cull the herds for want of fighting Chakthi. It would be a hard winter without their meat.

He marveled at the size of the herd and turned the paint horse around its farther edge as the guardian bulls lifted up their bulky heads and snorted challenge. He skirted the herd and went on across the plain. Low hills marked the far skyline, and he thought he would find those heights by dusk and make camp, setting out traps. If he could

not eat buffalo meat, then perhaps he might snare a rabbit or a part-
ridge.

Or perhaps go hungry: his life seemed all "perhapses" now.

As it was—a sign? He could not decide—his snares took two fat rabbits
and he ate well, and in the morning woke to find magpies chattering in
the trees. A flock swooped overhead and clustered around in noisy observance, which he decided was a favorable sign. But then, as he quit the
timber for the wide swath of open grass beyond—all rolling down off
the ridgetop to a sweeping valley that stretched across westward to another bundle of low hills that lay like a shadow across the horizon—he
saw a flight of crows. They swooped down toward him and cawed loud
and spun circles in the sky above so that he ducked in his saddle and
thought it must be a sign countering the good fortune of the magpies.

He reined in and studied the expanse of grass ahead. It was very
wide—likely a full day's riding to cross—and flat, devoid of timber. He
thought that if Tachyn found him there, he should have nowhere to run,
nowhere to hide, and should die.

And does that matter? he asked himself. He made obeisance to the
Maker and urged the paint horse forward.

The Tachyn came from the east: five horsemen riding hard to intercept
him.

They came up from a dry wash with whoops, and lances raised, and
he heeled the paint to a gallop even as he knew they must overtake him
and prick him from the saddle, his quest undone and wasted. He
thought a moment of the bow he carried and then as quickly discarded
the thought: he might take one or two—he was not so bad a bowman—
but still he'd die, and nothing be solved or resolved. So he left the bow
wrapped in its quiver behind his saddle and reined in his horse, waiting
for them.

"I am in your hands now," he said to the blue, unyielding sky.

White cloud streamed there, and the wind that blew it rustled the
grass and set his unbound hair to fluttering about his face. That was the
only thing marked him wakanisha, but he doubted Chakthi's men would
care even did they notice. As Racharran had warned, they'd likely kill
him easy as they slew the defenseless ones.

His horse fretted, snorting and stamping, and he reined it tight,
forcing it to stand even as his heart set to pounding and he felt the
breeze chill the hot sweat beading his forehead.

The Tachyn drew closer, slowing when he made no attempt to escape or use his bow. One man came out in front, his face and bare chest all banded with war paint, and raised his lance high and sideways so that the others slowed further until their horses walked, spreading in a wide circle around Morrhyn.

The leader came forward, the sun sparking brilliant off the Grannach brooches that fastened his plaits. He couched his lance and came on until the sharp-edged head touched Morrhyn's chest.

He said, "You are very brave. Or mad."

Morrhyn said, "I am very afraid, Dohnse. I do not know if I am mad, but perhaps I am."

Under the paint, Dohnse's eyes narrowed. "I gave you life once," he said. "Did you believe that was a lifetime's promise?"

"No." Morrhyn smiled tightly. "Neither did I think we'd meet again."

Dohnse leaned a little way forward in his saddle so that the lance point pricked through Morrhyn's shirt. The wakanisha held himself rigid. He felt a small trickling down his chest and belly and wondered if it was blood or sweat.

"I do not understand you," Dohnse said.

Morrhyn resisted the temptation to look down, to see what damage the lance had done; instead, he held the Tachyn's gaze. "I scarce understand myself," he said.

Dohnse frowned. "You *are* mad. Our clans are at war, and yet you ride alone? Why did you halt?" He waved his lance at the quivered bow behind Morrhyn's saddle. "Why do you not fight?"

"There's enough bloodshed already. I'd not deepen that pool."

Dohnse scowled and asked, "Are you a coward?"

Morrhyn only shrugged in answer.

Dohnse said, "When you came to us at the ford I thought you were brave."

Morrhyn said, "I was concerned for my clan. I am still: for the Commacht and all the clans."

"Ach! You speak in riddles." Dohnse spun his horse in a tight circle, lance indicating the warriors ringing Morrhyn, waiting. When he halted again, his lance stood poised. "You are concerned for the Tachyn?"

"For all the People," Morrhyn said. "For the Tachyn and the Aparhaso and the Naiche and the Lakanti and the Commacht. For the Grannach too. I fear a thing comes to Ket-Ta-Witko that shall destroy us all, save we face it together."

The lance point drooped a fraction and he felt a small flush of hope. Dohnse said, "You speak of the Grannach's warning? Of the dreams?"

Morrhyn said, "Yes."

Dohnse said, "Hadduth has explained that to us, that those dreams were dreams of *this* war."

"And Colun's warning?" Morrhyn asked.

"Of no account," Dohnse returned him. "The Grannach spoke of events beyond our borders. We place our trust in the Maker, in the Ahsa-tye-Patiko. We believe the Maker shall hold back these invaders—if they truly exist."

"Hadduth says this?" Morrhyn asked. And when Dohnse nodded: "Think you the Ahsa-tye-Patiko is not already broken? Perhaps that weakens our defenses."

"Rannach was the one defied the Will," Dohnse said.

"And Vachyr," Morrhyn said.

Dohnse looked a moment troubled. "Vachyr paid with his life. Rannach yet lives."

Morrhyn said, "In exile, banished. His life forfeit if he returns."

"But Vachyr lies in the trees," Dohnse said. "The ravens eat his flesh."

Morrhyn nodded. "And many more feed the ravens; it shall be a hard winter. And is the Will all forgotten, then perhaps these invaders *shall* come through the mountains. And what then?"

"We fight them. But first, we'll take blood-payment of you Commacht."

"There's blood already paid," Morrhyn said. "Ours and yours. Women weep in the lodges of my clan; children mourn their fathers, and husbands their wives. Is that all our future, Dohnse? To fight one another until your clan or mine is all destroyed? And do these invaders come—shall we fight them together or clan by clan?"

"I . . ." Dohnse lowered his lance somewhat, shaking his head. "I do not know. These are matters for the wakanishas and the akamans. I am only a warrior: I do Chakthi's bidding."

"I think that you are more than just Chakthi's liegeman. I think you are a man of honor. I thought that when you granted us the crossing of the ford."

"Ach!" Dohnse danced his horse. "I paid for that! It did not please Chakthi."

"But was still," Morrhyn said, "the honorable thing."

"Perhaps." Dohnse brought his horse to rest, and the lance back to Morrhyn's chest. "But it served me ill."

Morrhyn said, "But perhaps the Maker well."

"You weave words." The lance rose, pricking again. "You look to escape. Why should I not kill you? I should stand high in Chakthi's eyes did I bring him your head."

"Likely you would." Morrhyn wondered how he managed to speak so clear when his throat felt so dry and his tongue so thick with fear. He felt his body awash with sweat, but he was chilled and must fight the temptation to shiver. "Chakthi would likely take some pleasure in that."

Dohnse said, "Much pleasure. The head of the Commacht wakanisha? Chakthi would feast me for that, I think."

Morrhyn was surprised to hear himself laughing. Perhaps, he thought, I am mad. Aloud, he said, "A poor prize, my head. Empty of dreams: useless as a holed bucket."

Dohnse said, "You lie."

"No." Morrhyn shook the head in question. "I cannot dream. That's why I am here."

"Best you speak fast," Dohnse said, "because I tire of this word-weaving. I think I shall kill you soon."

"I've no dreams," Morrhyn said wearily. He wondered if it was not better that this Tachyn slay him: it should be an ending, a resolution of a kind. "Only darkness. I come here because I'd go to the Maker's Mountain. I had . . . a vision . . . The mountain called me. I left my clan to go there; I hope that the Maker will give me back my dreams. Perhaps give me answers to this madness."

"What madness?" Dohnse asked. "We fight in Vachyr's name, for Tachyn honor."

"Tachyn honor?" Morrhyn said. He felt a great weariness, as if he carried a tremendous weight that bore him down and set all his body to aching and numbness. All these words—those spoken by Dohnse now and those voiced by his own clan—they all seemed a wordy fog that swirled and turned and cried out meaninglessly, speaking of small things when larger events loomed, and none to see them clear or ward against them. For a moment he thought it should be a great relief to let it go: that Dohnse drive that point into his chest and take his head back to Chakthi. But he could not forget his duty, his responsibilities, and so he said, "And the Commacht fight for honor. And the defenseless ones die; and Ket-Ta-Witko stands like a blinded deer awaiting the invaders' arrows."

He sat back in his saddle, thinking that the blow must come now, wondering how it should feel to die. But the lance dropped and Dohnse said, "You speak all the time of these invaders, but say you cannot dream. How can you know?"

"What does Hadduth say?" Morrhyn asked. And saw Dohnse's eyes narrow again, and cloud. And heard doubt in the Tachyn's answer.

"What I've told you—that the dreams were of our war."

"*Were?*" Morrhyn looked at Dohnse's face, seeking to read it through the paint. "Those are old dreams, Matakwa dreams. What of now?"

Dohnse shook his head, braids flying, brooches glittering bright as the lance's point. He gave no answer.

Morrhyn's lips stretched in an unwilled smile that was less triumphant than resigned. "None, eh? Hadduth's blind as I?"

Dohnse said nothing, which was answer enough.

Morrhyn said, "Listen to me, Dohnse! Hear me out and then decide if you'll slay me. But in the Maker's name, hear me first."

Dohnse hesitated awhile, then nodded and Morrhyn felt a little spark of hope rekindled. Which was, he thought, like a sprig of dry moss lit in the teeth of a blizzard. But it was all he had, so he said, "I've lost my dreams, and from your silence I believe Hadduth's lost his. Am I wrong, then slay me—but first tell me that Hadduth still dreams. This I ask you, in the name of the Maker!"

Dohnse turned his face away. Morrhyn saw him swallow, then spit, and knew—horrid confirmation!—that he was right.

"So, the wakanishas of the Commacht and the Tachyn both no longer dream. Strange, eh? As if some black cloud blows over Ket-Ta-Witko, leaching out our gift. Perhaps from over the mountains, eh? Think on it, Dohnse! Is it not strange that the dreams are gone, and so soon after Colun's warning? And did Colun speak the truth—Have you ever known a Grannach to lie, Dohnse?—then they threaten the Grannach passes and might come against us. Not against only the Commacht, or the Tachyn, but against all the People! And what do we do? We fight —Tachyn against Commacht and Lakanti—and the Aparhaso and the Naiche go away, pretending this is none of their affair. The People stand in disarray, Dohnse! Like a deer herd scattered by wolves, all easy for the taking."

"Words," Dohnse said, but unconfidently. "Clever words to justify Vachyr's slaying. And to save your life."

"My life?" Morrhyn threw back his head and laughed. "My life is nothing! Take it if you will; it should be a weight off my shoulders. And Vachyr's slaying? I do not justify that, save to tell you Rannach's punishment was decided by the Council, in Matakwa, by all the akamans. Even his own father!"

A slow moment, then, as Dohnse sat his horse and a flight of summer geese winged overhead, the calling loud in the heavy silence. The grass rustled in the breeze and clouds stretched out like passing time above and the sun sat heavy and indifferent in the sky.

Then Dohnse nodded and said, "That was so."

He looked directly at Morrhyn, and the wakanisha saw a question in his eyes.

"I have no easy answers," he said. "Nor any promises or pleas. Only that I felt called to the Maker's Mountain and that is why I am here, alone. And if you must kill me, then do it."

Dohnse leaned sideways from his saddle to spit again. "You truly think this?" he asked. "That these invaders the Grannach warned of send their magicks to steal the wakanishas' dreams?"

Morrhyn said, "I think it may be so. I cannot say for sure."

"And you would go to the holy mountain to find out? To get back your dreams?"

Morrhyn nodded.

Dohnse said, "I think you are mad."

"Perhaps I am. How could I know?"

"It should be a sin against the Will to slay a madman. And I think you *are* mad."

Morrhyn shrugged.

Dohnse said, "This shall serve me ill when Chakthi hears of it, but I'll not take a madman's head."

Morrhyn thought: Maker, thank you.

Dohnse said, "Go! Ride hard and pray for me."

"I will," Morrhyn promised, and turned the paint horse past Dohnse's gray as the warrior shouted for the Tachyn to let him go, calling out that he was a crazy man and must surely earn them the Maker's displeasure were he slain.

There was yet some honor left, he thought, and therefore also hope.

The Fat Moon filled up and waned as he went on, replaced by the Red Berry Moon, and he wondered how much time was left or if it was all eaten up by Chakthi's hunger. He wondered how his clan fared, and if he rode into the arms of the invaders. That, he thought, should be a great joke: to come so far in search of answers only to die at the hands of the problem.

But he dismissed that thought: there remained in the hinder part of his mind the certainty he had known before Matakwa, confirmed by Colun and his Grannach—that terrible danger came against Ket-Ta-Witko. It was a certainty that nagged at him like an unhealing wound, and nightly he prayed the Maker give him back his dreams that he might know for sure and know how best to advise the clan and the People. But still no dreams came, only empty-minded sleep, so that he came almost to fear it, for it was like going down into blindness, and had his body and his horse not required the rest, he would have pressed on. He felt the attaining of the holy mountain was his only hope.

And so on he went, hiding whenever riders showed in stands of timber where he stood with hand across his horse's muzzle and his own breath loud in his ears, or crouched in washes and ravines as hoofbeats and shouts announced the passage of enemies he looked to save. He crossed rivers and passed by or through herds of buffalo. Often he went hungry: he relied on his snares for food and what he could forage from the land, and never looked to hunt the deer or wild pigs he saw. It was as if, dreamless, nightmare creatures bayed at his heels, propeling him forward, running desperately to a safety he could only hope existed.

He came up from the plains into the redrock country, where the land broke into barrens and all the comforting timber and grass gave way to wind-washed pines and dry bare stone that supported only moss and sorry grass that his horse compained to eat, and the streams ran rusty with the color of the soil. He pushed the animal and himself onward, both of them thinned, lean with travel, and passed through the redrock to the edge of the Meeting Ground.

Kinder country, in a way; and in another unkind, for it reminded him of all that had gone wrong at that Matakwa. He let his horse graze there, where the grass grew lush under the day's sun and the thin light of the fading Red Berry Moon painted the stream silver. He could see where the Council fires had scorched the earth and the lodges of the People had stood, all of them together, and wondered if he had seen the last Gathering. He prayed it not be, but that the Maker grant him insight and the People come back to the Ahsa-tye-Patiko and live again in harmony.

He got no answer and wondered if he was only vain in his quest.

"And if I am," he said, prompting the paint horse to glance up a moment from its grazing, "then I suppose I shall pay the price. I suppose I shall go up there and die."

He looked to where the Maker's Mountain loomed amongst the lesser peaks and could not decide whether it was promise of fulfillment or death. It seemed larger without the company of the People around him, a vast, stark pinnacle that stabbed the sky and dared him to climb its flanks. It would be hard going: he knew he could not take the horse much farther and must ascend that height alone and afoot. He might tumble down into a ravine, or fall beneath a rockslide.

"Or starve," he told himself aloud. "Or freeze, must I wait so long.

But . . ." He made obeisance to the Maker. "Wait I shall, for the one thing or the other."

He felt no other choice.

Five days he waited on the edge of the lonely Meeting Ground. The horse fattened and he had deer meat and rabbits to sustain him. Then he mounted the horse and rode it as far it could climb into the foothills. He thought the Grannach likely knew easier trails, but he lacked their help and must find his own way, up where none of the People—save, perhaps, Rannach and Arrhyna—had gone before. Then, where rock tumbled down like frozen stone water, and precipitous slopes of treacherous shale spilled loose from cliffs fragmented by time, he took the saddle off the horse, and the bridle, and turned the animal loose.

He felt sorry to part with the beast, and hoped it find its way back down to the good grazing. He shouldered it round to face the downslope and slapped its rump. The horse snorted in surprise and kicked a little, then swung its head to study him. The dark eyes seemed to accuse him.

He said, "I am sorry. You've served me faithfully, and I wish you well; but now I must go where you cannot. So . . ."

He slapped its rump again. The horse squealed and danced some few steps away, then halted again, looking at him. He took a shard of rock from amongst the shale and threw it.

The horse snickered and shook its head, then trotted off.

Morrhyn watched it go, a second piece of stone ready in his hand, but the horse appeared to have accepted its freedom and did not look back again. It went on down the narrow trail until it disappeared around a curving wall of reddish sunlit rock.

He felt very alone then. It seemed the breeze blew louder, whistling amongst the cliffs and crags, taunting him. He studied the heights above, and they seemed to radiate back a challenge. He felt small and afraid, and picked up those things he thought he could carry: a bearskin and his blanket, a weight of meat, a lariat; not much else. The saddle was useless now, and he left it, together with the bow and the quiver of arrows. Then he slung his makeshift pack across his back, secured it in place, and he began to climb.

Dusk caught him like a fly on a sheer rockface and he felt a terrible dread that he must lose his grip and fall, but he thought he had seen a cleft above and he willed himself to reach it, promising himself it be there.

It was, and that night he lay uncomfortable between narrow cliffs listening to the nightwind sing its sad song. He chewed on meat not quite properly cured and drank a little water. He wondered if he had slept when the sun touched his face, and crawled deeper into the cleft, seeking a path upward. He heard ravens calling overhead and wondered if they spoke to one another of the fool who dared the mountains alone, whose flesh they would soon pick. He found a place where stone had cracked and afforded him handholds, and climbed out onto a flank of the mountains where the sun warmed him and the wind blew out his hair and he looked out across a place where crag rose above crag and the Maker's Mountain lofted over all. He bowed to that monument and made obeisance to the Maker and then fixed his gaze on the pinnacle and went on.

He clambered like some atavistic thing that knew only its progress toward its goal, like a blind crawling creature seeking the source of heat, or a newborn pup mewling and struggling toward the bitch's teat, aware only of hunger's imperative. His hands grew bloodied, but he ignored the pain as he ignored the aching of his muscles and the nails that broke, or the sharp stones that stabbed him. He climbed: up cliffs and down slopes that set his head to spinning. He stumbled across ravines and over slides of shale that moved and shifted loose as the water of the streams he waded, too numb to know their chill. He fell and was bruised, and paid the aches no heed. He saw desolations of ravens swoop overhead, and lofty eagles spin circles in the sky. Sometimes he saw bighorn sheep watching him, their progress far surer than his across the rock. He slept by fires when he could find wood and cold when he could not. He became aware his supply of meat dwindled, and that the Red Berry Moon gave way to the Moon of Ripe Berries. His shirt and breeches grew tattered as his skin. Only resolution remained: the Maker's Mountain stood before him and he would reach it.

Almost, he forgot why; but always that peak stood proud against the sky and he went on, cold and hungry and blindly, until he had conquered the lesser obstacles and stood on the downslopes of his goal.

He looked up then and thought he must, truly, be mad.

The mountain rose majestic. Pristine, it touched the sky, and from where he rested he could not see its topmost heights, which were all lost in union with the heavens. He could only wince, his eyes dazzled by the great sweeping flanks of snow-clad rock that shone and glittered under the sun.

He crouched, shivering and small, awed by the mountain and what he thought to dare. No man could brave that: vanity and pride had driven him to this lost quest. Dreamless, he had sunk into insanity, attempting what no man had any right to attempt. He was less than an insect under that height: he was a presumption, insulting the Maker with his sorry presence.

But he was there, he had come thus far; so he began to climb again. And on the second day, when he felt no longer any pain or the absolute chill that pervaded his bones down to the marrow and he thought his teeth must break and shard for the drum-rattle chattering of his jaw, he found a cave.

He could scarce believe it, even as he crawled inside. It was a deep hole running back smooth-walled into the mountain. Moss grew on the walls and glowed as the sun went down and twilight overtook the slopes. It was warmed by a spring that bubbled up from a natural well, the water hot and pungent to the taste. He drank and thanked the Maker for the refuge, then spread his blanket and drew his bearskin over him and settled to sleep.

And that night he dreamed.

21 Terrible, Swift Sword

Colun rested his weight on the ax's haft as Baran chanted the wyrd. He felt mightily tired, as much in his soul as in his bones, and the golan's droning song sounded almost a lullaby. It would be a fine thing, he thought, to lie down and close his eyes, to sleep awhile. But there was likely no time for that, save he sleep forever. The strangeling invaders pressed too hard, and for all the golans' labors, there would be fresh battles ere long. Baran might close this tunnel, but it was not the only passage, and there were passes, clefts, and ravines the invaders would surely find and look to cross. Already they penetrated deeper into the Grannach fastnesses than any had believed possible, and did they reach the heartland . . . He grunted, rejecting that horrid contemplation. They must not! It was simple as that. It should be a turning of the world on its head, all topsy-turvy, and the Maker, surely, would not allow that.

Save . . . Was the natural order not already become disorder? Was the balance of the world not already thrown awry? These creatures had appeared from nowhere to conquer the Whaztaye, and now they broached the Grannach fastnesses, the sacred hills, like floodwater gushing into every cavity and channel of the mountains, seeping ever deeper, relentless as passing time or the grinding of stone. Could anything halt them?

He knew they could die—his bloody, blunted ax was proof of that —but hard, and they were so many; and the forces they wielded, the strangeling creatures they commanded . . . He spat rock dust at the memory and pushed it away. They *could* be slain: that was the important thing. And the Grannach were chosen by the Maker to keep the hills, and would not abandon that trust.

He shook his head, denying fatigue, and raised himself, lifting his ax to study the blade. The edge was dented, the clean metal fouled with the blood of beasts and men—if these invaders were men—and he took a cloth and spat and began to wipe away the foulness before taking out a whetstone and honing back a killing edge.

He achieved a satisfactory sharpness before he realized Baran's chant had ceased and rose quickly as the golan came running back. A wave of sound trailed the Stone Shaper, and Colun shook his head as pressure throbbed against his ears. Baran went past him and he began to trot after the Shaper, unable to resist a swift backward glance. There was a terrible rumbling, a wash of dust from which emerged a brief tongue of darting fire, then more solid, sharper fragments of the mountain hurled down the tunnel and the air was thick and filled with roiling darkness as the passage filled with all the mountain's terrible weight of stone.

The two Grannach crouched in the lee of a turn, their backs to the dusty, missile-filled gust, both deaf awhile as the mountain fell on the invaders. When the air was a little cleared they ventured out, and behind them stood a wall of solid rock. From it, like a questing hand, thrust a clawed, scaled paw all set with knifelike talons.

"Ha!" Baran grinned, wiping dirt from his beard, spitting dust and fragments of rock. "Some few died there, eh? That'll teach them!"

"Them perhaps," Colun allowed. "But the rest?"

Baran grunted, slapping at his tunic so that more dust rose. "The Maker knows." He shrugged. "I do what I can. Like you."

Colun spat dirt from his mouth. "Some say I delivered this." Curious, he walked back to the rockfall to study the scaled paw. "That bringing Rannach and Arrhyna to the mountains was defiance of the Order."

"I know, and I say—sheepshit!" Baran spoke thickly, a finger inserted in his mouth to scrub out the dirt of his rockfall. "No Javitz says such a thing, and the rest are fools. Whatever these creatures are, they came against us before that. And what difference can two flatlanders make?"

Colun shrugged, answerless.

"These creatures"—Baran leant closer to study the paw extending from the rockfall—"looked to our hills before you brought our guests. What they are, I've no idea—nor any other golan—but I tell you, you're not to blame for their coming. Those two in the valley are refugees. What difference can they make save we renege our duty to the Maker by refusing them sanctuary?"

"I don't know."

Baran wiped his hand against his tunic as if contact with the massive paw might have befouled him, and clapped Colun on the shoulder. "The world turns strange, my friend; and when that happens, folk look for easy answers. Blame this one, they say; blame that one. If Colun had not brought the flatlanders to our mountains, we'd be safe. Pah! Perhaps if Kratz had not lured Danske's daughter away, we'd be safe. Perhaps if Ogen had not fought Kyr, we'd be safe. Perhaps if the Maker had not put us down here, we'd be safe. Forget them and their foolish talk! What is is; and we must deal with what comes against us sooner than look for folk to blame."

Colun smiled. "But still some speak of sending the flatlanders back," he said. "And that should mean Rannach's death. I'd not see that: he's Racharran's son, and I've a certain fondness for him."

"No Javitz speaks so," Baran said. "And they live in a Javitz valley, no?"

"Yes," Colun said, and glanced back, toward the rockfall. "But how long shall they be safe there?"

"So long as we are safe in our mountains," Baran replied, and chuckled. "Hopefully long enough they can brew this tiswin you speak of. I'd taste that brew."

"You shall," Colun promised. And then, softer: "If there's time for its brewing."

Baran nodded, not speaking, and they went back along the quick-hewn tunnel to where it emerged on a face of precipitous stone, the egress so low only a Grannach might pass easily through. Beyond was a narrow shelf without a wall, rounded and sloped about its edges, the drop so deep it should hopefully break and destroy even the invaders' weirdling beasts; and if not, then the base was all set with jagged boulders.

The golans had worked hard since first the invaders entered the secret ways. All the Grannach had worked hard: they were the defenders, the wardens of the boundaries the Maker set about the world.

Below was a ravine walled tall at either end with tumbled stone, high shelves above all piled with boulders that might be pushed down on any strangelings trapped in the gulch. It was bright now, the sun directly overhead, spilling mellow light down the rockfaces so that they shone all warm as winter blankets.

Save, Colun thought, that they were blankets layered over sharp teeth that would bite and snag the unwary.

He followed Baran down the precipitous stairway that wound left-ward of the shelf: more of the golans' hurried work and none too smooth, but surely too narrow for the invaders' beasts to find a footing there. It ran steep awhile, then curved beneath a ledge and ended on a tunnel. They went inside.

Like all the golans' workings, the passage was lit by the stone magic, the rock itself glowing, curving, and turning with spurs like jagged daggers thrusting out so that even the two Grannach must duck and weave to avoid the serrated nubs and thrusts of the mountains' intestines. Colun could not imagine how any of the invaders' great beasts might pass such a maze, but neither could he resist thinking of the high passes and the lofty valleys, the wider tunnels. He felt a terrible dread that somehow none of these defenses should prove enough, and the strange-lings come through the hills like floodwater remorselessly seeking out all the small and indefensible crannies and cracks until it spills through and drowns all before it.

He shook off the feeling as the passage turned upward and curved and then ran down and curved again, emerging on a ledge above the Javitz home-cavern. The shelf there was walled, and warded. Young Grannach stood guardians about the entrance, armored and armed with axes, hook-billed pikes, and long spears, proud in their shining new armor. Not one had yet seen an invader, and all were eager to fight. Colun felt a terrible pride and a terrible sadness as he answered their salutes.

"They're young," Baran whispered as they went down the winding stairway, "and you're their creddan. They'd join you in battle, in honor. The young are like that—all brave and bloodthirsty. Were you not the same when you were young?"

"Ach!" Colun shook his head, sighing. "Was I? I cannot remember."

"You fought hard enough against the Kraj," Baran said. "At least, as best I remember. When Janzi brought his men against us . . ."

Colun silenced his friend with a weary hand. "That was then and, yes, I was young: I thought battle was glorious and honorable. Now I know better. And I know we face no such enemy as Janzi, but something worse. Far worse." He halted, resting his hands on the parapet of the descending stairway so that he might look out across the vast cavern below. "Look; what do you see?"

Baran said, "Home. The Javitz caves. Brave folk, worth defending."

"Yes." Colun nodded, then reached up to unlatch his helm. He dropped it at his feet and ran weary hands through his thatched and sweaty hair. "Brave folk: *my* folk, and yours. I am their creddan; they follow me. Sometimes I think they follow me like sheep, and perhaps even to the slaughter."

Baran frowned and asked, "What do you say?"

Colun shook his head. "I'm not sure. I know that these strangelings come against us and I am vowed to fight them. But the Kraj say that I bring the invaders on us because I side with the flatlanders. The Genji agree and the rest stand aloof."

"The Kraj would claim that," Baran said, "and the Genji? They are like mating worms, all wound together. But they still fight the invaders. As do the rest."

"Because the invaders trespass on our mountains." Colun's arm swept wide, indicating the vast cavern below, the mountains above. "But if they went by? If they passed through our lands into Ket-Ta-Witko and left us alone? I think some would allow that."

"No!" Baran shook his head, vigorous enough dust flew loose in a cloud, and chips of stone. "Perhaps the Kraj, the Genji, because of the old memories, but surely not the Basanga or the Katjen."

"Perhaps not." Colun set his elbows on the parapet and rested his chin on his hands, staring morosely at the cavern, at the serried ranks of houses that climbed the walls like honeycombs to where the topmost curvature of the vast cave swung over like some rocky sky to meet the rising houses on the farther side, the roadways between climbing up the walls and dangling in the moss-lit air between like spiderweb ladders. And down the middle, where the cave flattened, a stream there all boundaried with chuckling children and women washing. "But I thought that of the flatlanders. I thought that when I brought them news of the invaders they'd surely rally, but what happened? They fell to fighting amongst themselves!"

"You told me that," Baran said carefully. "But that was surely this matter of the maiden Arrhyna and the killing of—Vachyr, was that his name?"

"Yes." Colun nodded. "But do you not see?"

Baran said, "No. Those are flatlander affairs, and I do not understand them."

Colun sighed. "It seems plain enough to me. In some ways, at least; in others . . ." He shrugged. "I brought warning of the invaders to the flatlanders and they ignored it when they fell to squabbling amongst themselves. Racharran heeded me, and Yazte . . . But the rest." He shrugged again. "They'd sooner not know. They quote their Ahsa-tye-Patiko like a warding charm and believe that by ignoring the danger they dismiss it."

"They're flatlanders," Baran said. "They believe themselves safe behind our mountains."

"Yes." Colun ducked his head, slowly as a wearied horse. "And we Grannach, are we any better? We fight the invaders, but still argue that the fight is only for our own lands. That we are the Guardians of the mountains and nothing more. And the Kraj and the Genji argue one way, and the Basanga and the Katjen another, which is so much like the flatlanders, it frightens me."

"What do you say?" Baran asked.

"That there is a kind of horrid pattern in all this," Colun said, and sighed. "That invaders come against us and will doubtless move against Ket-Ta-Witko if we are defeated, and that our people and theirs seem equally divided. As if some fell wind blows over us all, to baffle us and confuse us, so that we dither and argue while all the time the enemy gains ground."

Baran turned his head to study Colun, frowning at the expression he saw. It seemed to him fatalistic, as if the creddan already accepted inevitable defeat. "We've always argued," he said. "It's our nature; but our arguments now are not about the invaders. All the families fight them."

"True." Colun smiled grimly. "But *how* do we fight?"

Baran wondered if the question was rhetorical and hesitated to respond. Then, when Colun said no more, he answered, "As we've always fought, family by family."

"Exactly." Colun nodded. "Each family to its own territory. As Javitz and Kraj and Genji and Basanga and Katjen; not as *Grannach.*"

"We are all Grannach," Baran said, confused.

"Which comes first," Colun asked, "Grannach or family?"

"Surely," Baran said, "they are the same thing."

"Are they?" Colun drew dusty fingers through his beard. "I am not so sure."

Baran said, "I do not understand."

"Suppose," Colun murmured, "that the invaders succeeded in breaching our tunnels, suppose they entered the Javitz cavern. Would the Kraj or the Genji come to our aid? Or would they leave us to our fate? Would they say the Javitz fall because I brought flatlanders into the mountains and the Javitz suffer for my sin and so our fate is none of their affair?"

Baran paused before replying. Then he said, "Surely they'd aid us . . ." But his voice lacked conviction.

"We'd aid them," Colun said. "But were it the other way around, I wonder."

Baran said, "Surely . . ." And let the sentence die unspoken, aware he had no sound answer nor any sound conviction.

"That's what I mean," Colun said, "about the pattern—about an evil wind. Listen. The flatlanders are bound by what they name the Ahsa-tye-Patiko, which is like the Order. But that all fell apart at their Matakwa; and for all I brought them warning, still they fell to squabbling amongst themselves and paid no heed to the larger danger. It was as if they could not see straight, but only see petty envies. And I fear the same might apply to us."

"Did you say the invaders ensorcel us?" Baran asked. "That they send some magic against us?"

Colun sighed and shrugged. "I do not know; I can only wonder. But I tell you this, my friend—I believe we must stand together, that save we fight as *Grannach*—as a people undivided—we shall likely fall. And also that"—he barked a harsh and humorless laugh—"the other families would dismiss that fear. Or bring it to debate so long the invaders come before any resolution be reached."

"We hold the tunnels still," Baran said defensively, not liking the turn of this conversation.

"We hold the tunnels," Colun agreed. "But for how long? The invaders are deep into the mountains now, deeper than any have ever penetrated, and they are so many."

"I don't know what to say." Baran shook his head. "You frighten me with this talk."

Colun said, "I frighten myself. Ach, perhaps I'm wrong. Perhaps I've dealt too much with flatlanders. So!" He pushed away from the parapet, grunting as he straightened his back, and clapped the golan on the shoulder. "Do we go find some beer to wash the dust from our mouths?"

Baran nodded eagerly: it was far easier to fight than contemplate his creddan's abstruse and frightening philosophies.

They descended the great stairway to the cavern's floor and followed the paved way beside the stream until they came to a curving road that lifted up past the honeycomb terraces to a vaulting bridge spanning a crack in the mountain's belly, then along another walled roadway to Colun's dwelling.

Marjia met them on the balcony with a smile that grew wider as she saw her husband was unharmed.

"It went well?"

Colun said, "They died. Baran brought the tunnel down on them. It was thirsty work."

Marjia laughed and bussed his cheek. "It always is. Come, I've a keg ready. And hot water."

She beckoned them inside, past the low-arched doorway to an antechamber where a steaming bowl rested on a shelf of rock, soap and cloths beside.

"You'll wash first," she warned. "Then slake your thirst."

Dutifully, they obeyed. Colun set his helmet and ax aside and they went through the inner door to a wide room that shone all gently golden save where a fire burned cheerfully in the hearth, lending flickering overtones of red to the light emanating from the rock. Bright rugs covered the floor and two deep and amply cushioned chairs stood before the fire, a wooden table between. Colun ushered Baran to one and crossed to where the keg sat inside a niche. He filled two mugs and looked inquiringly at Marjia. She shook her head and told him she'd business below, did he want his dinner, so he brought the mugs to the table and set them down, then sank into the empty chair.

Both Grannach drank deep, and neither spoke until the mugs were emptied. Colun refilled them and Baran ventured an opinion.

"These . . . fears . . . you have. Should you not voice them?"

Colun wiped foam from his lips. "I did," he said. "When I got back from Ket-Ta-Witko I sent word to all the creddans, speaking of my thoughts. The answer was they'd contemplate my words and give their answers in due course. Ach, Baran, old friend! You know what 'in due course' is to us."

Baran nodded. "We Grannach were ever a slow-moving folk."

"But now," Colun declared, "time moves fast. Perhaps too fast! I suspect we've not enough for lengthy contemplation."

"You sound," Baran said, "like a flatlander—all swift and hurrying."

Colun chuckled. "So Janzi claims. He says I'm tainted by contact with the Matawaye."

Baran shrugged: how to argue against time-honored tradition? The Grannach lived long, slow lives and were not given to swift decisions. That was the province of the flatlanders, all brief and hurried because they lacked the time to ponder things. They were fast-running water to the Grannach's stone. He wondered if Colun's stone had been worn down by the flatlanders' water.

"What do you think?"

Colun's question surprised him and he hid awhile behind his mug. Then, carefully: "I think we must fight as best we can."

"And does that mean breaking with tradition?"

Baran felt pinned by Colun's eyes; guilty for his doubts. He drained his mug and said to Colun's back as the creddan rose to fill both their tankards, "I think that these invaders are such a threat as we've not known before. I'd not see our mountains fall to them."

Colun sighed and was about to speak, when a clarion rang, belling loud through the outer cavern, softer in the chamber but nonetheless imperative. Both men sprang to their feet. Baran groaned. "Again? So soon?"

Colun said, "Things change apace, my friend. And do we not change as swift . . ."

He left the sentence dangling as he snatched up his helm and his ax and they both ran to the bridge, across that to the roadway and the battle awaiting them.

The tunnel was wide, a transport route between the different family caverns. It was not roofed so high the invaders' war beasts could fully raise their heads, and so they could not fight to fullest advantage. But still their slashing claws and darting, many-fanged jaws wrought terrible slaughter on the Grannach. And they came apace, slithering and scurrying so swift the golans had not enough time to bring down the rock but must fall back as they chanted their spells. And behind them, unhindered by the tunnel's roof, came the strangelings in their rainbow armor, like a bright flood intent on drowning all before it.

Colun swung his ax, sinking the blade deep into the paw that quested for his chest, and laughed as the beast screamed and snatched back the lusting claws. It limped on three legs then, and he saw his brave Javitz warriors run in to hack at the creature. He saw one taken by the fangs, and raised his ax high, swinging the blade down into the scaly snout, the jaws burst open by the blow so that the warrior was tossed loose. But he was still dead, his armor all pierced by the pressure of those dreadful teeth. Colun twisted his ax loose and struck again even as noisome breath gusted foul against his face. He felt the force of his blow in his arms and shoulders, as if he struck steel against stone. Then the ax was wrenched from his hand, the beast tossing its pierced head and screaming shrill as it writhed. He sprang back, but not quite fast enough to avoid the paw that caught him and flung him down—luckily, the Maker be praised, back clear of the creature's death throes.

He was hauled to his feet and dragged back down the tunnel. He struggled free of the helping hands and snatched up a dead man's ax. His head spun and his vision wavered, and in his ears he heard the Stone

Shapers' chanting all mingled in with the roaring of the living beasts and the screaming of the dying creatures. He saw the one he'd struck fall down, hind legs kicking, front scrabbling for purchase, even as the next came clambering over the body, and moved toward it. But hands clutched him and impelled him away, and then the roaring of the beasts was joined by the roaring of the mountain as the roof collapsed under the weight of the golans' chant and dust blew in a stormy cloud down all the remaining length of safe tunnel.

". . . little way. Likely not enough to halt them for long."

He shook his head, yawning to unblock the stoppage of his ears, and blinked until he saw Baran's mouth moving.

"What?" His own voice sounded distant.

Baran leaned close and said, "We could drop the tunnel only a little way! The Maker help us, but it was built too strong. They'll likely clear it before long."

"Then we fall back." Colun narrowed his eyes, forcing them into focus. Rubble spilled like a ramp from the bulk of stone plugging the tunnel, all hazy in the roiling dust. "Drop the rest while they dig that out."

Baran nodded and beckoned his fellow golans to him.

As they began their chant, Colun called up his warriors.

"We drop the tunnel." He saw their eyes all wide with disbelief and horror and mouthed a curse. "Fall back!"

They retreated down the tunnel, leaving the golans to their work as a youngling came running up.

"Creddan! Colun! They're coming in all over!"

"What?" Colun felt chill fill his belly. "What do you mean?"

The youngster said, "They're entering the cavern."

For an instant Colun rejected the news: it was too large to comprehend, too impossible. The caverns were inviolate, no matter what he'd said: surely the Maker would not allow it, *could* not allow it. Then he looked at the youngling's stricken face and knew it was so.

The world *was* turned on its head, all topsy-turvy.

He shouldered his borrowed ax and began to run, his fighting men on his heels.

And all the way he thought: Marjia, be alive. Maker, let her be alive.

He found chaos.

Rainbow-armored invaders spilled from the tunnels, pouring down the stairways like floodwater, all pushing one against the other in their haste so that some were pitched off to fall and crash onto the stone below. They seemed uncaring of their dead and wounded, for when one fell, none went to his aid but only past, often treading on the fallen so that the wounded were crushed under the weight of their fellows. Some halted on balconies and bridges, nocking long shafts to great bows and sending arrows down like rain on the Grannach below. And from several of the wider thoroughfares came the beasts, all snarling and slavering, their belling joining the battle cries of the Javitz and the howling of hurt folk and the screaming of women and children.

Colun halted his men where a wide, walled ledge afforded clear view of the cave, assessing the situation. He could not see Marjia, nor had the time to seek her, for a cluster of the invaders came charging at his position and he raised his ax to meet them.

They were tall as the flatlanders, these strangelings, and hard-armored. But height is not always an advantage and armor has weak spots: Colun need only duck his head to avoid the long sword that swung above him and then send his ax slicing against the invader's knee, all his Grannach strength in the blow.

The man—he supposed it was a man, but could not tell for sure—loosed a shrill cry and fell down as if kneeling before the creddan. Colun reversed his stroke and sent a scarlet helmet rolling away across the shelf, the head it protected still inside. Then he must spring back as the serrated blade of a pike stabbed at his chest. He turned, catching the pole between his left arm and ribs, and smashed his ax against it. The Grannach steel severed the pole and its user was pitched off balance. Before he had opportunity to draw the long knife he carried, Colun sank his ax into the bright yellow breastplate and roared in triumph as red blood spilled out. He shouldered the dying man aside and went in search of another victim.

There were none left: bodies littered the shelf, both invaders and Grannach, but where all the strangelings were dead, the Grannach had wounded they carried limping with them.

Colun ordered off the least hurt, leaving them to tend the worst, and led his remaining warriors at a run for the closest bridge, where invading archers stood. The Grannach swept them away, as many tossed down into the depths of the cavern as were slain by steel.

A pause then as he surveyed the cavern. There were not so many invaders as he had first thought. It was as if their shining armor, all so bright and light-reflecting, tricked the eye into a multiplication of their numbers. That, and perhaps the sheer fact that they were in the ancestral cave. Certainly no more emerged from the tunnels, and the Javitz drove those on the bridges back, or over, and all down the walks along the stream there were glittering bodies like poisonous beetles.

Some yet lived, fighting in tight groups along the terraces, surrounded by massing rings of Grannach. Colun thought they must soon fall, for they were heavily outnumbered by the Javitz.

He looked down and saw three of the dreadful beasts still living, and then a cry burst from his throat and he was running for the nearest descending road.

Marjia stood by the stream, a house at her back and a pike in her hands, a group of women with her, all armed with poles and swords taken from the fallen, presenting a steely wall to the creature that spat and snarled and pawed at them as if it were some monstrous nightmare cat confronting a hedgehog whose spikes were sharp steel. From the doorway and the windows of the house, children stared wide-eyed at the beast, and even as he raced toward his wife, Colun saw the invader lurking behind the creature and surmised something of their nature.

It was kind of symbiosis, he realized, the monstrous beast controlled in some fashion by the man, as if it were a fighting dog and the invader its handler, urging it on. His armor was not of the brilliant hues that marked his fellows, but only black, with bright crimson sigils on chest and back. He carried a tall pole that ended in a long spike from which protruded a recurved hook, and for all the beast needed no prompting in its bloodlust, still he poked at the hindquarters as if the carnage it wrought was insufficient to satisfy him.

Colun saw bodies littering the floor, some male but most women, slain in defense of the sanctuary, of the children hiding there. He saw Marjia thrust her pike at the beast and propelled himself desperately forward, his soul filled with a terrible dread.

He found the cavern's floor and charged the dark-armored invader. His ax rose and sank into the armored back. The invader jerked and stiffened, arms flung wide, the goad dropping from his hand. Colun swung the ax again, this time striking deep between the joindure of breastplate and tasset. He saw the man's head fling back and hooked it down as if he gaffed a fish. The armored figure was tugged onto its back and Colun sank his ax into the frontage of the jet helmet.

The beast roared then, and slowed as if it were struck, and turned from its attack to face the Grannach. It seemed confused and, as it roared and lashed its scaly tail, Colun darted past the wide-mouthed head to spring onto a shoulder as if it were a ladder and sink his ax into the backbone.

He was flung clear as the thing reared up, but his men were with him and attacked from all sides, hacking and cutting until the beast lay bloody and dead. He rose, wincing as bruised limbs protested, and said, "Marjia?"

"I'm here." She came to his side and put her arms around him, which hurt his ribs somewhat, but he said nothing. "That was brave."

He said, "You're safe."

"Yes." She nodded and he saw her eyes wander frightened about the cavern. "But how many are dead?"

He said, "I don't know; wait," and called up his men that he might tell them what he had guessed—that the beasts were each controlled by a single man and that they should seek the invaders in the dark armor and slay them, and after them their beasts. And then he said to his wife, "Stay here, eh?" and went back to the battle.

It was no easy thing to slay either the remaining creatures or the remaining invaders, but it was done and the Javitz looked to their hurt. There were too many, and Colun wondered how well they could withstand further attacks—and how the strangelings had succeeded in coming so far through the tunnels.

That was readily explained when scouts came back with wounded who told of a sudden massed attack, pressed home by so many invaders, they'd had no chance to send warning but could only fight and die where they stood.

"Then where are they?" Colun asked a Grannach whose face was forever scarred and whose left arm would never again bend readily. "Were there so many, where have they gone?"

That question, too, was answered as they licked their wounds and messengers hurried to the other family caverns to pass on and bring back news. Colun flinched when he heard it.

All the caves were assaulted, but that, for all the loss of life, seemed only a diversion designed to concentrate the families each within their own cavern, to draw them in from the high passes.

There, so word came, the invaders poured through, deep into the mountains, in such numbers as the Grannach could never hope to oppose.

"O Maker, stand with us now." Colun closed his eyes as he heard the news. Then opened them wide: "We must speak of this, all the families."

"You need rest." Marjia set a hand on his shoulder. "You've broken ribs and more bruises than I can count."

Colun patted her hand, though the movement cost him pain. "There's no time for rest," he said. "Save that last one the Maker gives us all, and I'm not ready for that yet."

"We Shapers can seal the tunnels," Baran said. "All of them, needs be. Lock the Javitz in safe."

"Ach, did we not speak of this?" Colun shook his head, and groaned. "Family by family, or as one people?"

"We'd be safe." Baran shrugged. "The Javitz would survive."

"And the world outside?" Colun began to move his head, thought better of it. "Shall we leave that go? Shall we Grannach all become moles—each family to its own sealed cavern? Shall we let these strangelings pass us by to conquer Ket-Ta-Witko?"

"What other choice have we?" Baran asked.

"To do what's right," Colun said. "To fight them as an army."

The creddans of the other families were of a different opinion.

All had suffered losses, not all were convinced the attacks were merely diversions.

"We fought them off," Janzi said. "We can do it again."

"Whilst they go through the passes?" Colun asked. "Into Ket-Ta-Witko?"

"Perhaps we're not so much in love with the flatlanders as you," said Gort. "Why should we fight their battles?"

"Is it not our duty to guard these hills?" Colun asked.

"We do," Janzi said. "We shall."

"Only that?" Colun looked from one creddan to the other. "I'd thought our duty extended farther."

"We guard the mountains," Gort said. "We do our duty by the Maker."

"The western tunnels are sealed, no?" Daryk said. "So they surely cannot attack again."

"Save they cross the mountains and turn back," Colun said, "from the east."

"Ach!" Janzi made a gesture of irritated dismissal. "How shall they pass through the hills? They'll die up there."

"How did they enter our tunnels?" asked Colun.

"We were not ready," Janzi said. "Now we are."

"Not ready?" Colun frowned. "We've been fighting them long enough, no?"

Janzi at least had the grace to look a moment ashamed. Then he said, "We were not ready for such numbers."

"Perhaps if we sealed all the tunnels?" Menas ventured. "Of east and west both?"

"And starve?" asked Colun. "Our meat come from the valleys, no? And our crops. Would you lock those off?"

Menas shrugged.

"What do you suggest?" Daryk asked.

"That we forgo our differences," Colun said. "That we fight as an army, all unified."

"And doubtless with you as our commander," Janzi said, and spat.

"No." This time Colun remembered not to shake his head. "I say only that we need act as one, are we to defeat these strangelings."

"We have," said Gort. "There are none left alive in the caverns."

"Ach, for now," Colun said. "But do they cross the mountains, think you they'll let us be? I tell you they'll come back against us."

"And I tell you that our caves are safe for now," Daryk said, "and it must surely take these strange folk time to cross the hills, if they can. So we've time to think on all this."

"We've no time at all!" Colun said.

"I think Daryk is right," said Menas. "I think we should ponder this."

"By the Maker!" Colun fisted an angry gesture. "What's to ponder? We are attacked! Invaders cross our mountains! What's left to ponder?"

"Much," said Daryk.

"Yes," said Gort. "I'm with Daryk. I say we think on all of this and not rush to decisions."

Menas nodded his agreement. "And the while, look to our family caverns."

Colun sighed and muttered a curse: he saw dark and bloody times ahead.

And so it went, in the Grannach way, slow as stone and as inexorable. And as they pondered, the invaders drove ever deeper into the mountains and into the high passes, moving relentlessly toward Ket-Ta-Witko. The Grannach fought them—not as Colun would have it, as a single unified army, but in the old way, family by family—and though many died, there seemed always more, the horde careless of its losses so that even when the Shapers sent avalanches down to bury the columns, or warriors tumbled boulders on them, still when the dust had cleared the horde pressed on, clambering over stone and corpses alike. The invaders seemed impervious to the cold of the high peaks and the rain that fell as the year aged, as if they were some mindless gestalt unlimited by physical considerations or any kind of sentiment save bloodlust.

Colun thought it could be only a matter of time before the enemy held the hills and the Grannach hid like rabbits in a sealed warren, awaiting their executioners. And then, he thought, the weirdlings would likely flood down into Ket-Ta-Witko to strike against the Matawaye, and the Grannach have no allies left in all the world. He thought he could not allow that, but neither was he sure what to do, what he *could* do.

22 Each in His Own Place

Morrhyn could not, during those brief interludes when he woke and understood where he was, understand how he lived. He had no food, and for all the hot spring warmed the cave a little, it was scarce enough to fend off the cold outside. Snow fell there—when he opened his eyes, he could see its drifting white curtain like a veil across the cave mouth—but he lacked the strength, or perhaps the will, to crawl so far as the entrance to see how deep it lay on the slopes or which moon stood in the sky, and so he only dragged himself to the well to sip the thick metallic water and then huddle again in the folds of bearskin and blanket and return to the dreaming. It was all he had. He hoped his horse survived; he doubted he should live, and could not care. His life was of no importance—one small spark amongst many, already sputtering as cold and hunger took their toll—and it seemed to him the Maker kept him alive only to dream, which he could not decide was punishment or reward.

It was strange to find his talent returned him only to reveal such horror. He supposed the Maker granted him final revelation, and that he would die in the cave when the last mystery was uncovered. He could not imagine climbing back down the mountain to speak of what he learned—did any still live below to hear it—for he was very weak and could not imagine making that descent. He thought that likely his bones would rest here forever, time stripping off the flesh with none to bring them home, for surely none other would be crazed enough to come here.

He wished he might bring back to the People word of what he dreamed, what he learned, but that was an old desire from another life: one he'd known before he came there, which was gone. His life now was the cave and the dreaming, nothing else, and his quest now seemed prideful and vain, the boasting of a dreamless Dreamer seeking some personal validation. It seemed to him a magnificent irony that his pride be answered with revelation, and that he then die alone with all that knowledge.

He drew the bearskin over his head and closed his eyes again, slipping on the instant back into the dream.

This must be how the Maker saw his creation, as if he looked out through his eyes, aware of all in all places, without time's barrier, but all contiguous. Save he was not the Maker, but only a man, and what he saw was so vast, he could not properly comprehend it or order it. It was larger and infinitely more complex than his poor mind might encompass, so that it seemed as if images of knowledge raced through his head too swift he could grasp it all, but see only parts.

But those parts!

He saw the folk who named themselves the Breakers cross the salt desert that boundaried the country of the Whaztaye. He saw their beastmasters drive their awful charges against the People Beyond the Hills, and the warrior horde come after. He saw the Whaztaye slain, and fleeing; and the Grannach succor them in the foothills. Uselessly, for he saw what the Breakers did (and stirred, horrified by the vision) knowing that should be the fate of the Matawaye, of his own People, as the Breakers came into the mountains and fought their way into the Grannach tunnels, and the high passes . . .

Where he saw Grannach slain by beasts and Breakers, and Colun fight them and argue for unity and be ignored so that he came to a decision even as the Grannach argued amongst themselves just as his own People had argued at Matakwa, and went each their own way, ignorant—or wilfully blind—to the larger danger . . .

Which set Tachyn and Commacht to fighting, which he saw as if he stood invisible in the midst of battle, watching Racharran charge a band of Chakthi's warriors alone, his men all spread about behind in defense of the helpless ones . . .

And Rannach in a valley with Arrhyna, where alders grew beside a river and Arrhyna swelled with child, and he knew that Rannach did not know, for Arrhyna was afraid as yet to tell him, fearing he'd bring her back to the lodges of the Commacht and die there . . .

Save that was already too late, for the Breakers crossed the mountains and would soon come against the Commacht, and all the People, and destroy them. Save . . .

There was a thing he did not understand, which floated on more water than he'd ever seen, swallowing wind in great squares of white l like flattened tents, and spat flame from metal pipes against creatures such as the Breakers used, and on the floating thing . . .

There was a Dreamer who . . .

Came to an unknown land, frightened of his talent (which Morrhyn could not understand) and denied it . . .

Because his world contained Breakers of a different kind, who . . .

Fire then: he woke drenched in sweat, and instantly shivered in the cave's chill, and drew the bearskin and the blanket tighter around his wasted body and dove back down into the dream . . .

Which showed the Breakers passing the mountains because . . .

The Ahsa-tye-Patiko was ignored when Vachyr stole Arrhyna with his father's blessing, and Chakthi was eaten by the black wind from the mountains . . .

And Rannach slew Vachyr when he might have taken the kidnapper alive, but did not because Arrhyna urged him to slay her abductor and he knew only hatred and pride . . .

Which drove Chakthi to what he did . . .

And Hadduth—worst of all—was tainted by the black wind and knew not what he did, save he was blinded as all the other Dreamers. But still . . .

The Tachyn would waste and destroy the Commacht even as the Breakers came down against all the People. Unless . . .

. . . It was as if that same black wind stirred cloudy over Morrhyn's dreaming, so that he wondered in his sleep if the Breakers were stronger than the Maker . . .

And saw them drive the People, all the Matawaye, all the Commacht and Tachyn, the Lakanti, the Naiche and the Aparhaso, before them as they had driven the Whaztaye . . .

And the floating thing find a harbor and folk come off the thing to a camp of wooden lodges . . .

And some of them shine like torches calling a lost rider home . . .

And flee from . . .

He was not sure . . . The Breakers or the People? There seemed no difference in the malign intent he sensed.

Only that those three shone like beacons in the darkness of his dreaming, and that . . .

He must find them, even as a rider lost in night and fog looks for the lights of home and asks the Maker his horse tread sure and not fall into hole or mire, but only come safe back . . .

But he could not understand how, for they were—he did not understand how he knew this, only that he did—not of his world, but of one of those contiguous with his, as if all the worlds spun around one another and nothing existed alone but all in perpetual coexistence so that all moved together and crossed and were the same and at the same time different . . .

And that, somehow, in a manner he could not understand, his world and theirs must come together to defeat the Breakers . . .

And that it was his task to make it so: and therefore to live . . .

. . . Which he could not understand at all, for he could not conceive of living: Surely he was destined to die here, in this cave.

Surely that was his fate . . . To dream these dreams that opened worlds to him and showed him past and future as if that were the Maker's last gift to him before he died . . .

But he had not seen it all; did not know it all.

He knew somewhat of things past and somewhat of things to come; but so much was yet veiled in mystery . . .

. . . Who were the Breakers? Where did they come from? *Why* were they so malign, so intent on destruction?

. . . And those strangers who shone so bright: who were they?

It seemed then that a light shone and he looked into its brightness and it spoke in words of flame that had no sound but what he heard inside the channels of his mind and the marrow of his bones and the core of his waning life: it said, *When the dream is done, go tell them. Go find them. Go do what you must, if you've the strength. That, or die with all your People.*

And he could not deny it, so he rose and hugged his bearskin to him and crawled to the cave mouth and looked out to where the snow fell over crags and peaks and far steep-walled valleys where lights moved that he knew were the lights of the Breakers as they wound their way to Ket-Ta-Witko, which they would conquer and leave waste after all the People were slain unless he obeyed the voice of the flame.

So he crawled back to the spring and drank and felt very afraid, for he still did not think he could survive the downward climb and that even if he somehow did, then still surely the Breakers must find him and slay him, and even did they not, then how could he, afoot, find his clan or any of the People in time to warn them?

You survived the journey here, the flame inside his eyes said. *You will survive the journey back, have you the courage.*

I am afraid, he answered. I am very afraid. And what good shall it do? Shall I tell them they are to die?"

No, said the flame. *Sleep and understand.*

So he slept, and dreamed again. Of an answer.

"Does he live?" Lhyn asked her husband. And then: "Be still, I must bind this."

Racharran sighed and held his wounded arm rigid as she wound a moss-filled bandage around the cut. "I don't know," he said. "How could I? He went away when we need him most. I'm not a Dreamer, that I can answer such questions."

"No." Lhyn tied off the bandage. "You're akaman of the Commacht."

"What does that mean?"

Lhyn set the remaining moss back in its pouch and faced him square. "We lose too many," she said. "First our son, and then Morrhyn. How many more?"

"This war is none of my making," he said. "It's all Chakthi's doing. I've looked to avoid it, but he sends his warriors all the time against us. What else can I do but fight?"

"You might have kept Morrhyn with us," she answered.

"How?" Racharran flexed his arm. The arrow had gone deep, but he thought he would not lose mobility; it was not the first cut he'd taken. "I did my best to dissuade him, but he'd have none of it. The Maker summoned him, he said—'I think I might find answers there,' he said— and would not be dissuaded."

"You could have held him," she replied. "Bade him remain."

"What is this?" Racharran asked. "You seem more concerned for Morrhyn than for Rannach."

"Rannach you sent off with Colun," she returned, "knowing he and Arrhyna would be safe with the Grannach. Morrhyn went alone, when Tachyn ride against us and he'd go where none have gone before."

"I could not stop him," he said. "How could I?"

"I don't know," she said. "Only that I am afraid for him."

"As am I," he said.

Lhyn said, "I know; I'm sorry. But . . ."

Racharran opened his arms and she came into them and he held her close, thankful for the comfort of her body. The year's events frightened him, disturbed all his notions and concepts of the world so that it seemed nothing was any more fixed or permanent but all blown about in disorder as if a vast and unfelt storm raged—but Lhyn's presence was an anchor in that gale.

"These are strange times," he said.

"I do not understand them," she said, and felt a pang of guilt that she felt greater fear for Morrhyn than for her son. It was as if his going had opened a hole in her, revealed only by his departure, his absence. She had not known it was there before, and she told herself that it was only because Morrhyn went into the unknown whilst Rannach went escorted by Colun's Grannach and must surely be safe with them. Whereas Morrhyn . . .

She hugged her husband tighter and said against his chest, "I am afraid."

"We are all afraid." He stroked her hair, watching the play of fire-light on the gold all threaded through with silver, and for a while pretended all was well: that they rested comfortable in their lodge and there was no war, nor any hunger, nor so many burial scaffolds in the trees, nor winter coming on.

But he was akaman of the Commacht, and such pretendings were not a luxury in which he could indulge. There were too many scaffolds in the trees and too many widows weeping in the lodges. The Falling Leaf Moon stood over the camp and soon the White Grass Moon would rise, and there were too few supplies stored up against the cold moons, for there had been no time for hunting with Chakthi's Tachyn always prowling.

He resisted the urge to sigh, looking past Lhyn's head to the fire, wishing Morrhyn were there. Even bereft of his dreams, the wakanisha had been a rock on which he might lean. But Morrhyn was gone away, and Racharran could not know if he was slain by the Tachyn as Lhyn feared, or lived, or starved, or . . . It was, Racharran thought, as if all the world had gone mad, all turned upside down and shaken by forces he did not understand. Chakthi pressed his war long past the time of fighting—no one fought after the Moon of Ripe Berries was gone—and surely the Tachyn must be as poorly set for winter as his own Commacht. Ach, even Yazte had called back his Lakanti warriors to cull the buffalo herds as they migrated, that his people have hides and meat and rich marrow to see out the winter. He had apologized, and Racharran could not argue. How could he ask the Lakanti to go hungry when the wolf winds blew and the grass was all hard and white, and the herds went away to the south? He could not; he could only accept Yazte's promise of charity, that whatever excess the Lakanti took would be gifted to the Commacht.

As if my clan is become a widow, he thought bitterly, dependent on charity.

And Juh and Tahdase, for all he had sent messengers entreating their aid, had done nothing. Save take their people far from the fighting, as if it were none of their affair but only a squabble between the Commacht and the Tachyn, which Racharran, even without Morrhyn's advice, sensed it was not. He thought then of what Morrhyn had said of a dark wind blowing over Ket-Ta-Witko, and shivered.

"What?" Lhyn asked, and he drew the furs up closer and held her and said in answer, "Nothing. Only a chill."

And thought, Such a chill as I've never known, as if the Wolf Moon rises and sets its cold claws in my bones.

He closed his eyes and thought of what folk said of Morrhyn: that the wakanisha betrayed his clan; that he was gone mad; that the Maker turned his face from the Dreamer. None of it to Racharran's face, but he heard the whispers and could do little to prevent them, for Morrhyn *was* gone away and even Racharran must wonder if that was wise. He must fight anger then, for he wanted the wakanisha with him, even dreamless. Morrhyn could at least interpret the Ahsa-tye-Patiko, which seemed to Racharran all sundered and forgotten, and help him hold the young men in check.

They chafed at his decision that the clan avoid conflict as best it could, arguing that it were better they fight fire with fire and attack Chakthi's folk as the Tachyn attacked them. Some had ventured to attempt that, and had ridden onto the Tachyn grass. Not many had come back. Rannach's comrades—Zhy and Hadustan—had been amongst them, and now their bones lay unhonored in the Tachyn country and Bakaan limped from a wound in his thigh where a lance had pierced him, and cursed and muttered that Rannach would make a better leader than his father.

It was hard to keep them controlled: they were like young buffalo bulls eager to test their mettle. But the Maker knew, there was surely fighting enough. It seemed that no matter where the Commacht went, even to the farthest reaches of the clan's territory, still Chakthi sent his warriors against them. It was as if grief made him mad, blind to the needs of his own people, consumed by a dreadful hatred that lusted entirely for destruction.

Racharran could not understand that. How Chakthi could ignore impending winter, when surely his folk must suffer, in pursuit of vengeance? He prayed that the rising of the White Grass Moon see an end to the fighting, but doubted, even as he prayed, that it should.

Then he thought of Rannach and Arrhyna and prayed they be safe, and Morrhyn, and into his mind came oozing doubt and accusation. Had Rannach only heeded his pleas and not sought Arrhyna for his bride, none of this would have happened. And then that had Rannach only come to him when he found Arrhyna stolen, Vachyr might still live and Chakthi have no cause to fight. He felt anger then, at his son's pride and wilfullness, and then guilt—for had Rannach not come back and honestly presented himself to the Council and accepted his punishment? Save Chakthi saw it not as punishment but salvation, and ignored his own son's sins and looked for blood.

The sigh that Racharran had earlier stifled burst forth. His wounded arm throbbed and a weight sat in his soul that so many suffered and died and he had no answers save to run.

"What is it?" Lhyn rose on an elbow. "Does your arm hurt you?"

"A little," he said. "It's nothing. I think we must strike camp tomorrow."

"Again?" She checked his bandaged arm as she spoke. "So soon?"

"We must make winter camp soon." He shifted as she examined his arm. He did not, at that moment, want her to see his eyes, the worry there. "We can't keep running."

"Surely Chakthi'll not fight through the winter," she said.

He said, "I hope not. But . . . When the snows come, we shall need a good place."

"The Wintering Ground?" she asked.

He shook his head. "Chakthi likely knows of that. Or has some notion of where it is. No: we need another place this year."

"We always go there," she said. "Every year."

"This," he said, "is not a year like any other."

Lhyn said, "No," and touched his face. "You carry a heavy burden, my husband."

"I'm akaman of the Commacht," he said. "What other choice have I?" Save, he thought even as he regretted it, that I run away like Morrhyn.

"Where shall we go?" she asked.

"I was thinking," he replied, "that there's that valley to the south, where the river bends. Sometimes buffalo winter there."

Lhyn nodded. "That would be a good place, I think."

"But not straight away," he said. "We'll move about awhile, in case. Then when the White Grass Moon rises, we'll go there. We should be safe there, the Maker willing."

"The Maker willing," Lhyn agreed, and pushed him down. "Now shall you sleep?"

Racharran said, "In a while. But not yet," and turned toward his wife.

Lhyn said, "Your arm . . ."

"Is not hurting," he lied, and moved under the furs as she opened her arms to him.

Perhaps for a little while longer he *could* pretend.

It was an answer Morrhyn did not properly understand, so perhaps it was not an answer at all but rather a possibility, dependent on him and those others who would heed his words. He could not be sure, and supposed that was the Maker's way—not to define certainly, but to open gates to possible paths for those willing to follow him, to follow his way, which was the Ahsa-tye-Patiko. Morrhyn wondered how many would listen; and then how he might reach them. He thought again that he could not, that he was too weak to attempt the climb, and that even did he survive, he must still cross the wide breadth of Ket-Ta-Witko to bring the word. And Ket-Ta-Witko was surely full of enemies now, both those born of the People and those born of that other race, the Breakers.

He shuddered as he thought of what the dreaming had revealed, of what they were and did and why. It was an evil so vast, he could barely fold his mind around it, and so vile he had sooner not contemplate it but only act.

Which seemed impossible. Surely better to seek the dream again, and in it find a surer answer: he bathed his face and drank and wrapped the furs around his skinny body and looked to sleep. But sleep was refused him. It would not come and so he could not dream, but only lie restless, his head all abuzz with horrid knowledge until it seemed the easier thing to rise and go out from the cave. And if he died attempting this gret task set on him, then that at least should be surcease from the awful knowledge he now owned. So he rose on trembling legs and stumbled to the cave mouth and stared out on a world gone all wintry white, with little prospect in it of survival.

Icicles depended from the arch of the cave, and where the spring spilled out across the ledge before, the warm water carved a narrow channel through snow for a little way and then became iced and glittery in the sun, which shone so bright against the snow, its light was blinding, a stab of pain against his eyes. He drew back, thinking that he must build a fire and paint his face with charcoal in defense against snowblindness; and then that he had no fire, nor the wood for its making.

And then it came to him that it was entirely impossible he could have survived his sojourn in the cave without a fire, without food. He should be dead—not on the climb down, but *now*. Indeed, long days past, for no man could survive these heights, this cold, without food and warmth. But he *was* alive. He did not believe he was become a ghost, for he could feel the heat of the spring and taste its mineral-laden water, and he shivered in the chill of the ledge. He could feel the wind on his face, and when he pricked his knife to his wrist—a final test—he felt the sting and saw blood come red from the wound. Surely ghosts did not feel such pain, or bleed. So he was not a ghost, but lived—and if he could not understand how that should be, then it was surely the Maker's doing: there existed a reason he survived.

A duty, he decided, albeit somewhat reluctantly. The Maker has kept me alive so that I might bring word to the People. Or, at least, granted me the chance to bring them word of salvation. So the rest is up to me and them. It seemed a vast and terrible duty, and likely impossible of achieving. But had he not come to this place in search of answers? And they were given him—so should he now renege that duty?

He could not: that should be a betrayal of the Maker and himself and all the People.

So he wrapped himself against the awful cold and made obeisance, and then began the impossible climb down.

23 Landfall

Had the exiles not been confined to the hold as the *Pride of the Lord* approached Salvation, they would have seen a coastline of humped yellow dunes sweeping away to north and south, the sand breaking against pine-clad ridges. Below decks, however, they could only wonder as the schooner heeled, Shipmaster Bennan aligning her bows on the opening of Deliverance Bay, knowing they should soon disembark, delivered to their final destination. They would have seen the headlands that embraced the cove, affording the bay calm anchorage, and the ominous bulk of Grostheim's wooden walls beside the mouth of the Restitution River. But all they knew was that the motion of the ship altered, and that above decks the sailors shouted cheerfully, happy to at last find safe landing. It was no easy thing to wait confined in semidarkness as their future loomed unseen, the place of their banishment no longer a distant prospect but now immediate, waiting invisible as they listened and wondered.

Peering up through the hatch, Arcole saw sails furled, and felt the schooner slow, drifting of her own impetus awhile. Then there were shouts and lines were tossed to unseen boats, the *Pride of the Lord* taken in tow until finally she lurched, her timbers groaning as they struck what he guessed must be a dock.

More noise then, and activity, as the ship was moored and the gangplank run out. The *Pride of the Lord* sighed and creaked, settling as if thankful her journey was done; and all the exiles could do was wait still.

Arcole smiled at Davyd and Flysse, essaying a confidence he did not entirely feel. "So, our future beckons, eh? It shall feel odd to tread dry land again."

Neither answered him, but smiled nervously, their eyes shifting from him to the hatch above. At last that hatch was thrown back and they were summoned to the deck, Militiamen shouting that they form orderly there.

The sun was bright after the gloom of the hold, and the wind that blew a welcome refreshment. Arcole looked about, seeing a gentle landscape: woods bosky in the distance, a wide river that ran all silvery inland, and, beside it, Grostheim. He had not known what to expect of this wilderness settlement—not a town such as graced the Levan, but surely not this fortress. It was a construction of wood, high walls daubed with hex signs and topped with watchtowers, the mouths of cannon there, and the glint of sunlight on bayonets where soldiers patrolled the ramparts. Whatever buildings accommodated the inhabitants were hidden behind the walls, those broken by heavy gates from which a timbered road ran down to the dock. There, he saw the red coats of the regular Militia mingling with the blue of Var's marines, a line of roughly clad men, each one wearing the brand of exile on his cheek, trudging back toward the fort. It was hard to think of that place as a town. He wondered why such fortification was necessary, if Salvation was indeed the empty land of popular supposition, but perhaps it was simply the Evanderan way.

On the dockside he saw Tomas Var and Captain Bennan conversing with two strangers. One wore the scarlet tunic of the Militia, its epaulets and braid announcing him a major, and Arcole guessed him to be the garrison commander. The other—presumably the governor—occupied a sedan chair, attended by four uniformed servants. As Arcole watched, all four glanced toward the schooner and he saw Var gesture, but what they said he could not hear, nor interpret their expressions.

Then Var returned on board to order the newcome exiles disembark. He met Arcole's eye but said nothing, only took his place at the head of the column alongside the red-coated officer and strode briskly toward the gates.

It was, indeed, odd to tread dry land again. It was immobile under Arcole's feet, and for a moment he staggered, become more accustomed to the constant shift of the deck. He felt Flysse clutch his arm and took her elbow, Davyd on her other side as they went unsteadily toward their fate.

Past the gates he saw walkways spanning the upper levels of the walls, connecting the watchtowers, and all around cannon and swivel guns as if Grostheim prepared for war or siege. Then there were build-ings—all wood, the only stone used in construction of chimneys. He supposed timber must be more plentiful here, and thought this settle-ment a strange place, quite unlike any town he had seen. It was impossi-ble to tell which structures were commercial and which domestic, for they all had the same rough-hewn uniformity, as if Grostheim were all one enormous barracks.

He turned his attention to the folk they passed. Those men inden-tured were easy to identify: all wore the brand upon their cheeks. Those who did not, nor were dressed in uniform, he assumed to be officials of the Autarchy or such adventurers as looked to make their fortunes colo-nizing this new world. The few women he saw appeared to fall into two distinct categories: there were some better dressed, who looked on the procession with a mixture of curiosity and distaste; others were poorer clad and watched incuriosly, or with expressions of pity. He guessed that those were marked upon their arms, like Flysse. He thought he had much to learn of this place.

They reached a square flanked on one side by a church—that edifice recognizable—the pastor studying them dispassionately, and were herded by, into a street that ended at a large building with the look of a warehouse or storage barn. Hex signs were painted across its frontage. At the head of the column, the major flung up an arm, halting them as he climbed the three steps up to the building's porch.

"I am Major Alyx Spelt," he announced. Arcole wondered why the officers of the Autarchy found it always necessary to declare their names. "I command the God's Militia in Grostheim, and for now you are in my care. This"—he gestured at the building behind him—"will be your home awhile. In time you will be assigned your owners, but until then you remain here. You will be fed and watered; there are blankets in-side."

He proceeded to outline conditions of behavior. Arcole listened with half an ear, studying the man.

Spelt was in his middle years, gray already streaking his temples. His face was deeply tanned and deeper lined, gray eyes peering from be-neath craggy brows. He looked, Arcole thought, to be carved from the same timber as Grostheim itself, weathered and harsh. He wore a saber and a brace of pistols, and all the while he spoke, his fingers drummed against the silver-chased butts. Arcole noticed that his fingers were stained dark with tobacco, the nails chewed down and ragged. He formed the impression that this Major Alyx Spelt hid tension behind a screen of discipline.

When the man was done speaking, two soldiers swung the doors open. Like cattle herded to a byre, the newcomers were marched inside. It was not unlike that warehouse that had been their last resting place in Evander, as if they were not human folk but only living cargo to be stored until dispensed. The floor was hard-packed earth, its only covering the blankets strewn carelessly about. Along two walls there were windows cut, glassless and set high, allowing just enough light the occupants might see one another. At the farther end stood a wooden partition separating the main area from what were, by the sour odor, open latrines. Two water butts flanked the doors, beside them stacks of earthenware platters and crude-fashioned mugs, none too clean.

Arcole led Flysse and Davyd to a place close by the doors. By dint of the reputation earned aboard the *Pride of the Lord,* none argued, and they gathered blankets for their beds. Arcole wondered how cold the night might be, and how long they would remain before they were— What had Spelt said?—"assigned your owners"? He hoped Var's promised intercession would favorably influence the governor. All well, he might find some comfortable position, learn about this place, and then . . . No, best not allow his hopes too free a rein. That should be too much akin to assuming a round of petanoye won on the first deal; wiser to b be patient, learn all he might, and then decide how to play the hand.

Tomas Var accepted the glass the servant proffered, waiting in dutiful silence as the governor ostentatiously tamped his pipe. They sat in what Wyme described as his "sanctum"—for sake of privacy, Var assumed. Captain Bennan waited in an outer room, entertained by the governor's lady, Celinda, and Major Spelt concluded his duties in the town. Wyme had expressed a desire to hear a summary of Var's report before they ate, so now Var sat in an overstuffed chair facing a massive desk, both items —like every other piece of furniture in the mansion—imported from Evander. He could not help but wonder at the cost of shipment, and think that it should surely have been easier to obtain pieces made locally. But that was not, he thought, Wyme's style.

He had met Andru Wyme only once before, and not much liked the man then, nor, as yet, found reason to change his mind. He supposed he was at fault in that, for Wyme was well regarded by the Autarchy. His appointment here was evidence of that, for only the most trusted of the Autarchy's officers were granted such position, effectively rulers of this western continent—but still he could not help thinking the man pompous. He thought now that Wyme made him wait deliberately, looking to emphasize his elevation over a mere captain of marines. And the way he dressed his servants—all brocaded waistcoats and silver-buckled shoes that seemed an odd contrast to the brands upon their cheeks—seemed to Var an affectation. While Wyme might love his duty, Var thought, he loved his comfort more. He smiled as an errant thought crossed his mind—Arcole Blayke would feel quite at home here.

"Something amuses you?"

Wyme touched a lucifer to his pipe and inhaled deeply as Var said, "I thought of an exile, a most remarkable man." He gestured at the room. "One I suspect is more accustomed to such quarters than the hold of a transport ship. I'd discuss him with you, by your leave."

"Later." Wyme shook the lucifer, the smell of sulphur a moment pungent, and tossed the spent match away. The waiting servant stooped to retrieve the stick. "First, your report."

Var nodded obediently: Arcole Blayke must, inevitably, play a large part in that.

When he was done speaking, Wyme grunted, thick brows arching over heavy-lidded eyes. "He impressed you, eh?" His tone was noncommittal.

"He saved the ship," Var said. "Were it not for his wits and courage, why, I believe the serpent must have sunk us. Surely far more lives would have been lost."

Wyme motioned for the servant to fill their glasses before he spoke again. "And yet he killed a man and damaged two others—all property of the Autarchy. That cannot be forgotten."

"He fought in defense of others," Var replied carefully, "who are also property of the Autarchy. And he was punished for that."

"Twelve lashes?" Wyme turned his glass between thick fingers, savoring the bouquet. "Hardly fitting for what he did."

"I deemed it adequate. I felt he acted honorably."

"Honorably?" Wyme's brows rose high at that, and he chuckled scornfully. "My dear Var, the man's an *exile*. Do you suggest these people possess notions of honor now?"

His tone, his expression, denied such a notion was acceptable. Not taking his eyes from the governor's face, Var watched the servant. The man's features remained immobile, his ears deaf to the insult.

"I'd say Blayke does. Certainly he's no common criminal. I understand that in the Levan he was regarded as a gentleman, even moved in aristocratic circles."

"In the Levan, perhaps." Wyme's hand described a dismissive arc. "But this is Salvation, and this fellow—Blayke, you name him?—comes here with the brand on his face like any other. Ergo, he *is* a criminal."

"Even so." Var hesitated, torn between fulfilling his promise to Arcole and fear of angering Wyme by pressing too hard. "That he saved the ship must count in his favor, no?"

"Perhaps," Wyme allowed. "But it would not do to give these people airs. God knows, they're the sweepings of humanity." He snorted disdainfully, oblivious of the branded man standing at his elbow. "You say he's some gentlemanly qualities?"

Var said, "Indeed, he has."

"Then I'll consider him for a manservant." Wyme raised his glass. "What think you of this wine?"

"Excellent." Var accepted the change of subject: he had fulfilled his promise and could do no more. "The vineyards flourish?"

"Largely." Wyme scowled, thick lips pursing. "We'll speak of them and other matters at dinner. Now, however, do you apprise me of events at home?"

Var wondered what occasioned the shadow he saw darken the governor's fleshy face. He began to speak of Evander and its subject lands, and by the time he was done, a gong belled, announcing the evening meal.

The governor's dining room was opulent, graced with crystal chandeliers and lace curtains, silverware on the long table and plates of fine imported china. Servants waited attentive behind each chair. Var found himself seated beside Celinda; Alyx Spelt and Captain Bennan faced him across the damask cloth, and Wyme took the head.

Their conversation was at first a disappointment to the marine. There was, he sensed, a topic that went undiscussed as they exchanged news, Celinda demanding he and Bennan tell her of Evander's latest fashions and what gossip circulated—both subjects of little interest to the two visitors. Spelt and Wyme made contribution, but all the while Var remembered the expression on the governor's face and wondered when it should be explained.

His curiosity remained unsatisfied until Celinda withdrew, leaving the men to their pipes and the port shipped over on the *Pride of the Lord*. The table was cleared of all but the decanter and the servants were dismissed before Wyme spoke, and even then softly, as if he feared eavesdroppers.

"We've alarming news," he declared. "It would seem we are not the only inhabitants of Salvation."

Across the table Bennan gulped in surprise, choking on port. Var gasped, setting down his pipe. "But I thought . . ." He gathered his wits, scattered by this unexpected announcement. "It's surely common knowledge none others lay claim to this land."

"That's surely the common *belief*." Spelt's voice was dry, and even though he spoke no louder than Wyme, it seemed his words rattled loud as musket fire. "But it would appear incorrect. We've evidence of others."

"Bloody evidence," Wyme said. "We share this land with savages."

24 Indenture

Like cattle herded to market, the exiles were driven through the streets to an open enclosure, where they were penned under the watchful gaze of Militiamen. The sun was hot and there was no shade. Folk gathered along the fence, studying the newcomers with calculating eyes, and to one side a pavilion afforded shadow to those Arcole assumed to be the aristocracy of Salvation. He saw Tomas Var there, with the major and the man he thought must be the governor; several others, as many women as men. All save the officers, whose uniforms were unchanging, were dressed in outmoded fashion. He wondered if Var had made good his promise, and what good it might do him. At his side, Davyd looked nervously about; Flysse fidgeted with her shawl, her eyes downcast. Almost, Arcole took her hand, for she looked so forlorn.

For those outside the fence—the free folk—this seemed a festive occasion. Their voices were loud as they discussed the likely merits of the exiles. Arcole was reminded of horse auctions he had attended, save now he was in the position of the beast. He liked the feeling not at all. Then the governor raised a hand and silence fell. He spoke a moment with Spelt, and the major barked an order that brought soldiers forward, urging the exiles to a circumnavigation of the pen. Like shuffling animals they were paraded before the onlookers: Arcole must curb his resentment, struggling to assume a docile expression.

As he passed the pavilion he saw Var lean toward the governor and the man nod, waving an indolent hand in his direction. A Militiaman tapped his shoulder, indicating he quit the circle. He heard Davyd's sudden intake of breath and the small cry Flysse gave. He found it difficult to meet their eyes as he followed the soldier to the side of the pen.

"You're in luck," the Militiaman murmured. "Governor's chosen you, an' that's an easy life."

Arcole said nothing in reply, only stood silent as the fates of his fellow exiles were decided.

It appeared the governor and his companions took first pick of the newcomers, for as the circle continued its round, soldiers removed several more to stand with Arcole. He was surprised to find himself so pleased that Flysse was selected, and when she came to his side he could not help returning her smile. Neither when Davyd joined them: he wondered if destiny kept them together.

Then it was the turn of Salvation's lesser citizens, who must bid for their servants.

Gradually the circle thinned, until finally all were accounted for and the ritual of indenture ended. The newcome exiles followed their masters into the streets. Arcole wondered if the governor had selected Flysse and Davyd too.

But then a tall, thin man emerged from the pavilion to beckon Davyd away.

The boy hesitated, taking Flysse and Arcole both by the hand. "I'll see you again," he said.

It was as much a question as a statement, and Arcole nodded, forcing a smile. "No doubt. This seems not so large a place, eh?"

Flysse said, "Take care, Davyd," in a tremulous voice.

"Well, lad?" The thin man beckoned again, though he seemed not overly impatient. "Do you say your farewells and follow me."

"Go on," Arcole urged. "Best not anger your new . . . employer." He could not bring himself to say owner.

Davyd nodded and swallowed, then released their hands and turned toward the thin man, who said, "I am Rupyrt Gahame. You will address me as 'Master' or 'Sieur Gahame.' Your name?"

"Davyd Furth," came the answer, "Sieur Gahame."

Gahame nodded as if satisfied, and walked away. He did not look back, as if he assumed Davyd must follow like, Arcole thought, a trained hound. The boy cast a last, lingering glance back, then squared his shoulders and trotted after the man. Arcole watched him go, quite unaware that Flysse now held his hand. It seemed curiously natural that she should.

He turned to survey the pavilion. The governor still sat in conversation with Spelt and Var, a red-haired woman in a gown fashionable some years past at his side. It was she waved a man forward, clearly issuing instructions, for the fellow bowed and came immediately to the pen.

His cheek marked him as indentured, his outfit as a servant of some kind. Over a shirt of coarse cotton he wore a garish red waistcoat, all brocade and frogging; his breeches ended at the calf, fastened over white stockings that descended to pewter-buckled shoes: Arcole surveyed the uniform with distaste.

"You're to come with me." He halted before Arcole and Flysse. "I'm Nathanial. How're you called?"

Arcole said, "I am Arcole Blayke, and this is Mistress Flysse Cobal."

Nathanial chuckled. "Not here you're not, my friend. You're plain Arcole and she's plain Flysse. For all she's not"—he studied Flysse with a lewd eye—"what you call plain."

He saw Arcole's face darken and his smile disappeared. "No offense, friend Arcole—if she's with you, so be it. But folk like us don't own second names. Just those the masters allow us. Now, come on, before Madame sees you dawdling. No good to upsetting her your first day."

He led the way out of the enclosure and they fell into step beside him, down streets lined with wooden houses, none more than two stories tall. Grostheim was, Arcole thought, a decidedly rustic place. "The governor chose us?" he asked.

"He picked you. You come recommended by that marine captain. Said you saved the ship, he did. Like to hear about that later, I would." Nathanial glanced speculatively at Arcole, then turned to wink at Flysse. "Flysse here, Madame took a fancy to. Reckons she's got the makings of a maid, she does."

So Var had kept his promise: Arcole decided the man was honorable, for all he was an Evanderan. "What am I to be?" he asked.

Nathanial shrugged. "I don't rightly know yet. Most likely a manservant, unless Wyme sets you to working the stables or some such."

"Wyme?" Arcole said.

"Governor Andru Wyme," Nathanial replied. "By God's grace, leader of this colony. That and a little help from his friends—he's a brother who's some sort of high-ranking officer in the Autarchy. Still, it's an easier life in his mansion than many another place. Save you upset him or madame, that is."

"Do you know a man called Rupyrt Gahame?"

Flysse's question surprised Arcole: he was for the moment more interested in discovering what he might of Wyme and his household.

"He's a trader," Nathanial said. "Got the licence to supply weapons and such to the inland settlers. Why?"

Flysse said, "He took a friend."

"That carrot-topped lad?" Nathanial nodded. "Then he's lucky. There're worse masters than Sieur Gahame."

Arcole frowned. Flysse's concern prompted a small pang of guilt that he had not thought more of the boy. "Gahame's an enterprise here?"

"Got a warehouse and an office in Grostheim," Nathanial agreed, "but he travels a good deal inland."

Arcole nodded, hiding his disappointment. It occurred to him that if Gahame took his indentured servants with him when he traveled inland, there might well be opportunity to escape—it might well have served him better had Gahame selected him rather than Davyd. "What lies inland?" he asked.

"Farms and vineyards, some mills. Then the wilderness."

"And what's there?" Arcole made the question deliberately casual.

"What's there?" Nathanial scratched a mop of dark brown hair. "I'd not rightly know. Forest, mostly, so I hear; wild beasts, folks claim. I've never seen it, nor want to. Only been past the walls once."

Arcole glanced up. The walls were clearly visible above the buildings, and on them the red coats of the God's Militia. They seemed suddenly the walls of a prison. "You don't go beyond the walls?" he asked.

"What for?" Nathanial favored him with a puzzled look. "I'd not want to work on a farm nor tend the grapes. No, not me. Born in Avanache, I was, and no wish to see the countryside."

"How long have you been here?"

"Close on eight years."

"And only once stepped past the walls?" Arcole was horrified.

"Not counting the jaunt to the dock, yes." Nathanial nodded cheerfully. "I'm happy enough here; I know when I'm well off. You'll learn that in time, my friend. You'll learn to make the best of it."

Arcole thought not; at least, not in the way Nathanial meant. The fellow appeared to have accepted indenture without thought of rebellion. He would not—by God, he would not! He smiled grimly and turned to Nathanial again.

"I saw the hexes on the walls. Are they to keep us in?"

"No point to that," Nathanial said. "No one escapes."

"None try?"

"No point," came the answer again. "There's nowhere to go, save the wilderness. And only a crazy man'd go there. Get eaten by the wild animals, likely, or starve. There've been a few, but Major Spelt and his redcoats brought them back and they were flogged, then set to hard labor."

"Then why hex the walls?" Arcole demanded.

"Habit, I suppose." Nathanial shrugged. "When they built Grostheim, they didn't know Salvation was empty, so they put the magic marks up there in case. But now, why, there's not even an Inquisitor here to renew the hexes. They've never been tested. For all I know, they don't even work."

"How do you know the wilderness is empty?" Arcole asked.

"Stands to reason, no?" said Nathanial. "They've been cutting back the forest since Grost's time, and there's been no sign of anyone else. The farmers and the wine growers never seen anyone; there's hunters go after game back in there, and they've never seen anyone. No, there's nothing out there save trees and wild beasts."

"No one explores?"

Arcole feared he perhaps plied Nathanial with too many questions, that the man should become suspicious, but he appeared not to notice, or not to mind. Perhaps, Arcole thought, he assumed the newcomers afraid and looked to comfort them, or such questions were usual from those just arrived.

"What for?" Nathanial gave him back. "The land already cleared provides us with all we need, so there's no reason. Leastways, not until more settlers come out." He chuckled with careless cynicism and touched the brand on his cheek. "Or Evander sends more of us folk to clear the forests."

Arcole laughed in response, unamused but seeking to encourage Nathanial. "And the farms and such?" he asked. "They employ indentured folk?"

"Who else'd do the work?" Nathanial favored Arcole with a pitying glance. "Like I say—you've landed easy."

"Don't they ever attempt escape?" Arcole wondered.

Nathanial laughed again. "Don't you listen, friend? *There's nowhere to go.* God, even if a man did flee—even if the redcoats didn't catch him, and he got away—there's nothing but God-knows-how-many leagues of wilderness beyond the farms. And then there're Wyme's hexes."

Sharp, Arcole said, "Wyme's hexes?"

"Aye, Wyme's hexes," Nathanial confirmed. "The governor's got the hexing gift. Not like an Inquisitor, mind you, but enough he can spell a man, or"—with a sidelong glance at Flysse—"a woman. Any of us go past the walls, the governor sets a hex on them. Then the major can hunt them down real easy."

Arcole felt Flysse's hand clench tight on his, and blessed her for asking the question that sprang to his lips: "Shall Davyd be hexed, then?"

"Does Sieur Gahame choose to take him out, yes," Nathanial answered, mistaking her tone for selfish fear. "But you needn't worry—it's only them who go beyond the walls that Wyme hexes. It tires him, I suppose."

This knowledge Arcole filed away for future reference: that Davyd might be hexed could affect his inchoate plans. He mulled the notion, falling silent as they continued through the streets.

Was Nathanial aware of his sudden quiet, the man gave no sign, but kept on talking, speaking of life in Grostheim and the benefits of indenture to Wyme's service as if he would deliver all the information at his disposal in the single lengthy address. There were, he explained, those amongst the governor's servants of higher rank than others, to whom the lesser servants must submit—to wit, the majordomo Benjamyn, the housekeeper Chryselle, the cook Dido, and the head groom Fredrik. He named assorted others, but Arcole paid scant attention: Nathanial's litany forced home the knowledge that he was become such a creature as he had always taken for granted—a servant, faceless. He rubbed at the scar decorating his cheek, anger welling anew so that he must struggle to maintain a bland expression, bite back the retort that he was no man's menial. Here he was exactly that, and did he claim difference he must suffer for his presumption. It sat ill, and in silence he swore that he would accept the indignity no longer than he must.

Then Nathanial halted before a chest-high fence trailed with roses; past the barrier lay lawns and flowerbeds, and a wide drive leading to a portico extending from the frontage of a sizable house. It was constructed in the style of an Evanderan country mansion, but all of wood, so that it looked to Arcole like a grandiose hunting lodge, a folly such as a rich man might order built in the forests.

Nathanial said, "The governor's mansion." And when Arcole moved toward the open gates, "No, no," hastily. "We're not allowed the front entrance. There's a servants' gate out back."

It seemed to Arcole strange to enter a house from the rear, but he steeled himself and followed Nathanial around the fence to a humbler gate that opened into a yard. Wash was hung there to dry, and three women, their rolled sleeves exposing the brands on their arms, labored over steaming tubs. They looked up as Nathanial led Arcole and Flysse across the yard, but did not speak or halt their work.

Nathanial brought the newcomers to a servants' hall, where more indentured folk busied themselves with the sundry tasks that fall to menials. Arcole had never before set foot in this part of a house; never before paused to wonder at a servant's lot. He gazed about, noticing that the men all wore outfits similar to his guide's, and that the women were dressed in uniform dirndls, the skirts white beneath green bodices.

At the farther end of the hall a white-haired man rose to his feet, an expression of inquiry on his lined face. He wore waistcoat and breeches like the others, but his shirt was of finer material, fastened at the neck with a silk foulard, and his shoes were buckled with polished silver.

"Benjamyn," Nathanial said, head bobbing, "these are the two the master's chosen. Flysse and Arcole, they're called."

Benjamyn nodded and waved Nathanial away. He looked to Arcole to be in his latter years, but his eyes were bright as they studied the newcomers, and he held himself rigidly erect. The brand on his cheek was so ancient it was barely visible. He took his time examining them, all the while making a little clucking sound, as if he ticked off mental points.

Finally he spoke: "I am Benjamyn, majordomo of this household. Nathanial has explained arrangements here?"

Arcole nodded. "Yes, he has." Then he frowned as he saw Flysse drop a curtsy. Old habits, he supposed, died hard; likely hard as the acquiring of new.

"Then you understand that after the master and his lady," Benjamyn continued, "you answer to me. Be always obedient, perform your duties, and you shall find this a comfortable home. What are your skills?"

Arcole hesitated. He had anticipated conversation with Wyme, the chance to outline his various abilities in a manner that would convince the governor he be placed in some suitable position—he was unsure how to answer this servant. He was not accustomed to speaking with servants beyond the issuing of requests that were, in reality, orders. He was grateful Flysse spoke up.

"I was a serving girl in a tavern," she said. "Before that I worked on my parents' farm."

Benjamyn nodded, tongue clicking vigorously. "Then perhaps you've the makings of a maid," he said. "But I think we'll start you in the kitchens, does Dido agree."

Bright black eyes turned to Arcole, brows raised questioningly. "And you, Arcole?"

"I . . ." Arcole shrugged helplessly: of a sudden his catalogue of accomplishments seemed of poor advantage. "I am accounted a fair cardsman; I play the harpsichord and the spinet; I can sketch and paint; I box quite well; and I can use a sword or pistol."

Arcole heard someone chuckle. Amongst the wrinkles furrowing

Benjamyn's forehead, two or three grew deeper. It was impossible to tell whether he smiled or frowned. "All very well," he said, "were you a gentleman. But what *useful* talents have you?"

Almost, Arcole said that he *was* a gentleman, but he bit back the claim—it was meaningless now, and he thought it could serve only to damage him in this strange new situation. Instead, he said, "I can ride. In the Levan I was considered a good horseman."

Benjamyn's tongue clicked louder. "Then I think," he said slowly, "that you shall begin your service in the stables. Nathanial, do you take him to Fredrik. Flysse, follow me."

He turned away. Flysse looked to Arcole with something akin to sorrow in her eyes. Arcole stood dumbstruck. A stableman? He was to be a stableman? He moved after Benjamyn, a protest forming—and was halted by Nathanial's hand on his arm.

"Don't argue," whispered the black-haired man. "Else old Benjamyn'll make your life truly miserable."

Arcole could think of few things more miserable than working in the stables, but heeded the warning. Surely in time he must be elevated to some more suitable position, and it would not do to rebel so early. He told himself that access to riding animals might well prove useful and, smarting beneath an expression of assumed docility, he allowed Nathanial to lead him from the hall.

They crossed the yard to another, redolent of the animals penned in the stables that stood against one wall. Two men in leather waistcoats sat on a bench polishing tackle; at Nathanial's shout, a third emerged from the stables.

"Fredrik, this is Arcole. Benjamyn sends him."

Fredrik eyed Arcole much as had the majordomo. He was some years younger, his face dark as old leather, a small, bowlegged man, his graying hair drawn back in a tail fastened with a blue bow.

"So." The bowing of his legs gave him a waddling gait. "You know horses, eh?" His accent belonged to the Levan.

Arcole nodded and said, "I've some skill."

Fredrik cocked his head. "You're Levanite?"

"I am," said Arcole, thinking to have found a friend.

The head groom dashed his hopes. "Don't look for favors on that account, eh? The Levan counts for naught here. We're all exiles, eh?" He tapped his scarred cheek in emphasis. "Show me your hands."

Arcole offered his palms for examination. Fredrik studied them and chuckled. "Ever groomed a horse?"

Arcole answered with a nod.

"Ever cleaned your own tack?"

Arcole shook his head.

Fredrik said, "You'll learn," and turned to the watching grooms. "Wyllem, do you see him kitted out, then put him to work."

Wyllem uncoiled a lanky frame from the bench and beckoned Arcole. "So what were you," he asked, "before you got sent here?"

Arcole said, "A gentleman."

"Well, you're no gentleman here, my friend," Wyllem chuckled. "What'd you do to earn your brand?"

"I killed a man in a duel," Arcole replied.

Wyllem appeared unimpressed. "I stole a pig," he said, and chuckled. "Then I killed it and ate it."

He seemed not much put out that his theft had delivered him to Salvation. Arcole wondered if all exiles accepted their fate so readily. He felt stunned, events moved with a numbing swiftness after the slow days aboard the schooner, and he followed Wyllem in silence as the groom brought him to an outhouse.

"We sleep in here." He pushed the door open, revealing a bare, dirt-floored shed containing four bunks, stabbing a finger at a section at the farther end that was walled off. "Those are Fredrik's quarters. Now, I reckon Bertran's gear'll fit you."

From a chest beside one bunk he produced breeches and a waistcoat the like of his own. Arcole asked, "What happened to Bertran?"

"He died," said Wyllem, grinning at Arcole's expression. "Of old age, be you afeared of fever."

Arcole hoped the clothing had been washed. At least he was allowed to keep his own shirt and boots; at least he need not wear the demeaning uniform of the house servants.

"Right," Wyllem declared when he was done, "now let's get to work."

They returned to the bench, where Wyllem introduced his fellow stableman, a taciturn Evanderan named Gylbert, whose only greeting was a grunt, after which he said nothing more.

As he scrubbed leather and polished harness, Arcole learnt that Wyme owned a stable of four horses and an equipage that was seldom used save when occasion demanded the ceremony of a carriage, or the governor made a trip inland.

"Then," Wyllem explained, "Fredrik handles the reins and we all get dressed up to play coachmen."

"He's no riding animals?" Arcole inquired.

"What for?" Wyllem shook his head, frowning, then chuckled. "Of course, you wouldn't know—the master's crippled, can't barely use his legs. He hobbles about on crutches in the house, and he's a chair and four big fellows to carry it when he goes about the town. Mistress, she's got another. Only sedan chairs in Grostheim, they are, shipped in from Evander."

He seemed proud of that monopoly, which seemed to Arcole very strange. It was as though the stableman felt himself somehow elevated by his master's prominence, and Arcole wondered if all servants felt the same reflected glory. The enormity of his situation sank in, perhaps for the first time: untold leagues separated him from his home, and he entered a world new in more than only geographic terms. He came close then to cursing Dom for that act supposed kind that had saved him from execution only to bring him here. But here he was, and now must make the best of it, even be he a stranger in a strange new world. He had, he recognized, much to learn—that what lessons he had accrued from contact with Flysse and Davyd were only a beginning.

"And does he hex you . . . us . . . when he travels abroad?" he asked.

"Nathanial told you about the master's gift, eh?" Wyllem smiled. "No, not us. Likely because he never goes past the walls without a squadron of Major Spelt's Militiamen along. No point to using his hex power when a musket ball can stop you from running, eh? Anyway, there's nowhere to go. Didn't Nathanial tell you that?"

"Yes," Arcole replied, "he did. He said there's only empty wilderness out there."

"Well then," said Wyllem, "there you are."

"Yes." Arcole sighed. "Here I am."

"You sleep here." Gahame indicated a corner of the warehouse, screened by crates, a mattress, and blankets on the floor. "There's a pump in the yard for washing, and you'll eat with the others. Those are your only clothes?"

"Yes, 'Sieur Gahame." Davyd nodded, surveying his quarters. He hoped there were no rats; at least there was a window looking onto the yard outside.

"Well, we'll have to see what we can find you," Gahame said. "I'll not have my indentured folk in stinking rags."

Davyd did not think his clothes stank, nor were they unduly ragged, but he said dutifully, "No, 'Sieur Gahame."

"As to your duties." Gahame paused. "Why were you exiled?"

Davyd hesitated. "I was caught trying to steal, 'Sieur Gahame . . ."

The thin man nodded thoughtfully. "Best not try such tricks with me, eh?" His tone was mild, but Davyd heard the threat beneath and shook his head vigorously.

"Oh, no, 'Sieur Gahame, I'd not do that. It was only that I was starving."

"Could you not find honest work?"

Gahame eyed him speculatively and Davyd shook his head, dissembling. "Work's hard to find in Bantar, 'sieur. Leastways when you're like me, and an orphan." He assumed what he hoped was a suitably crestfallen expression and added an element of truth, "I might've begged, but I didn't like to do that."

"A point in your favor," Gahame said. "But tell me: were you orphaned, why were you not placed in a workhouse?"

"I don't know, 'sieur," Davyd said, which was more or less the truth. "But I wasn't, and I had no money, and, well . . ." He shrugged expressively.

"To steal is to sin," Gahame declared. "Are you a believer, Davyd?"

Davyd nodded enthusiastically, omitting to say just what he believed in.

"Then," said Gahame, "you will be pleased to know that I allow my servants to attend church. In fact, I insist on it."

"Oh," said Davyd, "good. I shall enjoy that, 'Sieur Gahame."

Which was an absolute lie, for the idea filled him with renewed terror that he found difficult to conceal. In Bantar he had avoided churches as he avoided the Inquisitors and the Militia, for fear the priests owned the ability to sniff out his dreaming. Perhaps it was different here, but still the notion filled him with dread. It was a dilemma—he'd gain this man's goodwill, and could hardly refuse if Gahame insisted he attend services; did he protest, then it might be Gahame would suspect him and he be found out anyway. He wished Arcole were present to counsel him, but Arcole was gone and he must rely on his own wits.

"What's amiss?" he heard Gahame ask. "You're gone all pale, lad."

Davyd forced his mouth to parody a weak smile and mumbled, "You're too kind, 'sieur. I'd not expected such kindness."

"I do no more than any God-fearing man," Gahame said, though he appeared pleased with Davyd's response. "Now, tell me, have you any especial skills that might be useful in my enterprise?"

Not save you need locks picked, Davyd thought, or purses cut, but he shook his head and said, "I don't think so, 'sieur. What is the nature of your enterprise?"

"Of course, you'd not know." Gahame smiled, a benefactor proud of his success. "I've the governor's licence to supply the folk of Salvation with arms, also general hardware. Anyone in all this land requiring a musket, ball, or powder, also tools—ax heads, plowshares, and the like —must come to me. Or I go to them."

"You travel beyond Grostheim's walls?" That seemed to Davyd a somewhat unpleasant notion: he was familiar with cities, not the countryside, which struck him as a vaguely dangerous place. He had sooner remain safe behind the walls of this small city, even must he risk priestly discovery. It was an afterthought to add, "Sieur Gahame."

The trader seemed not to notice the lapse, though he was aware of Davyd's discomfort and chuckled encouragingly. "There's no danger in Salvation," he said confidently. "Save the odd wild beast come awandering out of the forest, and those we can easily shoot. No, lad, have no fear on that account—my weapons are used for hunting only. Besides, I'd not take you along yet. Until you're better seasoned, I'll find you work about these premises; you'll not be idle, I promise you."

Dutifully, Davyd nodded.

"Well, then," Gahame said, "follow me and I'll introduce you to your fellows." He strode away, Davyd at his heels.

Davyd thought this Rupyrt Gahame seemed a decent enough master. Save for this disturbing business of the church, he thought he'd landed on his feet. He wondered how Flysse and Arcole fared, and when he might see them again.

Flysse followed Dido, wondering how the woman could be so thin. Mistress Banlyn had ruled the cookhouse of the Flying Horse, and she had been, to put it kindly, an ample woman. But Dido, for all she was undoubted mistress of the mansion's kitchen, was gaunt. She looked to Flysse as if she hardly ate, her pale skin stretched tight over prominent bones so that she appeared all hollows and sharp angles that gave her a forbidding appearance. Her narrow face suggested asperity, but as yet she had shown Flysse only kindness.

Flysse had felt nervous when Benjamyn brought her to the cook— much as she had felt when first she approached the patroness of the Flying Horse—so she had curtsied and stood silent as the majordomo introduced her. But then he had left and Dido had given warm greeting, escorting her personally to the room she was to share with the three other scullions and the five housemaids. It had looked to Flysse neither worse nor better than her quarters in the tavern, and the underclothes and dirndl she must wear afforded her no embarrassment—it seemed to her quite natural that servants should be uniformed. She thought that

Arcole must find it far harder, for he was quite unaccustomed to that lowly station; she thought that in this respect she was likely better suited to her newfound station. It was, after all, not so different from what she had known in Evander.

She listened obediently as Dido outlined her duties, and told her something of the mansion's arrangement. She was to heed the cook in all matters, save when Benjamyn or Chryselle gave direct instruction—which, Dido explained, was unlikely, Flysse being at present the lowest of the low and therefore beneath their notice. She was to bathe regularly—Dido would not tolerate unwashed kitchen maids—and keep her clothes clean. She was forbidden the main part of the house, but might move freely in the kitchen and the yards behind. She was to be modest—there were six footmen and, now, three stablemen, and they would likely seek her favors, she being, Dido must admit, a pretty little thing. She was to ignore their blandishments, and did any invite her to their quarters, she was to refuse them and report their lewdness to Dido or Benjamyn.

She had asked then, "Does Arcole sleep there, by the stables?"

And Dido had studied her with a shrewd eye and asked in turn, "He's your sweetheart?"

Which had prompted Flysse to blush furiously and explain to the cook all that had transpired on board the *Pride of the Lord;* except, that was, for the fact that she now believed herself firmly in love.

Dido had nodded then, as if she understood, and said, "He appears a remarkable man. A gentleman, you say? Well, my girl, don't allow your heart to rule your head. It was the attentions of a *gentleman*"—she gave the word offensive connotations—"that got me sent here."

"Arcole's not like that," Flysse protested.

But Dido ignored her denial. "Men are men," she declared, "and your Arcole's just another. Nor's he a gentleman any longer, not here. Here he's just another exile, and whether he's better or worse than the rest remains to be seen. You'll not seek him out, d'you understand?"

"Yes." Flysse had nodded, blushing anew at the suggestion, but quite unable to resist asking, "But shall I see him sometimes?"

"Like as not," Dido had allowed, "for you'll be scrubbing pots out in the yard often enough, and we eat together. And then there's church."

"Church?" Flysse had asked.

"Indeed, church," Dido had replied. "This is a God-fearing household, and the master allows us to attend the early morning service each Sunday. You'll see him then. But there'll be no dawdling or such foolery, you hear me?"

"No," Flysse had promised. And then was struck by another thought: "Shall Davyd be there?"

"The lad from the ship?" Dido had ducked her gaunt gray head in agreement. "Master Gahame's a God-fearing man, so he'll be attending. Your young friend was lucky to find such a master."

That had pleased Flysse, and Dido's manner had seemed so kindly that she had ventured to ask if they might meet on other occasions. She thought it should be pleasant to find Davyd again.

"Other occasions?" Dido had seemed to find the question hard of understanding. "What other occasions?"

"I wondered . . ." Flysse had hesitated: the cook's seeming incomprehension disturbed her. "I wondered if I might not see him about the town."

"About the town?" Dido had echoed, and then laughed. "God knows, missy, you won't be going about the town for a long time. That's a privilege, don't you know? It'll be a few years before you earn that."

Flysse felt her heart sink. Was this mansion to be all her world for years to come? Abruptly timid, she said, "But Nathanial . . ."

"Is a manservant," Dido concluded, "and been with the master years now. Nathanial's earned the master's trust, so sometimes he's allowed out, like Benjamyn or me. But you? No, young Flysse, you won't be setting foot outside until you've earned the privilege. You just work hard and prove yourself, and then"—she smiled benignly, as if granting a gift—"why, in a few years' time perhaps you'll be allowed the odd trip to market or suchlike."

Flysse had swallowed, fighting sudden tears. This apparently kindly woman obviously saw nothing untoward or odd in such confinement. Indeed, she clearly considered the promise of a tiny measure of freedom a prize worthy of the striving. Flysse supposed that was the cost of exile, of indenture: it seemed a dreadful price. She endeavored to console herself with the thought that she shared this mansion prison with Arcole, and somehow—even be it at risk of punishment—she would contrive to see him, to spend what time she could with him.

She had wiped away her tears then and put on the dirndl, and followed Dido to the kitchen and the first day of her new life.

25 Events Unexpected

Autumn gave way to winter and the first snow fell on Grostheim. For Arcole it was welcome relief from the tedium of indentured life: as streets of hard-packed dirt were churned to clinging mud, Governor Wyme gave up his sedan chair in favor of his carriage. No longer was Arcole condemned to the endless round of stable duties, and if he must wear a uniform he found entirely ridiculous, at least he wore it outside the confines of the mansion. With Fredrik and his fellow grooms, he was required to accompany Wyme or the governor's wife on journeys about the town. He thought this likely saved his sanity.

The months had passed slowly for Arcole. He had given up immediate hope of finding himself promoted—he supposed that was the correct word—to a position within the house where he might catch Wyme's eye, and instead felt himself condemned to life as a stablehand. This he accepted with stoic resignation, employing all his wit and charm to befriend his fellow servants. He had come to realize a hierarchy existed amongst servants as rigid as the rankings of society, and he stood at the foot of the ladder. It was a hard lesson. He consoled himself—and was surprised he should—with the thought that he still saw Flysse. They met at mealtimes, when all the servants ate together, and often when she was given some menial task that brought her outside to the yards. They spoke then, and often as they might they contrived to sit together in church. Arcole found her company lifted his spirits, and with her his smile was genuine. Sometimes they managed a brief word or two with Davyd, but none too often and never at length. Arcole gathered the boy was content enough with his master and that his nimble fingers had been turned to the repairing of tools and weapons, which information he filed away for future reference. He no longer thought of finding like-minded folk amongst his fellow exiles, and had given up his vague dream of fomenting rebellion. The indentured folk seemed to him inured to their lot, as likely to rise against their oppressors as sheep against the shepherd. He thought now only of escape, albeit he could not yet envisage how. Still, did Davyd have access to weapons . . . Arcole wished he might find a means to speak at greater length with the boy.

Then, when snow blanketed the rooftops of Grostheim and the wind came howling chill out of the north, things changed. It seemed to Arcole as if he were dealt cards blind, to find on turning them that he held the Imperator and the Monarch and need only gain the Queen and the Duchess to obtain a winning hand—unlikely, but not impossible.

First came an influenza epidemic. It struck sudden and savage as the wind, and the servants of Wyme's household were not spared. Housemaids and manservants were confined feverish to their beds, those immune to the disease called upon to work the harder, their duties often as not doubled. Arcole was glad that Flysse did not succumb: more that Benjamyn summoned him from the stables.

"You've some social graces, no?" The majordomo sat with hands cupped around a mug of beef broth, a necklace of protective garlic bulging his starched shirt. "You understand the niceties of society?"

"I believe so," Arcole replied. "In the Levan, I moved in society." That seemed a lifetime away now.

Benjamyn's tongue clicked against his teeth. "You know the difference between a fish fork and a meat fork, eh?"

Sharp eyes studied Arcole, who said, "Of course."

"There's no 'of course' about it." Benjamyn gestured at a box of cutlery on the table before him. "Set those out for one."

Curious, Arcole did as he was bade. When he was finished, Benjamyn clicked his tongue in what might have been approval. "Now glasses," he ordered.

Arcole set out the glasses, and Benjamyn nodded. "You'll do, I think."

"For what?" asked Arcole.

Benjamyn said, "The house. We've too many sick and a need of manservants. Fetch your belongings from the stables, eh? From now on you'll sleep here."

Arcole suppressed a smile and hurried to the shed he shared with the other grooms. Fredrik grimaced when told of this sudden elevation, but offered no further comment as Arcole gathered up his meager possessions and returned to the mansion.

He was kitted out with the waistcoat and shoes of his new position, which irked him no less than his groom's clothing, and shown his new quarters. They were more comfortable—surely far warmer and spacious, the sick having been quarantined in separate rooms. That night he attended Governor Wyme and his wife; and though it sat ill to stand silent as they ate, springing to obey whenever summoned to refill a glass or remove a plate, he told himself this change could serve only to further his inchoate plans. He was, at least, closer to Wyme. And later, when master and mistress had eaten and the servants were allowed to take their dinner, he learned that Flysse, too, rose through the ranks of the indentured.

"I'm to attend the mistress," she told him. "Lynda fell sick and I'm to be a chambermaid."

"An honor," Dido advised them, "for all it must leave me short-handed."

"I only hope she'll hope do," said Chryselle. "If you let me down, missy . . ."

Arcole saw Flysse turn toward the housekeeper, her expression a mixture of submission and eagerness. He wished she did not look so servile, so eager to please. Almost, he spoke out on her behalf, but to his surprise Dido came to her defence.

"She's a good girl, is young Flysse," said the cook, "and does she work so hard for you as she has for me, then you'll have no cause for complaint, Chryselle."

The housekeeper said, "We'll see, eh? God knows, we've all our extra share of work with this cursed epidemic."

So it was they both found themselves raised swifter than would ordinarily have been the case, and Arcole found himself in a position to turn another card to his advantage.

He attended Wyme in the governor's study. The shutters were closed against the wind and heavy curtains drawn. A fire blazed in the hearth and Arcole stood awaiting his master's summons—to pour a glass of wine, or remove a spent lucifer. Such humble duty would have chafed the harder had he not been able to read the documents Wyme perused: it seemed not to have occurred to the man that Arcole could read and write. Arcole supposed that few, perhaps even none, of his fellow servants commanded those attributes; nor, he had come to learn, did indentured servants possess faces. To their masters, they were merely useful, anonymous creatures whose presence was taken for granted. He now felt a pang of guilt that he had once treated servants in like manner. But never would again, he promised himself as he let his eyes slant down to read the papers spread across Wyme's desk.

They dealt mostly with routine affairs—tables of figures concerning crops and vineyards, production reports, requests from inland farms for more indentured hands—but set to one side was a map of the known territory. Grostheim was marked, and the location of the inland hold-ings, the rivers that boundaried the cleared land, the wilderness beyond. Arcole determined that he must obtain a copy, did the opportunity arise. He thought that Wyme would not miss a page or two of paper, and could he only find the chance and the time to transcribe the map, he should own a useful tool.

Once, his musings were interrupted by the arrival of Major Spelt and a young lieutenant, whose name Benjaymn announced as Rogyr Stantin. The lieutenant looked to have ridden hard, and on his face Arcole saw writ alarm. Spelt appeared grim.

"There's ill news," he said, and favored Arcole with a scowl.

Wyme took the hint and said, "Arcole, do you bring us two glasses and then leave us."

Arcole brought the glasses, and thought to add a humidor. He bowed as Wyme waved a dismissive hand, and retreated to the kitchen. Bells hung there, to summon servants, each one marked with the loca-tion of a room. Arcole waited, wondering what ill news the Militiamen brought. He supposed it was most likely further word of the epidemic, or a request for labor to clear blocked roads. But were that the case, he mused, then why had Spelt indicated he be dismissed? He wondered what the major and the lieutenant had to say that need be kept from servants' ears. When the bell rang, he returned to the study.

Spelt and Stantin were gone, and Wyme sat grave-faced, a glass forgotten at his elbow. Three cold pipes lay on the desk and the room was thick with smoke. Wyme said, "Help me up," and Arcole bent to lift his bulk from the chair, passing the governor the crutches he must use to walk. He escorted the man to a sitting room and saw him settled in an armchair by the hearth.

"Wine," the governor ordered. "Then ask my wife attend me."

Arcole obeyed, setting a decanter and two glasses on a table. Before leaving he asked meekly, the thoughtful manservant, "Shall I tidy your study, 'sieur? Perhaps air the room?"

Wyme nodded absently. He appeared preoccupied, and Arcole sensed that news of grave import had been delivered. He hurried to find the governor's wife, conveying to her the message, and made his way back to the study. It was the work of only moments to gather up the glasses and pipes, which he set aside by the door, crossing to the desk. He began to rummage through the clutter there, seeking clean paper on which he might transcribe the map, when he noticed that the original was altered. Around a holding marked *Thirsk Farm,* Wyme had drawn a circle in red ink, and the figure 3. Sand still littered the inscription, and Arcole assumed it must be connected to the visit of the Militiamen. Curious, he bent to peruse the map closer. There were two similar notations—older, and ringed and numbered in like manner, marked *Defraney Mill* and *Clawson Farm.* Arcole wondered what the red rings and the numbers meant. He saw a sheet lying beside the map, that, too, sprinkled with sand, the ink not yet quite dry. He guessed the paper represented notes taken during the interview with Spelt and the lieutenant, and that were it known he could read, Wyme would never have allowed him in this room.

He forgot his original purpose as he began to read.

At the head, in a hand embellished with grandiose flourishes, was written the word *Attacks.* Beneath, Wyme had employed a personal code. It was easy to decipher—Arcole frowned, his heart quickening as he studied the governor's notes.

Beside the figure 1 Wyme had written *Clwsn Fm; Summer. Dstryd: all sls lost. No sign.* Beneath that entry was the figure 2 and the equally cryptic comments: *Defrny Mill; Summer. Burnd: no survrs. No sign.* A line was drawn across the page then, and under it the words: *Ptrls fnd no sign. Wilderness? Spelt suggsts svges.* Then a second line, below which was the figure 3 and the coded remarks, *Thrsk Farm, Autumn. Burnd: no survrs. No sign.* Then Wyme had inscribed a large question mark and the words: *What are they? Spelt suggsts Mil. expdtn.* The notes were then ended with a second outsize question mark.

Intrigued, not sure what he had discovered, Arcole set the papers in order. As best he could surmise, Wyme's notes indicated that three inland holdings had been attacked and destroyed, with all there slain. He looked to the map and saw that the three ringed locations stood close to the forest edge. It seemed that Major Spelt believed the attacks were the work of savages, and had suggested a military expedition be sent out. Were he right, Arcole thought, then Salvation was not the empty land folk supposed. Somewhere—likely in the wilderness forests—there were others, hostile to the Autarchy's colonists.

The idea was startling. Salvation was assumed to be Evander's foothold in this new world, the stepping-stone from which the Autarchy would eventually conquer all the wilderness. But if there were already inhabitants, and they opposed to the newcomers . . . Arcole whistled softly as myriad ideas ran wild through his head.

Were there folk in the wilderness, might they not welcome refugees? Perceive escaped exiles as allies in their struggle against Evander? Arcole moved from the desk, aware his absence might soon be noted. Playing his role of obedient servant, he drew the curtains open and threw the shutters wide. Cold air intruded, shocking as his discovery. He returned to the desk. There was no time now to copy the map, but that could be done later; now his head was abuzz with the implications of these attacks. They were, obviously, kept secret, likely for fear of panic. But how long should that secret be kept, did Spelt mount an expedition? Or were there further attacks? What effect might such news have on the citizens of Grostheim?

He tended the fire, wondering how he might use this knowledge.

Of itself, it seemed worthless, save that he became privy to information he was confident Wyme preferred be kept secret. Which would likely prove dangerous, were his knowledge made known—unless he could somehow contact these mysterious savages. Of a sudden all his suppressed resentment of Evander, of the Autarchy, came flooding back. He drove the poker hard into the hearth, raising a cloud of sparks. He thought of burning cabins, of Grostheim itself in flames. He was not alone! Even were his fellow exiles become docile, there were some in this new land who did not accept the authority of Evander. Surely he might find common cause with them. Save, he wondered, how? How might he contact them? And were they savages, how might he survive contact? He set the poker aside and went to close the shutters, draw the curtains, his mind racing.

He thought of Davyd. The boy was employed by Rupyrt Gahame, whose warehouse, by Davyd's account, was full of weapons. What if guns could be stolen? Surely weapons would make such a gift as must guarantee friendship. And knowledge of Grostheim—gleaned as a groom—could help, did these mysterious potential allies invade the citadel itself.

He took a deep breath, forcing his thoughts to slow. He ran ahead of himself, allowed that hatred of Evander he had believed controlled to flare up too fierce again. He counseled himself to patience: he had knowledge now, and knowledge was a weapon, did he but find the opportunity to use it. He must wait—God knew, servitude taught him how to do that—and amass more knowledge. And first he must find some means by which to speak at length with Davyd.

He collected the dirty glasses and the pipes and returned to his duties, once more the patient servant.

.   .   .

"Are you well?" Flysse studied him with solicitous eyes. "You're not ailing?"

"No." Arcole shook his head, dismissing her concern with a smile. "I was only thinking."

"Of what?" she asked.

They sat alone in the kitchen, the hour well past midnight. The mansion slept—soundly, Arcole hoped, for it was currently his duty and Flysse's to attend the governor and his wife, should they wake and require some service. It was an odious task, did Wyme demand his chamber pot, nor much better when he fretfully demanded mulled wine or hot chocolate. But so far neither bell had rung, and the thought had entered Arcole's head that this would be an ideal time to transcribe Wyme's map. As best he knew no hexes were laid on the study or its contents. What point, when the papers therein were only meaningless scribbles to the servants?

The idea had taken hold and grown, and almost he had gone. Then thought of Flysse had delayed him. He'd not announce his intention to her: in part for fear that were he discovered, she be punished as an accomplice; in part for fear that she seek to dissuade him or inadvertently blurt out what he did. He pondered what reason or excuse he could give her, and then that *did* Wyme summon him, she might come tell him and thus save awkward explanation of his absence.

He found himself caught in dilemma: unwilling to subject Flysse to risk, unable, quite, to trust her, and yet likely needing her help.

"So shall you tell me," he heard her ask, "or are they secrets, your thoughts?"

"No," he lied; and then dissembled, "I thought only how cozy this is, we two alone and all the household sleeping. As if this were our kitchen, and we some old wed couple."

He gestured at the dim-lit room, warmed by the great kitchen range. It was, indeed, a cozy scene. He occupied the armed chair that was customarily Benjamyn's preserve, a mug of chocolate steaming at his elbow. Flysse sat close by, where usually Chryselle would take her place. They might have been a married couple, enjoying the comfort of their own kitchen before retiring. He was not certain—it was perhaps only the stove's red glow—but he thought Flysse blushed.

She said, "Yes," in a small, soft voice, and he saw her lashes fall over lowered eyes.

She seemed suddenly nervous, as if his words and her response carried them to a place that was, if not dangerous, then somehow threatening, where she must tread carefully. He waited for her to say more, but she remained silent, busying herself with the repair of a skirt's hem, and would not meet his eye.

He frowned and asked her, "Flysse, what's amiss?"

She continued her needlework, not looking up, and only shook her head.

"Have I offended you?" he asked.

She answered, "No," in the same small voice, and he leant a little way across the table, enough that he saw moisture shining on her cheeks.

It was moment before he realized she wept, and then he acted without thinking. He rose from his chair and settled on the table at her side. He cupped her chin, to raise her face. For a while she resisted, but then let her head tilt back, and he saw the tears that trickled slowly down her cheeks. He moved to brush them away, but as his fingers touched her cheek she shuddered and drew back.

"What's wrong?" he asked. "Is my touch so offensive?"

She shook her head violently and sniffed, and said helplessly, "No, Arcole. Never that."

"Then what?" He set a hand against her cheek and this time she did not resist or move away, but only made a soft, inarticulate sound.

The skirt, part mended, fell to the floor as Flysse looked into his eyes. She could not help herself, but neither would she tell him clear what anguish his casual words, his touch, produced. That was for him to discover, for him to say the first words. She could not, for fear he dismiss her, that her declaration drive him away: that she could not bear.

Arcole stared at her. She was lovely in her grief. She was, it came to him, always beautiful. Did he not still think of himself as a gentleman, of her as a—what did he think her? Surely not a common servant, for Flysse was most uncommon. And was she a servant, then so was he in this place, and therefore they equal. Were she dressed in the finery of a lady, how would he perceive her? Save she lacked the affectations of the gentlewomen he had known, she was their equal; more, for she was courageous and kind, gentle, compassionate.

He realized he listed her attributes, and that she compared favorably with any woman he had known in the Levan.

He looked into her eyes and for the first time saw the truth, as if her tearful gaze drew back the curtains of his blindness.

He said, "Oh, Flysse," and could not help himself as he bent toward her.

Which was altogether far more than Flysse could resist. She closed her eyes as his face came closer, and then her arms, of their own volition it seemed, were around his neck. His breath was an instant warm on her mouth, and then lost there.

Arcole held her, for the moment oblivious of all save the pleasure of the kiss, of her body against his. It had been a long time since he held a woman; longer since he held one who loved him. And that Flysse loved him, he could no longer ignore. In some hinder part of his mind he recalled the signs—the looks, the words, her smiles—that should have told him earlier of her feelings. They had been there—on the *Pride of the Lord,* here in Wyme's mansion—and he had ignored them, been too preoccupied with his own fate, his plans, to read the signs aright. He was too used to the coquettish ways of the Levan's gentlewomen: Flysse was entirely honest, without artifice or devices. He was unused to such behavior.

When they moved a little way apart, he studied her face anew. The tears were gone, in their place a glorious smile. She said, "Arcole," and he could not help but draw her close again.

He had not quite known that his hands moved to the lacings of her bodice until she pushed them away. He was heated now: he wanted her, with no thought for the future, but only for the moment. Had they been in the Levan, were she kindred to the women he had know there, they would by now be undressing one another. But they were not and she was not; she was—it struck him with dazzling bemusement—too respectable.

As she said, "Arcole, no," he said, "Flysse, I'm sorry."

They laughed together, and though he still lusted for her, he knew he must wait.

For what? asked a seditious voice that belonged to that part of him that was still the gambler, the duelist, whose rakehell reputation had seduced grand ladies in another world. He knew the answer: marriage. That came from that part of him exile had changed, association with Flysse had changed. Flysse was respectable, she was not a woman of Levanite society whose favors were bestowed at whim, to whom a casual bedding meant no more than the saddling of a new horse. She was . . . unique. He drew her close again—careful now with his hands—as he accepted that he should have her only in the marriage bed, honestly; *respectably.*

Almost, he laughed at the notion. Arcole Blayke, swordsman and gambler, considering marriage to an exiled serving girl? That would surely afford his friends amusement. Then he thought: What friends? None save Dom risked taint when I was taken, but looked to their own skins. Laughter dissipated: Flysse saw him only as . . . what? Himself, he supposed: a man who wore exile's brand on his cheek. He thought Dom would approve of this woman. And marriage . . . Had the idea not crossed his mind? Should it be so bad? He pondered the alternatives, which appeared quite straightforward: he could have Flysse or not; he could wed her or not.

There came into his mind then a feeling of horrid loneliness. It surprised him: that it should be hard to bear, did he reject her now. To live so close, to see her daily, but never again hold her or kiss her? He thought he must find that intolerable now. She might turn to another. There were enough fellow servants present already cast lustful glances her way, had so far stayed their advances only because she dismissed them. Because—it dawned on him sudden as anything this revelatory night—it was understood she was bound to him. Only he had failed to see it: he could not help laughing then.

"What is it?" Flysse asked against his cheek. "Do I amuse you?"

"No," he told her, quite honest now. "I laugh at myself. At my blindness, that I could not see what was before my eyes."

"That I love you?" she murmured.

He answered, "Yes," knowing her question asked another, asked for an answer he was not yet—quite—sure he could honestly give.

Did she notice that hesitation, she gave no sign, but said, "At first I thought you haughty," and when he frowned: "I thought you too much the gentleman to notice me."

Guilty, he whispered, "I was."

"I thought," she said, "that you believed yourself too grand. That you considered me beneath your dignity."

He said, entirely honest now, "Oh, Flysse, you're not beneath my dignity, nor anyone's. You're fine as any lady. God knows, you're better than most I've met."

"I think," she said, smiling at the compliment, "that you did not always believe that."

"No," he admitted. "But you taught me better. You opened my eyes."

"It was when you befriended Davyd," she said, "that I saw you different. With him, and when you came to our defense."

And that delivered another pang of guilt, for had he not concealed his motives in befriending the boy? He thought that did he tell her that, then he must tell her everything—tell her of Davyd's dreaming and his unformed plans to escape, all of it. And then? He had dismissed the notion of taking her with him when—if—his plans came to fruition.

Another seditious thought then: married servants were granted their own room. Had he such privacy, it should be easier to study Wyme's map, to keep secret such papers and documents as he might need copy. But then he must surely tell her everything. And did she know, how would she react? Might she insist she go with him, perhaps under threat of revelation? Or insist, on the same terms, that he remain? She was brave—that he knew beyond doubting. But to ask she face the wilderness with him, to risk her life on a venture he must admit—should it even prove feasible—must be mightily dangerous, certainly arduous—did he want that?

He could not properly conceal his thoughts. He wondered if under her influence he lost his skills of dissemblance, of prevarication, when she said, "You're troubled again, my love."

He said, "Yes," and cursed himself and the unfair justice of the Autarchy that put him in this position, that he not deal honestly with her. She deserved honesty, but he could not yet bring himself to tell her what he planned. He told himself it was too soon; that it were better did he wait and come to know her better, and knew that for procrastination. He found himself once more caught on dilemma's horns.

"What is it?" she asked.

His answer was not entirely dishonest: he said, "I wonder what we do now."

Her response was entirely artless. She stiffened somewhat in his arms and her face lost a little of its radiance. She said quietly, "Is that not for you to say?"

"How do you mean?" he asked, afraid he flung himself headlong into a choice he had sooner not yet make.

Flysse pulled farther back, until he must hold her by the elbows else she withdraw entirely. He did not want that; neither did he want to choose.

"I know not how your society ladies do such things," she said. "I am only a plain woman . . ."

"Never plain," he told her, seeking to shift her direction, wondering how that should trouble him so. Wondering was this love, to feel so guilty that he deceived her? He wished she would not put him to the test: he doubted now he could hurt her. It seemed she commanded a power over him, in ways he could not properly comprehend. Surely he could not understand how it could come so sudden, that he feared to hurt her or dash her hopes. He wondered if somehow, without his knowing it, he *had* come to love her. He felt abruptly afraid: love was not a thing he was used to.

"No." She disengaged his hands, stepping a pace back. Her expression was both firm and frightened, and when he moved toward her, she raised a hand, silently bidding him keep his distance. "No soft, sweet words, Arcole. Please? Those are for your society ladies; I'd have only the truth of you."

He said, "Flysse," sensing where this conversation went, knowing he'd not venture there yet. Save neither would he lose her now: that should be too painful.

"No, please hear me out." She moved back farther, to where shadow touched her face and he could not properly read her expression. "I tell you—I am a plain woman, and decently raised. I've naught to my name, save I hold my honor, which brought me here. Because I refused the blandishments of a man . . ."

"Armnory Schweiz?" He spoke the name in genuine outrage. "Do you compare me with that animal?"

"No," she said, "and—forgive me—yes. He wanted but the one thing of me. Do you want different?"

"I am not Armnory Schweiz," he said angrily. "You insult me with that."

"I'd not," she said. "Save your intentions be no different."

"They are!" he protested. "They are not the same at all."

"What would you ask of me, then?" she demanded.

Were he quite honest, he would have told her, "I'd bed you. I'd have you now, and tomorrow, and for so long as I remain here, and not think of that decision I must one day make." But that, he knew, must surely lose her; and he knew with sudden clarity that he'd not lose her. It was as if he sat at a gaming table, his fortune to be lost or won on the turn of an unseen card. Well, he was a gambler, no? Perhaps even a man in love.

He said, "Flysse, I'd ask that you wed me." He was surprised the sentence came out so clear, so definite. He was not quite sure from where it came.

She said, "Arcole, I will," and stepped forward, out of the shadow that hid her face so that he could see her smile, which was bright with happiness and solemn in equal measure.

He moved toward her and this time she did not bid him back, but raised her arms to embrace him. He thought he had never been kissed like that before. Certainly he had never been in this situation before, and even as a part of him wondered what he did and where it should lead, another told him this was what he wanted.

The card was turned now, but he knew the stakes were changed. It was strange, how happy he felt.

Into her hair he murmured, "So, what *do* we do now?" Adding quickly, "I'd not besmirch your honor, but how do we go about this?"

The card turned, the step taken, he'd delay no longer than he must. Her kisses were sweet and full of promise—more, almost, than he could bear—and could he have her only in wedlock, then he'd turn that key soon as was possible.

She said, "We must go to Benjamyn, ask him. He then approaches the master for permission. Is that granted, a priest comes here to perform the ceremony."

"You've ascertained all this, eh?" He could not help but chuckle. "Were you so confident, then?"

She leaned back against his arms to look him in the eye and blushed prettily. "Not confident," she said, and smiled. "But hopeful."

"God, woman," he laughed, "you surely do speak plain."

"Would you have me otherwise?" she asked.

Arcole shook his head and said, "No, Flysse, I'd not. I'd have you just as you are." Which was the truth, and quite unexpectdly prompted him to answer that unspoken question he had earlier avoided: "I love you—just as you are."

It was, he realized, an honest declaration; or, at least, as honest as he was capable of. He was not sure precisely what love was, but if it meant such feelings as he entertained at the thought of losing her to another, or seeing her each day knowing he could not have her, then, yes, he loved her. If it meant this exhilaration he felt holding her, at the thought of their being together nightly, then, yes, he loved her. But if it meant staying with her, both their lives lived out as servants of Andru Wyme, indentured until death freed them, then—he must admit—he was not sure. He could not forsake his dream of escape. He could not tell her that, nor yet feel confident of sharing his dream. The guilt he felt at that surprised him, and if such guilt was a part of love, then again yes, he loved her.

Perhaps he would tell her. Likely, when they shared a room, it would be impossible to hide it from her. He decided he would wait, like any canny gambler, and see how the cards fell.

For now, with Flysse in his arms, he felt too happy to entertain such troubling thoughts for long.

26 A Messenger Cursed

Winter came early to the mountains. The valley lay under a mantle of snow that shone bright in the light of a sun that granted no warmth. The stream froze and Arrhyna must hack through the ice to obtain fresh water. Rannach had constructed a shelter for the horses and kept a fire burning close by their enclosure, lest the wolf winds that came howling out of the mountains freeze them where they stood. What hunting he did now was done afoot, treking laboriously through deep drifts to set traps for snowhares and whatever other creatures ventured out under the White Grass Moon, or huddling cold amongst the trees to put an arrow in an unwary deer come foraging down from the high slopes. At least it was fresh meat to augment the supplies he'd built up against the cold moons, but he could not help thinking that buffalo meat should be better, taken in the warm moons and stored ready for the cold. He could taste it, when he thought about it: the rich, fatty taste of ribs and haunches roasted over the embers of the campfire, the lodges of the Commacht all around, secure in the Wintering Ground. The men would be working on bridles and arrows, lances and shields; the women weaving blankets or softening the hides of buffalo and deer for tentcloth and clothing, sewing beads. He remembered the last winter in the lodges of his clan, when he had talked with Bakaan and the others of the spring's Matakwa and how he would claim Arrhyna for his bride.

Now he had his wish—Arrhyna *was* his wife—but he had never

thought it should be like this, the two of them all alone in the white wilderness of the valley. He worried about her: that she missed her parents, the company of other women, her moods. She seemed mostly content, but there were times when she grew sharp, her tongue cutting, and he did not understand those. Neither did he understand why Colun and Marjia no longer visited. Save . . . He dismissed that thought. Surely they could not be slain; surely the Grannach could not be defeated by the invaders. Surely the Maker would not allow that. For if he did, then Arrhyna was in terrible danger, and Rannach hated such ominous brooding. He pushed it aside and took the hare from the trap.

Three in one morning—a good catch. Enough that he felt justified in returning to Arrhyna; so he slung the carcass with the others on his belt and turned back toward their lodge, less needfully than only to see her and touch her and know her safe. He had done all he could, banished as he was, to make her life comfortable. Their lodge was warm and he had an ample supply of wood set by, no less sufficient meat. There were deer hides and the pelts of rabbits for winter clothing. They had furred boots and hardy garments to see them through the cold moons, and the stream still held sluggish fish for the hooking. But yet there was something about his wife that troubled him, as if sometimes she was about to speak of some momentous thing but then held back and kept it from him. He did not properly understand that, nor her appetite, which was large.

He supposed he did not much understand women; and they were, anyway, in strange circumstances. But he would have welcomed conversation with his mother, or with Marjia, that he might know better how to please and satisfy his wife. But his mother was far distant and forbidden him on pain of death, and Marjia . . . Marjia was not there, nor any sign of her coming.

The snowshoes he'd made crunched against the frozen crust. Lonely ravens clustered on the branches behind, optimistic that he left some tidbit. Overhead, the sky burned steely, like metal in flame save it was only cold, and when he looked to where the Maker's Mountain stood, the peak glittered, a blinding white pinnacle defiant of observation.

He was banished from Ket-Ta-Witko, promised death did he return to the lodges of his clan: this valley was all his world now, and Arrhyna, and he must be content with that. Which, mostly, he was; only sometimes he wondered how the Commacht fared, and missed Bakaan's jokes and Hadustan's laughter and Zhy's solemn comments. Even his father's stern face.

But he had Arrhyna: he smiled as he saw her.

She sat beneath the raised entry flaps of the lodge. The outside fire burned bright before her, and her hands moved deft over a hide, one of the needles Marjia had gifted her sparkling as she wove beads into the skin.

"What are you making?" he asked, even as she looked up and said, "Three hares, eh? Good hunting, husband."

He dropped the hares and bent to kiss her. She said, "A shirt. For you to wear when the New Grass Moon rises."

"Not until then?" he asked.

"It's deerhide," she said. "Until then, it will not be warm enough."

He smiled and sat beside her; set to gutting the hares. "Shall I wear it to the Matakwa?" he laughed, then stopped. "What's that?"

"What?" Arrhyna glanced up from her needlework.

"That sound." He looked from the open flaps of the lodge along the valley. "Like distant thunder."

The sky was all steely, neither quite blue nor gray, but colored at some midpoint between. There was no sign of any storm, neither clouds building nor lightning flashing, but when Arrhyna cocked her head and concentrated, she heard it—a faraway rumbling as if rocks moved, or some great force wended through the mountains.

She said, "I don't know."

It seemed to come from everywhere and nowhere. It was like the sound of the migrating herds, when the buffalo ran in all their glory and the earth shook under their hooves. But there were no buffalo here.

"Perhaps the Grannach move the mountains," Rannach joked.

Arrhyna thought it a poor jest. She looked to where the Maker's Mountain loomed, but that great peak stood silent and immobile.

"Or an avalanche," he said.

Arrhyna wondered if he entertained the same doubt, the same fear, she felt—that the sound was of no natural making but something else. But if he did, he kept the thought from her. Nor was she prepared to voice it, as if the saying of it might flesh out the fear, so they both held silent and only listened to the distant rumbling.

He could still not understand how he lived: he ate nothing, he drank only the snow that melted in his mouth. He had fallen down over rocks that should have shattered him, and into snowdrifts that buried him and should have held him frozen until the spring thaw, and dug his way out and found handholds where none existed with hands that no longer contained any feeling. He could only assume the Maker wished him to live and so kept him alive.

And so he went on, unthinking—driven by that memory of the

flame-voice that burned inside him and somehow sustained him—down the cliffs and the precipices, across the deep-drifted ravines and the fragile ice bridges, down to where the People were, knowing now that all were the People—the clans of Ket-Ta-Witko and the Grannach and the poor, lost Whaztaye, and all the other folk of all the other parceled worlds that were the Maker's creation, and all as important as each other and all threatened by the Breakers who would rend and destroy that fine fabric of coexistence, even those strange ones from the other world or time that he had glimpsed in his revelatory dreaming. And he was the only one in all the worlds to know, which was a terrible duty and a burden he labored under and would have cast off, save if he did, then all the Maker's creations must come unraveled and be destroyed, and he be as guilty as the Breakers for that undoing.

So he fought his way through snow-filled valleys, where the white powder caked his face and sometimes overtopped his head so that he must tunnel like some snow mole, and he walked over the ice that encased rivers, and through it when it lay too thin to support his weight. And he felt neither the cold nor any hunger, but burned with purpose, intent only on bringing that dread word which he could not be sure any would heed or believe. He did not sleep: it was as if the Maker shifted his limbs and drove him on, a container of purpose or a messenger, cursed.

And he came down from the holy mountain to where the Grannach lived and they found him there, moving like a blind horse through the wastes, driving only onward so that they must hold him and pin him down as they looked to minister to him, not knowing how any man so wasted could be alive.

"*Is* he alive?" Colun stared disbelievingly at the emaciated body. The Morrhyn he remembered was a hale man, tall and sturdy, with a head of thick, dark hair. This poor fellow was gaunt as a desiccated corpse, all jutting bones and sharp angles, his hair the color of snow. Was he truly Morrhyn, then he looked as the wakanisha surely would after he had been dead some little time. "Where did he come from?"

"We found him out on the snow," Nylj said. "He cried out and collapsed when we approached. I think he's blind."

Marjia knelt close, then glanced up. "He lives, though the Maker alone knows how. Look at him! He's starved."

"I do not understand this." Colun scratched a leathery cheek. "He looks like Morrhyn, but surely Morrhyn is with his clan."

"Be he Morrhyn or some other unfortunate, he still needs care."

Marjia rose, bustling past the curious menfolk to call the women to her. "See he's wrapped in warm blankets and build up that fire. Prepare broth."

Colun grunted, still intent on the skeletal figure. It was Morrhyn, he decided—the angle of those sunken cheeks, that ax-blade nose, those were Morrhyn's. But what in the Maker's name was the Commacht Dreamer doing here, and where had he come from? It was a mystery he supposed would be answered if the man lived—which, were he frank, seemed unlikely—and one he could have done without. The Maker knew, there were mysteries and troubles enough in these dark days.

He tugged at his beard as the women brought heated blankets and Marjia set to stirring the broth. There was little enough food and, despite their losses, too many Grannach to eat it. He let his eyes wander over the cavern, thinking they already had wounded enough to tend, and felt the darkness cloud his soul. It was no consolation to know his fears proven true, to know he had been right and the others wrong. The outcome was too dismal.

His people had debated as the invaders continued their advance, and long before any conclusion was reached, the strangelings had come deep into the mountains. They had swarmed into the high passes like some vast ant army, pushing remorselessly forward to sweep the defending Grannach from their path as a storm wind blows away chaff. The only unity the Grannach had reached was the agreement that the western tunnels be all sealed, but by then it was too late, for the invaders came in by the lesser entrances and the high, secret ways, and the Grannach were sealed up as he had prophesied like frightened rabbits in their warrens.

Too many had died, and too many more acted foolishly. Janzi and Gort had sealed their families in the ancestral caves, and for all Colun knew, they remained there, likely to starve. Daryk had died fighting the invaders as they came into the Basanga caverns, and scarce a hundred of his family had survived to flee to the Javitz: sad refugees in their own mountains. Menas, at least, had shown some sense at last and come with all his Katjen to join Colun's folk, but too late. Menas had been wounded, his side pierced by a lance, and was dead now. His last words had been a plea that his family accept Colun's leadership, and that Colun protect them as his own.

Colun had, of course, agreed, though he doubted he could protect anyone against the terror that stalked the hills. But he did his best, for all it cost him dear. When the invaders had come into the Javitz caverns, the Grannach were ready, and when it became obvious the strangelings came in numbers too great to defeat, Colun had made a terrible decision. He had planned it in advance, as a suicide plans his demise—in precise and horrid detail. The Javitz had been forewarned, and were ready with food and clothing, whatever they might carry easily. The refugees had less to carry, for all the Javitz shared with them what they had—and Colun had spoken long and forcefully on this, telling them they were no longer Javitz and Basanga and Katjen but only Grannach now, and did any argue, then they were free to return to their family caves. None did argue, but only obeyed him, hailing him as creddan of all the Stone Folk. It was an honor that sat sour as he called his people back from the advancing invaders and gave the word to the golans to do what they had reluctantly agreed upon.

It was a Pyrrhic victory: vast numbers of the invaders and their beasts had died as the Javitz cavern came tumbling down on them, burying them forever under such a weight of stone as must forever entomb them, and Colun had wept with his people to see the ancestral home cave destroyed—as if their past were taken from them, leaving only a bleak and homeless future. He felt an emptiness come into his soul as he fled, the tunnels all filled with the awful thunder of destruction, and he thought that wound should never heal.

He had led the decimated Grannach away to an uncertain future in the lesser caves and the high, hidden valleys, where they grubbed out a poor living as best they could and hid like nervous deer from the invaders' wolf packs that scoured the hills. But they did, at least, live, and Colun supposed that was something. And was he not sure how long they might survive or what dread fate descended on the world, then he could console himself with the knowledge that he had saved as many as he could and that there remained a remnant of the Grannach alive in the world who would otherwise have been dead. But that was small consolation, must they exist like rats, nibbling warily about the fringes of a world filled with only enemies. Sometimes he wondered if it had not been better to die fighting, but then he would look at the children and the women and the old ones and know that it was better to cling to life and hope, to ask the Maker to set right this awful imbalance.

He sometimes thought, in more cheerful moments, that perhaps the Matawaye would defeat the invaders, and then would feel that little optimism slip away as he thought of the awful fury of the strangelings and their numbers. He *knew* that the flatlanders were divided as his own folk had been, and would most likely fall like the Grannach before the incomers. And now Morrhyn was come, more dead than alive, and that was a very strange thing—that the Dreamer be here where he should not be, as if he were a corpse risen from the grave.

"I'd speak with him," he said. "When he wakes."

"No doubt." Marjia did not turn: she was too intent on spilling broth between Morrhyn's cracked and blistered lips. "But when that might be, I cannot say."

Colun turned to Nylj. "You found him in the valley, you say? Were there tracks?"

Nylj ducked his shaggy head. "The Maker knows how he came so far, but yes—his tracks came from the direction of the Mountain."

Colun frowned. Morrhyn had come from the Maker's Mountain? The mystery deepened.

"You're sure?" he asked.

Nylj looked a moment offended and Colun smiled an apology. "It seems impossible he could be there," he explained. "I cannot understand it."

"Nor I." Nylj allowed himself placated. "But there he was, like a snow-blinded hare struggling through the drifts."

"Did he say anything?" Colun asked.

"Only cried out. Were there words in it, I could not understand them."

Colun nodded and walked to the cave mouth. The snow had ceased falling a little after dawn and the valley lay silent and still, palisaded round by jagged peaks. The Maker's Mountain stood distant and aloof, and the winter sun outlined the tracks of Nylj's party like shadows on the snow. Colun could not understand it: Morrhyn had no right to be here, and still less to be alive. It was a further impossibility in a world become all impossible.

He went back inside the cave. Morrhyn slept now. Colun studied the wasted features and looked to his wife.

Marjia read the question in his eyes and said, "I don't know. He's no right to be alive, so perhaps he'll live. It's in the Maker's hands now."

Colun nodded and returned to his brooding. He thought he no longer understood his world; it seemed all turned on its head.

When he woke he was buried and began to tunnel from under the weight of snow, thinking all the while that it was oddly warm and that it should be far easier to sink down beneath that comfortable blanket and let it take him away to endless sleep. But he had a duty he must discharge, and so he chided himself and called on the Maker, and fought to reach the light. Then he felt himself clutched and fought the hands that held him and cried out, cursing, until he was forced down and knew himself lost. He was dead, or dying, and cursed spirits sought to drag him down, that he not dispense his charge, but all the world be given over to malignity and he be damned with them, a companion in despair.

Fire's glow then, and torches that revealed faces all craggy and bearded, and others that were hairless and smooth if no less craggy: he recognized them, dimly, from some distant place, another time. One, he thought he knew, but could not properly remember. Perhaps death played him a final trick, fooling his eyes and wandering mind. If so, he must fight it. He was not yet ready to die, not until his duty was done. And so he fought and cried out, looking for the light of the sky, that he might see the stars and take a bearing from them and go on.

"Morrhyn! Morrhyn, for the Maker's sake, don't you know me?"

He knew his eyes were open, but not that they saw, or what: he thought perhaps the spirits looked to trick him. The sky was black and starless and the only light came from flames which hurt his eyes. He sat up and wondered why he felt no cold but only warmth, as if he rested beside a fire. And indeed, when he squinted, he thought he saw a fire burning, and torches beyond, as if he rested within a cave whose walls reflected back the flames' glow, and in them saw squat shapes that were like the Grannach he remembered, who lived in the hills and were the Stone Guardians. Or tricksy spirits sent by the Breakers to lure him and lull him into failure.

He said, "Who are you? I charge you, in the name of the Maker, to speak true."

"I am Colun of the Grannach," said the closest shape. "Do you not know me?"

He looked at it and then away, at his body which he saw was all swathed in furs, and at the fire that burned close by, and the huddled shapes beyond. Then up to where only darkness was, shadows darting there, thrown by the fire and the torches. Then down again, to find a nervous, smiling face hung round with plaits of flaxen hair, holding out a bowl that steamed and gave off a most savory and appetizing aroma.

"This is Marjia, my wife," said the Colun-shape. "She's broth for you to drink."

He closed his eyes and voiced a silent prayer, and when he opened them again, shapes and shadows resolved into tangible reality and he knew he lay within a cave, surrounded by Grannach, and that it was not a spirit that spoke to him, but Colun, whom he knew.

He said, "Colun?"

And Colun answered, "Yes?"

"Where am I?"

"In a cave, deep in the mountains. Where the invaders are not yet come."

He said, "The Breakers. They are the destroyers of worlds."

"They surely look to destroy ours," Colun said.

And he said, "Yes. I must go on," and sought to rise. But he was too weak, and so must fall back as Colun said, "First eat. Build your strength, eh? Then we'll speak of what's to be done."

"There's no time. They'll be in Ket-Ta-Witko soon."

"Likely, they're there already," Colun said in a bitter voice. "They've crossed the mountains, and by now must be near the plains."

"I must tell the People. I *know* about the Breakers."

"Morrhyn, you're near to death. You cannot go on yet. You must rest and gather your strength, and then we'll go on together."

He said, "No! There's not the time. I have to go on."

"To die? That should be useless, no? Listen to me. You'll rest here and regain your strength, and then I'll take you on."

He frowned. The light hurt his eyes and he supposed he must have suffered the snowblindness, but now could see—praise the Maker!— which meant he had lain some time. "How long have I been here?" he asked.

"Seven days," Colun answered.

"Too long!" he cried, and sought to rise again.

Colun pushed him back, and he was too weak to resist. Marjia hung a blanket about his shoulders and held out the bowl.

"Drink this," she urged. "You're very weak and need food."

He studied her round face awhile, and then his hands. They seemed to him like sticks, the skin drawn taut and thin over the linkages of bone. They trembled, and when he attempted to take the bowl he could not, for his hands shook and the effort of closing his fingers was more than he could manage.

Marjia said, "Let me." And to Colun, "Do you support him?"

Colun nodded and set a thick arm around Morrhyn's shoulders, holding him up as Marjia spooned broth into his mouth. Some spilled down his chin, and inside him doubt laughed mockingly. He was the savior of his people, a man too weak to hold a bowl of broth who must be fed like a baby? He drank the first bowl and then another, and then sleep took him away again and he dreamed.

It was no clear dream, with no clear answers in it, but like those others a thing of possibilities: all pessimism and hope, intermingled, as if he saw all the multiple threads of myriad lives and myriad deeds spun out to conclusions that might or not be real, action and interaction confused, outcomes multiplied. He saw the remnants of the Grannach in their caves, and the Breakers' great army flooding down through the foothills onto the plains of Ket-Ta-Witko. He saw battles fought and the People die, slaughtered like the Whaztaye, and the Breakers claim all of Ket-Ta-Witko for their own. And come back into the mountains to hunt down the last of the Grannach, for they would leave none alive where they went, save it be for food or sport. And he saw them go on, beyond Ket-Ta-Witko into the other worlds, spreading destruction and death, conquering folk whose ways were strange and incomprehensible, and knew that if they were not halted, then they would take all the worlds for their and all the Maker's creation be undone and only darkness rule.

He saw Rannach and Arrhyna, snowbound in their lonely valley, and the horses they tended, and the new life swelling in Arrhyna's belly. And he saw himself, speaking with them, and Colun, and then himself mounted and riding with Rannach across a landscape all wintry and warring, bringing word of what he knew and what the People must do. And he saw himself ignored and heeded both, and the strands divide as complicated as a spider's web.

He saw the strange ones of his other dreams, afloat on a great river that he did not know, hunted. And warriors strangely dressed, with weapons he did not understand that spat fire and killed at distances greater than any arrow might attain. And in that was again hope and despair, the division of possibilities, so that he felt as must a leaf caught and tossed all about in a great wind, and all he knew was that somehow the three were the hope of the People, though why or how he could not comprehend.

And then, alternate to the destruction of all he knew and held dear, he saw again the answer—which was so enormous and frightening, it woke him.

He lurched up from his bed, crying out; and Marjia was there, and Colun, holding him, confused as he wept for the enormity of what he knew and the impossibility of its achievement. And the knowledge that he must attempt it, though it cost him his life.

"Soft, soft, eh? All's well." Marjia stroked his brow as she might stroke the brow of a child frightened by nightmare.

"You're safe here," Colun said. "The invaders go by and know nothing of this cave."

"Safe?" He heard his own voice croaking. Marjia fed him more broth and he added, "None are safe. I must go."

Colun said, "Morrhyn, you'd not last a night out there. The Maker alone knows how you survived this far."

He said, "The Maker keeps me alive, that I do his bidding."

ut that was as much to give the young men something to do as for
f attack. He did not, truly, think that even crazed Chakthi would
his war in such hard weather. But those Colun had spoken of . . .
y were another matter.

He drew his blanket tighter about his shoulders as he wandered,
ly, it seemed, about the new Wintering Ground.

The lodges of the clan sprawled back from the canyon's entrance,
the horse herds penned to the rear. He had seen to it that the lodges of
the younger warriors were pitched around the perimeter, interspersed
with those of older men, the defenseless ones toward the center. The
canyon walls were high enough protection, and he thought that did
attack come, then it must arrive from the mouth, where raiders must first
ford the river and then swing around the lake. They would be seen, he
thought, and easily fought off. But he prayed it not come to that: his
people needed time to recover from the ravages of that bloody summer.

Nor less, he thought, needed their Dreamer. Morrhyn, where are
you? I do what I can, but I need you still.

He felt a pang of guilt at that. It seemed not so long ago that he had
accused Lhyn of thinking first of Morrhyn, their son only second. Now
he did the same.

Save surely it's different, he thought. Rannach is safe in Colun's care
whilst Morrhyn is the Maker alone knows where, is he still alive. And
had we ever need of a wakanisha, then it has been these last moons and
now.

He smiled as folk called greetings, showing them a face that exhibited only confidence and reassurance even as the doubts whirled like
windblown snow about his mind. These were *his* people, his charge; it
was his duty as akaman to protect and guide them, and for that he
needed his Dreamer. Almost he cursed Morrhyn for that departure, and
wondered yet again at the wakanisha's warning, and Colun's.

He spoke cheerfully as he wound his way about the camp, but all
the time his mind tossed fears and doubts and hopes around like a dog
pack squabbling over a juicy bone. It was hard to be akaman, harder still
without the advice of Morrhyn.

"I've tea brewing."

He smiled with genuine pleasure as he came back to his own lodge
and saw Lhyn by the fireside, the kettle hung there, and nodded and
settled onto the fur she had spread, leaning back against the frame she'd
hung with a thick bearskin.

"That should be good," he said. "Then I think I'll ride out and
check the scouts."

Had he not been

Colun look to hi

He heard

been?"

He emp

second told th

Matawaye were o

and got back his dre

ment and wonder, and

again that he must now g

Colun frowned. "It wil

bound now, and these Breake.

"Even so." Morrhyn smiled

bowl of broth. "I must attempt it.'

"Not yet." Colun pointed a stubb

weak yet. You must regain your strength

Morrhyn said, "There's not enough ti

"Ach!" Colun waved frustrated hands. "

mountain. Drag you on a sled if needs be! But

"Rannach's horses, no?" Morrhyn returned.

Colun barked harsh laughter. "Think you you ca

it across Ket-Ta-Witko with all the invaders—and the

way? You'll die, man! Likely when you fall off and break

head."

"Rannach will ward me," he said.

"Rannach's banished," Colun gave him back. "His life forfei

ventures onto the plains."

Morrhyn said, "Bring me to him, eh? Only that."

Colun dug fingers through his beard and shook his head. He was

about to speak again, but Marjia forestalled him.

"My husband speaks somewhat of the truth," she said, ignoring

Colun's grunt. "Surely you are too weak yet to travel. You need to rest

and flesh yourself, else you *shall* die along the way. What good that, eh?

Shall you defeat yourself with manly pride, thinking you can do what

you're too weak to attempt? Listen—are you bound on the Maker's

journey, then you'd best equip yourself, no? Else you fail him."

"You believe me?" Morrhyn asked.

Marjia and Colun both nodded.

Colun said, "You're the wakanisha of the Commacht, old friend.

How can I doubt you after what you've told us? I like it not, but . . . Is

it the Maker's will, then so be it."

Marjia said, "It's promise of a new world, free of these Breakers. I'd

"Do you need to?" She poured the tea as she spoke.

"It will encourage them. They're young and they grow restless. It does them good that their akaman comes to take a part in their watch."

Lhyn shrugged. "You look tired," she said.

"I am." He sipped his tea and smiled. "I'm tired of fighting and hiding and wondering what tomorrow shall bring. I wish things had not changed so, and that we might pass this winter like all the others."

"It's not so bad." She gestured at the wide confines of the canyon. "This is a good place you brought us to and there've been no attacks since the moon rose."

"No," he agreed. "But . . ."

"But?" she asked.

"I cannot help thinking of what Morrhyn dreamed and Colun told us," he said.

At mention of Morrhyn's name her face clouded a moment. Then she nodded and said, "We'd best be ready."

"Yes," he said. And then, "I wish he'd come back."

Lhyn nodded, unspeaking, and Racharran emptied his cup and set it down, saying, "I'll go check the scouts."

Like all the fighting men, he kept his favorite horse tethered by the lodge. He pulled the horse blanket away and set his saddle in place. The roan stamped and snorted, eager to run as he set his quiver in place and picked up his lance. He loosed the picket string and swung astride, fighting the anxious horse to a sedate walk as he went out through the tents, and only when he was clear of the circle, did he let it run.

It was good to be mounted and galloping, with the wind in his hair, and for the little while it took him to reach the canyon's mouth he gave himself over to freedom, to carelessness: it was a rare luxury. He checked the watchers along the lake's shore, and then rode round to where the others sat about the feet of the bluffs. All gave back the same word: nothing moved on the plain beyond save snow, and all they watched was windblown white, wolves that dared not enter the canyon for the smell of men, and flights of hungry crows. They were bored; they'd go out ascouting: let them at least see what *was* out there.

Racharran listened to them and finally agreed. He feared that if he refused, they'd go out anyway—alone and of their own deciding—which must erode his authority at a time he felt he must hold that command secure. So he sent off a scouting party—a group of seven young men with Bakaan as their leader, in compensation for his wound—and gave strict instructions that they go no more than five days' ride beyond the canyon and come back swift with whatever news they had. They cheered his decision and galloped back to their lodges to collect food for the journey, and Racharran hoped they should return without news, only hungry and tired.

He was disappointed.

It was Bakaan who brought him the news.

He was the only one left alive, and the horse he rode was close to dying from the wounds it bore, as if some giant lion had scored its flanks with lethal claws. Nor was the rider much better.

They came back, both man and horse, all bloody and wearied from the fighting and the ride, and neither had the strength to ford the river, but the horse must be led across and Bakaan carried. And on the far bank, the horse stumbled and could go no farther so that a warrior took out his Grannach knife and slit its throat, which was a mercy, and shouted for women to come butcher the carcass for the camp's dogs.

They brought the man to Racharran, and when the akaman saw him, he had them bring him inside his own lodge and lay him down on soft furs beside the fire. He called Lhyn and other women to tend his wounds as all the clan gathered around, waiting to hear what word he brought back.

"I fought them," Bakaan said, the words slurred thick because his lips were divided by the cut that ran down his face from where his hair began to where his chin ended, and he spat out blood. "We all fought them."

"Yes, and doubtless bravely." Racharran knelt close as Lhyn bathed Bakaan's bloody face and glanced frightened at the hole in his belly that pulsed out blood in a thick and steady welling. "The Tachyn, were they?"

"No." Bakaan shook his head, his teeth rattling like the snakes on the summer prairie. "Not Tachyn: worse. They were demons! They ride creatures big as buffalo, but like lions, or lizards—all clawed and furry and scaled, together. And their masters! Oh, Maker defend us, they're armored like rainbows and trick your eyes so that you can't see them right. They were terrible . . ."

His voice faltered. A woman pressed a cloth to the hole in his belly. Lhyn called for another to bring moss to staunch the wound. Racharran did not think it could be enough: Bakaan was dying. Before that final ending came, though, he needed to know what the young warrior had fought, or who. He feared he knew, but still he must ask, even to drawing out Bakaan's last breaths. It was his duty as akaman of the Commacht.

"How far did you go?" he asked.

"Full five days' ride," Bakaan answered slowly through gasps of bloody spittle. "To where the oak woods begin, past that big river where the catfish are in summer. We thought to camp awhile there and scout around. Ach!" He closed his eyes and clenched his teeth as Lhyn set the compress to his wound.

She looked at her husband, and in her eyes he saw the plea he leave Bakaan to rest. He shrugged: he could not grant that luxury, not until he had all the information the young warrior brought.

"How many of them?" he said.

Bakaan's voice came fainter now, rising and falling like the wind. "Five, there were. Scouts, I think, but not such scouts as I've ever seen. Maker! They came on us so swift—those beast they ride are faster than our horses in the snow, and killers, like their masters. They came on us as we rode out. We fought them as best we could, and ran when we saw we could not defeat them. They came after us . . ."

"How far?" Racharran asked, suddenly afraid Bakaan led the strangelings home.

"They halted at the river. By then, only three of us lived. Debo and Manus died along the way of their wounds, and I killed their horses, riding them back." He turned his ravaged face to Racharran and smiled: it was a ghastly expression as his severed lips parted. "But I did not come straight back—I looked to confuse our trail. I rode toward the Tachyn grass." He attempted a laugh that coughed out blood. "Better they find Chakthi, eh?"

"Yes, you did well," Racharran said. "You were brave."

"Brave?" Bakaan grimaced. "I was very afraid. I think we all were when we saw them. But we looked to heed you—we tried to come back with word, but they chased us down. Oh, Maker, we were like hunted deer to them, and they the wolves."

"And you saw only these scouts?" Racharran asked. "None others?"

"No." Bakaan's teeth began to chatter. "Only those five. I . . ."

His voice choked off. The light went out in his eyes and his lips hung slackly open, dribbling blood that slowly stopped.

Lhyn said, "He's dead." The women with her began to chant the deathsong.

Racharran nodded grimly and reached out to shutter Bakaan's lids over the lifeless, staring eyes. "Prepare him for burial with all honor. He was a brave man."

Lhyn said softly, "Shall we all die bravely, like him?"

Racharran looked at his wife and answered, "The Maker willing, no." And to himself silently: Save the Maker turns his face from us and leaves us to this scourge.

"Are they what Colun warned of?" Lhyn asked. "What Morrhyn dreamed of?"

Racharran said, "I think they must be. What else can they be?"

"Then . . ."

"Yes." Racharran finished the sentence for her. "They've come through the mountains and are into Ket-Ta-Witko. And we had best prepare for such war as shall make this summer seem nothing."

She said, "Maker, defend us! What of Rannach, Arrhyna? What of Morrhyn?"

Racharran had no ready answer, and a problem of far more immediate concern—that these strangeling invaders approached dangerously close to the wintering clans. He pondered awhile in silence, staring at Bakaan's ravaged face, then said, "I must see them for myself."

Lhyn gasped and shook her head in mute denial.

Racharran sighed. "The People must be warned," he said. "I must see these invaders with own eyes, and send word to the other clans."

"Not you." Lhyn reached for his hand. "Why must you go?"

"I must know for myself," he said. "Can you not understand that?"

"I can understand that I've lost my son and Morrhyn," Lhyn returned. "And now, perhaps, shall lose my husband."

"How else can I tell them?" Racharran asked. "Do I go to Juh and the others with only the word of a dead young warrior, think you they'll believe me?"

"Why not?" she gave him back. "Shall they name Bakaan a liar? His dying words all untruths?"

"The way they've been, yes!" he said. "They'd likely tell me Bakaan fell to the Tachyn and only looked to glorify his defeat."

"Then they'd be fools."

"Yes!" he said. "Just as they've been fools this bloody summer. Think you they'll not look to turn their eyes the other way on this as on all else?"

Lhyn knew he spoke the truth. But even so . . . Must she now lose her husband as she'd lost her son and Morrhyn, about whom her feelings were all confused and mixed since his departure. She shook her head and sighed.

Racharran said, "I must! It's the only way I can be sure."

She said, not yet ready to admit defeat, "Sure? Are you not sure now?"

"Yes, but I am akaman of the Commacht," he said. "Shall I ask others to do what I will not? Besides, it must be my eyes see them and my word to the rest; else none shall believe it."

"Then let them not," she said.

Racharran smiled sadly and squeezed her hand. "And the People all go down before these strangelings? Save we fight together, I think we shall not survive—any of us. Did Morrhyn not say as much? Are we not united, then these invaders shall likely eat us up. I *must* go."

"And die alone?"

He shook his head. "I've no intention of dying. I intend only to *see*. To scout and bring back word."

"Like Bakaan?"

"Bakaan did not expect them. He had no warning. I do, and so shall be very careful."

Her fingers played in his, clutching tight as if she'd not leave him go, not chance another loss. She would not look at him, not meet his gaze for fear he see the tears brimming there.

"I shall be very cautious," he said, and squeezed her hand harder. "I've too much to lose, else."

"Ach, go!" She pulled her hand free so that she might cup his face with both, and draw him close and kiss him. "Go and be brave! But also careful, eh? I'd not lose you too."

Hadduth studied his akaman from under hooded lids. Chakthi's hair hung all unbound and tangled, dull with the ashes that he still daily scattered over his head; and would, Hadduth knew, until his lust for vengeance was assuaged. Which meant until Rannach was slain, or all the Commacht. The Tachyn Dreamer was no longer sure one death would satisfy Chakthi.

Carefully, he said, "We cannot pursue them in such weather. We're not even sure where they winter."

Chakthi looked up from his contemplation of the flames. His eyes were dark and cruel in the midst of the mourning paint he still wore. "We can find them."

"Not easily," Hadduth said. "Perhaps not at all."

"Dream of their Wintering Ground," Chakthi demanded. "Tell me where it is, where they hide."

Hadduth paused an instant, choosing the words of his reply. "I cannot command the dreams," he said slowly. "Only interpret what the Maker sends me."

Chakthi smiled, which made Hadduth distinctly uneasy, and for long moments fixed the wakanisha with his burning gaze. Then he asked, "What use are you, then?"

Hadduth swallowed, forcing himself to face Chakthi's accusing glare. "I am wakanisha of the Tachyn," he said. "I speak the Will."

"The Ahsa-tye-Patiko?" Chakthi spat into the fire. "What does that mean to me? Vachyr is dead, slain by the whoreson Commacht in defiance of the Will. And Rannach's punishment? To live, when the Ahsa-tye-Patiko demands his death. I've no more use for the Will."

"It was," Hadduth said very carefully, "a judgment I consider wrong. But even so, it *was* the judgment of the Chiefs' Council."

"The Council?" Chakthi said it like a curse. "I've less use for those toothless old women than I have for the Will."

Hadduth frowned, his eyes wandering about the lodge. Surreptitiously, he shaped a sign of warding: Chakthi voiced blasphemy now. "Perhaps he's dead," he suggested. "It cannot be easy to survive in the high mountains in winter."

"The Grannach aid him!" Chakthi snarled. "Colun was ever Racharran's friend, and he'll be friend to Racharran's son. Could I, I'd take the war to the Stone Folk."

Again, Hadduth made a gesture of warding: the Stone Folk were inviolate under the Will. Save, he thought, nothing was inviolate to Chakthi's lust, neither the Stone Folk nor the Ahsa-tye-Patiko. He licked his lips and said, "When the Moon of the Turning Year rises, we can go back to war. The Maker knows, we've fought hard this past year, but the clan is hungry. They've . . ."

"I know." Chakthi's hand chopped air, silencing the Dreamer. "They'd fill their bellies sooner than avenge my son."

"Hungry men make poor warriors," Hadduth said. "Let them rest awhile. Let them hunt."

"Hunt what?" snapped Chakthi. "Where's the game? There are no deer, nor buffalo. Save what they find dead."

Hadduth said, "Even so . . ." And fell silent as Chakthi's hand snaked to seize his wrist.

The grip was hard and he must fight not to struggle, not to show his discomfort. "Listen," Chakthi said, his voice hot and heavy. "I'll see Rannach and his whoreson father dead for what they've done. I'll have Racharran's wife for my pleasure, and Rannach's traitorous bride too. And when I tire of them, I'll give them to my favored men. I'll have my revenge, and I care nothing for what the Ahsa-tye-Patiko says or what people think of me. And who is not with me is against me. Do you understand?"

Hadduth nodded, frightened. Vaguely, in that part of his mind that stood aloof from Chakthi's fury and observed dispassionately what they said, he wondered if he did not fear his akaman more than the Maker. Surely Chakthi's anger was the more immediate: he saw vividly the punishments Chakthi had ordered for those who argued with him or disobeyed him. He thought of Dohnse, stripped of all he owned and banished to the farther edges of the Wintering Ground for allowing Morrhyn to ride free. Dohnse's life was hard now: Hadduth would not see himself consigned to such ignominy. He said, "I understand, and I am with you."

He wondered if in that moment he forsook the Maker. But Chakthi loosed his wrist, and as he massaged his numbed hand, he knew he feared the instancy of Chakthi's rage at least as much as he feared the disapprobation of the Maker. Later, he thought, he could make apology.

Chakthi said, "Good," and smiled. "I'd have my wakanisha with me, and have him dream for me."

"I can try," Hadduth said.

"You can do better," Chakthi returned. "You've pahé root?"

Hadduth nodded.

"Then go build a sweat lodge and eat your pahé and dream for me. I'll not see your face again until you've answers."

Hadduth nodded again. "As my akaman commands."

Chakthi flicked dismissive fingers and the Dreamer quit the lodge. He tugged his wolfskin cloak tight about his shoulders as he emerged from the warmth into the cold outside. Great soft flakes of snow fell out of a dark and starless sky. The White Grass Moon was hidden behind the overcast that delivered the snow, and the lodges of the Tachyn huddled like some great crop of mushrooms over the Wintering Ground. A dog barked and was challenged by others. Hadduth thought the sound mocking, perhaps even condemnatory, as if the Maker spoke through the throats of the dogs. He *had* made a choice, he realized: he had chosen Chakthi's service over that of his calling, and for a moment he contemplated turning back, telling his akaman that he could no longer dream and the pahé root would make no difference because the Maker turned his face from the Tachyn for their betrayal of the Ahsa-tye-Patiko.

Then he saw Dohnse, out toward the farthest edge of the Wintering Ground. The warrior shuffled across the snow, hunting for wood, and when others saw him, they presented him their backs or flung balled handfuls of snow at him. None spoke to him; some urged dogs to attack him, children pointed and jeered. Hadduth thought he could not endure that: he found his own warm lodge and the pahé root and set about Chakthi's business.

28 Endings and Beginnings

Rannach saw them first. He was out on his snow-shoes with a deer slung across his shoulders. He let the carcass drop and nocked an arrow to his bowstring before he recognized them against the glare of sun on snow. When he did, he set arrow and bow back in the quiver and began to shuffle his way over the hardpack toward them, wondering why so many Grannach came when before only Colun and Marjia had ventured into the valley.

He saw those two at the head of the little column, four more behind, and wondered what it was the others dragged on that sled.

When he saw the fur-swathed burden, he gasped, scarce able to believe his eyes.

"Morrhyn?"

"Rannach." The wakanisha was hard to recognize, he was so thin, his skin burned dark as old leather in stark contrast to the white of his hair, but his eyes burned bright as if lit by some inner fire. "Is Arrhyna well?"

"Yes." Rannach nodded dumbly, gaping at the Dreamer. "You?"

His voice begged a question filled with doubt. Morrhyn smiled and said, "My friends would not let me walk, for all I'm quite capable."

"He's weak," Marjia said disapprovingly. "Perhaps weak as he's obstinate."

"You see?" Morrhyn raised a hand to gesture at the Grannach

woman. Rannach saw how the skin clung taut to the bones. "I told them I could walk, but there's no arguing with this one."

"Hush, you," Marjia said. "Save your strength. You'll need it, are you to do what you insist you must."

"She's a tyrant," Morrhyn said, his fond tone belying the words. "Nor her husband much better."

"We'd have kept him longer," Colun said. "But he insisted—"

"And he is obstinate as all men," Marjia interrupted, "and as foolish, so we bring him. Now, shall we see him warm in your lodge?"

"And tell you all that's happened," Colun said.

"And what must happen now," Morrhyn added.

Rannach frowned, confused, then nodded and fell into shuffling step alongside the Grannach as they strode onward, hauling the sled.

Like her husband before her, Arrhyna was surprised to see so many Grannach, and wondered what it was they dragged with them on the sled. But she set aside the trout she cleaned and washed her fishy hands with snow, then rose to greet them as they came up.

"I bring guests."

Rannach smiled as he called to her, as if this were all quite normal, but behind his cheerful humor Arrhyna saw concern. She called back, "And most welcome," but still she felt the ugly prickling of presentiment. And when she saw Morrhyn, she could not help but gasp at his appearance.

"I've changed somewhat, eh?" The Dreamer thrust aside the furs covering him and clambered from the sled. "But you've not. You're lovely as ever. Even lovelier."

He waved back the Grannach, who looked to support him and stepped toward her. She thought him vastly changed yet somehow the same, as if he were transformed. She thought his eyes burned, and when they fell toward her belly she knew, even though she did not yet swell, that he was aware of the life she carried there.

She said, "You flatter me," and wondered what he did here, where he had come from. And what his arrival presaged. She felt suddenly frightened.

He said, "No, I speak only the truth," and put his arms around her in a friendly embrace that succeeded in bringing his mouth close enough to her ear that he might whisper, "Does Rannach know?"

"Not yet," she said, not needing amplification.

"Perhaps you should tell him," he murmured. "You've both decisions to make."

Arrhyna felt her smile freeze. For an instant she felt an unwelcome future rush upon her, then Morrhyn let her go and she looked to the others. "I bid you welcome, and enter our lodge in friendship." She sought stability in the formal greeting.

Marjia said, "It shall be crowded."

"No matter." Rannach stepped out of his snowshoes and hung the deer on the gutting frame. "Friends can never overcrowd a lodge."

Even so, there was little clear space when all entered and settled around the fire. The Grannach were short but bulky, and seemed to take up more space than the three Matawaye. Arrhyna thought that Morrhyn, thin as he was, took up less than any other. She could not help but study him even as she set a kettle to boiling and prepared tea. She anticipated Colun asking after his promised tiswin, but the creddan made no mention of the brew and that disturbed her further. She waited for someone to speak, aware they brought news she doubted would be good.

All, it seemed, waited for Morrhyn, whilst he appeared only to luxuriate in the lodge's warmth.

He beamed, stretching his hands toward the fire, and said, "Ach, but it's good to sit in a lodge again. Not"—with an apologetic glance at the Grannach—"that it was not fine in the caves. But this is somewhat like coming home."

Rannach said, "This *is* home."

"Yes." Morrhyn looked around. "And a fine place you've made of it. You prosper here."

Arrhyna lifted the kettle from the fire and realized she lacked cups enough for all. Marjia saw her discomfort and went bustling outside to return with cups that she held as Arrhyna filled them and then passed around.

When all were served, Colun said bluntly, "Do we get down to it? Or shall we sit around talking small, while . . ."

"Hush, you." Marjia dug an elbow into his ribs. "This is for Morrhyn to say, no?"

Colun grunted and ducked his head and looked to the snow-haired wakanisha. Arrhyna felt her mouth dry. It seemed a draft found a way through the lodge's hides, dancing cold fingers down the length of her spine. She touched Rannach's hand, staring at Morrhyn.

He sighed, no longer smiling, and said, "I've news, and not much of it good. Ket-Ta-Witko stands in danger, and all the People; terrible danger . . ."

He spoke then of the war Chakthi pressed, and the attacks the Commacht had suffered, the indifference of all save Yazte's Lakanti. He told of his quest, of finding the cave and surviving there, and the dreams that came to him. From time to time he broke off, allowing Colun to describe the ravages suffered by the Grannach, and how the invaders came through the mountains, and the Stone Folk were slain and now become a single people with him their leader. Arrhyna listened and felt her heart grow chill. Her fingers entwined with Rannach's and held them hard.

"They've not come here," Rannach said when the awful telling was done.

"Not yet," Colun returned him. "This valley is out of their way; they go to your plains. But when they're done there . . ."

"Are they successful," Rannach said. "Are they not defeated."

"The People stand no chance against them." Morrhyn's voice was a cold wind blowing down the night, unwelcome as it was unavoidable. "This I have dreamed, and I tell you it is true. The clans are all divided, and save they unite . . . Even if they do unite . . ."

He shook his head helplessly, hopelessly. Rannach said, "Then the Maker delivers the People to these . . . Breakers, you name them? He turns his face from us?"

Morrhyn looked awhile into the fire and then shrugged. "Surely the People are tested," he said lowly. "Surely they have erred, and—I believe—earned his displeasure."

"What's that to do with me?" Rannach asked, and glanced sidelong at Arrhyna. "With us?"

Morrhyn raised his head to face the younger man. Arrhyna thought she saw pain writ there. "Nothing," he said, "and everything. Do you not see it?"

Arrhyna believed she did, and liked it not at all; but she kept silent, waiting for her husband to speak.

Rannach frowned. "I am banished," he said at last. "Accounted no longer of the People, but an outcast."

Colun snorted then irritably, and asked, "Think you these Breakers shall make such fine distinctions when they come back to scour these hills? What shall you do then? Go to them crying, 'I am not of the People. Leave me be?' I think they'll not care much who or what you are, but only slay you and your bride. I'd thought Racharran's son made of better stuff."

Rannach scowled and Arrhyna tightened her grip on his hand, fearing he'd take such offense as to strike at the Grannach.

"Soft, soft." Morrhyn spoke again, his narrowed hands gesturing placation. "Shall we friends fall to quarreling and disagreement like all the rest? Are we no better than Chakthi, or those others who pretend there's naught amiss?"

He looked from one to another, his eyes lit with such inner fire as to still them all. Arrhyna thought she saw the Maker looking out from those orbs—how else could Morrhyn know she was pregnant, save all his dreams were true? And if they were all true . . . Again she felt those chill fingers trail her spine, tingle over her heart.

Rannach met Morrhyn's gaze awhile, then lowered his eyes. "Tell me what it is I should see," he said, his voice gruff with confused emotions. "I am only a plain man, a simple warrior. I do not see these things so clear."

"The Ahsa-tye-Patiko is more than just a set of rules," Morrhyn said, his voice soft but yet seeming to ring loud as any clarion. "It is our covenant with the Maker, the thing that binds us to him and him to us. And it stands broken, forgotten or ignored by many. Thus are those wards he set about our land weakened, and the Breakers able to come through."

Rannach frowned. "You say the sins of men deliver this scourge?"

"Yes." Morrhyn nodded solemnly. "The Maker forgives much, but when men forsake the covenant of the Will . . . Why should he remember us when we forget him? Listen—Chakthi's was the first sin, that he was akaman of the Tachyn but still agreed to Arrhyna's kidnap. No less Hadduth's, for he was wakanisha and should have dissuaded Chakthi from that course . . ."

"Ach, dissuade Chakthi?" Rannach waved a scornful hand. "He's as likely to try dissuading Chakthi as attempt to milk a bull buffalo."

"And so perhaps his sin is the greater," Morrhyn said. "For it was Hadduth's charge to define and interpret the Will, and he did not. Like Chakthi, he turned his face from the Maker in pursuit of only human profit: that was the second sin. And then—the third—Vachyr took Arrhyna, which was a sure breaking of the Ahsa-tye-Patiko."

"And I slew Vachyr." Rannach's voice was defiant, his eyes no less so. "I slew him within the aegis of the Meeting Ground."

Morrhyn said, "Yes," looking directly at Rannach. "That was the fifth sin."

Rannach said, "The fifth? Surely the fourth, if it *was* a sin—he gave me no other choice."

Morrhyn said, "Did he not? Truly?"

Rannach hesitated. Arrhyna drew in a deep and frightened breath, clutching his hand hard. Morrhyn knew all that had transpired: she saw it in his eyes, all fiery with the dreams the Maker had sent him. She summoned up her courage and said, "I urged Rannach to kill him. I told him what Vachyr had done and told Rannach to slay him for it. So is there sin to be apportioned here, then I must take my share."

Rannach said, "No! What sin there is is mine alone. I chose to slay Vachyr; I was mad with rage. Leave Arrhyna out of this."

Morrhyn said, "I cannot. She's of the People, as are you. You are both the Maker's children, parts of his creation and so bound by his Will. Arrhyna's was the fourth sin, that she urged you to the fifth."

"Then are we guilty as Chakthi?" Rannach asked defiantly. "Guilty as Vachyr and Hadduth?"

"No." Morrhyn shook his head and stretched out his lips in a wan smile. "Your sins were those of reaction, not commission. And you suffered banishment, by agreement of all the Council."

"Then what is all this about?" Rannach demanded.

"Atonement. And the saving of the People. Forgiveness; salvation, all well."

"I do not understand."

"I must go back to Ket-Ta-Witko," Morrhyn said.

Soft, somehow knowing what should come next, Arrhyna gasped, "No!"

Morrhyn smiled at her—gently, apologetically—and said, "This is a hard duty, but I've no other way, no other choice."

"Rannach cannot go back," she said. "On pain of death, he cannot! They'll execute him, does he go back."

"Why should I?" Rannach asked.

"Because I must," Morrhyn answered. "And because you love the People. Because you are a brave, good man. Because I need you."

Arrhyna said again louder, "No!"

"I'll willingly gift you a horse; two," Rannach said. "But go back? That's my death. Even my father would command it."

"Not with the word I bring," Morrhyn said. "The word I *must* bring, else all the People fall to the Breakers. And the last of the Grannach, and all the worlds beyond, unending until nothing is left save destruction and ruin and chaos, and all the Maker's works brought down and only sad, dark night left ruling."

Rannach sat openmouthed, his eyes haunted. "So bad? Truly?"

"Truly."

Arrhyna, all cold now, said, "Must it be Rannach? Why not . . ." She looked, ashamed, at Colun.

Morrhyn smiled sadly and said, "The Stone Folk saved me when I might have died in the snow, and they've fought battles enough with the Breakers and have their own wounds to tend. They've done their share, with more to come. Now I need someone who can ride hard and bring me safe to the People. The Grannach do not ride—I've no other choice but to ask Rannach." His sad smile went away, only remorse left behind. "Could it be otherwise . . ."

Arrhyna closed her eyes tight against the tears that threatened, and in that self-willed darkness heard Morrhyn add, "But there's a thing he should know before he chooses. Shall you tell him, or I?"

She opened her eyes to face that future she had sensed approached since first Morrhyn embraced her, and she knew he saw her as only a wakanisha could. Almost, she hated him for that knowledge, but not quite. How could she, when in his burning eyes she saw only unwelcomed truths and the pain that seared him for what he knew, and knew he must do?

She heard Rannach say, "Tell me what?" and turned her face to her husband.

"I carry your child," she said.

Rannach's jaw dropped. His expression was comical enough that Arrhyna almost laughed: would have, had other and weightier matters not pressed her lips tight together. Then Marjia said, "Why are men always so surprised?" And she could not help but chuckle.

Rannach asked, "A boy or a girl?"

Which seemed to Arrhyna so foolish, she began to giggle, and say, "How can I tell?"

But Morrhyn said, "A boy. A fine and healthy boy."

And all the laughter ceased as they looked to the Dreamer, who essayed an almost shamefaced smile and shrugged, saying, "I saw it in my dreams. It's a boy, who—"

He broke off, his smile disappearing.

Arrhyna said, "What? Tell me, Morrhyn."

The wakanisha licked his lips nervously, and ran a hand over his gaunt face and said, "There are threads to dreams, like all the threads that weave out a blanket. Some go one way, some another; others are broken . . ."

Arrhyna felt the fingers again, dancing chilly down her spine, as if all the possible futures plucked at her. She reached slowly for the kettle, filling her own cup and then passing the receptacle on. Bad manners, she knew, but knew she had no time now for manners, only the terrible dread urgency that filled her. She voiced a question even as she felt convinced she knew the answer, as if she owned the powers of a Dreamer.

"Does Rannach not go?"

Morrhyn took a cup and sipped, then he looked her sadly in the eye and said, "It must be his choice. I cannot say."

She drank tea and felt an emptiness open inside her. She said, "That's no choice, is it?"

He shrugged. "There are always choices."

"Poor choices sometimes," she said. "And sometimes no choice at all."

Rannach looked from one to the other, confused, and asked, "What do you say?"

Arrhyna tore her eyes from Morrhyn's solemn gaze and turned to face her husband. "The horses are healthy, no?"

Rannach nodded.

"And there's a deer to butcher?"

Rannach said, "Yes, you saw it."

She nodded. "You'll need meat, are you to travel fast."

"I've not agreed to go yet," Rannach began.

"If you do not, then our child will die. Likely I shall too. And you, and all the People. Is that not right, Morrhyn?"

Morrhyn nodded. "That's one trail the future takes."

Arrhyna could not understand how she was able to speak so firm, so clear. "Rannach, do you go ready that deer. You'd best leave soon."

He said, "And leave you alone? With child?"

Marjia said, "She'll not be alone. She'll be with us."

Rannach hesitated.

Arrhyna said, "Go, husband. I'll be safe with our friends. Safer than if you remain."

Rannach frowned, staring at her, and she took hold of both his hands and smiled as best and warmly as she could and said, "There's no other choice. I wish there were, but there's not. So go and do as Morrhyn bids you, then come back safe."

For a while he only stared at her, reading the truth in her eyes. Then he swallowed hard and ducked his head and kissed her, and went out from the tent to butcher the deer.

Racharran took only five of his most reliable warriors with him, men proven in battle who would not panic or run at the sight of what he feared they'd encounter. All well, he hoped they would spot the strangelings only at a distance—locate the placement of their forces and assess their strength that he have some clearer idea what the People faced—then come back safe with such information. That was what he hoped, and what he told Lhyn would happen as she held him tight and fought back tears, but they both knew that hope was one thing and reality another.

He was no Dreamer that he could foresee the future, but he could not forget Bakaan's wounds or the dying warrior's words, which seemed clear portent of things to come. He wished Morrhyn were there to advise him—he felt he became akaman and wakinsha both, and that was a terrible weight to carry. But he put on a brave face and led his little party out from the canyon across the snow fields, in the direction of the catfish river Bakaan had described.

The snow was hard frozen and relatively easy to travel. The White Grass Moon waned, and with its going the snowfalls ceased, replaced by only bitter cold and winds that cut to the bone. Icicles hung glittering in the watery sunlight from trees that thrust out naked branches like the clutching fingers of nightmares. Rivers and streams were locked beneath thick crusts of ice, their water black as night and cold as death's kiss beneath. There was little game: deer sought the shelter of the woodlands, and the few buffalo herds they saw huddled disconsolate in close-packed, defensive groups where trees or terrain afforded some shelter. It was not a time to travel. That, at least, was some consolation, for Racharran thought not even crazed Chakthi could persuade his warriors out from their Wintering Ground in such harsh weather.

He led his men on. All wore furs—bear, buffalo, and wolf—with more for the horses, and blankets and skins for shelter at night when men and animals both might freeze to death. They each carried a lance and a bow, spare strings and quivers filled with arrows tipped with sharp Grannach steel; also knives and tinder and packs of dried meat, and fodder for the horses—the equipment of a raiding party. They wore no paint, but each man daubed his eyes with black against the snowblindness; and all rode cautious, as if they *were* out raiding.

They came to the catfish river and walked their mounts over the ice to the oakwood beyond. So far they had seen no sign of the invaders. They camped inside the wood and chanced a fire. Racharran calculated the timber should hide the smoke, and without that heat they might well die. Before the light went, he checked the forest trails for spoor, but found only trunks scratched deep and high, as if lions had tested their claws against the wood. The score marks were level with his head as he sat his horse, and he guessed them made by the beasts Bakaan had described. He marveled at their size, and wondered if such creatures might be slain.

The forest was a day and half's ride across. It would likely have been swifter to skirt around, but the trees afforded shelter from the relentless wind and cover from unwelcome observation. It ended on the rim of a wide and shallow valley edged on its farther side with broken hills, drumlins that scattered in a hundred directions, the gulches between all wide and deep enough to hide a raiding party.

On the far side of those breaks, where the land flattened again to a broad plain dotted with stands of winter-bared trees, they saw their quarry.

Bylas was out ahead, and came cantering back with his lance held up horizontal in sign of warning. Racharran halted the rest in the shelter of a low ridge.

"The Maker blind me if I lie," Bylas said even as he dragged his horse to a panting stop, "but I've never seen such creatures. They're all Bakaan described and worse." He shaped a sign of warding.

Racharran asked, "How far away?"

"Just out of bowshot," Bylas said. "Out on the flat where the stream turns past a wood. They're hunting buffalo. No!" He shook his head and spat onto the frozen snow. "Not hunting—slaughtering. Ach, I've not seen the like of it."

His eyes were wide and his face drawn. Racharran knew him for a phlegmatic man, not given to excitement or fear: now he looked horrified.

"Wait here." Racharran passed his rein to Bylas and swung to the ground. "You others, come with me. Bylas has seen them—I'd have us all witnesses."

Bylas said, "Carefully, eh?"

Racharran nodded and drove his lance into the ground, then took up his bow and looked to his companions. "We only watch, you understand? Not fight, save they attack."

Bylas muttered, "The Maker grant they don't."

"The wind's in our favor," Racharran said more confidently than he felt.

"What if . . . ?" asked Bishi, and had no need to end the sentence.

"We run," Racharran said. "We are watchers now. We need only to know their strength and what they are, and bring that word back to the clan and all the People."

"But if they see us or scent us," Zhonne asked, "and attack?"

Again Racharran said, "We run. This is not war with the Tachyn—brothers though we be, we do not go back for any fallen. We run, that some, at least, live to take back the word."

"That is not our way," said Lonah. "To leave a fallen brother?"

"I think," Racharran said, "that these are not such enemies as we've ever faced. I believe it our duty to warn all of the People, and to do that we must survive."

"And if you fall?" asked Motsos. "Are we to leave you?"

Racharran said, "Yes," and stabbed a finger at each of them in turn. "I charge you with this duty—that no matter what happens here, you will endeavor to go back. Not look to save a fallen brother or boast your prowess, but only take back word of what these creatures are, and the threat they are, to the Commacht and all of the People. Do you swear to this?"

They liked this not at all, but one by one, under the ferocity of his gaze, they agreed.

"Then let us go," Racharran said, more cheerfully than he felt, "and see what Bylas has seen."

"You'll not enjoy it," Bylas said, nor did they. The buffalo were in a small draw—a herd of thirty or so, half that number already dead, their bloodsmell panicking the rest so that they milled about and charged uselessly up the ridges or toward the entrance. Racharran could not decide which he found the more disgusting—the creatures that attacked or the creatures that paced the rims and the entrance. The latter he supposed men: they wore the shapes of men, the heads and arms and legs all encased in bright armor that shone and glittered and tricked the eye so that it was just as Bakaan had told him. They were hard to see, to define, and they carried swords and lances that seemed possessed of their own power, so that when only a single strangeling sprang out before the terrified buffalo brandishing his weapon, the beasts snorted and turned away, driven back toward the other predators.

And those were no less horrifying than Bakaan had said—each big as a buffalo bull, but not such creatures as Racharran had ever seen. They ran on wide and padded feet that sprouted claws large as daggers, and their bodies were fur and scales combined, with lashing tails like those of rats. They had massive shoulders and heavy heads, sharp-eared and longly jawed, with savage fangs and hot red eyes. They seemed to Racharran abominations, as if different and unrelated creatures were joined in horrid amalgamation. And their appearance was matched, even surpassed, by their bloodlust—Racharran must hold himself back from crying out at what they did to the buffalo.

The People hunted the buffalo. Like the Matawaye, they were part of life's circle, creations of the Maker, set down in Ket-Ta-Witko that they might multiply and grant their bounty to the People. Their skins made robes and tents, their bones implements and glue, the sinews cords. All was designated within the Ahsa-tye-Patiko, and the People took no more from the herds than met their needs: that was the Maker's Will.

This was not. This was wanton slaughter, neither for meat nor shelter but only for lust of killing, of destruction. The strangeling beasts clawed and bit and roared as the buffalo bellowed in terror and pain, and stumbled in the tanglings of their own entrails. Racharran saw a cow brought down and gutted and left kicking behind; a bull tossing helpless horns and running as two of the beasts mounted its back and chewed away its spine, and then left it to course and gut another. A yearling died at a single bite.

It was all he could do not to flight arrows against them. But he fought that impulse and made himself still and watched, even as bile rose in his throat and he felt such hatred as he had never felt, not even against Chakthi. He heard a sound and turned to see Lonah spitting vomit. At his side, Bishi thrust a finger between his teeth and bit down, that he not cry out in disgust. Zhonne and Motsos lay white-faced as the snow under them.

The buffalo died, all of them, and their slayers gorged on some and left the rest all bloody and ruined and pointlessly slain. Then the man-things came down and carved off steaks and ribs and set to eating the meat raw.

They were easier to define against the dark shapes of the buffalo carcasses, and Racharran saw that there were no more than seven of them, and seven of the creatures. For a moment he thought of re-scinding his own orders and attacking, but he knew—for all his outrage prompted him to believe otherwise—that such monstrosities as these could not be defeated by six Commacht. They were too terrible, too given to wanton slaughter: what they did had nothing in it of humanity, but only . . . *otherness*, such strangeness as spoke of generation out-side the Maker's creation. He felt he looked on blasphemy incarnate, as if all the darkness and ugliness of the very worst of sins were released into the world and become rapacious flesh.

He watched aghast, scarce daring to breathe for fear these things sense it and slay him before he had chance to tell the People what he had seen. He watched them end their feast, and the man-things call up the beasts and set saddles on them, then mount and ride away. He was ashamed he felt so glad when they went away from where he lay.

"What now?" Zhonne asked, his voice harsh with disgust.

Racharran thought a moment. Then: "I think those must be scouts." He did not want to say what he knew he must, but he was akaman of the Commacht—he had a duty. So he said, "We must go after them and see where they go. Likely they join a larger band. We need to know how large, and where it is."

"Likely we go to our deaths," Motsos said.

Racharran said, "Perhaps. Would you turn back?"

Motsos glanced sidelong at Zhonne and Bishi, then shook his head.

"But a long way behind them, eh?" Lonah said. "And very wary."

"Yes," Racharran said, and forced his mouth to smile. "But look you, they go toward the Tachyn grass. Shall we dare that?"

It was a poor jest, but it elicited smiles, albeit grim.

"I think," Lonah said, "that after what I've seen this day I am not much afraid of Chakthi's wrath."

"Then we go," Racharran said. "And see what worse things lie ahead."

The strangelings' stranger mounts ran swift and sinuous, their wide paws better equipped for traversing the snow than the smaller hooves of the Commacht horses. Racharran held his men back—those paws left a clear trail, and he'd not risk battle with such beasts. At least, not yet, for in his soul he knew that fight must sooner or later come. But not yet, he prayed. Not until all the People understand and join together to face this threat. So he waited as the invaders disappeared into the snowy distance and only then took his men out.

They crossed the flat and, as the light began to fade, came to a band of low hills bearded with windblown pines. The tracks went into a gully that shone with harlequin patterns of shadow and starlight. Racharran halted at the entrance. He did not know if these creatures traveled by night or would make camp, but he was loath to stumble on them. He bade his men wait and himself went forward on foot. He saw, as he tracked them, that his own feet were easily encompassed by the massive paw marks: he clutched his bow tighter and willed his pounding heart slow down. Then, where the gully turned, he saw the reflection of fireglow on the snow and heard the rumbling growls of the beasts interspersed with guttural voices. He tested the wind. It was tricksy amongst the hills and dividing channels, but came mostly from ahead: he decided to chance it, and crept closer.

Hugging shadow as if it were Lhyn's body, he moved into the angle of the gully and saw ahead a widening, a shallow bowl where the strangelings made their camp.

The riders sat about a fire, still armored save for their helmets, and he saw they were not, in the generalities of their shaping, so very different from men. He was surprised to see that three were female. This he assumed from the angling of cheekbones and lips, for all of them were of similar physiognomy and length of hair. He was even more surprised that they were so . . . the only word he could think of was *beautiful*. Their hair was long and fair, falling in soft, smooth folds about faces that, even planed and shadowed by the fire's light, were lovely, as if physical beauty were cynically contrasted with horrid nature. Their brows were wide and smooth above large, gently slanted eyes, their noses straight, their mouths generous, their teeth broad and white, tearing at raw chunks of buffalo meat that dribbled blood down their chins so that they wiped and licked it from their fingers, laughing.

Racharran stared at them awhile, fascinated and horrified, and then to where their monstrous mounts lay on the snow. They were not tethered, and from time to time one rose and paced and growled before lying down again. He thought them all weird and horrible, and thanked the Maker the wind blew as it did and that they set out no guards. He supposed them too confident for that.

He crept away with held breath and returned to his men.

That night none of the Commacht slept nor lit a fire, but only sat huddled with their horses close at hand, praying the wind not change direction or the animals betray them with a snicker. When cold dawn came up, Racharran once more ventured into the gully. The invaders' fire was only embers, their trail leading out. He called up his men, and they continued their wary pursuit.

Beyond the hills lay open plain, then forest, and they must hang back for fear their quarry sight them. But the tracks ran clear, as if the invaders had learned what they would and now returned to report.

It took them three days to traverse the forest, and when they reached the edgewoods they could see the pinnacle of the Maker's Mountain far off in the distance, shining brilliant under the winter sun. Save for brief obeisance, they paid the peak scant attention, for their eyes were entirely occupied with what lay between the woodland and the mountains.

An army such as Ket-Ta-Witko had never seen camped there, spread bright and brilliant across the snow. Racharran stared in horrified wonder. These invaders did not put up such lodges as the People used, but rather great pavilions that might hold whole families and were all rainbow-striped and hung with gaudy banners that bristled and crackled in the wind. And amongst them, down the wide avenues between, went folk armored in colors to match the kaleidoscopes of the pavilions, so that the vast area covered seemed to shimmer and glitter with a myriad of hues that hurt the observing eye. Fires burned there, but seemingly only for their heat. Those invaders who ate consumed meat taken raw from the buffalo that stood penned and terrified to one side of the camp. On the other side were the riding beasts, not penned but watched by folk in black armor who wandered the perimeter of the unmarked enclosure with long goads like strange-bladed lances.

Racharran watched from the shelter of the trees and endeavored to calculate their numbers. He thought they must amount to more than three full clans.

"So do the People unite," Motsos said, "we shall outnumber them."

"*If* the People unite," Racharran answered in a whisper. "And do not forget those beasts."

"Do they fight as they slaughter buffalo," Zhonne said, "then they must at least double the numbers."

Racharran said, "Yes." And then: "We go back. We must warn the clan."

"And the others?" asked Lonah.

"We must warn all the People," Racharran said, and sighed. "Save we unite, I think we are all lost. I think the worst is come upon us all."

They moved back into the timber and mounted their horses, and then rode hard away.

29 Dark Dreams, Dark Promises

If it was strange to dream again after so long without
such revelation, the dreams that came to Hadduth
were stranger still.

It was as though a hand other than the Maker's shaped the images.
He could not say whose, but knew only that they were not, after a while,
such dreams as he had ever known; and behind them, like fleeting movement caught in the eye's corner, was such power as terrified and intrigued him both. At first, when he began his vigil, he thought he
suffered them as he would suffer nightmares; then he reveled in them,
for they held out such promise as he had never known.

He dreamed first—as had all the wakanishas of the People before
that last, fateful Matakwa—of strange riders mounted on stranger
steeds, whose paws left prints of fire across the grass, whose mouths
gaped wicked fangs, and whose eyes burned as they drove the People
before them like buffalo driven crazy by a prairie fire. He woke frightened then, crying out into the darkness of the sweat tent, and would
have gone out and warned Chakthi that such danger as neither he nor
the akaman could imagine came upon them and would destroy them,
but he knew that was not what Chakthi wanted to hear and so forced
himself to a semblance of calm and set more stoneso on the fire and ate
more pahé root and returned to the oneiric world.

Then he dreamed that he stood before the awful riders and
crouched in terror as they came down on him, save they did not trample

him but turned their mounts around him in a circle and dipped their lances in recognition. Then from out of the circle came a figure mounted on the strangest horse Hadduth had ever seen, horns curling from its head, its coat the color of blood, its eyes blazing as if fires burned within the sockets. On its back, straddling a great ornate saddle, sat a figure clad in armor that shone like the sun, who leveled a gauntleted finger at the cowering Dreamer and beckoned to him. Hadduth whimpered in terror, and the figure laughed and rode away. As Hadduth rose and watched them go, he wondered how he lived and why they spared him, because between him and them stood a wall of fire that ate up the grass as if it would devour all of Ket-Ta-Witko, leaving nothing behind save he.

The next time he dreamed, the rider halted and beckoned Hadduth to join him again, and when the wakanisha at first demurred, the figure laughed and set his awful horse to prancing so that Hadduth cowered and cried out and woke.

That dream came again and again, until he was afraid to resist and instead bowed his head and asked where the rider would take him.

The armored figure did not answer, but only beckoned him to ride with them, and he—afraid of what refusal might bring—agreed. And then he dreamed the Tachyn rode with them and they moved against the Commacht, and he saw Racharran taken and slain, and Racharran's wife brought to Chakthi, who hailed his wakanisha as a brother and a great Dreamer, and vaunted him above all others in the clan.

From that dream he woke filled with pride, and after he had eaten the food brought him and drunk a little water, he took more pahé and returned more eagerly to the dreaming, which now showed him Rannach brought before Chakthi and slain, and the woman Arrhyna delivered to Chakthi, who thanked him and heaped praise on him, and gifts, so that he became greater than the greatest of the favored Tachyn warriors.

And then he dreamed he stood upon a hill and looked out over all the land that was Ket-Ta-Witko, and at his side was the warrior armored as if with the sun, all bright and glittering, who swept out a hand in which was held a great and burning blade and spoke. And though Hadduth could not understand the words, he knew they were of conquest and the elevation of the Tachyn over all others. He saw Chakthi climbing the hill, laboring, and looked to the shining warrior, who nodded his agreement that Hadduth reach out to aid Chakthi and bring him onto the hill to stand with them.

And Hadduth realized the hill was the Maker's Mountain and that he stood higher than any man had stood before, and that Chakthi stood with him only by his leave. And the sun-bright figure gestured all around, at all of Ket-Ta-Witko and all that existed beyond, down the passages of time and dreaming at worlds beyond, and worlds that might be, and told Hadduth all should be his, all ruled by the Tachyn, if he would but heed the import of the dream and do that which should raise up his clan in conquest of all its enemies. None should stand before him, or higher than he, but bow and hail and fear him.

Hadduth woke, tempted and afraid. Such pride, such promises, flew in the face of the Maker and was contrary to all the Ahsa-tye-Patiko meant. But still, even so . . .

It was a heady seduction.

Were it possible, it must surely please Chakthi. He remembered vividly those other dreams, of Chakthi's praise, his own elevation, the aggrandizement . . .

He ate more pahé and slipped once more into the dreaming.

When at last he emerged from the sweat tent he was gaunt and hollow-eyed, but he had Chakthi's answer now: he told the akaman what Chakthi wanted to hear, and Chakthi was pleased, and feasted his wakanisha; and together, secretly, they prepared.

Racharran and his men came back to the Wintering Ground weary and alarmed. It was no pleasure to find his worst fears confirmed, and still less to see the faces of his people as he told them the disturbing news. When he was done, a long, deep silence filled the camp, and all the Commacht stared at him as if he were diseased and threatened to infect them with his plague. He waited for comment, but it seemed his news was of such moment, none could find their tongue.

"It's as Morrhyn warned," he said, and instantly regretted mentioning the absent wakanisha, for out of the crowd a man called, "Morrhyn? What's Morrhyn to do with this? Morrhyn deserted us."

"No!" Rachrran answered. "Morrhyn lost his dreams—likely under the influence of these strange folk—and looks to get them back, that he might aid us. He risks his life for that."

"But still he's not with us;"said another.

All Racharran could do was shrug, for that was true.

"Even so," he said, "this horde has come through the mountains. These are the people Colun warned us of, and if they're on the grass of Ket-Ta-Witko, then I fear the Grannach are defeated."

"Come the year's turning," a warrior called, "we'll defeat them."

"I think we cannot." Racharran shook his head slowly and sadly.

"Surely not alone. They are many—far more than us Commacht—and the beasts they ride are ferocious as blood-mad lions. I wonder if they'll even wait for the Moon of the Turning Year."

"No one fights before," the man said. "Not even Chakthi."

"These are strangeling folk," Racharran replied, "and not like us. I think they may not wait."

Behind him, the chosen five nodded grim heads in agreement.

"Then what shall we do? You are akaman of the Commacht. Tell us what we should do."

He recognized Lhyn's voice and struggled not to smile his thanks for that support. Instead, he waited awhile as others took her cue and voiced the same question.

"We must prepare for war," he said. "Even be it under the eye of the Wolf Moon or the Rain Moon, we must be ready. Also, we must seek the support of all the clans. We must—".

A voice interrupted him. "The support of the Tachyn? Ach, that's not so likely, eh?"

Racharran shrugged. "What comes is enemy to all the People, to the Tachyn no less than us. I'd ask Chakthi to set aside his . . . differences"—that elicited laughter, albeit cynical—"but first I'd send messengers to the Lakanti and the Aparhaso and the Naiche, to tell them what we saw and what we fear, and ask that they oin with us. That might persuade Chakthi. I'd send out messengers with tomorrow's dawn."

He saw Lhyn's face tense at that. She knew he must be one, albeit he was not yet a day returned. He held his own features still as voices buzzed, warriors speaking one with another, husbands with wives. A child cried and was hushed to silence; dogs paced fretful about the edges of the throng, as if they sensed the import of this meeting. In the sky, the sun observed them with a pale and indifferent gaze. Faint from the farther depths of the canyon came the belling of a bull buffalo, and overhead a flight of nine crows swooped low and unusually silent. Racharran wondered if that was a sign. Morrhyn could likely interpret it, he thought, but Morrhyn is not here. Perhaps Morrhyn is dead. He caught Lhyn's eye and silently thanked her for her smile.

Then, slowly, the hum of conversation ceased and the clan looked again to their akaman.

"What is your decision?" he asked.

There was a silence that hammered on his ears. Then a man said, "You are our akaman and we cannot doubt your word. Tell us what you'd do."

Other voices rose in agreement. The crows began to caw and wheel in circles above.

"I'd go to Juh," Racharran said, "with Bylas. I'd send Zhonne and Lonah to speak with Tahdase; and Motsos and Bishi to Yazte. We have all seen these strangelings and can say what they do—and what we fear they shall do."

"And Chakthi?" a man asked.

"Yes, Chakthi. He might not take my word, eh?" Racharran smiled, encouraging their support; encouraged himself by their laughter. "I'd first look to convince the Aparhaso and the Naiche and the Lakanti, then ask them, each of them, to send messengers to the Tachyn. Do you agree?"

His answer came shouted: "Yes! You are akaman of the Commacht and we follow you!"

He felt proud of his clan then; he hoped their trust was not misplaced and that he did the right thing. Surely he could not think of another course.

He wished Morrhyn was not gone away.

"You'll go to Juh?"

Lhyn stirred the pot suspended over the lodgefire, her eyes downcast. The flames set red lights in her hair, and Racharran thought she looked beautiful and young. He felt old and tired. He wished he need not go; he wished there was no horde massing below the mountains. He shook his head, dismissing futile wishes: what was was, and he must face it.

He said, "Yes. Can I convince Juh, then Tahdase will likely follow. Yazte will believe Motsos and Bishi, do they go with my tokens of authority."

"And you'll ride out again?" she said.

"What other choice have I?" he asked.

Lhyn sighed and said, "None. I only wish . . ." She shook her head and fell silent.

He asked, "What do you wish?"

She looked up then and met his eyes, saying, "These are not such times as allow us wishes, eh? Only duty."

He said, "Yes," and reached for the flask of tiswin she'd set beside him.

"Will they agree?" she asked.

He filled a cup and drank before he answered: "I don't know. The Maker willing, yes; but . . ."

"It should be better were Morrhyn here," she said, staring at the pot.

Racharran said, "Yes, but he is not. And so . . ."

"You must do what you can," she finished for him.

"What I can think of," he said. "And hope it's enough."

Lhyn said, "Yes. I'll pray it is."

The Aparhaso wintered in a thick-timbered valley, wooded down all its length with beech and birch and hemlock. No buffalo sheltered there, but Juh's clan had no need of such provision, for they had fought no war that year and had enjoyed the time to hunt and stock themselves well against the cold moons. They had a well-fed look, all plump and content, which contrasted with the two thin Commacht who rode in on horses not much fatter than their owners.

Juh was surprised to see them; Hazhe no less. Racharran saw alarm on both their faces as he reined in his horse before Juh's lodge and waited on the Aparhaso akaman's invitation to dismount.

It came slower than it might, for Juh seemed not quite able to believe his brother chieftain had come avisiting in the Wolf Moon, but then he beckoned them down and offered formal greeting. He looked a moment at the crowd that had followed them, then bade them enter his tent and called for men to tend their horses. Inside, he gestured them to settle on the spread furs and offered tiswin as Hazhe closed the lodge-flap.

The wakanisha piled more dung on the fire and took his place beside his akaman. Both studied the two Commacht with sympathetic eyes.

Racharran sipped the tiswin, thinking that he had rather been offered food and tea, but Juh's wife appeared to have gone off somewhere, and the silver-haired akaman gave him no other choice.

There was a lengthy and cautious silence as they drank. Then Juh said, "It is my pleasure that you visit us, but it is . . . In such weather?"

Racharran set down his cup and said, "These are unusual times, my brother. I've such news as cannot wait the year's turning, but must be decided now."

Juh motioned that he continue, and Racharran told of his scouting and what he had seen—what he believed it meant for the People.

When he was done, Juh looked to Bylas, who ducked his head and said, "It is all as Racharran has told you."

Juh looked then at Hazhe. The Dreamer frowned and asked, "What does Morrhyn make of this?"

Racharran said, "Morrhyn is not with us. He went away to the mountains to get back his dreams."

The two Aparhaso exchanged a glance, and Juh said, "Then this is all your thinking?"

"What else can I think?" Racharran asked. "I have seen what I have seen. What do you think?"

Juh drank tiswin and said, "That no one fights in winter."

"Not the People," Racharran said, echoes of his own folk's response ringing in his head. He had hoped—prayed!—that Juh think deeper and wider. "But these strangelings are not like us."

"No," Juh agreed. "But even so—to attack when the Wolf Moon rides the sky? Surely none do that."

"They are not like us," Racharran said again, and looked to Hazhe. "What do you dream, wakanisha?"

Hazhe's face gave him all the answer he needed, and before the Dreamer had a chance to answer, he said: "Like Morrhyn, eh? No dreams at all?"

Hazhe shrugged shamefaced, glanced sidelong at Juh, and shook his head.

"It's as Morrhyn said," Racharran declared. "There's a dark wind blows across Ket-Ta-Witko to cloud the minds of the wakanishas and confuse us all."

"But Morrhyn is gone away," said Hazhe. "In such dark times, should he have not stayed with his clan?"

"He did what he thought best," Racharran said, aware he sounded defiant, "what he believed he must. He will come back." If he can, he thought. If he's not already dead.

"Be he with you or not," Juh said, "still you ask much of us."

"I ask you to defend Ket-Ta-Witko," Racharran said. "I ask you to face this enemy that shall surely destroy us do we not unite."

Juh raised a hand mottled with age and said, "Slowly, slowly, my brother. I do not doubt what you tell us you have seen; I do not doubt some great horde has crossed the Grannach mountains, perhaps even defeated the Stone Folk. I do not doubt they are terrible—remember that I heard Colun speak at Matakwa and I know the Grannach speak true. But . . ."

"What?" Racharran ignored all protocol: he heard prevarication in Juh's voice—all *but* and *but*—and feared his warning should go ignored. "But what?"

Juh sighed and raised his silvered head to the lodge's smokehole. "That the Wolf Moon is up," he said, "and my people are content in their Wintering Ground. That none fight across the snow, and it should be hard to persuade my warriors to leave their warm lodges and their wives. Not until the Moon of the Turning Year, at least."

"That is the Will," Hazhe said. "The Ahsa-tye-Patiko."

Racharran ground his teeth, biting back his rising temper: was he to persuade them, he must not lose it, not show the anger their complacency roused. They seemed to him as men who looked on building storm clouds and told themselves the sky was clear and no rain would fall. He took up his cup, afraid his hand should break it, and sipped tiswin and said, "Morrhyn suggested the Ahsa-tye-Patiko is broken, by all that happened at this last Matakwa and after."

Hazhe looked at Juh, who said, "That is a matter between you and Chakthi. What bearing has it on what you ask?"

Hazhe said, "That argument were better explained by Morrhyn. Had he not gone away."

Racharran said, "But he has, and so you've only my word."

"Which we do not doubt," Juh said. "Only your estimate of the time."

Racharran fought his face and voice to calm. "I think that do we not band together, then these invaders shall come upon us like a storm wind and blow us down like dead trees. All of us!"

"That is your opinion," Juh said, nodding solemnly. "And I respect it. I shall think on it and speak of it, and give you my decision."

Harshly, Racharran asked, "When?"

Mildly, Juh replied, "When I've thought it over and discussed it with Hazhe and my people."

Racharran said, reining his frustration as he would an unbroken horse, "How long shall that take?"

"As long," Juh answered, "as it does. Until then, you are my guests, and welcome here."

Racharran nodded, knowing he could get no better answer, fearing what it should be. He looked at Hazhe, praying the Dreamer came to his side, and got back only an impassive gaze that offered him neither answer nor hope.

"They're blind!" he said, his voice harsh with anger. "They choose it, like children tugging the blankets over their heads to fend off the night fears. They'll not listen! They close their eyes and hope the night stalkers will go away."

"You're angry," Lhyn said. "Because they'd not heed you."

"Yes!" Racharran leaned forward to take up the flask and pour more tiswin. "I'm angry because they ignore the threat, and because they'll die for it. Because we all might die for it."

"You've done what you can," Lhyn said. "What more can you do?"

He said, "I don't know. The Maker help me, but I don't know."

Lhyn came to rest beside him and filled his cup. "Perhaps Morrhyn will come back with answers," she said.

"Perhaps." Racharran gusted bitter laughter. "And perhaps the Maker will burn up the strangelings. Perhaps he'll wipe them off the grass before they slay us all. Or perhaps we shall all die under their blades, and the Maker turn his face away and condemn us for our stupidity."

The news had not been good: no better from the others than what he had brought back from Juh's Aparhaso.

Zhonne and Lonah had returned from the Naiche's Wintering Ground with word that Tahdase would follow Juh's lead—which meant that the Naiche would not consider fighting until Juh gave the word, until the snows were gone.

Most surprising had been Yazte's response.

Motsos and Bishi had told Racharran of warm welcome and promises of food and support for the Commacht—but no promise of warriors until the Moon of the Turning Year rose. They said that Yazte had lost men to the Tachyn for his support of the Commacht during the summer's war and would not lose more, nor go out bellicose before winter's end. Not until his clan was fat-fed and rested, he said. But then, did Racharran call him to war with the Tachyn or any others, he would come with all his warriors and drive either Chakthi's people or any others from off the grass of Ket-Ta-Witko.

That hurt Racharran the most: he had believed that Yazte, of all the akamans, would see the awful truth and come to unity. Without at the least the Lakanti, he doubted any of the People could survive what he was convinced must soon come against them. Without any agreement, any unity, he thought the Matawaye must soon fall to the invaders, and his heart turned sour at the ignorance of his brothers.

"I must send scouts out," he told Lhyn. "To watch for what comes."

"Yes," she said, doing her best to hide her own fear, wanting to lend him strength. "What you think is best."

He said, "I'm not sure what that is anymore."

"You'll do what's right," she said. "You always do."

"Do I?" he asked.

She said again, "Yes. You lead the Commacht."

"It used to be," he said. "With Morrhyn's guidance."

"It used to be." Her eyes closed a moment. "But not now. Now only you lead us."

"I wish," he said, and closed his own eyes as she touched his face, "that I had his guidance now."

She said, "Yes, but he's gone."

"I wish," he said as she touched him and her hands moved from his face to his chest, "that he were not. I wish he were here."

Rannach draped a blanket over the stallion's head and passed the rein to Morrhyn. Arrhyna's paint mare, which she had given the wakanisha to ride, was already masked. Either animal might panic at the sight or scent of what lay ahead, and that must surely bring their desperate journey to a swift ending.

"Be careful, eh?" Morrhyn asked.

Rannach nodded without speaking and slipped away through the trees, to the edge of the copse, where he could better see the obstacle across their path.

Colun had brought them out of the valley, through the Grannach's secret ways, to the very edge of the Meeting Ground. There he had left them, reiterating promises that Arrhyna should be safe with his people who would await Morrhyn's return—if he survived—in readiness for what the Dreamer hoped to achieve. None of them as sure it could be accomplished. It was, as Morrhyn explained, one possible path amongst the multiple branchings of all the possible futures, the reality of its success dependent on frail men making the right choices.

And were they to have any hope at all, then Morrhyn and Rannach must survive the journey.

They had ridden swift as weather and terrain allowed from the Meeting Ground, and struck out directly for the Commacht grazing. Rannach would have taken a more circuitous path—it occurred to Morrhyn that the young warrior matured and grew more cautious with the knowledge that Arrhyna carried his child—but the wakanisha had pressed him to speed. It was a gamble. Rannach's preferred way would have skirted well clear of the Tachyn lands, which should surely be the safer trail, but longer, more consumptive of time, which Morrhyn knew they lacked. Did they not come timely to the Commacht, then they might as well fall to Chakthi's men; it would make no difference. Death was death, no matter which the hand that dealt it.

So they chanced the Tachyn and rode hard across the snow, pushing their horses to the limits of their endurance, comforted by their one advantage: Morrhyn had back his dreams.

It was Rannach who chose the details of their path and Morrhyn who set the general direction, warning when they need slow and when they need hide, when to skirt around and when to wait. He dreamed each night now, and daily thanked the Maker for the return of his talent.

It was as if a strong, clean wind blew through his dreams, sweeping away the obfuscating darkness. The last night had told him they should go cautious through this hurst, for danger lay ahead.

Now he held the blanket-blinded horses and waited for Rannach's return. The trees stood bare-branched and draped with icicles that shone in the morning sun. Small birds darted scavenging about, and through the latticework of naked boughs he could see the sky all cold and wintry blue. It prompted thoughts of objective eyes, that studied him judgmental and indifferent. His breath came out in steaming clouds, and even through the furs he wore he could feel the terrible cold. He drew the two horses closer, seeking their warmth. He could not remember so harsh a winter, and wondered if that were somehow connected to the coming of the Breakers into Ket-Ta-Witko. Surely they commanded powerful magicks: perhaps they brought bad weather with them. But if they did, he thought, then surely the Maker fought them, for the sun shone and the snow was frozen hard enough that it did little to slow the animals. It should be worse were there blizzards, or the ground all muddy. And then he thought that the Breakers must be no less able to travel fast over the frozen landscape, and smiled unhappily: what favored him and Rannach must also favor their enemies—it seemed all balanced on a knife's edge, the outcome yet to be determined. He shivered, leaning against the paint mare's neck, wondering.

Then Rannach came back. Under the hood of the furry cape he wore, his eyes were wide with wonder and horror, and it seemed a measure of blood had drained from his dark skin. He held his bow with an arrow nocked, as if he needed the comfort of the weapon.

"The Maker alone knows," his voice was hushed and harsh, "I've not seen such things, such creatures!"

Morrhyn said, "I know."

"How?" Rannach asked, then shook his head. "Of course! In your dreams."

Morrhyn nodded.

"There was a column," Rannach said. "Thirty of them, all riding . . . *things*."

Again Morrhyn nodded, and said, "Like giant lions, lizards, and rats, all together, eh?"

"Yes." Rannach stared at the Dreamer. "And the riders were all armored. They looked like bright beetles. I think it should be hard to fight them. Those creatures they ride would likely terrify our horses."

"Likely," Morrhyn agreed. "But the Maker willing, we'll not fight them. Only escape."

Rannach lowered his eyes to the bow he still held, as if he'd forgotten it. He eased the string down and set the shaft back in his quiver, then looked again at Morrhyn.

"Is that the only way? To give up Ket-Ta-Witko?"

Morrhyn shrugged, the movement lost under the furs he wore. "That or die."

"None other?"

Morrhyn shook his head. It was a hard answer, but all he had to give. The dreams had shown him that.

Rannach looked awhile at the bleak and sun-bright sky, and then shook his head and sighed. "It shall be no easy task to persuade the People. The Commacht shall surely take it hard; the rest . . ."

"Shall listen or not," Morrhyn said. "The world turns, like"—he smiled cynically—"like a stone that exposes the dark, grubbing things beneath. Save we cannot turn the stone back, only go away from it."

"Or fight them," Rannach said. It was hard to know whether he made a statement or asked a question.

"You've seen some few of them," Morrhyn said, "and know they must be hard to fight. You've heard Colun speak of them, and know what they do. It's too late even to try turning the stone back. They are here now, in Ket-Ta-Witko, and they'll overrun it all save we can convince the People of the Maker's promise."

Rannach drew a hand across his mouth. His eyes were haunted as they found Morrhyn's. "Is this my doing?" he asked, low-voiced. "The reward of my sin?"

Morrhyn wished he need not answer, but truth was truth, and it was a time for such honesty else all be lost. So he said, "It's as I told you back in the valley, an accretion of sins. Yours was one."

"Then am I damned?"

"The Maker's kinder than that," Morrhyn said. "He offers redemption, forgiveness. You atone for your sin by what you do now in bringing me back. Bringing the promise of salvation."

"And Arrhyna?" asked Rannach. "What of her? You said she'd sinned also."

"In small measure, I think," Morrhyn replied. "And was it not Arrhyna who persuaded you to guide me? Had she not spoken up, would you have quit the valley?"

"No." Rannach shook his head. "Not save she told me to go."

"Then I think she also atones."

"And Chakthi?" Rannach asked.

Morrhyn hesitated. He'd known no dreams of the Tachyn. He'd seen in sleep the Commacht and the Lakanti, the Aparhaso and the Naiche, find that salvation the Maker offered—would they but listen and heed—but nothing of Chakthi's clan. Remnants of the dark wind's fog still hung about them, as if the Breakers' magic clung stronger there. He said, "We must bring the word to Chakthi also. What he does after . . ."

He shrugged, and Rannach barked a sour laugh and said, "I'd never thought to save Chakthi."

"But you'll try, no?" Morrhyn asked urgently. He could not say it clear—that should be too great a revelation, such as might upset all his hopes—but he willed Rannach to agreement.

The younger man looked into his eyes and nodded. "I must try, no? I must atone for what I've done, else . . ." He shuddered. "I've the feeling that do I fail you, Arrhyna and our child must die; and the Grannach and the Commacht, and all the People. It's as you taught us the Ahsa-tye-Patiko says, no? All's balanced, and is that balance disturbed, then compensation must be made, else the scales swing wild and all suffer."

Morrhyn felt his heart lift. Not far, for far too much still hung upon those scales, but did the headstrong Rannach recognize his debt and show willingness to compensate, then there *was* hope. He smiled and said, "You grow up. You show your father's wisdom."

Rannach's face clouded a moment at mention of Racharran, but then he essayed a tight-lipped smile and said, "I dealt my father unfair, eh? I was angry with him for my banishment; I thought he should have supported me better. But now I think I see that what he did was all he could do, to keep the balance."

Morrhyn said, "Yes. It was as he told you—he is akaman of the Commacht, with a duty to his clan and all the People, and he could not do else. You could learn much from Racharran."

His face clouded as he said it, remembering a dream that showed one of the many paths—one he had sooner not take. Save he wondered if it was not one forced upon him.

"What's amiss?" Rannach asked. "You've the look of a man troubled."

Morrhyn shook off the memory. His way was clear and must it lead to that—to what he'd sooner not think of—then still he had no choice were the People to have any hope. Racharran would not turn away, he thought.

He forced a smile and said, "Should I not be? I worry that we'll not reach the People in time. So, tell me what you saw."

"Thirty Breakers," Rannach answered, "moving across our path from south to north. They're gone now."

"Then we proceed," Morrhyn said. "No?"

Rannach took his horse's rein and lifted the blanket from the stallion's head, swinging lithely astride the big horse. Morrhyn took the blanket slower from the mare's head and mounted stiffly. He felt frail, and as they rode out from the hurst he could feel the mare's spine thud hard against his withered buttocks even through his fur-lined breeches and the padding of his saddle. It was a sorry thing, he thought, to lose so much flesh that riding became so arduous a task. But then again, it was as he had told Rannach. All was balanced by the Maker, and had he lost flesh, still he had gained much else in compensation.

He had hope now, where none had been before; and promised answers to the awful threat of the Breakers. So he turned his face to the sky and offered the Maker his thanks—and his heartfelt wish the People listen to him—and followed Rannach out across the snow, refusing to heed the doubt that came as they crossed the tracks the Breakers had made.

30 The Wind Blows Cold

Bylas saw them first: a column of twenty, weirdly mounted on those strange beasts, all armed with bows and blades and great hook-headed lances, their eye-bedazzling armor sparkling and shimmering like twenty different rainbows in the hard light of the winter sun. They came in single file down the draw, the creatures they rode padding swift and sure over the snow. He saw the beasts were not reined like horses, but only saddled, and guided by the rider's knees and shouts. He remembered the wounds Bakaan and his horse had worn, and tested the wind. It blew from off the invaders, carrying a faint stench of meat and blood, as if they breathed out the memories of their carnage. He held his breath and slithered down from off the ridgetop. Racharran had given clear orders that he was only to watch—no more—and bring back word of what came against the People.

He found his horse and looked to his fellow scouts, motioning them to hold silent as he murmured what he had seen.

Motsos whispered back, "So do we return? Or do we trail them?"

Bylas thought a moment and then said, "I think we'd best follow them and see where they go."

"And do they go toward the Wintering Ground?" Motsos asked.

"Then we ride ahead," Bylas answered, "and warn the clan."

"Can we outrun them." Motsos stroked his horse's neck. "We've seen them move, eh? Should they find us on open ground . . ."

Bylas grinned sourly and said, "Yes. But even so, we must try. Do they find the Wintering Ground . . ."

He left the sentence unfinished and Motsos nodded. They both knew there was little chance of outrunning those strangeling beasts over the snow, nor much better of defeating them; not five scouts against twenty.

"So we ride." Bylas turned his horse's head to parallel the draw. "And carefully, eh? Lest they hear or see us."

The snow was hard enough that their hooves made little sound, and in a while Bylas lifted his mount to a canter that he might reach the timber beyond the draw and use that cover to see where the invaders went. He looked at the bleak sky and wondered if this was his day to die.

Like all the warriors of the Commacht—like all the warriors of the People—he was prepared to give his life in defense of the helpless ones, in defense of Ket-Ta-Witko. That was a man's honor, his understood duty. But he had seen the invaders before and could not help but doubt his chances against them. If it came to it, then he would fight, but he could not help but think it should be a useless battle that must leave him dead and the invaders go on to overrun the canyon and the clan, and leave nothing living.

He prayed it not come to that, and heeled his horse to a faster pace, eager to reach the trees and see where the twenty strangelings went before they saw or scented his scouts. He hoped the Maker would forgive him for hoping they turned toward the Tachyn grazing. Even with what he felt for Chakthi, he could not, honestly, wish such fate on the Tachyn, save it were better visited on them than his own clan.

"Can you go on?" Rannach studied Morrhyn with worried eyes. "We can rest awhile longer if you need."

"No." Against the protests of his body, Morrhyn forced himself upright. "We go on."

Maker, he thought. You gave me back my dreams and showed me what I have to do, and for that I thank you. But could you not also have given me back my strength? I feel weak as a babe.

But he got no answer, only the dull, numb aching that possessed his knees and sent pain stabbing down the length of his spine as he rose from his blankets and straightened his back. He felt old, and wondered if that was the payment demanded for the visions, for the knowledge of the many paths and the one true hope.

If so, he thought, then so be it. I will pay it. I will pay my life if need be. Only let me bring the word to the Commacht and all the People, and they survive. If I must die for that, then I shall, willingly. Only let we who believe in you live and not be destroyed.

He watched as Rannach shoveled snow over the embers of their fire, tugging his furs closer about his shivering body. Maker, how could he feel so cold? It sank into his bones and set his ears to drumming with the ache of it, his teeth to chattering hard enough he feared they might splinter. His scalp, even under the fur-lined hood, felt as if needles dug into his brain. He supposed it was because he had lost so much flesh, living in the cave and then on the descent, but . . .

If that was the price . . .

He willed his legs, his feet, to walk, one step after another until he had reached his borrowed horse and could lean against the mare's warm strength. Set a hand on her neck and find the rein, swing up onto the saddle Rannach had already—young and strong and not at all exhausted —placed there.

He fell down.

Rannach lifted him from the snow, setting him tottery upright, lean-ing against the paint mare who snorted and shifted, threatening to spill him down again.

"By the Maker, you cannot even mount a horse! We must wait and rest."

"No!" He shook his head. "We've not the time. Help me up."

"You're too weak." Rannach looked at him, eyes wide even as he frowned. Doubt was writ there in his gaze. "We'll wait and eat. Gain strength, eh? I can hunt us food."

"Help me up," Morrhyn said. "We've no time."

"But you'll die. You're skin and bones."

"I can still ride: I must. Help me up and I'll ride. I'll eat along the way."

"Eat what?" Rannach asked. "We're safe here. I can hunt here."

Morrhyn held tight to the saddle, hoping the mare not move else he'd fall down again. He said, "And wait for the Breakers to find us? No! We must find the clan and tell them. Now help me up. We've meat enough to keep us going."

"You need a winter's eating," Rannach said. "Just to put the flesh back on your bones."

"I'll eat my fill when we're safe. Now shall you help me mount, or shall I leave you here?"

"Ach!" Rannach picked him up and threw him astride Arrhyna's horse. "I should know better than to argue with a wakanisha."

Morrhyn gritted his teeth against the pain of unfleshed buttocks meeting horse's spine, and smiled. "Yes, you should. Now let's go on. The valley ahead is safe. But after . . ."

"There were fifteen men," Perico said, "after a herd of wintering buffalo. It should have been a good hunting—extra meat, and winter-thick hides. Only . . ."

"Only?" Juh asked.

"None came back," Perico said.

Juh looked at Hazhe: "What do you think?"

The Aparhaso Dreamer looked at Perico and asked, "What did you see?"

Perico said, "A herd of buffalo slaughtered, and our hunters with them. Tracks in the snow, amongst the blood, as if great lions had fallen on them all."

Hazhe looked at Juh, not saying anything.

Juh said speculatively, "Was Racharran speaking the truth?"

Hazhe shrugged. "Perhaps. I'd not doubt his word, save . . ." He turned toward Perico. "Those tracks. Like lions, you said?"

"Like giant lions." Perico nodded urgently. "Tracks larger than any horse's hoof. And"—he looked from wakanisha to akaman—"there was so much blood. It was not a hunting, it was a slaughter. The buffalo were all torn apart, and our hunters with them. I saw horses with their bellies ripped out, and men without heads. As if . . ." He shook his head, the telling too enormous to comprehend.

"As if Racharran spoke only the truth," Hazhe said. "The Maker help us."

"The Maker help us," Juh echoed. "I should have listened to him better."

"We could not know," Hazhe said. "Not then."

"But now?" Juh asked.

Perico looked from one to the other. He was only a warrior, and they the guardians of his clan: he assumed they spoke of matters beyond his ken, and trusted them to decide favorably for the benefit of all. Save he'd heard, like all the Aparhaso, of Racharran's visit and what the Commacht akaman had said to his own chieftain of strangeling invaders such as the Grannach had warned of at Matakwa. He cleared his throat and spoke.

"We must fight them," he said.

Juh and Hazhe turned toward him.

He swallowed breath and summoned up his courage. "I saw our

people slain," he said. "And buffalo slaughtered not for meat or hides, but only, it seemed, for sport. If it's as the Commacht akaman said, then I think we must ready for war."

He feared he had earned Juh's displeasure, but the white-haired akaman smiled—albeit sadly—and said, "Yes. I was wrong to disregard Racharran. You see it out of younger eyes. So—you will take my promise to him: that the Aparhaso will listen to what he has to say, and fight these invaders with him."

Perico said, "Me?"

Juh nodded and said, "You. You will go out tomorrow to the Commacht Wintering Ground and tell Racharran that I shall listen to all he has to say of how we fight these invaders. Bring him back if he'll come. If not, bring back his word of what he'd have us do."

Perico nodded, thinking he'd bought himself an unwanted duty—it was a long, cold ride to the Commacht's new Wintering Ground. But even so . . . He thought of the animals and the men he'd seen slaughtered. Might that journey defeat the invaders . . .

"Before the sun rises," he said, "I'll be on my way."

The column seemed in no hurry. Bylas supposed that was because they scouted ahead of the main force, and then wondered how far behind that great army was. Did it follow after these twenty strangelings, or did it remain below the hills, awaiting the scouts' reports? He stroked his horse's winter-shaggy muzzle, murmuring softly, that the animal not give away his position. He thought the invaders' own eyes magically gifted if they could see him through the trees, but perhaps they were. How could he know? How could anyone? Such folk had never before ridden the plains of Ket-Ta-Witko.

He saw they came toward the wood, and made a swift decision.

"We pull back. We'll put the wood between us and them, and seek the shelter of the ridges."

"And do they come to the ridges?" Motsos asked.

"Then we pull back farther. The canyon's what, three days' riding?" Motsos said, "For us. But for them . . . ?"

"Save they see us and chase us," Bylas said, "I think they'll ride slow. But listen, all of you. Does it come to a chase, we do not go back. You understand? We must not lead them to the canyon, but away." He thought a moment. "You've the fastest horse here, Motsos. So, are we spotted, we run and look to confuse our tracks. When you safely can, break off and take word home. Warn Racharran."

"Leave you?" Motsos looked offended.

Bylas said, "Yes! That the clan know is the important thing." He set a hand on his friend's shoulder. "And your horse is swift, eh?"

Motsos nodded reluctantly. "As you say."

Bylas smiled. "As I say. Now, let's mount and ride while we've the time."

They swung astride their horses and rode fast as snow and low-hung branches allowed. None were cowards, but all felt mightily wary of being found on open ground by what came after them.

Tahdase's lodge was warm, the fire merry as his young wife took the kettle from the flames and filled her husband's and Isten's cups. That duty done, she retreated demurely and set to decorating a shirt with brightly colored designs of summer flowers. Tahdase glanced at her and smiled fondly, wondering if he'd have the opportunity to wear the shirt or she have the time to finish it. He turned his face toward his wakanisha and motioned that Isten speak.

The Dreamer looked aged. Crescents of shadow hung beneath his eyes, and those had a haunted look. He sipped his tea and voiced polite thanks before he spoke of what brought them together.

"They say strange riders have been sighted. Such folk as Racharran's men spoke of. They say there are buffalo slaughtered and left to rot." He smiled a twisted smile and snorted sad laughter. "If anything *can* rot in such a winter."

Tahdase said, "I know this; I have heard what they say. What I need to know is who these strangelings are, and what they do here."

Isten stared at his akaman as if Tahdase were a child who should know better. "They are who Racharran's men told us they are, I think. They are the folk Colun spoke of at Matakwa."

His tone prompted a brief narrowing of Tahdase's eyes, a flash of anger that was instantly replaced with embarrassment as the young chieftain ducked his head and said, "Yes, all I've heard is as Racharran's men told us. But . . ." He raised his head so that Isten saw the plea his gaze expressed. "What are we to do about them?"

"Are they scouts," the wakanisha said, "then they are the vanguard of that horde Racharran saw. Likely they seek the Wintering Grounds."

"And if they find them," Tahdase said softly, "and they are all Colun and Racharran said they are, then we are in terrible danger."

At the rear of the lodge his wife gasped and pierced her thumb with the needle. Tahdase glanced briefly in her direction and returned his gaze to Isten.

The wakanisha nodded gravely and said, "Yes."

"So what shall we do?" Tahdase asked.

Isten met his gaze, thinking he seemed very young and frightened. The wakanisha felt very old. He said, "Had I my dreams . . ."

"But you don't," Tahdase said sharply. "The Maker turns his face from you." He saw the hurt in Isten's eyes and added softer, "He turns his face from us all, no?"

Isten nodded. "It would seem so. It would seem what happened at Matakwa blights us."

"Then it's the fault of the Commacht and the Tachyn?" Tahdase sprang on hope like a starving dog on a carcass.

"Perhaps." Isten gestured helplessly. "Surely the wards are broken, can these folk cross the mountains. Perhaps the Ahsa-tye-Patiko is broken."

"Not by us," Tahdase said.

Isten said, "I wonder," in a slow and thoughtful voice. "I wonder if it matters any longer who owns the blame. Is the Ahsa-tye-Patiko broken, then it is broken, and I think that who broke it matters little in the Maker's eyes."

Tahdase frowned. "How can that be? Was it broken by the Tachyn and Commacht, then surely these newcomers must descend on them."

"Our people die," Isten said. "And have these strange folk come through the mountains, then surely the Grannach also die. Are they guilty? Were the Whaztaye guilty?"

"I know nothing of the Whaztaye," Tahdase said—defensively, Isten thought. "Nor much of the Grannach. My father knew them, but I . . ." He shrugged.

"The Grannach do not lie," Isten said. "They are the guardians of the hills, and they do not lie. But they did warn us . . ."

"Yes, yes." Tahdase nodded. "And have these invaders come through the Grannach's passes, then no doubt Grannach *have* died. And Naiche die, and likely other clans suffer. But what are we to do?"

"I think," Isten said, "that perhaps we should send riders to the Commacht and ask what Racharran does."

"Perhaps." Tahdase stared awhile at the fire, rolling his cup between his hands. He seemed not to notice the hot tea that spilled out. "But first let's send riders to the Aparhaso and ask what Juh does."

"Why not send them to both?" Isten asked.

"No." Tahdase shook his head. "First to Juh. Then, when we've word of what he thinks, to the Commacht."

"Are you sure?" Isten asked.

"This is my decision," Tahdase said.

Isten nodded. "You are akaman of the Naiche: it shall be as you wish."

They crossed the valley and topped the wall beyond. From there, looking out from behind the screen of pines that hid them, they could see the broken country stretching away to the width of the icebound river that curved slow and lazy across the flat. The river was too broad that ice had locked it yet, and the farther bank devolved onto a wide beach that ran smooth to the stands of hemlock, beech, and maple that scratched at the cold sky with naked branches.

Rannach turned to Morrhyn and pursed his lips. The wakanisha looked, if anything, worse than that first day in the valley. Strands of white hair straggled from the hood of his cape, and his cheeks were sunk in, the bones prominent as a dead man's. His lips were thinned and cracked by the cold, moving as his teeth chattered. Had he not known better, Rannach might have thought him a ghost, a revenant spirit come back to haunt him for his sins. In all of Morrhyn's face, only his eyes seemed alive, and they burned with such awful determination, Rannach could not look long at them for fear they'd suck out his soul and bind him forever to the Dreamer's purpose.

Save, he thought, he was already bound.

The Maker knew, but he felt no choice but to deliver Morrhyn safe to his father who—being the man he was—might likely execute the sentence agreed by the Council should his son return from banishment. "Just" was a word people applied to Racharran; "hard" was what came to Rannach's mind. He thought it not impossible his father thank him for bringing Morrhyn back and then order his execution: justly.

But he had given Morrhyn his promise and he would not renege on that, no matter the cost.

"I see no danger," he said. "There's neither smoke nor any other sign. Nothing moves out there."

"Even so." Morrhyn leant against a pine, an arm around the trunk as if without that prop he must fall down.

"Even so?" Rannach queried.

"It's there," Morrhyn said, the syllables distorted by his jangling teeth. "Small, but even so . . ."

"We can follow this ridge," Rannach offered. "It shall delay us—the next ford is three days distant—but if you say we must . . ."

"Three days?" Morrhyn frowned, which contorted his face horribly. "And after?"

Rannach stabbed a finger in the direction of the river. "Do we cross here, then we're in line for the Wintering Ground. Five more days?"

"And that way?" Morrhyn waved a glove at the ridgetop.

Rannach said, "Three days to the ford, then a stretch of river breaks that shall likely take us three more. After that, perhaps nine or ten. The horses are wearying, remember."

Morrhyn nodded. Rannach thought, And also you. Can you last so long? Can you even last five days?

"There's not the time." Morrhyn spoke into the gnarled bark of the tree. "Maker, there's not the time." He pushed away from the tree, shuffling across the snow to where the paint mare waited. "We must risk it. But listen, eh?"

Rannach nodded as he heaved the Dreamer astride the mare. He no longer asked if Morrhyn needed help: it was too obvious, and he only gave it.

"There's danger down there." Morrhyn raised a hand to point in the direction of the breaks. "No great force, but . . . something. I cannot dream it clearer."

"And if we ride around this danger?" Rannach asked.

"Then we shall come too late," Morrhyn said. "Oh, Rannach! The Maker forgive me, but I lead you into peril."

Rannach smiled. "My life's forfeit, no? Every step I take into Ket-Ta-Witko I'm in peril. So what more is this?"

Morrhyn smiled back. "You've courage," he said. "And you grow wiser. But listen, I think that what we face cannot be met with honest lance. Your bow should be the better weapon."

"Then I'll ready my bow." Rannach mounted his stallion and heeled his lance in the saddle sheath, drew his bow from the quiver and nocked a shaft. "Do we go on?"

"Yes." Morrhyn nodded. "But carefully, eh?"

Bylas heeled his horse to speed for all the animal was already running fast as it could. He could hear the baying of the lion creatures behind him. They sounded close, but he had sooner not look back: better to fasten his eyes on the broken country ahead, where he might lose them. Better not to see them at all.

He turned his face in Motsos's direction and shouted, "When we reach the gulleys, you turn off and ride for the canyon."

Motsos waved a hand in acknowledgment. Bylas breathed a hasty prayer to the Maker that they all survive. He doubted they would. But Maker, he asked, let Motsos at least live to take word back.

They came in amongst the ridges and galloped hard along the widest draw. Then, deliberately, waving Motsos on, Bylas slowed his horse and motioned the others up around him. In a group they followed after Motsos until he turned away in the direction of the canyon. They followed awhile, until Motsos split off and the snow lay all churned behind him so that pursuit must surely be difficult.

Then Bylas shouted over the pounding of the desperate hooves and the roaring of the lion-things behind, "We fight! For the Commacht, eh? And all the People!"

"We should have wintered with the Commacht." Yazte loosed a string of curses that elicited a reproachful glance from his wife. "Together, we might be strong enough."

"'Might' is a loose bridle," Kahteney said. "And from all Motsos and Bishi told us, two clans alone should not be enough."

"No." Yazte shook his head, reaching for the tiswin. "But had we listened, looked to persuade the others—"

"We did not and they did not," Kahteney interrupted. "And now it's too late."

"I know." Yazte grunted, like some hibernating bear disturbed out of winter slumber. "I know all the things we should have done and did not; what I want to know now is what we should do now."

Kahteney looked him in the eye and gave bleak answer: "I don't know."

"Ach, you're my wakanisha," Yazte grumbled. "You're supposed to advise me."

Kahteney chuckled softly, the sound as grim as his worried face. "I've no dreams to guide me," he murmured, "nor much advice to offer. Save what hindsight grants."

"Hindsight!" Yazte gestured irritably, splashing tiswin unnoticed over his breeches. "Hindsight's no use to me. I've a clan looking to me for guidance—I must look ahead."

Kahteney nodded. "Those we've sighted are surely scouts. Scouts go ahead of a war band—"

Now it was Yazte who interrupted: "And therefore that horde Racharran sent warning of comes into Ket-Ta-Witko. Yes! I know this, and that even the scouts are formidable. I know that if they find our Wintering Ground and bring that horde against us, we've little chance. Oh, by the Maker, I know this! But what am I to do?"

Did he expect a response, he got none. He continued: "Shall I tell my Lakanti we must strike our lodges and quit the Wintering Ground?

To go where? To the Commacht? Would they welcome a whole clan in that canyon? What should we all eat? And if these strangeling invaders find the canyon? In the Maker's name, Kahteney, I tell you I don't see any answers. Not save we wait here and pray; and likely die."

Softly, Kahteney said, "Perhaps that's the Maker's wish."

Yazte said bitterly, "Then he's unkind."

"Or just," Kahteney said no louder, "and delivers the People to punishment for the breaking of the Ahsa-tye-Patiko."

"All of us?" Yazte drained his cup, refilled the vessel. "That's a hard judgment, no? Should he not limit his ire to those closer concerned?"

Kahteney shrugged, offering no answer.

"I'd not," Yazte said sullenly, "just sit here and wait for death. But the Maker help me, I cannot think of what else to do."

"Perhaps . . ." Kahteney hesitated. "Perhaps you should send a messenger to Racharran."

"To what end?" asked Yazte. "If anything, the Commacht are worse off than we. Morrhyn's gone away, no? And the Commacht suffered all summer from Chakthi's raids."

Kahteney shrugged again. "I can offer no better advice."

"Ach!" Yazte emptied another cup. "He's hard, our Maker."

"But just," Kahteney said. "Perhaps he'll offer us a chance to survive. I cannot believe he'd destroy all of the People for the sins of the few."

"Think you so?" Yazte sighed hugely. "I see little chance for any of us. I think perhaps we are all doomed."

"Perhaps we should pray," Kahteney suggested.

"You've not already?" Yazte pantomimed surprise.

Kahteney knew his akaman too well to take offense, so he only nodded and said, "I have. But perhaps we should hold a Prayer Ceremony."

Yazte sniffed. "If you think it might do some good. But meanwhile I think I'll take your other advice."

"Which?" Kahteney asked.

"The messenger," Yazte answered. "I shall send a rider to the Commacht to find out what Racharran does."

They came down off the ridgetop cautious as wolves with man-scent on the wind. Rannach took the lead, guiding the stallion with knees alone, his hands on bow and shaft, his eyes alert for sign of promised danger. Morrhyn followed behind, one hand holding the mare's rein, the other locked in her mane. He feared he'd otherwise fall, and cursed his weakness. A bow and arrows hung quivered on his saddle, but he doubted he had the strength to flight a shaft. If what he dreaded did wait below, then it should be Rannach's fight alone, and he like some invalid, one of the helpless ones. He prayed his dream was wrong and knew it could not be. Had he any power now, it was oneiric, prophetic. *Something* awaited them.

He clung to the mare as she plunged through the snow drifted amongst the breaks. Perhaps, he thought, the danger lay in the river. Even with the ford, that must be perilous to cross. Frozen along its banks, the water was snow-gorged, running cold and swift, with sizable chunks of ice racing on the flood. It should be easy for a horse to lose footing there, or panic at the onrush of floes. He shuddered at the thought of finding himself unhorsed in midstream, doubting he could hold his seat if the mare bucked; sure that he must die if he fell into the icy water.

He turned a head that ached with the cold toward the walls of the break they descended. Snow glittered there, under a hard blue sky, the sun watery above. Ahead, its rays layered veins of gold on the black water of the river, the floating ice all gemlike—silver and blue. Ahead, Rannach's stallion snorted and began to plunge against the rein.

Rannach came out of the saddle in a single fluid movement, leaving the stallion to wade back to Morrhyn.

"He scents something." As he spoke, his eyes moved across the terrain below. "Hold him and wait here. Keep them both quiet if you can."

Morrhyn nodded and urged the mare closer to the nervous stallion. "Be careful, eh?" He took the stallion's rein. The horse snapped yellow teeth and he wondered if he *could* hold both animals: the mare sensed her companion's unease and began herself to shift under him. He wound both reins in his left hand and promised himself that if he should be unseated, he would lie in the snow and hold them until Rannach came back.

If Rannach came back.

The younger man was already scrambling up the side of the break, his head bared now so that the warrior's braids flung loose. Pale sunlight shone on the fastening brooches. Morrhyn remembered they were Arrhyna's gifts, and how proud Rannach was to wear them.

Then Rannach was gone, cresting the break's wall to find cover behind a snow-clad boulder. It was a vantage point that afforded him a large view across the surrounding network of ravines and washes. They angled down like the scratchings of some gigantic beast to the river, all dips and hollows that radiated from off the ridge. He tested the wind—

it blew from off the river to his right, but when he chanced rising enough that he could scan the banks for some distance in both directions, he saw nothing.

So, whatever scent the stallion had caught came from the right, but not along the river. Therefore, from one of the dips and gulches in that direction. He eased his bowstring down and began to crawl on his belly across the crest.

The depression on the farther side was empty: he slithered down and worked his way on cautious feet to the riverside end, then slunk along the descending slope to the next break.

Fox-wary, he eased around the wall, and saw what had frightened his horse.

It frightened him.

He had seen the Breakers at a distance, from a safe position, but now he looked close on one, and on the creature the Breaker rode. He knew he must kill them both, for they must surely sight him and Morrhyn at the ford and come after them. And he knew they could not outrun that great *thing*, with its massive, clawed paws and hugely muscled legs, not even were his stallion unweary. And Morrhyn would likely fall off Arrhyna's mare, or both horses panic. And there was the river to ford, and Morrhyn said there was no time to waste.

So . . .

He drew his bowstring tight and sighted down the shaft, trying hard not to think of Arrhyna or the child she carried, for such thoughts urged him to turn and flee, go back to them and leave Ket-Ta-Witko and the People to their fate. But he had made a promise: he could not flee. He swallowed a breath that would be released with his shaft, and hesitated as the beast coughed out a sullen grumble and raised one great paw, licking at the pads for all the world like some enormous cat worrying at a splinter or a cut.

So that was why the Breaker and his beast were alone: the creature was hurt. Rannach might have smiled had he truly believed that afforded him some advantage, but he did not think it did. Even wounded, that thing could slay him. And did he slay the beast, then he must surely face the other, whose armor shone rose-pink as a summer flower and seemed to shift and shimmer so that his eyes could not properly follow its outlines.

But he had made a promise, and he was a warrior. He drew the bowstring until fletchings brushed his cheek, and stepped around the break's concealing wall to loose his shaft.

The lion-thing roared loud enough to wake the dead as the arrow pierced its eye. Its head lurched back, jaws spread wide so that Rannach saw all the dreadful panoply of its fangs even as he drew a second arrow and nocked it to the string. He bent the bow and let fly again.

The shaft drove into the throat and over the furred scales there, blood darkening the pale flesh. The creature dropped its hurt paw and fell as it clawed at the missiles embedded in its eye and neck.

Rannach drew and fired three more shafts as the awful howling filled up the break and echoed off the walls. He had always been good with a bow, and each arrow struck where he aimed: one drove into the belly, another lanced the remaining eye, the third went in between the jaws.

Then he dropped the bow as the Breaker closed on him.

The invader came fast across the snow, leaving him no time to use that weapon again, so that he let the curved bone drop and snatched hatchet and knife from their scabbards.

Good Grannach steel those blades, the ax mounted on a pole of fire-tempered hickory wrapped round with soaked leather that had hardened like a second skin. Nor less the knife, its haft secure in his left hand, the blade half an arm's length of pointed metal honed sharp on both its sides.

He ducked under the longer blade the Breaker swung and took the reversing stroke with the hatchet, turning to drive the knife against his opponent's ribs. Had he fought one of the People, his counter would have driven the blade deep through hide and flesh, and hurt and weakened enough he might turn his hatchet and stove in the skull. But the Breaker was armored, and he felt his arm jarred by the impact, a hard metallic elbow slammed against his cheek. He staggered, retreating as the sword reversed and came threatening toward his chest.

He danced back, hampered by the snow, grateful it was not drifted and deep but stamped down by the paws of the screaming beast he prayed was dying, else he was surely lost.

The Breaker's blade glittered, darting in sweeping arcs at his head and chest. It was not such a combat as he was accustomed to, and he sprang farther back, wary as he gauged the reach of his enemy. The sword was twice the length and more of his knife, and he saw the Breaker held it in a double-handed grip and knew that one blow must cut him down, or take off his head.

And then he saw that each sweep turned the Breaker a little to the side. Not long, for the man was very fast and the sword came hurling back even before he exposed his armored ribs—but there *was* a moment. No more than an instant, an eye's blink of time, but perhaps enough.

Rannach wondered how far away were the Breaker's companions. He thought this solitary beastrider must be one of some scouting party, separated from the rest when the lion-thing went lame. He wondered how far those agonized screams carried, how long before the rest heard them and came back.

"No time," Morrhyn had said: he could not delay.

Once, he had slain a Tachyn raider with a thrown hatchet. He doubted even Grannach steel, thrown, would pierce the armor the Breaker wore. But close, could he get past that scything blade . . .

He feigned a stumble, feinted under a vicious, sweeping cut, and dove forward, rolling headlong over the trampled snow to rise inside the Breaker's reach, his hatchet rising and falling even as his knife drove up.

The hatchet hammered against the Breaker's concealing helm; the knife found flesh between the helmet and the armor's collar. Rannach turned the knife, twisting the blade even as he thrust it deeper, even as he smashed the hatchet against the helm.

He felt warmth on his knife hand and knew it was the heat of blood spilling out. He felt the Breaker's arms close around him and the man's weight fold against him, dragging him down onto his knees. Still he pounded the helmet with his ax, and saw the helm buckle and split. For an instant, through the concealing faceplate, he saw blue eyes staring at him in naked surprise. Then the light went out of them and the Breaker gusted a sigh that sounded weary, and was only deadweight.

Rannach pushed the body away and looked toward the dead man's mount. The lion-thing still moved, but its cries were softer now—pained mewlings rather than roars. He climbed to his feet and walked toward it.

It was no pleasanter to observe close up than at a distance. It seemed to him an abomination, neither one true creature or another but some horrid amalgamation, as if some malign creator had taken the parts of several animals and worked them together in obscene parody of what was true. But it was a beast of some kind, and for all that he had wounded it unto death, still he felt a kind of sorrow for its suffering and thought of it as a horse hurt in battle. He lifted his hatchet and brought it down against the rolling skull.

The thing coughed blood and ceased its mewling. Rannach went back to the fallen Breaker.

The man lay on his back on the snow. Blood oozed from under the helmet, dark in contrast with the rose-colored armor. Rannach wondered how a Breaker's face should look. Evil, he supposed, as weirdly distorted as the beasts they rode. He kicked the fallen figure, tapped the lolling head with his hatchet.

It did not move, save to roll and flop in that manner that only the dead possess, so he reached down to find the fastenings and pull the helmet loose.

He started back at what he saw, gasping, for he had revealed the face of a beautiful woman, her eyes wide as they stared sightlessly into the oblivion of the sky. Her hair was long and the color of honey, tumbling loose about perfect features, the bones delicate, the flesh smooth and soft and tan.

Rannach stared at her awhile, then spat and wiped a hand over his face. He rose and found his bow, then went back to where Morrhyn waited.

The Dreamer said, "Praise the Maker, I feared you were slain. I heard screaming . . ."

"Her mount," Rannach said. "I killed it."

"*Her* mount?"

"Did your visions not tell you that?" Rannach said. "She was a woman!" He took his horse's rein and shook his head. "I slew a woman, Morrhyn. A woman! What does that make me? Am I now a woman-killer? Am I now like Vachyr?"

Morrhyn looked out from under the hood of his cape and fixed Rannach with the heat of his burning eyes. "She was a Breaker," he said.

"She was a woman!"

Morrhyn nodded. "And did she plead with you? Did she ask your help? Ask you to aid her as you would a woman of the People?"

Rannach shook his head and said, "No, she attacked me. She'd have taken my head were I not swifter."

"Then she was your enemy," Morrhyn said. "Do you think women are weaker than men? I tell you, no. Listen! Would Arrhyna not fight were she called? Do you think your mother would not take up a blade to defend your father? Do the women of the People not take up arms to defend the clans?"

Rannach nodded. "But not like that. Not all warlike."

"She was a Breaker," Morrhyn said. "And they are not like us." Save they be our other side, he thought. Was that not a part of my dreams? That the Breakers *are* that other side, like shadow to sunlight?

"Even so." Rannach swung astride the stallion. "I cannot enjoy killing a woman."

"Likely she'll not be the last." Morrhyn pointed a finger toward the river. "They'd take Ket-Ta-Witko and lay it waste, feed the People to their beasts—those who survive. So, do we go on? Or shall you mourn her and give her honorable burial, and we wait here until her comrades come for us?"

Rannach looked at him out of troubled eyes. "Are you become so hard?" he asked.

Morrhyn looked him back and answered, "Yes. Now take me to the Wintering Ground, else your conscience destroy the People."

They forded the river and nighted in the timber on the flatland beyond, then traversed the plain and rode toward the Commacht's ancestral Wintering Ground. Morrhyn's dreams spoke of no further danger along their way, but troubled him nonetheless, for they seemed to promise a homecoming that was somehow not there.

He could not understand that, only advise Rannach that they continue onward. He wondered if the Breakers now owned larger magicks that clouded even the dreams the Maker sent him, or if the Maker himself denied that final promise.

When they came to the Wintering Ground and found it empty, he felt very lost and very afraid.

31 Until Death

It was a simple ceremony, held in the church in the presence of those few servants Wyme granted leave from their duties. Benjamyn attended with Chryselle, and Dido looked on beaming as if it were her daughter who stood before the pastor. Flysse was radiant, and did she wear only her customary dirndl, still her smile and obvious happiness seemed to Arcole to clothe her in brilliance. He took her hand when the pastor nodded and set the plain brass ring—Dido's gift—on her finger, repeating the vows. She answered in a firm, clear voice and with a slight shock he realized he was wed. It was a curious sensation, both exciting and somewhat alarming, and he hoped he did the right thing. Then Benjamyn declared they'd best return, and they went back through the snowbound streets, Flysse clutching Arcole's arm all the way.

Surprises awaited them in the mansion: Dido had prepared a small wedding cake and Wyme had decreed that the servants might each enjoy a mug of ale to toast the married couple. Flysse's fellow maids teased her, and the male servants offered Arcole their congratulations. Then, to his amazement, Benjamyn announced they were spared all duties until the following morning and to a chorus of good wishes, and not a few lewd comments, the majordomo brought them to a room that was now theirs alone. Fleetingly, Arcole thought that this was in part why he had married Flysse. But as the door closed and she turned toward him, he forgot that reason and the pang of guilt the memory induced, aware only of her happiness and his own. Whatever motivations had once moved him, he knew now that he loved this woman, and that he truly wanted her for his wife. He opened his arms and she came into them, and this time when he began to unlace her bodice she offered no resistance but laughed and kissed him, and then, blushing somewhat, led him to the bed.

Later, as they lay together, their arms entwined, Arcole knew that he had never been so happy. "I love you," he murmured into her hair. "I love you."

Flysse turned so that her mouth was against his and, as he began to kiss her again, said, "And I love you."

David was elated at the news. Indeed, had it not betrayed his thief's freedom, he would have shouted it at the sky as he sat atop Rupyrt's Gahame's roof. But that should have curtailed his clandestine lease on Grostheim's night-dark streets and earned him punishment, so he stilled his eager tongue and only sat chortling at the thought of Arcole and Flysse wed. It was almost as much happiness as he could imagine. He threw back his head and laughed—softly—into the darkness.

It was a wide night here, wider than any he'd seen in Evander, as if the sky were scraped clear of human grime so that all the stars shone through like promises. He could sit up here and imagine the country beyond the walls: it would be wide as the sky, and white with snow, the Restitution River glittering with ice-pack, and in the distance the forest edge, mysterious and—he frowned as he realized it—strangely enticing. That was most odd: he was a child of the city, a denizen of the streets and alleyways, accustomed to high walls and close rooftops, not that unknown country Sieur Gahame named the wilderness. God knew, Grostheim was curious enough, with its buildings all of wood and its streets either split timber or plain dirt, not at all like Bantar; not at all like the world he had known, far away across the sea. Yet it seemed almost he felt . . . He could not put it properly in words; Arcole would know how, but Davyd had not had the time to discuss it with his friend and could only struggle to comprehend his inexplicable feelings. It was as if the wilderness called him. The notion of it, of a land all trees and hills with not a building around, no streets or roofs but only such countryside as he'd not the experience to imagine even, was terrifying. And simultaneously . . . he shook his head, frowning as the word took shape . . . appealing. Yes, that was it: appealing. As if he were a child again, lonely, longing for the warmth of Aunt Dory's embrace—save in his head, Aunt Dory was replaced by that strange country beyond Salvation's boundaries. Sometimes he dreamed of it, of sunlit trees and plashing streams all filled with fish, high hills and grassy plains—which was most odd, for he'd no knowledge of that place, nor any love of things bucolic. When Flysse had spoken of her childhood in Cudham he'd thought it curious she loved the land so well. Yet now . . . He drew his borrowed furs closer as he pondered the mystery.

At first he'd thought not at all of the land beyond Grostheim's walls, perfectly content to remain within the city. Indeed, he'd not been unhappy to remain confined within Sieur Gahame's enclave. The master was not unkind, and Davyd had, if anything, a greater degree of security than he'd ever known. He had listened to the older men—who'd accompanied the master on journeys inland—speak of the wilderness. They had seen the forests only at a distance, usually from the yard of a farm or the deck of a barge, but they spoke of it as a place of menace, of wild beasts and trackless ways, and Davyd had shivered with them and agreed that was no place for decent folk. He was grateful for Grostheim's solid walls: they held out the unknown.

Then, as the year progressed, he had grown more confident and more curious. Then, he had soon enough discovered, those skills that had earned him a living in Bantar could be put to use here.

It was not difficult for a thief and a lockpick to find a way out of the warehouse.

He had his corner; the four other indentured men occupied a shed in the yard. Sieur Gahame lived in a cottage built against the wall surrounding his property, which consisted of the warehouse and the yard, the buildings and the palisade wall. Davyd was the only one in the warehouse: and the fastenings of the windows and doors were easy to pick.

He thought the inhabitants of Grostheim—the unbranded inhabitants, at least—assumed the rest too cowed to risk such venture, and that they were likely right. Surely his fellows in Sieur Gahame's enterprise were a docile lot, content with bed and board and those small luxuries the master allowed. Certainly, they made no complaint; rather, sang the master's praises for the good food they got and the pint of ale come a Saturday night. Laurens and Godfry were even grateful for church of a Sunday. (Davyd was, to some extent, equally grateful for that devotional duty: he had realized the priest owned no magical talent and could not guess his own ability, and the visits afforded him his only chance to speak with Arcole and Flysse.) He supposed Sieur Gahame was a good master. He supposed that was why no hexes were set about the property —that absence allowing his freedom—for why should contented slaves object to decent food and warm beds? And did they, where could they go? Grostheim was locked tight as any prison, and past its walls was only the larger prison that was Salvation.

He was not sure why he objected, save the dreams woke something in him. Sieur Gahame treated him well enough: he was fed and clothed, slept dry and warm, and his future was surely more certain than it had been in Evander. He need only serve the master and earn his trust, and in time he would be allowed out past the walls of the Gahame property, even be allowed to accompany Sieur Gahame on journeys inland—he was not sure he wanted that, but it should be a greater degree of freedom than most branded folk got. But he was not happy with his lot. He thought perhaps Arcole had sown some seed in him, unrecognized, that taught him better to object to the scar marking his cheek and the limitations of exile.

That and, perhaps, the dreams.

They had come more frequently since his discovery of the roof's freedom, and stronger. Not all were benign. Indeed, there were some terrifying as those he'd known on board the *Pride of the Lord;* he huddled inside his furs as he thought of those.

The dreams had begun this winter, as if in company to the influenza epidemic. He could not interpret them clearly, not decide whether they warned or promised. He was only sure that they alarmed him in ways he could not understand. Had his brief meetings with Arcole allowed the time, he would have discussed them, but the few short minutes stolen from church services did not allow, and Flysse was always there, close to Arcole, and she did not know, so he had only his own interpretation.

And that was hard.

Sometimes he dreamed of carnage, as if he floated in the sky, an unseen observer of the awful slaughter below. They were all bloody, human folk slain by faceless, formless beings, less shaped than shadows. In those it seemed the wilderness forest folk had told him of spewed-out monsters that came in the night to slay whatever—whoever—claimed the land. In those, he dreamed of fire and swords and insensate massacre. He saw women clubbed, or burned; men shot with arrows, or pricked all bloody with knives and lances.

And were those horrid images not enough, the dreams were permeated with such a sense of naked hatred, of a palpable intention to murder and destroy, he was thankful when he woke that he slept alone in his warehouse corner, for he woke all sweaty and often as not screaming, and thought that had he been observed then surely he must be guessed for a dreamer.

In some the forest was ominous: all dread and terror.

In others it was benign.

In some it called to him, as if the trees he had never seen beckoned, promising him hope and freedom, a life he had not known or imagined. Then it was as if a mother opened her arms to a lost son, and when he went into that embrace he woke smiling, comforted, and reassured. He dreamed of mountains, then; all tree-topped and craggy, and a place beyond where the sun shone on grass and rivers that ran blue, save where fat fish that he knew should be good to eat burst silver ripples across the surface. It was a landscape that filled him with a delight he could not, waking or asleep, comprehend.

He had lived all his life in the close gray city of Bantar and knew nothing of blue rivers or grass: he could not understand the dream, nor much better the other in which Grostheim rang loud with screams and howling shadows paced the streets in wanton slaughter, and he could not know if he was a shadow or a victim, only that he was very afraid.

He knew in the marrow of his bones, born of his talent's certainty, that *something* was going to happen. But he could not say when, or what. He wanted to discuss it with Arcole and could not. It curdled his joy that his friends were wed, and tainted that pleasure with threat. And yet, as he huddled closer inside his borrowed furs, he could not help smiling still. Arcole and Flysse were wed: they were man and wife, and shared—so they had whispered this last Sunday—a room now. Small, they had said, but theirs alone; with a door they might lock and a window that afforded them a view of the stableyard: Governor Wyme was a God-fearing man and allowed his married servants a degree of privacy.

Davyd thought of how much he should like to see his friends.

He turned his eyes from the sky to the streets below. They were empty, churned mud and dirtied snow lit by infrequent lanterns and the random gleam of unshuttered windows, none abroad so late save prowling cats hunting the rats that belonged to every city.

He thought of how he would like to speak with Arcole about his dreams. And if Arcole had married Flysse, then surely she must be privy to her husband's knowledge, no?

He surveyed the streets, an idea forming.

"What are you doing?"

Arcole said, "Nothing. I stole some paper and ink, eh? I'd not forget my penmanship. Shall you tell Wyme, or Benjamyn?"

Flysse said, "No, of course I'd not," sharply. "But you're not writing."

Arcole said, "Then what?"

Flysse drew her shawl closer around her and went to where her husband sat. They had a chair, of which she was proud, and Arcole had begged a barrel that served for a table. Those, and the trunk Dido had given them for their few clothes, were all the furniture they possessed apart from the bed. But though sparsely furnished and barely larger than a closet, the room was *theirs*.

"I can write my name," she said. "And some other letters."

Arcole turned from his "penmanship" and kissed her cheek. "Shall I teach you more?" he asked.

Flysse said, "One day, perhaps. But now—what's that?"

He shrugged and said again, "Nothing."

Their single candle painted his face with shadow, and Flysse could not see his expression, but his evasive tone, the set of his shoulders as he hunched over his work—those she could interpret. It saddened her that he kept secrets.

In all other respects he was an ideal husband, and these past weeks had been amongst the happiest Flysse could remember. She supposed that was a small happiness, to be content with a tiny room in another's home, shared with the man she loved, who—of this Flysse was confident —loved her. She supposed it was a meager existence to one such as Arcole, whose tales of salons and ballrooms, of grand hotels and lavish parties, had amazed and delighted her. To him, she supposed, this room was not much more than a cell, the mansion a prison. She knew it grated on him, his indenture, and that he did his best to hide his resentment. With others he succeeded, but she was his wife and loved him—she knew him better. So when he scowled and only grunted in response to her voice, she told herself he would come eventually to acceptance and make the best of his lot, and did her best to cheer him. Usually she succeeded, for it seemed he took honest pleasure in her company. But sometimes . . . She frowned and stroked his hair.

He had begun to steal, which most of the branded folk did in small ways such as Benjamyn and Chryselle and Dido chose to overlook. There was a scullion she knew sucked eggs and claimed them broken or addled; Nathanial was wont to sample the wine he served; most took their little tithe of food—one of the benefits of indenture to the governor. But Arcole stole the most unlikely things. Hidden beneath the boards of their room was paper, an inkpot, two pens with metal nibs he had labored to repair, and when Flysse asked him why, he answered only vaguely—that he'd not forget his penmanship, or that he intended to sketch her. But he never had, and while Flysse could write little more than her name, she knew what words looked like. She knew that the lines he drew were not words, save where he set his tiny squiggles down against a mark, and the sheet he labored over surely bore no resemblance to her. It hurt that he seemed not to trust her in this, whatever it was.

He arched his head back against her hand and turned toward her, smiling. She noticed that first he carefully set down his pen, and when he put his hands upon her hips she decided she would not, this time, be circumvented.

"What is it?" she asked, and before he could dissemble with words or his lips, "Arcole, I am your wife. Shall you lie to me?"

He looked an instant shamefaced, then shook his head. "Not to you, Flysse."

"So?"

"I'd not lie to you," he said with a terrible sincerity. "So better I say nothing."

Flysse stood awhile silent, shocked. The room was chill, but when she shivered it was not from the cold, save what curdled in her belly. "What do you say?" she asked at last. "I don't understand."

Arcole took her hands and kissed them. "Is it not enough I love you?"

"But keep secrets from me?" It hurt to say that, so stern. "Is it so in the Levan that husbands and wives hold secrets from one another?"

He chuckled then, which confused her. "As it happens, yes," he said. "But we're not in the Levan, eh? And even were we, I'd not. There'd be no cause."

She guessed he spoke of such matters as he had described to her, which seemed most scandalous—that married men kept mistresses, and wives entertained lovers as if the marriage vows meant nothing. Was that how society behaved, she'd have none of it. "No," she said, "we are not in the Levan."

"Were we," he responded, "there'd be no cause."

Flysse felt confusion grow. Did he say he'd not give her cause to doubt him, but be a faithful husband no matter where they be? Or did he say that were they in the Levan, there should be no cause for any secrets? She was a plain woman, and preferred plain speech: she said, "Arcole, do you speak honestly to me?"

He sighed and said again, "It were better I say nothing, Flysse. Better you not know what I do."

Anger grew, or was it fear? She faced him square and said, "I am your wife, our lives are as one now. You should not hold secrets from me."

He said, "No," and sighed again.

"So?" she prompted.

"So," he said, "I have stolen paper and pen and ink from Wyme's study, and am I found out shall be punished. I'd not see you suffer for what I've done."

Flysse sensed there was truth in that, but that it was not all the truth. She withdrew her hands from his grasp and stepped past him to stare at the sheet of paper. From the corner of her eye she saw him move, and wondered an instant if he would block her or remove the mysterious document. She was pleased when he did neither but only stood watching. Still, she could not understand what it was she studied.

"I know what you've taken," she said, "and where you hide it. And that you often work on this . . . whatever it is. Were it discovered, think you the master would not assume my knowledge and punish me?"

Arcole said softly, "Perhaps you should report me." Then he gasped as Flysse's hand struck hard against his cheek, stinging across the brand there.

"How dare you!" There was genuine anger in her voice. "Have you so low an opinion of me?"

"No." He shook his head, smiling as he rubbed gingerly where her blow had landed. "No, Flysse, I've not. God knows, I've only the highest opinion of you."

His smile was genuine, his tone apologetic. Flysse felt outrage dissolve, regret form in its place, and again confusion. She said, "Arcole, forgive me."

"No." He took a pace toward her, hand rising to touch her lips, silencing her apology. "I deserved that reminder I wed an honest woman. What I said was unwarranted, unforgivable. Flysse . . ." He took her hands again, his expression solemn, "Do you forgive me?"

She said, "Yes, of course." And then, "But I still fail to understand what it is you do."

He had known he could not keep it secret, and with his gambler's instinct decided to chance whatever transpired.

Sleeping in a room shared with Nathanial and the other single men allowed no opportunity work to work on the chart. One or the other would inevitably have seen what he did, and even had they not recognized it, they would surely have known he could read and write. He could not risk their telling, either by a tongue's casual slip or deliberate malice. He knew there were some who resented his elevation and would likely seize the opportunity to advise Benjamyn of his project. Then doubtless Benjamyn would investigate and inform Wyme, and all his hopes be dashed.

Sharing this tiny chamber with Flysse had given him the privacy he needed to hide his stolen materials and work unseen—save by her—on the chart. It was impossible to believe she would not sooner or later learn what he did, but—cowardly, he supposed—he had avoided this inescapable confrontation as long as possible. He knew Flysse would not betray him; he had no idea how she would take the truth.

He said, "It's a map."

"A map? A map of what?"

Arcole found her tone difficult of interpretation. He was suddenly very afraid: he loved this woman, and knew himself ashamed he had thought to deceive her. He said, "Of Salvation."

She stepped by him, leaning over their barrel-table to study the hard-won chart. "Do you explain?"

He ventured to set an arm around her and was relieved she did not shake it off as he indicated his work.

"This is the coastline; Grostheim's here, this line is the Restitution River. These are inland holdings. It's not done yet."

"How can you know all this?" she asked, her gaze still fixed on the sheet.

Arcole wished he might see her eyes. He said, "Wyme keeps maps in his study. When I have the chance, I study them; memorize them."

"You're very clever," she said.

Her voice was carefully modulated, the warmth that had been there earlier cooled. Arcole said, "Not really. I make mistakes, working solely from memory. Often I must start again."

Flysse said, "This looks complete. What's this?"

She touched the line indicating the forest edge, and Arcole told her, "The beginning of the wilderness."

"And these?" Now she dabbed a finger's tip at the crosses he had drawn.

"Holdings that have been destroyed," he said.

She turned from the map at that, and her face was grave. "Destroyed?"

He nodded. "There were three when first I saw the map. There have been six more marked since then. And the Militia patrols the boundaries —I think there shall be more when they return."

"How do you know?" she asked. "That there's patrols, I mean?"

"Wyme talks," he said, and shrugged, grinning. "He thinks we branded folk have no ears. He's careful—I think some great event unfolds—but still he lets things slip. And he leaves papers about: I think he forgets I can read and write. If he ever knew."

Flysse heard the bitterness in his voice and nodded thoughtfully. "Destroyed, you say. By what?"

Arcole shrugged again. "I don't know for sure. I think no one knows; only that farms have been found burned, and all the folk there slain. Wyme'd not have such news get out."

"No wonder you'd keep this secret," she said. "Did any learn you know . . ."

She shivered, and Arcole drew her close, but she set a hand against his chest and pushed him back a little. "They'll not have it from me." It was a promise he accepted with confidence. "But still—Arcole, what is this *for?*"

He said, "Something is happening in this land that Wyme does not understand. Something is killing the farmers. Or *someone.* I think there may be folk living in the wilderness. See?" He touched the map swiftly, counting the crosses there. "The attacks began close on the forest edge, on the most isolated holdings; but they move closer to Grostheim. I think Wyme is afraid—surely, he keeps this news from all but the Militia."

"It frightens me," she said.

"You've no need to fear." He hoped she spoke of the map, not of all it portended. "I doubt whatever is out there would dare attack this place. There are too many soldiers . . ."

"No." Flysse shook her head. Her eyes were suddenly lonely. "It's not that I fear."

"Then what?" he asked.

Almost, Flysse could wish she had not begun this: it led toward a destination that did, indeed, frighten her. But she was on the path now and could not turn back—her innate honesty would not allow her. Suspicion grew: of what the map meant, not only in immediate conclusion but also in terms of her marriage. A horrid question shaped in her mind, and for all its possible answer terrified her, she knew it must be asked. So she squared her shoulders and looked her husband in the eye and voiced her fear. "You contemplate escape, no?"

His expression was all the answer she needed, but still he ducked his head and said, "Yes," in the tone of a man caught out in some misdemeanor.

He began to amplify, but Flysse waved him silent. The room's cold seemed now to permeate her and she folded her arms, hugging her shawl close. Her throat was abruptly dry and she must force out the words she had no choice but to speak. "Alone? Or did you intend to take me?"

"Flysse," he said, his voice hollow, "I love you."

"But?" She studied his face. Was it the shadowplay of the candle, or did she see anguish there?

"As yet I see no way I might escape," he said in the same dull tone. "Even could I, it should surely be perilous."

"You evade my question, 'sieur." The cold inside her seemed to gather, focusing on a point deep in her belly, and there grew hot: she felt anger kindle afresh. She had believed she knew this man, believed he loved her. Suddenly she was no longer certain. "I ask you: is it your intention to desert me, or have I a place in these designs of yours?"

Arcole said, "Flysse," helplessly, and shook his head.

"You do not answer, 'sieur," she said coldly.

"Flysse," he said again, and moved toward her.

She stepped back. "Is your silence my answer?"

He swallowed, ran frustrated hands through his hair, and met her icy gaze. "This"—he gestured at the map—"is no more than a vague dream as yet. I learn what I can, against a possibility likely hopeless. It may well come to naught . . ."

"But does it not?" she pressed. "Have I a place in this dream of yours?"

"I'd not bring you into peril," he said. "I'd not see you harmed. I love you too much."

"I had thought love required honesty," she said. "I had thought love meant sharing; being together."

"We are together," he said, "and I do tell you honestly what I do."

"We are together, yes." Flysse laughed: a short, sharp snort, devoid of humor. "I had believed we were together because you wanted that. Now I must wonder if it was only the privacy marriage affords you, this room that allows you to weave your plans. And your honesty? It seems that must be drawn out of you, no?"

"I'm sorry."

"Now, doubtless." Flysse smiled, the curving of her lips no warmer than her laugh. "But had I not discovered your intent?"

Arcole could only shrug. It was difficult to meet her eye. Her gaze was so cold now, and he knew he hurt her. He wished he had not; of a sudden, he wished he had told her everything from the start. Had any doubt lingered that he loved her, it was gone now. He had not realized she might hurt him so much, not realized her pain could cut him so deep. He wondered how he might heal the wound. He knew he would not lose her; and feared she was already gone.

"Well?" she prompted.

He sighed and rallied his thoughts. "I know not where this leads," he said, indicating the map again. "I stumbled on this knowledge and found some hope there. I'd not be a damned servant all my life, Flysse! I

was unjustly charged, unjustly branded! Evander sent me to this godfor-
saken place, and I'd not die a servant of Evander. I . . ."

He fell silent as her eyes blazed like blue ice. "And I was fairly
condemned?" Her voice was low, throbbing with barely contained fury.
"Did I deserve exile? Am I only a 'damned servant'?"

"No!" he said fervently. "Oh, God, Flysse, you're my wife because I
wanted that. *Wanted* it! I tell you honestly—I love you; and I'd live out
my life with you, proud you name me husband."

"Save," she said, "the opportunity comes to escape."

"No." He shook his head. "I hadn't thought so far. Once, perhaps,
but no longer! Never since that night. I'd not thought past the making
of the map."

"And now you must." She wondered she did not weep. Surely she
felt tears threaten, but also the heat of anger still, the outrage his betrayal
delivered. "Think carefully, Arcole."

He nodded. "It may not be possible," he said slowly, choosing his
words with infinite care. "To flee this house, get past the walls. Wyme
should surely send soldiers after"—he almost said "me," caught himself
—"us. And then we'd need to cross Salvation. We'd need supplies;
weapons. I'm not sure where we'd go. Into the wilderness, perhaps.
Or . . ."

He hesitated and Flysse urged him on with tilt of her chin.

"Or go to the savages Wyme writes of," he said. "Seek sanctuary
with them."

"Who slay farmers and branded folk alike?" she said. "Who burn
farms and leave none living? Think you they'd welcome us open-
armed?"

"I said it should be dangerous." God, this woman cut to the meat of
it! He supposed it was one reason he loved her. He wondered how he
could have contemplated leaving her. And how he could not.

"I think that should be rank foolishness," she said. "To think to find
common cause with this unknown folk who burn and kill? Shall you go
to them and they wait while you explain your purpose ere they slay
you?"

He grinned shamefaced and shook his head, shrugging. "I told you
it is, as yet, no more than a vague dream. Think you it should be better
to run for the wilderness?"

"Were escape possible," she said, "yes. It should not be easy, but I
suspect the forests are kinder than these mysterious savage folk."

"Likely you're right," he said. "But even then—to make a life in the
wilderness? That should be no easy thing."

"No," she agreed. "And likely harder for you than for me."

"Eh?" he gasped. "What do you say?"

"That all your life has been lived in cities," she replied. "That did you flee to some metropolis you'd easily find your way around its streets, its salons. But the country? I was born in the country, Arcole."

"The wilderness," he said, "is hardly the *country*."

"But more akin than city streets," she gave him back. "Can you find food in a wood, Arcole? Can you recognize those mushrooms good to eat or tell which are toadstools that will poison you? I can. Can you dress a deer, or has your venison always come on a plate, out of the kitchen? Can you cook, or has some 'damned servant' performed that duty for you? I suspect I am likely equipped better for the wilderness than you, *husband*."

He stared at her, his jaw dropping. Flysse felt her anger cool a trifle: his expression was so dumbfounded she might have laughed had the circumstances been different. Obviously he had not considered such matters: she began to think he told the truth when he said he had not thought past the making of his map. But even so . . . He had clearly considered the possibility—the likelihood, even—of leaving her behind. She could not, yet, forgive that. She was no longer even sure she could trust him, and that was a sad notion.

"I suppose . . ." he muttered. "No—I've not the least idea how to dress a deer. And mushrooms?" He grinned. "Mushrooms come sautéed, no? Or in a sauce, from the kitchen."

Flysse refused to be mollified, although her anger shifted direction somewhat. It seemed he set his plans afoot without sufficient thought, as if desire for escape overcame his reason. That was foolishness, and such lack of common sense irritated her. "Best to consider such matters, no?" she asked. "There shall be no restaurants in the wilderness. No 'damned servants' to wait on you."

Arcole wished he'd not used those words. They had come careless: he did not think of Flysse as a servant. He said, "I'm sorry."

Flysse shrugged dismissively, not yet ready to be placated. "And the supplies you mention," she said, "the weapons. Where shall they come from?"

His expression changed, the hopeful grin disappearing behind a veil of uncertainty. Flysse saw on the instant there was more he held back, and her anger flared anew.

"No more secrets, eh?" she demanded.

He said, "Flysse, I made a promise."

She said, "As you made promises to me, *husband?*"

"No," he said, torn, and, "yes. I gave my word I'd not speak of it."

Arcole winced as she snorted that awful laugh again. "Your word, eh? Who's had your word now?" Realization then: "Davyd?"

Arcole nodded helplessly.

"Of course! Davyd is indentured to Sieur Gahame, who's a warehouse full of weapons. In God's name, Arcole, did you plan to take the boy with you?"

His face answered her, and she must struggle not to strike him again. "You planned to take Davyd with you, but leave me? You'd see me safe, eh, but carry the lad into danger?"

"Flysse," he said, "you don't understand."

"Then make me." She was not sure whether she demanded or pleaded. It seemed her world was turned upside down, nothing any longer fixed or sure. "Tell me."

"I cannot," he moaned. "I gave my word."

"On what?" she snapped. "You admit you'd enlist his aid. Because he was a thief? Because he's access to Gahame's stores? Because Gahame has other maps?"

"In part." Arcole wished she did not guess so much, so acutely; wished, too, he could explain that promise given Davyd. But that must break his word and impugn his honor: he could not.

"Only in part?" Her voice was scornful. "Then what else, *husband?* What more do you hold back?"

He said, "God knows, Flysse, I'd tell you had I not made a promise. *But I did!* I gave my word, and I'll not break that."

She said, "No, of course not," and he winced at the contempt he heard. "You'll lie to me, but your word to Davyd—that's sacred, eh?"

"It's not the same," he protested. "I made a promise on board the ship, when Davyd . . . told me what he told me."

Flysse stood a moment silent, perplexed. Arcole seemed genuinely ashamed of his deception, but nonetheless determined in this matter of his promise to Davyd. For all she no longer felt she knew him so well as she had believed, still she believed she knew him well enough to know him obstinate in matters of honor. And even though it irked her, she must grudgingly respect him in this: a promise, after all, *was* a promise.

At last she said, "So then, I'll ask Davyd what this promise is when next I've the chance. Does he not tell me, well . . . so be it. But understand this, Arcole—you'll not bring the boy to harm. You'll not endanger him, or—" She shook her head. "Fear not I'll betray you; you've *my* word on that. But you'll not harm Davyd!"

"No," he promised. "I give you my word."

She looked at him awhile. Then: "And does escape prove possible, you'll take me with you."

"Flysse," he said.

"You'll take me with you," she repeated.

Her tone brooked no dissent: Arcole ducked his head. "We go together," he agreed.

"I'll have your word on that," she said. "Your solemn promise before God. Your word of honor, Arcole."

He was surprised she should accept it still; and pleased: it left him room for hope not all was lost between them. He bowed his head and faced her. "My word on it. Before God, and as I love you."

Flysse nodded. "And henceforth you'll make me privy to your plans, eh? There shall be no more deception, no more secrecy. I'll have your word on that also."

"You have it," he said.

"Then we've a bargain." She turned away. "And I'll to bed for what's left of this night."

Arcole said once more, "Flysse, I'm sorry," but got back no reply.

He watched her climb beneath the quilt. He no longer had any stomach for his cartographic efforts and, after ensuring the ink was dry, stowed the map and his few tools in their hiding place and pinched out the candle. He yawned: the night, indeed, had aged and he felt drained, as if their argument leached out his energy. He shucked off his jacket and clambered into their bed. Flysse presented him her back, and when he put a hand upon her shoulder, she shrugged it off without a word. He lay lonely beside her, contemplating his errors.

32 Preparations

Those services attended by the branded folk of Grostheim took place soon after dawn, that the indentured be allowed their devotions without disruption of their duties or discomfort to their masters. Not all attended—cooks must prepare breakfasts and the lowest of the low lay fires and clean stoves—but from Wyme's mansion each Sunday Benjamyn and Chryselle led a shivering procession through the ice-rimed streets to the wooden building grandiosely described as a cathedral. Few free citizens were abroad so early on a winter's morning, and none shared the church—they'd not stoop to worship with common exiles. It afforded the branded folk a rare opportunity to exchange news, albeit in whispers as the priest intoned the prayers and led the ragged chorus of hymns.

Davyd knew something was amiss as soon as he set eyes on his friends. Flysse's cheeks were red with cold, and he thought she had been weeping though her pursed lips suggested contained anger. Arcole looked wretched, and Davyd saw that whilst he stood close beside his wife, they did not, as usual, hold hands. For all their proximity, he sensed a distance between them, and inched through the worshippers to find his usual place beside them, asking softly, "What's wrong?"

It was Flysse who replied, and her response startled him: "What was Arcole's promise, Davyd?"

Her voice was pitched low that only he might hear, but still was

edged with pain and anger. He frowned, confused, and looked past her
to Arcole, who shrugged and sighed.

"Arcole made you a promise on board the ship," Flysse whispered.
"He keeps his word; he'll not tell me its nature, so I ask you. What did
he promise, Davyd?"

He did not immediately respond, save to gasp and glance with nervous eyes toward the priest. The vicar was reading from a book of
prayer, his voice a drone, his gaze intent on the page. He appeared
disinterested in his flock, least of all in Davyd.

"How do you know?" asked the boy.

"I discovered . . . certain things about my husband." Flysse cast
a sidelong glance at Arcole. Davyd thought the man flinched. "He
had no choice but to admit a promise was given. I'd know what it
was."

Davyd swallowed the lump that seemed to abruptly clog his throat
and licked his lips nervously. He felt Flysse's hand close around his
wrist, squeezing. The urgency of her grip was matched by the urgency in
her eyes.

"I'd not pry out your secrets," she murmured, "but this affects us
all, I think. I'd not see you come to harm, Davyd; and I fear you may. So
I ask you, as a friend—what was the promise?"

He looked from her face back toward the priest, then warily around
the church. There was no Inquisitor present to sniff out his secret, nor
had the priest such power, but even so . . . He felt very afraid. Might
not the voicing of it in this place somehow reveal him? He shuddered,
his eyes darting about as might a rabbit's when a predator's wings
shadow the ground.

"Shall you tell me?" Flysse asked. "I swear it shall go no farther,
only—" She shook her head and Davyd saw a tear moisten her cheek.
"We've a difference, Arcole and I, that needs be settled."

There was such anguish in her voice that Davyd momentarily forgot
his own fears. He looked at her and saw pain in her eyes; past her,
Arcole stood miserable. Davyd wondered what had gone on that they
seemed so sad. Wondered, too, how that promise Arcole had given him
could so affect them. Was he somehow responsible for their distress? He
could not understand how that might be, surely hoped it was not. He
thought of all the kindness Flysse had showed him: surely he could trust
her with his secret. Indeed, had he not wished he could discuss his more
recent dreams with Arcole, so why not also with Flysse? But not here,
not in this place.

Low, he said, "It's important you know?"

Flysse said, "It is," and then: "Do you not trust me, Davyd?"

He nodded. "Yes, of course. But . . ." His eyes roamed the church. "I'd not speak of it here. Please?"

"Then where?" she asked. "Where else might we speak?"

Decision then, sudden, prompted by her obvious distress. He said, "Your room, it's on the mansion's yard, no?"

"Yes." Flysse nodded, confused now. "But how . . . ?"

Davyd hushed her. "You've a window? Tell me where it is, exactly."

She did, and then he asked: "Describe the yard, and whatever walls there are. Does the governor have dogs?"

As she told him, he felt a mounting excitement. It should be an adventure, and did it heal the rift between his friends, then it should be worth the risk. He had already, after all, contemplated the enterprise: now it assumed a far greater importance.

Flysse said, "I don't understand. How can this help?"

Davyd smiled and told her, "Trust me, eh?"

The day was chill. Spring approached, but winter was reluctant to give up its hold on the city. The sky was a steely blue, the sun denying warmth, a cold wind skirling the streets, where icicles hung from eaves and braziers were set out on porches, smoldering charcoal scenting the frosty air. Arcole considered the day far warmer than his wife.

Flysse had said little to him since that night—indeed, no more than she must, and the other servants cast curious glances their way. Nathanial whispered about lovebirds falling out until Arcole threatened to box his ears, thereby earning himself a reprimand from Benjamyn. She refused to tell him what Davyd had said, only that the boy had agreed to reveal the content of the promise. He could not understand how, and when he asked, Flysse favored him only with cold looks and bade him wait.

It was worse for the need to perform those duties assigned him. That he had sooner taken Flysse aside and pleaded with her, seek to reconcile their differences, was of no account to Benjamyn, or to Governor Wyme or his wife. In this household Arcole was but another servant; his problems were of no relevance to those concerned with its smooth function. He had never thought before how servants were expected to go about their business regardless of their personal circumstances. Save some illness afflict them, their masters took their presence for granted. Wyme had no interest in his indentured folk save they fail in their duty —and below stairs Benjamyn was the governor's representative, and no kinder. So Arcole must hide his feelings and play out his role as if naught were amiss. It fueled his resentment.

Nor were the nights any easier than the days. Flysse remained taciturn, watching in silence when he brought out his cache to add some new detail to the map. When she did speak, it was usually to demand he explain just what he did, and when he attempted blandishments, they were met with cool disinterest. It was, if anything, worse in bed. There, Flysse turned from him so that to his catalogue of woes was added frustration. He knew that he had offended her deeply, hurt her badly, but he thought himself punished enough and he wondered when she might decide to end his suffering. And then if she ever should, or if that happiness they had known was forever lost. That thought chilled him to the marrow of his bones: he came to realize how deeply he loved her and how selfish he had been. But when he tried to tell her, she only faced him with stony indifference or turned her back.

Arcole was not at all accustomed to such treatment, or to such misery as it delivered. It was an object lesson: he was better accustomed to success with women, and on those few occasions he had been spurned, there had always been another to whom he could turn. Here, there was only Flysse—nor would he have it otherwise. But still he cursed himself for his mistakes and wished he might undo the past, for all he knew that country was locked and he must look to the future instead. Yet it was not easy to hope when he lay sleepless, Flysse cold as a statue beside him.

Then one night when a waning moon hung like a crescent of ice over Grostheim, there came a tapping on their window.

Arcole was instantly alert, Flysse not much slower to wake. He shivered as he rose, clad only in his nightshirt. The yard outside was dark, and he thought for a moment gusting wind had rattled the frame or an icicle fallen, but then the tapping came again and he set his face to the glass. Frost rimed the edges of the pane, and at first he did not see the shape, but then darkness coalesced out of shadow and a pale face was revealed. Arcole started back, shocked a moment before he recognized Davyd. Then he slipped the catch and swung the window open. Davyd clambered in on a draft of chill air; Arcole closed the window, gaping.

The boy looked like a savage, or some weird shaggy beast. Furs swathed his body, tied with cords. One spread across his shoulders, the boneless legs wrapped about his throat, the head, still sprouting snarling fangs, surmounting his tousled red hair. His legs, too, were wrapped, and on his feet were hairy boots more like the paws of some wild creature than any footwear Arcole had seen.

"I told you I'd come, eh?"

Davyd addressed them both, grinning hugely. He seemed immensely pleased with himself, but his smile faltered as Arcole shook his head in bewilderment.

Davyd turned to Flysse: "You didn't tell him?"

Flysse shook her head, her expression confusing the boy. "No, Davyd. But is this safe?" Her expression changed to one of concern. "None saw you, eh? How shall you get back?"

Davyd's grin returned. "It was easy to get out; the return should be no harder. Remember, I was a thief."

"Even so," she said. "I didn't expect . . ." She gestured at his furs, at the window.

"How else?" he asked. "We've not time in church. Nor would I speak of it there. In case . . ."

Now Flysse grew confused, and Arcole smiled. Davyd settled on the bed; Flysse drew the quilt about her. Arcole donned a coat and took the solitary chair.

"Best we not delay," Davyd said, loosening his furs. "Sieur Gahame has us wake early, and I'd not chance the streets come light."

"This is dangerous," Flysse said.

"Yes." Davyd could not help but preen a little at his own daring. "But I'm used to danger, no? And you asked me to speak of Arcole's promise."

Flysse nodded. "We've much to speak of, all of us."

Davyd wondered at the glance she gave her husband then, but she waited for him and so he said without preamble, "I'm a Dreamer, Flysse." He paused as she gasped, a hand flying to her mouth. "You know what that means, eh? That was why I begged Arcole he hold it secret—I'd not be burned at the stake."

"No!" Her eyes were huge with wonder.

"Arcole guessed it," Davyd continued, "when I dreamed of the sea serpent on board the ship. And when it came, he saw my secret."

He looked from her to Arcole, aware still of distance between them, sensing it was, somehow, to do with him. So he added, "I swore him to secrecy, Flysse, even to keeping it from you. Do you forgive me?"

She said softly, "Yes. Yes, of course I do. God, what a thing! How have you survived?"

"By telling no one," he said. "Save Arcole, and now you. Before this, only Aunt Dory knew."

Flysse reached out to take his hand where it emerged from the swathing pelts. He liked that. Pretending an insouciance he had learned from Arcole, he said, "I've been dreaming again."

Arcole leant forward. "Of what?"

Davyd shrugged. "The forests, sometimes, as if the wilderness calls me." He pushed back the skull grinning atop his head and frowned. "Sometimes it's as if the forests want me to go there, as if they promise . . . I'm not sure . . . safety, perhaps. But sometimes they seem to threaten me." He shuddered. "I see things . . . shadows . . . that kill folk. They come out of the forests and slay. I've dreamed of them coming here, to Grostheim. They roam the streets like . . . like monsters."

Flysse said, "What does that mean?"

Davyd shrugged again. "I don't know. The dreams aren't . . ."

Arcole supplied the word: "Specific?"

"Yes." Davyd nodded. "Before—in Evander—they'd warn me of danger. If I planned a robbery and I dreamed of danger, I'd call it off. Save that last time." He grinned ruefully. "I dreamed of danger then, but I was short of coin and took the chance—and got caught. On the *Pride of the Lord,* I dreamed of danger from the sea."

"And the sea serpent attacked," Flysse murmured. "So what of these new dreams?"

Davyd said, "I don't know. Only that there's danger here, and likely in the forests too."

"Save you spoke of the wilderness calling you," Arcole said.

"Yes." Davyd saw Flysse and Arcole exchange a look he could not interpret. "As if . . . as if they are dangerous, but also safe. I don't understand."

"Coming here was dangerous," Flysse said. "Might it not be that?"

"I don't think so." Davyd's face was pale and small inside his furs. "Those dreams are of the . . . the shadows that come out of the trees, only they roam the streets."

"God!" Arcole stared at the youth. "I wonder . . . Davyd, when you dream of these monsters, do you see aught else?"

"Killing," Davyd said. "Sometimes here in the city, sometimes . . . other places. Like farms."

Arcole said, "The attacks Wyme's noted."

Davyd looked at him uncomprehending. Flysse said, "We've things to tell you too, Davyd."

She gestured that Arcole speak, and he told Davyd all he'd learned —of the map and the governor's coded comments, and what he believed they meant.

When he was done, Davyd studied him awhile through narrowed eyes. Then, astutely: "You plan to escape, no?"

"I . . ." Arcole hesitated, glancing at Flysse. "I hope it might be possible."

"You'll take me with you?" Davyd looked from one to the other, eyes urgent as his words. "I can help you, I know I can."

Flysse said, "I'd not see you come to harm, Davyd."

Arcole said, "It's only a vague hope as yet."

Davyd heard reluctance in both their voices. He could not believe they planned escape without him; could not believe they'd leave him behind, alone. They were his *friends!* They were as family to him! Mustering his thoughts, he said, "If I've dreamed of these creatures roaming the streets like . . . like wild animals, then Grostheim's dangerous. And I can steal from Sieur Gahame's warehouse. And in the wilderness, my dreams must be useful, no? I'll know when danger threatens, so we'll have warning. You can't leave me behind, you *need* me!" He stabbed a thumb into his furs, his voice urgent. "I can get clothes; muskets, even. I can get you a sword, Arcole. I can steal powder and shot. I've heard Sieur Gahame speaking of Salvation—I know something of the land. I can be useful."

He thought that Arcole, alone, would have agreed, but Arcole looked to Flysse, as if she held the yea or the nay of it. He said, "Please, Flysse," and when he saw her hesitate, he pressed on: "I'll not be safe in Grostheim. My dreams warn of that. I'll be safer with you."

Flysse offered no immediate response, and Arcole appeared still to await her decision. At last Arcole said slowly—cautiously, Davyd thought—"Are the dreams true, then likely he's right. Surely he could be in no more danger."

"Save there are soldiers in Grostheim," Flysse said, "who can likely beat any savages, or monsters, or whatever they are. Save we might all starve in the wilderness, or freeze. Or be caught by the Militia. Or be captured by these creatures. Arcole, he's but a boy."

"I'm nigh sixteen," Davyd lied. "And you'll need my help."

Arcole's face was impassive. It seemed to him that Flysse used the same arguments against Davyd's going as he had set regarding her accompanying him, but he'd not risk pointing that out. Davyd looked from one to the other, sensing that Arcole subjected himself to Flysse. When she remained silent, he said, "If you don't take me with you, I'll go alone. I swear it! I'll escape on my own!"

He heard his voice rise and was abruptly afraid he sounded only petulant. He had claimed years he did not own: he must act them, else he be left behind. He thought he could not bear that. Gentler, he said: "Please, Flysse. Take me with you."

Still she refused a straight answer, but instead asked, "You truly believe there's danger in Grostheim?"

He nodded. "Truly," he said, and saw her glance again at Arcole, who ducked his head and said, "I've heard of Dreamers. The Autarchy fears them because they've that power—to know something of the future. Davyd foresaw the sea serpent. If he's dreamed of Grostheim under attack, then I believe it shall come."

"And he should be useful, eh?"

Flysse's tone was bitter: Arcole winced.

Davyd said, "I shall be safer with you than alone."

Flysse looked him in the eye then. "You'd truly attempt to escape alone?"

He nodded solemnly.

Flysse sighed. She studied Arcole with eyes that seemed to Davyd like blue ice. Then she said: "God knows, Arcole, but you've much to answer for," and turned to the boy. When it fell on him, her gaze was not much warmer. "So be it, then. Davyd, you shall come with us, does the opportunity present itself. *If* it's possible."

Davyd beamed: he had no doubt but that it must be possible. Had not Arcole planned it? Happier, he asked, "What do we do?"

Flysse shrugged beneath the quilt and indicated her husband with tilted chin. "He's the mastermind of this venture," she said.

Davyd saw Arcole wince again, as if Flysse's tone cut him deep, but his excitement burned too hot for him to spend much time pondering what troubled them. He waited for Arcole, impatient.

"I draft this map." Arcole tapped the sheet he held. "So far, it indicates the attacks are from the northwest. See?" He indicated the sites of the burned holdings. "All have been north of the Restitution. So do we run due west, perhaps south of the river, then we may avoid these mysterious raiders. I'd thought to make alliance with them, but . . ." He glanced at Flysse as if seeking her approval; it was denied. ". . . . But Flysse told me better, and I agree it should not be safe. So best we head west."

"Along the river!" Davyd could not contain himself. "Listen, Sieur Gahame trades all over Salvation, and when he travels farthest afield he takes barges. The river's swifter than a horse, he says."

"Indeed." Arcole nodded approvingly. "Can we steal a boat of some kind . . . Davyd, what do you know of the Restitution?"

"It's a river." Davyd shrugged, searching his memory. "Sieur Gahame calls it a waterway—Salvation's heartline, he names it. He hires barges for his longer trips."

"Yes, yes." Arcole waved the boy to crestfallen silence. "But it feeds into Deliverance Bay, so it's a tidal river—the ebb and flow of the ocean govern its currents. Do you understand?"

Davyd shook his head and Arcole reached out to touch his hand in apology. "Forgive me. How should you? It means that the river currents are governed by the sea's tides. Did we take a boat on the ebb, we'd find ourselves fighting the current running east. Hard work, eh? We need the incoming flow to speed us on our way, and there you can help."

Mollified, Davyd smiled and asked, "How?"

"Likely Gahame owns charts," Arcole said. "Tables that detail the shifting of the Restitution's flow. Could you obtain them, or copies of them?"

"I can't read, Arcole."

"Dammit! Of course not." Arcole struck his own forehead, grinning that Davyd not feel embarrassed. "I'm a fool. So—do you but keep your ears open and learn what you can of the river. Without"—he glanced warily at Flysse—"making obvious what you do."

"That I can." Davyd nodded solemnly. "Some of my best scores were won by listening."

"No more than that," Flysse admonished. "And only carefully."

Davyd nodded again. "What else?"

Arcole looked first to Flysse, then said, "How easy is it to obtain those supplies you spoke of?"

"I sleep in the warehouse," Davyd replied, "and there are neither guards nor hexes. It would not be hard to steal, am I careful. Take only a little at a time. How much time do we have?"

Arcole shrugged. "I cannot say. God knows, I cannot even say if this shall prove possible. It's no more than a dream as yet."

"The forests call me in my dreams," Davyd said, "so I think it *shall* be done. What should we need?"

Arcole thought a moment. "At least one musket," he said, "and better three. Also pistols, and powder and shot for all. Can you get me a sword, then good."

"I can do that," Davyd said. "What else? Furs? Knives?"

"Knives, yes," said Arcole. "And hatchets. Not furs, I think. I'd not risk the snow, but wait for spring."

"Would the snow not slow pursuit?" Flysse asked.

"And us," Arcole returned. "Besides, this shall all take time, I think. We shall not likely be ready ere winter ends. Even were we, then we'd need furs and tents and food—more than Davyd might safely steal, eh?"

Now Flysse looked embarrassed: Davyd thought he saw Arcole conceal a furtive smile.

"No," Arcole continued, "we'd best travel light. Save the weapons, we'll take only a little food and—" He paused, thinking. "Does Gahame's enterprise run to clothing, Davyd?"

Davyd nodded.

"I've boots," Arcole said, "and those clothes I came here in. But were it possible, I'd prefer sturdier gear. And Flysse can hardly travel in skirts and such."

"I can get us all gear," Davyd said confidently. "Breeches and jackets; boots. Shall we need topcoats?"

"Blankets shall serve as well," Arcole said. "But sturdy boots for Flysse and yourself; also breeches, a shirt." He looked to Flysse. "You and Davyd are of a size, no?"

She ducked her head. Davyd thought some of the ice had left her eyes when she looked at her husband.

"Then such gear as Flysse shall need," Arcole said. "And you. For me, only a good jacket; and those other things."

Davyd nodded vigorously.

"But all of it," Arcole said as Flysse opened her mouth preparatory to speaking, "carefully. Is there risk involved, or the chance you be found out, then leave it. You'll not put yourself in jeopardy, eh? I'll have your word on that, Davyd. You do these things only safely."

Davyd gave his word. He felt a tremendous excitement now, and absolutely confident that all should be as Arcole planned. He would, bit by bit, accumulate what they needed. He would plumb Laurens and Godfry and the others for knowledge of the river—even Sieur Gahame, who was not averse to speaking of his ventures—and prove himself worthy of Arcole's trust. And then, when Arcole deemed the time right, they would go away together. Arcole and Flysse and he, like a family, to freedom. His talent should be no longer a burden to be concealed but a gift to be vaunted, used for their protection. It was an exhilarating notion.

"So then, carefully, eh?" Arcole's voice cut through his thoughts. "And slowly, so none suspect."

Davyd grinned. Then straightened his mouth when Flysse asked, "Shall it truly be so easy?"

He wondered if she asked it only in argument. He felt the question was addressed to Arcole, but still, afloat on optimism and excitement, he said, "Yes. I can do all that."

Arcole said, "No," bringing him somewhat down to earth, "it shall not. It shall be hard waiting, and harder doing. Perhaps even impossible. But what else shall we do? Live out our lives as slaves to the Autarchy? Run hither and yon like trained dogs on our masters' bidding? Die old and weary in servitude? No, Flysse, it shall not be easy. It will be dangerous—for which reason I hesitated to involve you; because I'd not see you come to harm. Neither you or Davyd; but I tell you this—I'll not die a servant of Evander."

"Nor," said Davyd, mightily enthused, "shall I."

Flysse said nothing. Only tugged the quilt tighter about her, as if a colder wind blew through the little room.

"So," Arcole declared, "for now we've plans enough. Best you return, eh, Davyd? We'd not want you caught out."

"No." Davyd turned instinctively toward the window, assessing the hour. Dawn was not now far off and he gathered his furs about him. "Shall I come back?"

"Best wait a while." Arcole glanced again at Flysse. "We'll meet in church come Sunday, no? Tell us then how your part goes, eh?"

Davyd nodded, busying himself with the cords that held the furs about his body. There was something here he did not understand, but neither was he sure he wanted to examine it. That differences stood betwixt Arcole and Flysse troubled him, and he'd not now entertain troubles, only hope. He supposed they argued as he understood wed people sometimes did: he had no experience of such matters and trusted that their love should iron out the differences. He settled the bear's skull —should he have told them the forests contained such creatures?—over his head, and turned to the window.

"Be careful," Arcole said; and Flysse: "God ward you, Davyd."

Then he was gone into the windblown night, thinking he must not be so different to those things he had dreamed of as he scurried across the yard and jumped the fence to run shadowy and all befurred through the streets.

"Is there anyone you'll not use?"

"What do you mean?" he asked.

"To use Davyd." She hugged the quilt about her body; Arcole still occupied the single chair. "Since learning he was a Dreamer, no?"

Arcole gestured: he felt helpless under her implacable gaze. "God, Flysse," he said, "I didn't love you then. I guessed what Davyd was, and then he swore me to keep his secret. I thought—yes—that his talent might be useful if . . ." He shrugged and wiped a hand across his mouth. "If the opportunity to escape ever presented itself. I didn't know if it would, but . . . God! I never planned to fall in love with you. But I did! *And I am!* What can I say?"

She offered no reprieve from his misery, only stared at the frosty window.

"I told you true," he said wearily, "when I said I'd not see you come to harm. I thought at first I might escape; and I'd not then deliver you into such peril. Now . . ." He set a hand against his chest as does a man taking a vow. "Now I'd not leave you, ever. Those vows we swore hold strong. You're my wife, Flysse. I love you. Does this dream come true, then I'd have you with me always. Can you say different?"

Flysse studied the patterns the ice made across the window. Beyond, the yard stood white with frost. The sky spread lightless above, the moon and stars hidden beneath the gloom preceding dawn. And that, she thought, cold and cheerless as the chagrin of her soul. She could not say different: she loved this man. But could she trust him any longer?

Once—no doubt of it—she'd have put her life in his hands. Her life and all her hope. *Had*, she told herself, done just that. Was that not what marriage meant? To trust, to believe in someone, placing your fate in their hands, confident it be well tended? But Arcole had held things back he should have told her. He had kept secrets from her—thought even of leaving her. She was not sure she could forgive that—even knowing she loved him—and it drove a knife into her heart that she could not say the words she knew he wanted to hear, that she wanted to say. It would be so easy to turn toward him and open her arms, knowing he should come into them with gratitude—with love—but she could not. There was, to her surprise, a cold, hard part of her that required more.

Commitment, she supposed; that absolute bonding she had assumed was naturally a part of marriage—that coherence of purpose and resolution she had seen in her parents, that she gave herself. She was no longer sure—could no longer be certain—that it was there in Arcole. He loved her, yes. But did the chance to escape present itself, would he take her with him, save she force him to it, or would he—be it easier, or more opportune—leave her behind? She could no longer know, not for sure, and that pained her. She wished she had his way with words—that she might trick out honest answers from him—but she did not, and could rely only on her own judgment.

She sighed and closed her eyes that he not see the doubt and hurt there.

Arcole said, "Flysse? Hear me, Flysse."

She opened her eyes and turned toward him.

"I've hurt you," he said, "and for that I'm shamed. Now I tell you honestly—do you forbid me, I'll forget all this—all my thoughts of escape. Do you tell me it must be so, I'll be a servant all my life. Only so long as I live it out with you."

"Truly?" she asked, not yet ready to believe but wanting to.

He ducked his head. "This map?" He tossed the paper to her. It landed by her feet. "Tear it up. Come Sunday we'll tell Davyd to forget it all. I'll forget it all. Only that I not lose you."

Flysse took the chart from where it had fallen and held it a moment. "Truly?" she asked again.

Arcole nodded again: "Truly. You're more important than freedom. God, you own my freedom! I'd not care to live without you."

She held out the map and said, "Keep it."

He took it and asked, "Are we reconciled, then?"

"Not yet, Arcole."

And he must be satisfied with that, as she must be. And they both wonder what the future hold.

33 Events Pertaining

Captain of Militia Danyael Corm had never expected to find himself leading an armed column into Salvation's hinterland under such circumstances. When he had applied for posting to Grostheim, he had thought the transfer an astute career move. In Evander and the lands conquered in the War of Restitution, advancement depended overmuch on connections and social ties. He had few connections and no social ties, and consequently believed he might look forward to a slow—and likely limited—rise through the ranks. The new world offered opportunity to climb higher—without, he had thought, much risk.

But now he rode through the mud of early spring at the head of fifty mounted infantry, with two mule-drawn supply carts and the distinctly unpleasant belief he might well die. Had he been able, he would have left this duty to another officer: he had much rather remain in Grostheim, behind the city walls and cannons. But Major Spelt had left him little choice, and had he looked to evade the commission, he knew he must consign himself to remaining a captain until he died. Which, he could not help thinking, might now not be long off.

He had known there were what Spelt referred to as "problems." All the officers had known that since last summer; there was talk in the mess —muted, but nonetheless fervent—and it was impossible to avoid speculation. It went no farther—the major had made clear that loose tongues would earn his displeasure—but amongst the higher ranks it had been a topic of excited discussion.

Farms were burned out and all the inhabitants slain. Animals had been slaughtered or driven off, crops wasted, vineyards torched. Like most of his fellows, Corm had arrived in Salvation confident the land was empty—a vast fallow field for the Autarchy to plow with indentured labor. Now it seemed all that was wrong: Evander was not alone in staking claim—there were others. But neither Spelt nor Governor Wyme could say whom, or what. Only that folk died, and that the attacks be kept secret.

And Captain Corm was elected to a most unpleasant duty.

He must make a patrol of all the holdings north of the Restitution, to where the river disappeared into the wilderness timber, then north along the forest edge to the Glory River as far as the coast, and southwest from there back to Grostheim. It would take—assuming untroubled passage—the better part of two months. Was there what Major Spelt named "difficulties," the duration could not be locked to any chronology.

In plainer words, Corm thought bitterly, they—or more particularly *he*—might never return.

The thought chilled him, and he shrugged his coat closer about him. It was a good bearskin, purchased from Rupyrt Gahame—warmer than this softening spring weather required, but he took comfort from its bulk. It held him warm, and he thought it might well be thick enough to slow an arrow's progress. Rogyr Stantin had told him they used arrows —whoever, or whatever, *they* were.

The lieutenant had found the wreckage of the Thirsk farm—the first to fall—and he had said there were stone-tipped arrowheads in the charred timbers. Captain Corm wondered what manner of savages would head their weapons with stone, and why the lieutenant did not lead this column. He was surely better suited to the task: he seemed quite unafraid.

Corm turned in his saddle and waved Stantin alongside.

"So, Rogyr, shall we find these monsters of yours soon?"

It was easy to make his question brave: far worse to admit his fears.

Stantin shrugged. "Who can say, Danyael? I know only that I found a farm slaughtered. But . . ." He turned his face toward the forest's edge. "I think they came from there. God, I'd sooner the major sent us into the woods to find them and punish them. A major expedition, eh?"

"Yes!" Corm returned with feigned enthusiasm. "Go in and teach them a lesson! A full column—with cannon in support—should learn them."

Stantin nodded, his polished tricorn glancing sparks of sunlight.

"Still," Corm said, not quite able to contain his uneasiness, "I wonder what they are."

Stantin shrugged again. "Who knows? Does it matter?"

"I'd think," said Corm, "that it might be good we know our enemies."

"Godless creatures," Stantin replied. "Wilderness things out of the forests. Not born of God, and therefore to be destroyed. No?"

"Yes," said Corm dutifully, glancing back along the column.

It spread in a regimented line behind him. Horsemen two by two, the wagons at the rear, warded by ten riders. All armed with muskets and sabers. Shot and powder and food and tents on board the wagons. They had checked nine holdings so far, and none with report of attack.

But they drew close to the forest now, and he could not help shifting in his saddle as his gut stirred uncomfortable.

"Are you well?" asked Stantin.

Corm said, "Yes, of course," and hid his hatred of the younger man's senseless courage.

They bivouacked along the Restitution's bank that night, in a meadow damp with spring rain and ripe with snowdrops, and the next day found the Defraney holding burned down.

It was not as Stantin had described the Thirsk farm. It was far worse: Corm spewed when he saw the skulls—the farmer and his wife mounted on poles alongside pigs and cows and dogs, the indentured folk beside.

In two more days they came on the Cateham mill. It was only charred rubble, save for the waterwheel: Anton Cateham and his wife were pinned to that and spun on the river's turning. Fish nibbled at their flesh and Captain Corm threw up again.

They found nine more ravaged holdings as they traversed the wilderness rim, all burned; all destroyed as if something emerged from the woods to deny Evander's supremacy, and then went back, hiding until the time to strike came again. There was no sign of where they came from, or where they went after, only what they left behind.

Corm felt his life draw close to ending, as if a malign shadow fell dark across his future: he felt the wilderness waited to strike him down. He decided he had better resign himself to remaining a captain and stay in Evander, but he was an officer and could neither discuss nor show that fear. He must act out his role, feigning a grim resolution he fortified with furtive sips from his hip flask. He must join Stantin in condemnation of the demons, blustering about bloody revenge, God's will, and each day go on as Major Spelt had ordered him.

He took his column north to where the Glory River fed the forests, and turned east. By then even Lieutenant Stantin was nervous. He rode with musket primed across his knees, his finger on the trigger; all did. And all the time they watched the land around, anticipating. Along the banks of the Glory they found seven more burned holdings, all of them mounted with ghastly totems—as if the demons Corm no longer doubted existed threatened Salvation and vaunted their defiance of Evander's rule. Captain Corm wished wholeheartedly he had never left Evander: ignominy should be better than this.

And then . . .

The sun stood high in a sky of pure azure, like a burning eye surveying the earth beneath; indifferent. Spring came apace, driven on the fresh wind that billowed clouds across the blue. Buttercups and daisies sprouted eager from the meadows bordering the river, and the Glory ran urgent with spring flood, bubbling and burbling between the wide grassy banks. It was a day such as the poets of the Levan described in their sonnets, or the minstrels of Tarrabon sang of.

And Captain Danyael Corm and his troop were caught between the river and what came out of the wilderness.

There was no warning. The last ravaged holding lay some nineteen days behind. Three back they had passed the night comfortably at the Payton farm, and since then the land had spread empty. Corm began to relax, thinking the worst was over, never guessing it awaited them.

He called a halt when the sun still stood a hand's span above the western horizon. The river stood to their left, grass stretching beyond it to the ominous line of the forest edge, blue-gray at the day's ending. He ordered the horses grazed and picketed, saw their tents pitched in orderly rows. He felt almost safe—the Glory was a reliable defense and in better than two weeks there had been no sign of the demons—but still he kept his watch doubled and longed for the day he should see Grotheim's strong walls; preferably at his back, with gates closed and barred.

He sighed as he found the refuge of his tent, settling on the camp bed to bring his flask from his tunic and sip eagerly. Payton had refilled it with brandy, and he smacked his lips gratefully as he drank. Then he swiftly hid the flask as Stantin came in.

"All's well." The lieutenant gave no sign that he smelled the spirit on Corm's breath. "The cooks have fires started, and I've stood down those not on watch."

"Excellent." Corm stood up, straightening his tunic. He glanced at his musket and decided to leave the gun: he wore his sword and a brace of pistols. "Think you we've seen the worst?"

Stantin shrugged. "God only knows, Danyael. Or the devil." He crossed his fingers and spat delicately. "We deal with demons out here, and they defy all reason."

"Even so." Corm frowned, not wanting to be reminded of what he could not forget. "We've seen no sign of attack since the Jaymes farm. I think we've left them behind."

He settled his tricorn squarely on his head, afraid he showed Stantin his fear; afraid the junior officer might report it to Spelt. He nodded sagely and said, "We've much to report, eh?"

"Indeed." Stantin smoothed his hair. "It's my thinking these demons grow braver. I'd see a major expedition mounted against them."

"Major Spelt shall doubtless hear your thoughts," Corm said. "But have we the forces?"

"We should send word home," Stantin gave him back. "Ask Evander for more men."

Corm ducked his head. "My thoughts precisely," he declared. "I shall communicate all this to the major on our return. But now—do we find our dinner?"

They quit the tent for an evening painted glorious by the setting sun. It seemed that fire lit the sky, as if the wilderness woods blazed above and smoked blue below. The slender crescent of a new moon stood to the east and a few brave stars vaunted the dusk. Swallows darted overhead, and in the grass pipits sang shrill. The Glory ran like molten metal, and the air was appetizing with the smell of roasting venison. Corm looked around: surely they were safe now?

They ate, as was customary on such patrol duty, with the noncommissioned officers. The two sergeants and five corporals were cheerful: Corm thought they lacked his imagination.

When they were done, he benevolently suggested that Stantin take the first watch and he relieve the lieutenant at midnight. That, he thought, should give him a while alone with his flask. He returned to his tent with the sun gone all the way down behind the trees and the sky stretched like blue velvet studded with silver above. He took off his belts and his tunic, his boots, and laid himself down with his pistols close to hand, his flask closer. He was not sure when he fell asleep, nor when he woke, only that it was a scream that roused him. It seemed to hang on the air, palpable as the earlier smell of roasting meat. He sat up, quite unaware of the flask that fell and dribbled across his legs.

He swallowed the horrible dryness that clogged his throat and snatched up both pistols. Those first, his boots after, then his belt that held his saber. He buckled it on, all the time aware that his heart beat wild against his ribs and all his worst fears came to meet him. He heard more screams. He thrust the pistols into their holsters and took up his musket.

"God," he asked as he left the tent, not knowing he spoke aloud, "please let it be nothing. Please, let it be nothing."

It was not: it was his nightmare fleshed.

He saw shapes moving amongst the tents. They were like shadows, indistinct and fleeting, and when he fired his musket at one he could not see whether it fell or only blended back into the night. He felt a terrible temptation to dart back to the useless refuge of his tent, to find his flask and drain it, but he saw flames and had no wish to die by fire. He cursed as he flung the musket away and drew both pistols.

A shadow presented itself before him and he saw the gleam of white teeth snarling, eyes that seemed to burn with unholy fire. He discharged both pistols and the thing—the demon—fell. Moaning, he took his powder horn and dribbled a charge into a muzzle, wadded cloth and rammed it in, added a ball, more cloth, knowing all the time that something was coming out of the night to kill him. He cocked the pistol and stared around. The bivouac was lit bright now, tents were burning. he heard the horses shrilling terrified, and the shouts of dying men. He holstered his loaded pistol and drew his sword, thrust it into the ground, and reloaded the second pistol.

Then—his terror suddenly so deep he no longer felt afraid—he took up his saber in his right hand and a pistol in his left and ran for the camp's center.

Stantin was there. An arrow jutted from his left shoulder, decorating his scarlet tunic with a darker color. Like Corm, he held sword and pistol. Then a figure erupted—Corm could think of no other way to put it—out of the burning shadows, and sunk a hatchet into Stantin's skull. The lieutenant voiced no cry as he died: only gaped as if in surprise, and fell down with his face all curtained with blood. It was not possible through the shouting and the rattle of discharged muskets, the screaming of horses and men, the angry creaking of the burning tents, that Corm could hear the sound of the hatchet striking Stantin, but he did and it galvanized him.

He screamed himself and pounded forward, saber lifted high. He fired his pistol at the shadow as it stooped to lever its ax from the lieutenant's skull. The lead ball struck the shadow in the shoulder and spun it away from Stantin. It made a sound and rolled onto its belly, struggling to rise. Corm swung his saber down and laughed as the steel blade cut deep across the ribs, then hacked again, against the shoulders. The shadow squealed and flattened: Corm drove his sword down straight, as if he pinned an insect.

The shadow grunted and was still. God! Dear God, thank you, he thought. They can be slain. Corm dragged his blade loose and holstered his empty gun, drew the other.

"Rally to me, men! Hold hard and fight!"

He looked around. He was not sure how many men he had left—he was, it seemed, inside a ring a fire. He could hear men dying beyond the flames, and some in them, their screams the worst. About him were no more than twenty of all his troop. He saw a sergeant and shouted, "Brystol, report!"

He had no time left to wonder why his fear was gone: only whether he survive this.

Sergeant Brystol came up. "Demons, sir! Just like the lieutenant said. Never saw them coming, sir; couldn't tell they was here until . . ." He ducked an arrow that sang out of the flames. "Devil's spawn, sir. Horrible shadowy beasts come from the night."

"They can be killed," Corm yelled. "Demons or no, they *can* be killed."

"God's on our side, sir," said Brystol, "so that's not surprisin'. Only it seems there's an awful lot o' them."

"Yes, God's on our side," Corm answered. "Praise be, and form a square."

He had not fought in the War of Restitution but he had studied the manuals, had attended the academy classes. He knew the correct procedures by rote.

Dear God, please let those procedures be right, he prayed. Please let them work against the devil's minions.

He reloaded as his men formed around him.

They were a solid square. He checked them—five or so to each side, kneeling with muskets cocked and aimed.

"They've shot and powder, sergeant?"

He was aware of arrows whistling by: they seemed somehow far away.

"They do, sir," said Brystol.

"Then volley," Corm said.

"On my order, lads!" Brystol yelled. "Fire!"

From around the square, black powder smoke billowed. From past the flames there came screams, then arrows. Corm saw a trooper fall back, a shaft embedded in his throat; another swore volubly as he tugged at the pole driven into his side.

"Again! Fire at will!"

Corm spent his pistol into the flames. He could see the targets no better than his men. They all of them fired at shadows—at demons—that came out of the nighttime wilderness and faded back into that flamelit gloom. He wondered if their dead rose up. He glanced at the one he had killed and was thankful it still lay there. Perhaps they were mortal, if demons could be so described.

More arrows fell: more Militiamen died.

The square was down to fifteen men.

Then ten.

Corm saw Sergeant Brystol fall to his knees, an arrow in his chest, another in his belly. Then a third sprout from his throat.

Sergeant Brystol lay dead and Captain Danyael Corm was suddenly aware he stood with only five men.

He watched them die, and was alone.

A shape came out from the flames, whooping. Corm dropped his empty pistols and raised his saber. He was ready to die now. Dying was preferable to wondering, to waiting. The demon swung a hatchet at his head and he met the blow, turned it with his sword and delivered a cut that opened the devil's belly. He laughed and took the hand from the wrist of the next attacker. Spun and sliced flesh as the thing went past him, then split its skull.

As you slew Rogyr Stantin, he thought.

"I'm God's man, " he shouted, hardly knowing he did. "I'm Danyael Corm, and I'm a captain of the God's Militia. I defy you to kill me! God's on my side and I renounce your black master!"

He swung his blade at the next attacker, and was confused. The demon ducked lithe under his stroke and only touched him with the short lance it held.

He saw another coming and pointed his blade at the thing's belly, but that, too, evaded his saber and struck him as it ran past.

The blow was hard and he twisted, anticipating the return, but the demon was gone into the surrounding flames and he faced a third.

That, like the others, hit him and darted by.

Then more, until his head swam and his sword arm grew tired. A blow struck his back and he staggered. Another took his knees from under him and he fell down. He waved his saber and felt it struck from his grasp.

I am going to die, he thought. Now they'll kill me.

He tried to climb upright, but could not: too many blows landed on him. Blood ran into his eyes and he could not find his sword. He tasted dirt in his mouth and waited for death. He felt too weary to pray.

Then hands were on him, turning him roughly onto his back so that he flung up both arms, protective about his face, anticipating the hatchet he knew must descend. He felt his wrists gripped, and weight upon his ankles, as if the demons stood on him and pinned him down. He waited for the final blow, vaguely surprised he was not screaming. He thought he no longer cared, that death was preferable to wondering at its arrival.

Powerful fingers clasped his jaw then, digging deep, and he opened his eyes. The sky was red and silent save for the sounds of burning. Sparks rose in whirling flood, climbing up to falter against the stars, and Danyael Corm saw the demon clearly. It knelt beside him, its left arm extended, its hand a vise about his face, compelling attention. No less the eyes that studied him. They were dark, reflecting flame so that they appeared lit by fire. They sat beneath a craggy brow, divided by a broad, hooked nose. Across the eyes and nose ran a band of black, dark as the braided hair that framed the awful visage. The mouth was wide and full-lipped, and Corm could not tell whether it snarled hatred or beamed triumph; perhaps both.

He did not, at first, realize the demon spoke. It seemed only to snarl and grunt, but then he recognized words amongst the grumbling.

"I let you live, redcoat, so that you go back and tell your people to go. We are coming against your walls to kill you all. Tell them that! Stay, and none shall live. The heads of your men shall stand on poles for the crows to pick, and your women shall weep as we take them. This is our land and you have no place here. Go away or die."

Corm stared aghast as the creature rose. It wore leather and furs, and he smelled it—an earthy, musky odor. It seemed a thing of the land, of the wilderness. That it spoke in words he could understand seemed inexplicable—save it was a demon and so could, presumably, speak in tongues. He saw that it held a short lance that appeared to be decorated with hair: not knowing how, he knew the hair was human. He saw a hatchet tucked beneath its belt, and a knife. He felt a foot drive hard against his ribs and gasped.

"Stand up. You are not a man, but stand like one."

Corm rose slowly to his feet, groaning as his bruised back protested. Warily, he looked around. He stood surrounded by demons. They seemed to him all alike: skin-clad and horrible, with the band of black across all their faces. He could not yet accept they gave him back his life. He was not sure he wanted it: he could see his command dead beyond the creatures. Some already lacked heads, and he must swallow bile as he saw a demon slice off Sergeant Brystol's scalp and lash the bloody scrap to its lance.

"Come."

The demon chief—he supposed this must be the leader—took his arm and thrust him toward a horse another brought out of the flames.

"Get up."

Corm tried hard to mount, but he was shuddering now and the horse pranced, scenting his fear. Now that it seemed he might live, he felt once again terrified. The demons laughed; one struck him hard across the buttocks. God, dear God, he prayed, only let me live. Grant me my life, please. That and my dignity. Grant me the strength to set my foot in the stirrup and ride away as befits an officer in your Militia.

Shaking, he took the stirrup and raised his leg. The horse snickered, eyes rolling, ears flattened. Corm lost the stirrup, stumbling helplessly back. He wept bitter tears as he was picked up and flung into the saddle, clutching desperately at the reins as the animal bucked and the demons whooped and laughed, capering in mimicry of his helplessness.

"Remember my words." The demon chief locked a steely hand about Corm's knee. "This is our land and we share it with no one. Go away or we shall kill you all."

One of the creatures must have prodded the horse then—Corm did not see it, knew only that the horse shrilled and began to gallop, maddened, away from the fires.

Away from the demons—and that was enough for Danyael Corm. He stretched along the beast's neck and let it run, wanting only to be gone.

34 A Grim Future

Rannach stared at the empty valley with eyes bleak as the land itself. When he turned them to Morrhyn they grew no warmer, save with the cold fire of accusation.

"Where are they?" His voice was hoarse and harsh. "Have we come so far for nothing?"

Morrhyn, in his turn, stared at the Wintering Ground. Snow lay deep along all its length, the stream that spilled from one wall frozen in a bright downward-curving arc, the pool it formed iced thick, the runoff only an indentation in the pure white blanket. There were no tracks: the snow lay pristine. Where lodges should have stood there was emptiness; the sky hung blue and chill above, not at all sullied by the smoke that should have risen from the lodgefires. Silence reigned, as if even the wind held its breath. He shook his head helplessly, blinking against the tears that threatened to cloud his eyes and freeze upon his cheeks. He thought that in this awful moment of utter disappointment he could easily give up his life. Simply drop from the paint mare and crawl away into the snow to die; to close his eyes and willingly enter the cold's embrace. It was too much: he had endured too much, come too far, to find his goal deserted and empty as lost hope.

"Well?" Rannach's angry voice cut through his misery, sharp as a knife. "You're the Dreamer: where are they?"

So low he must repeat himself at Rannach's irritated request, Morrhyn said, "I don't know."

"Ach!" Rannach sawed his rein, prompting the stallion to curvet, snorting its irritation. "Was it all for nothing, then? Did I leave Arrhyna for this?" He gestured at the empty landscape. "What do we do now?"

Morrhyn slumped even lower in his saddle. It seemed his hope seeped out like blood from a wound. Was it all presumption, his daring hope that he might save the People? Did the Maker punish him for such ambition, such vanity? Was all his quest only a mockery?

He wiped a glove across his mouth and stared silently at the sky as Rannach waited impatiently for answers. The sun westered, and soon it would be dark. He had no ready answers: he had, now, no answers at all.

He sighed and said, "Do we make camp here this night? Perhaps I'll dream."

"You'd best," Rannach said curtly. "Else we shall likely die."

"So you dream again," Chakthi said, and filled Hadduth's cup with tiswin, "that's good. But do you dream true?"

"I dream of the Tachyn," Hadduth answered, then corrected himself: "I dream of you conquering your enemies. That is only just, so surely it must also be true."

"Yes." Chakthi nodded, old ashes falling from his lank hair. "What is just must surely be true. But tell me again."

Hadduth told him, and the akaman thought on it, then smiled, the curving of his lips no more than a baring of teeth, like a wolverine's snarl. "I must play Racharran at his own game, no?"

"Yes," Hadduth told him, "if you—if we—are to have our just revenge."

"And that I'd surely have. So I must play the diplomat, eh?" Chakthi's mouth spread wider. Hadduth could not tell whether he smiled or grimaced. "That shall not be easy."

"But you can do it," Hadduth said.

"Oh, yes! I can do it," Chakthi agreed. "To see Racharran and his whoreson child destroyed, I'd pledge my soul."

Hadduth saw no reason to tell him that he likely did; his own, he thought, was perhaps already bought. But by what power! The Maker was as nothing to the masters of his newfound dreams. The Maker sent him none; he turned his face away from his People and gave them over to the strong. Surely that must mean his new masters outreached the Maker, and who stood early with them must surely be vaunted and enlarged over all others; and it gave him the means to please Chakthi.

"It shall not be easy," he said. "Racharran can bear us Tachyn little love after this year."

"But can it be done?" said Chakthi. "Tell me it can be done."

"It can," Hadduth promised. "So long as we are careful, and play the role of penintents."

"Promise me what I want," Chakthi said, "and I'll take any part you say."

Hadduth nodded. "Then best," he said, "that you wash your hair and bind up your braids; take off the mourning clay."

"Vachyr's not yet avenged. I swore a vow . . ."

"Which to honor requires that you play your part. Or . . ."

"I'll do it." Chakthi ran fingers through his filthy hair. "Vachyr would understand, no?"

"He would," promised Hadduth. "Shall I help you?"

Chakthi nodded, and the wakanisha set water to heating on the fire, that his akaman might cleanse his hair and take the clay from his face, and deliver the Commacht to his masters.

"Well?" Rannach asked again. "Where do we go? What have you dreamed? Or do we sit here and wait for death?"

Morrhyn leant closer to the fire. It seemed not to warm him. He sat swathed in furs, a blanket around him, food—albeit only the last of the dried meat the Grannach had provided—in his belly, but still felt the cold pervade his bones—and no less his soul. He felt alone, bereft as that other, awful time when he had recognized that his dreams were taken. He wondered if that was come again, and the Breakers' dark wind blew so strong over Ket-Ta-Witko that it held off the Maker's benefit?

But how? he wondered. He had dreamed all down the long road from the Grannach's valley. The dreams had been strong, enough that they had evaded the Breakers' scouts, come safe to where the clan should be. But now . . .

This last night he had not dreamed at all, but found only sleep—dreamless and sound—under the shelter Rannach had constructed. And he had woken to chagrin and Rannach's accusatory eyes.

For a moment he thought of lying to his companion, then dismissed the thought: Rannach deserved better than that. He had risked his life to bring Morrhyn to the clan, to the People. He had left his wife behind, where he might have remained safe, and had given himself wholeheart-edly to the quest, to the hope Morrhyn had promised.

No, Morrhyn thought, I cannot lie to him. I owe him better. Even if all of this has been futile.

"I did not dream," he said. And before Rannach had a chance to voice the anger that flashed in his eyes: "I know not why, only that I did not. Perhaps the Breakers command magicks that defeat even the Maker."

Rannach's eyes grew wide at that, and he closed his mouth on his accusations and anger and only said, in a hushed voice, "Can that be?"

"Perhaps." Morrhyn shrugged his thin shoulders. "They are surely powerful."

"But they die," Rannach said, the statement reaching for hope. "I slew one."

"Yes," Morrhyn said. "And bravely as any warrior of the Commacht. Racharran would be proud of you."

And found in that a straw at which he might clutch.

"Listen! You're your father's son—had Racharran his way, you'd be the next akaman of the Commacht . . ."

Rannach's bitter laughter echoed off the valley's snow-clad walls.

Morrhyn ignored it, motioning the younger man to silence. "Heed me, eh? Can I not dream, then we must rely upon other senses. Were you akaman of the Commacht and had fought all year against an enemy whose anger ignores the Ahsa-tye-Patiko—and would likely seek you out even in winter, even to your Wintering Ground, which he'd know of— where would you go?"

Rannach's frown deepened. "You speak of Chakthi and his Tachyn, no?" he said. "So did I wish to hide the clan, I'd not come here. Morrhyn!" His face brightened. "That's why, eh? That's why the clan's not here! My father took them to some safer place, where Chakthi should not find them."

"I think it must be so," Morrhyn said. "But where?"

The frown came back. Rannach tugged awhile on a braid, the movement setting the brooch Arrhyna had given him to sparkling as it caught the early morning sun. Morrhyn thought of Arrhyna and felt sorrow for all that he forced on her and her husband, save there were far greater issues at stake than only their happiness. But still, even so, he could not help that pang of guilt.

"There's a canyon," Rannach said, and paused.

"Think!" Morrhyn urged him.

"South of here," Rannach said. "Sometimes buffalo winter there. There's a river—shallow—across the mouth. But that would slow raiders; and there's timber. My father showed it me once, and said it might be a good Wintering Ground—did we not already own the finest."

Morrhyn sighed again, this time with relief, or expectation of hope —it was all he had now. "Let's go there," he said.

"It's only a memory," Rannach said.

"Even so."

"And if they're not there?"

"Then we look elsewhere," Morrhyn said. "No?"

Rannach said, "Yes," and smiled, and set to piling snow over the fire, all bustling optimism again. "And if they're not, then we can go ask Yazte and his Lakanti. They'll surely know, eh?" He chuckled. "I doubt Yazte shall order my execution."

Morrhyn shook his head and wished he felt as much cheered; but darkness and doubt tugged like claws on his mind, holding him back from such effervescent optimism. He could not forget his dreamless sleep, or his wonder that the Breakers owned far worse magicks than he feared. He told himself there *was* an answer, there was still promise of salvation for the People. But when he looked out onto the empty valley, he could not still the doubt that filled him, chill as the cold that numbed his bones.

The Hard Frost Moon saw Motsos home, unyielding as the snow under his horse's weary hooves. He leaned along the animal's neck as the crusting ice that spanned the river before the canyon broke, and dark water trammeled around the creature's fetlocks. Warriors watched him with nocked bows so that he must lift up and shout his name before they slew him.

That should be ironic—to be slain by his own brothers as he brought them warning. He laughed at the thought, then leaned down again along the horse's neck. The Maker knew it was warm, and he was so very tired.

But he was still a warrior of the Commacht, so he rubbed his eyes and forced himself upright as the watchers helped him from the saddle and promised his horse be groomed and fed, then led him, all tottery as a child, to Racharran's lodge, where the akaman stood ready to meet him, alerted by the scouts along the river.

He squatted on warm furs, leaning toward the fire as Lhyn set a cup of warm tiswin in his hand, and smiled as Racharran himself draped a blanket around his shoulders and asked what news.

"There were twenty of them," he said. "Scouts, Bylas supposed; and I agree with him. I'd have stayed to fight, but he told me to bring word. I'd the fastest horse."

"Yes." Racharran nodded. "That horse of yours can outrun the wind. My favorite is slow, beside."

Motsos beamed at such praise, then frowned. "I'd have fought them," he said, "had Bylas not asked that I come back."

"It's for the best," Racharran said, "that we know where the enemy is. So—tell me what you saw."

"A column of twenty," Motsos said. "All on those things they ride, those . . . *creatures*. We could smell their stink and hear their howling, coming arrow-true across the plains. I think their horde cannot be far behind."

"No," Racharran agreed. "But where?"

"You know that river where the breaks are?" Motsos said. "All flat before, and then a wood? And then the jumbles?"

Racharran nodded.

"They chased us to the gulleys." Motsos drank the hot tiswin as if it were some elixir. "I left them there. That's only three days' ride in good weather, but those beasts they ride." He sipped more tiswin, his homely features thoughtful. "I think they'd travel faster than any horse."

Racharran nodded, his face grim. "And were they the outriders of the horde . . ."

He left the sentence unfinished. Motsos said, "Our scouts ride five days ahead, even seven."

"Yes. *Our* scouts." Racharran smiled darkly. "But these people are not like us."

"Even so." Motsos shrugged. "That great horde we saw—surely it cannot travel so fast."

"Perhaps." Racharran found a twig and broke it. The snapping rang loud in the silence. "Say they travel faster than we can, say those you saw could reach this canyon in three days. Say they ride—what?—five days before the rest. Then it might take them no more than eleven days to take word back." He paused, calculating; when he spoke again, his voice was low and grim. "Their entire force could be on us as the Rain Moon rises."

Motsos raised his cup to his lips and found it empty. Lhyn reached to fill it and he downed the liquor in a single gulp, so alarmed he forgot to even thank her. When he remembered and murmured the words, she shook her head. Her eyes were fixed firm on her husband, and in them Motsos thought he saw a fear that must surely mirror his own. He stared at Racharran, waiting.

The twig Racharran held was in splinters now. He threw the pieces into the fire. "We must prepare to fight," he decided.

"Perhaps they'll not find us." Lhyn's voice was soft, as if she feared to say it aloud lest she betray them.

"The Maker willing, no," Racharran said. "But I think we'd best prepare. Surely they look for us. Likely they look for all the clans."

"Can they fight all the People?" Lhyn's eyes were large with wondering horror.

"Were there enough of them." His mouth curved in parody of a smile. "Eh, Motsos?"

Motsos nodded, wishing he might find argument; knowing he could not.

"Could we not move on? Flee them?" Lhyn asked.

Racharran barked laughter like an angry dog. "And go where? Here, we've at least the canyon's walls at our back. I'd sooner not fight, but we may have no choice; and I'd sooner not wait to find out but be ready. So . . ." He threw back his head a moment, as if he shook off doubt, and when he looked again at Lhyn and Motsos, his face was all stern purpose. "We prepare to fight. Meanwhile, I'd see how Bylas fares. And"—this softer—"how close these invaders are."

"I'll take you back," Motsos said.

"There's no need." Racharran shook his head. "I can find the place you decribed."

Motsos said, "I'd also know how Bylas fares."

Racharran smiled more warmly then and ducked his head. "So be it. But rest this night, eh? We'll go out at dawn."

Perico wished he were not charged with Juh's message: it was an honor he could easily have done without.

The Hard Frost Moon was no time for traveling, and worse in this unusually harsh winter. He had sooner spend his time warm in his lodge with his young wife than out on the open snow with the air so cold that each breath struck his lungs like a lance and dusted his horse's mane with ice; so cold it was a danger to touch metal for fear he leave skin behind.

And worse for all he saw along the way.

He scarce dared build a fire for the fear it betray his position, and had it not been a surety that he freeze in the night, he would have slept without. But that was surely death, and so he sought out hidden places, where trees or rocks should hide the light and smoke, and even then slept restless, waking through the nights in fear of invaders.

He had seen them.

Oh, by the Maker, he had seen them! And they filled him with such dread as stirred his bowels and urged him go back save that should earn him Juh's punishment and mark him a coward. So he went on, frightened, and by day and night prayed to the Maker that he come safe through to the Commacht, and that they send him back with an escort.

Preferably a hundred or so warriors, for he doubted he could face those creatures with less.

They were such things as nightmare spawned, and he wished Juh had listened earlier to Racharran and heeded the Commacht akaman who was, he decided, a wise and foresighted man.

Had Juh only listened, then he would not be here alone, hiding from creatures that surely blasphemed the Maker with their very existence.

"You're sure Juh said that?"

Kanseah nodded, concealing the affront he felt. Surely it was hard enough that Tahdase sent him out in such foul weather without the Naiche akaman questioning the word he brought back. He let his eyes wander sidelong to Isten's face, and found it set in a frown that matched Tahdase's.

"He told me—himself!—that he sends a rider to the Commacht to ask what Racharran does."

"And?" Tahdase asked.

"That was all," Kanseah said. "He sends a rider. I think . . ."

He hesitated, not wishing to put words in the mouth of an akaman.

"What do you think?" Isten asked, his voice soft so that Kanseah felt a little mollified. "I'd hear what you think Juh will do."

"I think," Kanseah said, "that Juh will listen to Racharran's words and likely heed them." Almost, he added, "This time," but he held that thought back and said only, "That was my feeling."

Isten looked at Tahdase and said, "I think the time has come to do the same."

Tahdase studied the fire awhile, then ducked his head. "Yes. We shall send a rider to the Commacht."

Silently, Kanseah asked the Maker fervently that it not be he.

"They slew one, at least."

Racharran angled his lance in the direction of the horrid body sprawled frozen in the snow. It was pin-pricked with arrows and its blood was a shadow over the white. A broken lance protruded from the chest. Not far beyond lay an invader, arrows in the bright armor and the marks of hatchet blows on the helm. Farther down the break lay a Commacht, his left arm near sundered from the shoulder, his furs divided by a sword's cut. Farther still lay his horse, dead from its wounds.

Motsos said, "Bylas took them away from the Wintering Ground, as he said he would."

"Yes, he was brave." Racharran nodded. "Now let's find him, eh?"

It was not difficult: the winding pathways of the breaks were all marked with blood and bodies. Horses lay clawed and gutted and the Commacht warriors were cold in the snow, their weapons clutched in frozen fingers and the armored corpses of the invaders strewn around them. Their courage made Racharran proud, but even so . . . For all the Commacht dead, there were only three invaders slain, and two beasts.

Bylas was the last.

His horse lay under the body of an invader's mount, whose jaws were closed around the lance driven deep into its throat. Some way beyond, where the break twisted back on itself in a direction opposite to the Commacht's Wintering Ground, Bylas lay locked in the embrace of a figure armored in sunny yellow. His hatchet was buried in the invader's helm, his knife between the joindure of breastplate and tasset.

Racharran said, "He died well."

Motsos grunted sorry agreement and asked, "Shall we gather them for burial?"

"No. There were twenty of them, you said, no? Three are slain, so the rest go running back. I'd know where; and where the horde is now."

"They deserve honorable burial," Mostsos said.

"Surely they do," Racharran agreed. "But we've not the time, are we to defend the clan."

For a while Motsos stared at him as if he'd argue, but then he shrugged and said, "Yes, I suppose it must be. But the Maker knows, I do not like this—to leave brave men unburied?"

"Think you I do?" Racharran answered.

He waited until Motsos shook his head then said, "So we go on; and see what danger comes against the clans."

Hadduth said, "We must play this careful. Racharran will be slow to trust your word, I think."

"Yes." Chakthi nodded, his newly wound braids falling about a face scrubbed clean of mourning white but dark with contained anger, and ugly anticipation.

"You cannot go," Hadduth said, "nor I."

"No." Chakthi smiled, which was like the snarl of a cornered beast. "But who shall we send?"

"Who might they trust?" Hadduth mused. "Amongst all our people, who would they believe?"

Chakthi thought a moment, and his feral smile stretched wider.

"There's one," he said, "who's aided them in the past. They'd trust him, no?"

"Dohnse?" Hadduth matched his akaman's smile with his own.

"Twice now he's met the Commacht wakanisha and let him go," Chakthi said. "Surely they'd trust him."

"Yes!" Hadduth chuckled. "Let it be Dohnse."

"Is it much farther?" Morrhyn studied the bleak white plain ahead. Nothing moved there save skirling snow, tossed by the wind: it was as if they were the only living things in all Ket-Ta-Witko. Had he not known better, he might have believed the Breakers were already come and gone, and the People left slaughtered behind. But that surely could not be. The Maker could not be so unkind and no army had passed them, nor had they come on scenes of battle—he did not count the sad corpses they'd found where warriors had skirmished and died. Had the true slaughter begun, there would have been more, far more: he shivered at the thought and turned toward Rannach.

The younger man shrugged. "It was long ago—I was a boy. But . . ." Like Morrhyn, he stared at the empty plain. "I think it cannot be far."

"I pray not," Morrhyn said, and drew his furs tighter, his face lost under the shadow of the hood. And silently, for he'd not let Rannach hear his doubts, I pray we be in time.

He turned his face toward the sky. Its blue was like ice on a river, the sun a watery eye that sank too rapidly westward. The Hard Frost Moon rose in the east, narrowed almost to disappearing. Soon the Rain Moon would be up, but he doubted it should deliver its promise. This awful winter had too strong a hold, as if it locked white fingers on the land and would not let go.

"So, onward." Rannach heeled the stallion out from the trees. Morrhyn followed, staring glumly at the horse ahead. It was mightily thinned, ribs visible and head bowed down. Arrhyna's mare was in no better condition, and he added to his prayers the hope the animals lasted. Without them there was no hope at all.

"Should we become separated, it is as before." Racharran fixed each man with a commanding stare. "We leave the fallen."

He waited until they had all given reluctant agreement. They liked the order not at all, nor he any better—but the word they carried outweighed the importance of any one life.

"One of us at least must get back," he said, "and tell the clan what we've seen."

"And then?" Motsos asked. "And what if you are . . . ?"

He paused, unwilling to speak his fear. Racharran voiced it for him. "If I am slain," he said, "then as many of you as can must get back, to warn the clan. We'll need brave warriors, if . . ."

Like Motsos, he let his voice trail off, eyes shifting to the sheltering timber, his mind carrying his sight past the trees to the horde encamped on the snow beyond the forest. Even did that great mass advance slowly, still it must come down on the Commacht soon after the Rain Moon rose. Did it move swift—he pushed the thought away. Surely it could not: surely so vast a horde must come slow, seeking food along the way. They were not such warriors as he knew, but still they must eat—as must their horrid beasts—and the need to provide for such an army must surely govern its pace . . . Surely?

He forced a smile. "Do they find the Wintering Ground, we must be ready."

Motsos said, "Perhaps they'll not." But his voice was low and his face expressed no belief in his own words.

Racharran said, "The Maker willing. But best we prepare, eh?"

Motsos nodded and showed his teeth in an answering smile that was patently false.

"So let's ride." Racharran stood. "I'd be home fast as we can."

Though what good speed should do them, he did not know; save they get back to die amongst their loved ones. Even did that horde divide to attack the clans one by one, there were still enough to overwhelm the Commacht and the clan die like animals cornered in their lair. He spoke of defending the canyon, but that could be only a brief defense against such numbers, against the savagery of the invaders. The canyon was as much trap as refuge, but he could think of no other course—this snow was no battleground for the warriors of the People, who fought off horseback, running and raiding. This snow—this Maker-cursed winter—favored only the invaders. He wished Morrhyn were there to advise him; he wished his fellow akamans had listened to his wakanisha. But wishes were no more tangible than the wind and he must face the grim reality that before long he should likely see his people all slain, and the best he dared hope was that they give a good account of themselves and take no few of the invaders with them into the spirit world. It seemed a sorry hope, and he could not dismiss the anger he felt that Juh and the rest had chosen to ignore his warnings and had sat back complacent as the invaders came through the mountains into Ket-Ta-Witko.

But that, like ephemeral wishes, was pointless: they *had,* and now it seemed they would pay the price. He wondered if the Maker truly turned his face from the People, for all that had happened that last year. Did he consign his creations to destruction for the breaking of the Ahsa-tye-Patiko? Were Morrhyn there, he might explain it; but he was not, and Racharran could not. All he could do was lead his people in such war as he knew they could not survive.

His heart sat heavy as he mounted and led his men away, back toward the canyon.

None spoke as they rode, and he thought likely they shared his own gloomy vision of the future. It would be, he thought, a sorry homecoming.

They were two days out from the canyon when they saw the riders. There had been no sign of the invaders' scouts—as if they'd learnt all they needed and drew back to the horde—and what slowly crossed the snow ahead were two figures on horses whose gait told of near exhaustion. Racharran saw no need to halt, nor need of caution, but rather felt a great curiosity. Perhaps the other clans had learned of the horde and sent messengers. Surely too late, but even so . . . He urged his mount to a faster pace, closing on the riders.

They turned to face the oncomers as if readying for fight, and as they did, Racharran gasped and shouted, "I know that horse! By the Maker, that's Rannach's stallion!"

"And that pretty mare he gave Arrhyna," Motsos called back. "Do they come home?"

For an instant, Racharran wondered if he would welcome that, or if he rather preferred they remain in the mountains. He supposed this meant they at least lived—albeit surely for only a while longer.

He closed the distance and saw his son raise a lance in greeting. Then the second figure threw back the hood of its cape and he wondered who rode with Rannach.

When Morrhyn said, "Greetings, Racharran. Do you not know me?" he could only shake his head and gape.

35 Messengers and Doubts

Lhyn came to meet them as they rode in from the canyon mouth, her eyes bright as she saw Racharran come safe home, then starting wide in unalloyed amazement as she recognized her son. Unthinking, careless of dignity, she broke into a run. She was not alone—most of the clan came with her, eager to hear their akaman's news, no less surprised than she to see Rannach with him.

And Arrhyna? Surely that was the paint mare Arrhyna rode, but could it be Arrhyna slumped there, all swathed in concealing furs? A measure of trepidation tainted Lhyn's joy, for that second figure sat the horse like one at the limits of exhaustion. She glanced back and saw Nemeth and Zeil hurrying forward.

Then she gasped as the figure pushed back the concealing hood and she saw the snow-white hair framing a face that even so emaciated she knew. Her steps faltered as eyes that seemed to burn from out of the dark and skeletal features fixed on her, and the thinned mouth stretched out in a smile.

"Morrhyn?" She came on slow, looking from one to the other. "Rannach?"

Around her the Commacht fell silent, staring fixedly at the men they had likely thought dead, surely never to be seen again. Racharran halted his horse and slid from the saddle.

"We've unexpected guests," he said. "And much news."

It was hard to tear her eyes from her son, from Morrhyn, and she glanced sidelong at her husband. "Good or bad?"

Racharran said, "Both. But we'll speak of that later."

She nodded and went to the two men, still mounted. Morrhyn, she thought, because he needed help to climb down, Rannach because he seemed unsure of his welcome. She had no thought of the Council's decree then: only that her son was come home. She raised her arms and he came off the weary stallion into them. His embrace was strong, but she thought him very thin, even gaunt.

He said, "Mother, it's good to see you."

She only shook her head, lost for words, and held him, her cheek against his, her hands touching his face as if she'd reassure herself he lived and was real, and not some phantom come to taunt her. When she was satisfied, she let him go and looked to Morrhyn.

The wakanisha was dismounted now. He looked smaller, sunk in on himself, yet somehow larger. That, she decided, was his eyes—they blazed with such purpose as she'd not before seen, as if their light alone animated his wasted body. She embraced him as she had embraced her son, and against his chest said, "Morrhyn, I am happy to see you back. I am happy you live."

He smiled—she could not help but think of a corpse's grin—and said, "As am I."

Then Racharran was there, and Nemeth and Zeil, asking of Arrhyna; and the wives of the dead scouts, inquiring of their husbands.

Racharran spoke to them, and to Arrhyna's parents Rannach said, "Arrhyna is safe—or was the last I saw her. I left her in care of Colun's Grannach, in a valley where no Breakers have come. Also . . ." He hesitated, grinning, proud and embarrassed both. "Also she carries a child, a son."

They laughed and beamed their pleasure even as the widows of the dead began to keen. Lhyn wondered if she had not sooner known her son remained safe there, and then . . .

"How can you know it's a boy?" she asked.

Rannach said, "Morrhyn told me," as if that were the most natural thing in all the world.

She looked again at Morrhyn then. He stood tottery as an old man. Had Racharran not supported him, she thought he must fall down in the trampled snow. She looked again at his burning eyes and saw the truth there.

"You dream again," she said.

He nodded. "I've much to tell you; to tell all the clan. And not much time for the speaking. We've none of us much time; none of the People."

It was as if a wolfwind blew icy through the warmth of a lodgefire, and Lhyn shivered. Racharran said, "I've the gist of it, but we must talk in clan Council."

Lhyn stared at him and was afraid of what she read in his eyes. She looked at Rannach and Morrhyn and said firmly, "Tonight. These two needing feeding first."

Morrhyn said, "It should be better now."

"No." She shook her head. "First, warmth and food. Tonight you can address the clan."

For a moment she thought he'd argue, but then Racharran nodded and turned toward the encircling crowd and raised his arms for silence —which was scarce necessary for they all hung on every word—and said, "Our wakanisha is come back with much news. But he is weary and hungry, and would rest awhile. So—build up the fires, and when the moon rises we shall speak of the future and what we must do."

Lhyn noticed that Morrhyn raised his face to the sky then, as if he'd check which moon might rise and the time before its coming; and felt again afraid.

The lodge was warm, which was an unfamiliar sensation, and his belly was full, which was no more familiar. Had his body its way, he'd have slept—just closed his eyes and rested back against the luxury of the furs and drifted off into sleep: it should be so easy.

And so hard: the clan waited on him and he owned a duty to the Commacht and to all the People, entrusted him by the Maker. Enough had fallen to the Breakers—Racharran had told of Bakaan's death, and Bylas's, and all the others—and he'd lose no more.

He wished his body were not so frail and waved off Lhyn's offer of tiswin for all he thought it might vitalize him. He took tea instead, and summoned up his thoughts and said, "It's as I told Racharran along the way—save the People leave, we shall all be destroyed."

Lhyn asked, knowing she need not but still compelled: "You're sure? It's much the Maker demands of us."

Morrhyn said, "Yes: I am sure. Save we do this, we are all lost. The Commacht and all the People."

Racharran said, "Leave? It's surely hazardous here; but even so . . ."

Rannach said, "They defeated the Grannach. They came through the mountains."

"I've seen them," Racharran said. "But . . ."

Sharply, Rannach said, "What?"

His father shrugged and answered, "I've looked to band the clans—after Matakwa; after the first killings by these . . . Breakers, you name them?"

"They name themselves so," Morrhyn said, "because they break worlds, because they break the Maker's Will."

Racharran nodded, turning to his son. "Even so. I believe you—trust you!—but still you were banished by the full Council. Shall the other clans trust you? Or call for your life, for breaking that edict?"

Rannach threw back his head and laughed. "My life, Father? I've chanced that coming here. Not against warriors of the People, but against the Breakers! I left my wife in the mountains! I—"

Morrhyn clutched his angry, outflung arm, silencing him. "I asked Rannach to bring me back," he said. "And Arrhyna urged him go, because it was the only way. He chanced his life for the People."

Racharran ducked his head. When it lifted, he said, "Forgive me, my son. I am proud of you: I welcome you back, and shall fight any who seek to execute that sentence."

"Save," Rannach said, "it shall likely be the Breakers who slay me, do you not listen."

"I listen," Racharran said. "It's the others I fear are deaf."

Morrhyn sighed and said, "Are they, then so be it. But the Commacht can survive! If . . ."

Racharran waved him silent. "I know. But to leave . . . everything? That's a hard departure, no?"

Morrhyn said, "It's the only way, else we all die. Do the rest listen, then good. But if they refuse—the Commacht, at least, might live."

Racharran nodded. "Yes, so be it. But I'd make this offer to the rest."

"If there's time," Morrhyn said.

It had not been easy to convince the Commacht that flight was the clan's only hope. There were no few who still saw Morrhyn's departure as betrayal, and those who could scarce envisage the journey west in such bleak weather; others claimed that journey could only leave them easy prey to the Breakers, and more could not believe the promise.

The talking had gone on well into the night before the cold had driven them to their lodges, and had resumed the next day. Morrhyn had spoken as eloquently as he could, and his fierce words and penetrat-

ing eyes had persuaded many. Then Rannach had spoken, of his sojourn
in the valley and the sad news the Grannach brought. Racharran had
told of his own encounters with the Breakers, and had summoned those
warriors who had seen the enemy and lived to speak. Another night and
another day were spent debating it, but finally, as the sun fell behind the
canyon walls, the last doubters allowed themselves convinced and it was
agreed.

And then the messengers began to arrive.

Perico came very slowly across the river with his right hand lifted up and
the fingers spread wide in sign of peace, or the Commacht he knew
watched from the slim moonshadows of the trees might slay him else.
He thought few might be welcomed here, in so well-armed a camp—
which, he thought, was unusually abustle. Indeed, almost as if the Commacht prepared to move.

Save no clan moved from its Wintering Ground in such weather;
not with the Hard Frost Moon barely faded and the Rain Moon yet to
come.

Unless . . .

He heeled his mount faster through the ice-strewn water and
shouted, "I am Perico of the Aparhaso! I come with word from Juh, for
the akaman of the Commacht."

And to himself and his horse: "And I am very cold and afraid, and I
think I shall not like taking Racharran's word back to my akaman."

Kanseah wondered if it was a sin against the Ahsa-tye-Patiko to resent
the duty his akaman and his wakanisha set on him.

An honor, they had told him, but he found scant honor in riding
alone through the bone-cold night, wondering if strange creatures might
pounce upon him and slay him and leave his body unburied; or
worse.

He had seen the remains of past battles strewn along his path: bared
bones of men and horses, all stripped and shattered. He would have
howled—had he not feared the sound bring down those . . . things
. . . upon him—and urged his horse to a swifter pace: the Commacht
Wintering Ground offered safety.

He preferred to think no farther than that: it was all too large for a
simple warrior who'd sooner lay warm with his wife than carry messages
that might shift the shape of the world.

*   *   *

Jach thought it should be good to see the Commacht again; and was it on such a mission as Yazte had said, then he must surely be acclaimed a hero on his return.

He had been surprised when his adaman had summoned him and invited him to sit beside Kahteney, and the chieftain's wife had poured him tea, and both had praised the speed of his favorite horse and his equestrian skill, and he had listened carefully to what they told him to say and felt only pride that he was entrusted with the message for Racharran.

Yazte's own words, emphasized by Kahteney so that each one was burned clear on Jach's memory: The Lakanti will follow you now. Give us word by this messenger, who can be trusted, and we go with you.

It was a great mission—a matter of great honor—and it almost warmed Jach's heart enough that he no longer felt the cold.

Dohnse came in wary as a cur dog.

The Commacht had poor reason to welcome any Tachyn, and he doubted many might recognize him as the man who'd let the clan cross the river unattacked, or any as the one who'd let Morrhyn ride free. Indeed, he could not properly understand why Chakthi had sent him with a message he could not entirely understand or believe.

He had seen the Tachyn akaman scrubbed clean of mourning's white clay with his hair bound up again, and surely Chakthi had smiled and said his rage was gone and such threat came against all the People that old sorrows need be set aside and all band together against the newcome enemy. He had sounded sincere; and Hadduth had been with him, and lent his voice to Chakthi's, and both had given Dohnse the message.

But even so . . .

Chakthi was not such a man as to readily give up his anger, no matter what else threatened. And there was something about Hadduth . . .

But even so: it was better to ride free than skulk foraging about the Tachyn Wintering Ground like some homeless hound, so Dohnse approached the Commacht with his hands raised high so that they see he carried no weapons, his shield reversed and his lance slung point-down in sign of friendship, and was unsure whether it be his alone or also Chakthi's.

He would deliver his message, he thought, and afterward decide.

When the lookouts brought him to Racharran, he was mightily surprised to find Perico of the Aparhaso, and Kanseah of the Lakanti, and young Jach of the Naiche come there before him; no less to see the banished Rannach at his father's side.

But it was sight of Morrhyn that surprised him most.

The Commacht Dreamer greeted him as a friend, which set him a little more at ease as he nervously faced the suspicious eyes that studied him as if he were a scout for a raiding party. That he could understand, but there was something more, something in all their eyes, on all their faces, that he could not quite define. They seemed to share some secret knowledge. And the camp he had just crossed had looked to him as one readying for travel.

"I am sent in peace," he said when the formal greetings were done. "By Chakthi; with his word of friendship."

Rannach frowned at that, mistrust cold in his eyes. Nor did Racharran look much better convinced.

It was Morrhyn who beckoned him to sit and said, "I know this man. Dohnse, is it not? It was he agreed our fording of the river, and again when I went away he let me pass unharmed."

Softly, Dohnse murmured, "And paid for that."

Racharran said, "And now Chakthi sends you with his word of friendship?"

Dohnse nodded.

Rannach said, "Why you?"

Dohnse shrugged, forcing himself to look at the younger man, not into Morrhyn's bright and burning eyes. Rannach seemed older, less headstrong. "Because of what I did, I suppose," he said. "Because of all the Tachyn, you might trust me."

Rannach said, "Trust Chakthi? That's much to ask."

"Still Dohnse comes in peace." Racharran frowned at his son's bluntness. "And we shall hear him out."

Dohnse bowed his head and said, "My thanks. You've little enough reason to trust any Tachyn, but this I tell you—I bear you no ill will, nor do I seek to trick you."

"And Chakthi?" Rannach demanded, ignoring his father's angry grunt.

Dohnse hesitated. Things went on here that he did not understand but sensed were momentous. Rannach was come back from exile, and Morrhyn returned looking as if he'd seen the face of the Maker. All the clans were represented, and he supposed Perico and the others came like him, as messengers, with words from their leaders concerning the invaders. Likely their messages were much as his. But still—there was that about Chakthi and Hadduth that sat ill with him. Did they seek to play him as a pawn in some secret game, he would not lose his honor: he had little enough else. He decided to speak only the truth.

"Chakthi and Hadduth bade me come," he said, "and tell you that they believe such danger comes against all the People as to make Chakthi forget his anger. He says that it is set aside, and revenge forgotten. He says he would know what the Commacht intend, as it was Morrhyn and Racharran who spoke most strongly in Matakwa, when he had better listened than allowed his grief such rein. He says that surely the akaman of the Commacht must understand what it is to lose a son, and know that pain; and that his grief made him mad. For this he apologizes and asks forgiveness. He says he will pay whatever blood-price Racharran asks in compensation for this past summer's war."

That, all of it, was exactly what Chakthi had told him, and he fell silent, awaiting Racharran's answer.

The Commacht akaman looked at Morrhyn and raised his brows in silent question.

Morrhyn said, "Do you believe this, Dohnse?"

Again Dohnse shrugged. "He has washed the white from his face, and braided up his hair again. He smiles now, and says he waits for Racharran's word."

Rannach spat into the fire. Morrhyn repeated: "Do you believe this, Dohnse?"

"I tell you," Dohnse said, uncomfortable, "what my akaman bade me say."

"What Chakthi says," Rannach muttered, "is not always what he means."

Dohnse shifted on the furs. The lodge felt very warm and he knew he trod a thin line that hung above a gulf of dishonor. "I tell you what I was told to say." He looked at Rannach, at Racharran; then into Morrhyn's eyes. They made him think of ice pits, could fire burn blue in ice.

Those eyes locked hard on his and he could not look away. Suddenly the others faded—the fire gone, and the shadows it cast across the lodge. There remained only Morrhyn's eyes, which seemed to look deep into him, into his soul, and demand the truth, absolute. It was as if the Maker himself stared at him.

From out of that blue burning he heard a voice say, "I believe you are an honorable man, Dohnse. I believe you have told us what Chakthi says, each word true as he said it. But . . . what do *you* believe?"

"I?" He stared into the blue fire. His mouth went dry, and at the same time he felt a great desire to spit. It seemed a lump lodged in his throat and he wondered, under that penetrating gaze, if it was potential dishonor he coughed out as he said, "I do not believe him. I do not believe Hadduth. The Maker forgive me, but I believe they intend to betray you." He could not help himself: those eyes drew out the truth like fish guts. Perhaps the carcass left behind would be clean, and he be only honorable, not stinking of treachery and lies. "I believe they would know what you do and use that against you. I know not how, but that is what I believe, the Maker help me."

Morrhyn said, "He shall, my friend," and the lodge came back in focus and Dohnse shook his head, swaying where he sat.

Morrhyn set a hand on his shoulder, steadying him, and passed him a cup that he gulped down, not knowing what he drank, save it was hot and wet his parched throat.

"Have I betrayed my clan?" he asked.

"No!" Morrhyn shook his head, more vigorously than a man so frail had right to do. "You uphold the honor of your clan, and your own."

Dohnse smiled gratefully, and said, "Thank you."

Morrhyn nodded, pausing awhile, as if measuring the Tachyn. Then he said: "The Commacht go to the Meeting Ground. The Maker promises us another land. A place free of the Breakers, where we can live peaceful."

Dohnse gasped. This was not at all what he had expected to hear: no wonder those others wore such thoughtful faces. But there was no doubting the confidence in Morrhyn's voice. Slowly, he said, "That's a long trek in such snow. And with these . . . Breakers . . . across the way?"

Morrhyn said, "It shall not be easy. But still, it's the Maker's promise. Otherwise, all the People shall die."

Dohnse hesitated, glancing from one to another. On the faces of the Commacht he saw only certainty and resolution; on those of the other messengers, a mixture of wonder and doubt. He cleared his throat and asked, "How shall this be? How *can* this be?"

Morrhyn said, "When you let me pass, I went to the Gate Mountain and the Maker sent me visions—promises. The Ahsa-tye-Patiko has been broken, and so the People are denied Ket-Ta-Witko, which shall fall to the Breakers. Do the People remain, then they, too, shall fall to the invaders.

"But the Maker does not entirely forsake his people. He offers us the chance of salvation. He offers us another land, do we but heed him. There, we may start anew."

Dohnse looked into the Commacht wakanisha's eyes and wondered why he could not see such truth in Hadduth's: there was no room left for doubt in Morrhyn's and so he nodded, accepting. But even so, the enormity of what Morrhyn said spun his mind around as if he rode an unbroken horse.

"How?" was all he could think to ask.

"The *how* of it I do not know," Morrhyn replied, "only that it must be so. Are the People to live, they must go to the Meeting Ground. The Grannach who survive shall join us there, and the Maker deliver us safe to a new land."

Dohnse licked his lips. He could not doubt Morrhyn's words, but still it was as if the wakanisha told him to reach into the fire and take out a burning log, and that his flesh should not be seared. He looked again around the circle and saw that same mixture of confidence and doubt reflected in all their faces.

"The Commacht ready now," Racharran said. "We go before the Rain Moon comes up."

Morrhyn said, "The Breakers cross the plains even now, and in the season of the Rain Moon shall come against all who remain; but those who come with us to the Meeting Ground shall find the new land. This is what the Maker told me—that those who believe and accept his redemption shall be saved."

"Even," Dohnse asked, "my clan? After I've told you . . ." He paused. It was one thing to hear Morrhyn assure him he retained his honor, another to accept it. ". . . That I believe Chakthi would betray you?"

Morrhyn said, "All the People. Do the Tachyn come honestly, then they shall find the new land too."

Dohnse said, "I . . ." and glanced around again. "I do not know how Chakthi shall take this. Or Hadduth."

"They will take it as they take it. Like all the akamans, like all the other clans." Morrhyn looked at each messenger then, fiercely. "Take that word back to your akamans—that the Commacht go to the Meeting Ground to find a new land, free of the Breakers. Tell them we leave soon, and they had best join us."

Dohnse watched as Perico nodded. The Aparhaso, he thought, believed. Kanseah frowned as if he were unsure; or uncertain how Tahdase should take this news. Jach looked dumbfounded. And likely, Dohnse thought, his own face reflected that same startlement.

"You might remain with us, do you wish." Racharran's voice brought the Tachyn's eyes to the Commacht's face. "You need not go back."

Dohnse frowned and shook his head. "We've spoken here of honor," he said, "and though I thank you for that offer, I refuse it. Is all

that Morrhyn's said true—which I believe it is—then how could I keep
my honor did I stay? No, I must go back to my clan with this promise.
Do Chakthi and Hadduth listen is their affair; but I shall bring this word
to the Tachyn. I must, else I am entirely without honor."

"Well said." Racharran nodded, smiling approval.

"Take back the word, Dohnse," Morrhyn said. "Tell Chakthi and
Hadduth; and do they not tell your clan, then *you* advise the Tachyn of
the Maker's promise."

Dohnse nodded and said, "I shall." Then frowned again and added,
"But there's little time."

"The Maker willing, there shall be enough," Morrhyn returned.
"Do we act swift."

He gestured that Racharran speak, and the Commacht akaman said,
"We prepare to leave now. All well, the Breakers shall find this canyon
empty when they come. All others should strike camp and join us along
the way. In such weather it shall likely take us all the Rain Moon to find
the Meeting Ground, but . . ."

He turned to Morrhyn, who said, "The Moon of the Turning Year
should be a fitting time to find a new land, no?"

"All well." Rannach's voice was edged. "But is there not a thing we
should consider?"

"What?" his father asked.

Rannach gestured at Dohnse. "That this Tachyn owns honor I
would not dispute. But he's warned us he mistrusts Chakthi and
Hadduth—that he believes they intend to betray us. Is this not
true?"

His face, planed hawkish and fierce by deprivation and fireglow,
swung toward Dohnse, who could only nod agreement and say forlornly,
"Yes."

"Then do we send him back with word of all we intend," Rannach
said, "might Chakthi not attack us along the way? Or even at the Meeting Ground?"

Racharran's stern face expressed no emotion as he looked from his
son to Dohnse and said, "There's that, yes."

"And if Chakthi uses this? And halts us on the way? How many
shall die? Shall we ever reach the Meeting Ground, or shall we be
destroyed by Chakthi and the Breakers?"

Morrhyn's answer was calm. "It is a chance we must take."

Rannach opened his mouth to reply, then closed it and nodded his
comprehension.

Racharran said, "It is decided." His voice was firm.

...ed at the sky and saw an eagle, spinning high circles over th... the Commacht as the clan straggled across the snow. He... what the gallant bird saw: live hope, or sorry eating? ...e deliver salvation or damnation? ...eagle offered no answers; nor the Maker.

Morrhyn wished again he dreamed.

...looked Hazhe in the eye and said, "You did not see him; I did. ...oked"—he shrugged, spreading his hands wide—"like a man who ...spoken with the Maker. Like a man . . . changed! His hair is all ...te now, and his eyes . . . his eyes burn! They look into you and see ...ur soul. And Rannach came back to guide him."

"Rannach was exiled by the Council," Juh said.

Perico said, "Yes, but he risked his life to bring Morrhyn home. And Morrhyn's message; I think we must be mad do we ignore it. The Commacht prepared to leave even as I departed." He took his courage firm in both hands and said it out loud: "We had best go with them."

"Still, it defies the Council." Juh's ancient face creased deeper as he frowned. "Rannach was forbidden Ket-Ta-Witko: he should not have come back."

Almost, Perico shouted his frustration. Could his akaman not see that what mattered here was Morrhyn's promise, not the manner of its delivery? He forced himself to impatient calm and said, "Morrhyn was wasted; had Rannach not escorted him, he'd not have made it back."

Juh's frown deepened until his eyes were almost lost, flashing irritably at Perico, who wondered if he had overstepped the line. What matter? he thought. Shall we dance around petty protocol now, when these Breakers threaten us and all the People?

Hazhe said, "Perhaps he was not meant to come back."

Perico gasped and could not stop himself from blurting out again, "You did not see him! I tell you, he's . . ." He raised his hands helplessly, shrugging. "Had you only seen him—heard him—you'd understand. You'd believe!"

"But we have not," the wakanisha returned. "Only you have heard this fabulous promise."

Perico's face darkened in a scowl and Hazhe raised an apologetic hand. "It's not that we disbelieve you," he said soothingly. "But what you tell us is so . . ." He glanced at Juh. "So large a thing."

"These Breakers are also a large thing," Perico snapped. "Racharran has seen their full force, and he says it is such as shall crush us all. Do you doubt his word too?"

One by one the messengers nodded their agreement and went to find their horses, beginning the journey back to their Wintering Ground with the promise of salvation or destruction—none sure how their akamans might take it, or even if the People should die under the beasts and blades of the Breakers before they could find their redemption.

36 Flight

The Commacht wasted no further time: the camp was struck and the clan moved out. Scouts ranged ahead and warriors flanked the defenseless ones. Youths with their hair not yet braided herded the horses, and a band of the older men rode in rearguard. Racharran headed the column, Morrhyn and Rannach alongside, but in truth it was the wakanisha who guided them all.

He hoped the clement day was a sign of the Maker's favor. Surely, it seemed the sun shone a little warmer, sparkling bright on the snow that crunched under the many hooves, the poles of the travois gliding smooth and easy. And the crows that had circled the Wintering Ground with the rising of the sun had not followed them, but descended on the empty camp to pick over the leavings like the dark shadows of nightmares left behind. The camp dogs ran eager beside the plodding horses, and children laughed to be off on a great—albeit not understood—adventure. Even those who had argued against going now wore smiles or, at least, determined expressions, as if, once committed, they would make the best of things.

Morrhyn prayed fervently that it *was* the best of things they did: the road ahead was long and hard, and undoubtedly dangerous. And though he did not doubt it was the only way, still he could not entirely dismiss the creeping tendrils of unease that curled insertive into his mind.

The journey alone should surely claim some. The oldest and the weakest should likely die before they reached the Meeting Ground, for

food was sure to run short
to be found, and the supplies
to see them through. The nigh
hide from enemies; nor would th
And did the Breakers find the
That thought he preferred to s
tragedy if that happened.
It was a desperate race, run slow
neither he nor Racharran would abande
should be a forsaking of all, and without
Honor—that was the thought which pro
Dohnse and the Tachyn, a thing both marvelo
had said, seemed to him an honorable man wh
truth as he saw it. But was he right, then Chak
bored some fell design against the Commacht. W
clan along the way? And what, did that happen, wo
He felt a responsibility toward the Tachyn warrio
sparing of his life somehow bound them together. And w
kind of sadness, that he had laid such a burden on Dohn
as the bringing of the promise to the Tachyn. He wondered
would take it—(and thought that in the telling he had advise
of the Commacht's route)—and what Hadduth would make of
they grasp the promise, or look to use it for their own ends? He
they should be sensible—surely they were no less threatened b
Breakers than any other clan—but wondered if Chakthi were not, th
mad; and Hadduth . . . Perhaps that dark wind the Breakers sent o
over Ket-Ta-Witko had stolen the Tachyn wakanisha's soul.
Perhaps; but even so: what other choice had he owned? He could
not deny the Tachyn the promise of salvation for fear of Chakthi and his
Dreamer; for fear, alone, of betrayal. That would have been to deny such
honest folk as Dohnse the promise, which must surely have been a
denial of the Maker. Not all the Tachyn, he told himself, were like
Chakthi, like Hadduth.
But still . . . He looked out across the sparkling snow fields and
wondered; and thought that he was a frail and doubtful vessel for the
Maker's promise, for the hope of his People.
Maker, he said into the brightness of the snow and the warm musti-
ness of the horse's mane, Only guide me. I'd do what you would have
me do. But I need your help because I am only frail flesh and doubt
myself. I've not dreamed lately; and I need to dream if I am to bring my
people—all the People—safe through. So give me back my dreams,
please?

Now Hazhe frowned disapprovingly. Perico could not care: he saw his akaman and his wakanisha prevaricating when action was required, urgent and immediate. But he held his tongue as Juh spoke.

"Morrhyn would have us quit our Wintering Ground, eh? And go out through the snow to the Meeting Ground; in hope of a miracle?"

He stared at Perico, who ducked his head and said, "Yes."

"Which should be a great upheaval," Juh said. "And not much welcomed, I think. Folk would surely die along that trail, in search of Morrhyn's promise."

"The Maker's promise!" Perico insisted.

"Perhaps." Juh looked to Hazhe. "What do you think?"

"I think," the wakanisha said, "that we must ponder this between ourselves and decide how best to advise the clan."

Juh nodded. Perico said, "The Breakers draw ever closer. By the full of the Rain Moon, at the latest, they'll be upon us. There's little time for debate."

Juh's answering look was angry, as if Perico were some upstart speaking out of turn. He said, "Perhaps. Or perhaps they'll not find us. Perhaps the Maker sends them to scourge the Commacht for their sins."

Now Perico gaped. "What sins?" he asked.

It was Hazhe who answered: "That Rannach slew Vachyr when the laws of Matakwa held sway, and then defied the judgment of the Council to return to Ket-Ta-Witko."

Perico ground his teeth. It seemed to him they were willfully blind, willfully deaf: like Sand Boy turning his back on the flood, hands covering his ears that he not hear the water that drowned him.

"We shall think about all you've told us," Juh said. "You may go now."

Perico offered the old man formal thanks and quit the lodge. Outside, the night was dark, stars hiding behind low cloud, the newborn crescent of the Rain Moon peeking briefly from the rack like a flirtatious maiden from under her blanket. Fires burned cheerful through the camp and folk watched him curiously as he trudged to his own lodge. He hiked his blanket over his head and went with face downcast: he felt no wish to speak with anyone save his wife. Ahwandia would listen to him; she always gave sound advice. He needed that now, for he felt he was about to make such decisions as might set him at odds with Juh and Hazhe.

They had not looked into Morrhyn's eyes, nor heard the surety in the Commacht's voice. He had, and he believed; in his soul he knew what he would do—what he knew he must do. But it would be good to have Ahwandia's approval.

• • •

The clan moved slower than a war band; slower than Morrhyn and Rannach, for there were so many, with horses and dogs and travois to draw, and the teeth of the old ones and the youngest chattered in the cold and babies cried, and late-born foals foundered in the snow so that their mothers turned back to nurse them and ignored the shouts of the unblooded herdsmen, and all the time the Commacht rode cautious, wary of attack.

"At this pace we'll not reach the Meeting Ground before the New Grass Moon." Rannach halted his borrowed horse, turning in his saddle to look back along the sprawling line. "And the Maker help us if we're found."

"Would you leave them?" Racharran reined his own horse to a stop. "Any of them?"

Rannach took his eyes from the clan and turned them on his father, shaking his head: "No."

"Well said." Racharran smiled, albeit grimly. "You begin to think like an akaman."

Rannach snorted laughter. "Me? An akaman? Father, I am exiled by the Council—I am under a sentence of death at this moment."

Racharran frowned and shook his head. "We've spoken of that, and I stand with Morrhyn—what comes against the People now transcends all else, and that judgment was negated when you brought Morrhyn back."

Rannach nodded, the buffalo head that topped his robe bobbing with the movement so that the curved horns shone in the rays of the setting sun. "So you believe—and I thank you for it. But—"

"What else should I believe?" Racharran interrupted.

"I had wondered . . ." Rannach hesitated, and smiled from under the horned cowl. "I had wondered if you would not deliver that sentence."

His father stared at him, eyes wide. "Truly?" he asked.

"Truly," Rannach answered.

"Am I so hard, then?" Racharran's brow creased, and he fidgeted with his horse's rein so that the animal pranced, curveting in the snow.

"Yes, father; you are a very hard man. You are a stern, stiff man; and it is not easy to fulfill your expectations."

Racharran said, "I . . ." and shook his head, licking his lips. Then he spat and squared his shoulders. "I am sorry. I never meant . . ."

Rannach laughed again, this time cheerfully, and reached to touch his father's wrist. "I know—now. I've learned much in my valley, with

Arrhyna; and more from Colun and Morrhyn. I know it cannot be easy to guide the fate of a clan. Nor to have such an enemy as Chakthi. Coward though he be . . ."

He left that sentence dangling, and Racharran narrowed his eyes and asked cautiously, "How mean you?"

Rannach grinned and said, "Colun spoke of a bear, and a man in a tree."

"That?" Racharran smiled even as he frowned. "Colun swore to hold silent on that."

"He deemed it wise to tell me," Rannach said. "That I might understand you better; and why Chakthi resents you. Is it true?"

Racharran threw back his head and roared laughter into the sunset. "Yes!" he said when he drew breath. "In the name of the Maker, it's true. Chakthi hung there like a ripe fruit, with his breeches all stained and dripping with no juice any would want! It took us a while to persuade him down. And when we did, he stank. Even his horse shied away."

"I wish," Rannach said, "that I'd seen that."

Racharran shrugged. "Some things are best unseen." Then he grinned. "But surely Chakthi was a sorry sight that day."

"And for that he hates you?" Rannach asked. "For that he hates all the Commacht?"

"Does it take more?" Racharran's face grew sober. "What makes a man your enemy? Some petty slight? Some knowledge of weakness? In some men these things grow, like a festering wound, until the poison spreads through all the body."

"You saved his life," Rannach said. "You and Colun—he should be grateful!"

"Perhaps." Racharran shrugged again. "But it is not always like that: some men resent the favor. They see it as a debt they'd sooner not owe."

"But still a debt." Rannach frowned. "He owes you better than what he's done."

"Yes." Racharran nodded. "But Chakthi is Chakthi, and not much like other men; and so that old wound festers."

Rannach lowered his head and set both hands on his horse's neck, and asked from under the shadow of the buffalo hood, "Do you trust him now?"

Racharran said, "I trust Morrhyn, and I trust Dohnse."

"But Chakthi?" Rannach asked. "And Hadduth?"

"No." Racharran waited until his son looked him in the eye. "I trust them not at all."

"And yet you let Dohnse go? You think larger than I, and farther."

Racharran smiled wearily and said, "I am akaman of the Commacht, and I believe that Morrhyn has spoken with the Maker. You've listened to him, no?"

Rannach said, "Yes, you know I have. I'd not be here else."

"Go on listening to him," Racharran said, "for you'll be akaman one day."

"I?" Rannach laughed as he shook his head.

"Yes: you," Racharran said. "You learn wisdom daily."

"I think that Morrhyn spoke only the truth," Kanseah said, looking from Tahdase's face to Isten's. "And that if we do not act on his words, we shall be destroyed by these Breakers."

"Who have not yet come against us," Tahdase said.

"But soon shall, I think," said Kanseah.

"Racharran said this?" Isten asked.

Kanseah nodded. "Yes. Racharran spoke of a great horde moving across Ket-Ta-Witko; and Morrhyn spoke of visions given him by the Maker himself, on the mountain. He says that the Breakers are come into Ket-Ta-Witko and shall slay all the People, save we go to the Meeting Ground."

"Where the Maker himself shall lead us to a new land?" Isten asked.

Kanseah ducked his head in agreement: "That is what Morrhyn said, yes."

Tahdase said, "That's a long journey, no? To quit our safe Wintering Ground for the hills?"

"Safer than waiting here for the Breakers to come," Kanseah said.

"Do they come," said Isten.

"We've seen the signs," Kanseah said. "Dead buffalo and dead men. And Racharran has told me what he's seen. Shall we ignore all that?"

"And are they meant for us?" Tahdase turned his inquiring face to his wakanisha.

Isten shrugged. "I cannot say. But to journey to the Meeting Ground? With the Rain Moon barely risen?"

Tahdase said, "I'd know what Juh decides. This is not a matter to determine quickly."

Isten nodded and said, "A hard road, that. I wonder what Hazhe makes of all this?"

"It would be best," Tahdase said, "if we acted in concord, the Naiche and the Aparhaso together. It should be safer that way—must we go."

"Yes," Isten said. "Best we send a rider to the Aparhaso and learn what Juh does."

Kanseah said, unthinking, "Not me. I've carried messages enough of late."

Akaman and Dreamer, both, looked at him as if he'd lost his mind. He wondered if he had—and knew he believed everything that Morrhyn said, and that he would not go out again save to join the Commacht—which likely, he thought, made him the sanest man present.

"No," said Tahdase, "you've done your share. We'll send another, eh?"

"Tomorrow," said Isten. "And when we know what Juh and his Aparhaso do, then we'll decide."

Kanseah nodded and quit the lodge.

His mind whirled as if he were caught in the eddies of the river that ran through the Naiche Wintering Ground. That swift current shone bright and cold under the hibernal sun, and all down its length stood the lodges of his clan which, he thought, might likely all be slain by the Breakers if cautious Tahdase and wary Isten failed to act.

He looked at the sky and asked the Maker to judge him as he reached his own decision. He had heard Morrhyn and knew what the Commacht did; he had told his akaman and his wakanisha—dispensed his duty. He knew in his soul that Morrhyn was right: he did not believe there was any other choice.

He raised his arms and shouted, "Listen to me! Listen to me, all you Naiche! Listen to what I tell you!"

Lhyn set the kettle over the fire and turned her body to the wind to break the gusting that threatened to extinguish the flames. Even through the furs she wore she felt the cold out here, where nothing stood to break the blast save frail humanity. She rubbed her hands together and held them closer to the fire, listening to the buffeting of the wind against the hides of the lodge.

She felt afraid and hid her fear, for she'd not let her husband or her son—or even Morrhyn—see it. They needed the strength of belief, and she knew—she'd looked into Morrhyn's eyes, and theirs—that none of them entirely trusted what they did was right but did what they believed was best; the only thing.

And she believed it, sure in her heart, and knew she must support them.

What else was there?

So she smiled as the wind took her breath away and flung iced splinters of frozen snow against her cheeks, and sheltered the fire that they'd have tea to drink and warm food, and wondered how the defenseless ones fared.

Later, when Racharran and Rannach and Morrhyn had eaten, she would go see how the others faced this storm wind, and if they had enough to eat.

And how many had died in the cold.

She started as a hand touched her shoulder and looked up to find Morrhyn standing over her.

"This is not easy." His smile was like a ghost's; she remembered him younger, when . . . She shook the memory off with the ice on her furs, and said, "No," not quite sure whether they spoke of the cold and the wind or things long past but there still, unforgotten.

He said, "Tea?"

She nodded and said, "Soon. When the water boils."

He squatted and she looked at him, wondering how he came to be so gaunt, his hair turned the color of sun-washed snow, and his eyes so burning blue. She knew, of course: he'd told her; but even so she remembered the young man who'd called her to his blanket and asked her to decide between him and Racharran. And her answer.

"I'd welcome warm tea," he said, and smiled; and touched her cheek. "Once, eh?"

She said, understanding, "Yes."

"But now," he said, "I'm no woman's. I'm wed to another."

She said, "Yes."

"I've no choice," he said. "But if I had . . ."

Lhyn said, "Yes; I know," and took the kettle from the flames and poured him tea.

He drank it and looked around, at the lodges erected swift against the night and the snow, and said, "This is no easy thing any of us do. I wonder . . ."

She asked when he fell silent, "What?"

"If," he said, "it is all in vain. If we shall reach the Meeting Ground; the promise."

"Do you doubt it?" She took his hand. "You brought us the word. How can you doubt it now?"

He shrugged and smiled, and said, "Easily. I wonder every day if I bring the People to salvation or destruction."

She said, "Salvation, Morrhyn! You guide us to a new land, and rescue us from the Breakers!"

"I hope it is so," he said.

She said, "It is! It must be so!"

He held tight to her hand and smiled, and said no more.

Jach accepted the tiswin Yazte offered gratefully. The Maker knew, but this must raise his standing amongst the Lakanti—Yazte's chosen messenger, and now come back with such incredible news and welcomed to the akaman's lodge to sit with his chief and Kahteney. The warriors and the maidens, both, would surely look at him anew now; he sipped the tiswin and smiled hugely.

"And the Commacht go?" Kahteney asked.

Jach nodded. "They were readying for departure when I found them, and it was Racharran's word that they decamp even as I left."

"To the Meeting Ground," Yazte said in a tone pitched somewhere between question and statement.

Jach nodded and said, "Yes, to the Meeting Ground. Morrhyn said . . ."

"You've told us what Morrhyn said." Yazte raised a hand to silence the young warrior, smiling that Jach not feel slighted. He looked to Kahteney. "What do you think?"

The wakanisha stared awhile into the fire, then said, "I think that Morrhyn went to the Mountain and spoke with the Maker."

Jach's head bobbed vigorously. "You should have seen him! He was . . ."

"Yes, yes." Again Yazte halted his enthusiastic description. "We do not doubt what you've told us, but we must decide what we are to do about it."

"What's to decide?" Jach could not rein his tongue. "Surely we go with them?"

Yazte studied him with fond eyes. "There's more to it than just striking camp, young Jach. Have you thought about the journey?"

Jach's smile flattened into a frown. He shrugged and said, "Do you doubt Morrhyn's word?"

"No." Yazte shook his head. "But even so . . ."

"There's many would surely die along the way," Kahteney said. "This cold is enemy enough, but did these . . . Breakers, Morrhyn names them? . . . come upon us, then likely none should survive."

"And if they come on us here," Yazte said, "then likely none shall live."

"It's a difficult choice," Kahteney agreed.

It did not seem so to Jach: he had spoken with Morrhyn and seen the truth. He *knew* the only choice was between destruction and the promise of a new land, but he was only a simple warrior and not long with the braids, and he supposed Yazte and Kahteney saw a wider picture. He looked from the wakanisha to the akaman and waited.

Yazte said, "I wish we both might have spoken with Morrhyn, and with Racharran."

Kahteney shrugged. "Jach here was sent in our place, no? And with instructions to learn what the Commacht do, concerning these . . . Breakers. So he's done that and we know what the Commacht do."

Yazte nodded ponderously. "And what shall *we* do?" he asked, absently scratching at his wide belly.

Kahteney looked at Jach, his eyes contemplative. Jach felt himself weighed, and elevated when the wakanisha said, "I think we should heed him. He's our trusted man, no? And he tells us Racharran takes his clan to the Meeting Ground."

"With the Rain Moon filling," Yazte said, "and hard snow still on the ground."

"And these Breakers moving against us all," Kahteney said. "On which subject I cannot doubt Racharran's word."

"It's a long way," Yazte said.

"Yes," Kahteney said. "Shall we fight them? It should be alone, I think."

In his turn, Yazte studied Jach. The young warrior held his face composed under that scrutiny, then gasped when his akaman said, "What would you do, Jach?"

He said carefully, "Were it possible, I'd gather up all the clans and ride against the Breakers. But . . ." He shrugged. "It's too late for that, no? The Grannach warned us at the last Matakwa, and we paid that warning no heed. Now it's too late: we cannot gather, and the Breakers come into Ket-Ta-Witko like . . . like . . . some prairie fire that rushes on and devours everything before it, all unheeding." He broke off, nervous, fearing that he spoke too forward. But Yazte gestured that he go on, and so he told them, "I listened to what Morrhyn said, and Rannach, and Racharran; and I think we had best go with the Commacht. Else, I believe that we shall die. I believe the Maker sends the Breakers to scourge us and, do we not heed Morrhyn's promise, then we are surely doomed."

He fell silent, eyes lowered, embarrassed: he presumed to advise men greater than he. But still he believed all he said was true.

Softly, Kahteney said, "Out of the mouths of the young comes wisdom."

Yazte said, "Do you truly understand what you say, Jach? Are you right—and Morrhyn, and Racharran—then you say that the People must quit Ket-Ta-Witko and go to some other place? That we must up and leave this land we know for some unknown country? Are *you* ready to do that?"

Jach looked his akaman straight in the eye and said, "Yes!"

Kahteney reached out to set a hand on his shoulder and asked, "To go out in winter? When so many shall die along the way? And perhaps these Breakers find us?"

Jach met the Dreamer's gaze firm as he'd met Yazte's and said, "I think it is the only way. I think that if we do not follow the Commacht, we all shall surely die."

Kahteney smiled approvingly and turned his face to Yazte. "I hear him," he said. "I hear truth in his voice."

"Yes." Yazte heaved a huge sigh and reached for the tiswin; poured them all a cup before he said, "I hear the truth. So! We join the Commacht, no?"

He looked at Jach. "This a great decision you bring us to."

Jach met his gaze and said earnestly, "The only true decision, my akaman."

Yazte laughed. "I'll tell all those who complain that you are the culprit, eh? That it was you convinced us to go?"

Jach said, "If you must," and shrugged his embarrassment.

"Tomorrow, eh?" Yazte looked at Kahteney. "Do we strike camp tomorrow, we can find the Commacht in a day or two."

The wakanisha nodded and smiled at Jach. "You did well. Perhaps the Lakanti owe you their lives."

There were already victims: colts taken by the cold, and horses wearied past endurance; oldsters who could not survive the rigors of the road, some babes.

They left them in the trees when trees were available for burial, and in the snow when they could not. When stone was there, they cairned the dead; but most were left alone and bereft of proper ceremony, for whatever scavengers haunted the ice-clad plains to find.

Wolves flanked their way, which was both blessing and curse, for whilst the winter-hungry packs took the weakest horses and the weakest, or bravest, dogs, still they gave assurance there were no Breakers.

For where the Breakers came, nothing lived.

This the dreams Morrhyn had lost as he approached the clan's Wintering Ground now told him were true. The dreams came back as the Commacht moved out from under the aegis of the invaders' sendings, or perhaps it was that his clan was moved to purpose and, with the word of promise sent out to all the People, the Maker showed a more favorable face. Or perhaps again it was that the clan's belief raised up a bulwark against whatever magicks the Breakers employed. He did not understand how it could be—nor much cared—only that the dreams came back and allowed him to guide the Commacht toward the promise. He knew again where the long, slow column should turn aside to avoid the strangeling beastriders; which draw might shelter their fires; which wood hide them from the searching Breakers; which valley offer them safe progress, where the Breakers not see them, and that was enough for now: must be, for it was all he had.

His dreams did not reveal the outcome of the perilous trek and he supposed that was not yet decided, and could not help but think on those visions he had known in the cave and that one awful image of a possible future in which all the People were slain and only the Breakers remained.

That he tried to ignore, seeking to focus his mind on hope, and on that other image of the promised land; but it remained always there, like a skulking ghost that whispered all was pointless, useless.

Nor could he deny that he was afraid. To dream of danger when only he and Rannach had been threatened was one thing—two men could easily hide—but to conceal the entire clan from the Breakers, that was so large an undertaking, it seemed a near-unbearable weight newly set on his shoulders. But these dark thoughts he kept to himself, and showed the Commacht only a confident face; and when hearts sank he repeated the promise and raised them up. He wished his own might rise, and asked the Maker's forgiveness for his weakness.

They traveled south at first, toward the Lakanti grass, and then swung west, a course that would bring them ever closer to the boundary of their grazing and the Tachyn's.

"To the Meeting Ground?" Chakthi stared at Dohnse from out of eyes opened wide in astonishment. "In such weather?"

Dohnse nodded, his own eyes flicking sidelong from akaman to wakanisha. "That is what Racharran said. Morrhyn says that we can all find a new land there, free of the Breakers. The Maker will take us there."

"Which can be no bad thing," Hadduth said, addressing Chakthi. "Eh? These invaders are surely a plague to us all."

"And the Commacht are gone?" Chakthi frowned, as if the idea were too large to encompass. "Quit their new Wintering Ground now?"

"They struck their lodges even as I left," Dohnse said. "Had all the messengers not come together, I think they'd have been gone before. Perhaps they waited for us—to give the word."

Hadduth said, "Morrhyn's word."

"His promise," Dohnse said. "Got from the Maker."

The Tachyn Dreamer looked hard at him and asked, "You believe that?"

"I do."

He trusted neither of them any longer, but perhaps there was still hope. Surely he believed what Morrhyn had told him, and if that were true, then the Tachyn must follow the Commacht or be slain and damned. If he could persuade them to join the exodus, then perhaps his people might live and he retain some vestige of honor.

He opened his mouth to speak, ready to persuade, to convince; but Hadduth silenced him with a raised hand and said, "We'd best join them, no? Should they meet the Breakers along the way, they'll need friends."

Chakthi stared awhile at his wakanisha and then nodded: "Yes. We'll speak with the clan this night, and in the morning go out."

Dohnse looked, frowning, from one to the other. It seemed to him that decision had been reached too easy.

37 A Promise Given

Yazte and his Lakanti found them as they toiled up out of a valley that hid them well, but was thick along all its length with deep snow. The Commacht scouts saw the newcomers first and signaled back to the column, which clambered slowly to the egress to find the Lakanti waiting before the edgewoods of a winter-bared forest. It heartened the Commacht to see friends again and strengthened their belief in Morrhyn—even the doubters found it convincing that the Lakanti akaman should believe and bring his clan to join them. And the doubling of numbers was no bad thing, nor the supplies the Lakanti brought, for that summer's war had left the Commacht poorly provisioned for the trek.

Racharran smiled as he saw Yazte all swathed in furs like a great bear astride his horse and went forward with Morrhyn, leaving Rannach to see the clan safely up from the valley.

"Well met." He reached to clasp Yazte's hand.

"Are we?" Yazte frowned grumpily from under his cowl. "I could be sitting warm and comfortable in my lodge if not for . . ." He looked past Racharran and his eyes grew wide. "Morrhyn?"

"Yes." Morrhyn smiled.

Yazte said, "Jach told me you'd changed somewhat. But . . ."

Morrhyn shrugged and looked to Kahteney. "We must talk, my brother."

Kahteney nodded. Himself slender as his akaman was plump, he looked fleshy beside Morrhyn. "I'd hear everything," he said.

"You shall," Morrhyn promised. "But later. Do we halt now?"

Racharran looked at the forest, then out across the snow. The sun westered fast and the light began to fade, the temperature dropping as the wind sent ghostly clouds swirling over the flatlands, rattling the bare branches like clattering teeth.

"Is it safe?"

"As best I can tell." Morrhyn in turn studied the woods. "I've not dreamed of any peril here."

"You dream?" Kahteney's voice was shocked.

"I do." Morrhyn's smile was a mixture of gratitude and ruefulness. "Not always of pleasant things, but later we'll speak of this, eh?"

Kahteney ducked his head slowly, as if he'd discuss it all on the spot, but Yazte raised his voice over the gusting of the wind and said, "Do we set our lodges inside the wood before night finds us? Or shall we sit here talking until my old ones freeze?"

Racharran turned in his saddle to watch the tail of the column come up out of the valley. Rannach sat his borrowed horse beside a pillar of stone shining blackly with frozen meltwater, urging on the youngsters herding the loose horses. "There's something you should know," he said, angling his lance at his son.

"That Rannach's come back?" Yazte looked at the mounted figure and shook his head. "Jach told me. Brought Morrhyn back, he said."

Racharran nodded. "The Council's judgment?"

"Ach!" Yazte turned his head to spit into the snow. "You knew my feelings when that was delivered—they've not changed."

Racharran said, "Even so. Do the others find us . . ."

"We spoke of this." Yazte glanced sidelong at Kahteney, who smiled his agreement. "And it seems to us that Rannach's exile must be abrogated. Morrhyn needed him, no? And the People need Morrhyn's promise. And save for Rannach, we'd not have that. So? Do any object to his presence, they've you and I both to argue with. Now, can we, for the Maker's sake, set up our camp and open a flask of tiswin?"

Racharran laughed and said, "Yes!"

The trees broke the wind somewhat, even if their skeletal branches swung and swayed and rattled so that the night was filled with their chattering—as if it were the Spirit Night and all the dead of that year come wandering back. But still it was warmer than the open prairie, and the lodgefires burned bright with friendship's heat and shared purpose.

Lhyn smiled as she worked with Roza, readying food for the men who spoke so earnestly of what had been and what might lie ahead. Yazte's wife was plump and cheerful as her husband, and her company alone lifted Lhyn's spirits. She felt better at ease than she had since quitting the Wintering Ground, encompassed by friends whose presence strengthened her—not to mention that the Lakanti had shared out their food and furs so that all were now better kitted for the journey.

She and Roza, with an escort of young warriors, had seen to the distribution, and she knew now that her people stood a better chance of finding Morrhyn's promised land with fewer losses, and that was enough for her. So did the men speak of manly things whilst the women readied the food that should fuel them for those endeavors, she did not mind. Anyway, even did he not ask her advice now, Racharran would talk it all through again and seek her thoughts when they lay under the blankets and she give them and—usually—be heeded. So she cooked and listened with half an ear to Roza, and half to what the men said.

Most of it she knew, and stirred the pot as Morrhyn told of his journey to the Mountain and the visions gotten there, and Rannach spoke of the Grannach's secret valley and all Colun had told him. They both told of the journey back—which filled her heart with pride, that her son was so brave—and Racharran spoke of the Breakers he'd seen, and the messengers sent from all the clans.

She pricked up her ears as Yazte asked, "Shall they join us, you think?"

And saw her husband shrug and answer, "I cannot guess. They were told . . . But do they hear is in the Maker's hands."

Kahteney looked at Morrhyn then, with something akin to wonder in his eyes, and asked, "Have you dreamed of this?"

Morrhyn shrugged; Lhyn frowned to see him so thin, his shoulders like sticks under his shirt. "No. At least, not clearly—I've told you, there are branching paths that lead to different futures."

Yazte studied him with awe in his eyes—and, Lhyn thought, something close to fear—and asked, "And this one? This path we take?"

"Is safe," Morrhyn said. "And brings us to the Meeting Ground, where the Maker will bring us to a new land."

Softly, Kahteney said, "I still cannot dream."

Lhyn let go the spoon she held: there was such sadness in his voice. She wondered if a wakanisha's loss of dreams was harder or worse than a mother's loss of her son. But Morrhyn had gotten back his dreams; and she had gotten back her son: she felt sorry for Kahteney.

Morrhyn said, "Mine were lost awhile. When I came back into Ket-Ta-Witko, toward our Wintering Ground, I lost them."

"Ach, yes!" Rannach laughed and reached for the flask of tiswin. "And that frightened me. Think of it—we'd come out of the hills with Breakers all around and Morrhyn guiding us past them. Until he came to our own grazing! Then he lost his dreams. The Wintering Ground was empty and he could not tell me where the Commacht wintered. Ach, I had to remember a thing my father told me years ago. That was lucky, eh?"

Lhyn said, "Rannach," and waited as he turned his face toward her. "The tiswin goes to your head."

He frowned, and then looked shamefaced and ducked his head and said lowly, "Yes, Mother."

She said, "You have done brave things, but Arrhyna waits for you to come back, no? And she bears your child. Shall you go back to her a drunkard?"

Rannach shook his head and said, "No, Mother," and set his cup between his knees.

Lhyn nodded and went back to her stirring of the pot, then looked again to where the men sat and wondered why Morrhyn faced her with such . . . she could not tell . . . suspicion, perhaps, in his eyes. Or guilt, or fear.

Their eyes met and he looked away, but not before she saw him compose his features in an expression of deliberate calm that hid those fleeting emotions she'd seen there. Abruptly, a terrible wondering filled her, as if his glance had lit a fire of ugly doubt. It had been at mention of Arrhyna and the child that he'd looked so troubled, and she could conceive of only one reason. Vachyr had raped Arrhyna—might the child then be his? Surely Morrhyn would know, but he had said nothing and clearly Rannach believed it was his seed that grew in Arrhyna's womb. Morrhyn's silence seemed confirmation of that, but if he only hid the truth from Rannach? Lhyn frowned and set such unpleasant notions aside. Better not to think of that: better, were it true, that Rannach not know. She stirred the pot and smiled at Roza and listened to the men talking.

"Can we trust Chakthi?" Yazte asked. "Might he not attack us in revenge for Vachyr?"

Her husband shrugged and laughed. "The Commacht and Lakanti, both? I think not—and does he believe, he'll surely bring his clan to join us. What else has he, save destruction?"

Yazte said, "I don't know; only that he fought you all this summer."

Kahteney said, "Morrhyn, what do you believe? What do you dream?"

Morrhyn said, "As I've told you—of branching paths and many futures. But nothing of imminent danger."

He lowered his head, not wanting to speak of all the paths, or all the futures: they were too diverse, and too dangerous. If he spoke of all of them, of all the fates that might, or could, befall the People; of all the fates that might, or could, lead them to destruction, then surely it must be too much and they founder in the wondering of it all like a horse mired in quicksand, kicking every which way to escape with nowhere firm footing. So he shrugged and hoped he did the right thing and faced Kahteney with a rueful smile that mirrored the one he gave Rannach when the young warrior asked how Arrhyna fared, and the unborn child.

Racharran said, "We must go on anyway, or the Breakers shall destroy us all."

Yazte said, "Them or the Tachyn. Save now Chakthi might feel afraid . . ."

Racharran said, "We'll find out, no? When we pass them; and all well, Chakthi has listened to Dohnse and will join us. Like Juh and Tahdase, the Maker willing."

Yazte smiled and grunted like a bear, echoing, "All well. But you're kinder than I, brother; I'd have left Chakthi and his Tachyn to these Breakers."

"They're not all like Chakthi," Racharran said. "Dohnse has honor."

Dohnse was praying fervently as the Tachyn quit the Wintering Ground and rode out across the snow that Chakthi and Hadduth acted decently: because they believed Morrhyn's promise, not for selfish reasons.

He had listened to the Commacht Dreamer and did believe, but his akaman and his wakanisha?

Of them he could not be sure—not in his heart; not with the utter truth he had seen in Morrhyn's eyes, heard in the Commacht Dreamer's voice.

He believed; and had Chakthi not summoned up the clan and ordered it quit the Wintering Ground to join the exodus, he wondered if he might not have called rebellion against his akaman and led the Tachyn out alone.

If they would follow him.

He thought they'd likely not: truth was no sure thing when larger forces governed belief. And he was nothing: only a warrior disgraced and excused by his akaman.

He was glad that Chakthi and Hadduth had listened to him, and still not sure but that they kept some hidden design to themselves, and he the unwitting pawn in their game.

But even so, the Tachyn struck camp and moved to join the Commacht; and he thought by now they must have met the Lakanti, so did his akaman intend some subterfuge or ambush then it must be against a clan doubled and strong—Commacht and Lakanti together—and he doubted that either Chakthi or Hadduth would risk so much.

He asked the Maker it be so, and rode on across the snow.

It was at that same river crossing where Morrhyn had first encountered Dohnse that they met again. The Commacht and Lakanti came on in a long, wide column across the plain, ahead of them the water flowing too swift to freeze, and past that the broken, ridged country, still snow-clad even as the year grew older. The scouts halted at the ford, and when a lone Tachyn appeared, sent a man back to bring up the akamans and the wakanishas. They came with an escort of armed and wary warriors and halted on the east bank.

Morrhyn narrowed his eyes against the wind's fist and the glare of sun on snow and said, "That's Dohnse."

"And the rest?" Yazte grunted suspiciously, peering about as if he momentarily expected attack. "Hiding in ambush?"

"And send a man to warn us?" Racharran shook his head. "Likely they shelter, or are not yet arrived." He turned to Morrhyn. "What shall we do?"

Morrhyn said, "Speak with him: I trust him," and beckoned Dohnse forward.

The Tachyn heeled his horse, splashing across the ford, and halted before them, offering formal greetings. He eyed them somewhat nervously, as if unsure of his reception.

"Are you come alone?" Morrhyn asked. "Or is your clan ahead?"

"Ahead," Dohnse replied, "sheltering in the breaks. Chakthi was . . ." He shrugged, his face expressing uncertainty. "He was unsure of his welcome."

Racharran said, "You gave him the message?" And even as Dohnse nodded, "Then what doubt has he?"

Dohnse shrugged again and said, "He's a cautious man. And . . ." His gesture seemed to encompass the summer's war and all the ill feeling between his clan and the Commacht.

"Yesterday's trouble." Racharran raised a hand in sign of peace. "Tell him we'll—"

He broke off as Yazte touched his wrist. "Tell him," the Lakanti said, "to come meet us here; him and Hadduth. They can lead us to your people."

His wide smile belied the mistrust implicit in his words, and Dohnse smiled grimly back and nodded. "As you wish."

He turned his horse and went back across the river, cantering in amongst the breaks.

Yazte's smile became genuine. "Does he set an ambush, he'll not come. And should he think to trick us, we'll have hostages."

Morrhyn said softly, "There's no ambush. Not here."

"Even so." Yazte shrugged, then frowned as Dohnse came back with Chakthi and Hadduth.

All three Tachyn forded the stream and reined in. Hadduth sat silent on his horse, his eyes fixed curiously on Morrhyn, widening somewhat as the gaunt Dreamer returned his own blue stare, and then turning away as if the Tachyn could not meet that penetrating gaze.

Chakthi greeted them and made the sign of apology. "You've cause enough to hate me," he said, "but it's as Dohnse told you—Vachyr's death drove me awhile mad, and I knew not what I did. I ask your forgiveness; and do you name blood-price, I shall pay it."

Racharran studied him a moment. His face was clean of mourning's white and his hair was braided. Also, he bore no weapons and his eyes met the Commacht akaman's unflinchingly. Racharran glanced sidelong at Morrhyn, who ducked his head a fraction.

"What threatens now outweighs all that's gone before." Racharran ignored Yazte's eloquent sniff. "I'd see no more slain. Neither by the Breakers nor any other. Do you accept the promise Morrhyn brings us and swear truce, then we've peace between us."

Chakthi nodded solemnly and raised a hand in pledge. "I swear truce, to peace between your clan and mine. This I swear in the name of the Maker, and do I renege, may he damn me."

Racharran in turn raised a hand and said, "Let there be peace between us . . . brother."

Chakthi smiled and said, "Peace, brother."

"So be it." Racharran glanced at the sky. The sun stood close on its zenith, bright against the steel-hard blue. "We've a ways yet to go, and slowly with so many. Do you call up your people and we go on?"

"As you command." Chakthi lowered his head submissively. "Where do we station ourselves?"

Yazte said quickly, "To the rear," and favored the Tachyn with a bland smile. "Our people are already on the move."

Chakthi's features expressed no resentment, but still Racharran thought to say diplomatically, "Shall you be our rearguard?"

Chakthi said, "As you wish. Shall you come with me?" His eyes encompassed all the warriors standing in audience: tacit acceptance that he was a hostage.

"No." Racharran shook his head before Yazte had chance to speak again. "Best that you organize your people and we ford this river."

Chakthi nodded and turned his horse. Hadduth moved to his side, but Dohnse hesitated an instant, as if doubtful, then shrugged and went with them.

"I'd sooner have kept them," Yazte murmured.

"He swore on the Maker's name." Racharran watched the three Tachyn riding for the breaks. "There's peace between us now."

Yazte spat and grunted.

Racharran said, "We need trust, are we to survive. And he gave his word."

"Yes." Yazte's response was ambiguous. "He did."

They crossed the river and went on into the breaks where the Tachyn sheltered. There was no ambush, and, as the column passed, the Tachyn fell in docile at the rear. The Commacht and the Lakanti were all mingled, and Racharran had thought to station Rannach in their midst, that his son and Chakthi not meet. Both had sworn vows of peace, but even so . . . Both, he thought, were hotheaded, and he'd no wish to test the new-made truce. He sent a rider back, to call Rannach up to the fore. Did all three tribes stand between them, they need not meet. At least, not yet.

He brought his horse closer to Morrhyn's and said, "It went smooth enough, no?"

The wakanisha ducked his head inside his cowl and said nothing.

Racharran frowned. "You've dreamed of trouble?"

"No." Morrhyn shook his head and sighed.

"Then what?" Racharran asked. "Do you think of what Dohnse told us? Do you expect betrayal?"

"No." Morrhyn turned briefly toward his akaman and smiled thinly, then looked ahead again.

Chakthi had given his word, no? Had pledged his very soul, which surely must be proof enough of his honest intent. Surely; save . . .

Why had Hadduth seemed so hesitant? Kahteney had been full of questions when he learned that Morrhyn had back his dreams, but the Tachyn wakanisha had voiced none. That seemed to Morrhyn strange—that a Dreamer stripped of his talent not question another newly blessed by the Maker; and after that initial observation, Hadduth had refused to meet Morrhyn's eye.

Perhaps he was ashamed; perhaps he regretted the summer's war; perhaps he felt guilt for his part in that trouble. Morrhyn thought that was likely the reason—that Hadduth felt embarrassment in his presence.

Perhaps; but he could not shake off the lingering doubt that behind Hadduth's veiled gaze lurked something else, as if the man's blank face hid secrets. What, he could not say, and shook his head in frustration. Likely it was only embarrassment, or guilt; and his dreams warned of no danger from the Tachyn along the way.

He realized Racharran studied him with worried eyes and forced a warmer smile. "I've not dreamed of betrayal," he said. "And we've Chakthi's promise, no?"

Racharran nodded. "Was that a lie, you'd know." His tone hung midway between question and statement. "You'd have dreamed of that."

Morrhyn said, "Yes," more confidently than he felt.

The Maker's promise belongs to all the People, he told himself, to the Tachyn as much as any other clan. It cannot be denied them for fear of nebulous doubt.

"And likely Dohnse would warn us," Racharran's voice intruded on his musings, "did Chakthi plan anything."

"Yes." Morrhyn agreed with an eagerness born of suspicion. "Dohnse's an honorable man."

Racharran said, "Then all's well," and turned as Rannach came up.

"The Tachyn fall in behind." Rannach's voice was flat. "And people say Chakthi's sworn truce."

"Good." Racharran smiled. "Now ride with us."

Rannach grinned and dutifully brought his horse into line.

They went on, clearing the breaks to climb the rising plain ahead, where the land lay all open save for little stands of timber and folds that might conceal the Breakers had Morrhyn not promised them safe passage. Word spread fast amongst the refugees that the Commacht wakanisha dreamed again, and soundly. They had heard it, of course, the news delivered by the messengers, but to hear it said was not the same as *knowing* it: that sensate belief came with the reality of their situation, and the many who followed only because their akamans led them began to accept the promise, and to trust in Morrhyn.

By now the Commacht entertained no doubts, but the more recently come Lakanti and the even later-come Tachyn at first rode wary, knowing that if the Breakers came on them, they were surely lost. But the days passed and they moved inexorably, if furtively, toward the distant mountains without attack. Sometimes they hid, seeking the concealment of draws or woodland, or setting high ground between themselves and the searching enemy Morrhyn warned of. But always his warnings proved sound and, must they hide—cold and hungry for want of fires that would betray them—then that was a small price to pay for survival and the promise of salvation. They began to call him Prophet, which embarrassed him greatly, for whilst he was confident his dreaming protected them from discovery, still he felt an irritating doubt that nagged, like a dog barking far off, at the hinder part of his mind.

He could not clarify it or properly explain it. Nor—for fear of disturbing the harmony that grew—would he speak of it. He sought out Hadduth and was met with smooth apologies for past disagreements and the Tachyn's assurance that his own dreams were not yet returned. Neither were Kahteney's, and so Morrhyn must accept Hadduth's word, and only wonder at his undefined misgivings.

When the akamans met—from which conferences Rannach was tactfully banished—Chakthi was all submissive contrition, bowing to the suggestions of Racharran and Yazte as if he were newcome to his station and they the senior chieftains. He seemed all repentant, and held his clan in its rearward position without argument. Even the Lakanti akaman softened toward him and, almost, Morrhyn came to believe his and Hadduth's good intentions.

But still not quite: there yet remained something he could not define hidden behind their smiles and earnest eyes.

And daily the dark bulk of the mountains came closer, until, between the setting of the Rain Moon and the rising of the Moon of the Turning Year, they sighted the Maker's Mountain shining in promise under a sun that grew steadily warmer.

The snow that had blanketed Ket-Ta-Witko for so long began to thaw, which slowed them somewhat—for the rivers grew fierce with meltwater and the ground muddy. But the Maker's Mountain rose before them, and in the sheltered places trees put out buds, and birds sang louder, as if in recognition of the coming spring, and that filled them with renewed hope.

And then, with the Moon of the Turning Year gibbous in the sky, they reached the Meeting Ground.

.   .   .

"What now?" Racharran asked, and five pairs of eyes turned expectantly to Morrhyn.

He paused a moment before replying, gathering up his thoughts. "We must wait awhile. We must give the Aparhaso and the Naiche the chance to join us, and allow Rannach time to bring Arrhyna and Colun's Grannach down from the valley."

Kahteney asked softly, "How much time?"

Morrhyn shrugged and said, "The Maker will tell us when."

"Tell you." Kahteney's voice was rueful. "I've not yet gotten back my dreams."

"They'll come." Morrhyn smiled encouragingly and looked to where Hadduth sat, his brows rising in question.

The Tachyn wakanisha shook his head and muttered, "No. I still cannot dream."

He met Morrhyn's stare only briefly before lowering his eyes.

"How shall it happen?" Yazte asked.

"I don't know yet. The Maker will doubtless tell me."

"Before too long, I hope." Yazte scratched a chin. "Do the Breakers pick up our trail . . ."

"*When* they do," Chakthi said. "So large a trail cannot go long unnoticed."

Yazte's expression suggested he found it irritating to agree with the Tachyn, but still he ducked his head and said, "That's true."

Morrhyn shrugged again. Racharran said, "Even so, we cannot leave the Aparahso and the Naiche."

Chakthi said, "Perhaps the Breakers have found them. Perhaps they cannot join us."

"Still, we wait." Racharran's voice was firm, brooking no dissent. He looked to Morrhyn, smiling. "Morrhyn shall tell us when the time comes."   .

"Forgive me." Chakthi lowered his head, hands spread in sign of apology. "As you say—we wait."

Three days they had been on the Meeting Ground. The lodges stood close-huddled, for none felt entirely safe with the hills ringing them and nowhere to run if worse came to worst. The warriors of all three clans grouped daily about the approaches, and at night remained on guard, constantly alert. Their supplies dwindled apace, and even though the sun shone warmer each day and the snow melted, still there was little grazing for the horse herds. Nor any game to be found—the buffalo were not yet come back, and it seemed the deer and smaller animals had all fled or been slain by the Breakers.

Morrhyn was assailed daily by those who dared approach him, and always with the same question: "When?"

To all he gave the same answer: "In the Maker's good time. When he brings us to salvation."

Most accepted, trusting him—was he not become, after all, their Prophet?—but there were yet others who began to wonder, and murmured cautiously amongst themselves that he was changed, that he was the wakanisha who had deserted his clan in time of trouble, that perhaps the exodus was a terrible mistake.

None of this was said in his hearing, but still he heard it; and could not help but wonder if it be true—in his dreams, he got only the suggestion he wait, that all would be well.

But he knew that food ran short in the lodges, and that the animals fared no better. He could not help but entertain the terrible doubt that perhaps he was a false Prophet, tricked by the Breakers' magicks and duped by them into leading the People to destruction. He prayed each night for strength, for revelation—and got back comforting dreams of salvation. But when he woke and went out from his lodge into the warming sun and saw the expectant faces that turned his way, the doubts came back. He ate the pahé root given him by Kahteney—his own all gone—but that allowed him no clearer dreaming than before: only *Wait!*

It was hard to be a Prophet, for folk expected clear and instant answers that he could not give. He did not—honestly—know how or when the Maker would show them the way to the new land. He could only pray, and trust the Maker; and pray again that he was not duped into becoming the Breakers' instrument.

Two more days passed and hope—or its loss?—arrived with the dawning sun: Perico rode in with two hundred weary Aparhaso; and before the same sun set, Kanseah brought a smaller group of the Naiche.

Their explanations were echoes, like two voices chanting the same sad song:

"Juh would not listen," Perico said. "I told him everything; him and Hazhe. *But they would not listen!* What else could I do? They said we were safe—that what came against us was come against the Commacht and the Tachyn for the breaking of the Ahsa-tye-Patiko—that they'd think on it and in time decide."

His face was haggard, near-gaunt as Morrhyn's with fear and hunger, and his eyes roamed round in search of absolution.

Racharran said, "I warned Juh, and he'd not listen to me."

"I told Tahdase and Isten that our people were dying," Kanseah said. He was not in much better condition than Perico. "And that the buffalo were slaughtered, and Morrhyn had told me why—and by what. But they closed their ears!"

"They heard all of it," Perico said. "And still did nothing!"

"Tahdase would know what Juh did," Kanseah said, addressing himself to Morrhyn. "And until then, wait."

Perico said, "Juh only listened to Hazhe—and Hazhe said it was the sins of Vachyr and Rannach brought the Breakers into Ket-Ta-Witko, and therefore they alone were likely to suffer."

"I told them of the promise," said Kanseah. "Everything you told me, but they blocked their ears."

"What else could I do?" Perico asked. "Those who believed are with me."

"I defied my akaman and my wakanisha," said Kanseah. "I told all those who'd listen of the promise, and brought them out to join you."

"They came with me," Perico said. "All those who believe. Juh and Hazhe wait to die. They think they're safe, but I know they're not. The Maker forgive me, but I looked to save who I could."

Their eyes searched out forgiveness: the assurance they had done the right thing. The lodge grew silent.

Morrhyn felt their pain and knew their doubt. It seemed to him much akin to his own. He prayed he be right as he said, "Those who hear the Maker's promise shall be saved. Those who ignore it . . ." He smiled sadly. "I think they shall die for their disbelief. What you did was right—you have saved as many as you could. Those who refused the promise . . ."

He shrugged. Kanseah said, "Then we're not damned?"

Morrhyn shook his head and answered, "No more than I."

That night Morrhyn dreamed of approaching danger.

He rode a great white stallion that raced toward the Maker's Mountain whilst from the opposite direction came the figure he had seen in his earliest dreams of the Breakers, armored in sun-bright gold, and mounted on the strange and horrid horse with burning eyes and curling horns. Who reached the pinnacle first should be the winner and decide the fate of the People.

He woke before the race was ended and hurried from his lodge to warn Racharran, his heart filled with awful dread.

Around the mid-part of the morning, with the sun shining warm on the muddied, trampled dirt of the Meeting Ground, Motsos, who had ridden out farther than most scouts, came back at a gallop to report sighting a column of twenty Breakers riding their strangeling mounts along the incoming line of the Aparhaso and the Naiche.

He'd no doubt, he said, that they followed the tracks. Before the day ended, he thought, they must find the Meeting Ground.

38 Time Running Out

It was easy to steal the shot, and no harder to conceal bags of powder. Sieur Gahame trusted his indentured folk—what use would they have for such things? But the muskets, the pistols, and the swords—Davyd had decided he should carry a blade, like Arcole—were more difficult. Such obvious thefts would be noticed, and so he elected to leave them until the last minute, when their absence would be noted too late.

Besides, folk had been purchasing more weapons recently, and Sieur Gahame was likely to spot any missing.

It was not a matter the master discussed with his branded servants, but none in his employ could help but notice that muskets and pistols and blades were suddenly in great demand: Sieur Gahame was delighted with the trade, of course, but even so, Davyd noticed he often wore a frown and spoke at length—and in whispers—with his customers. And when the boy spoke with Godfry or Laurens or Prestyr, they muttered darkly of unforeseen events and told him he was too young to understand.

But Davyd thought he knew the reason. He was, after all, a Dreamer; and of late his dreams were more vivid, more alarming. He had believed Grostheim a safe enough haven, but now, as spring advanced, the dreams of winter took on a starker note. They came more frequently, and bloodier, as he saw his oneiric shadows rampage through the streets. Often he woke sheet-tangled and all awash with sweat after finding himself ringed with hairless skulls that grinned from atop poles and warned him of his own death. He dreamed of burning walls and shrieking women, and always the sneaking, deadly creatures.

And then, as if in compensation, he would dream again of the wilderness as a haven, a succoring comfort that called out to him, promising safety. He understood those, if anything, less than the nightmares. He was, if not accustomed, then at least reconciled to dreams of danger. Dreams of safety he understood not at all. But still, somehow, they reshaped his thinking, and he no longer feared the wilderness beyond Grostheim's walls. He saw it as both hazard and promise, and was ready to go there.

He would not remain behind when Arcole and Flysse fled.

That frightened him most of all—that they go without him. There was no longer any doubt in his mind that they *should* go. He knew Arcole planned it, no matter his friend's hesitancy, and he retained that absolute belief in Arcole won on the *Pride of the Lord:* somehow, regardless of the odds, Arcole *would* find a way. Of Flysse he was less sure. She was, by nature, more cautious; and there remained, on those careful occasions he met them, that coolness, as if disagreements remained unsettled. He had tentatively asked of it, and got back bland responses that gave him no clear answers, only ambiguity and doubt. So he had done his best to shut it from his mind and concentrate on his own part in their great adventure.

It should have been easier had Arcole set a date, but he would not—or could not—and Davyd must be satisfied with "When the time is ripe" and "It depends on circumstances." His dreams warned him those circumstances drew ever closer and he chafed at the delay, fearing Arcole waited too long.

And all the while, rumors grew to confirm his fears.

In a settlement the size of Grostheim it was hard to keep secrets, especially when farmers came in through the spring mud to buy guns and shot and powder. The masters spoke in whispers, but the indentured folk had ears and heard. And though it was not said openly, still it spread—like rot through wood, or a smoldering spark that takes hold on a carpet and burns its way to the curtains and then begins to eat the house's walls.

There were holdings burned, they whispered. A neighbor had gone visiting and found only charred timbers and all the animals driven off.

Another had failed to visit as promised, and on investigation his neighbor had found heads mounted on poles. The governor had sent out a patrol that had not returned . . .

Davyd traded his news with Arcole and Flysse, so they were better informed than most. Theirs was the surer news. Yes, the governor *had* sent out a patrol; and no, it had not returned. It was a column of fifty mounted infantry, commanded by a Captain Danyael Corm, and Arcole awaited his return when he might add the captain's findings to his map and better assess the situation. And, yes, it seemed the column should have returned by then.

Davyd told them of his dreams, and Arcole told him to stand ready. They none of them said it aloud, but all thought it: the time loomed close, and they all grew afraid.

And all the while Grostheim buzzed lively as a beehive with rumor and more obvious signs of trouble. Folk began to come in from the outlying holdings, seeking the security of the city's walls. The inns and rooming houses filled with refugees, and tents and lean-tos sprouted over every open space. The masters took to wearing blades and pistols in the streets. Major Spelt increased the guards along the walls, and Militia patrols tramped their rounds in greater numbers. And the indentured folk whispered when they might of what their fate should be did the unknown come. The presence of demons in Salvation was no longer a secret whispered by the masters, but common knowledge bruited about wherever folk met. Those brave farmers who had elected to remain on their land were considered doomed—if not already dead—and those who sought the safety of the city's walls bemoaned the loss of their property and demanded to know what the Autarchy, in the form of Governor Wyme, intended to do.

The governor's hands were as full as the streets. He must find the means to feed the newcomers, lest riots break out. He must organize accommodation, sanitation, and persuade reluctant owners to leave their animals outside the walls, lest the streets become impassable. He must sit in judgment over the inevitable quarrels of crowded, frightened folk.

And more—he must, with Major Spelt, ready for the attack.

He had worn himself close to exhaustion with the renewal of the hexes warding the city, and could not help but wonder if they should be strong enough. He knew only that Grostheim faced an enemy none had suspected, creatures that came, it seemed, silent as shadows to wreak bloody slaughter.

He doubted Evander could send help before the summer—if the Autarchy decided to send help at all. He had sent word back with

Tomas Var on the *Pride of the Lord,* but then he had had only suspicions, not the dreadful certainty of more recent events. And the *Pride of the Lord* must cross—God grant it did!—the Sea of Sorrows and all the wide ocean between this land and the Old World. He had requested that the Autarchy send reinforcements, troops, and, at the very least, one Inquisitor.

As that spring aged, Grostheim became a frightened city.

"I see no way to pass the walls." Arcole turned from his most recent work: a copied map of the city. "There are but the two gates and both locked at dusk, always guarded. God, this *is* a prison! It needs no hexes to hold us, only wood and soldiers."

Flysse watched as he pushed back his hair and almost went to him, he looked so hangdog. But not yet; she was not yet quite ready, not yet quite certain he'd take her with him did the chance present. She needed that reassurance, so she said, "And Davyd's dreams? What of them?"

Arcole shrugged. "I don't doubt them. This place will be attacked. But shall that help us?"

Flysse shrugged in turn. It had come to this between them: to this shrugging and cold discussion of tactics; it hurt her, but she could do no different. She was not yet ready to accept his apologies and protestations: she must *know* that he loved her as she loved him, and bear the hurt the while.

"It would occupy the guards." Arcole frowned and rubbed his eyes. "We might go over the wall."

"As it's attacked?" Flysse shook her head. "Won't the Militiamen be more alert then?"

"Yes, there's that." Arcole nodded and grinned ruefully. "But perhaps also somewhat preoccupied."

"With attacking demons who'd likely kill us soon as the guards?" Flysse shuddered. "Surely there's a better way. What if Davyd's owner went out? Are the farms attacked so, then shan't they need supplies? Might we not . . ."

"No." Arcole waved her silent. "The farmers come in, not go out. God! There are whole families seeking the protection of Grostheim now, coming in like refugees from a war. Gahame's not going to risk his neck, and even did he, he'd not take Davyd with him. Nor might we easily find passage on his wagons."

"Then it would seem," Flysse said, "that we are caught."

"Yes, like pet rats in a trap. And I'd not see you caught so."

He looked at her with sad and weary eyes, and she saw lines on his face that had not been there in the summer and felt her resolve waver. "Truly?" she asked.

He said, "Truly. What must I do, Flysse? What *can* I do? I'd give up my life for you. Do you not know that?"

She said, "I . . ." and shook her head, unsure of the answer. Afraid of giving up her resolve, afraid of what that secession might bring, its outcome.

He said, "I've spelled it out, no? I've told you I'll give up these plans, do you command, and you said no. I've promised I'll not flee without you—nor would I want to now! I've given you my word I'll not deliver Davyd to needless danger. What more do you need? What more can I do? Can you not forgive me?"

He closed his eyes and sighed, breath gusting exhausted from his mouth. He spread his arms, then closed them across his chest, his head fallen. As if, Flysse thought, he hugged his pain. He seemed so far from the proud man she had known on the *Pride of the Lord*—the gallant she had fallen in love with and never thought could notice her—she felt her eyes water. It was almost too much to bear; almost.

She said, "Perhaps," and hesitated as she saw hope light her husband's eyes. He rose a little from his seat, as if he'd come to her, and she held up a preventive hand. "Perhaps soon, Arcole."

"But not yet?" Hope faded; his smile was ragged.

"But not yet," she echoed, wishing she might honestly tell him otherwise.

Captain Danyael Corm arrived tramp-ragged at Grostheim's gates. He wore a beard and a rank odor of sweat, and his hair was turned all white. His uniform was lost and he could barely speak his name, nor was his horse in much better condition. They both stood haggard under the startled eyes of the watch.

When he succeeded in making himself known, he was brought swiftly to Spelt's quarters. There, brandy eased his tongue, and he made his dazed report and was allowed to bathe. Dressed in a clean uniform, he accompanied the anxious Spelt to Governor Wyme's mansion.

Arcole attended the governor as the two officers were ushered in. He served them brandy and pipes, and was dismissed by Wyme with a curt wave. He knew, from his clandestine investigations, that Corm had led the column of mounted infantry. He thought the man looked shocked, as if he had witnessed horrors his mind could not encompass.

On Spelt's grave face he read concern. He closed the door and contemplated eavesdropping, but Benjamyn was abroad and worrying about dinner: Arcole returned to his role of dutiful servant.

Wyme would add to his records, he thought, as he set places at the table, and all well unwittingly share them. He placed the silver platters and the crystal glasses with a smile that his fellow servants attributed to a settlement with Flysse.

They were not entirely wrong in their assumption.

The two officers sat late with the governor, and Wyme sat later still in his study. Arcole was required to help him there and bring a cushion for his withered legs; see the brandy flask filled and a glass set near, a pipe primed. Celinda was long abed, attended by Flysse.

Arcole stood rigid behind the crippled man as Wyme arranged the papers on his desk. He struck a lucifer as Wyme picked up his pipe and was rewarded with an absent nod.

"Thank you, Arcole. You may go now."

Arcole bowed—God, it was still so hard to do that!—and asked, no harder, "Shall I await you, 'sieur?"

Wyme ducked his head: "I'll ring, do I need you."

Like summoning a dog, Arcole thought, but I'll wait and read those papers when you're done. And then I'll know what you know—and use your knowledge.

He bowed again, though Wyme did not look up, and quit the room.

Flysse was alone in the kitchen and he told her, "Something's afoot. Corm and Spelt are gone, and Wyme's greatly troubled. I'm to wait for him, but once he's abed . . ."

Flysse nodded and said, "Mistress Celinda was much troubled." Then her eyes clouded and she asked, "What think you?"

"That we stand ready," he said. "Tell Davyd to prepare us those guns."

"Save only it be safe for him," she returned.

"Save that," Arcole agreed. "But things go on, Flysse. Corm wore the look of a man bearing bad news."

"And you'll go find it out, eh?" She startled him then, when she reached across the table to touch his hand—a triumph, that—and said, "Take care."

It was hard not to snatch up her hand, to kiss it, but he thought he could not bear further rejection. When she was ready, she would open her arms to him, and then he would go to her eagerly. But for now he only nodded and waited.

Long past midnight the bell rang, and Arcole went to Wyme's study.

Grostheim's governor was in his cups, and even had he not needed crutches to walk, still he should have needed a hand. Arcole lifted him onto the sticks and held him upright as he staggered bedward.

Wyme muttered, "Bad news; very bad. Measures must be taken. Strict measures, I tell you."

Arcole thought that he would regret such admissions—did he remember them—come morning. He saw Wyme to his chamber and settled the drunken governor on his bed. He tugged off Wyme's boots and helped the man out of his clothes—the while wondering how many times servants had done the same for him, and he as unthinking as the sodden baggage he now undressed. He felt ashamed, for what he did now and what he had done then.

As soon as Wyme began to snore, he left the governor and hurried to the kitchen.

"Are we the only ones awake?" he asked Flysse.

She said, "I think so. I've seen none else."

"Then I'm to the study," he said. "To discover what news Corm brought."

"Take care," she said. "I'd not see you caught. Not now."

It was hard to resist the concern in her blue eyes. Easier to turn back and hold her, and make better what grew again between them; but what lay ahead might depend on what he found, and he'd live free with Flysse. He grinned and went away.

It was stark news Wyme had noted down: confirmation of Davyd's dreams, Arcole thought. He studied the scrawled notes with a frown, snatching paper and pen from the governor's desk. So many holdings ravaged. A troop of fifty mounted infantry slain, save for Corm. And worst of all, the final ragged notes:

The demons vow to attack us. Slay us all. They shall come, they say, and kill us because it is their land. I do not doubt it. Too much has happened—we are not alone here. I must send to Evander for more soldiers. An Inquistor; my hexes are not strong enough. Surely and Inquisitor can defend us.

Arcole stared at the alarming comments. The time had come, he thought, and they could delay no longer. No matter how difficult, they must find a way out of the city. He would discuss it with Flysse and set a date, and when next they spoke with Davyd, he would tell the lad to take the last of their provisions and stand ready to flee. He recorded Wyme's commentary and the placements of the attacks, then dusted the paper and folded it into his tunic, set the desk in order, and pinched out the candle.

As he went toward the door, it opened and Benjamyn said, "What are you doing here?"

The majordomo held a candle in a brass holder. He wore a night-shirt and a tasseled sleeping cap. His legs were spindly and very white. He should have looked ridiculous were it not for the outrage on his lined face. Arcole saw Flysse standing a little way behind, her eyes wide with alarm.

"Well?" Benjamyn demanded, advancing a step.

Arcole took a pace back. His mind raced—this could mean the downfall of all his plans. He said, "I was tidying the governor's study, Benjamyn." It sounded unlikely to his own ears.

To the majordomo it obviously sounded wildly improbable.

"At this hour?" Benjamyn came another step into the room. He raised the candle, eyes darting around, returning accusingly to Arcole. "Did the master order it?"

Arcole said quickly, "He did," hoping Wyme's memory should prove too fogged with brandy to contradict.

Benjamyn's tongue clicked vigorously. To Arcole it sounded like the ticking of a clock that measured the time to his sentencing.

"What's that?" Benjamyn pointed at Arcole's chest.

Arcole said, "Nothing."

Benjamyn said, "Show me."

Arcole looked down, and saw a corner of paper protruding from beneath his tunic. He cursed silently. As best he knew, Benjamyn could read no more than a few words, but the paper alone should be sufficient to undo him. Doubtless the majordomo would show it to Wyme, and Wyme would immediately know his secrets stolen. Arcole had no idea what punishment that might entail, but he was certain it must unravel all his plans and likely see him parted from Flysse forever. He hesitated, racking his mind for some plausible excuse.

Benjamyn came another step closer, hand extended. Arcole saw Flysse framed in the doorway behind the majordomo.

"I stole a sheet of paper," he extemporized. "I thought to make a sketch of Flysse."

Benjaymyn's tongue clicked louder. "Then show me," he insisted.

Arcole shook his head.

"You augment your troubles," Benjamyn warned. "I find you ransacking the master's inner sanctum, and now you refuse to obey me? This shall go hard for you."

"It's only a sheet of paper," Arcole said.

"Then show me," Benjamyn repeated. "Or is it more?"

Arcole was a gambler, but it was difficult to hold his expression calm. Perhaps it was lack of practice, perhaps it was the import of the occasion, but Benjamyn saw something that prompted his eyes to widen and his lips to thin.

"It is, no?" he barked. Then: "God, of course! You lay claim to having been a gentleman. You can read, eh?"

Arcole heard Flysse gasp. Benjamyn ignored her, his gaze intent on Arcole's face. "You read the master's papers!" His expression was horrified. "God, you spy on the master!"

He darted forward, snatching at Arcole's tunic; Arcole raised a hand to fend him off.

This, even more, it seemed, than the original crime, offended the old man. He shouted as Arcole's palm struck his chest, and swung the candle holder at Arcole's head. Arcole deflected the blow, and the brass holder was knocked from Benjamyn's grip. The candle came loose, rolling across the floor to drip wax and flame on the carpet. Arcole took hold of Benjamyn's wrists, twisting aside as a bony knee rose toward his groin.

He called, "Flysse—the candle!" And to Benjamyn: "For God's sake, be silent."

The majordomo's reply was a shriek of unalloyed rage. Arcole let go one wrist and struggled to clamp a hand over Benjamyn's mouth. Benjamyn promptly employed his free hand in an attempt to claw Arcole's eyes. Desperately, Arcole wondered how long it could be before the whole house was woken and come looking for the source of the disturbance. No less—and no less desperately—he wondered what to do with Benjamyn.

Flysse stamped out the guttering candle and took up the holder. The room was dark now, save for the dull glow of the banked fire and what little light intruded from the hall. Benjamyn's white nightshirt lent him the appearance of a specter, attacking her husband. She saw Arcole clutching the majordomo's arm with one hand, the other seeking to shut off the old man's outraged yelling even as Benjamyn sought to rake his face.

She acted without premeditation. It was as it had been when Armnory Schweiz looked to steal her honor, save now it was Arcole—her husband—she saw threatened. She raised the candle holder as she had raised the pewter mug, and brought it down against the back of Benjamy's head.

There was an ugly sound, sharp and soft at the same time, like an ax falling against rotten wood. Benjamyn's shouting ceased abruptly, he grunted, and then the grunt became a failing whistle of breath. Flysse felt wetness on her hand.

She stepped back, staring as Benjamyn went limp in Arcole's grip. Her husband clutched at the majordomo, no longer fighting to hold him off, but only to hold him up. Benjamyn's head lolled forward onto Arcole's chest, and for a horrid moment Flysse saw the stain that spread across the wool of his nightcap. She dropped the candle holder. As it fell, she saw with terrified clarity that the edge was dented and turned back on itself.

She said, "Oh, God, what have I done?"

Arcole lowered Benjamyn to the floor and touched gentle fingers to the old man's neck. "Killed him," he said.

Tears formed and began to spill down Flysse's cheeks. A sob took shape in her throat, cut short by Arcole's hands on her shoulders.

"No!" His voice was soft, but nonetheless urgent. "Flysse, don't cry! We've not the time."

She stared at him, then down at Benjamyn. She began to tremble.

Arcole put his arms around her and pulled her tight against his chest. "Listen to me," he said. "Flysse, do you listen to me? Our lives depend on it, and all our plans."

It was hard to stem the shaking that gripped her, but she heard such urgency in his voice, she did her best. She raised a tearful face to his, and when he kissed her—gently—she did not resist, only held him close, seeking the comfort of his arms.

"I killed him," she moaned.

"You had no choice," he said firmly. "He left you none. Besides, you didn't mean to do it."

She said, "No," as if the single negative were a prayer of forgiveness.

"But if he's found like this," Arcole said, "we'll both be blamed, both suffer. Listen to me, Flysse, we've likely not much time."

He put his hands on her shoulders again and pushed her back. She had sooner he held her close, but he kept her at arm's length. Reluctantly, she looked into his eyes.

He said, "First, we must carry him to the kitchen. Do you understand, Flysse?"

Not sure she did, she nodded.

"None must suspect we were here." He loosed his grip just long enough to gesture at Wyme's study. "All well, we can claim he fell. Yes! We'll spill some grease on the floor and say he slipped."

Dully, Flysse said, "The floor's clean, Arcole. It always is; Dido has the scullions scrub it each night."

He cursed softly and said, "Then he only slipped. God, he's old enough—and waking, he was likely doddery. But"—his grip tightened on her shoulders and he shook her gently—"does it come to accusations of murder, then I did it."

"No," she said. "I killed him. The sin is mine."

"No sin!" Arcole snapped. "An accident, no more. Did you intend to kill him?"

Flysse shook her head. "I saw him attack you. I wanted to stop him, only that."

"Then in the absence of intention," he said, "you cannot be guilty. *It was an accident!* Is there sin, then I claim it. I came to Wyme's study, I involved you in my plans. What sin exists, Flysse, is mine. And do any suggest it was murder, then I claim that too."

She stared at him aghast. "Do you love me so much?"

Solemnly, he ducked his head. "Yes. Have I not told you? You own my life, Flysse. My life and my heart and my soul."

"But it was I hit him," she said. "I cannot let you take the blame for that."

"God!" He smiled at her savagely and tenderly. "Think you I'd not have slain him? He left me little choice, eh? But do you say aught to contradict me in this, then we shall both likely go to the gallows, or be sold off apart to wilderness farms. And then what shall become of Davyd, eh? He needs the one of us, at least. Far best only I be blamed for this. And better still if we can conceal it."

She stared at him through eyes so filled with tears, his face was hazy. Could he truly love her so much? There now seemed little doubt. She said, 'Arcole, I'm sorry."

"No time for apologies now," he said. "And I've my share of those, beside. Shall you do as I . . ." Almost, he said, "Tell you"; amended it to "Suggest?" And when she nodded, let her go and said, "Then pick up that candle holder and the candle."

As she did that, he lifted Benjamyn. The old man's corpse was light as he carried it toward the kitchen. Over his shoulder he said, "Close the door. And do any come, we were neither of us near the study."

Flysse obeyed as if she were a puppet, her strings tugged by his voice. A dreadful numbness gripped her. Her limbs felt heavy, her heart seemed to beat sonorous against her ribs, filling her with sluggish blood. Like that, she thought, that welled from Benjamyn's shattered skull. She marveled at Arcole's calm, and at his sacrifice. She thought she could not let him make it.

She followed him to the kitchen and watched as he set the corpse upon the clean-scrubbed floor. A welling of blood came from the head, pooling slow and thick.

Arcole surveyed his handiwork and said, "So. He came in and slipped. You"—he gestured at Flysse's chair— "were sitting there. You dozed, and when you woke, it startled him. He slipped and fell." He took the candle holder from her and set it close by Benjamyn's head. Then thought to light the candle and drip wax over the floor; pinch out the candle and drop that nearby. "It may be enough."

"And is it not?" Flysse asked.

"Then he found me at Wyme's brandy." Arcole crossed to where that was kept and swilled a mouthful. "He threatened me and we struggled. He fell."

"Arcole, I cannot let you do this."

He took her face in hands then and said, "Flysse, you can. You must! Do you not see it?"

She shook her head. He took the incriminating paper from his tunic and gave it her. "Is this found," he said, "then all is lost. *We are lost.* You and Davyd and I, all our dreams. If Wyme suspects we were in his study, then, like Benjamyn, he'll likely remember I can read. And then he'll find those other papers, the maps, and we shall both be found guilty. And Davyd will have no one, nor hope of escape from this place."

"Should that be so bad?" she asked.

"Do you forget Davyd's dreams?" he asked in return. And when she helplessly shook her head: "No? Then I beg you do as I say."

"You're sure?"

He nodded. "I've killed enough men that my hands are already bloody. Can I not escape this charge, then perhaps it's a kind of justice. But I can at least know you and Davyd go free. And do you follow our plan, then you can likely use those maps to escape."

"Not without you," she said.

"If you must," he replied. And when she shook her head: "You once extracted promises from me, no? Now I ask the same of you. As you love me, I'll have your word you *will* flee this place if you safely can, and with Davyd. Your word, Flysse?"

Brown eyes locked with blue: his intense, hers blurred by tears. Finally she nodded and said, "Is that your command, Arcole?"

"No. My wish."

"Then," she said, "I shall seek to fulfill your wish."

Then Chryselle entered the kitchen and began to scream when she saw her husband's body.

"Coffee, by God!" Governor Wyme gestured irritably and Nathanial sprang to fill the extended cup. "And brandy."

Wyme took the decanter and spilled a generous measure into his coffee. He sipped, then closed his eyes and sighed gustily. His head hurt abominably; and as if Danyael Corm had not delivered sufficient bad news the preceding night, he must now face the demise of his major-domo. He did not appreciate the disruption of his sleep or his household, and that did no more than the throbbing of his skull to improve his mood. He tugged his dressing gown tighter across his ample belly and surveyed the scene.

It was, he thought with irritable amusement, rather like one of those tableaux the common folk found entertaining. *The Death of the Old Retainer,* or some such trite title. Benjamyn was the centerpiece, and most assuredly dead. Chryselle sobbed—the sound threatening to hurt Wyme's ears—in Dido's arms. Young—what was her name?—yes, Flysse, stood pale-faced beside her husband. Fredrik, Wyllem and Gylbert stood like guards to either side. Nathanial stood wide-eyed, staring at the corpse. The other servants hung back, still and silent as waxworks.

Most definitely, Wyme decided, a tableaux. But of whose making?

He studied Benjamyn's body and the candle holder close by. Arcole had offered an explanation that was superficially plausible, but Wyme was not a stupid man and by nature suspicious. He hooked a finger in Nathanial's direction and said, "Bring me that candle holder."

Nathanial obeyed, wincing as he saw the blood that discolored the dented edge. Wyme took the thing without qualms and turned it in his hands.

Then he pointed at the corpse and said, "Fredrik, turn him over."

The head groom obeyed, his face impassive. Wyme said, "Drag him over here."

He ignored Chryselle's renewed weeping as the corpse was hauled across the floor and leant forward to survey the wreckage of Benjamyn's skull. Then he turned the candle holder around again and looked at Arcole.

"He slipped, eh?"

Arcole nodded.

"And fell?"

Another silent nod.

"Onto this?" Wyme held up the candle holder.

"I suppose so." Arcole shrugged.

"Because he was startled when Flysse woke."

Arcole nodded again.

"And where were you?"

"I was . . ." Wyme saw Arcole's eyes dart round, and Flysse stiffen beside him. "I was . . . sampling your brandy." He gestured to where the decanter was usually kept.

Wyme sipped more of the fortified coffee. There was more to this affair than met the eye, but for now he had troubles enough to occupy him. It was definitely time Grostheim had an Inquisitor, he thought. An Inquisitor could unravel this in moments: his own magic did not extend so far. God, he was not even sure his hexing powers extended to protecting the walls from the promised arrival of the demons. But those were thoughts for another day; he shook his head and groaned regret of the movement. If he settled this affair swiftly, he might manage an hour or two's more sleep.

"You were stealing my brandy," he said. And even as Arcole voiced an affirmative: "And Benjamyn caught you at it. You killed him, no?"

Arcole said, "No. He slipped and fell."

"Either way." Wyme reached under his dressing gown to scratch his chest. "You are responsible."

Flysse said sharply, "No!"

Arcole said, "Flysse . . ."

Wyme looked from one to the other. The woman was involved in this, and by God she was a pretty thing. He wondered he'd not noticed her before. Likely Celinda had, and kept her from him. He glanced at Chryselle and a notion shaped: Had Benjamyn perhaps come seeking Flysse? And Arcole objected, and the two men struggled, and Arcole slain Benjamyn? Or perhaps it was all about stolen brandy. God knew, old Benjamyn was—*had been*—a disciplinarian, likely to castigate a man for small theft, but a most excellent majordomo. It would be hard to replace him—which irked the governor; and the more for the notion that Arcole should have been ideal as a replacement when Benjamyn died of natural causes or grew too old. He had the finesse, the manners: Wyme had entertained high hopes of Arcole.

And now they were all dashed at the worst possible time. God, who could take Benjamyn's place? The household would be in chaos; Celinda would undoubtedly blame him.

The governor scowled and said, "I believe you killed him. I pronounce you guilty . . ."

"Without trial?"

Wyllem and Gylbert grasped Arcole's arms as he lunged forward. Fredrik stood before him, a hand raised ready to strike. Praise God for loyal servants, Wyme thought.

"Take him." Wyme looked to Fredrik. "There's a secure place? A shed or suchlike, that can be locked?"

Fredrik nodded. "Do I clear out some tack, 'sieur."

"Then take him there and lock him in," Wyme said. "Make sure he can't break out, and I'll deal with him later. Now the rest of you go to your beds. Nathanial—my crutches."

Nathanial hurried to obey as Wyllem and Gylbert took firmer hold of Arcole and Flysse began to sob. She clutched at him and Fredrik pushed her away. She could only watch and weep as he was led out.

She turned to Wyme as Nathanial lifted him onto the crutches. "What shall happen to him, 'sieur?"

Wyme halted, looking at her, and smiled. "Why, my dear," he said, "having been found guilty of murder, he must be hanged."

39 Gambler's Luck

Flysse could hardly believe what had happened. She had known Arcole took risks in his clandestine mapmaking, but she had never thought it might come to this—to sentence of death. She wept as he was taken out and locked in the tack room, and wept as she returned to their chamber. She latched the door and flung herself on the bed, her mind racing. It seemed that all their dreams of freedom were shattered and she must stand helplessly by as her husband was hung. She thought she could not bear that, especially not now, when they had mended their love.

She could not, and so she would not: there had to be something she do. She dried her eyes and willed herself to think calmly, and as the sun rose pale in a hard blue sky, she knew what she would do. It should be dangerous, but she could not leave Arcole to his fate.

As Dido prepared the mistress's breakfast tray, and those servants not engaged in their duties ate, Flysse approached Nathanial.

"What shall happen now?"

Nathanial wiped crumbs from his chin and shrugged. "Why, he'll be hung, of course. In the town square, most likely." He smiled speculatively. "I expect we'll get time off to watch."

"When?" Flysse asked, thinking that she'd like to strike him.

Nathanial glanced at Fredrik, who said, "When the gallows is ready."

Flysse gulped, blinking tears away. "When shall that be?"

Fredrik drank tea, studying her quizzically, then turned to Nathanial. "How long d'you think?"

"For God's sake!" Dido turned angry eyes on the two men. "Must you torment the poor girl? Surely she's suffered enough."

They had the grace to look somewhat embarrassed then, and Fredrik said, "Well, there's not been a hanging in a long time, and the old gallows was dismantled. I suppose the master'll order a new scaffold built, and that'll take a day or two."

"It's Saturday today," Nathanial said, "an' the master won't ask the carpenters to work Sunday, so I'd reckon it'll be Monday."

Fredrik nodded in silent confirmation; Flysse swallowed and took the tray Dido proffered. There might be enough time. She prayed there be enough.

When she returned to the kitchen, she asked Dido if she might visit Arcole. The cook hesitated, then patted Flysse's hand and said, "Well, I suppose he is your husband. But not long, eh? Just a quick visit, and then it's back to your duties."

Flysse blurted out her thanks and hurried away.

The tack room was located at the rear of the stables. There were no windows, and the door was padlocked from the outside. The floor was hard dirt and the room smelled of ancient leather and horses. Fredrik grudgingly allowed she might spend a few moments with her husband and locked her in, promising to return in a while.

Arcole was disheveled, but his smile was bright as he took her in his arms.

"You've not suffered? Has Wyme said anything to you?"

"Only sour looks, and I've not seen the master."

"I shall miss you," he said, and sighed.

"Listen"—Flysse drew back so that she could see his face— "Fredrik says you'll be hung on Monday. He thinks the master will order the gallows started today, but tomorrow's Sunday . . ."

Arcole laughed. "And a God-fearing man like Wyme wouldn't hang anyone on Sunday, eh? Shall he allow me to attend services?"

She thought he put on a brave face, but there was no time for bravado now. She motioned him to silence, saying, "I'll have a chance to speak with Davyd in church."

"Bid him farewell for me," Arcole said, "and tell him I'm sorry our plans end this way."

Flysse said, "Perhaps they don't. Listen . . ."

*   *   *

Their conversation was necessarily brief. Before long, Fredrik came to unlock the door and advise Flysse she'd best return to her duties, and she must hug Arcole and turn away, praying all go well. It seemed to her that a clock ticked in her head, marking out the moments left them.

It was almost impossible to attend to her tasks. She was unusually clumsy, earning reprimands from Celinda and even Dido, though the cook's were gentler than the mistress's, and she showed Flysse a degree of rough sympathy.

Around the mid-part of the morning, Wyme ordered his carriage be readied. "He'll be goin' to order the gallows started," Nathanial declared, then fell silent under Flysse's scowl.

"You'd best say a special prayer for him tomorrow," Dido said.

Flysse nodded, thinking that she most definitely would, albeit not the kind Dido had in mind. That night she could barely sleep, and when the servants assembled for their walk to the church, she was the first ready.

As they crossed the square to the church, she saw that Nathanial's guess had been correct. A platform was already built, and timber lay about its sides, long beams that would support a man dangling from the shorter cross-piece. Flysse stared at the half-finished construction and shuddered, then grit her teeth and walked straight-backed into the church.

Davyd found her as usual, and she thought at first he must have heard the grim news, for his face was pale and drawn, reminding her of his expression aboard the *Pride of the Lord.*

"You've heard?" she asked.

He shook his head impatiently, speaking in an urgent whisper before she could amplify. "Flysse, we must go soon. My dreams are worse, and I think the demons are coming fast. I think they'll be here before long." He broke off, frowing. "Where's Arcole?"

"Locked in, and sentenced to death."

"What?" Davyd gaped at her, and she gestured him to be cautious, telling him what had happened.

"No," he muttered when she was done. "Not now. God, not now!"

Flysse said, "We must get him out. Tonight!"

Davyd was silent for a moment, as if digesting this news. Then he nodded and asked, "What kind of lock is on the door?"

As best she could remember, Flysse described the padlock.

"I can pick that," he said confidently, "and I've all the stuff we need."

"We must still get past the walls," she whispered back. "How can we get past the guards?"

Davyd grinned and said, "I think I know of a way. It won't be pleasant, but I doubt anyone will look for us there. You know how many folk have come to Grostheim these past weeks? Well, there are tents set up for them, and the governor ordered trenches dug to carry off their waste. They go under the walls . . ."

"If it's the only way," Flysse murmured. "But it must be tonight."

"Yes." Davyd nodded. "I'll come tonight, with all our stuff."

"I'll await you," Flysse said. "And God help us."

Davyd took her hand. "I'll not let Arcole down," he said, "nor you."

Flysse sat at the kitchen table, stonily ignoring Nathanial's attempts at flattery. Arcole was imprisoned across the yard, but still the dark-haired servant paid her unseemly court, and no matter how often she told him she was wed, still he pressed her.

"I am married," she said, "Arcole lives, and I am still his wife."

"But when . . ." Nathanial pantomimed hanging.

"He is not yet dead," Flysse said.

"But shall be soon." Nathanial was undeterred. "And besides, you'd had a falling-out, no?"

"We argued." Flysse nodded wearily. "And settled all our differences. Can you not understand? I love Arcole."

"No point to loving a dead man." Nathanial would not be put off. "A woman like you, you'll want a man. And I'm likely to take Benjamyn's place now."

"Please, Nathanial," Flysse said, "do you leave me be? My husband is alive, and even is he . . ." She shook her head, unwilling to say the words. "Then I should be in mourning."

"But after that," said Nathanial.

Flysse started as a bell rang, thankful for the interruption. Even the emptying of madame's chamber pot should be preferable to hearing out Nathanial's ceaseless cajolements. But it was not Celinda: the governor rang from his study.

"Likely in his cups again." Nathanial rose, winking. "Has he left a glass or two, we can share it after I've got him settled, eh?"

Flysse offered no response, only watched as he quit the kitchen.

The gasped as Davyd came in.

"God!" She rose swiftly, eyes darting to the door that had only just closed on Nathanial. "Davyd, you startled me."

He motioned her to silence. "No time," he whispered. "Are you ready?"

She nodded, thinking that he seemed fevered, his green eyes burning. She saw he wore a knife on his belt.

"You've the maps Arcole drew?" The way he glanced around made Flysse think of hunted animals. "Where are they?"

"In our room," she said, pointing at the relevant door. It seemed her feet were rooted now that the moment had come. Davyd's strength surprised her as he drew her forward. "Show me," he urged. "And quick!"

She moved ahead and he set a hand against her back, pushing her. She prayed that Wyme keep Nathanial occupied; did he not, then perhaps the servant would think she had been summoned to madame. She felt her heart beat wild against her ribs.

They found the room, and Flysse took the maps from their hiding place.

Davyd said, "I've left our gear in the stables. Now bring me to Arcole."

He unlatched the window and thrust it open, peering out a moment before climbing through. Flysse followed, encumbered by her skirts and petticoats. She thought it should be hard to flee in the dirndl.

They crossed the yard. Flysse noticed the night was moonless. It seemed unnaturally quiet, or perhaps only their footsteps sounded loud. Inside the stable, three bulky packs stood by the door.

"There." Flysse pointed to where Arcole was imprisoned.

"Wait here." Davyd halted her as she moved to accompany him. "Does anyone approach, call out. But softly, eh?"

She nodded and took a vantage point beside the door. Davyd faded into the shadows.

The lock was of a model he had picked before, and it took only moments to trip its tumblers, even with unsteady hands. He eased the door open, not wanting creaking hinges to give the alarm. The tiny chamber stank, but Arcole greeted him with a smile.

"Well met, Davyd."

Davyd marveled at the man's calm: he could only nod and whisper, "Yes."

"You've brought everything?" Arcole emerged from the makeshift cell as if his liberation were no surprise at all.

Davyd repeated, "Yes."

"Excellent." Arcole grasped his shoulder. "Done well."

"We've a ways yet to go." Davyd endeavored to match Arcole's insouciance, then shuddered as his dreams flared bright inside his mind. "And tonight we'll have a diversion; I'd stake my life on it."

"You do," said Arcole as if it were the most natural thing in the world.

They reached the door and Flysse flung herself into her husband's arms. Arcole gently disentangled himself, kissed her once. "I'm hardly fit to be embraced," he murmured. Then grinned: So, shall we be gone?"

Davyd bent to the packs, tugging two cloaks loose. Beneath, all was wrapped in oilskin. "These will hide your uniforms," he said. "All well, we'll look like refugees seeking a place to sleep."

He was gratified by Arcole's smile of approval. As they donned the cloaks, he eased his head around the door—and jerked it back.

"Someone comes!"

Arcole beckoned him away. "Fredrik, damn him. He must have heard something. Wait; and silently, eh?"

Davyd and Flysse moved back into the shadows. Arcole lowered his pack, taking station where the door should hide him. As Fredrik came in, he stepped forward, his left hand dropping onto the groom's shoulder. He spun the startled man around, and struck him once on the jaw. Fredrik made a whoofing sound, like one of his beloved horses, and fell unconscious. Arcole dragged him to the tack room and locked the door.

"So I've not forgotten how." He rubbed his knuckles. "Now shall we depart?"

He shouldered his pack and motioned that Davyd lead the way.

Wyme's mansion stood silent as they climbed the fence, and no one witnessed their furtive departure. Farther into the city, the streets were crowded. Flysse clutched Arcole's hand.

"We're no more than three newcomers," he whispered, "just as Davyd said. Three poor lost souls seeking a bed for the night. God knows, I at least look the part."

Flysse forced a smile and drew a little closer, then gasped as Davyd halted abruptly, waving them back.

"A patrol!"

He turned, bringing them into an alley. It was littered with bodies, and as they picked their way along, folk grumbled sleepily that there was no room left. The patrol marched briskly by as they reached the farther end, where the alleyway gave onto a wider thoroughfare, its sidewalks lined with wagons.

"Down here," Davyd said.

Then a line of fire, like a sparkling rocket, arched across the sky and cannon boomed from atop the walls.

Flysse screamed and Davyd shouted, both sounds lost in the roar of cannon fire. Arcole gestured that Davyd lead the way, and they began to run down a street thrown into sudden chaos. People emerged from the wagons, some in nightgowns, most of the men clutching weapons, all yelling. They gaped, milling like nervous cattle, as more flames soared overhead. Arcole looked to where one fiery line ended on a rooftop and shouted, "Fire arrows!" Neither Flysse or Davyd heard him, for the artillery along the walls kept up a relentless din, and between the cannon's booming there was the rattle of musketry. A handful of the flaming arrows had fired roofs, and here and there folk flung up ladders, passing buckets from hand to hand to douse the flames. A column of red-coated Militiamen came pounding down the street, cursing the refugees who impeded their progress, the sergeant waving his saber and threatening to use it on any who got in his way. Davyd beckoned his companions, falling into step behind the soldiers. The column cleared them a way and they ran to the end of the street, where he led them off at an angle, shouldering through the crowd there.

A man grabbed at him, demanding to know what transpired and where they went. Davyd evaded his grasp and the man turned to snatch at Flysse. Arcole knocked his hand away and bellowed, "Demons! God preserve us, the demons are come!"

The cry was instantly taken up, adding to the tumult, and the street became a seething mass of panicked folk. Davyd ducked between two houses, leading them clear of the chaos.

They paused to snatch a breath. The sky over Grostheim blossomed red, the screaming of the inhabitants vying with the thunder of the cannon and the crackling of musket fire for supremacy.

"We've our diversion, by God," Arcole chuckled. "Even do they notice our absence, they'll not come looking for us in a hurry."

Flysse stared at him, alarmed by his expression. It was one of . . . . *glee* was the only word she could think of, as if he took pleasure in the city's panic, as if he saw impending destruction as a personal revenge.

"We've yet to get past the walls," Davyd said, then shuddered as he added, "and past the demons."

"We shall," Arcole declared confidently. "Have faith."

Davyd nodded and attempted an unconvincing grin. "This way, then."

They climbed a fence and hurried across a yard, into a second, where a large dog barked madly; along a path littered with garbage to an avenue they crossed into another alley. Folk poured from buildings, joining the refugees in the streets, and though all were armed, they were disorganized, standing in knots or shuffling back and forth, uncertain what to do, so that they only jammed the thoroughfares and hindered the Militiamen running for the walls. Arcole added to the confusion by repeating his warning of demons as he went by, but, save for that, the passage of three more panic-stricken refugees went unnoticed.

The crash of cannon fire grew louder, and the air heavy with powder smoke. Flysse saw the walls loom, red-lit, above. She could see the soldiers there, manning the artillery pieces or leaning out to discharge their muskets. She could not see what they fired at, but she thought she could hear an unearthly yammering from beyond the walls, as if hell's own hounds bayed at Grostheim's gates. Then a more pungent odor intruded on her nostrils, and she winced at the stench.

"Here." Davyd pointed, and grimaced. "It's the only way."

They stood in the shadow of a warehouse. Its bulk formed one side of a rough square, more large buildings the other two, and the wall itself the third. Between lay a patch of open ground—likely the only open space in all the city now—bisected by a trench lined with makeshift canvas screens. The trench ran to the wall and disappeared beneath.

Flysse hesitated. "I'm not sure I can."

"You must!" Arcole hung an arm about her shoulders, urging her forward. "We've come too far—there's no turning back now."

Davyd was already moving, crouched over, across the open space. Arcole pushed Flysse on. Her eyes began to water and she could not help but struggle.

"As Davyd says," Arcole shouted into her ear, "it's the only way."

She shook her head helplessly and he took her hand, dragging her forcibly after him. "You will," he said. "God, Flysse, do you hesitate now, I'll—" He halted, turning to face her. "I'll go back to Wyme and give myself up. I'll hang because you don't want to dirty your feet!"

It was unfair, but all he could think of to persuade her. Save, perhaps, knocking her out and hauling her through, and he was not sure she would survive that, nor even certain it was possible. He was by no means sure he could bring himself to strike her, no matter the reason.

She looked at him through tear-blurred eyes and forced a small smile. "I'd not see you hang, husband. So—lead on."

"My brave Flysse." He answered her smile and touched her cheek. "We'll soon enough wash away Grostheim's filth in the river, eh?"

She nodded and let him lead her to the screens.

The smell grew worse, and worse still past the canvas. Davyd stood waiting for them, a kerchief wound about his mouth and nose. He brought two more from his pockets, passing them over.

Arcole said, "God, Davyd, your plan stinks," and laughed. "But it's a good one."

Davyd nodded. Above the kerchief his eyes looked no happier than Flysse's. "It goes under the wall," he said. "The governor had it dug when the streets filled with refugees."

"It's fitting, no?" Arcole knotted the cloth in place. "We're no more than waste to Wyme. Do I lead now?"

Without awaiting an answer, he began to pace along the line of canvas, toward the wall. Flysse followed, Davyd bringing up the rear.

The screens ended just before the wall, and Arcole stepped into the trench. Filthy water climbed above his knees, disturbed insects rising in a horrid, buzzing swarm around his head. He offered Flysse his hand and she followed him, fighting the urge to vomit, trying to ignore the things that floated in the latrine. It was easier to ignore the cannonades thundering above.

Between the screens' edges and the wall lay a few feet of open ground. They ducked down, gagging on the miasma, and reached the opening. The wall's timbers were cut ragged here, splintery stumps ending scant inches above the foul water.

Arcole said, "Keep low until we reach the river."

Davyd touched Flysse's shoulder and said, "It's not too far."

She smiled her thanks, and voiced a silent prayer they all survive.

Arcole said, "Ready?" And when she nodded: "Stay close."

He went down on hands and knees, lowering himself until only his head and back stood above the fetid stream. As he crawled under the wall, he must duck down, all his body sinking beneath the flow.

Flysse wished she might take a deep breath, but knew that if she did she would surely empty her stomach. She closed her eyes and clenched her teeth tight, then followed her husband. She feared she would panic as she went under the wall, crawling blind through a clinging mud she had rather not think about.

It seemed to last a ghastly eternity, but she still had breath in her lungs when a hand grasped her shoulder and lifted her up. She gazed at Arcole, unspeaking, as she dragged the befouled kerchief from her face and spat, staring about as Davyd's dripping head emerged.

Arcole stood to her left, flattened against the wall. The trench curved rightward ahead, meeting the river a hundred feet or so distant. The Restitution glimmered red in the cannon's discharges, and the sound of gunfire on this side of the wall was deafening, as if they stood in the heart of a storm.

Indeed they did, Flysse thought, for in the awful light of the cannonades she saw Grostheim surrounded by demons.

They stood in groups, some along the riverbank, some close to the walls. Some ran back and forth, as if to draw the defenders' fire; others capered, waving weapons in challenge. All screamed; and all of their faces were leering, painted masks. They seemed careless of the volleys from the walls, even when canister shot tore through their ranks. Their hatred seemed almost palpable.

Flysse could not see how it might be possible they reach the river safely, how they might then escape. She thought they must die here.

Speech was pointless in the din, and Arcole grasped her elbow, indicating they must crawl again. Mindlessly, numbed by the terrible sounds, she obeyed. She glanced back at Davyd and saw his eyes huge with barely controlled terror, in a face gone ashen under its coating of filth. She reached back, taking his hand and squeezing, then began to crawl.

Perhaps it was the stench—perhaps it was good fortune—but none of the demons stood near the trench, and none came close as the three pressed onward. They reached the river and Arcole turned westward, hugging the shallows. A wooden jetty lay in that direction, designed to accommodate barges plying inland. Five burned at their moorings, and the flames had taken hold of the jetty that favored the desperate enterprise—the demons kept clear of the conflagration.

All three ducked low as they moved upriver, shedding their cloaks and letting the Restitution wash off a measure of the encrusting filth. Flysse wondered if she would ever feel clean again, or safe.

The air grew warmer as they approached the burning barges, and a film of ash drifted over the water. Arcole motioned that they halt. The riverbank stood high enough that they were hidden from view as he gestured at the blazing jetty.

"We must swim to get past that." He looked to Davyd. "Can you manage that?"

Flysse felt embarrassment that she had entirely forgotten Davyd's dread of water, and proud of Arcole that he had not. Davyd reached down to splash his face. Cleaned of filth, it looked wan, the bonfire night drawing deep shadows beneath his eyes.

"Have I a choice?" he asked hoarsely.

"Not really," Arcole replied, and gestured at the bank. "Save . . ."

Davyd grinned: Flysse thought she had seen such smiles on dead faces. "I can try," he said. "But . . . I can't swim."

"You wrapped these well." Arcole lowered his pack into the water. "See? It floats. Do you hold on to yours and let me pull you."

Davyd swallowed, spat, and nodded. Arcole turned to Flysse, brows raised in silent question. She said, "I can swim. But these skirts hamper me."

"There's fresh clothing in these?" Arcole gestured at the packs, and when Davyd nodded again: "Well, we all need a change, no?"

Flysse understood his meaning: she unlaced her bodice and shrugged it off, then the skirt and petticoats. She was not sorry to see them drift away, though Davyd's blush prompted a match that warmed her cheeks. Modestly, she hid herself in the river.

"Come, then." Arcole set Davyd's hands on the oilskin parcel. "Hold tight and trust me."

Davyd closed his eyes as he felt himself towed out into the current. Panic threatened as he felt the river tug at him, but he rested his chin on the pack and clenched his teeth, telling himself he had no choice.

He kept his eyes tight shut, his hands rigid on the pack's cords, until his feet touched bottom once again. Then, warily, he opened an eye and looked around. He was sure a demon must loom over him, or the hulk of a burning barge collapse on him, but he saw only the Restitution's south bank and the dinghies moored there. He began to chuckle hysterically.

Arcole clapped a hand across his mouth, silencing him, and reached to help Flysse. Davyd blushed anew as she came out of the water: her underthings clung to her so that she seemed like some scantily clad water nymph. He looked away and asked, "What now?" He thought his voice echoed his unwilled excitement.

Arcole said, "The tide's turned, I think," and gestured at a dinghy. "So we take one of these and float away."

40 Waiting for the Dream

The ambush was swift and furious: none sought battle honor in this fight, only to destroy the Breakers that the People might survive.

Racharran led fifty warriors out, Yazte the same number, and also Chakthi. Their strategy was quickly decided and they rode hard, guided by Motsos, split into two groups where the incoming tracks ran between a thick stand of timber and a low ridge. This, all well, would be the killing ground. The Commacht concealed themselves amongst the trees as the Lakanti and the Tachyn hid behind the spur.

The Breakers appeared around the mid-part of the afternoon, their weird mounts padding swift over the muddy ground, wide heads lifting as their nostrils flared to test the breeze. As they came abreast of the ridge's downslope, the foremost pair roared, baring vicious fangs. The riders slowed them, hands rising in warning.

Racharran set a buffalo horn to his lips and blew a long clarion.

His Commacht broke from the shelter of the trees, flighting arrows as they raced down the line of Breakers. Simultaneously, Yazte led his warriors in a charge down the ridge to hit the head of the column as Chakthi brought his Tachyn out to attack from the rear. Shafts feathered beasts and Breakers alike, and the afternoon grew loud with pained and angry roaring.

Racharran spun his horse around and charged back. Briefly through the confusion, he saw that Yazte blocked the way ahead, the Lakanti riding the war circle, from which they sent arrows directly into the Breakers midst. Behind, the Tachyn pushed forward, denying the invaders' scouts escape. But the enemy seemed not to think of that possibility and only fought, driving beasts that sprouted arrows like the quills on a porcupine at the Commacht and the Lakanti. Chakthi's men had an easier time, firing at armored backs and furry, scaled rumps.

The difference in numbers was great enough that it should have been a brief contest. But such was the strength of the Breakers' rainbow armor—and such the power of their strange beasts—that even though half their number fell in the first charge, still the survivors claimed a toll. The fallen slowed them, but they counterattacked with grim ferocity, beasts clambering over the dead and dying to reach the ambushers, tearing at their own in their bloodlust when the wounded hampered them. All was confusion. Horses shrilled as talons ripped them or fangs closed bloody on necks and hindquarters. The Breakers' long swords and ugly pikes swung and thrust: not all the unseated warriors fought clear.

Racharran fired his last arrow into the gaping maw of a beast already decorated with shafts and barely avoided the claws that reached for him even as the creature roared and died. Its rider, armor hung with shafts like battle trophies, sprang clear of the dying thing and hefted a long blade at the Commacht akaman. Racharran swung his horse clear and drew his hatchet. The way ahead was blocked with bodies and he wheeled his mount toward the timber, circling back even as Motsos sent a shaft into the Breaker. The armored figure—man or woman? Racharran cared not—staggered and then came on. Racharran charged back, knees urging his horse sideways, away from the swinging sword, as he brought his ax down against the helm.

The Breaker fell onto hands and knees, and Motsos rode it down, spinning his mount in a prancing circle that smashed hooves against the Breaker until the body lay all broken on the ground, blood welling from the armor's joints.

That was the last; there were no more left alive, and those beasts that still spat and snapped their fangs were dispatched with shafts fired from safe range.

Five Commacht were dead and five more wounded. Three Lakanti were slain and seven bore cuts. Two Tachyn had fallen and three boasted wounds. It was a fearsome thing that so few of the enemy made such claim. Racharran thought on what should happen did all the horde come to the Meeting Ground, and his face grew somber.

"We slew them!" Motsos wiped beast-blood from his face, laughing triumphantly. "Ach, but we slew them all! We taught them a lesson, no?"

Racharran nodded and forced himself to smile. Twenty scouts killed —how far from the main force and how long before they were missed and others sent? How long before the Breakers found the Meeting Ground?

How long before Morrhyn fulfilled his promise?

The council lodge was crowded. Perico and Kanseah sat in awkward representation of their clans, unaccustomed to such elevation, for they now found themselves treated as akamans, equal to the rest. Mostly, they stayed silent and only listened.

"Our scouts must range farther." Racharran looked around for confirmation. "Theirs got too close. And should the whole horde come . . ."

"Shall those we slew be missed?" Yazte asked, his question echoing Racharran's fear. "Will they send others?"

Racharran said, "I do not understand these people. They are not like any warriors I have fought."

He smiled brief apology to Chakthi for that, and the Tachyn waved a dismissive hand, answering the smile with his own. Since the fight he was better trusted; even fat Yazte spoke civilly to him now. He looked to Morrhyn and said, "You dreamed of this—can you not tell us what else might come?"

Morrhyn sighed and shook his head. "I know only that we must wait for the Grannach." He made no mention of Rannach: for all Chakthi had led his warriors in this day's battle, still he could not entirely believe the man was honest, that behind his newly mild demeanor there did not yet lurk resentment. "I think that until they come, the Maker will not reveal his plans."

Chakthi shrugged. "I think they'd best come soon."

"That's true." Yazte nodded ponderously and said aloud what they all knew: "Food's short, and folk grow restless. They wonder if all our flight was useless."

He raised a hand, signing apology to Morrhyn. The wakanisha nodded. "I know," he said softly, "and had I better answers, I'd give them. But . . ."

There was silence awhile, ominous. Then Racharran said, "Two days' ride, at least." He glanced sidelong at Morrhyn. "With so many defenseless ones, we'll need ample warning."

The others grunted their agreement. Morrhyn lowered his head. He felt wretched: a prophet with insufficient answers, only his faith to sustain him—and that beset with horrid doubt.

Across the fire Kahteney favored him with a supportive smile. Hadduth sat expressionless, his narrow face a mask that gave away nothing.

"If," Yazte said, and hesitated; coughed as if reluctant to go on, "if they do attack, this is not a good place to fight."

"We've no other choice." Racharran shrugged. "I've thought of that; I've a plan of sorts."

Chakthi said, "To what end?"

"They can come only from the one direction," Racharran said. "The hills ring us here, so they must come in through the pass."

"Shall we meet them there?" Yazte kept his eyes on Racharran, not looking at Morrhyn. "That should mean fighting mostly afoot."

"True." Racharran smiled grimly. "But are the Grannach with us, their stone magic should work to our advantage."

"To block the pass?" Chakthi asked. "Send the stone down on the Breakers?"

"That, yes," Racharran said, "And our warriors on the heights."

"And the defenseless ones?" asked Yazte.

"They run for the high hills." Racharran gestured to where the mountains rose. "Hopefully, with Grannach guides. We can, at least, give them some time; and we go after."

Chakthi said quietly, "If the Grannach come."

"Yes—if." Racharran looked at the Tachyn out of troubled eyes. "If not, then we must fight alone. But still, there's Morrhyn's promise. And I've faith in that yet!"

Morrhyn smiled his thanks, but he saw that the rest only looked at him with the same closed expression Hadduth wore.

That night he dreamed again of the white stallion racing for the Mountain. And as before, that goal was contested by the armored figure on the weird horse. Sometimes it seemed he ran ahead of the Breaker, sometimes that the Breaker ran faster. It was as if they galloped the sky, for the hills that ringed the majestic pinnacle of the Maker's Mountain were as nothing to their steeds, no more than ruts and furrows. He heeled the stallion to ever greater efforts, and the great horse responded willingly. But the Mountain seemed no closer, and he could not tell who might reach it first.

He woke nervous, his mouth dry and his head throbbing with a dull ache that reverberated against his eyes. He thought he still heard the stallion's hooves pounding, the gusting of its breath, but then he realized those sounds came from beyond his lodge and felt a rush of terrible panic.

Had the Breakers come?

He threw off his sleeping furs and, naked, unlaced the lodgeflap to thrust out his head.

The sky was yet dull, dawn no more than a faint promise on the eastern horizon, but the Meeting Ground woke noisy. Dogs barked and he heard people shouting. His heart beating fast, he tugged on shirt, breeches, and boots, and draped a blanket about his shoulders as he hurried out.

Then he shouted his joy as he saw the line of Grannach moving through the lodges, Rannach and Arrhyna leading their horses at the head, Colun and Marjia striding beside them.

There were too many for the Council lodge, so they all sat as if in Matakwa, circled within a ring of guardian warriors, all others—both the People and the Grannach—standing beyond and listening eagerly. What grim news there was was swiftly exchanged, and they settled to discussing the future.

Colun said, "The Breakers own the mountains now. There is nowhere safe."

"Nor the grass," Racharran said. "Nowhere in all Ket-Ta-Witko."

Colun grunted as if this were no more than he expected and combed his beard with stubby fingers. "So, Morrhyn?"

All eyes turned toward him: those of the men seated about the inner circle and the ring of guards, and all those beyond. Silence descended; even the dogs fell quiet. The morning was yet young, the sun barely above the treetops, the surrounding hills still shadowy. But when he turned his face toward the Maker's Mountain, he saw the pinnacle bright-lit, shining like a burnished golden blade raised against the sky. The eternal snow still decked the uppermost heights, but it was lit all golden, and glittered so that it was hard to hold his eyes open against that illumination. But he did, even as he felt tears stream down his cheeks, and so he saw the white stallion that reared up over the Mountain, hooves pawing the heavens, and felt all his faith come flooding back, washing doubt away.

For long moments he stared, watching the burning Mountain and the ethereal horse, and then both were gone. The horse shook its head and became a drifting cloud; the Mountain became again a looming peak not yet touched by the sun.

He wiped his face and said, "You saw?"

Colun stared at him. Racharran shook his head. Kahteney asked, "Saw what?"

He pointed toward the Mountain and saw incomprehension on their faces. He felt his mouth stretch in a triumphant smile.

When he spoke, his voice was confident.

"The Grannach are come," he said, "and now the Maker will reveal his promise. This I know."

Blunt as ever, Colun said, "When?"

He shook his head, smiling still. As if forever imprinted on his eyes, he saw the vision still. "Soon," he promised. "The Maker will show me soon." He looked to where Kahteney sat. "You've pahé left?"

Kahteney nodded solemnly.

"Good." Morrhyn stretched. "Do you give it me, I think I shall dream well."

He was deep in dreams when the scouts came in on lathered horses, their reports all the same.

The Breakers were two days' ride out, approaching from all directions. Like the migrating buffalo, they came fast, following the trails of all the clans, converging on the Meeting Ground which they must surely reach even as the Moon of the Turning Year reached its fullest.

Morrhyn lay dreaming as the news spread like wildfire through the camp. Racharran thought to wake him, but Kahteney warned against that.

"The pahé owns him now," the Lakanti Dreamer explained, "and it should be dangerous to interrupt him. Likely you could not, anyway. And does he dream the means of our salvation . . ."

He shrugged, his eyes troubled as he faced Racharran. In them the Commacht akaman saw his own fear, his own dread doubt—*and if he does not, then what point to waking him? We are doomed, so let him sleep on and die in his sleep.*

Racharran nodded and turned to Colun. "You've Stone Shapers with you?"

"Yes." Colun's eyes narrowed under craggy brows. "Baran's the strongest, but there are some seven others."

Swiftly, Racharran outlined his plan.

Colun frowned and tugged at his beard and said, "I don't know if the golans can work their magic here."

Racharran fought to hide his frustration at the slow, deliberate Grannach ways and asked, "Why not send for them, that we might find out?"

Colun grunted and shouted for a man to bring Baran.

When the squat Stone Shaper was put the question, he chewed on his luxuriant moustache awhile and gave the same answer. Then he grinned through his beard and said, "But we can find out, no?"

"The Breakers will be on us within two days," Racharran said. "Two days at the most, and likely less."

Baran nodded as if this were all the time in the world. "Then we'd best set to work, eh? This shall be interesting."

He ambled away, voice raised in a bellow that summoned his fellow golans. Racharran turned back to Colun.

"Can your folk take the defenseless ones into the hills?" His voice was hoarse, his expression desperate. "Does Morrhyn not wake . . ."

"There's no point." Colun shook his head, his own face rueful. "We sealed our passages when we left."

Racharran said, "Even so."

Colun shook his head again. "The valleys are all sealed off, and nowhere else for so many. This Maker-cursed winter's not yet all gone up there, and you've not enough food for all of them. Also"—he turned to glance mournfully toward his lost mountains—"the Breakers have left their foul beasts roaming up there."

Racharran's hands stretched wide and closed into fists. Almost, he shouted curses at the Maker, at Morrhyn. Almost, but not quite: a spark of faith still burned. He opened his mouth to speak, but Colun forestalled him.

"There's no escaping into the hills. They'd die up there; better they die here. It should be easier."

"At the Breakers' hands?" Racharran stared at him, aghast. "Under the teeth of their beasts?"

"No." Colun took a deep breath; sighed. "Remember, I saw what the Breakers did to the Whaztaye. It should be better if the defenseless ones took their own lives. Better none live if the Breakers prevail."

That "if" sounded to Racharran most horribly like "when." He nodded. "Then so be it." He looked around, at the somber faces surrounding him. "We fight here. The Maker willing, we shall survive."

Softly, Yazte said, "The Maker grant Morrhyn wakes and fulfills that promise."

"The Maker grant." Racharran ducked his head in earnest agreement. "But meanwhile, best we ready for the worst."

They set to planning their defense, which did not take them long:

there was little enough to decide. Less, could Baran and his fellow Stone Shapers not block the entrance; and even if they did, it could still be only a matter of time before the Breakers climbed the hills.

Rannach faced Nemeth and Zeil and bowed his head, saying solemnly, "I'd ask your forgiveness."

Husband and wife exchanged a look, and Nemeth said, "For what?"

"For the unhappiness I've brought her."

"Unhappiness?" Nemeth frowned, gesturing to where Arrhyna sat, her belly larger now. "Our daughter is unhappy?"

"I am not," Arrhyna said.

Rannach said, "Had I not slain Vachyr, perhaps none of this would have happened."

"Ach!" Nemeth chopped air. "Vachyr *stole* your bride, our daughter." He shaped a sign of warding. "The Maker forgive me, but I was glad when I saw Vachyr's body across your saddle."

"Even so; Morrhyn has told me that sin was a part of what delivered this." His hand indicated the camp, all abustle with preparations for war.

Zeil said gently, "And also Morrhyn has said that he could not have survived the journey back without you."

"And that he believes the Maker must forgive you, no?" Nemeth said. "Then how shall we not?"

"Still, it seems that we all shall . . ." Rannach shrugged, glancing at his wife.

Arrhyna smiled calmly and ended the sentence for him: "Die?" She turned, still smiling, to her parents. "Sometimes my husband's faith wavers. He forgets Morrhyn's promise."

Rannach frowned. "Morrhyn lies adreaming." He sighed and took Arrhyna's hand. "Likely he'll be dreaming when the Breakers come."

Arrhyna said to her parents, "You see?" and set a hand on Rannach's cheek so that his face was turned toward her. "You must believe, my husband. You *must!*"

Rannach said, eyes wide and loving, "Do you? Truly?"

Confidently, she answered, "Yes."

He touched the hand that touched his cheek, and a darkness filled his eyes. "Even so—are you wrong, and I not with you . . ." His hand fell, a finger tapping the hilt of the small knife she wore.

She said, "It will not come to that. But should it, then I'd not live on without you."

.   .   .

"It can be done." Baran beamed as if proud of that knowledge. "I'd wondered if our magic would work here. But—yes: we can do it."

Racharran sighed and offered silent thanks to the Maker. That must buy them a little time at least.

The Stone Shaper perched himself like a hairy rock on the very edge of the pass, peering curiously up and down its length, with Colun squatting beside him. Racharran, none too easy so close to the drop, watched them.

"How much?" Baran asked. "We can seal it all now, or just the egress." He turned, grinning wickedly. "We might allow them entry and then bring down the stone. I should enjoy that."

Racharran looked past him to where the lodges covered the Meeting Ground. They could be struck in moments. The horses were already gathered into one great herd. The People knew what came against them, and the defenseless ones wore blades now. Warriors were chosen to dispatch those too infirm to slay themselves. They waited: for Morrhyn to wake or the Breakers come, none—even those strongest in their faith —any longer certain which should come first.

The sun shone bright, warmer than ever, and the Moon of the Turning Year would reach its fullness in two more nights.

And the Breakers be on them before then.

Morrhyn, he thought, wake up!

He looked to Yazte and Chakthi, who stood a little way back from the rim with Perico and Kanseah, and asked, "How think you? All now, or as they enter?"

Colun said, "Seal the farther end now. Let their vanguard enter this end, and then . . ." He clapped his hands.

Baran nodded enthusiastically.

Yazte said, "Our bowmen might wait here."

"And my Grannach," Colun added.

Racharran sought Chakthi's response: the Tachyn shrugged as if the decision were not his to make.

Kanseah said nervously, "Might it not be better to block all the pass?"

Colun grunted, twisting to eye the Naiche warrior. "They come in their thousands, no? Do they find a wall of stone before them, they'll halt and look to climb it. And that shall not take them long."

"And if it's done as you suggest?" Perico asked.

Colun smiled. "We slay no few of them on the first day, perhaps that shall give them pause." He rose, staring to where the Maker's Mountain shone in the sun, and gestured obeisance. "Perhaps pause enough that Morrhyn wakes."

Racharran said, "The Maker grant it be so."

Yazte said, "It might at least surprise them."

"And kill them," said Baran.

"Your way." Racharran touched the Stone Shaper on one broad shoulder. "With bowmen and Grannach stationed to the sides. Slay as many as you can; and when the rest attempt the climb, we'll be waiting."

The two Grannach exchanged a look of triumph and rose to their feet. Grinning, Colun said, "I told you these flatlanders would see sense."

Baran chuckled and cupped his hands about his mouth. A long, loud wailing rang out.

"What's that?" Racharran asked.

"The signal," Colun replied. "The magic's readied—now the walls go down."

"The People!" Racharran clutched the Grannach. "They'll not be harmed?"

"None, my word on it." Colun's smile spread like a crack splitting a rock. "My folk stand guard and hold yours back. We decided all this last night."

Racharran began to speak, but his words were lost under the thunder of breaking stone. Where the pass fed onto the Meeting Ground, the walls shifted, bulging outward as if the stone lost its solidity, becoming for a moment elastic. Then great shards and boulders fell away from the walls to tumble down in one great, rumbling descent. Dust filled the afternoon air, darkening the sky like the smoke of a forest fire, hiding the Meeting Ground awhile. The cliff shuddered under Racharran's feet and he sprang back, clear of the rim, where Colun and Baran stood grinning proudly. The others stood wide-eyed. Kanseah looked afraid, as if he doubted the safety of their position.

When the pall settled and the earth had ceased its trembling, Racharran saw the Meeting Ground was sealed off by a wall of jagged stone that stretched across the pass from rim to rim. A few last boulders still dropped, bouncing down the near-vertical face to shatter at the foot.

"That was well done!" Colun clapped an enthusiastic hand to Baran's shoulder. "The rest?"

"We'll work it now." Baran pointed along the rimrock, to where his fellow Stone Shapers came running. He smiled, the expression prompting Racharran to think of wolves. "When they come, it shall be to a Grannach welcome."

"We'll leave you to it, then." Colun beckoned the Matawaye away. "This is Stone Shaper work, and best left to them."

Racharran nodded. His ears still rang with echoes of the avalanche. This surely shall buy us time, he thought. But how much?

"When Baran and the others have set their spells, we'd best set our guards." Colun spoke as if toppling passes were an everyday event. "Meanwhile . . . has anyone a flask or two of tiswin?"

"You look weary." Lhyn's fingers were deft as they tied off her husband's braids. "Shall you rest now?"

"I am weary." Racharran flexed his shoulders, sighing. "I am weary to my soul. But no, not rest—there's no time. Do the Breakers move by night . . ."

"The guards are set, no?" Lhyn fastened silver brooches in his hair, pinning the warrior's braids. "Men watch, and the Stone Shapers are in place. What more can you do?"

"Be there; wait," he answered. "Pray."

"Wait here," she said. "Pray here. With me."

He smiled a slow, sad smile and took her in his arms, wondering all the while if it was for the last time. "I cannot," he said against her cheek. "Better the People see me; see all their akamans. We must go strutting about and pretend that all's well. Besides, I'd be there on the cliff if they come."

"Yes, I know." She kissed him. "I am selfish—I'd have you to myself this night."

He met her kiss and held her close a moment, then loosed his hold. "Have you any regrets?"

She smiled and stroked his cheek and shook her head. "None."

"Good; nor I." He reached for his weapons. "The Maker be with us all."

"He is." She rose with him, going to the lodgeflap. "Perhaps Morrhyn shall wake soon."

Racharran nodded and tried to smile. "Perhaps."

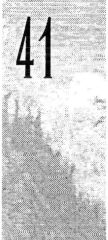

41 The Promise

Cloud scarred the moon's face and curtained the stars. A wind gusted chill along the clifftop, whispering mournfully. A dog barked, was answered, and then fell silent. The night was filled with a palpable tension, as if the darkness possessed its own weight and pressed down upon the watchers.

Out on the flat beyond the hills, fires burned, myriad points of light that stretched out and back in a great mass that moved inexorably forward, toward the Meeting Ground. It was as if, Racharran thought, some vast funereal procession came to the People. He looked to the right and left, checking the warriors and the Grannach he knew were in place. It was hard to wait: the People fought on horseback, swift; not like this, nor by night. He spat, and glanced westward, to where the Maker's Mountain stood. The peak was cloud-shrouded, only a dim bulk against the sky.

Morrhyn, wake!

He turned his face back to the plain. The lights were closer, massing until they seemed a solid line of fire, like a river of flame that ran in flood toward the pass. He checked his arrows, knowing they were sound: needing something to do. He glanced at his son. Rannach sat stroking a stone along the edges of his hatchet, his eyes fixed firm on the blade. To his other side, Colun squatted with Baran and three of the Grannach Stone Shapers. All carried battle-axes and wide knives; Colun was humming tunelessly. Spread out along the cliff's rim were some two hundred

Commacht, Perico with his Aparhaso warriors, and Kanseah with his
Naiche. Across the width of the gap, invisible in the cloudy night, Yazte
and his Lakanti waited with Chakthi and his Tachyn, four Stone Shapers
with them. More men waited behind: reinforcements. Kahteney and
Hadduth were amongst the lodges; and Morrhyn.

The fires came on: so fast. By the midpoint of the night they must
surely reach the pass. Racharran felt a terrible certainty the Breakers
would attack, not waiting for dawn but commencing their onslaught
immediately, like the dark, shadow creatures they were. He murmured a
prayer: that Morrhyn wake, and then that the People defeat these monstrous invaders. He asked the Maker's forgiveness of his doubt, and
prayed Lhyn die easily, and he with honor.

It was hard now to believe that any could survive.

He saw Rannach looking at him and smiled, wondering if the expression was truly as sour as it felt.

Rannach said, "Father, I'm sorry."

Racharran nodded, his smile warmed by that, and clasped his son's
shoulder. "And I. But that's in the past now, eh?"

Rannach ducked his head and touched his father's hand. Then his
face grew fierce and he indicated the waiting men, the cliff's scarp. "We
shall not die alone. They'll not easily take the Meeting Ground."

"No, not easily."

"Arrhyna believes Morrhyn will wake." Rannach's smile was both
tender and sad.

"Perhaps." Racharran shrugged. It was momentarily harder to hope.

The lights drew closer, bobbing and dancing through the expectant
night as if all the fireflies in the world had gathered, or a wall of scourg-
ing flame rushed at the People. Soon it was possible to see that each was
a torch held aloft by an individual rider. There were so many, Racharran
thought, so very many, and all with the single, awful purpose. His mouth
felt dry and he spat again; and wondered if he was afraid, or only sad
that soon the People should be slaughtered, and Ket-Ta-Witko lost to
them.

The wind got up and blew the cloud away to the east. The Moon of the
Turning Year emerged huge and bright, a single night from its full girth.
It lit the Maker's Mountain with a silver radiance, the pinnacle blazing
eerily above the lesser peaks. Stars pricked the sky; fewer, it seemed,
than the approaching torches.

Colun said, "Good. We can see them clearer now."

The great burning column slowed, bunching so that it became a single, vast mass. And still it moved forward, but now a group of riders came charging on ahead, almost to the ingress of the pass.

Men nocked arrows, and Racharran called softly, "Hold! Not yet! Wait on my word," hoping that Yazte and Chakthi gave the same command.

The breakers halted and he saw two dismount. Their torches burned atop long poles that they drove into the ground, one to either side of the pass like guiding beacons. Faces hid by garish helms stared at the opening, at the heights above, and then the Breakers swung back astride their weirdling mounts and with the others raced back to the main horde.

Now that the cloud was gone and the night was grown silvery, the watchers on the cliffs could see that each pole bore a crossbar, from which things were hung, swaying slowly, turning: heads.

From one pole, Juh and Hazhe gazed blindly toward the Meeting Ground; from the other, Tahdase and Isten fixed blank eyes on the pass.

Racharran heard Perico cry out softly, and when he looked in that direction, he saw Kanseah shape a sign of warding.

Then a single horn sounded and all the torches were doused.

By the moon's light the Breakers' bright armor glittered and shone ethereal, as if phantom rainbows spilled across the plain.

The horn sounded again and they charged.

Racharran heard Baran chuckle, and saw the stoneshaper begin to move his hands, chanting lowly.

The foremost Breakers entered the pass. Their beasts growled and snarled now, the sound like the rumble of falling stone or the grumbling of floodwater filling up the passage. Twenty abreast they came, racing their mounts onward, urging them to the slaughter, more than Racharran could count.

They filled the pass and he turned his head to where the Grannach's new-formed wall blocked the egress. He saw the vanguard haul their animals to a stop, the lion-beasts rearing, pawing the air, roaring their frustration. The riders struggled to turn them back, shouting to those who followed. But the beasts' howling dinned too loud and the press came on too eager, driving the forerunners up against the wall. The strangeling animals fought one another as they were forced together, rearing up to claw and bite their fellows, even the riders.

Then Baran's chanting, and that of his companion Stone Shapers, grew louder, rising to a guttural crescendo. And ceased.

It seemed then that the earth itself moved. Racharran felt himself lifted up and dropped as the pass caved in. The sound of it deafened him—not even the running buffalo herds made such a thunder. He saw the rimrock shudder and bulge, then fragment and topple down. Vast blocks of stone rained onto the Breakers, crushing riders and their mounts like bugs under the terrible fury of the Stone Shapers' magic. It was a brief vision, fragmented as the rock that rained down to fill the pass along all its length. And the sound lasted far longer, as if the stone bones of Ket-Ta-Witko roared in triumph. That seemed to echo off the sky itself, so that men covered their ears and flattened on the ground, awed by this demonstration of Grannach power. A cloud rose, hiding the stars and the moon, and small shards of rock exploded upward, as if the broken walls ground ever deeper onto their prey, expelling the lesser pieces.

Beyond the entrance to the pass, the horde halted as boulders tumbled outward, bouncing and rolling across the grass to claim more victims.

The poles that dangled the severed heads of Juh and Hazhe, Tahdase and Isten, were broken and buried, and where the pass had stood, there now existed only a barrier of stone. It blocked the ingress and its face was unsound, all filled with treacherously loose rock and spills of shale. Before it, spread in a wide fan, the ground was littered with boulders.

The dust cloud fell back and the thunder ground to a reluctant halt. Then the night filled with a new sound as the Breakers raised their heads and howled their anger. Their beasts roared as the advancing army pushed those closest to the wall against the tumbled rocks, and for a while confusion reigned.

Then the lone horn sounded and slowly order was imposed on the milling throng. The snarling, fighting creatures were forced to snapping obedience as the riders drew them back, regrouping. Once more they clustered in a solid mass and, by the light of the burgeoning moon, the watchers on the rimrock saw armored figures dismount, stripping their beasts of harness as others, carrying poles that ended in long spikes with recurved hooks, came forward. These wore night-black armor painted with sigils on chest and back that glowed the dull crimson of old, dried blood.

"We've fought these," Colun said. "They're beastmasters of some kind."

There was no need of further explanation: the jet-armored figures drove the beasts forward through the toppled boulders, goading the creatures to the wall, to the foot of the cliffs.

Like enormous cats, they began to scramble upward.

"Our work, this." Baran rose and shouted across the length of the new-formed wall. "Do you call your men back from the rim."

The Stone Shapers began their chanting again. Racharran watched the Breakers' beasts climb. Fifty of them, he guessed; less as some lost footing on the unsure rock and fell, yowling furiously, to the ground. Those limped and licked at hurts, and snarled irritably as the beastmasters drove them back to their task.

Fresh stone came loose from the wall and the cliffs' edges, and it seemed the rock shifted under the weight of the clambering creatures, no longer packed solid but become suddenly impermanent. The beasts screamed and fell, and from above them boulders tumbled, flinging them away or crushing them until none remained on the slopes.

Twice more the dark-armored beastmasters forced the surviving animals to attempt the climb; and twice more Baran and his fellows sent stone against them, thwarting the attempts.

The horn belled and the beastmasters fell back, bringing the animals with them. Only nine lived still, and they limped, favoring wounds.

"A lesson taught them, eh?" Colun's voice was triumphant. "I doubt they'll try that again."

"Likely not." Racharran smiled wearily. "But what shall come next?"

He realized the sky grew light. The moon was gone away to the west, and along the eastern horizon a band of brightness presaged the sun's rising. The disc came up red-golden as fire and sent long lances of brilliance across the plain. It shone bright on the Breakers' rainbow-hued armor and on the furred and scaled hides of their mounts. It seemed to Racharran they covered all the grass, and he knew they were not defeated; would not give up. He knew they must, sooner or later, overcome by sheer weight of numbers.

And tonight the Moon of the Turning Year would reach its full.

Morrhyn, wake!

For want of occupation, Lhyn spilled leaves into a pot and set the tea to brewing. Through the hides of the lodge she could hear the sounds of battle, distant but yet horribly clear. She wondered if Racharran lived— and Rannach—and prayed they did and were not wounded. She prayed that Morrhyn wake, and fought to still the doubting voice that whispered he would not, or if he did, it should be too late.

She looked at the sleeping man, his snowy hair spread loose on the furs, and saw him shift, turning this way and that, the lids of his closed eyes moving, twitching.

Kahteney said softly, "He dreams. Surely, he dreams."

Lhyn turned to the Lakanti wakanisha, but said nothing. There seemed nothing to say that had not already been spoken. Kahteney smiled wanly and shrugged.

Hadduth only sat, his lean-planed face unmoving as his dark eyes, which neither blinked nor shifted from Morrhyn's face.

Lhyn wished he were not there. No matter Chakthi's vow, no matter the Tachyn fought with the rest, she could not feel comfortable with Hadduth. There was something indefinable about the man, something secretive and hidden. She thought his eyes were bland and unyielding as a snake's.

Maker, she prayed, let him wake in time.

And stirred the tea and waited.

"We can do no more." Baran gestured angrily at the jagged rimrock. "Do we bring down more, there'll be no cliff left—only a slope they can climb."

Racharran nodded, accepting. The cliff's edge was no longer a regular line but all indented and broken where the Stone Shapers had sent it down onto the Breakers. The ground below was spread with rocks and shattered bodies, those of armored attackers and beasts alike. He nocked a shaft. Colun and his Grannach, warriors and Stone Shapers alike, drew heavy axes.

"We bowmen will look to shoot them as they climb." Racharran addressed the Grannach creddan. "Do you take those who reach the rim."

Colun smiled and Racharran called out the order to the Matawaye.

The sun stood high now, the sky all blue and cloudless, marked with the wheeling shapes of the crows and ravens that gathered in anticipation of carrion feast. At least, Racharran thought, we've the advantage of height. The Breakers' arrows fell short of the rimrock, and the breaking of the cliff edge crenellated the stone so that the warriors enjoyed some small measure of cover from which to fire their shafts.

Even so, he thought, it can be only a matter time.

At his side, Rannach tensed his bowstring and grinned. "This is a good day to die."

Racharran answered, "Yes," and wished they might live.

"They come again!"

Kanseah's shout brought him to the edge. More Breakers attempted the ascent. They seemed like brightly colored insects as they clambered upward, limber for all the weight of their armor. Racharran angled his bow and drew the string to his cheek, let fly, and saw his shaft pierce an armored shoulder. The Breaker slowed, a hand falling free of its hold, and Rannach's arrow drove down between pauldron and helmet. The Breaker jerked, arching back from the slope, and fell away. The body dropped and was trodden down as more rushed to the climb, careless of their dead. They seemed to Racharran not at all like men, but entirely insectile in their grim determination. He thought that did the warriors slay enough, the rest would likely use the bodies for a ramp and climb the cliff on a ladder of corpses. Save the Matawaye would run out of arrows before that, and it come to hand-to-hand fighting. He nocked a second shaft and took aim.

"Look! What do they do?"

Rannach pointed to where Breakers turned their weirdling beasts from the mass. Two groups there were, each of hundreds, riding off in opposite directions along the line of hills.

"They seek to flank us," Racharran answered grimly. "They look to find an undefended place to climb."

He turned, shouting for Colun, and indicated the departing Breakers.

"Leave them to us." Colun bellowed for Baran to join him. "We'll crush them like bugs."

He summoned his Grannach and sent a runner across the blockage of the pass to advise those on the farther side. Soon two parties of the Stone Folk went trotting to meet the flankers. Racharran sent a hundred warriors with each group.

And still the Breakers continued their assault.

"Shall we win?"

Arrhyna stroked absently at her rounded belly, staring toward the pass, her head cocked as she listened to the clamor.

"It's in the Maker's hands now." Marjia stroked a stone against the edges of a blade. "I pray he favors us, but . . ." She shrugged.

Arrhyna looked down at her, seeing a face so calm, it seemed carved of stone. "I'd know how Rannach fares," she said. "I'd go to him."

"No!" Marjia looked up from her sharpening. "That's warriors' work up there. And you've a child to think of."

"You fought." Arrhyna scowled her frustration. "You told me of the fighting in the caves."

"That was necessity." Marjia inspected the blade and found it satisfactory; sheathed it on her ample waist. "And do they get past the men, I'll fight them again. But they've not yet, and so we've hope still."

"Have we?" Arrhyna sighed and made herself settle beside the tranquil Grannach woman. "I told Rannach to have faith, but the moon shall be full this night. And Morrhyn said that was when . . ." She, in her turn, shrugged.

"Then there's still time, no?" Marjia took Arrhyna's hands. "Perhaps Morrhyn shall wake soon and show us the way."

Arrhyna clutched the comfort of the hard, warm hands and looked into Marjia's blue eyes. "Even does he," she said softly, ashamed her faith faltered, "how can so many escape? He spoke of a new land but, even does he wake, I cannot understand how we shall reach it."

"The ways of the Maker are mysterious," Marjia said. "And not always for us to comprehend. That's the duty of your wakanishas, no? Perhaps our duty is only to believe, to have faith even where it seems impossible hope can exist."

"Like here?" Arrhyna smiled sadly.

"Yes, like here." Marjia answered her smile with one more confident. "Now, do we prepare food? Our men will grow famished—fighting's hungry work."

Arrhyna nodded: better to work—to do what she could—than wonder if Rannach lived, or if at any moment Breakers should appear.

Motsos grunted as the arrow struck his shoulder, then cursed as his hand went numb and dropped his bow. The Maker-bedamned Breakers should not have the range—surely their bows could not flight shafts so far.

Unless . . .

He jumped back as a second arrow whistled past his head, and cursed again. Along the line he saw an Aparahso stagger, a bright yellow shaft protruding from his throat. Then a crimson shaft, and a black, sprouted from the man's chest and he fell down.

"Magic!" Motsos risked standing to shout his warning. "There's magic in their arrows!"

He heard his call taken up and passed along, and others scream out the same as they realized a new power was in play. He sat down and twisted his head to study the arrow thrusting from his shoulder. It was a pale blue, very much like the color of the sky, and as he grasped it, he wondered if the head was barbed.

When he tugged, he got his answer: yes. Fire ignited in his shoulder and he cursed some more and let go; drew his knife and gritted his teeth and set to cutting through the shaft. When he was done, his left arm hung useless by his side and he could no longer feel his fingers or move them: he hoped the head was not poisoned. He stretched on his belly and crawled back to the rim, intent on retrieving his bow. It was too good a weapon to leave—a full winter in the making; the work of a peaceful winter when the world turned as it should and Ket-Ta-Witko had been safe.

The bow was fallen into a gap made by the Grannach. Motsos bellied his way forward and reached out.

His fingers were closed tight on the bow when the arrow pierced his eye. His last thought was that now he would see Bylas and the others again.

"Get back!" Racharran took a fistful of his son's shirt and yanked Rannach from the cliff edge. "There's magic in their shafts!"

Rannach struggled free, his face dark with anger. "Then how can we fight them?" He nocked an arrow even as he spoke. "Must we stand back and let them climb?"

Racharran clasped his arm lest he go back. "We fire only from cover! Only from safety!"

"And grant them the rim?" Rannach shook his head, breaking free. "They'll be on us like ants over honey. They'll take the hills and enter the Meeting Ground."

"And swifter are we dead." Racharran moved in front of his son. "Listen! Use your bow—yes! But only from a safe place, eh?"

Rannach smiled sourly. "Where's safe here, father?"

"Use the broken stone." Racharran stepped aside and looked around. The cliff top was wide, and where it ran back toward the Meeting Ground there were stunted trees and scrubby bushes. The reinforcements waited there, watching the Breakers' bright arrows loft above the rim. He ran to them, thinking the Grannach's battle-axes should be useful now, and wondering how his allies fared.

His orders were swiftly issued and as swiftly obeyed: the waiting men were grateful for occupation and set to work eagerly.

Soon screens of bush and ramshackle bulwarks of felled timber were set along the rimrock. Little of it was sound enough to halt the bright shafts, but it provided some measure of cover for the People's bowmen. And Rannach was right: did the Breakers reach the rim, all was lost.

Racharran took up his own bow and found himself a place. The sun was warm on his back, and when he glanced up he saw the bright burning disc was gone past its zenith and moved toward the west. Soon the Moon of the Turning Year would climb above the eastern horizon, and then night fall.

He wondered how long that night might be.

He loosed an arrow and ducked as three shafts tore into the screen of bushes. They were so colorful, like the armor the Breakers wore. He thought of those he'd seen, and how beautiful they were, and wondered at that—for it seemed somehow an obscenity that people so handsome should be so evil.

He fired again and risked a downward observation, cursing aloud at what he saw.

Too many of the Matawaye were forced back from the rim, and the Breakers climbed easier now. More were on the scarp, moving inexorably upward, and soon it must surely come to hand-to-hand fighting. And then . . . Racharran cursed again, for then surely all was lost.

Save . . .

Morrhyn, wake up!

His mouth and throat were dry and his eyes awhile unfocused. He felt both horribly weary and invigorated, as if he returned from a long and arduous journey and must soon begin another. He groaned and pushed the furs away and felt hands on him, a wetness on his parched tongue.

He swallowed and groaned and forced his eyes to see.

Lhyn's face hovered above him and he smiled. She looked so lovely; and also afraid, as if hope tantalized her and she not quite dare believe it.

He said, "We shall be saved," and wondered if that was his voice croaking. He raised a trembling hand to the cup and drank again, and then spoke clearer, louder: "I've seen the way and we must be ready."

Lhyn smiled as Kahteney's face appeared above her shoulder. "How?" the Lakanti asked.

Morrhyn shook his head and said, "There's not the time for the telling; later."

Lhyn asked, "When?"

And he told her with absolute certainty, "When the Moon of the Turning Year shines on the Maker's Mountain."

Kahteney said, "That might not be soon enough."

Morrhyn frowned. "How so?" Then gasped. "How long have I dreamed?"

Lhyn said, "Days."

"The Breakers are come," Kahteney said. "They're beyond the hills now and coming up the cliffs. They've magic in their arrows and our warriors lose the advantage."

Morrhyn pushed the furs aside, careless of modesty. "What's the hour?"

Kahteney said, "Dusk. Soon the moon will light the Mountain."

Morrhyn looked about for clothing. "Then we've truly little time." He felt his heart race.

Even now, when the Maker had shown the fulfillment of his promise, there was still doubt, still that sharp knife edge of time to walk.

No, he told himself as he dragged on breeches, I cannot doubt now. I must not! He showed me the way—he would not be so cruel as to show me that and then take it away.

Through the folds of his shirt he heard Kahteney ask, "What shall we do?"

He answered as his head emerged: "Strike camp. Ready the People for departure. Send word to the warriors—tell them they must hold the Breakers awhile longer and then fall back as the moon lights the Mountain. They must be *here*"—he struck the ground in emphasis—"when the time comes; else they'll be left behind."

Hadduth spoke for the first time: "I'll take that word."

He rose on the saying and ducked through the lodgeflap and was gone before Morrhyn had further chance to speak.

Morrhyn grunted, tugging on his boots. Doubt's dog barked as the skin fell down on Hadduth's retreating back. He had sooner kept the Tachyn Dreamer with him, but it was too late now—he could only hope his fears not be realized.

Lhyn said, "Shall you eat something?" And he smiled at her and shook his head, saying, "I've not the time. Nor you—we must tell the People, that they be ready."

She nodded and he rose, hesitating a moment as his legs trembled and threatened to give way under him. Lhyn took his arm and he rested against her for a moment, and briefly thought of all the things that might have been and now never could. Then he stood erect and pushed the lodgeflap aside and went out onto the Meeting Ground.

Bats fluttered in the dying light, and already stars showed overhead. The moon hung massive above the hills, huge and bright and yellow, paling the fires that burned. There were folk outside, waiting, all their faces lit with expectation as he appeared; waiting for the Prophet whose word perhaps came too late.

He raised his arms, even though the only sounds were those of battle and the barking of excited dogs and the whickering of horses that wondered why they were not ridden in the fight.

He began to speak, telling them what they must do.

▪   ▪   ▪

"There are too many!" Colun rested panting on his grounded ax. The crescent head was bloodied and his shirt and breeches were all dark with gore. "The Maker damn them, but they forced us back!"

"The Stone Shapers?" Racharran asked.

"Did what they could." Colun wiped a hand through a beard all matted and bloody. "They sent the cliffs down, but still the cursed Breakers came. When Baran toppled stone on them, those still living rode farther along the foot, and we cannot match those beasts they ride for speed. They outdistanced us and found a place."

"They're on the rim?" Racharran peered into the darkening night. "How far away?"

"We slowed them somewhat." Colun smiled grimly. "The Stone Shapers cracked the hills—put a ravine between us and them they'll find hard to cross. But sooner or later they will; and the Shapers are exhausted. There's a limit to how much stone magic they can work before it drains them." He gestured to where Baran squatted. The golan sat with down-hung head, his shoulders heaving as he breathed.

Racharran mouthed a curse and asked, "How many?"

Colun answered, "Hundreds, and more coming. They bring their beasts up now."

"The Maker help us." Racharran sighed and clapped a hand to Colun's broad shoulder. "You did well, my friend, but now . . ."

"Save the Maker aid us, save Morrhyn deliver his promise . . ." Colun shrugged, glancing up to where the full moon climbed the sky. "We're lost."

Racharran cursed again, then shouted for Rannach.

When his son came, he said, "Listen, the Breakers are on the cliff, and before long . . ." He imparted Colun's news. Rannach scowled and asked, "What do we do?"

"You," Racharran said, "take our reinforcements and fall back on the Meeting Ground. Take Perico and Kanseah with you, them and their men."

"Perico's dead," Rannach said. "I saw him fall."

"The Maker accept his soul." Racharran took his son's hand. "You take the Aparhaso. Form a battle line around the Meeting Ground."

"I'd sooner stay here," Rannach said. "With you."

"No." Racharran smiled. "I need a man I can trust down there."

Obstinately, Rannach said, "Send Yazte. Or Chakthi."

Colun shook his head. "The Breakers will come from that direction too."

"The Lakanti and the Tachyn will hold that side," Racharran said, urgent now. "And I'll hold this with our Commacht."

"And we Grannach," Colun said.

"And the Grannach," Racharran allowed. "But I'd know the defenseless ones are warded. I charge you with this duty, Rannach. Do you hold the Meeting Ground secure."

For a moment it seemed Rannach would argue, but then he ducked his head and said, "As my akaman commands."

Racharran said, "As your father asks, eh?"

"Yes," Rannach said. "And you?"

"I'll hold here," Racharran said, "as long as we can. Then we'll fall back. The Meeting Ground shall be our last line of defense."

"Save," Colun said, "that Morrhyn wakes."

Racharran said, "Save that, yes."

Rannach only grunted and clutched his father's hand. Then he turned and ran to where the reinforcements waited, shouting for them to follow him.

"He grows up," Colun said.

"Yes." Racharran's smile grew melancholy. "But not likely to old age."

"Perhaps Morrhyn shall wake." Colun shrugged. "Even now."

"Perhaps." Racharran looked at the moon. Its light planed his face with shadows. "But he cuts it fine."

He nocked his last arrow and went stealthy to the rim, intent the shaft should count. The defenders ran short now, and even did they employ the Breakers' shafts, those were fashioned for longer bows and clumsy fired from the shorter Matawaye bows. Soon there would be no more arrows—nor Stone Shapers to send falling rock—and the Breakers would gain the rim and it come to close fighting.

Racharran tossed his bow behind him and did the only thing he could think of now, which was to shoulder loose the woody barricade and send it tumbling down the cliff. Then he moved back, drawing hatchet and knife, and waited for the first Breakers to surmount the rimrock.

Dohnse saw Hadduth crouch down at Chakthi's side, his mouth close against the akaman's ear. He wondered what news the wakanisha brought, and felt a sudden rush of hope when Chakthi's mouth stretched out in a smile and he nodded vigorously. Akaman and Dreamer clasped hands and then Hadduth went scuttling away, back toward the Meeting Ground. Chakthi, still beaming, beckoned Dohnse to him.

"Morrhyn has woken!" Chakthi's hand grabbed hard on Dohnse's wrist. "When the moon lights the Maker's Mountain, he says we shall be saved!"

"Praise the Maker!" Dohnse smiled: there *was* still hope. "Praise Morrhyn!"

"Yes, praise them both." Chakthi loosed his grip and pointed across the walled pass. "Go tell Racharran. He trusts you, no?"

Dohnse nodded. "I think he does. But what do I tell him?"

"That—" Chakthi paused a moment. He smiled still, and it seemed to Dohnse a smile of triumph, of promises met and prayers answered. Dohnse wondered why it made him think of bared fangs. "Tell him that we must hold the rimrock that long—until the moon lights the Maker's Mountain—and then fall back. It must be done swift—Morrhyn will see the defenseless ones safe through—" Chakthi paused again, as if gathering his thoughts. "I know not how, only that Hadduth told me Morrhyn knows the means, and we must hold until then. So—tell Racharran that I shall hold this side until then. And does he hold the other, all shall be well."

Dohnse nodded. Inside his head he voiced a prayer of thanks to the Maker, and to Morrhyn. Aloud, he asked, "And Yazte and his Lakanti; the Grannach?"

Chakthi's smile flattened. "I'll tell Yazte to take them back," he said. His smile widened again. "Tell Racharran I'd make good all our past differences. I'd earn back my honor: that I claim that right! Tell him we Tachyn shall hold this side alone—so that the Lakanti and the Grannach have a better chance at Morrhyn's promise. Now go!"

Dohnse said, "I'll come back to fight beside you."

Chakthi shrugged carelessly: "If you can. If not, go with the Commacht."

Dohnse nodded and ran to where the Commacht stood.

The Moon of the Turning Year climbed the sky. Morrhyn watched, unsure whether he willed it to rise faster or slower—to bring swifter the promise, or delay the departure that more might live. He knew it could not be long before the Breakers gained the hills and came down onto the Meeting Ground; he prayed there be enough time.

He clutched his furs closer as the night wind skirled sparks up from the fires and brought the sounds of combat to his ears. He wondered if he truly heard so clear, or if it was only imagination that belled out the roaring of the Breakers' weirdling beasts and the clatter of steel, the shouts and screams of dying men.

Around him in a wide, expectant mass, the People waited. The lodges were struck and packed, the horses eager, the dogs darting and barking, knowing some great movement was afoot. Children cried, unnerved by what they felt and could not understand.

Rannach and Kanseah and all their men stood in a wide ring about the Meeting Ground, and it seemed to Morrhyn that he could smell their anticipation like sweat on the wind.

The moon climbed up—so slowly. It lit the Meeting Ground and spread its light over the hills and slowly, slowly, carried that light toward the Maker's Mountain, which stood yet faint against the stars.

Lhyn touched his elbow and he smiled at her, seeing how the moonlight shone on her hair. Arrhyna was with her; and Marjia, with all the Grannach women and their rocky little children; and Nemeth and Ziel; and all their belongings with them, horses and dogs and loaded travois.

Waiting.

He prayed they all come safely through.

And watched the moon pursue its slow ascent and listened to the sounds of battle.

And the distant barking of doubt's dog, which—now, when all hung poised on the moment of the promise—he had no time to listen to.

"Tell Yazte to go." Racharran smiled gratefully at Dohnse. "Tell him to take his Lakanti and all the Grannach down. Does Chakthi wish to gain honor, then let him. Tell him I'll hold here as long as I can."

Dohnse said, "I'd stay with you."

Racharran clasped his hand. Said: "You honor me with that; but, no. Better you take back my word."

Dohnse said, "I'll take it and come back. Save you forbid me."

Racharran said, "I'll not forbid you. But why?"

Dohnse shrugged. "We'll not all leave this place, eh? I think that I shall likely die this night, and I'd sooner die amongst the Commacht than with Chakthi."

Racharran said, "As you wish. But listen—not all of us shall die, and do you live, you've a place amongst the Commacht. If you wish."

Dohnse said, "I do," and smiled and ran away, back to where Chakthi waited for his message.

The Breakers gained the cliff top now, and for every one that fell it seemed three more clambered over the rimrock.

They came relentless, careless of their own dead, and the defenders grew weary. Matawaye and Grannach fell, and still bright arrows flew, and the defenders of Ket-Ta-Witko fell back—and fell dead—and fought the invaders down every bloody footstep pacing out the invaders' advance toward the Meeting Ground.

Racharran's arms ached, his muscles throbbing as he wielded hatchet and knife against armor that deflected his blows, save when he chanced his life and went in close to strike where armor joined and left an opening through which he could drive a blade, or drive his hatchet down on helm or upswung, sword-bearing arm.

But he fought on—all the warriors fought on—even as the roaring of the Breakers' beasts came echoing down the night to tell him they'd crossed the Grannach's ravines to attack from the flanks and came down out of the hills to close around the Meeting Ground.

Colun fought beside him, and he knew the Grannach creddan wearied no less than he. It was odd to see a Grannach wearied, but Colun's ax swung slower and, more often than not, his blows failed to cut the rainbow armor that came flooding over the rimrock so that he must hack and pound, and grunt and gasp at the effort.

"Fall back!" Racharran shouted as best he could out of lungs all robbed of wind, and a throat parched dry. "Fall back to the Meeting Ground!"

His people needed not much urging: the Breakers supplied that goad, like a floodtide ramming against a fragile dam. Like some terrible, inexorable force that washed and ground down anything standing against it. Racharran ran with them, back from the cliff edge over which Breakers now clambered unhindered, away from the approaching roars of blood-hungry beasts.

He looked at Colun and said, "Go back. I'll hold them."

Colun said, "No! I'll die here with you."

"No!" He set his knife to the Grannach's chest. "You're creddan of all the Grannach now. Take your people to Morrhyn's promise! You owe them that! They'll need you, where you go."

Colun said, "And you? Shall the Commacht not need their akaman? Your People not need a leader?"

"Rannach is akaman now." Racharran pricked his knife harder against Colun's chest. "Tell the People that, eh? Tell my son; and tell Lhyn. But go! *Now!*"

Colun stared at him, ignoring the blade, and asked, "Is this truly your wish?"

Racharran said, "Yes! Now do you go, or shall it all be a waste? Look—you see the moon?"

Colun raised his eyes: the Moon of the Turning Year shone yellow above them. The disc stood high now and its light struck the Maker's Mountain bright as the sun at noon.

The snowcapped pinnacle glittered, shining pristine. It blazed under the moon's brilliance like a torch defying darkness. Its peak shone as white-hot against the Grannach's eyes as smelting metal, its flanks all lit like white bridal robes: all full of promise.

Racharran said, "Go!"

And Colun ducked his head and took his old friend's hand and said, "Yes, do you command it."

"I do. Take your people to safety; and can I not join you, watch over my people. Be the Stone Guardians again."

Colun said, "I will," and called his folk to him and led them toward the Meeting Ground and the promise.

42 Exodus and Betrayal

Morrhyn raised his arms, wide spread, as if he'd embrace the moonlit Mountain. Limned bright now by the Moon of the Turning Year, the pinnacle appeared larger than ever, rising vast and majestic against the sky. It seemed to swell, inflated and enlarged by the moon, climbing the night so that its bulk hid the stars and all the surrounding hills. It seemed that only the Mountain and the moon existed, twin promises of escape, of refuge and salvation. And between those enormities, under them as if quelled by their majesty, there was silence. The light that descended from above and which reflected off the Mountain seemed to leach out all sound. The clamor of the battle faded and the animals fell silent, and none of the waiting People spoke.

Morrhyn began to chant, soft at first but then louder, his voice rising in a shout that echoed over the Meeting Ground, and all the People took it up and raised their voices in unison, in prayer to the Maker that he grant his promise and take them away.

Then it seemed white fire burned about the peak, as if the eternal snow ignited and blazed, a beacon so bright that even the moon was dulled beneath its radiance. Morrhyn fell silent, and the People with him, as if that enormous light stole their voices. But none took their eyes from the Mountain, even as tears formed and it seemed they must be blinded.

So all saw the beacon swell and from it come a great arcing ray of brilliance that fell on the Meeting Ground and all the people there. Shadows flung long, and men and women clutched one another in hope and fear. It was if a gate opened where no gate could be, nor any opening that men understood, for it was an opening in the very fabric of existence, as if within the light the air itself was rent, exposing a wide hole—at first black within the radiance, but then clearer, so that through it they saw . . .

. . . Another land: a new and promised land where mountains rose under a sky of pure blue and the grass stretched out lush, and clean rivers ran. It was at first as if the gate afforded such a view as an eagle might own, high and wide. But then that vista hurtled closer, as if the eagle stooped, and through the gate they saw the grass as if it were but a few short steps away, and they needed only pace out that distance to be there.

None moved. The light burned from off the Maker's Mountain, and at the center of the Meeting Ground the gate stood, white light arching over the earth of Ket-Ta-Witko, over the soil of the new land beyond.

Sound returned: the dreadful roaring of the Breakers' beasts and the clatter of steel, the shouts and screams that spoke of dying.

Morrhyn shouted, "Go! Go through!"

But still none moved, only stood awed.

Morrhyn took Lhyn's shoulder and pushed her forward. "Go!"

She shook her head.

"The Maker fulfills his promise!" He shouted into her face. "Shall you ignore it now?"

Again she shook her head and softly said, "Let yours be the first foot to tread that place."

"I cannot." He let go her shoulder. "I must wait here for the last to come."

She said, "Then I'll wait with you."

He looked to Arrhyna, but she in turn shook her head and said, "I go with Rannach."

He turned about. All around, faces paled and stark in the brilliance stared at the gate. A horse stamped and whickered as if impatient with the awestruck People. Almost, Morrhyn cursed them for their reticence, fearing their reverence should delay them and even now see them fall victim to the approaching Breakers.

He turned to Kahteney. "Shall you be the first, brother?"

Kahteney smiled and shook his head. "I wait for Yazte."

Hadduth stood watching and Morrhyn turned to him. He'd sooner not see the Tachyn Dreamer be the first, but someone had to take that step and he knew it could not be he. He did not understand how he knew, but still the knowledge was there: he must wait until the last moment, else the gate close. He gestured to Hadduth.

"No." Hadduth stood rigid, his eyes dark pools that held no expression. "I am not worthy."

"In the Maker's name, what is that?" Morrhyn turned as Yazte came puffing up, his battle-bloodied Lakanti with him.

"The new land." Morrhyn clasped the akaman's wrist. It was slick with blood. "The Maker opens the way for us. Shall you lead the People through?"

Yazte frowned. "That's surely your honor. Or Racharran's. Save . . ."

Lhyn saw his expression and asked, "Where is he?"

"Holding the line." Yazte gestured with a hatchet whose blade was all stained dark. "Falling back. Chakthi fights with him."

Morrhyn pointed at the gate and the Lakanti shook his head. "Let the defenseless ones go through. I'll wait here until they're safe; wait for Racharran."

High across the night the gate burned white. Through it the grass shifted, rustling softly as wind rippled the luxuriant growth. Morrhyn groaned—this was unexpected agony, that the Maker open the way and the People prevaricate.

Then Colun came trotting at the head of his Grannach. He stared at the gate, and then at Morrhyn.

"Why do you wait?"

"I must," Morrhyn said. "And the rest . . . afraid, I think. None will take the first step."

Colun frowned and muttered, "Flatlanders!" Then shouted: "Marjia?"

His wife came forward. In the gate's light her yellow hair was silver. Colun said, "Our possessions?" and she turned slightly that he might see the bundle she carried, which was all they had brought out of their hills.

Colun looked at Morrhyn, a question in his deepset eyes.

Morrhyn nodded and said, "Do you go through, then?"

"Is this your wish?" Colun asked.

"Do you go through, then perhaps the rest shall follow." Morrhyn smiled. "And it seems fitting the Stone Folk be the first, no?"

"First or last." Colun peered through the gate. "Save someone goes it would seem you flatlanders shall stand gawping until the Breakers come. So . . ." He hefted his ax. "Grannach, to me! We go to a new land, praise the Maker."

He took Marjia's hand and walked into the gate, his Grannach behind.

For an instant their shapes wavered, like figures blurred in heat haze. Then they were solid again, walking out onto grass that crushed beneath their feet, staring around with growing smiles, their eyes wide with wonder and delight.

When all the Grannach were through, Colun looked back and shouted, "Can you hear me?"

His voice came as if from afar, but nonetheless clear. Morrhyn called back, "Yes. What do you see?"

"A fine new land." Colun swept his ax out in a wide gesture. "A land like Ket-Ta-Witko must have been when first the Maker birthed us. There are mountains over there."

Morrhyn could not see where he pointed. The arch of the gate allowed only a limited view, as if a lodgeflap were raised on a new morning, on a new world.

"So?" Colun bellowed. "Do you flatlanders come on? Or shall you deny the Maker's gift?"

Morrhyn turned again to Yazte. "Go through. Lead the People to salvation."

Yazte hesitated and said, "Racharran?"

Morrhyn said, "I'll wait for him. But you—for the Maker's sake, for his love!—take them through!"

Yazte puffed out his plump cheeks and shrugged. Then he beckoned Roza to him and raised his hatchet. "Bring up the horses!" His voice was a roar. "We go to find Morrhyn's promised land! Ware, Colun —the horses come!"

The Grannach scattered as the Lakanti drove the horses through. The herds were gathered together, and the animals of the Commacht and the Aparhaso and the Naiche and the Tachyn went with those of the Lakanti in a great running mass that spread out across the sunlit prairie, galloping as if glad to be free of the Breakers' threat, charging with tossing heads and a great thunderous pounding of hooves to where a river curved blue across the green. Yazte raised his eyes to where the Maker's Mountain shone in the night and made gesture of obeisance, then walked under the white-blazing arch with Roza at his side and Kahteney close behind, and all his warriors and their women and children and dogs following.

It was as if his safe passing shattered the People's fear: they surged forward, vying now to pass under the arch of the gate and find salvation.

For a while all was tumult. Dogs barked joyfully and children, woken from restive sleep, began to howl. Morrhyn watched them go, and gave thanks to the Maker for this great and impossible gift.

The Meeting Ground emptied. He looked about and saw Lhyn and

Arrhyna, only; waiting still. He supposed Hadduth must have gone with the rest.

He said, "You can do nothing here. Go through."

They hesitated, watching his face.

He said, "The rest will come soon. Rannach and Racharran with them, the Maker willing."

Lhyn said, "And if they are not?"

He smiled tentatively. "I'll wait for them. But you must go through. What point to delay? Better you go set up the lodges, eh? They'll be hungry when they come."

Still they hesitated, and he said: "The Maker opens us a way, but there's not so much time. This gate must close, lest the Breakers follow us."

Lhyn said, "And does it close before they come? What if Racharran and Rannach are trapped here?"

He looked into her frightened eyes and said, "Shall you deny the Maker, then? Shall it all be for nothing? All Racharran's done; and Rannach? Think you they'd want you to wait and risk your lives? I tell you—no! Better you be safe and they not have that concern, eh?"

She stared at him, unmoving.

"When they come," he said, "it shall be swift. I'll see them through —my word on that. You go, and await them there."

He stabbed a finger at the gate, where laughing Matawaye and Grannach raised their faces to a blue and sun-bright sky. Some knelt to kiss the ground; some went to free horses of the travois; others set to capturing the loose animals.

He said, "Do you love them, go!"

Arrhyna glanced at Lhyn. The older woman looked past Morrhyn to the hills surrounding the Meeting Ground. Behind the radiance of the Maker's Mountain and the bright brilliance of the burning gate, the hills were indistinct. But the wind carried the sounds of fighting now. Morrhyn took Lhyn's arm and turned her away from that: turned her toward the promise. She struggled against his grip and he thought how much he loved her; and took her other arm and pushed her bodily toward the gate.

He said, "You'll not die."

And shoved her through.

She cried out, tottering and falling onto her back on soft green grass. For a moment she stared indignantly. Morrhyn turned away and took Arrhyna's hand and led her to the opening. She looked at him a moment and said, "Send Rannach safe through, eh?" And he ducked his head and loosed her hand and watched as she stepped under the arch into the new land.

Then he looked away, narrowing his eyes against the brightness, and waited for the rest, praying they come timely.

The Breakers owned the hills now.

They came up over the rimrock in a kaleidoscope flood. And out of the deeper hills spreading back around the Meeting Ground, they came with a wave of their beasts driven before them by the beastmasters, the bright-armored warriors behind. The fangs and claws and hides of the beasts were stained with the blood of the defenders, and the swords and pikes and spears the Breakers wielded shone no cleaner under the moon.

Rannach withdrew: he had no other choice—save to die—and runners had brought word the promised exodus was begun.

He could see the Maker's Mountain shining godly against the sky, and the great lance of light it sent down onto the Meeting Ground. It seemed a vast white bonfire burned there, lofting up from where once the Council fires had burned and he been judged and exiled. It seemed the People walked into that fire and did not emerge. Gone to Morrhyn's promised land, he supposed. And wondered if he should find that place, or die in Ket-Ta-Witko.

Were he not wed, he thought he would choose that latter: it was a sorry thing to give up the land to the Breakers.

But he was, and Arrhyna carried his child, and that imposed on him another duty. So he gave up notions of honorable death and its consequent atonement for his sins and shouted that all fall back on the Meeting Ground, on the light that burned there and the white arch that blazed and swallowed the People into the Maker's promise.

"So, brother, we fight together at last."

Chakthi wiped a bloodied knife against his breeches and smiled at Racharran.

The Commacht akaman smiled back. "In defense of Ket-Ta-Witko, brother. Is this not better?"

The Maker's burning promise set shadows about Chakthi's eyes and whitened his smiling teeth like a wolf's fangs. He nodded, then shouted, "Ware, brother!"

A Breaker, armor red as fresh-spilled blood, charged from the bushes. Racharran ducked under the sweeping sword and swung his hatchet against the plated belly. The Breaker grunted and bent, and Chakthi darted in to thrust his knife through the divide of helmet and neckguard. The Breaker gasped. Racharran struck again with his hatchet and the red armor darkened as blood spilled out.

"And we fight well, eh?" Chakthi worked his blade in again and the Breaker stilled.

Racharran said, "We do. But"— he gestured at the undergrowth— "best we fall back, eh?"

"As you command," Chakthi said.

The bushes swayed as bodies armored, and bodies furred and scaled, pushed through. Down the steep slopes of the hills lay corpses: more of the People than the Breakers. Racharran shouted the order and the defenders withdrew.

Dohnse spat, thinking that his mouth was surely too dry to form saliva, and wished they might just turn and run for the promise blazing at the center of the Meeting Ground. But he had sworn allegiance to Racharran and could not, now, quit the akaman. Nor, was he honest, would he: not until all the People were gone safe to the new land Morrhyn promised. It seemed only right he be amongst the last, and hoped he might be.

Nor could he, even now, forget those looks Chakthi had exchanged with Hadduth, or the doubt he had expressed to Racharran. He hoped —prayed, even—he was wrong, but he could not forget; or quite trust Chakthi.

He clutched his hatchet and the pike he'd taken from a slain Breaker, and moved back toward the tempting light of the Meeting Ground.

Rannach brought his men onto the trampled grass and ringed them around the gate.

It was strange, that blazing white archway, that from one side looked onto springtime plains lit by a friendly yellow sun, and from the other was only a white flickering in the noisy night, as if the moon were reflected off water. Through the one side he could see Arrhyna and Lhyn staring hopefully back at him; and Yazte and Colun, and the People already gone through. He smiled at his wife and his mother and waited for his father.

Morrhyn said, "They come! Look!"

The wakanisha pointed across the Meeting Ground, and Rannach saw the last of the warriors come spilling down from the foothills. Racharran and Chakthi spurred them on, the last of the last, shouting for the men to group on the gate.

He gripped his weapons tighter then, for close behind came beasts and Breakers, rushing down the slopes swift as charging buffalo, or avalanches in winter. He shouted encouragement and wished his arrows were not all spent, or that all the horses had not gone through the gate, that he might charge to the attack.

But he could not—only hold and wait and pray.

Morrhyn said, "Go through!" and Rannach shook his head.

"Now!" Morrhyn grasped his shoulder, propelling him toward the gate. "You've a wife waiting for you there, and a child to be born. The first in the new land! Go!"

Rannach said, "My father . . ."

"Comes!" Morrhyn thrust a hand to where Racharran ran for the gate. "See? Now go! Call up your men and take them through."

Rannach looked into the Dreamer's blue stare and opened his mouth to argue. Morrhyn set a finger on his lips and said, "The People shall need leaders in the new land, and you shall be one. Now go, for the Maker's sake!"

Rannach wiped his mouth, stared toward where his father came, and said, "What of you?"

"The gate closes after me." Morrhyn's face was urgent as his voice. "I'll see them safely through and none of the Breakers."

Rannach nodded and turned toward the gate. Arrhyna stood there, beckoning. He shouted for his men to join him and pointed at the arch.

"Go through! Now!"

They went and he clasped Morrhyn's hand. "Your word my father shall be safe?"

"The Maker willing." Morrhyn nodded.

Rannach looked a last time to the running figures and then flung himself through the gate. Arrhyna came into his arms, careless of the blood that decorated his shirt and breeches, his skin, and she held him close. Lhyn touched his arm and stared back through the opening of reality's fabric. He put an arm around his mother's shoulders, and all three watched what they could of Ket-Ta-Witko's final drama.

It was flight only now, and what defense they put up desperate and running. Ket-Ta-Witko was lost to them, but the new land waited beyond the gate. It was the promise of the lodgefire's warmth on a winter night when the wind howled and flung blizzards at the wanderer, save the blizzard was the Breakers and the howling that of their beasts. It was the log a drowning man clutches in the flood, save that log burned white and was a gift to all, and the flood was rainbow-armored and furred and fanged and scaled and clawed. They ran, spurred on by Morrhyn's shouts to efforts greater than seemed possible, when limbs wearied and ached from the fighting and breath came short. Commacht held up limping Tachyn, and Tachyn with streaming wounds supported injured Commacht. There was but the one shared purpose: to reach the gate.

None hesitated—only went through as Morrhyn pointed the way and fell thankful into the arms of loved ones and brothers, or simply collapsed onto the grass and wept thanks to the Maker and his Prophet.

Racharran and Chakthi were the last. Them and Dohnse, so that in the confusion he was the only one to see what happened.

They all bore wounds. The pike Dohnse had taken he used as a staff: his breeches hung tattered about his left leg, where claws had scored deep lines that filled his boot with blood, and the sword cut across his shoulder and chest burned like fire. Chakthi's face was blood-masked and he limped on a cut leg. Racharran supported him, for all the Commacht akaman was in no better condition. His shirt was severed crossways over his ribs and flesh flapped loose there, his right arm leaving a trail of droplets, and one eye was swollen shut, blood coursing from the cut to paint his cheek.

The Commacht akaman glanced around, scanning the slopes as best he could to be sure none were left behind.

Chakthi said, "Come, brother, we're the last."

Racharran said, "You're sure?"

"Yes! There are no more left alive."

Racharran turned his damaged face to Dohnse and asked him the same question, and Dohnse nodded and said, "I see no others."

Morrhyn shouted that they come and Racharran turned his head one last time to peer all bloody at the hills. "Then best we go, eh?"

They began to run as best they could toward the light of the promise. Racharran held Chakthi up; Dohnse came after, casting swift glances back over his shoulder.

He saw the first of the great lionbeasts come snarling down through the trees and bushes that footed the hills and shouted a warning. Racharran grunted and forced his legs to faster pace, holding Chakthi's left arm across his shoulders, his right supportive around the Tachyn's waist. Chakthi hobbled beside; Dohnse brought up the rear.

He saw the weirdling beast come charging over the open ground and shouted, "Go on! I'll take it!"

The creature ran slavering and snarling at them, and he marveled at how large it was—big as a horse—and took the pike and grounded the butt, shouting his defiance.

The beast saw him and its jaws gaped wide, all filled with knifeblade teeth, and he knelt, groaning as his wounded leg blazed pain, and held the pike firm.

The beast roared and sprang. Dohnse watched stark-eyed as it rose up against the light the moon and the Mountain threw across the Meeting Ground, and saw it fill the sky.

He rolled aside as it came down on him; down onto the blade of the pike, which pierced its chest and drove through its ribs under the beast's own weight and came out from its back.

Wincing, he clambered upright, clutching his hatchet. The beast curled about the pike, snapping at the shaft, legs clawing. Blood stained its hide black under the brilliance of the Maker's Mountain and the burning moon. Dohnse turned and stumbled after Racharran and Chakthi.

And thus saw.

Morrhyn waited by the white arch that rose above the center of the Meeting Ground. Racharran carried Chakthi toward him.

The Prophet turned as if answering some shout from beyond the gate.

And Chakthi drew a knife and stabbed Racharran.

The Commacht akaman jerked upright. His arms let go of Chakthi and he staggered a little way aside. He stared at the Tachyn he had called his brother out of eyes that opened wide in pain and disbelief. Dohnse saw his mouth move but could not hear what he said because the moonlit night was too loud with roaring and the shouts of the Breakers. But he saw Racharran clutch the blade protruding from his ribs and pull it loose, and then fall onto his knees with blood coming out his mouth. And Chakthi laugh and—limping no longer—kick Racharran in the chest. Then resuming his limp, go to the gate and speak a moment with Morrhyn before going through.

Dohnse went to where Racharran lay.

He cradled Racharran's head, staring aghast at eyes that had already lost their light and dulled. Racharran coughed, barking gouts of red and pink-stained bubbles out of a mouth that stretched back from his teeth, which chattered even as his legs kicked and drummed against the ground of Ket-Ta-Witko. His body stiffened in Dohnse's arms, arching up, spine curved so that only his heels and shoulders touched the soil. Then all his body went limp and he loosed one last shuddering sigh that whistled into Dohnse's face. And he was dead.

"Dohnse!" Morrhyn's voice seemed to come from a long way off. "Dohnse, come! Hurry!"

He closed Racharran's dully staring eyes and took up his hatchet.

"Dohnse! Now!"

He rose, shaky on his hurt leg: worse for what he had witnessed. And thought to pick up Racharran's body and carry it to the new land. But beasts and Breakers came over the Meeting Ground like a flood, like a blizzard, and Morrhyn shouted at him to come. And so he only made Racharran a promise and turned away.

And went through the gate.

It was warm there—as it should be in the Moon of the Turning Year —and he smelled the sweet scent of the grass and felt the wind on his face, and saw all the People gathered in a great wondering mass. And looked back at the arch of white light that rose over the prairie and saw Morrhyn step through.

The gate closed behind the Prophet.

He came through with beasts and Breakers howling on his heels, and the gate closed.

It was like the snuffing of an ember. There was an arch of brightness that rose over the grass, white as moon-washed snow against the sky's blue, and through it could be seen Ket-Ta-Witko's night, lit by the Moon of the Turning Year, and the invaders charging, hungry to gain entry.

And then there was nothing. Morrhyn stepped through and the gate ceased to exist.

Past where it had stood, the grass ran out wide and wind-ruffled. A river turned and twisted lazy blue under the sun. In the distance mountains bulked shadow across the horizon. Birds sang and insects buzzed.

Dohnse stood, favoring his wounded leg, and saw Chakthi deep in conversation with Hadduth. Rannach sat with his arms around Arrhyna. Lhyn stared at the gate, her face stricken, tears coursing unheeded down her cheeks.

Dohnse turned to Morrhyn and said, "There's a thing I must tell you. About Racharran's murder."

43 New Land: New Judgments

"He lies! The Maker damn his soul—he lies!"

Chakthi turned like a cornered wolverine, spinning and spitting at the faces surrounding him. Night was fallen over the new land, and the fires of a new Council painted his lupine features red and shadowed, as if indignation and guilt played there in equal measure.

The light of a moon akin to that of the Moon of the Turning Year hung westward in the sky, not far off its setting. It joined the fires' light to decorate the faces of the watchers judgmental. They sat—Rannach and Morrhyn, Yazte and Kahteney, Colun, Kanseah; Hadduth: all those vested with the authority of Ket-Ta-Witko—alert and listening. Past them, the People; hushed and waiting.

Chakthi stabbed a finger in Dohnse's direction and said again, "He lies!"

Morrhyn raised his face to the moon. It shone so bright, so new and fresh—a welcome to this new land. He sighed, wishing such doubts had been left behind.

And wondered if the barking he heard was doubt's black dog mocking him or only one from the vast encampment shouting its joy to be safe. He looked to Dohnse and gestured for the Tachyn warrior to speak.

Dohnse said, "I do not lie. I saw what I saw—Chakthi took out his knife and put it between Racharran's ribs."

"Liar!"

Chakthi spat at Dohnse.

Dohnse said, "I do not lie; you lie. I'll fight you to prove the truth."

"No!" Morrhyn raised his hand. "We came to this new land to escape bloodshed. Now shall we begin our life here by spilling blood?"

They looked to him: he was the Prophet now, undoubted. His word was law. He looked to where Lhyn sat and saw the trails of tears down her cheeks. He felt a terrible sadness, and wondered what he should say, knowing it would be accepted.

Kahteney voiced it: "How do you judge, Morrhyn?"

He sighed: the weight was not gone, even here. He looked at Rannach and saw anger stretching the younger man's features tight. He thought it all began again—the enmity and the killing—and that perhaps it was such emotion that had opened the ways between the worlds for the Breakers to come through and slake their thirst for conquest and destruction. The breaking of the Ahsa-tye-Patiko had, he knew, brought them to Ket-Ta-Witko. Now was it to begin again, as if the People left behind them guilt's spoor to be followed by the destroyers of worlds?

He voiced a silent prayer to the Maker and said, "I shall sleep on it. The Maker willing, I'll dream of the answer."

Dohnse stared at Chakthi and then at Morrhyn and said, "Racharran promised me a place amongst the Commacht. I'd have that, be it your will."

Morrhyn shrugged and looked at Rannach. "You're akaman of the Commacht now—how say you?"

Rannach said, "I'd honor my father's promise. Nor"—he stared at Chakthi—"do I doubt what Dohnse says."

Chakthi glowered, his eyes lit red and savage as any wolverine's. Morrhyn watched him and heard the dog bark louder. Over and over, he thought, like dirt thrown up from the hooves of a running horse. Can we not put this aside?

But Racharran had been his friend and Lhyn sat silently weeping, and he knew he must decide. He prayed the Maker give him answer and said, "Let the akaman of the Commacht choose whether or not he accept Dohnse amongst us."

Rannach said, "He's welcome."

Dohnse smiled his gratitude and Morrhyn said, "For the rest, I'll give my answer in the morning. Now do we give thanks to the Maker for this new land?"

The dream was very clear, showing him precisely what he must say. But even so, behind it—like shadows thrown by bright fire—there was an element of doubt, as if what was just and right hung balanced by darker emotions, retribution and revenge to be later delivered.

But he knew what he must say, and went out from his lodge to the waiting People.

They gathered in nervous silence—all save the worst hurt and the youngest—their joy in the new land tainted with doubt and suspicion. It was, in a way, the first Matakwa in this new and unnamed place, and it seemed to Morrhyn not so different from that last in lost Ket-Ta-Witko.

He walked into the circle and said, "I have dreamed," and turned his face to Chakthi. "Do you speak of what happened?"

Chakthi glanced sidelong at Hadduth and rose. His wounds were cleansed and sewn, the stitched cuts lending him a ferocious aspect. He said, "I fought to the last beside Racharran and we came together to the gate. We both were wounded, and my brother held me up—he was a brave man and a great warrior."

There came a murmur of approval at that, loudest from those Tachyn still loyal to their akaman. Chakthi paused, favoring his hurt leg, rubbing as if absently at the wound.

Morrhyn said, "Go on." His voice was impassive, expressing nothing.

Chakthi nodded and said, "The Breakers and their beasts came close on our heels. I felt my brother Racharran falter . . ." His voice trailed off and he closed his eyes a moment, as if pained by the memory. "I tried to hold him, but I lacked the strength. I saw an arrow in him—a Breaker's shaft—and he said to me, 'I am slain, brother. Go on.' I did my best to bring him to the gate, but the life went out of him fast and I could not—I could only leave him, and ask the Maker accept his soul." Slowly he turned around, his eyes roving the circle as if defying any there to contradict him, falling finally on Dohnse. "And does any here say different, they lie."

A murmuring then, soon swallowed by silence. The morning sun shone warm on green grass that whispered a faint song under the wind's gentle caress. Crickets chattered and high overhead a hawk hung black against the cloudless sky.

Faces turned expectant to Morrhyn. Rannach whispered, "Do you deliver judgment?"

Morrhyn whispered back, "That is not my place. I am not akaman of the Commacht, but only wakanisha."

Rannach said, "You're the Prophet," in a puzzled voice.

Morrhyn motioned him to silence and said, "This tale has another shape and we should hear that. Dohnse, do you speak?"

He stared fixedly at Chakthi, but the Tachyn akaman ignored his blue gaze, seating himself and whispering with Hadduth. Dohnse rose.

He clutched a pole, resting his weight on the stick for fear he collapse. For all his leg was sewn and bound, it still throbbed as if a fire burned where the claws had scored him. He cleared his throat and said, "I was with them—Racharran and Chakthi—and we were the last. A beast came after us and I slew it, and when I rose I saw Chakthi take out a knife and drive it between Racharran's ribs. Then he kicked Racharran and went on through the gate."

Chakthi shouted, "Liar! Who else saw this?"

Dohnse shrugged and said, "None, I think."

Chakthi smiled and said, "Where was Morrhyn, then? He waited by the gate, no? But he saw nothing."

Dohnse said, "Morrhyn was turned away. He spoke through the gate and did not see what you did. But I saw it."

Chakthi curled his lip and spat.

Morrhyn said carefully, his eyes again firm on Chakthi, "So this tale has two tellings; and very different. Which do we believe?"

Chakthi said, "I am akaman of the Tachyn and this man only a warrior."

Morrhyn said, "Does that make his word any less?"

"Than mine?" Chakthi nodded. "Yes."

"Akaman or warrior," Morrhyn said, "still the Maker judges. And on his scales, all are equal." Still he locked his eyes on Chakthi. "Have you aught else to say?"

Hadduth whispered into the akaman's ear and Chakthi shook his head.

Yazte said, "Morrhyn, you are the Prophet. You brought us here, and you say you've dreamed. Then do you tell us your dream? What *is* the truth here?"

Morrhyn sighed and looked at the hawk. The bird still rode the wind, lofty and arrogant in its freedom. He thought perhaps he had none any longer, but only duty, which was a hard burden. It would be easy to speak of the dream and deliver judgment: the Maker had shown him what had happened; and what should happen did he take the role of decider. He could make it easy for the People—shout out the truth and order sentence. But then he would be forever the Prophet, and they always look to him for answers when those solutions were better found in their own minds, their own spirits. The Maker offered hope—their presence in this new land was proof enough of that—but also he looked to men to do right of their own volition, not be only guided like herded horses.

So he said, "The truth? The truth is what Dohnse tells us, that Chakthi slew Racharran."

Noise then: a great shouting. Knives appeared, bright in the sun. Colun was on his feet, a hand extended in angry accusation, his voice roaring for sentence of death. Morrhyn saw Lhyn staring at the Tachyn, her eyes spilling out tears and her lips writhing back from her teeth. Yazte rose ponderous, hand on his belt knife. Rannach remained seated —which allowed Morrhyn some measure of hope—but his face was dark with rage and disgust.

Morrhyn climbed upright and raised his arms: silence fell—he was the Prophet.

"We are come to a new land," he said, "which is a gift of the Maker, when else we might have died. But it seems we bring with us all the troubles of Ket-Ta-Witko. Do you all think about that? Think about how much this Council is like the last Matakwa, when that which drove us from our homeland began."

Yazte said, "Tell us what to do."

Morrhyn shook his head. "No. That is not for me to decide."

Yazte opened his mouth to speak again, but Kahteney took his arm and spoke to him, and the Lakanti chieftain shrugged and scowled, and fell quiet.

Rannach asked, "Then who? Who decides if not you?"

Morrhyn looked at the young man and said, "You."

It hung on this, precarious as an egg balanced on a knife's blade, delicate and deadly as that hawk riding the unseen currents of the sky. The dream—the Maker—had shown him that: Rannach must decide; or . . . He had rather not think of that "or," and so he held his tongue and stared at Rannach, waiting.

"I am not fit," Rannach said.

Morrhyn said, "You are akaman of the Commacht now. It was your father Chakthi murdered." It was hard, that, with Lhyn's eyes wide upon him, all tear-tracked. "Yours, then, the decision."

Yazte said, "That's fair."

And Colun, "Yes! Let Rannach decide."

Chakthi said, "Is this Matakwa as the Prophet claims, then *all* must have a voice, and the decision be reached by all."

"This is our way and has always been our way." Hadduth rose to his feet and spoke loud. "At that last Matakwa—when Vachyr was slain— Racharran had no say because it was his son accused! Now accusation of murder is made against Chakthi, and Racharran's son asked to decide the verdict. How can that be fair? Racharran himself would not agree to it."

Voices murmured, "No!" Others murmured, "Yes!" And some said, "Execute him!"

More called for Morrhyn to decide: because he was the Prophet.

He raised his arms again. It was somewhat embarrassing to own such repute that that simple gesture delivered silence. He said, "I will not."

Kahteney rose. "Perhaps there's another way. The Prophet says that Rannach must decide; Chakthi and Hadduth say no. So—shall this Matakwa elect the judges? Or the judge?"

Morrhyn said again, "I'll not be the judge. This is for the People to decide."

Kahteney said, "Then I give my vote to Rannach."

Yazte said, "He's mine also."

Colun said, "And mine."

Hadduth said, "The Grannach have no voice in the Council of the People."

Kanseah said, "The Naiche shall abide by Rannach's judgment."

There was no one yet to speak for the Aparhaso, so Morrhyn said, "Shall it be so? Shall Rannach judge?"

And there came an answer that matched the bellowing of the Breakers' beasts in its volume: *"Yes!"*

"So be it." Morrhyn beckoned Rannach to stand. "The judgment is yours to make."

Chakthi shouted, "No! This is not the way. This is not how the Ahsa-tye-Patiko has it."

Hadduth joined him in his protest, and no few of the Tachyn; but all the rest—which was the great mass of the People—shouted them down and they were forced to angry silence.

Rannach stood. He looked around the circle: at Morrhyn and his mother, at his wife, at Yazte and Kahteney and Colun, at Dohnse and all the rest waiting for his word, and finally at Chakthi.

"I believe Dohnse speaks the truth," he said. "And Morrhyn. I believe that Chakthi slew my father."

Shouts came: calling for Chakthi's death. Morrhyn waited, hanging like that hawk on the currents of Rannach's words. All hinged on this: the dreamed future, which might go the one way or the other, dependent on men, on one man—Rannach.

Rannach said, "This year past, I slew Vachyr. I believed that what I did was right. But had I let him live—had I brought him back alive to judgment—then perhaps the Breakers would not have come to Ket-Ta-Witko. Perhaps there would have been no war between the Commacht and the Tachyn. Perhaps we should all live still in that old land the Maker gave us. But I did not think then; now I do."

He paused, staring round. His eyes were fierce, defying any to argue him. Morrhyn waited, patient as the hawk; nor any less hungry.

"Blood was shed then," Rannach continued, "when blood should not have been shed. Morrhyn taught me that it broke the Ahsa-tye-Patiko and delivered the Maker's wrath against all the People. It delivered the Breakers upon us."

The hawk folded its wings and stooped: salvation or damnation?

Morrhyn waited with the rest. The dream spread out down its intricate paths, like a spider's web—mazed and fragile and strong until broken.

And Rannach said, "I'd not chance again the Maker's wrath. We are brought to a new land, which is good." He gestured at the rolling grass, the blue-running rivers, the distant mountains. "I'd not again chance breaking the Ahsa-tye-Patiko. I'd not spoil the grass of this new land with blood. Listen! My wife grows large with a child—shall he be born to war? Or shall we live peaceful? We are exiled from Ket-Ta-Witko by what I did, and Vachyr, and Chakthi. But I'd not see that strife again. I'd see a peaceful land where my son might grow up without war.

"So—I claim no blood right against Chakthi. He slew my father, but I'll not claim his life."

Yazte said, "No payment? He murdered your father—my brother! —and you'd let him go free? That I cannot accept."

Shy Kanseah, even, said, "I believe the Prophet; I believe Dohnse. Can you let your father go unavenged?"

Rannach looked at Morrhyn, who gave back no clear answer save an enigmatic smile, and said: "I would not soil the grass of this new land with blood. Does Chakthi confess his sins and swear repentance and fealty to all the People, then I say he and his Tachyn live with us; and let our coming here wash away past sins."

He turned his eyes challenging on Chakthi. Morrhyn fought a smile —it went well so far: one path the dream had shown him. But there were yet more to be taken, to other destinies.

And Chakthi took one as he stared at Rannach and shook his head and said, "Swear fealty to you? *No!* I confess no sins; neither accept your right to judge me."

The hawk rose up and Morrhyn was not sure whether its claws hung open or closed.

"Then I give judgment," Rannach said.

Chakthi said, "You cannot."

Yazte said, "He can—we sit in Chiefs' Council and we have all agreed. Rannach's is the final word."

"One day, old man," Chakthi said, "I swear I shall kill you."

Yazte laughed and said, "Dream on, murderer."

Chakthi surged up, but Hadduth grasped his arm and pulled him down even as the Lakanti and the Tachyn again drew weapons.

Kahteney said, "What is this judgment?"

And Rannach said, "That we of the People who are true to the Ahsa-tye-Patiko cannot live with such as he, or any who follow him. I say that we send them away, where they not soil us with lies and envy and hatred. I say that they go"—he flung out an arm to where the line of distant mountains stretched all shadowy and cloud-hung across the eastern horizon—"there! Beyond those hills; and find themselves a place and never come back to where the People live."

Chakthi scowled, and Hadduth whispered again into his ear. Morrhyn smiled, glad that path was taken.

Colun said, "Those look like good mountains. I'd take my Grannach there and build our tunnels again. How think you, Baran?"

Baran nodded and said, "Yes. Let's go there."

And Colun said, "We'll be the Stone Guardians again, eh? And forbid Chakthi and any fools who follow him passage back."

Baran grinned through his beard and glowered at the Tachyn and said, "Yes. We'll seal off the hills and never let them through."

Rannach said, "So be it. Let all who follow Chakthi strike their lodges and go with him. They shall go in peace—unharmed!—and cross the hills and never come back on pain of death. Save"—he stared fierce around—"any who come here like us—like exiles fleeing destruction and oppression—shall be welcomed. Any who come seeking that refuge the Maker gave *us* shall be welcome amongst the People.

"How say you?"

His question was answered with a roar of approval and agreement from all save those still loyal to Chakthi.

Morrhyn felt pride swell, and bright hope: Rannach had learned well in exile, and in the long, hard moons that followed. He had chosen a path that seemed to the Dreamer the best—the one that led to peace and a future fruitful to all the People. He seemed to inherit his father's wisdom, and—hopeful—the wakanisha smiled at Rannach.

Who said, "Those who'd go with Chakthi shall quit this place tomorrow, before the sun stands noonday. Is that fair?"

Yazte said, "More than fair. I'd send them out now."

Rannach said, "They need time. They've wounds also."

Morrhyn blessed him for that.

Yazte shrugged and Colun asked, "Shall we Grannach go with them and guard their passage?"

Morrhyn waited again for Rannach's decision, and was no less pleased when Rannach said, "Let them first take out their horses from the herd and all they own, and then warriors from all of the People escort them to the hills; those who'd go. All others are welcome to remain. But those who go with Chakthi shall be taken there by all the clans—the Commacht and the Lakanti, the Naiche and the Aparahaso, the Grannach—that all see them gone across the mountains, nor ever return save to swear loyalty to all the People and the Ahsa-tye-Patiko. That"—he looked to where Morrhyn sat smiling—"is my judgment."

Chakthi scowled and climbed halfway to his feet, but Hadduth held him back again and whispered to him, and the Tachyn akaman, still sullen, acquiesced and began to smile.

And Morrhyn remembered another path is dreams had taken, and wondered again about the weight and the burden that duty gave him. But he closed his mouth on the warnings he'd shout because he knew this was a thing to be determined by men who were not Dreamers, and must decide their own fates. He was the Prophet and saw the many paths, but did he outline them all, then none had choice—which was the balancing of the Maker's scales.

Yet still he wondered, as he looked at Chakthi and Hadduth, if it had not been better he told all he knew. That, or take a knife and drive it into both of them as they, together, had driven that blade into Rachar-ran.

But he did not, only bowed his head and agreed with Rannach's judgment.

It was the best he could do: the only thing he could do, and leave the People themselves.

The Tachyn still loyal to Chakthi struck their lodges not long after the sun rose. They gathered up their horses and their dogs and all else they possessed. They set their worst wounded on travois and began the long trek to whatever awaited them pas the mountains.

Colun and his Grannach went with them, and an escort of all the warriors Rannach had decreed.

They were not so many—Dohnse was believed, and the Prophet's dreaming—and for those who went with Chakthi and Hadduth, there was an equal number that remained behind.

They were welcomed into the clans still loyal to the People, though it was a sad welcoming, for much was lost. Not only Ket-Ta-Witko, but also those things that had made them what they were—and all of them knew those things were changed.

Chakthi and all who followed him seemed no longer of the People, but tainted by the sin of the Breakers' dark wind, and all those who watched them go wondered at their fate, and what their anger might bring.

Morrhyn watched the long column go out and thought of what his dreams had shown him: if all was now well, and the People safe, or the Breakers come again because . . .

He set that doubt aside and asked, "What shall we call this land?"

Rannach said, "Ket-Ta-Thanne."

Which meant in the language of the People *The Promised Land.*

Morrhyn nodded and said, "That seems fitting."

And so it was named: Ket-Ta-Thanne.

And the People settled there—the Commacht and the Lakanti, the Aparhaso and the Naiche and the Grannach—and spread across the grass and into the mountains, and set up their lodges and built their tunnels, and dwelt in harmony, all of them—save Chakthi's Tachyn, who had gone across the mountains the Grannach guarded to whatever lay beyond.

And while all remembered Rannach's vow that Ket-Ta-Thanne should be always a refuge for exiles, it seemed they were the only folk in all those wide spaces, and none realized how soon they would be called upon to honor that promise.

44 A Desperate Enterprise

Arcole saw Flysse and Davyd settled safely in the dinghy, the packs amidships, and used Davyd's knife to cut the mooring line. He shouldered the rowboat out into deeper water—all the time praying the tide was turned enough it should carry them upriver—and hauled himself on board.

"Keep low," he warned. "Are we seen, hopefully they'll think this only an empty, drifting boat."

Obeying his own instruction, he crouched beneath the gunwales, endeavoring not to breathe in his own odor. God, but he smelled foul! And surely no chance to strip off his reeking clothing and bathe until dawn, at least. By then, were his calculations right—did the tide favor them, and the demons not halt them—they should be far enough from Grostheim that they might risk a brief halt. He thought their escape must go unnoticed for some time: even did the city withstand the siege, there would be confusion in its aftermath. Fredrik would doubtless report their flight to Wyme, but the governor would be fully occupied reorganizing his city. Likely he'd not consider the possibility of his servants fleeing into the arms of the demons, but rather think them hiding within the walls. Even did he reach the conclusion that they had fled past the walls, then surely he would think them dead at the demons' hands. Pursuit by Militiamen seemed definitely unlikely.

But pursuit by the demons . . . That was another matter.

Arcole wondered what they were. His clandestine studies had suggested they were savage beyond belief, and the little he had seen of them supported this. But he had somehow supposed they should look other than men, yet the figures he had seen capering under the walls had appeared, at least relatively, human. They were not giants or deformed, as best he could tell, and whilst their faces had seemed unearthly, he thought that the result of paint rather than any demonic malformation. Still, he hoped he would not be presented the opportunity to study them at close quarters.

He felt the dinghy rock gently, and risked a swift glance at the riverbank. The twin landmarks of Grostheim and the blazing barges lay astern now—the current *did* carry them inland—fading slowly into the moonless night. Stars shone above, their light replacing the fiery glow so that the Restitution glittered as if sprinkled with quicksilver. They drifted closer to the bank than was comfortable, but he dared not ply the oars yet, for fear the demons spot them.

"I think we're safe." He reached back to stroke Flysse's ankle. "In a while, I'll use the oars."

Then he cursed as something moved across the water behind them.

"What is it?" Flysse's voice was husky with fear and nausea.

Arcole said, "I spoke too soon," and looked forward across the packs to where Davyd lay. "There are muskets in these?"

Davyd said, "Two, wrapped in oilskin, with powder and shot. Also three pistols."

Arcole began to feel at the packs, seeking the weapons. His fingers found the hard outline of a musket and he cut the securing cords, dragging out the gun.

Flysse asked again, "What is it?" Her question was more urgent now.

Arcole slit the oilskin wrapping the musket and began to load. "Pursuit." He looked back, ignoring Flysse's gasp as she turned and saw what came after them.

It was a canoe. It sat low in the water, prow and stern curving up and over like the horns of some malign river beast. Four demons paddled the craft with a dreadful vigor; a fifth crouched in the nose. Arcole thought he held a nocked bow.

"Davyd!" He tossed the boy the knife. "Find the second musket and load it."

Davyd began to slash at a pack. "I've never fired a musket," he said.

"I have," Arcole returned. "Only load for me. Flysse, stay down."

"I can row," she said.

"No." Arcole shook his head. "They've four oarsmen. And"—he cocked the musket—"I need a steady hand for this."

He settled back on the packs, sighting sternward over Flysse's body. The musket was of cheap production, no more than a trade weapon, and he was accustomed to the finest: he prayed the thing fired true. He squeezed the trigger.

Water fountained ahead and to the left of the canoe. Arcole cursed and began to reload. The canoe gained: it seemed to leap across the surface. Arcole saw the demon at the prow loose an arrow; felt its passage past his face. He fired again.

The heavy lead ball burst splinters from the canoe's curving bow. Davyd said, "Ready!"

Arcole took the offered gun and passed Davyd the spent weapon.

The shot landed to starboard of their pursuers, an arm's length clear. Arcole cursed.

"Ready."

Davyd's voice was hoarse with terror, and his hand trembled as he gave Arcole the musket. Arcole said, "Gahame should sight in his guns better," and was rewarded with a nervous laugh.

This one pulls to the left and fires short, he reminded himself, and that damned canoe is closing on us fast. He adjusted his aim, then paused as a shaft struck hard against the dinghy's stern. Flysse gave a little scream and Arcole took a deep breath. The bowman nocked a fresh arrow. Arcole fired as he drew his string.

The demon screamed and fell back amongst the oarsmen: Arcole whooped gleefully as the canoe slowed and veered off course.

He took the second musket—this pulls right—and fired again. Chips flew from the canoe and a second agonized cry rang out.

"So demons can be slain!" Arcole shouted. "Davyd?"

The boy had the gun ready. The canoe turned farther into the river as the rowers lost their stroke, presenting a broader target. Arcole's next shot sent a demon spilling overboard. Only two remained now, and it seemed they gave up the chase. One rose, sending a hatchet whirling toward the dinghy. It struck the stern and sank. Arcole fired again, aiming for the craft now, blowing a hole in the thin side, close on the waterline. Davyd held out a loaded musket, but he shook his head.

"Best we save our shot." He gestured cheerfully at the canoe. "I think we've dissuaded them, and there's but the one came after us."

The canoe took on water now, settling deeper, and the surviving demons seemed more intent on avoiding a swim to the bank than continuing the hunt. They set to paddling shoreward, falling steadily astern as the dinghy drifted upstream.

"Flysse, you're not hurt?" Arcole set the musket down. "Davyd?"

Flysse said, "No," in a small voice. "Only afraid."

Davyd said, "I'm hale," as steadily as he could.

"You did well," Arcole declared, "and we're surely safe now."

Flysse rose to find a bench. Reproachfully, she said, "You told me that before, no?"

"I did," Arcole agreed solemnly. "But this time I think I'm right."

His smile was infectious and Flysse began to laugh; soon Davyd joined in.

"And," Arcole chuckled, "I told you I'd use the oars in a while. See how I keep my word?"

He found the oars and began to row.

By daybreak his hands were blistered and he thought his spine must soon crack, but he continued at his task until the sun was up and the river shone golden all around. Grassy banks drifted by, and stands of timber, but they saw no one, nor did any demons appear behind them. Arcole deemed it safe to rest and take stock: he turned the boat to the shore.

They beached on a strand of dark sand overhung by willows, their arrival sending a flock of twittering birds skyward. A heron squawked a protest and took lumbering flight. Arcole slumped at the oars and it was Davyd who sprang overboard to drag the dinghy ashore.

Wearily, his body aching, Arcole joined the boy, and with Flysse's aid they manhandled the boat under the cover of the drooping willows. For a while they all three slumped on the sand, scarce able to believe they looked on a morning not bound by Grostheim's walls. The river ran empty before them, and behind, past the willows, the bank rose higher than a man's head.

"Are we safe?" Flysse asked.

"I'll check." Arcole made to rise, but Davyd motioned him back, saying, "I'll go. You rest here."

Arcole gestured his assent, and Davyd clambered up the bank to peer over the top.

"Grass," he reported. "For as far as I could see, except for some trees. There are no houses, nor any people."

"Good." Arcole lay back against the dinghy. "I suggest we rest here awhile. Do we have any food?"

Davyd said, "I brought none. Only clothes and the weapons and such."

"No matter." Arcole grinned. "We shall feast on freedom, and perhaps tonight hunt our dinner. Meanwhile, the river shall be our bath.

God!" He plucked at his shirt, grimacing. "I stink. A change of clothes will be a blessing."

Flysse was abruptly aware of her undressed state. Arcole seemed too tired to notice, but Davyd kept his eyes averted, and when he did look toward her, his cheeks grew red. After all they had been through, it seemed almost amusing that her dishabille should embarrass him so, but his obvious discomfort was unnerving and she found her herself eager to be more modestly dressed.

"There are clothes in the packs?" she asked. And when Davyd nodded—not looking at her—she said, "Then I'd take mine and bathe."

Arcole said, "Don't go far, and be careful," as Davyd opened the three packs and sorted out the contents.

He handed Flysse a sturdy linen shirt and a pair of buckskin breeches, a belt and a pair of high, soft boots. "I'm sorry." His eyes darted about, looking everywhere but at her as his face flushed bright pink. "There are no . . ." He gestured vaguely. "No . . . um, small things."

"No matter." Flysse smiled as she took his offering. "These are ample."

She carried the gear away, down the beach to where the willows screened her from the two men. Then all modesty was forgotten as she tore off her undergarments and splashed into the water.

Back at the dinghy, Arcole forced himself to examine their supplies. The map he had so painstakingly constructed was blurred from its watery journey, the ink badly run and most of his annotations now indecipherable. Even so, aided by his memory, he thought it should serve them well enough; and Davyd's loot was invaluable.

In addition to shirts and breeches and boots the twins of Flysse's outfit, there were the two muskets, three holstered pistols, several horns of powder and bags of shot; three knives complete with sheaths, and two smallswords in plain leather scabbards. Also three tinderboxes, two canteens, and a collection of wire snares and fishing lines; the tarpaulins would serve as cloaks and tents both. Arcole voiced his appreciation.

"Sieur Gahame carries no . . ." Davyd coughed nervously, blushing, and in a mumbled rush, "Underthings. Nothing like that . . . So I couldn't . . . I'm sorry."

"Sorry?" Arcole grunted as he leaned forward to slap the boy on the shoulder. "God, Davyd, you've done us proud. I marvel you were able to gather all this."

Davyd's blush was replaced with a smile. "I am—was—a thief," he murmured.

"A most excellent thief." Arcole chuckled. "The finest thief I've ever known. How could we have won through without you?"

Davyd basked in the praise, embarrassment and fear fading. He felt Arcole treated him like a man, and that filled him with pride. Even better, the dream voice that had echoed in his head was silent now, gone with the terror he seemed to have left behind along the Restitution. He rose to his feet.

"Shall I make a fire?" he asked.

"Perhaps not yet." Arcole shook his head and yawned. "The smoke might betray us, and the sun's warm enough, no? Indeed, I think I shall lie here awhile and enjoy it—after I've washed off this stink."

Davyd nodded, and they waited until Flysse returned. Her wet hair hung like liquid gold about her fresh-scrubbed face, and in her home-spun shirt and buckskin breeches she looked like some soldier-maid. The more when Arcole had her affix a pistol and a knife to her belt.

"I know nothing of guns," she protested. "Neither how to fire nor to load."

"I'll teach you," Arcole promised. "I'll teach you both. And Davyd how to use that fine blade."

It was not, in truth, a very fine blade, but serviceable enough; and the pleasure on Davyd's face was ample reward for the lie.

"And now." Arcole clambered stiffly to his feet, groaning as his aching back protested. "I shall bathe. And then sleep awhile."

"Shall that be safe?" Flysse asked.

"Likely," came the answer. "Surely necessary, for I doubt I can row again until I've rested."

"I can," Davyd said eagerly. "I can row while you sleep."

Arcole felt no wish to dampen the boy's enthusiasm, but neither did he trust him to handle the dinghy successfully. Once, he would have said it plain—careless of Davyd's mortification—but now he was changed and looked to avoid giving the boy hurt. Indeed, he thought as he studied the earnest young face, Davyd was no longer a boy. Perhaps not yet quite a man, for all he took a man's part in this venture, but surely no longer a boy.

"I suspect," he said gently, "that we shall all benefit from sleep. Do you stand guard, that I may sleep easy?"

"I will," said Davyd, and took up a musket.

Arcole said, "Well done," and went to bathe.

The river ran chilly and the sand he used to scrub his body was abrasive, but to be once more clean was pure joy, augmented by victory. Although that, he reminded himself as he ground sand into his hair, was not yet full-won. He was confident no Militiamen would come after them, but the demons were a different prospect—he had no idea whether the creatures would leave them go or mount a pursuit. He knew —or at least guessed—they came out of the wilderness: therefore, the wilderness might well hold more. Perhaps they fled one band only to reach another, and the wilderness itself might well prove hostile.

Nor did the territory claimed by Evander offer refuge. Not all the homesteaders had come in to Grostheim, and those still occupying their holdings—were they not slain by the demons—would hardly welcome three branded exiles. The map would guide them, show them where the holdings lay so that they might go cautious and unseen, but true liberty must inevitably lie in the very jaws of danger—in the wilderness itself.

No, he told himself, we have not won yet. One victory, perhaps—to escape Grostheim—but surely more battles ahead. Perhaps with demons, perhaps with the wild creatures of the forests, perhaps with the elements themselves. And then they must make some kind of life in the wilderness: survival would be no easy thing.

But, he told himself as the enormity of their venture loomed huge in his mind, threatening to douse his optimism, we *did* escape. We fought off demons, and we have weapons, snares Flysse knows how to use; and Davyd's dreams. His spirits rose again as he thought of that. Davyd's dreaming had shown them the time was come, had warned of the attack; and Davyd had spoken of dreams that suggested the wilderness could be a friendly place. So they must rely on that strange ability to ward them and guide them, and go on. After all, they had no other way to go save onward.

Cheered, Arcole sank his discarded clothing in the shallows and dressed, then returned to the beach.

He sent Davyd off to bathe and settled himself on the sun-warmed sand. Flysse came to sit beside him.

"There's danger still, no?" she asked quietly.

He took her hand and said, "We knew that when we planned this venture. That was why I had intended to leave you behind. Save," he added quickly as he saw her stiffen, the pain that flashed in her blue eyes, "I wonder if I truly could have done that. And now? Whatever we face ahead, I am glad I face it with you."

Flysse smiled and bent to kiss him. He put his arms around her and drew her down: it had been so long since they lay together. Their caresses grew more ardent, and then Flysse pulled back.

"Remember Davyd," she said reluctantly. "He'll return soon, and he was embarrassed enough when I stood in my underthings."

"I thought you looked charming," Arcole murmured. And sighed: "But, yes, I'd not upset him."

Flysse stroked his hair. "Perhaps tonight," she whispered. "Surely soon; but now, do you sleep?"

Arcole offered no argument, but stretched out, closing his eyes as he murmured, "Tell Davyd he's on watch, eh? He'll like that."

Flysse nodded and continued to gently stroke his hair as his breathing slowed and became sonorous. The furrows that had etched his brow faded as he relaxed, and his lips parted in a slow smile. She thought how much she loved this man, and put aside contemplation of the perils ahead. Whatever they might be, she and Arcole, and Davyd, would be together. She refused to believe they could fail now.

"He sleeps?" Davyd came up softly, his stolen boots silent on the sand. When Flysse nodded, he stooped to take a cord and pull back his hair. He said, "I'll take the watch."

"He asked you do that," Flysse said.

She smiled as Davyd nodded gravely, thinking that he grew apace; that with his sword and pistol, his knife and his musket, he looked like some youthful frontiersman. Then she thought of his dreams and wondered if he, more than any of them, had a truer inkling of what lay ahead. Almost, she asked him, but decided not. He was intent on his duty now, and the memory of his face when he had spoken of his dreams lingered. She had sooner not remind him of those nightmares.

Davyd cradled his musket and strode to the farther end of the beach. He hoped no demons came paddling up the river: he knew how to load the gun—could repair it, given tools—but he had never in his life fired a musket. It was tempting to try it out, but that would wake Arcole and frighten Flysse—and perhaps give warning of their presence—so he only raised the weapon to his shoulder and sighted down the barrel, carefully cocking and lowering the hammer. Then he stopped, angry with himself: he was behaving like a child, as if the musket were a toy, but he was no longer a child and the musket a real and dangerous weapon. He blushed and glanced back to where Flysse lay with Arcole, hoping she had not witnessed his infantile game.

Then blushed anew as memory of her in her underthings kindled. She was Arcole's wife, and he should not entertain such thoughts as lurked on the heels of the memory. Arcole was his friend—his savior— and Flysse was wed: decent folk did not think of their friend's wives in such a fashion. He scowled and climbed the bank, high enough he might peer out across the grasslands.

It was, to him, a strange sight; for an instant almost as disturbing as the open sea had been. He was not accustomed to open places, and this spread wide and clear as any ocean. He thought the grass like water, the stands of timber like islands. The horizon shimmered in the rising heat —summer, he thought, could not be far off. Evander seemed a lifetime distant, even Grostheim now, for they could never return. He wondered if the city stood, or if the demons had prevailed. If so, then Sieur Gahame was surely dead, Laurens and Godfry with him. He could not decide if he was sorry. He thought that at least no Inquisitor would ever find him here, and turned his eyes to the west.

The forest edge was no more than a dark blur, shifting like distant smoke in the haze. He had no idea how long it should take them to reach that . . . refuge? He was not sure. There was that element in his dreams that had suggested safety, but also threat. He closed his eyes and for a moment endeavored to conjure up the horror of his recent dreams. It was entirely gone, and he breathed a sigh of relief. Perhaps tonight— or whenever he slept—he would dream again and prove his usefulness. He had, after all, warned of the demons' attack, and he was the one who had secured the clothes they wore and the weapons they carried. Without his skills Arcole would still lie caged. In fact, he decided, they owed him their lives: pride rose. Then guilt. Had Arcole not befriended him, *he* would be in Grostheim now. Perhaps his skull would decorate some demon's trophy pole; and did he live, it should be as an indentured exile, all his life. No, whatever he had done for Arcole, Arcole had done as much and more for him. These were not things for tallies, such columns of loss and profit as Sieur Gahame totted, but matters of comradeship, of shared purpose. It was as if they were a family—he and Flysse and Arcole. He only wished he could forget how Flysse had looked.

Arcole woke around noon. Flysse lay asleep beside him and Davyd prowled the beach like some soldier eager for battle. He yawned and rose, his aches somewhat abated now, and went to the river, splashing his face.

"What now?" Davyd asked.

"We'd best be gone." Arcole looked east, down the Restitution. "All well, there'll be no pursuit. But even so . . ."

Davyd nodded. "How far to the forest?"

"Some days, at least." Arcole flexed his hands. They were not soft, but neither was he accustomed to rowing a dinghy for so long. "Can you handle an oar?"

"I don't know," Davyd answered. "I've never tried."

"There's a skill to it." Arcole looked at his palms and winced. Then chuckled. "Something else I must teach you, eh?"

"Now?" Davyd asked.

"Perhaps not yet." Arcole shook his head, and saw disappointment cloud the young face, prompting him to add, "You've had no sleep as yet. God, you must be exhausted."

"I can stay awake," Davyd promised.

"And you would, I've no doubt." Arcole set a hand on his shoulder. "But I'd sooner you slept. Do you dream, you can warn us or guide us to safety. That's your duty for now, eh?"

Davyd accepted and they gathered up their gear, stowing it in the dinghy. They filled the canteens and Arcole was about to launch the boat, but Flysse bade him wait, tugging her shirt loose. The tails were long, and she cut strips that she bound about his hands.

"Thank you." He bowed elegantly, and bussed her cheek. "Now, westward ho, eh?"

They pushed the little craft into the river and took their places—Arcole at the oars, Davyd at the prow, Flysse in the stern. The tide had turned and they were not yet so far from Deliverance Bay that they escaped its influence: Arcole must work hard to keep them headed upstream. Sleep had restored him somewhat, but soon enough he felt his back and shoulders protest anew at the unfamiliar effort, and must endeavor to ignore the ache that grew and spread until it seemed all his body throbbed. He gritted his teeth and continued rowing.

Davyd closed his eyes—he did, indeed, feel weary—but he was far too excited to sleep. What if demons lay ahead? Arcole faced backward and would not see them, and Flysse might miss them: Davyd felt he had a duty to remain awake, watchful. He settled his musket across his knees and adjusted the unfamiliar length of the smallsword across the bench, scanning the river ahead.

The Restitution remained empty of other traffic, though as they moved steadily westward they saw indications of landward habitation. The signs were not encouraging. There was a burned-out building close to the water: perhaps once a stopping place for barges, it was now only a collection of charred timber. Later, where the banks flattened, they saw a farm in the distance—like the first structure, now razed. Farm animals watched them go by—cattle and pigs, chickens, some horses. Milch cows lowed mournfully, protesting their swollen udders.

"I could milk those," Flysse said.

"And I could shoot one," Arcole returned. "Or a hog. Perhaps tonight."

"Why not now?" Flysse asked.

"I'd sooner put more distance between us and Grostheim," he replied. "And find some sheltered spot to spend the night."

"What if there are no animals?"

"I've the map, remember." Arcole grinned. "The farms are marked and we can scout them, halt each night near a holding and hunt our dinner."

Davyd said nothing, but the thought of roasted meat set his stomach to grumbling. He wished he had been able to steal food of some kind. Escape, he decided, would be far more flavorsome on a full belly.

As the sun approached the faraway forests, the Restitution swept in a leisurely bend to the north and woodland came down to the river on the flanks of a little knoll. Grass spread wide around the timbered hillock, and they could see cattle grazing. Arcole checked the map and saw a farm marked: the Danby holding, destroyed by demons. He elected to make camp for the night. He was, anyway, not sure he could row any longer.

They beached the dinghy and warily scouted their surroundings. The wood was small, and concealed—as best they could tell, none being expert in these matters—anything hostile. There was ample dry wood for a fire, and the sky held no threat of rain. Arcole unwrapped his hands. The palms were tender, but not so bad he could not shoot. He took a musket, announcing his intention of finding them beef for their dinner.

"It should not be difficult," he said. "Do you wait here?"

"The both of us?" Flysse asked.

"Yes," Arcole replied. "I'll not be long."

Flysse smiled mischievously and asked, "And when you've shot our dinner, what then?"

"Why," he said, "we eat it, of course."

"Roasted whole?" she asked with deliberate innocence. "Or shall you cut us tender steaks?"

Arcole frowned, forced to realize his mistake.

Flysse laughed and said, "You've no idea how to butcher meat, eh?" And when he shook his head: "I've seen it done. I'll show you how."

"What about me?" asked Davyd. He felt none too happy at the prospect of being left alone.

"Best you guard our camp," Arcole said. "Do you see anything, fire a shot and we'll return. We'll not be far away."

Davyd nodded dubiously. Arcole said, "I doubt I shall need more than one shot to kill a cow, so—do we find anything amiss, you'll hear two shots, fired close."

Davyd ducked his head again. Flysse took a canteen and went with Arcole.

"Is it such thirsty work?" Arcole asked.

"No." Flysse shook her head. "But you'll need this. Wait and see."

They walked out onto the grass. Dusk was not far off, and the light of the descending sun shone clear and brilliant over the plain. Flights of birds winged overhead, homeward bound, and crickets buzzed loud in the warm air. Shadowy in the distance, Arcole thought he made out the shape of the destroyed farm. He supposed that if demons lingered, they would make fires—if demons had need of fires—but he could see no smoke. He hoped there were none; elected to take the risk: fresh meat would be a boon.

The cattle stood grazing or chewing the cud, watching the approaching couple with curious, placid eyes. They showed no sign of fear and, almost, Arcole felt guilty as he raised his musket and sighted on a piebald cow.

She grunted as the shot struck, and fell down on her forelegs. It seemed she bowed to inescapable fate. Then she toppled onto her side, kicked awhile, and lay still.

Arcole motioned Flysse down as he reloaded the musket, waiting. Save for the nervous lowing of the other cattle, he heard nothing, nor did anything move on the plain, save for a flock of small, startled birds that burst into flight at the detonation. In a while he rose and went forward.

"Wait," Flysse said. "Best take off your shirt."

Arcole frowned but did as he was bade.

Flysse smiled and said, "You've never seen your dinner prepared." And when he shook his head, "It's bloody work."

"I'd sooner eat in a civilized dining room," Arcole sighed, then drew his knife. "Tell me what to do, eh?"

He set to work, following her instructions even as he frowned his distaste of the bloody task. His arms were soon painted with red, splashes decorating his chest, but inexpert though his carving was, in time long steaks lay on the grass, and a haunch.

Flysse uncorked the canteen that he might sluice off the gore. Arcole studied the remains of the cow, thinking that enough was left to feed them for a week. "Is that all we take?" he asked.

"Save we stay here to smoke it," she advised him. "We've easily enough for a day or two, and more would only spoil. Are there loose herds all along the way, we can find more."

He bowed to her superior wisdom, aware that she knew far more about such matters than he. Were Flysse not there, he would have simply hacked at the carcass, taking whatever he could cut. He could hunt —handle a musket—but in this area Flysse was the expert. We make a fine couple, he thought, and told her so.

"We've all our different skills, I think." She handed him his shirt. "Now, how do we carry this meat back without we get all bloody?"

The steaks they skewered on the musket's ramrod; Arcole shouldered the leg, and they returned to the beach.

Davyd had gathered wood, piling it where the bulk of the dinghy would conceal the glow from the river. "I thought it better to wait until dark before lighting it," he said. "So the smoke won't show."

"Well done." Arcole applauded. "You learn fast."

Davyd grinned, and they settled in companionable silence to await nightfall.

It seemed wise to set a watch, and in light of his hard work that day, Flysse and Davyd insisted Arcole take the first turn, that he might then sleep the remainder of the night. He offered little argument, and it was agreed Flysse take the middle watch and Davyd the last. Unspoken went the thought that Davyd might dream of what lay ahead.

It was a wide and starry night, as if the heavens celebrated their first day of freedom, and Arcole sat watching the river slide silvery and empty by. He heard the calling of owls in the little wood, and bats swooped about his head. His belly was full, and for all he knew they faced hardship in the days to come, he felt content. Were he only able to lie with Flysse, he thought he should be entirely happy.

He turned as he heard a muffled cry, seeing Davyd twist about on his canvas bed, throwing up an arm as if in defense. Almost, he went to the lad, but then held back. Did Davyd dream of their future, it should be better to leave him lie, better they have warning. He cradled his musket and sought to block out the faint sounds.

When Flysse came to relieve him, she said, "Davyd dreams."

He said, "I know," and pulled her down beside him. "As do I, save mine are all of you."

She said, "Arcole . . ." and then lost her ability to speak under the pressure of his lips. It was hard—very hard—to resist, but she was a modest woman, and Davyd lay nearby—might wake and see them. So she took her hands from his neck and set them against his chest and pushed him back.

"Not here," she gasped. "Not where Davyd . . ."

Arcole sighed and lowered his head in acceptance. "God, Flysse, but this is not easy." His voice was throaty with desire.

"No," she murmured. "I know; nor for me. But . . ."

"But I understand," he whispered, and touched his mouth to her cheek. Then took her hand and grinned. "It shall spur me on. I shall row as no man has ever rowed before, that we reach the forests and . . ." He was not quite sure what should happen then. He extemporized: "I shall build us a cabin, and Davyd another—a decent distance off!—and we shall have privacy to . . ."

His grin spread wide. Once Flysse would have blushed at the innuendo, but now she smiled and nodded eagerly. "I pray it be so, husband. And soon."

"It shall be," he promised. "Wife."

"And are you to row so hard," she said, "then you had best sleep now, eh?"

Arcole had sooner remain with her, but she spoke the truth and he nodded, passing her the musket. "This is primed," he explained. "You need only cock the hammer—thus—then squeeze the trigger. Your pistol works the same way."

Flysse took the musket gingerly. "You must teach me how to load," she said.

"As I promised." Arcole rose. "And how to shoot. And you must teach me how to butcher meat and set a snare."

"We'll teach each other," Flysse said.

"I think," he murmured, "that we already do."

He found his bed and stretched out, listening to the small sounds Davyd made. He wondered what they augured; but not for long—he was incredibly weary, and even as Davyd groaned and thrashed, he drifted down into welcome sleep. All well, the morning would be soon enough to discuss the future.

45 The River

"There was the river, running into the forest. It went toward mountains, and I knew I must reach them, but not how." Davyd shook his head, struggling to find the words that might accurately describe his dream. It was not easy: words were too precise for such amorphous things, too limiting when the oneiric images flickered and shifted and were, anyway, composed more of emotion than any substantial matter. "I had to leave the river, and then I was in the forest. It . . . *felt* . . . dangerous, as if it watched me. Or something in it watched me. Then there was fire, and I thought it must devour me, but then a wind blew down from the mountains and made a way through the flames. I went that way, and the fire reached for me."

He broke off, shuddering at the memory. Flysse set a hand on his shoulder, her touch a solace; Arcole passed him a canteen. He drank, and sighed, smiling ruefully.

"It's hard to describe, but . . . Anyway, the fire reached for me, and then the wind blew stronger and drove it back a little. I walked into the wind—toward the mountains. I knew I should be safe there if I could only reach a place—a special place—but I didn't know where it was. I just had to go into the mountains to find it. The fire came after me, chasing me. I ran, and then I woke."

He shrugged. It felt strange even now, even with these good friends, to talk about his dreaming. It was a matter kept secret for so long—on pain of horrid death—it still unnerved him to discuss it so openly. He raised his head, reassuring himself they sat beneath the open sky, beside the Restitution—far from Grostheim and the Autarchy. That calmed him a little, but still it was not a thing with which he felt entirely comfortable.

"What do you think it means?" Arcole looked from the smudged map to Davyd's face. "You're our guide in this, no?"

The words were designed to encourage Davyd, and he smiled his thanks. "I'm not sure," he said slowly. "Before I came to Salvation, the dreams were never so clear. They warned me of danger—as I've told you —but never so . . . so . . ."

"Specifically?" Arcole supplied.

Davyd supposed that was the word and ducked his head in agreement. "Never so specifically," he said. "It was like . . . Well, if I were planning a job and dreamed of burning, or Militiamen, I knew I shouldn't try it. But since I came here, I've dreamed of . . . specific? . . . things, like the forests and the demons."

"Were there demons in this dream?" Arcole asked.

"No." Davyd shook his head. "Only the fire—which means danger —and the wind and the mountains. I suppose that means the mountains are safe. If we can find the special place."

"Perhaps as we get closer to the mountains," Flysse said, "you'll know."

"Perhaps," Davyd allowed cautiously.

Arcole studied the map. "The river isn't charted past Salvation's boundary." He turned his head, staring to the west. "It comes out of the wilderness, and past the forest's edge there's nothing drawn. But rivers rise in high ground, so . . ."

"We follow the river," Flysse said.

"As far as we can." Arcole frowned. "But the closer we get to the mountains, the stronger the downstream current gets. There has to come a time we can't row against it, and we must proceed on foot."

Flysse said, "Isn't that what you planned?"

He nodded. "But I confess my plans were mostly concentrated on escaping Grostheim. After that, I was relying on Davyd."

That seemed a tremendous burden, but Davyd squared his shoulders and said, "I'll do my best."

"I know you will," Arcole declared. "I've faith in you. So, we know there's danger in the forest." He folded the map. "That much we knew already. Also that Davyd's dreamed of safety there. Now we know there's a specific place—we head for that."

"How?" asked Flysse. "Davyd doesn't know where it is."

Or if it really exists, Davyd thought.

"I trust him," said Arcole, smiling. "If he's dreamed there's such a place, then it's there and we only need find it. Davyd will dream the way for us."

His confidence was flattering, but still Davyd could not help the disturbing thought that his dreams warned of danger in equal measure with safety: they did not tell him which should prevail. It was hard, this burden of trust.

"So, do we go?" Arcole rose businesslike to his feet, retying the bandages about his hands. "Are we to reach the safety of the mountains, we've some way yet to go."

He kicked sand over the fire and turned toward the dinghy. Davyd thought he likely sought to occupy them all, that none brood overlong on the bad part of the dream. Well, he was happy enough with that. He gathered up his gear and followed Arcole to the boat.

That day, around noon, they saw a band of demons on the north bank.

In the sun's bright light the creatures seemed somewhat less terrifying than the fire-lit shadow-shapes of Grostheim's night, but nonetheless menacing. There were six of them, barbarically clad in leather and animal skins, their hair woven in long braids. Their faces were distorted by bars of paint, black and white and red, so that it was difficult to discern clear features. Their hostility was obvious: they raised bows and sent arrows arcing across the water as Arcole turned the dinghy to midstream. They wore the shapes of men, as best he could tell, but he had no wish to study them close and bent to his oars, propelling the little boat out of range.

The demons promptly mounted horses and for a while paced the boat, howling, but the river was wide, and turned, and timber showed more frequently along the banks. In time they fell away behind.

Arcole wondered if they would continue the pursuit. It was an alarming thought—mounted, the creatures might well catch up. He decided that their camp that night should be on the southern shore.

"I think," he gasped, "that I must teach you two how to shoot as soon as we've time."

Flysse nodded from the stern, her eyes fixed nervously on the north bank. In the bow, Davyd clutched his musket with white-knuckled fingers, little more color in his face.

"We've lost them," Arcole declared with far more confidence than he felt. "And tonight we'll have the river betwixt us and them."

"What," Davyd asked in a low voice, "if there are others on that side?"

It was not possible to shrug as he plied the oars, so Arcole only grunted and said, "We'll pick our spot with care, eh?"

Davyd frowned and said, "I didn't dream of them."

None had explanation for that, and so neither Flysse nor Arcole gave answer, only looked at each other.

"I should have," Davyd continued. "God! If my dreaming is to be useful, I should have dreamed of them."

His voice was plaintive, and Arcole said, "Perhaps your dreams are of the great events only. Like the attack on Grostheim, or the sea serpent."

"No." Davyd refused to be mollified. "My thieving was no 'great event,' but I dreamed of danger when I did that." He shook his head and asked, "What use to dream of 'great events' if some band of six come on us in ambuscade and I don't give warning?"

"Perhaps," Flysse said, "you must concentrate."

"How so?" asked Davyd. "What do you mean?"

Flysse's brow wrinkled as she thought, seeking to define her notion. "Before, in Bantar," she said at last, "did you *try* to dream?"

Davyd thought a moment, then shook his head. "Not try." He smiled wanly. "I was always afraid I might be discovered. That an Inquisitor . . ." He fell silent, shivering at the memory. "No, I never *tried* to dream. Until . . ."

"Until?" Flysse prompted him.

"Until I came to Grostheim." Davyd spoke slowly, as if realization were dragged unwilling from his mind. "When Arcole spoke of our escape and looked to me for warning . . . Yes, then I tried. It was not . . . pleasant. I was afraid."

"But you made the effort," said Flysse. "You sought to dream. You concentrated on it."

She waited until Davyd nodded. Arcole went on rowing, waiting himself to see where this led.

"There are no Inquisitors here." Flysse's hand gestured at the river, the empty landscape beyond. "Nor hexers or priests. Only we three, and the danger of the demons."

Davyd pondered awhile, then ducked his head in reluctant agreement.

"And the demons," Flysse continued, "are a danger like the God's Militia. It's as if you were planning a—" Almost, she said "robbery," but amended that to "job. Yes, it's as if each day, each night, you plan a job. It's like that, save now there's no need to fear discovery by the Autarchy."

"No," Davyd agreed. "I suppose not."

"So perhaps," Flysse said, "if you *try* to dream . . . If you lie down determined to dream . . ."

"It might work," Davyd finished for her. "Yes, it might."

He sounded doubtful still, or wary, so Flysse said, "It worked before, no? When Arcole asked that you warn of the attack, it worked then —when you tried."

Davyd said, "Yes."

Flysse said, "And it should be without risk of burning. It should be in a good cause." She smiled encouragingly. "It should be in defense of us all, no?"

"That's true." Davyd's nod was more enthusiastic now. It was hard to resist Flysse's smile, harder to think of some demon taking her head. He was, after all, their guide in such matters: Arcole had said so. It remained a frightening responsibility; but he would not—could not, he thought—deny Flysse. He said, "Yes, that's true. From now on I'll try."

Flysse said, "You are very brave." And though he did not think it so, he basked in the accolade and endeavored to set his jaw in a stern and manly line. He could not bear to think that harm might come to her for want of his efforts. Yes, he would try hard; he would be their dream guide, if it lay in his power. He liked that—Dream Guide. That, he decided, was his title now, though he blushed to say it out loud. He nodded solemnly and returned his attention to the river ahead.

Arcole caught Flysse's eye and beamed his approval. God, to think that he had once considered her beneath him— a tavern wench, a farm girl. She was so much more than that, he felt ashamed of those old, near-forgotten thoughts. God, but he loved this woman!

By mid-afternoon he could row no longer. His arms lost strength and his back protested each sweep of the oars. He thought that did he not rest, the dinghy must drift on the current. And that was now all downstream: they were long past the influence of Deliverance Bay's tidal flow, the Restitution turning its power to the east. Did they drift, then it must be back the way they had come.

"We must halt," he said. "I can row no more."

Flysse said, "It's early yet."

"Even so." In unintended emphasis he missed his stroke, the starboard oar sweeping clear of the water so that he pitched backward, almost tumbling from the bench. "No, enough."

"We'll take over," she said. "Davyd and I."

Arcole could do no more than hold them steady against the current. "You don't know how," he said. "And it's hard work."

"Then it's time we learnt," she replied. "Nor am I a stranger to hard work."

He hesitated, and Davyd lent his argument to Flysse's. "You said you'd teach us," he reminded Arcole. "And can we all take turns at the oars, then surely we must make better time."

"Very well." Arcole bowed to their persuasions. "But first, bandage your hands, or they'll be raw by dusk." He held the dinghy stationary as they cut strips from their shirts. "Then we must change places. But carefully, eh? Else we all find ourselves in the river."

The dinghy rocked precariously as they shifted position. Arcole went to the stern, where he might watch them and issue instructions; Flysse and Davyd settled together on the rowing bench.

"So, you must do this in unison."

"What's that?" asked Davyd.

Arcole said, "Together. Each oar must land at the same time, or you'll be fighting each other and we'll zig and zag and go nowhere. Now, this is how you do it . . ."

Their progress was at first erratic, and more than once one or the other tumbled backward off the bench. Flysse was glad she wore breeches: in skirts she'd have no dignity left. Twice, oars were dropped, and caught only by dint of speed and good fortune. For some time they did no more than hold station, but then they began to move—slowly—upstream again. Arcole voiced his approval, and was answered with two triumphant smiles.

He brought the map from his shirt and set to calculating the distance traveled. By his reckoning they should reach a holding before dusk. Wyme had not marked the farm as visited by the demons, but, he thought, the map was drawn some time ago. He decided they could not risk discovery, and blessed Flysse for her butcher's skill—there was ample meat they could eat well again. And, he thought, eyeing the sweaty faces of the two rowers, we all shall need sustenance tonight.

He rose a little, studying the river ahead. Wyme's maps had not run to such details as the marking of woods or highlands, and he thought to find a suitable resting place, hopefully sheltered from observation.

One appeared in a while. The terrain grew rougher, and a low bluff showed where the Restitution meandered southward. Loblolly pines grew tall on the crest, running down the steep flanks to form a screen between the river and the land. He pointed, advising Flysse and Davyd of their destination, then must explain how the boat might be turned in the desired direction.

It took some time before they reached the bench beneath the bluff and got the dinghy beached. Neither Flysse nor Davyd was reluctant to halt their labors, and Arcole could not resist chuckling as they groaned and stretched their backs.

"Hard work, eh?" Flysse scowled; Davyd grunted. Arcole, somewhat rested now, told them, "Do you take your ease here and I'll climb up that headland, see what's beyond. Do we have . . . visitors . . . then fire a pistol, and I'll return."

Flysse plucked her shirt away from her breasts and asked, "Can we safely bathe? I'm . . ." She grimaced her distaste.

"When I return," Arcole said. "When we know it's safe."

She nodded and said, "Be careful."

"Yes." He took his musket and set to climbing.

From atop the bluff he could see the Restitution sweep away in wide curves to north and south, thankfully empty. The far bank was a heat-hazed blur, and for a while he checked the sky there for sign of smoke. None showed, and he moved warily through the pines until he might see what lay inland.

At the edge of the hurst he perused the map again. As best he calculated, the closest holding was the Bayliss farm, a good league or more to the west. He wondered if he stood on Bayliss land, and if the farm survived still. He could see no signs of habitation; no cattle grazed the vast expanse of grass spread out before him, and there was no smoke to indicate fires of any kind. Faint in the distance he saw the glitter of a stream, and dotted over the plain were stands of timber. He hoped none hid demons, and decided that their watch this night should be set upon the bluff: that would afford a better vantage point than the bench.

As he returned it came to him that he fell back into a way of thinking he had believed lay behind him. This sense of ever-present peril, the need to set a guard each night, the endless vigilance—it all reminded him of the conflict Evander named the War of Restitution, the Levan the Conquest. Evander had won that struggle, he thought, but shall not win this small fight. No, neither Evander nor the demons—whatever they may be—shall defeat us.

He was grinning as he approached the others.

"The land stands empty," he reported. "And the river. Flysse, do you wish to bathe, it's safe enough."

Flysse said, "Praise God," in a voice so earnest, Arcole could not resist taking her in his arms and kissing her soundly.

"And we'll get a fire ready," he promised, then glancing at the sky: "Though lighting it must wait, I fear."

"No matter." Flysse lifted hair rendered heavy by her efforts from her neck. "The sun is still warm—I'll bask awhile."

Davyd could not help the image that flashed into his mind at that, and turned away so neither she nor Arcole could see him blush. "I'll gather wood," he declared gruffly.

"There's plenty up there." Arcole stabbed a finger at the bluff.

"Fresh pine?" Flysse shook her head. "That spits and smokes. Better search along the shore for drifted wood, or fallen branches. It's dry stuff we need."

Arcole exaggerated a bow. "I learn apace," he laughed. "God, what would I do without you? Without the two of you?"

"Go hungry without me," she answered, chuckling. "And without Davyd . . ."

Her laughter died. She shook her head and turned away. Davyd watched her, thinking, I'll do my best. Is it in my power, I *shall* be your Dream Guide and see you safe from harm. Then added guiltily, Yours and Arcole's both, and set to searching for suitable kindling.

That night Arcole insisted he take the first watch, that he be able to sleep the remainder and, hopefully, dream of any danger ahead. Davyd took his musket and scrambled up the cliff to take station on the rim. The river ran smooth and dark as oil below him, and the banked fire was a dim red eye between the boat and the bluff. He could barely make out the shapes of Flysse and Arcole—and did not like to look too hard—but when he did, he thought they lay together and felt a sudden flush of . . . He was not sure, it was a feeling compounded of mixed emotions: envy and embarrassment and guilt. For a while he wished he were Arcole, and could not help imagining how it might feel to lie with Flysse in his arms. Then, angry with himself for such thoughts, he rose and patrolled inland, creeping stealthily through the pines until he reached the edge and looked out across the grass. Far off, he thought he saw faint light, as if from windows, or perhaps a group of close-spaced fires. He wondered if he should return to the river to report the sight. But what if Flysse and Arcole still lay together? He felt his cheeks grow warm at the notion of interrupting them, and decided that if folk—settlers or demons—sat around those fires, they could not know they were observed, neither were they close enough to represent any immediate threat. He stood awhile, watching, then returned to the bluff's rim.

All was silent below, save for the soft whispering of the river. Stars spread overhead, brilliant as jewels scattered across a velvet cloth, and the slender crescent of the new moon drifted leisurely westward. Davyd squatted, musket across his thighs, fighting against the images of Flysse that threatened to intrude. I must not, he told himself sternly, but still there came the insidious thought: What if Arcole were not with us?

He was grateful when Arcole came to relieve him. "I thought I saw lights," he reported. "A long way off to the west."

"The Bayliss holding's in that direction." Arcole seemed in a great good humor; Davyd felt a rush of guilty envy. "It might be that: I'll take a look. Meanwhile, sleep well."

Davyd nodded and climbed down to the river.

Flysse stirred sleepily as he found his bedroll. He saw that hers and Arcole's were laid together. He took his own a little way off and stretched out, telling himself, I am the Dream Guide. I must do my duty and not think of her.

He doubted that should be possible, but his efforts at the oars and the tension of the day seeped suddenly into him, so that he slept before he knew it. And dreamed.

"There was no danger in it," he said around a mouthful of roasted beef. "I dreamed of a meeting, no more than that. I saw no faces, but I don't think they were demons."

"Can you be sure?" Arcole said.

"There was no sense of danger." Davyd shrugged. "I can't be *sure,* but before . . ." He scratched at his cheek, where the brand stood pale against his growing tan. "There was always the feeling of danger before."

Flysse said, "You slept undisturbed." And when he frowned, amplified: "You've always tossed and turned, cried out."

He nodded thoughtfully and said, "I suppose I did. Surely when I dreamed of the attack on Grostheim, I woke frightened. This was not like that at all. This was quite peaceful."

"So." Arcole wiped grease from his beard. "We're to have a meeting, eh? Likely, a peaceful meeting."

Davyd spread his hands in an equivocal gesture. "I suppose so; I don't know for sure." He smiled apologetically. "I'm sorry."

"Sorry?" Arcole laughed, and reached to slap his shoulder, turning to Flysse. "D'you hear him? He predicts our future and then apologizes."

"It's not very clear," said Davyd. "I'd hoped to do better."

"You do the best you can," Arcole returned. "I'd ask no more of any man."

Davyd liked that: that Arcole named him a man. He felt better. "I'll practice," he said, not sure how he would do that, but nonetheless determined.

Curious—and not a little wary—they loaded the dinghy and continued on their way. The sun was not long risen, but still it lit the river as if the water were molten gold. The sky was a pristine blue, the breeze that came out of the west refreshing. Herons stood, patient fishermen, along the banks, and an osprey stooped to snatch a plump trout. Magpies chattered, and from a stretch of woodland a great black flock of crows took noisy flight.

Before midmorning, as they drew level with the Bayliss farm, Davyd's dream was proved true.

He crouched in the bow, scanning the shore and the river ahead, so he was the first to see them. He gasped, settling a thumb on the musket's hammer, then said, "People!"

Arcole backed water, turning the dinghy that he might see.

Flysse said, "Not demons, I think."

"Evanderans are no less dangerous." Arcole craned around, squinting shoreward. "Does some farmer see our brands, he'll look to take us in."

"I think they're all indentured folk." Davyd shaded his eyes against the brilliance of the sun. "They look all ragged."

Arcole asked, "Are they armed?"

"They've axes and such," Davyd replied. "I can see no guns."

Arcole turned the dinghy closer to the shore and held it stationary as he surveyed the watchers. They crowded on a little jetty, studying the approaching boat. They appeared a sorry lot, four women and three men, unkempt and dressed in dirty homespun. They waved at the boat. He saw no firearms, but as Davyd had warned, they held axes and other tools. He brought the dinghy closer still.

"Flysse, do you pass me my musket?"

She obeyed even as she said, "Surely they offer no harm. Look, I can see their brands."

"Even so." Arcole nodded. "Davyd, do I give the word, fire over their heads."

He let the dinghy drift a little nearer and called out, "Greetings, friends. Who are you?"   .

They seemed nonplussed as they saw the trio in the dinghy clearly. The oldest man shouted, "You've come from Grostheim?"

"We have," Arcole replied. "And you?"

"Where are the others?" The man scanned the river as if he anticipated a flotilla. "Where are the soldiers?"

"Busy defending the city," Arcole called. "We're all alone."

A woman wailed at that, clutching a screaming child to her breast.

"No soldiers?" asked the man. "Oh, God save us! Did the master send you?"

"Who's the master?" Arcole shouted.

"Sieur Bayliss," came the reply. "Him and the mistress quit the holding weeks back. Told us to hang on, he did. Said he'd have soldiers come to bring us in."

"Grostheim was under siege when we . . . departed," Arcole called. "I know nothing of this Bayliss."

The man gaped. He turned to his companions, an expression of bewilderment on his bearded face. A younger fellow pushed to the fore and shouted, "You're exiles, no? Indentured folk like us?"

"Exiles, yes," Arcole called back. "But no longer indentured. We chose to quit our . . employment. We're headed west."

The young man turned slowly in that direction, staring at the distant shadow of the forests as if he struggled to comprehend Arcole's words.

"You're runaways? You're going into the wilderness?"

"To live free," Arcole returned.

"And you don't bring help?"

"I fear not."

"The masters'll hunt you down." The older man spoke again, goggling now, as if their presence might somehow contaminate him. "The governor'll send Militiamen after you."

"The Militiamen are otherwise occupied," Arcole gave back. "Or were when we left. The demons came in force against the city, and I doubt we'll be missed."

"No soldiers," a woman cried. "No help. Oh, God, we're done for."

The young man said, "You've a boat."

"A very small boat," Arcole said. "Barely large enough for us three. Surely too small for ten people, or even seven. Besides, you're safer here than in Grostheim."

The young man looked set to argue, but the older put a hand on his arm and said, "He's right, Gerold. We'd swamp that little thing. And if he speaks the truth about Grostheim . . ."

"He does," Flysse called. "The demons are all around the city—we fled in the confusion."

"Then what shall we do?" asked the oldster.

Arcole said, "You've not yet been attacked?"

"Not yet," came the answer in a tone of despair.

"Did Bayliss leave you weapons?" Arcole asked.

The man frowned as if the question were nonsensical and shook his head. "We're indentured folk, not allowed weapons." He touched his brand to emphasize his words. "The master took all the muskets and pistols with him."

Arcole said, "A kindly master, eh?" in a tone of contempt.

The young man said, "You've guns."

"Only these," Arcole replied. "Which we shall need, I think."

Gerold hefted the ax he carried; Davyd raised his musket across his chest. Surely it could not come to a fight? His dream had suggested no danger. He caught Gerold's eye and for a moment they stared at each other, then the ax was lowered and Gerold muttered, "God, does it come to this? We all wear the brand, no? Shall we fight one another?"

Davyd said, "I'd not."

Arcole said, "It's the masters to blame—the Autarchy of Evander. They use folk like us as they will, but when danger threatens—then they run, looking only to save their own skins."

Gerold said, "That's true, but of little comfort. What's to become of us?"

"Have the demons not yet attacked this farm," Arcole said, "then perhaps they never will. You may be safe here; surely safer than did you try for Grostheim."

Gerold spat and said, "So we're to remain; tend the master's herds and fields while he hides behind the city walls. And then, does he return?"

Arcole said, "You might keep the place for your own. Or you could follow us into the forests."

"The wilderness?" Gerold shook his head vigorously, spitting and crossing his fingers. "That's where the demons come from, no? I'll not go there."

"Nor I," agreed the oldster. "Nor any of us. But, friend, might you not stay? We'd stand a better chance with your muskets."

"Would you fight the Autarchy?" Arcole asked. "When Bayliss comes back—if he does—would you claim this farm for your own?"

It was as if he suggested some great obscenity. The old man stood with dropped jaw, and Gerold stared at Arcole as if he were crazed. The others shook their heads and voiced denial.

"Then what of us?" Arcole pressed. "You ask us to stay—to risk our lives, perhaps, in your defense. But when Bayliss returns, you'd welcome him—and hand us over?"

Gerold, at least, had the grace to blush. The old man shrugged and said, "That's the way of the world, no? The masters rule and we serve. What else can we do?"

Arcole said, "Save you've the courage to stand up for yourselves, nothing. But we go west, to freedom."

"More like to your deaths," the old man grunted.

"Perhaps." Arcole smiled. "But is that our fate, we'll die free."

"At least rest here awhile," the old man suggested. "We've food aplenty."

Arcole shook his head. "I think not. The day's young yet, and we've a way to travel. Fare you well."

He wasted no more time, but set to propelling the dinghy out into the stream, away from the dock. The exiles stood watching, their expressions hopeless.

"Might we not have stayed?" Flysse asked.

"Why?" Arcole returned. "There's nothing for us there, save likely they'd seek to take our guns. And should Bayliss come home, hand us over."

"Think you they would?" she asked. "Truly?"

Arcole nodded. "Those were defeated folk. They've accepted their lot—Evander's beaten them down."

From the bow, Davyd said, "I was afraid that Gerold was going to attack us. I feared I'd have to shoot."

"I didn't," Arcole replied calmly. "I trusted your dream."

Davyd pondered that awhile, then grinned. "Yes," he said. "I dreamed true, no?"

"You did," said Arcole. "You did, indeed."

They floated on, the days steadily warmer as spring gave way to summer, pulling to midstream where Arcole's map showed holdings—they none of them felt any desire to repeat their sad encounter with the hapless folk of the Bayliss holding. When their food ran low, Arcole shot—he could not think of it as hunting—a cow or a hog from the herds now roaming loose over the empty farmlands. Flysse demonstrated her rustic skills, filling the canteens with fresh milk, or finding vegetables to supplement the meat. Twice, she brought them eggs.

Davyd tried his hand with the fishing lines, but had no luck, and Arcole would not yet permit him to fire the musket for fear of wasting shot. Had he not dreamed, he would have felt useless; but the dreams came often now, and he grew more adept in their interpretation. It seemed that his ability increased as they drew closer to the wilderness.

Three times he warned against the danger of landing, and they duly saw demons on the shore, pushing on until night hid them and they deemed it safe to beach the dinghy. Three more times he urged they hold to midstream, and demons appeared along the bank, pacing the boat until the terrain or the sweeps of the river denied them further pursuit. And all the time the shadow line of the forests grew more distinct, no longer a faraway goal, but daily more real. The wilderness began to assume a looming physical presence, and Davyd spent more and more time each day scanning its nearing edges, seeking to find the mountains beyond.

When his surveillance was rewarded, he doubted the evidence his eyes gave him. Ahead, it was as though a vast brush had painted a line of darkness across the horizon. The pale, bright green of the grasslands gave way to darker hues, green and blue and black: the wilderness forest. That enormous swath was wide enough, but it in turn was dwarfed by what stood beyond and above. It seemed the forests climbed to meet the sky, save a wall of stone stood above the timber as if supporting the heavens. He could scarcely believe anything so massive existed in all the world as those great peaks. They ran as far as he could see to north and south, cloud shrouding the summits, their flanks all blue and gray above the green darkness of the treeline, sparkling white higher up. He thought that if safety lay there, it should be certainly very hard to find, for he could not envisage how anyone might climb such a barrier.

But on more nights than one, it was if a voice whispered from the mountains, calling him, summoning him to them. He could not understand it, but he believed—in his blood and the marrow of his bones—that he must go there, must bring Flysse and Arcole to that refuge. That he must play his part of Dream Guide.

As the forests loomed ever closer, so the signs of habitation fell away. Arcole's map showed no more holdings, and the animals grazing the riverside pastures thinned. They held a council and decided to rest awhile, long enough that Flysse might smoke meat for them to carry with them. Arcole was loath to chance the forest's hunting: he feared all their shot might be needed against more savage creatures, and indeed Davyd's dreams now suggested great peril lay ahead. It was as if they must pass a test of some kind before they could hope to gain the promised sanctuary, and often as he dreamed of the mountains and safety, he dreamed of fire and demons. But did he wake sweating, gripped by remembered terror, still there was a boon to the delay. Arcole taught him and Flysse to use their weapons, and began to teach Davyd the rudiments of swordplay.

The lessons were, of necessity, sparse, the use of powder and shot limited, but the basics were conveyed and afforded them both a small sense of security. Davyd thought that at least, did the demons fall on them, they might now give a fair account of themselves. Even so, as nightly he dreamed of threat, he longed to be gone. To face whatever lay ahead must surely be better than this waiting. He felt only relief when Flysse announced their supplies ready, and Arcole declared it time to go.

46 The Wilderness

Timber flanked the Restitution now, and the current grew daily stronger. The banks narrowed, rocks began to show, and when the first cascade appeared, Arcole declared it time to leave the dinghy and proceed on foot.

It was strange to walk again; stranger still that their way wound amongst vast trees, branches spreading wide and leafy overhead so that the sky was more often than not hidden and they marched in shadow dappled with harlequin patterns of filtered sunlight. Birds sang but were seldom seen, and startled beasts—deer and boars and bears—surprised them, fleeing half glimpsed from their approach. They none of them felt at ease. They had Davyd's dreams to set their nerves on edge, their ears straining to discern the unfamiliar forest sounds, their eyes scanning the crepuscular woods. They momentarily anticipated the onslaught of demons, coming screaming out of the trees.

Arcole took the lead, Davyd the rear, and they followed the river because it led them westward toward the mountains, and that was the direction Davyd's dreams told them to go. It was hard traveling, for the land soon rose, the river tumbling down over steep falls or cutting a way through rocky gorges, the banks often impossible to traverse, so that they must meander deeper into the forest and trust their ears to tell them where the water ran. But westward, always westward, the tree-shaded sun on their backs in the mornings, on their faces come the afternoons.

And did Arcole head their little column, it was Davyd who guided them now.

The content of the dreams still frightened him, but he was at peace with the ability. Indeed, he was proud of his role as Dream Guide and grew daily more confident. When he urged caution, Arcole listened, and Flysse studied him with wide and wondering eyes. Davyd could not help luxuriating in her admiration any more than he could resist the pleasure he felt at Arcole's trust, but it was easier to resist his guilty thoughts under the burden of responsibility. When he took his turn on guard and images of Flysse came hot into his mind, he pushed them away—there was too much danger here to allow such distractions. And when he slept, it was not Flysse who invaded his dreams, but images of demons and peril, and the sense of a hazardous maze to be traversed before they might reach safety.

That remained a promise. When he dreamed of flight from yelling monsters or of raging flames, there was always, behind the nightmare images, that vision of the mountains, and the sense of a cool wind, protective against the fire. He could still neither explain nor understand it, only *know* that sanctuary lay ahead. He thought the wilderness changed him; surely, he felt, he was no longer a frightened boy looking to Arcole for protection, but now a man. He thought, even, that he felt hair on his chin, and was proud of that.

Four days into the forest he dreamed that they should hide, and consequently they passed the next day huddled in a cave beside a waterfall. Arcole, spying from the rimrock, advised that a band of some twenty or more demons went east along their backtrail. The following morning Davyd announced it was safe to continue, and they clambered cold and damp from their hiding place.

Soon after that he urged they detour, away from the river, and Arcole agreed without demur, even though the going was hard and they neither saw nor heard demons.

One night he forbade them a fire. It had rained that day and they were soaked, but still Arcole concurred and they found a place where pines had toppled, one bringing down another across a shallow bowl, roofing the hollow so that it was hidden from casual sight: had Davyd not dreamed of such a place, they would not have found it. They gathered deadfall branches, constructing a shelter that was as much camouflage as protection against the night's cold, and leant against one another for warmth. Arcole and Davyd sat to either side of Flysse, close, and it was impossible for Davyd to ignore her proximity until voices sounded soft through the darkness.

Then he only held his musket tight and ransacked his memory for precise recollection of the dream that had warned against a fire.

It had been a jumbled affair, of savage hunters and cowering prey, and his only certainty was that they must not risk discovery. He clenched his jaw then, for his teeth threatened to chatter, and he could not tell if that was the cold or the chill of the dreadful fear that gripped him. He turned his head and saw Flysse's face a pale shape in the gloom. Almost, he took her hand, but then he saw she clutched at Arcole's arm and envied his friend that touch. He had thought such impulses banished: he turned his eyes away and cursed silently, not sure whether he cursed Arcole or himself.

Outside, beyond the sheltering trunks, the voices came closer. Soft calls went back and forth. Davyd strained to hear them clear. It seemed he could almost understand what they said, but that was impossible; and he told himself his imagination ran wild. He hooked a finger about the musket's trigger, his thumb on the hammer. He vowed that no demon should take Flysse whilst he still lived.

The voices came closer, until they sounded from just outside the makeshift shelter. The moon was filled, drifting cold, indifferent light over the forest, and its illumination granted Davyd brief glimpses of feet and legs clad in buckskin. He saw the boots the demons wore were decorated with colored beads, and flinched as the fallen pines vibrated under a demon's weight. Dead needles and shards of moldering bark cascaded down, crawling things dropping. One landed on his face and he must fight the urge to slap it away. He felt Flysse, rigid beside him. Her eyes were wide and staring and her lips were clenched. She held a pistol. Past her, Arcole held his musket upright, angled at the treacherous roof. Davyd thought his pounding heart must surely beat loud enough that the demons hear it, or some crawling, biting thing prompt him to involuntary movement. His hands began to ache as they gripped his musket: he forced himself to relax his hold. He struggled to breathe evenly. Dear God! The dream had warned of danger, but not like this, not so close. He could not understood how the demons could fail to see them.

The pines shuddered some more, creaking as the demon walked across them. It said something in its odd, almost comprehensible tongue, and then a fresh downpour rained over the three as it sprang clear. The voices receded, fading away, and finally were gone.

No one moved or spoke. Davyd felt sweat run hot down his face, cold down his back. An owl hooted, then some large animal shuffled past. Deep in the forest a beast snarled, and another screamed.

In a voice so soft it should not carry past the shelter, Arcole said, "I believe they're gone."

Davyd was surprised so low a tone could sound so tense. He turned his head slowly sideways, shuddering as something with too many legs fell down his chest and began to crawl over his belly. It was more than he could bear: he pressed a hand to his wet shirt, crushing the insect.

"Careful." Arcole's warning was still pitched low. "Best, I think, that we stay here. How say you, Davyd?"

He nodded, not trusting his voice. He thought that if he spoke at all, he would likely scream. He felt horribly cold and thrust a hand into his mouth, biting, that his teeth not rattle announcement of their presence. Arcole's teeth flashed white in a brief smile. Then Davyd flinched as Flysse's hand touched his.

She put her mouth close to his ear. Her breath was warm and made him shiver. "Praise God for your dreams," she murmured. "Without you we'd surely be dead."

He stretched his mouth in what he hoped was a gallant smile, though it was more likely a grimace. Flysse answered his smile and touched her lips to his cheek. It was a cruel kindness.

Arcole said, "Do you two sleep now, and I'll watch the night."

Flysse said, "I doubt I can. My heart races too fast." But she rested her head against his shoulder and closed her eyes.

Davyd wished it were his shoulder cradling her head. He wished the confines of their shelter did not press them so close. He doubted he could sleep. The last thing he remembered was Arcole's low voice: "None snores, eh?"

That night he dreamed the wind blew warm and strong out of the mountains, and there was no fire nor any demons—only the wind, like summer sunlight on his face. In the morning he knew it was safe to go on.

"Think you they hunt us?" Arcole asked as they prepared to leave.

Davyd stretched, flexing cramped muscles. "I don't know," he said. "How can they know we're here?"

"Perhaps they've some way of sending messages." Arcole shrugged. "Perhaps those bands we saw along the river send word. Perhaps they hunt us because we slew their fellows."

"I think perhaps they claim all this land for their own, and name any who come here enemy. I think they are filled with hate."

The words were no sooner uttered than Davyd wondered why he said them; they seemed to come involuntary, from that part of him that dreamed. Surely it was not a thing he had considered before: survival was enough. He frowned, confused, and brushed bark and bugs from his hair.

Arcole nodded thoughtfully. "And how much do they claim?"

"Likely all of Salvation," Davyd answered, but it seemed another spoke, his mouth only the tool of utterance.

Arcole studied him a moment, then: "And the mountains? Beyond the mountains?"

"Safety." Suddenly Davyd was entirely himself again. He shook his head, shrugging, wondering if the frightening night had deranged him. "I don't know, only that the mountains are our one chance."

Arcole fixed his pack across his back. "They'll not be easy to climb." He smiled. "But perhaps you'll dream us up a pass."

Davyd nodded. "Perhaps."

The mountains were invisible now, lost behind the curtain of trees. They seemed very far away, and he could not imagine climbing such heights. For an instant he wondered if escape was only an impossible dream, the wind that promised safety only a subterfuge, a trick. Perhaps his dreaming would bring them all safe through the forests only to see them die amongst those gigantic peaks. For a moment he doubted.

Then he gasped, his vision blurring. It was as if he dreamed awake: he felt the wind on his face, and through the timber saw a light that burned off doubt. In a voice he was not sure belonged to him, he said, "The mountains are safe. We must go there."

He staggered and felt Arcole's hands on him, holding him upright. His friend's face was etched with concern.

"Are you fevered?"

"I'm . . ." He shook his head. "No . . . we're safe now. We must go on . . . To the mountains."

Arcole let him go, said, "Yes. But are you hale?"

For a moment he stared at Davyd as if he were a stranger; for a moment Davyd felt he was a stranger. Then he swallowed, ducking his head. His vision cleared and he saw only the forest again. He said, "I am," and grinned. "Save that I'm wet and cold and would sleep a week or so, all's well."

Hesitantly, Arcole said, "It should be dangerous to chance a fire now. Those creatures might see the smoke."

It sounded like an apology: it was odd to hear such indecision from so confident a man, and Davyd frowned. "I'll dry out as we walk," he said. "And tonight we can build a fire."

"As you say." Arcole looked to his priming as if he could no longer meet Davyd's eyes.

.   .   .

Flysse had retired into the trees to perform her ablutions, and halted
within their shade when she heard the curious conversation. She did not
intend to eavesdrop, but there was that about Davyd's manner that
prompted her to wait and listen. He was so much changed from the
frightened boy she had comforted in Bantar, she scarce recognized him
any longer. He had seemed so young then, so skinny and afraid, she
could not help but mother him. Now he was a young man. He had
grown tall and muscular, and between their arrival in Grostheim and
now his voice had deepened. And there were other changes. She wished
she had not kissed him—she feared it should stoke the fires she sensed
burned within him, and that could lead only to difficulties.

It was no longer possible to ignore the fact that he harbored feelings
for her. She supposed that was not so unusual, and thought that had
they remained in Grostheim, he would, in time, have transferred that
infatuation to some girl of his own age. But they had not remained—
they were three folk fleeing into the wilderness, and that forced them on
ever more proximate. She wished she could find some way to damp his
ardor without hurting his feelings. Perhaps when they reached the
promised sanctuary of the mountains . . .

Which prompted fresh wonderings. That Davyd was a Dreamer, she
accepted—was grateful for his talent—but even in that he changed. She
had urged he endeavor to employ his gift more precisely, and since that
day it seemed the ability increased apace. He dreamed nightly now.
Indeed, did she interpret what she had just heard aright, he now began
to dream awake. She understood the look Arcole had given him: it was
as if Davyd entered some strange transitional phase, as if the butterfly
began to emerge from the cocoon. He remained the youth she knew,
and at the same time seemed a stranger. She wondered what he would
be when finally grown to maturity.

She rested a hand against the gnarled bole of a pine and looked to
the sky. The sun came out now, the clouds that had delivered the rain
blown off on a high westerly wind. Light came down bright through the
branches, warm as a lover's promise, and the forest seemed a tranquil
place. It had been since they reached these woods, she thought, that
Davyd's prophetic dreams had grown so much stronger. Along the river,
as they closed on the wilderness, the ability had burgeoned, but now it
was stronger than ever. It was as if he saw each day mapped out, and
was no longer at all hesitant in his predictions. He told them where to
walk and where to camp, when they might forage for food and—most
important of all—when they need hide. Without him she doubted even

Arcole could survive for long, and even as she was grateful, she felt a little frightened. Almost, she thought, Davyd became something more than human.

Then, as she came out from the timber and he saw her approach, he was only Davyd again, smiling and then blushing, busying himself with his gear. He was bedraggled, his lengthening hair a lank red curtain about his face, his shirt stretched wet across his broadened shoulders. She smiled, but he was aping Arcole, checking the priming of his musket, and did not see.

"Do we break our fast?" she asked for want of something to say. "Or do we flee?"

Arcole said, "Our guide tells me we're safe for now. But best we go on, look forward to a fire tonight. Eh, Davyd?"

Flysse knew her husband well enough to recognize he sought to heal whatever breach that earlier strangeness might have opened, and smiled her approval. Davyd did not look up, only nodded absently and murmured, "Yes; tonight."

"Then onward we go," Arcole declared, then looked at Davyd and asked, "Do you take the lead?"

Davyd stared back, momentarily perplexed. "Me?" He pushed wet hair from his forehead, which furrowed now.

"It seems only fitting," Arcole replied. "You guide us, no? Your rightful place is in the lead."

Davyd thought a moment, then nodded. "I suppose so," he allowed, seeming not entirely convinced. "But I don't think it really makes much difference."

Arcole said, "Even so," and bowed, gesturing that Davyd set himself to the fore.

Davyd straightened his back, squared his shoulders, and grinned as he braced his musket across his chest.

"Follow me, then."

Arcole saluted and motioned Flysse ahead of him as he took station at the rear.

That night they found a clearing cut by a little rill that bubbled through the grass. They built a fire and Flysse set out snares, winning them four plump rabbits. They still set a watch, but just as Davyd had promised, no danger came—only a black bear that snuffled down to the water, then lumbered off grumbling as it caught their scent.

It had by now become their accepted custom that Davyd take the first watch, that he have the remainder of the night to dream. Flysse waited until he slept, then crept to where Arcole sat: she felt a need to express her thoughts.

"He changes," she whispered. "I saw what happened this morning."

"That was odd, no?" Arcole returned her. "But to our good, I think."

"Yes." Flysse nodded against his chest. "But why? He was not like this in Grostheim."

Arcole shrugged. "I've not met a Dreamer before, only seen them burned. Perhaps the hexes on Grostheim's walls prevented him. Perhaps danger brings out the talent, or it's to do with the wilderness. Perhaps it was your suggestion."

"How could the wilderness make him dream?" she asked. "And if it does, do the demons dream also?"

"I don't know." Arcole shrugged again. "Perhaps they do. I'd hazard the guess they've magic of some kind. How else could they creep up on the city so?"

Flysse said, "Do you think it still stands?"

"Perhaps." Arcole nuzzled her hair. "The walls were strong, and hexed; the Militia had weapons aplenty. Wyme might have sent back to Evander, asking for reinforcements."

Flysse said, "Do the demons prevail, we shall be all alone."

Arcole laughed softly and said, "That was our plan, no? And does Davyd bring us to this 'safe place' of his . . . Perhaps we shall find folk there. Hopefully of kinder disposition."

Flysse lifted her head to look into his eyes. "Think you it could be so?" she asked. "Can there be other folk here, kinder?"

"Who knows?" Arcole bent to kiss her gently. "All I know for sure is that we must go on. We've little other choice, eh?"

"If the demons have magic," Flysse murmured, "shall they not find us?"

"They've not so far," Arcole said. "And we've Davyd for our guide. We must trust *his* magic to bring us through."

"Yes." Flysse was silent awhile, then: "He changes in other ways."

"He grows," Arcole said. "And fast."

"He grows and . . ." Flysse hesitated to say it.

Arcole finished the sentence for her: "He harbors a barely concealed passion for you. Yes, think you I've not noticed that?"

"It's . . . difficult." Flysse looked to where Davyd lay, glad that he slept soundly. "I'd not hurt him, but it is sometimes . . . embarrassing."

"I cannot find it in me to condemn him for finding you desirable."

Arcole spoke with exaggerated solemnity. "After all, I share that passion. But do you wish me to speak with him . . ."

"No!" Flysse shook her head. "That should only make it worse. He'd feel guilty—God, he already does! Sometimes he'll not meet my eye, but only blushes and turns away—and I'd not come between you. But when we reach his 'safe place'—when we halt—what then?"

"Perhaps," said Arcole slowly, "we must share you."

" 'Sieur!" Flysse punched his chest, hard enough he winced. "I am your wife. Yours! I'll not be passed about like some doxy. Is that the way of it in the Levan? Be it so, it is not mine!"

She heard a strange sound then, coming from her husband's throat. It was as if he choked, and for an instant she feared her blow had wounded him. Then she realized he suppressed laughter—and struck him again.

"Think you I'd share you with anyone?" he asked. "God, Flysse, were Davyd not my friend, I'd call him out just for the way he looks at you!"

Flysse smiled, mollified. "Even so," she whispered, "he becomes a man, and it shall likely become a problem, no?"

Arcole nodded, thoughtful now. "If there are folk in his 'safe place,' " he said, "then surely there must be women there. If not . . . Well, perhaps he and I shall go back to Salvation to steal him a wife."

"Steal a woman?" Flysse was shocked.

"Do the demons leave any alive," Arcole said. "He becomes, after all, a handsome enough young man. Perhaps some branded girl dreams of freedom and would welcome a handsome young rover to satisfy her dreams."

Flysse wondered if he was serious, and if she could approve. "Would you do that for Davyd?" she asked. "Truly?"

"For Davyd," Arcole replied, "yes. Sooner than come to blows over you."

"I hope," Flysse said earnestly, "That there *are* folk in the 'safe place.' I'd not see you go back, husband. Not leave me again."

"Nor I." Arcole spoke no less fervently. "But for now, all we can do is hope, eh? Let us reach this promised sanctuary, and then discuss Davyd's future."

Flysse said, "Yes," and snuggled against him, drowsy now.

The forest rose steeper as they progressed westward, spurs of stone beginning to thrust through the timber as if the mountains clawed an anchorage in the lowlands. Often now they could see the heights like an enormous wall before them. Their passage slowed in consequence, for often they must clamber up vertiginous slopes or detour around those too precipitous to climb. Sometimes there were gorges so sheer they could only traverse the cliff edge until gentler terrain allowed them passage. The high waters of the river were left behind, lost in the maze of timber and undulating land, and they relied entirely on Davyd to guide them and still they must hide when he ordered.

It seemed there were fewer demons roaming the woodlands now, and days passed when Davyd announced it safe to hunt, or delay as Flysse found mushrooms and wild onions and other plants that flavored the deer Arcole brought down, or the grouse and rabbits she snared.

Davyd enjoyed those days, for Arcole taught him to stalk and—finally—allowed him a shot at a deer. He was mightily proud of his kill, and could not resist telling the tale of the hunt in great detail to Flysse. No less did he enjoy his continuing lessons with the smallsword, the more for Arcole's praise of his burgeoning skill.

"You've the makings of a fine swordsman," Arcole announced to his delight. "Do you only practice, I think you shall be very good indeed."

Davyd beamed his pleasure. Flysse, watching them, was somewhat less pleased. It occurred to her that if her worst doubts were realized—if Davyd's infatuation did not wane—he might make some indecorous approach and Arcole take offense. It might, she thought, come to a fight; and her husband taught Davyd his talents. As yet, the young man would stand no chance against Arcole's superior skill, but if Arcole taught him well enough . . . Flysse prayed events not reach that turn—she'd see neither of them harmed.

They continued to climb, the forest thinning as they moved ever deeper into the foothills. The beech and maple of the eastern edges gave way to spruce and tamarack, balsam fir, and their route lay often over open ground, across high shoulders of rock and slopes of littered scree. The mountains were no longer hidden, but always in sight, vast buttresses rising overhead, the peaks beyond misty with cloud. They seemed as much a barrier as sanctuary, for as their enormity was revealed, so it dawned on the travelers that the conquest of such monoliths was impossible. They would surely freeze or starve or fall to their deaths did they attempt to ascent that sky-challenging wall.

But Davyd led them unerring as a scented hound. It was if a lodestone lay inside his skull, guiding him to the unknown refuge of his dreams. He did not hesitate, and neither Arcole nor Flysse offered argument as he urged them onward, though their muscles protested the climbing and their bellies grew hollow as the game grew scarcer.

The deer and rabbits of the lower forests did not venture there, and the great horned sheep that traversed the ledges defied hunting, too often leaping agile away before Arcole or Davyd had the chance to fire, those shot too often tumbling down into inaccessible ravines. They went often hungry and often cold, for kindling was harder to find and the nights grew chill; but Davyd insisted they must go on, and his companions followed.

They went up through the foothills to the flanks of the true mountains, where only bare stone rose above and the only food was the fish they caught in lonely tarns. For days Davyd had dreamed only of the wind, of its promise, then one night, on a shelf that shone like polished onyx under the moon, he moaned and tossed about, and woke wide-eyed and sweating.

"They're close!" he gasped, staring around, his hands instinctively finding his musket, clutching the gun to his chest. "Oh, God! We may not have time!"

He sprang to his feet, ignoring his companions as he ran to the shelf's edge, scanning the slopes below. Arcole bade Flysse secure their packs and hurried to join him.

"What did you dream?"

Davyd turned fevered eyes on the man. "Fire met the wind," he moaned. "Always before, the wind has turned the fire back. This time it couldn't! I stood between, but when I tried to walk into the wind, hands of flame reached out to pull me back. Arcole, we must hurry!"

"Yes." Arcole surveyed the heights. "But to where?"

The shelf was reached up a near-vertical slope, backed along most of its length by a sheer wall of impassable stone. To the north, it curved and fell down in a rocky jumble to a ravine where white water foamed. There, the cliff was climbable—but barely, and only with time-consuming difficulty. Were they on that ascent when the demons came, they would have no chance: the demons need only stand below and pick them off.

Davyd said, "Up! It's the only way."

"If they catch us there, we're dead." Arcole surveyed the cliff, the shelf. "Do we stand here and fight, we've surely a better chance."

"No!" Davyd shook his head. "We must climb. Do we stay here, we're lost."

Arcole said, "Caught on that climb, we're lost."

Davyd faced him. His eyes were wild and red with tortured sleep, shifting about as if he momentarily anticipated the arrival of the demons. "Trust me," he croaked. "Arcole, you *must!*"

Arcole looked at his face and nodded: it was impossible to argue with such fervor. "So be it." He spun, calling to Flysse. "We must climb. Now!"

Urgency was palpable as they ran toward her and she handed them their packs, fixing her own across her back. They thrust their muskets through the rolled tarpaulins and slung them in place. None spoke as they hurried to the farther end of the shelf.

Then Arcole said, "Flysse, do you go first. That way . . ."

He fell silent as a yammering shriek disturbed the morning. More rang out, as if wild dogs came running hot on their scent. They began to climb.

It seemed madness to attempt the ascent. Leisurely, it should likely have taken the better part of the morning to reach the rimrock. It needed care, the cautious checking of hand- and footholds. Yet now they went incautious, swift as strength and rock allowed. Flysse had a brief wild image of frightened spiders running up a wall.

The howling grew louder. She heard Arcole curse. An arrow clattered off the rock above her, sparking chips that fell like sharp rain against her face. She dared not look down, only climb and pray.

Arcole lodged the fingers of his left hand on a jut of stone and tugged his pistol loose. It was difficult to cock the hammer without losing the priming, without loosing his precarious footing. He twisted round as far as he was able and saw a snarling, painted demon below, sighting down the length of an arrow. He fired, and the demon screamed, falling back. He jammed the spent pistol into his belt and went on climbing. He could not believe—did Davyd dream it, or no— that they could survive this.

Davyd only climbed. A dreadful fear ˙gripped him, far worse than the thought of crashing to the shelf below or any contemplation of an arrow striking. He would prefer that to falling into the hands of the demons—he *knew* his death should be slow at their hands. He somehow knew, as surely as if he dreamed it, that those creatures would recognize him as a Dreamer and punish him for that damning gift in ways worse than even an Inquisitor might invent. He damned himself for a failure— he was the Dream Guide! He should have anticipated this. He could not understand how he had failed, save all had been some weird, oneiric design to bring them to this impasse. Perhaps the demons had played with him, driving him to this place. Perhaps they had put the dreams in his head.

Then, suddenly as it had come before, he felt the wind touch his face, and—as before, when he had doubted—he felt he saw a light like a welcoming lantern at the mouth of a long, dark street. Almost, he lurched back, but his fingers and his toes held their grip and he clung only a moment to the sheer rock, not knowing he smiled. He felt once more confident—this *was* the only way. Had they remained on the shelf, the demons would have overwhelmed them with sheer weight of numbers. It still seemed entirely impossible, but this way—this fly's climb—*was* their only hope.

He heard Arcole grunt, "Climb, for God's sake!" and realized he had halted. The crash of an arrow galvanized him and he went limber upward, strong now, as if the wind had toned his muscles, washed away fatigue. It remained hideously dangerous—likely still impossible—but hope drew him on, sure as baited hook to fish. Were he to die now, it should be in strength, not fear.

Then panic threatened as he heard Arcole cry out and craned his head around to see his friend's face contorted in a grimace of pain. A shaft jutted from his waist, above the hip. He feared Arcole must lose his grip and tumble down. He reached toward the man even as Flysse screamed.

"No!" Arcole's lips stretched back from gritted teeth. "Go on, both of you. It's not so bad."

Davyd hesitated, and Arcole mouthed a foul curse. "Go on, I say. You can't help me. Go on!"

Still, Davyd hesitated. Arcole spat against the stone and eased upward until he was level with Davyd.

"Do I fall, then I charge you with Flysse's care." His voice was hoarse, his breath labored. "She'll need you. Now go on."

He began to struggle past, and Davyd saw the red stain spreading across his shirt. Flysse began to climb again: Davyd saw no choice but to follow.

They clambered up, Davyd's warning dream delivered just soon enough that they rose past the arrows' range. The shafts clattered about their feet, then below them. Flysse and Arcole both climbed with grim determination, their faces to the rock, not looking back. Davyd risked a glance and saw demons mounting after them—three, then five, then seven; twenty or more below, shrieking as they watched the vertical pursuit.

Up: fingers wearing ragged against the stone, leaving bloody smears where they found niches, toes scrabbling for footholds, lungs searing with the effort. And still the cliff lofted above, the demons swift behind. Flysse thought of slow bugs chased by lithe spiders.

Then a shriek; another. Rocks fell. They flattened against the stone. More missiles went by them: demons were smashed away.

Flysse screamed again, pushing back from the cliff as a face appeared above her. Almost she fell, but strong hands grasped her wrists and snatched her up, inward: into the stone.

Arcole looked up at her cry and saw her disappear. It was not possible—no ledge or cave existed there, but still she disappeared. He fought the pain of his wound, shouting her name as he willed his exhausted body to fresh effort. Wildly, he wondered if the arrow had slain him, and now he clambered through that limbo the priests spoke of, punished for his sins. If so, he still felt pain—the arrow burned a fiery shaft at every movement. He had not known such agony since his branding. He shouted "Flysse!" again, and gaped as a face showed where no face could be. It was a round, thick-bearded visage that looked as if some mossy rock were carved in semblance of human physiognomy. He wondered if this were some other kind of demon. No matter: it had taken Flysse and he would go after her.

Davyd felt more confident, but even so it was bewildering to see Flysse drawn into the rockface. And then Arcole, as he achieved the place. He climbed with a fury that took him past Davyd, and an odd face appeared, framed in shimmering dark light, as if it peered out from a night-washed cavern mouth. It smiled, exposing wide and craggy teeth, and reached for Arcole with large, knobby hands, and Arcole was gone.

Davyd stared, wishing for the reassurance of the dream wind, the light, but all he saw now was empty stone.

Then the face again, another beside, like clumsy clay effigies, both grimacing and beckoning. When they appeared, so did the shadow of the impossible cave. Their hands opened to take him, fingers powerful as the manacles he had once worn closing about his wrists. He felt his feet torn free of the cliff, and for an instant he hung in empty air. Then he was hauled, ungainly as a filled sack, into a cave.

He landed gasping. Large, booted feet surrounded him, descending from sturdy legs clad in tanned leather. When he looked up, he saw a ring of bearded faces that made him think of the gnomes Aunt Dory had told him dwelt inside the hills and came out by night to steal away human children. They wore wide swords, and several carried battle-axes, the blades like lethal crescent moons. Their eyes were large and luminous, peering unreadable at the refugees. Davyd lay panting, turning his head to find his companions. Flysse crouched against a wall of stone, her gaze intent on Arcole. He lay on his face, the shaft of the demon's arrow rising from his back. Davyd could see his shirt and breeches stained with blood; he could not tell if his friend still breathed. Behind them, where he and Arcole and Flysse had been pulled into the mountain—where the cavern's mouth should be—there was only smooth dark stone.

47 Under the Hills and Far Away

Davyd stared at the blank stone, wondering for a moment if he lost his mind. Or perhaps he dreamed all this—the attack, the desperate flight, the impossible rescue—and would in a while awake. But he *felt* the rock against his back, and when he dragged a hand over the floor he felt his skin abraded, so he decided it was not a dream but only impossible. He caught Flysse's eye and saw amazement and disbelief on her face before she returned her attention to Arcole.

Davyd said, "This cannot be," less in belief than for want of hearing his own voice, the reassurance that they were safe, if that were the case and they not hauled from the frying pan to be set in the fire. He looked at the odd, gnomic creatures and asked, "What are you?"

They smiled—that baring of the teeth a comfort, for their expressions were friendly—and one tapped his chest and said in a guttural voice, "Colun," and then a string of syllables Davyd could not understand, though it seemed they stood on the edge of comprehensibility.

He said, "Davyd," and touched a shaking hand to his own chest; then pointed at Flysse and said her name, and then Arcole's.

The one called Colun nodded and spoke again, gesturing the while at Arcole, and though Davyd could not understand him, the sentences had a reassuring sound, so when the craggy little man knelt beside Arcole to study the arrow, Davyd said to Flysse, "They mean us no harm, I think."

She seemed not to hear him but hovered protectively over Arcole, and when Colun touched her shoulder she flinched and swung desperate eyes to Davyd.

He said again, more firmly now as conviction took hold, "They mean us no harm, Flysse. They saved us from the demons, no? And my dreams brought us to them, so surely they cannot intend harm."

She looked at him, and then at Colun. Tears ran down her cheeks as her eyes returned to Arcole, but she allowed herself removed from his side and took position at his head, cradling him and stroking his hair.

Colun gently touched the arrow and spoke, gesturing with a knife he drew. Davyd gathered that he pantomimed the removal of the shaft and nodded and said to Flysse, "I think he'd take out the arrow."

"Is that safe?" Flysse asked. "Can he?"

Davyd had no idea, but he thought that Arcole should likely die if such surgery were not performed; and knew it was beyond his capability. He nodded and said, "Can you remove it?" And when Flysse shook her head, "Then best we let . . . Colun?"

The little man nodded enthusiastically, seeming somehow to comprehend the exchange. He beckoned two of his companion gnomes forward, indicating that one hold down Arcole's legs, the other his shoulders. Then he smiled reassuringly at Flysse and slit Arcole's shirt that it might be removed. Arcole groaned and stirred, but the little men held him firm as Colun examined the wound. Another of his kin approached with a torch and he turned his knife blade in the flame. Then, with a delicacy surprising in one who appeared carved from the rock itself, he applied the blade to Arcole's skin.

Arcole cried out; Flysse gasped as he bucked, her eyes wide and intent on Colun. Davyd winced in sympathy as blood welled from the cut. Colun bent closer, working the blade cautiously into Arcole's back. Then he set one gnarly hand around the shaft and tugged it clear. The head came out all bloody and he studied it a moment, then said, "Chakthi," which sounded to Davyd like a curse, and flung the arrow away.

Another picked it up and broke the shaft in two, then went to where the cave mouth had been and set a hand flat on the stone and murmured softly. Davyd gaped as the opening reappeared and the broken arrow was hurled out—as if, he thought, they'd not have it contaminate this place of sanctuary. He watched bemused as some reversing cantrip was uttered and the hole once again sealed itself.

He looked to see if Flysse had witnessed this fresh marvel, but she was focused entirely on Arcole. Nor did any of the gnomes heed the magic, as if it were to them mundane, and Davyd returned his attention to his wounded comrade.

Arcole's breathing was for a while ragged as a mossy compress was set on the wound and bandaged in place, but then it grew even, and when a gnome moistened his face and brought a cup to his lips, he murmured faint thanks. Davyd exhaled a sigh of relief; Flysse smiled gratefully.

Colun shrugged and spoke, gesturing at where the cave mouth had been, his rocky features expressing distaste. Davyd understood none of it, save that several times a word that sounded like *Tack-in* was spoken, and *Chakthi*. He supposed they referred to the demons, and thanked whatever power sent him his dreams and had brought them there, for the rescue. He could no longer doubt that these odd, underhill folk were friends.

Colun rose then, wiping his blade clean, and barked orders that sent two of his fellows scurrying off into the depths of the cavern, which was, Davyd now saw, not a cave but a tunnel that ran back deep into the mountain. He studied it closer and wondered dazedly what produced the sunny light, and then thought again of the opening appearing in the impervious cliff—closed now as if it had never existed—and realized his saviors commanded magic. He hoped they entertained no animosity toward Dreamers: he recognized there could now be no turning back.

Then the two gnomes Colun had dispatched returned with a litter, and Arcole was lifted gently onto the makeshift stretcher. Colun beckoned, indicating Flysse and Davyd rise and accompany him, and they obeyed unquestioning as he set off into the mountain.

Colun's men bore the litter and Flysse and Davyd took station at either side. Flysse took Arcole's hand, but he seemed unaware of her touch, gone away into restful unconsciousness. She kept her eyes on him, only occasionally glancing up to see what lay ahead, whilst Davyd—confident Arcole was in good hands—stared awed about.

It was a journey of wonder to walk that passageway, its floor smoother than a city pavement, the light radiating from the walls and roof bright as summer's noon, the air flinty crisp, seeming to smell of the rock itself. More marvelous still was the knowledge that they traversed the mountains, that this tunnel ran straight and true through heights impossible to scale. As they progressed steadily deeper, Davyd felt growing inside him the absolute conviction that they came to sanctuary. He smiled, confident now that his dreams had guided them well, that he *was* the Dream Guide and had not failed his comrades. He looked across Arcole's supine body to Flysse and saw her smile, albeit wanly, before her attention was returned to Arcole.

They went on through the perpetual light, which shone always around and ahead of them, though when Davyd glanced back he saw that it faded behind them, as if their passage allowed the glow to subside into twilight. He guessed—it was not possible to reckon time accurately on this subterranean journey—that they walked away the morning. Surely he felt weariness pervade his limbs, muscles strained by the desperate climb beginning to protest this further exertion. Flysse, he saw, began to limp, her breath laboring, and he quickened his pace so that he drew alongside Colun.

"Is it much farther?" he asked, then snorted laughter and shrugged as he realized that Colun likely understood him no better than he comprehended the gnome's language. He pointed back at Flysse and then pantomimed exhaustion.

Colun nodded sagely and then shook his head, uttering a burst of the guttural syllables. Davyd frowned, thinking that the small man's words seemed clearer now, almost understandable. It was as if they each spoke some oddly distorted version of the same language, denied interpretation only by accent and emphasis. But that, he thought, could not be: he spoke Evanderan, and Colun was surely not of that country—save Aunt Dory's tales had all been true and gnomes did exist. But not, he quickly told himself, as Aunt Dory had described them—not child stealers, but benign. Still, some growing measure of communication was reached, for he gathered they had not much farther to go before they could rest. Perhaps, he thought, whatever magic gouged this tunnel and lights our way also gifts us with tongues, that we come to understanding.

He nodded to Colun, smiled, and fell back to speak with Flysse. "I think it's not far," he said, "before we can rest."

Flysse smiled wearily. "You speak their language now?"

Davyd shrugged. "It's as though"—he shook his head helplessly, grinning in mild embarrassment, for he'd not appear presumptious in her eyes—"as if I *almost* understand. And Colun seems to understand me."

"Perhaps," Flysse returned him, echoing his own thoughts, "magic unites us. Why not? God knows, there's surely magic here."

They halted where the tunnel expanded into a circular stony chamber, openings gaping in the rock as if this were some kind of under-mountain crossroads. At the center was a well, and around the walls were benches wide enough to sleep on, with mattresses and brightly colored blankets. An oven was cut into the circular wall, set ready with kindling, and with niches to either side from which food was produced and set to cooking.

Arcole was lowered carefully to the floor, and Colun examined his bandages and his face, grinning delightedly as his patient opened bleary eyes and asked hoarsely, "Where am I?"

Flysse was at his side on the instant, clutching his hands and stooping to kiss his cheek even as she said, "Safe! Oh, God, Arcole! I feared you were slain."

"I too," he croaked. "Davyd?"

"We're all safe. Davyd's warning came timely. He was right about everything."

"Did you doubt him?" Arcole attempted to rise, but Colun set an irresistible hand on his chest and pushed him back. Arcole gaped as he saw the craggy features. "I thought I'd dreamed you," he muttered, "but whoever you are—or whatever—you've my thanks, 'sieur."

Colun beamed as if he understood, and with words and gestures indicated that Arcole rest.

Davyd came to his side with a cup of water—this place was well equipped, as if it were some kind of dormitory—and brought the cup to Arcole's lips.

Arcole drank and nodded thanks and said, "You did well, my friend. I'd not have thought to come here, wherever this is."

"We're under the mountain." Davyd waved an excited hand, indicating the chamber. His words came tumbling out, impelled by the delight he felt that Arcole survived. "The cliff opened and the gnomes pulled us in. Then the cave closed and they dug the arrow out of your back and carried you here. Their leader's called Colun, and I think the demons are their enemies."

Colun glanced up at mention of his name, and Arcole said, "Well, Sieur Colun, you've my gratitude. Indeed, my undying gratitude."

He chuckled at the pun and then began to cough. Colun came quickly to his side, indicating he should not speak, but lie still. Flysse stroked his hair and mopped his sweat-beaded brow.

"Rest," she urged. "You were sore hurt."

Arcole said, "I know," and grinned. "But it appears I am in good hands now. Surely, I've a pretty nurse. And"—he reached to take Davyd's hand—"a true friend to guide and guard me."

"I was afraid," Davyd admitted. "I feared I was wrong, and that you were slain."

"You saved us," Arcole replied. "I'm the more in your debt now."

Davyd grinned and shrugged. Flysse said, "As Colun tells you, rest. They prepare food, but after you've eaten you must sleep."

"As you command"—Arcole's eyes fixed on her worried face—"my lovely wife."

She smiled and stroked his cheek and for a while it was obvious that they saw only each other. And so relieved was he that Arcole lived, Davyd could not envy that communion but feel only a tremendous gratitude that his friend was alive.

He withdrew a little way, settling on a bench as the chamber grew redolent of cooking, reminding his stomach it was a long time since last any of them had eaten. He smiled his thanks when a gnome handed him a bowl of beaten metal filled with meat and vegetables, and hungrily set to consuming the tasty food. Colun, he saw, mashed a bowl for Arcole, sprinkling the resultant soup with herbs of some kind before passing the dish to Flysse. The gnome nodded approvingly as she began to spoon the mixture into Arcole's mouth, watching awhile as the man ate. Davyd assumed the little man satisfied with his patient's progress, and that was a further comfort. Davyd realized he trusted Colun without reservation, as if his dreaming talent spoke on the gnome's behalf.

When they had finished eating, Colun allowed them to rest awhile longer. Arcole was gone to sleep, and both Davyd and Flysse welcomed the respite. Flysse's eyes drooped shut as she leant against a bench, still holding Arcole's hand; and for all his wonderment, Davyd felt sleep's curtains drawing closed. He could, he thought drowsily, sleep away days —now that he felt safe.

But soon enough Colun was shaking them awake, indicating that they press on. Davyd went to the well and splashed cool water on his face, realizing the while that only Colun and the two litter bearers remained. He wondered where the others had gone, and with much gesturing, Colun succeeded in advising him they were returned to the cave mouth. To keep watch, Davyd thought; and wondered if that was a thing these strange folk always did, as if they were guardians of these mountains.

As they marched on, the tunnel grew wider and branched in places, and in others revealed openings, large and small, that suggested a labyrinth of passageways. Davyd thought of the vast and widespread heights he had seen from the wilderness forest, and marveled anew that those massy crags and peaks were all criss crossed with tunnels like an ant's nest. What magic Colun's people must command to have built these secret ways. He wondered how long they had inhabited the hills, and wished he spoke their language that he might learn more about them.

But were the tunnels marvelous, still they did not prepare him for what he saw at the journey's end.

They emerged under a wide and intricately decorated arch onto a broad balcony that seemed suspended in space. Davyd and Flysse gasped in unison, halting as they stared at the wondrous panorama spread before them. Colun, it would seem, had anticipated this, for he, too, halted, allowing them awhile to gape.

They were in a cavern so vast, it seemed the entire heart of the mountain had been carved out, the stone rendered a hollow shell containing as many, or more, folk as Grostheim. Indeed Davyd's impression was of a city hidden in the hill, all bustling with industry and lit by that same magic as illuminated the tunnels.

To either side of the balcony, wide stairways descended to the cavern floor—save, Davyd thought, "cavern" was too small a word to encompass this place—where silvery springs filled pools and wells around which were constructed pathways, ramps, more balconies, and stairways. About the edges of the cavern stood houses that appeared less built than grown from the stone itself. They climbed the walls like martins' nests, connected by arcing bridges and intricate walkways. Distant along the enormous hollow the glow of fires could be seen, the clangor of beaten metal echoing as if smiths worked there. Then Davyd saw the most wondrous thing of all. Peering down, he saw a gnome standing before an outcrop of jagged rock, his hands raised and his mouth moving. It was as if he worshipped or spoke to the stone. Davyd could not hear what was said, but as the tiny figure performed its strange ritual, the rock began to move like butter set too close to flame. Davyd's jaw fell open as he watched the stone melt and flow, oozing viscous until the outcrop was become smooth, and steps formed in its side. The distant figure stepped back, arms akimbo as it surveyed its handiwork, then turned and called something that brought more gnomes to survey the magical construction.

Davyd started as Colun touched his elbow. The little man was smiling as if amused, and pointed at the Stone Shaper, saying a word that sounded to Davyd like "golan," then pointed at the houses and back at the reformed stone. Davyd guessed he said the "golan" began work on a new house.

"This is . . ." Davyd shook his head, lost for words.

"Incredible," Flysse supplied, her own eyes wide with wonder.

Colun chuckled and beckoned them on, down the stairway.

They were met at the foot by a group of the small folk, the men dressed, like Colun, in sturdy leathers, the women in wide-skirted dresses that gave them the appearance of fabulous animated dolls. One whose hair was a striking yellow stepped forward. Her face was round and friendly, her smile at first for Colun alone but then encompassing the bemused newcomers. Colun touched her cheek and said, "Marjia," which Davyd assumed must be her name, and then spoke theirs.

Marjia nodded and repeated the names, then her smile faded as she drew close to Arcole. She bent over the sleeping man, gently touching his brow, then speaking swift words which set Colun to nodding gravely. He beckoned again, and Davyd and Flysse followed their hosts along a pavement of seamless stone to an ascending stair. The litter bearers carried their burden to a walled balcony fronting one of the rock-houses. Marjia led the way inside, clearly bidding the two gnomes wait as she gathered bright cushions and patterned blankets that she spread over the floor of an inner room. Arcole was set down on that bed, the packs and weapons to one side, and Marjia glanced inquiringly at Flysse, leveling a stubby finger at the taller woman and then at Arcole. Flysse nodded, and Marjia waved her closer, then made a shooing motion that hastened the others from the room.

The litter bearers departed and Colun led Davyd to a larger chamber, where glassless windows looked onto the balcony. He indicated that Davyd seat himself on a bench that was, it seemed, grown from the wall. It was too low a seat for Davyd's height, and he found his knees raised uncomfortably close to his chin. Colun chuckled and found cushions that he tossed to the floor. Davyd sat there, watching as Colun went to a niche from which he brought two cups and an earthenware flask. He grinned as he brandished the flask, smacking his lips enthusiastically, and said, "Tiswin."

Davyd accepted a cup, toasting his host.

It had been more than a year since alcohol had passed his lips, and the tiswin tasted fierce. It was, he thought, akin to gin but sweeter. Surely it warmed his belly and eased away his aches, so that a pleasant languor spread through his body, and before he had emptied a second cup he felt his eyes grow heavy and saw the room blur and dim. He was vaguely aware of Colun setting a cushion behind his head and taking the cup from his hand; he mumbled thanks and then fell sound asleep.

Flysse could make no sense of Marjia's words, but she understood the woman's gestures and obeyed as Marjia indicated she turn Arcole onto his belly. Marjia frowned when she saw the scars striping his back, then motioned that Flysse aid her in removing the bandages. She lifted the compress from the wound and studied Colun's rude surgery. Flysse was much reassured when the gnomic woman nodded and smiled, and patted her hand: she seemed to be telling Flysse that the wound was not poisoned.

Then Flysse must wait as Marjia bustled out, returning in a while with a bowl of steaming water and an assortment of jars, vials, and cloths. Arcole stirred drowsily as they stripped him and Marjia bathed his wound. When it was clean, she ground up an ointment that she smeared liberally over the red-lipped gash. A fresh compress was set in place, and together they bandaged him. Marjia dribbled a dark liquid into his mouth, then spread a blanket over his body and gestured that Flysse follow her out of the chamber.

Flysse was at first reluctant to leave Arcole, but Marjia pantomimed that he would sleep on, and that Flysse might wash and eat, and she allowed herself to be persuaded.

She followed Marjia to a chamber that was clearly a bathroom, for water flowed out of the wall into a basin, and off to one side was a stone tub. Marjia indicated that she avail herself of the facilities and pointed back the way they had come before leaving Flysse alone.

Flysse was too concerned for Arcole to do more than quickly bathe her face and drag a comb through her tangled hair before she quit the room and went back to where he lay. He did sleep on, and for a moment she feared he sank into coma, but when she checked his breathing and his pulse, both were steady, and when she touched his brow, it was unfevered. She assumed the medicines of their curious hosts took effect, but even so she was loath to leave him, and had Marjia not reappeared, she would have settled by his side to wait impatiently for him to wake.

Instead, she went with the little doll-like woman to the outer chamber. There she found Colun seated at a wooden table with a flask and cup at his elbow. Davyd lay sprawled on the floor, snoring softly, and Colun pointed at the young man and then at the flask in explanation. Marjia shook her head in what was clearly a fond exaggeration and pantomimed her husband—Flysse assumed they were wed—drinking to excess. Colun laughed softly and said something in their strange language, at which Marjia smiled hugely and cuffed him gently on the ear.

It was so domestic a scene, so *normal,* Flysse burst into tears.

Marjia was instantly at her side, a comforting arm encircling Flysse's waist, leading her to a bench, where she slumped with helpless tears coursing her cheeks. Marjia passed her a kerchief and she mopped her eyes and blew her nose; Colun filled a cup, and after a moment's hesitation she took it. Davyd's condition persuaded her to sip cautiously, but the tiswin was comforting and her weeping gradually subsided.

She wiped her face anew and said, "Forgive me. I owe you thanks, we all owe you thanks. You saved our lives and you tend my husband. I . . ." She gestured helplessly, smiling now as she saw their faces intent on hers, their eyes sympathetic and uncomprehending.

Marjia spoke, but Flysse could understand the woman no better than Marjia understood her, and wondered how it was Davyd believed he almost interpreted their words. Certainly on the journey there it had seemed he and Colun attained a degree of communication denied her. She wondered if that might be something to do with Davyd's talent for dreaming, and smiled fondly at the soundly slumbering youth. Were they to remain for any time with these little folk, she thought, she must attempt to learn their language.

Marjia grew busy again and, before Flysse had emptied her cup, food was set on the table. The savory odors roused Davyd, who opened somewhat bleary eyes and yawned hugely, then grinned and clambered to his feet.

"How's Arcole?" His grin faded, replaced with an expression of concern. "Where is he?"

"He sleeps," Flysse told him. "Marjia tended his wound, and now he sleeps. I think that's likely for the best."

"Yes" Davyd nodded owlishly and yawned again.

Marjia asked with gestures and words if he'd sooner sleep than eat, and he shook his head, saying, "Eat first, then sleep," which both she and Colun seemed to understand.

"This is good," he declared as he wolfed mouthfuls. "Have you tried the tiswin yet, Flysse? That's good too."

"In measure," she answered, thinking that his youth lent him recuperative powers greater than her own. She felt almost too weary to eat, and had she not wished to build her strength that she be ready when Arcole woke, she would have forgone the meal to stretch out by his side.

"I drank only a cup or so," Davyd protested, somewhat crestfallen. "It's that I've not had liquor in so long."

He seemed at that moment so like a child caught in some naughtiness that Flysse could only laugh. Marjia and Colun—for all they likely had no idea what was said—joined in.

When the meal was finished, their hosts jointly indicated they should sleep, and Flysse returned to Arcole, Davyd following Colun to a separate chamber. Marjia spread the floor with more cushions, and handed Flysse a blanket, then quit the room. As she went through the low doorway, she touched the wall and murmured soft words that dimmed the light, leaving Flysse in a gentle twilight. Flysse arranged the cushions and lay beside Arcole. She'd have held him in her arms but feared disturbing him or aggravating his wound, and so contented herself with taking one outflung hand, which she held against her cheek. It was her intention to remain awake, to watch over Arcole, but food and tiswin and the comforting knowledge they were safe combined with weariness to betray her: she hardly knew her eyes closed before she slept.

．　．　．

Arcole opened his eyes and moved to rise. Then grunted a curse as pain lanced his back and confused memory flooded in. Of course—he'd taken a shaft and then been rescued by . . . Images of small, muscular men appeared, one named Colun, who had fed them and . . . He could recall no more. Cautiously, he lifted his head. He lay in a window-less chamber that appeared as much cave as room, lit by a soft, source-less radiance. He saw Flysse beside him and felt reassured, then gently disengaged her hand that he might examine the bandage around his waist.

His movements woke her and she sat up, her smile bright as the risen sun as she saw him awake.

"Oh, Arcole!" Her arms enfolded him and he winced, so that she held him gentler, asking, "Does it hurt?"

"Somewhat," he told her honestly. "Where are we?"

Flysse explained all that happened, and when she was done he said, "By God, we're fortunate, no?"

"Yes," she agreed. "But still you took a bad wound."

He said, "I've taken worse, I'll mend soon enough."

Flysse nodded, and held him until he fell asleep again.

For long days he lay slowly recovering in the chamber, tended by Marjia and Flysse, who refused to go farther from his side than the balcony. Davyd visited him when he woke, and regaled him with tales of their saviors and the fabulous cavern. A whole people dwelt here, Davyd explained, who called themselves—as best he could tell—the Grannach. Colun was their leader, their creddan in the Grannach tongue, and the cave and the houses and the myriad tunnels were magically fashioned by Stone Shapers who were called golans. They had furnaces and forges in which they made weapons and the metalware they used, and some of the tunnels led to mountain valleys, where they pastured animals and some-times hunted. They had fled there after a great battle—with other folk of a different race, Davyd gathered, some of whom lived west of the moun-tains, and some to the east. The latter, Davyd believed, were the de-mons, whom the Grannach named *Tack-in*. He thought their leader was called Chakthi, and he was despised by the Grannach.

"God, but you've learned much," Arcole declared after one such report. "How can you understand them? Their speech sounds all barks to me."

"I don't know." Davyd shrugged, frowning. "I don't understand all of it, but it's as though . . ." He shrugged again. "As though the more I speak with them, the better I understand what they say."

"And do they understand you?" Arcole asked.

"Not much." Davyd shook his head. "Colun learns a few words, but mostly I learn their tongue."

"That's as well." Arcole rested back against a pile of cushions. "One of us had better communicate with them. Now, do you tell me what you know of the western land and its folk? Are they also . . . What are our saviors called, Grannach?"

"No, I think they're like us." Davyd's excited face grew speculative and he raised a hand to indicate greater height. "They live out in the open and they're called something like *mat-ah-why-ee.*"

"Like us, eh?" Arcole smiled. "And fled here too? Is everyone here an exile?"

"I think it must be so." Davyd nodded. "I think that Colun plans to take us to them when you're well enough to travel."

"That shall not be long now," Arcole said, smiling as Flysse murmured a warning, "for I heal apace." He paused, then asked, "Do you dream of what lies ahead?"

Davyd nodded again and told them of his dreams.

They had begun soon after his arrival in the Grannach cavern. Dreams of safety at first, as if whatever power shaped his oneiric visions would reassure him this sanctuary was sound. Then they had grown stranger, but slowly clearer and more precise. It was as if, he thought, another mind reached out to communicate with him.

He dreamed of rolling plains, great forests and wide rivers, and of tall, handsome folk mounted on horses; of villages comprised all of painted tents, filled with laughing children. And yet, encompassed within those images, he had felt a sorrow as if something were lost or left behind; and also a great hope, as if the people of his dreams put doubt behind them and looked to a brighter future.

Gradually a single figure had emerged—that of a man whose hair was white as snow, though he was not yet old, and whose face was clearer than any other. A kind and gentle face that smiled out of the dream and spoke in silence, a hand raised to beckon Davyd to him.

"I think," Davyd said, "that he greets me. I think he welcomes us to his country."

"Then," Arcole declared, "it would be churlish of us to refuse, no?"

"Not," Flysse said firmly, "until you are quite well."

Time had little meaning in the cavern. That the Grannach controlled its light seemed to confuse the natural pace of the days, as if the exiles' bodies missed the regulation of sunrise and sunset, and as Arcole's wound slowly healed, he began to chafe at this new confinement. Davyd, too, began to express impatience. His dreams grew more imperative, as if the white-haired man would have them come to him before the summer ended. Only Flysse was content to linger, and that because she'd know her husband fully recovered before they embarked on fresh adventures.

At last the wound *was* full-healed. Marjia no longer insisted Arcole wear a compress, nor that he swallow the recuperative drafts, and one day Colun told them—through Davyd—that it was time to go.

They said their farewells and gathered up their packs. The Grannach had already gifted them with fresh clothing, sewn to their sizes, and now added food. With an escort led by Colun, they quit the fabulous cavern.

Colun brought them through the winding tunnels to a mountain valley where sheep and deer grazed under the benign light of a late-summer sun. It was a joy to walk once more under blue skies, to see clouds sail the winds and feel the fresh breeze on their faces.

Stranger still to find a welcoming party camped in the foothills, as if they were not refugees but expected and welcome guests whose arrival had been somewhat delayed.

Arcole and Flysse gazed in wonder as tall men clad in buckskins, their hair tied in long braids, hailed the Grannach. Arcole fingered his musket, murmuring, "They look like the demons."

"They're friends," Davyd said confidently.

He stepped forward, his gaze locked firm on the white-haired man who opened his arms and said, "Well met, brother. I am Morrhyn."